Breaking the Line Books Presents

Victoria's Journey

The Four Book Compilation of the
Victoria's Journey Series by
Bestselling Author, A'Mera
Frieman

BREAKING THE LINE BOOKS

Victoria's Journey
Copyright © 2015 by Breaking the Line Books
Cover design by A'Mera Frieman

ISBN – 13: 978-0692439524

This title is also available in e-book and audio formats through Amazon and other retail outlets.

Visit www.breakingthelinebooks.com for more information.

Printed in the United States of America

Victoria's Beginning

Book 1

It is always better to start a story at the beginning. As many would agree, the beginning of a story is like the foundation on which a house is built, without a solid foundation, the house will fall apart. This story begins with the foundation of a journey. It is a rather lengthy and hard journey; however, the difficult and ultimately fulfilling road that is travelled is definitely fascinating. The blessings that can be received by the lessons that are learned are abundant. Some who read this series might say to themselves that this story sounds a little like their grandmothers', mother's, or even their own. And, that is essentially the point. In writing this story, the goal is for those who read it to connect in some way to the characters and feel their hardships and blessings as their own.

Prologue

"Push!!"

Dr. Herbert yelled.

Tess was so tired after the long ride to the nearby country hospital and the long, painful labor that she didn't think that she could push anymore.

"Push now, girl!"

The doctor raised his voice again in his impatience.

Tess pushed with all of her might and out came her squalling baby. The nurse gave the doctor a strange look and did not pick up the squirming infant.

"Doctor Herbert, maybe we should get one of the colored nurses to swaddle the child."

The doctor took one look at the baby and realized the reason for the nurse's reaction.

"Don't be silly, Rebecca, pick that baby up and start the clean up. Don't you know that's Paul Roberts' grandchild?"

Dr. Herbert shook his head because everyone knew that Paul Roberts was more White than Negro and wealthier than most folks around town. That was the only reason that his son and daughter-in-law were allowed in the White part of the hospital.

By now, Tess was concerned and wanted her husband very badly, but husbands weren't allowed in the birthing room.

"Is something wrong with my baby?" she asked anxious because of the nurse's attitude.

Dr. Herbert finished his work on Tess and sought to allay her fear.

"No, child, nothing is wrong with your baby except she shows her grandfather's White blood proudly. What will you name her?"

"Her name is Victoria Alicia Roberts."

Tess had to raise her voice to be heard over Victoria's demanding cries.

Dr. Herbert laughed.

"With lungs like that, I would say her name is strong enough to suit her."

Finally, the nurse gave Tess her baby who was now swaddled and quiet. Tess took one look at the tiny white face and smooth red hair and burst into tears.

"Why are you crying, girl?"

Both the doctor and nurse spoke at the same time.

Dr. Herbert confused but familiar with post birthing emotions tried again to calm the beautiful dark-skinned Black girl.

"She's eight pounds and nine ounces of healthy baby. What could possibly make you cry about delivering a healthy child? Did Clyde want a boy that bad? Well, you're both young and healthy, you'll have plenty more chances to have a boy."

Tess worried her bottom lip and sobbed.

"No, we didn't care if it was a girl or boy."

"Well, what is it then, girl?"

Dr. Herbert could feel his impatience rising and tried to tamp it down. Nerves, it's just nerves, he said to himself.

"She's doesn't look Black! She won't have a normal life living with us, and I hate that God is punishing me like this!"

"Why would you say such a thing? Tess Roberts, I'm ashamed of you! Your family is a strong root in this community, and a healthy baby girl is not a punishment," replied Dr. Herbert raising his voice in anger.

By now, Tess was beyond reason and shouted back. Her anger made her forget that she was yelling at a White man.

"You're ashamed of me? Well, I'm ashamed of myself because I just had a White baby, and I am as Black as your boots! I'm ashamed for her that she will never be able to live like regular Negro people because she won't be accepted, and people will stare at me. She won't be able to associate with White people either because her mama and daddy are Negros! I am being punished, and I hate her and myself!"

The doctor grabbed the now crying baby from Tess before she could hurt her.

After she flung her final statement, Tess passed out on the bed. Dr. Herbert called in Clyde, Tess' husband, and told him of his beautiful, healthy baby girl and nothing of his conversation with Tess. Clyde looked stunned when he saw his tiny daughter and left without even holding her. Dr. Herbert shook his head and felt that it was all just the post birthing emotions. He figured that when Tess woke, she would have changed her mind about her child.

He took one last look at Victoria, and his chest filled with pride to have delivered such beauty. Victoria opened her eyes and stared directly at the doctor at the precise moment. The beautiful white rose skin and blue eyes matched perfectly with her auburn red hair. Again, Dr. Herbert felt a swell of pride. Then, he called over the nurse to take Victoria to the White nursery and a Negro orderly to take Tess to her room on the Negro side of the hospital.

1

I was born in the early 1940's, and I looked more White than Black like my parents. Many in the small town of Carson and the outer country community whispered that I was not my father's child. Sometimes, they would whisper that I wasn't my mother's child either because my mother was a very dark skinned Negro woman, but my father had a very fair complexion. It was said that I looked just like my grandpa, Paul Roberts, whose father had been White.

Since my parents couldn't stand the rude stares and comments from White and Black people, I was sent to live with my maternal aunts, Charlotte and Mary, in Dallas before my first birthday. My aunts were fairer skinned than my parents and used to the attention from looking closer to White than Negro.

Aunt Charlotte had fallen in love and married a wealthy White man named Jake St. Francis from California who had left her a very rich widow two years after they married. When she inherited all of her husband's wealth, Aunt Charlotte bought a big house in a secluded North Dallas neighborhood and took Aunt Mary in to live with her so that she wouldn't be alone. When I came along, it was a blessing to Aunt Charlotte because she and Jake had not had any children. As I grew up in her home, she would tell me that she never would betray Jake's love, even to have children. Then she would tweak my nose and tell me that I was more than enough.

Aunt Mary was a little different. She could look at someone and tell the future. When she moved in with Aunt Charlotte, she began to have wealthy White people come to hear their destiny. The more Aunt Mary's "sight" produced results, the more people sought her out so that Aunt Charlotte built her a private salon where her clients could come. My earliest memories were from my Aunt Mary telling me in her soft voice that I was special, and that I would one day be given a special choice. I'd giggle, and she'd smile and send me back to Aunt Charlotte.

I always felt so loved with my aunts. My parents continued to have more children without the income to care for them. So, as I grew to understand what this meant, I was only too happy to be where I was the center of attention.

From the time that I was given to them, my aunts invested time and money to see that I had a good elementary education and nurtured my musical talents in singing and piano. I learned to speak proper English, even better than my aunts. I learned so fast that my teachers and tutors would get frustrated trying to find things to challenge me.

Sometimes, my aunts would stare at me and tell me that I was the most beautiful child that they had ever seen. Well, they were my aunts. But, I thought they were the beautiful ones with their smooth latte skin and deep dark eyes. I felt ugly next to them with my White skin and red hair. My aunts were tall and with curves in the right places. I knew that only from hearing one of the church deacons say this to Aunt Mary when he asked if he could come over and sit awhile with her. She said no.

However, with all the attention, I never thought myself better than anyone or spoiled because my aunts kept up our family's Christian upbringing by being involved in the local Baptist church. And since my piano teacher was also the choirmaster, it seemed that I was at the church everyday. The loving feeling that I had grown with my aunts continued there, and praising God and Jesus with my talents became second nature.

On my seventh birthday, the choirmaster pronounced to my aunts that he could not teach me any more because I had learned so quickly that I had surpassed even his musical skills. My aunts were amazed and bought a piano and several music books for me to learn more and play at home. At seven years old, I was playing and singing for the church choir, which amazed the pastor so much, that he spoke to my aunts about more formal training in the New York. My aunts knew that I needed to train, but declined because I was so young.

One night, I heard Aunt Mary speaking to Aunt Charlotte.

"Charlotte, she has an old soul. She understands like an adult, and she learns fast. This is how it should be with her."

"Yes, I know, Mary, but she is my baby and I cannot let her go."

Aunt Mary sighed heavily.

"One day, you will have no choice."

I didn't know what Aunt Mary meant because I never wanted to leave Aunt Charlotte and Aunt Mary, not even to get married. And since my parents didn't want me, I knew that I would be with them forever.

That summer, my aunts decided to visit their parents, the Daniels in June instead of July like we usually visited. My aunts had made the trip to my grandparents' farm once a year since I was four. I was so excited because I loved going to the country.

I loved my Big Mama Chandra and Grandpa Ed. They made me feel so good. Big Mama was so beautiful. She was tall with light peach colored skin and long beautiful dark hair and deep dark brown eyes. She always smelled like vanilla and mint when she hugged me, and she always told me that I was her little mirror. This was our game, so I would smile and tell her that I looked like my Grandpa Paul. Big Mama Chandra would just shake her head, smile, and send me to Ms. Sadie for teacakes.

Ms. Sadie was the housekeeper, and she made the best teacakes.

Grandpa Ed was tall and dark. His skin looked like warm coffee, and he had the straightest and whitest teeth I had ever seen. And when he smiled, he really smiled. I always liked for him to smile at me, and since he was so quiet and serious all the time, a smile from Grandpa Ed was something else.

I loved visiting my mama's family because they had accepted me when my mama didn't want me. My mama and daddy started to visit Big Mama and Grandpa Ed the summer I turned six, and I got the feeling then that something was wrong and that they hated me. Sometimes, my Daddy would look at me real hard and squint his eyes like he was looking for something. Then, he would go argue with Mama right in front of Big Mama Chandra but never in front of Grandpa Ed.

When I heard Daddy's raised voice during their second visit, I ran to the kitchen, grabbed a bunch of biscuits, and took my little brothers and sister into the fields to play so that we wouldn't have to hear the hateful words that Daddy said to Mama. I always felt like I was the reason that they fought so much, but whenever I would ask Big Mama Chandra about it, she would just grab me up in a big hug and tickle me. I knew that she did this to keep from answering me, and I still wondered if it was all about me.

That summer, Grandpa Ed took me to the fields with him in the mornings of my first week so that I could learn how the farm was run. We went to the cotton fields first, and I met all of the workers, drifters, and their children.

One of the children was a little older than the rest, and I heard Grandpa Ed call him David. He looked to be taking care of all the children in a cleared part of the field. He was tall for his age, and he had a nice face but he was very thin. He smiled at me and asked if I wanted to play with him and the other children. Grandpa Ed told him that I was learning the farm, but if I wanted, I could come play later. I grew happy because I would be able to play with other children instead of my siblings. It's not like I didn't like playing with my siblings, it's just that if my siblings were around so were my parents. Anyway, somehow, I knew it was going to be nice playing with David and the other children.

My grandfather took me to the other crops that were the farm's livelihood: the corn, cotton, and the wheat. I looked across all of the land and I felt so connected. Grandpa Ed told me that he rotated the crops every year so that the soil would never be ruined. He also shared with me that it was part of his Native American heritage to take care of the land and repair the harm done so that the land would always give plenty.

"The Adams want part of our land, but they don't take care of what they got, so I'll never sell to them or anyone who doesn't know the land like we do, Victoria," said Grandpa.

The Adams' were the White family down the road that owned several acres of land next to my grandparents. Mr. Bob and Ms. Sophie weren't nice people, and everyone knew they were greedy spiteful people who hated to see my Black grandparents have more than they did. I just stayed quiet and slipped my hand into Grandpa Ed's while we stared across the land. Somehow, even, at seven, I knew how Grandpa Ed felt. I reached down and grabbed a handful of the rich soil and put it to my nose. It was a smell that made me feel good.

When Grandpa Ed brought me back to the farm on the field wagon, Big Mama Chandra came running down the steps.

"Ed, I can't believe that you kept this young'un out in the wagon with you all day! Poor little mite! That pretty skin is all burnt up! Now, you come with me and Big Mama will fix you right up. Ed, you go on round back and wash up for your piece of vinegar roll."

Grandpa Ed just shook his head, clicked his tongue, and drove the wagon to the back. Big Mama Chandra made the best vinegar rolls, and if Grandpa Ed wanted a piece, he knew he had to move faster than my Aunt Charlotte and Aunt Mary. They loved Big Mama's vinegar rolls.

As soon as Big Mama Chandra was done rubbing me with her cream, I wiggled out of her grasp and tried to run off to find David and the other children.

"Where you off to, my little mirror?"

"Grandpa told me that I could play with the worker and drifter children," I replied, trying to inch closer to the door.

"Well, your new little friends might not want to play with you just now after I've rubbed you with my special sunburn cream, but go right ahead. Maybe, you can keep yourself occupied so I can talk with your grandpa and aunts."

With that said, I took off like lightning to find David. I found them all at the end of the cotton row next to the house playing Red Rover. I ran over to join them. David and several of the children saw me and gave a little wave. As I stood there, one by one, the children started holding their noses and looking around at each other. Since David was farther off, he wasn't holding his nose.

"What's that stink?" asked the little boy next to me.

"I don't know, but it's nasty!" cried the little girl on my other side.

"It smells like fish and lemons!" cried the little boy.

"My grandma just rubbed cream on me because she said that my skin was burnt. I think that's the smell, but all I smell is lemon."

"Lemme see, " said David as he walked toward me. He leaned down and sniffed," UGH! Dat's got to be her sun cream!"

"I'm sorry! I can go back to the house if the smell is too bad," I cried and tears started to fill my eyes because I was really ashamed by then.

"Hey, it's okay. Yo' Big Mama done rubbed stuff on us too that stunk to the high heav'ns." C'mon!"

David grabbed my hand, and all of us ran to the freshly plowed dirt on the other side of the cotton row.

"Here roll around, and the stink will be gone," advised David.

I threw my body into the dirt and rolled around. As I rolled the other children grabbed handfuls of the soil and started to rub me with it. Soon, we were all laughing and covered in dirt. I didn't care if I got in trouble because my new friends accepted me.

That afternoon, we played and played until the other children's mothers started to call them home to supper. David never got called so he stayed with me.

"Aren't you going too, David? Where's your Mama?"

He looked really sad, and I wanted to take back the words.

"She died while she was birthin' me, so it's just me, my Uncle P, and Aunt Addy. My daddy left me with them because he wanted to go see the world without a young'un taggin' along. My uncle and aunt took me in and gave me a home because Aunt Addy couldn't have no babies."

"I'm sorry, David," I said quietly, "my mama and daddy don't want me either. Are your aunt and uncle good to you? Do they treat you right? My mama and daddy are mean to me."

I felt the tears in my eyes.

"I don't know why they don't like me. I wish I did then I would stop doing what makes them mad at me, so they would love me like Aunt Charlotte does."

"Yes, my aunt and uncle take good care of me. Aunt Addy was a school teacher, so she teaches all of the worker and drifter children wherever Uncle P takes us to help with the crops."

He laughed.

"Uncle P, says that he's the only one that she can't teach 'cause he set in his ways."

Then, David saw my tears and touched me on the arm and said, "you're it!" then he ran off for me to chase him. I immediately forgot about my tears and began the game of "you're it".

It had started to get dark and the shadows were getting longer. It was kind of hard for me to see him, but I saw him run toward my grandparents' house.

When I caught up with him standing beneath the side living room window, he caught me and put his hand over my mouth before I could yell, "you're it!" He put his finger over his lips and nodded toward the open window. I nodded back, and he took his hand from my mouth.

"What do you mean, they want her for the rest of the summer, Pa?" asked Aunt Charlotte.

"They have not even sent her a letter or come by to see her and she has been here two weeks! You know what people have been saying to Clyde about her color and looks! Y'all know how he feels about her!"

"Hush, now, Charlotte!" Grandpa Ed said firmly. There was immediate silence.

"Clyde and Tess have told us that they will be coming to pick her up on Saturday, and they will bring her back at the end of July," Grandpa Ed said in his quiet manner.

"Mama have you or Mary seen or felt anything about this?"

"I have not, child," said Big Mama, "have you Mary?"

There was a long pause, and Aunt Mary said quietly, "She has to go Charlotte. I have only seen misery in my visions of her little face, but I know that she has to go to them for this time."

"Misery? That's too much for y'all to expect for me to let her go to them now!" Aunt Charlotte sobbed.

She was weeping out loud, and it made me want to go to her because I knew that they were talking about me. I didn't want Aunt Charlotte to cry anymore, but when I moved, David shook his head and grabbed my arm tightly.

"Calm down, Charlotte, we will be able to visit her everyday if we need to see how she is doing," said Big Mama.

"Remember, Charlotte, they are her parents, and they wouldn't sign the papers to give her to you through the law. Maybe that's a sign that they really do want her."

"All I know is that she is mine, and they are not going to treat her like a little slave like they do when they visit her here and expect for her to take care of their other children. She is only seven!" Aunt Charlotte cried.

I heard movement, and I knew that Aunt Mary was hugging Aunt Charlotte as she did whenever Aunt Charlotte was upset.

David looked at me, grabbed my hand, and ran to the edge of the fields.

"See, your parents do want you!" said David excitedly. When he saw my face, he calmed down, and asked, "Why aren't you excited?"

"Because I told you that my mama and daddy don't like me, and I don't know what is going to happen," I said quietly. "Don't worry, Victoria, nothing is going to happen to you. Ever. I won't let it."

"Do you promise, David?" David puffed his chest up, and said, "Yes, I do."

It was then that we heard a deep voice singing, "I sing 'cause I'm happy, I sing 'cause I'm free, his eye is on the sparrow, and I know he watches me."

David smiled, "That's my uncle coming from the Adams'. He always comes late to get me and my aunt."

David's Uncle P came from between the rows of corn. He was tall, big, and dark skinned, and he had the biggest eyes Victoria had ever seen.

"C'mon now young'un, yo' ainty is a'itch'n to stuff som'n down our gullets," said David's Uncle P.

Then he glanced at Victoria and smiled.

"Well, lookee, it's a lil Ms. Chandra! How do, lil ma'am?"

He held out his hand.

I looked at a hand that was bigger than my Grandpa Ed's and hesitated afraid. He looked at his hand and took it back quickly.

"That's alright, lil 'un. My hand is a mite filt'y."

I hadn't been thinking that at all, so I piped up.

"I'm sorry, mister, I was just scared for a minute. Can I shake your hand now? See, my hand is dirty too."

I held up my hand for him to see, and he laughed and shook my small hand. I felt my hand swallowed up in his large one. And then, I felt a peculiar warmth run through my hand across my chest.

"Yo'r special lil 'un. You have an old spirit. Be strong and stay good," said Mr. P.

"Uncle P, you're going to scare her," David said rolling his eyes.

I looked at Mr. P's face, and it looked like it was shining especially his eyes. I wasn't scared only curious.

"I like it, David, it's okay. Thank you, Mr. P."

"Now, now, lil 'un, you call me Unca' P too, ok?"

I nodded my head.

"It's past time I was in the house, David. Will I see y'all tomorrow?"

"Yep!"

He jumped up and down.

Then I turned and ran to the front door of the house.

When I looked back, David and Uncle P were watching me. I waved, and they waved back. Then they turned and disappeared into the cornfield.

As I was trying to sneak back to my room, I heard Big Mama shout.

"Come in here, child, why are you sneaking around in your own house?"

I put my head down knowing that I was in trouble and walked into the living room.

"Victoria Alicia Roberts! Why are you so filthy?!" exclaimed Aunt Charlotte.

Big Mama chuckled.

"I know why. The homestead children told you to roll in the dirt to get the stink of my cream off, didn't they?"

"Yes ma'am."

I kept my head down and picked at the crusted dirt on my elbow.

"Well, run tell Ms. Sadie to get you a bath ready."

"Mama! She needs a spanking with all that dirt she's tracked in here," said Aunt Charlotte.

"Now, this is my house, Charlotte, and I'll pass the discipline here, understand?"

Aunt Charlotte looked down.

"Yes, ma'am."

I ran out of the living room as fast as I could, but I still heard Big Mama when she yelled.

"And as soon as you get out of that water, you come in here, Victoria."

I kept running to find Ms. Sadie because I was scared then. Big Mama never called me by my name.

When I return to the living room, Grandpa Ed called me to him.

"Come here, my dear, grandpa needs to talk to you."

I sidled over to his chair with my head down. He put his finger under my chin and raised my head up to look him in the eye.

"Never carry your head down, my sweet, always hold your head up high no matter what."

"Yes, sir," I replied.

"Victoria, your parents want to take you to live with them for the rest of the summer. They will be here day after tomorrow," said Grandpa Ed.

"Pa, at least ask her is she wants to go," pleaded Aunt Charlotte.

I didn't want any more fighting about me, so I looked at Aunt Charlotte.

"I'll go with Mama and Daddy, Auntie. That way you and Aunt Mary can do other stuff with Grandpa and Big Mama."

Then I smiled really big so that she wouldn't see how hard it was for me to go away from her.

"Oh, sweetie, Aunt Mary and I don't need to do stuff with Grandpa and Big Mama. If you really want to go, I'll let you go. We will visit you as much as we can. I'm sure that Big Mama will keep us busy while we are here with her, so that the time will fly by until you're back," Aunt Charlotte promised.

She got up, came over to me, and hugged me.

As she held me to her, she turned her head and whispered.

"Don't worry, a short time with them will be alright, then you'll be back with your Aunt Mary and me."

I nodded my head and she stepped back.

Big Mama came over to me then.

"Come now, little mirror, and I will make sure that you get the first of the supper biscuits."

I felt happier since no one was fighting anymore and because Big Mama made the best biscuits. It took my mind off of the little time that I had left before going to my mama and daddy's house.

2

By the time Saturday morning came, I was so scared that I all I could do was stare at the top of my grandparents' house. I don't think that I slept at all. I thought a lot about the day before when I had played with David. We had a lot of fun, and he gave me a big hug and told me that he would visit me at my mama and daddy's house. It made me feel a little better and gave me something to look forward to when I left.

My Aunt Charlotte had stayed with me all night in the rocking chair by my window. I don't think that she slept much that night either. Her normally bright eyes were dull, and her long dark hair was loose and tangled. When she saw that I was awake, she got me out of bed and had me wash off in the hallway washroom. She dressed my hair, told me to put on my best play clothes, and go sit in the front room.

While I was waiting on the edge of the divan, Big Mama Chandra walked in and sat beside me.

"Don't look so afraid, child, it's your Mama and Daddy coming to get you."

"It's not that I'm afraid, Big Mama, I just don't know what will happen to me. Sometimes, I feel like my Daddy doesn't like me."

"Of course he likes you, girl! He loves you and so does your Mama!"

I felt a little better after she said this, but I still felt a deep fear that I couldn't explain to my grandmother. Big Mama Chandra grabbed me up to her chest and gave me a big hug. I forgot all about the fear in her strong arms. I could hear her heart beating and sniffed the fresh smell of baking powder on her apron probably from baking biscuits. I felt like I was imprinting a memory to savor in the time with my mama and daddy. I began to wonder where my aunts and Grandpa Ed were and if I would get to see them before my parents came to take me away with them.

Like a prompt from my mind, Aunt Mary came through the front room door.

" They're here, Mama," she said in a hushed voice.

"Well, Mary, don't just stand there, tell them to come into the house like the civilized person that I raised you up as."

Aunt Mary left the room, and a few moments later my parents walked into the room.

Now, if I had been only a little scared before, the look on my parents' faces made me want to run into my room and hide under the bed.

My daddy, Clyde had such a mean look on his face that he didn't even look like the handsome man that I knew as my daddy. My mama, Tess, well she stood behind my daddy with her eyes squinted looking around the room until she zeroed in on where I sat with Big Mama Chandra's arms around me.

From that point she just stared at me with her mouth tightened into a line. Her dark beauty was striking even though she looked a lot older than she really was. Her belly was large which meant that I was going to have another brother or sister soon. The thought crossed my mind that I didn't want another sister or brother, and that my parents shouldn't have more kids. I felt bad after the thought and prayed that I wouldn't be punished for it.

The tension in the room was so thick that I felt like choking as if the air was full of smoke instead of bright summer sunshine.

"Didn't I raise you to speak when you walk into a room, Tess?"

My mama stopped looking at me and focused her tightened features on her mother.

"Yes" she said as if tasting something nasty.

By this time, my grandmother had risen to her full height from the divan where we were sitting.

"Yes what?"

I had never heard Big Mama Chandra use that voice on anyone, and I stared at her in awe.

My mama looked down at the floor under my grandmother's scrutiny and said, "Yes, ma'am."

Meanwhile, my daddy had been moving into the room closer to where I was sitting. When my mama gave into Big Mama Chandra, my daddy turned to my grandmother.

"I guess I wasn't raised with manners either, huh Chandra?"

"I don't know how you were raised Clyde, and I don't care, but you are my son by marriage which means you will act like you have manners in my house even if you weren't raised with them."

"We just came to get our "daughter" and spend some time with her since no one seems bothered to bring her to see us."

But it was the smug way that he said "daughter" that had got my attention and Aunt Charlotte's as well as she walked in the room.

"Why did you say "daughter" like that, Clyde?" she demanded.

My daddy swung around to face Aunt Charlotte, and the look on his face completely changed. Before, he had looked mean and twisted, but when he looked at Aunt Charlotte, his eyes brightened and the biggest smile broke out on his handsome face.

"Charlotte," he crooned, "I thought that you would come to see Victoria off with us."

"Yes, I wanted to give her some treats to share with my other niece and nephews. How many is it now?" she said looking in disgust at my mama's belly.

"You know damned well how many we have, Charlotte! You make me so sick with all of your judgments. You don't know nothing, you bourgeois bitch!"

The room became hushed as my mama spat her last statement at Aunt Charlotte. All eyes except my mama's had turned toward the door that was now occupied by Grandpa Ed. Even my daddy was quiet.

"As long as you live, Tess, you will never use that kind of language in front of your mother or child. You have become disrespectful and uncouth. It does not sit well on you. Now, you and Charlotte will stop your bickering, and you will apologize to Chandra and Victoria," said Grandpa Ed in a hard voice.

Mama turned to face Grandpa Ed while he was speaking, and her mouth quivered as if she wanted to cry.

"Yes, sir," she said quietly.

Then she turned to me and Big Mama and with her mouth twisted like she had again tasted something nasty.

"I'm sorry, Mama and Vicky."

I hated to be called Vicky, and Aunt Charlotte knew it.

"Tess, please don't call her that. She doesn't like it."

"I will call my child whatever I want, Charlotte, because she is my child. And, I gave her that name."

At that point, I didn't think that Big Mama wanted any more fighting so she settled it.

"Tess, I think Charlotte would know what the child likes and doesn't like, so call her by the name that she uses all the time which is Victoria."

Mama didn't look she liked having to accept this, so she just stayed quiet.

"Well, get your things, 'Victoria', so that we can get to your other grandpa and grandma's house to get your sister and brothers," said Daddy rubbing his hands together.

He was close enough to me by then to reach down and grab my arm in a tight hold. I felt him squeeze my arm, and I stood up quickly to avoid another squeeze.

"Why didn't y'all bring the other children to see us, Tess?" asked Aunt Mary.

"Would it matter, Mary? Don't act like you or Charlotte care about your other niece and nephews because I know that you don't."

"Now, Tess, what did your pa just tell you?" asked Big Mama gently.

Mama glanced at Big Mama and said nothing else. She held her full lips together so tightly they looked like a thin line.

Aunt Charlotte came over to me with a small brown paper bag.

"Here are some rock candies and root beer licorice for you and your brothers and sister, Victoria. Now you make sure and don't eat too many before supper, okay?"

She was about to hand over the bag when my daddy leaned down and snatched it away from my grasp.

"I'll take those and issue it out to the children, Charlotte. Don't you worry your pretty little head about them getting any before supper."

He finished this statement with a wide smile at Aunt Charlotte.

Aunt Charlotte looked him in the eye.

"You never answered my question, Clyde."

Daddy didn't even pretend not to know what Aunt Charlotte meant.

"I didn't mean anything by it, Charlotte. I know that you have been taking on our burden, and she's more your daughter than ours. I was just teasing."

This seemed to satisfy Aunt Charlotte, so she leaned down and hugged me so tight that I almost couldn't breath.

She whispered in my ear.

"It won't be long, and we'll be back home in Dallas, ok? And remember, I love you."

She stepped back quickly, and it was then she noticed the grip that my daddy had on my arm. She frowned but said nothing else. Daddy was looking at Aunt Charlotte from head to toe and especially at her chest. Mama cleared her throat and frowned at Daddy who then glanced at Mama's face and then returned his gaze at Aunt Charlotte.

"Let's go, Clyde," Mama said tightly.

Grandpa Ed picked up my little suitcase that Aunt Mary had placed by the door.

"Come here, little one, and give old Grandpa Ed a hug and kiss before he heads to the field."

I ran over to him glad that Daddy had to release me as his grip had started to hurt.

When I hugged Grandpa Ed, he slipped some paper in the small side pocket of my dress.

"Take this and hide it from your mama and daddy. Use it when you can but not in front of them."

I nodded slightly to let him know I understood, he let me go and I slipped my hand in to feel the papers in my pocket. I knew that it was money.

Then Aunt Mary and Big Mama Chandra came over and gave me a hug as well. Aunt Mary didn't say a word, but I felt the weight of her dark eyes on my face.

As I looked up at her beautiful beloved face, she sighed sadly and told me to be a good girl until I returned. Big Mama Chandra gave Mama a big linen covered wicket basket that had the most delicious smells coming from underneath it.

"Here is some food for y'all so that you won't have to worry about cooking today, Tess. It should be enough to have for supper today and dinner tomorrow."

Daddy stepped up and gave the basket back to Big Mama.

"I can feed my family, Chandra."

Big Mama just looked from him to Mama.

"I don't doubt that you can feed your family, Clyde, but this is something for my daughter as she is in the family way. She doesn't need to be on her feet that long, and if I can help her with only that part, I will."

Big Mama then walked outside to Daddy's big white Chevy car and placed the basket in the backseat. Aunt Charlotte walked past us and stood beside Big Mama who still had the car door open. Mama turned around and walked through the door of the house. Daddy grabbed my arm again in his hard grip and walked up behind Mama. I watched in horror as he put the hand that he had fisted the candy filled brown paper bag into the small of her back and push her roughly through the front door. Mama stumbled but she caught herself on the front porch post. Big Mama and Aunt Charlotte had gasped and ran forward a little when they saw Mama fall forward.

"Goodness grief, Tess, are you okay?" cried Big Mama.

"Yes, Mama, I've just become a little clumsy with this baby," said Mama breathlessly.

I opened my mouth to tell the truth, and Daddy squeezed my arm painfully. I looked up at his face, and he was looking at me and shaking his head. I got the message and didn't say a thing. I felt so weak because I knew what he had done and to protect myself, I didn't tell the truth.

Daddy walked forward and down the steps almost dragging me behind him. He let go so that he could open his door and he nudged me roughly toward the back door where Big Mama and Aunt Charlotte were standing.

Aunt Charlotte gave me another hug and leaned into the open window.

"Clyde, I will be by early next week to visit."

Daddy turned his head around to the back seat and smiled widely at Aunt Charlotte.

"I would love for you to come by Charlotte. I'm sure that Tess would love it too. Wouldn't you, Tess?"

By that time, Mama had opened her own door and sat silently in the front seat. She glanced over at Daddy.

"It'll be too early for such a visit, Charlotte, why don't you wait a couple of weeks so that "Victoria" can get settled in with us?"

Daddy put his arm along the back of the seat and pinched Mama's neck hard. She put her head down and bit her lip but she didn't cry out in pain.

"What Tess means Charlotte is why don't you let us spend some time with Victoria, and then you are welcome to come over and see me, I mean us, when you are ready."

Aunt Charlotte hadn't heard the last part of Daddy's statement because Grandpa Ed had started up his field tractor.

When Grandpa Ed had driven into the fields, Aunt Charlotte turned around, and said that she would give mama and daddy time with me before she visited. Then she stood back when Daddy started the car and started driving slowly around the circular driveway.

I looked back through the rear window and wanted to cry out, "Please don't let them take me now! He's mean to Mama!" but I just raised my hand and waved at Big Mama and Aunt Charlotte who stood waving back at me.

As Daddy's car made its way down the lane, I saw David and the other children running through the rows of corn on Mama's side of the car. I slid over and waved at them as we drove past. They were running to keep up with the car and waving back at me too.

Daddy looked back at me and yelled viciously.

"Quit all the silly waving like you're leaving on a ship or something, Vicky! You look stupid!"

"I'm just waving at my friends, Daddy."

"Did you just back talk me, girl?" he continued to yell.

I was afraid after seeing what he did to Mama, so I looked down and shook my head.

"You will look at me when I'm talking to you!" he shouted.

I looked up then and noticed that he had slowed the car down and was almost leaning into the backseat.

"When I tell you to do something or not to do something, you better listen and do as I say, do you hear me "Vicky?""

Tears filled my eyes as I replied a quiet, "yes, sir".

"And we will call you "Vicky" if we want to whether you like it or not!"

I didn't know what to do or say, so I kept quiet and tried to shrink myself into the corner so that he wouldn't notice me anymore. He turned around in his seat and sped up a little.

I looked out the window and saw that my friends had heard everything through the open windows of the car. They had stopped running in the corn and come out to the side of the field next to the lane. They were like silent statues lining the lane with David at the end.

"Dirty field children," grumbled Daddy, "you don't need to be around children like that anyway. Don't you know who your grandpa is? He's Paul Roberts, the wealthiest black man around here. Your Grandpa Ed needs to remember that when he's giving my wife orders. I mean who does he think he is? My pa has ten more acres than he does and more hands. Why, more people respect his word than Ed's!"

On and on Daddy went about what Grandpa Paul had that Grandpa Ed didn't.

I stopped listening and started to think about Aunt Charlotte and Aunt Mary and all the things that we would do when we went back to Dallas. I tried to wipe the tears falling down my face slowly so that my daddy wouldn't notice and do something worse than yell at me. And all the while he had been yelling, Mama had not said a word.

When we arrived at Daddy's wealthy father, Paul Roberts' house, my brothers, Clyde Jr. and Steven came running out of the long one-story stone ranch house. My little sister, Ruth was trying to run but as she was only three, so she was stumbling over her feet to get to the car.

As we go out of the car, Daddy held up the candy bag.

"Look what Daddy bought y'all! Candy!" then he handed both of the boys a handful and when Ruth came to stand beside him, he gave her a smaller handful.

I stood at his side waiting for my handful, but he only crumpled up the bag and put it in his pocket. I felt left out but I didn't want to gain Daddy's attention. Little Ruth came over to me and held out her arms for a hug. I reached down and squeezed her little body as she was my favorite of my little siblings. Ruth noticed when she pulled back to grab my hand that I didn't have any candy. She held out her bounty of sweets and said, "Huh, huh," while trying to push the candy into my hand.

Mama came around to stand by Ruth.

"No, no, Ruth, Vicky can't have any candy now."

She looked at me meanly, picked up my little sister, and walked toward Grandpa Paul's house. I felt like someone had hit me in the chest, and I wanted to turn and run all the way back to my Aunt Charlotte, Aunt Mary, and my grandparents. I saw Daddy staring at me, and I put my head down and shuffled my way to the house.

As I looked up at the door, I saw my grandmother, Betts, who never let us call her Grandma. It had to always be Betts. She was pale skinned with long auburn red hair like mine. Her eyes were a light brown that sometimes looked gold in the sunlight. And she was covered in freckles. Betts was not as pretty or shapely as my Big Mama Chandra, but she was a handsome woman that knew she was. Many people whispered that Betts was not faithful to Grandpa Paul, but none would ever say that to his face.

Betts doted on her sons though, especially my Daddy. She had sent her daughters away to live with her aunt in California. Her explanation to everyone who asked why she kept her sons and sent her daughters away was said laughingly, "Why I sent them off because there will be only one hen in this nest."

No one quite knew what it meant, but no one who knew Betts wanted to ask her more questions than necessary as she could be a downright mean and nasty. Since she was Grandpa Paul's wife, she was respected and held in awe even if people whispered behind their hands about her.

Betts saw me walking up to the door.

"Well, it's about time that we got to see little Miss High and Mighty. Clyde, however, did you drag her away from those uppity folks across the creek?"

"Well, Mama, I just walked in and gave them what for. Why, they was so scared that they packed Vicky's stuff and had her out of that stankin' house so fast that my head was swimming," Daddy laughed out to Betts.

"That's right! They better respect my son." Betts had a malicious gleam in her light eyes.

"Come on, girl, you and your mangy mama can get to the kitchen to start serving dinner."

I looked up at her when she called Mama a name, but Betts wasn't looking at me. She was looking at Mama with a frown.

As Mama glanced back at the car, Betts looked at Daddy.

"Why does it take your lazy wife so long to move? And why is she looking back at that Chevy?"

"Her ol' Mama gave her a food basket, and I guess she wants to go get it."

Then he turned to Mama with a sly grin.

"Is that right, Tess? Do you want to go get the basket?"

I saw Mama start trembling and she replied haltingly.

"Uh, no, no. I was just checking to see if any of the little ones were at the old well."

Daddy laughed again.

"And what if they were? It wouldn't hurt to lose one or two of the little piggies. Takes more money to feed them than Daddy's livestock."

"Hush now with that, Clyde," said Betts, "you don't want any bad hoodoo on you."

"Hoodoo, Mama, can't touch me because I'm your child," replied Daddy.

"It can touch anyone, boy, never forget that."

Betts looked hard at Daddy.

And with that statement, Betts turned and walked farther into the house. I followed her curious about what hoodoo was, and what it did. The cool interior of the house was a welcome relief to the summer sun but it seemed too cold. I hesitated in the doorway and found that there were lines of salt under each window. There were two large square mirrors on each of the walls that had sprigs of sage hanging at each corner. There were small tables under each mirror that had a black and silver bowl on the top right in the middle. I glanced into the bowl closest to me and found that there was a small mound of salt sitting directly in the center.

When I felt movement behind me, I moved quickly into the large front room of the house. This room felt very dark and cold as if the sunlight that streamed through the windows was afraid to come inside. The divans and chairs were heavy with all of the dark wood and dark dyed cotton pillows. They were placed in an exact square around the stone fireplace. I didn't like the room at all, and I felt as if something was watching me from the dark corners where no light from the windows could reach. I felt stunned as if I couldn't move.

I jumped when I felt the small hand of Ruth placed in mine. I glanced down at her tiny face that was almost blocked by the thumb in her mouth.

"Sced, Vic-kee," she whispered.

Her expression became frightened as she looked in the dark corners.

"It's okay, Ruthie, God won't let nothing hurt us."

I gave her hand a little squeeze that made us both feel better.

Daddy came into the front room with Mama trailing behind him.

"Don't you go filling her head with all that God nonsense, Vicky. You hear me?"

Ruth and I both lowered our heads at his voice.

"Yes, sir," I whispered.

Mama came over to us, looked down at our hands, and yanked Ruth away from me.

"Go help your grandmother," she said pushing me toward the hallway.

I wondered what I had done to make her so angry with me, but I did as I was told and followed the smells of food down the hallway to the kitchen.

As I walked into the kitchen, Betts turned around from the brick oven, and pointed to the counter by the icebox.

"Take that possum out of the pan, and put it on a big plate," she said before turning back to the oven.

I was disgusted that she had cooked a whole possum, but I again did as I was told.

"Betts? Where is the big plate?"

"Oh my! You mean to tell me, that cow, Chandra, didn't teach you how to set a plate? Ugh! Look in that cabinet behind you and take one of the plates from the second shelf. Or do I need to show you what that is too?" she said snidely without turning around.

I turned, followed her directions, and found the shelf with big plates. I placed it on the counter then I grabbed a cheesecloth off of the worktable and went toward the possum pan.

"No you don't use my cheesecloth for that," she yelled, "grab that big fork and use it and your hand to move it."

I dropped the cheesecloth back on the table and picked up the big fork. I went to the counter with the possum and looked down at it. Since it was whole, it looked like skinned cat that had been cooked in a big pan of grease. It didn't smell good either, but I didn't want to get in trouble again. I placed the big fork in the mouth of the possum, put my hand on the rear of it, and lifted the creature. As soon as I lifted the possum, it started to slip.

"Ouch!"

I grabbed the bottom of the creature to keep it from falling, and the hot grease burned my hand.

"Don't you drop that meat," Betts shrieked when she saw me jump at the burning heat.

My hand was hurting and burning, but I refused to drop the possum. I slowly shuffled to the counter with my disgusting burden.

When I was finally able to place the creature on the plate, I let out a painful but relieved breath. I turned to go to the large tub sink to wash the heat and grease from my hands.

"Take your lazy behind outside to wash that off! I don't want none of that stinky grease in my sink."

"There is no need to speak to the child like that, Betts. Calm your common ways."

I froze at the sound of that low voice coming from the now opened back door. I wanted to turn to see who had the nerve to chastise Betts that way, but I already knew.

3

"It's about time that you came to eat. I've been trying to keep everything warm and tasty for you, Paul," stated a somewhat chastened Betts.

"I can see that you have been keeping some things a little too warm. Victoria, as good as it is to see my grandchild, I think we need to get some cool water on your hands."

My Grandpa Paul then walked into the kitchen where I stood frozen, picked me up in his muscular arms, and walked into the bright sunlight of the backyard. He didn't seem to mind that possum grease was getting all over his plaid chambray shirt and denim jeans. He hurried over to the well and tested the water sitting in the bucket.

"Too warm for what I have in mind, Victoria. Let's draw up some cool from underground, okay?"

I just nodded my head as I was still in shock from his sudden appearance.

As he busied himself trying to help me, I took the chance to stare at the man that people say gave me my looks. As he was bending over the well, I saw the blue of his eyes reflected in the water as well as the rich auburn color of his hair and eyelashes. His skin was smooth and white but had a slight golden tint to it from the sun. He was not a tall man but he seemed to be, and he wasn't fat at all. Just moving slightly, I could see all of the muscles in his arms and neck.

Grandpa Paul had poured the water out of the bucket into Betts' vegetable garden, placed the empty bucket on the wench, and lowered the bucket into the well all while I was looking at him. I could do nothing else but stare at his actions, and he didn't seem to mind that I was a little statue beside him.

"Well, let me look at you. Why you look like one of the small calf's after their gas bath, but you are still my beautiful oldest grandchild."

He clicked his tongue when he grabbed my hands and turned them over.

"Those little mitts will need to be rubbed with some herbs and aloe."

Then he leaned close with his blue eyes twinkling and whispered, "After we wash off all the grease, I have some cream that we can use that I got from your Grandpa Ed that he swears will cure anything. Maybe we can use that instead, huh? But we cannot tell anyone that we have it or used it, okay little one?"

Again, I couldn't find my tongue to speak, so I just nodded. Grandpa Paul called out to one of the little Mexican boys pushing a wheelbarrow of corn across the yard.

"Juan, come here, and pull up the well bucket."

The little boy ran over to us and started to crank the bucket up out of the well. I was amazed at how easily he handled the heavy bucket. My shock must have shown on my face as Juan looked at me with a smirk on his dirty little face, gave the bucket to Grandpa Paul, and ran back to pushing his wheelbarrow.

"Okay, Victoria, hold still with your hands open to the sky," commanded Grandpa Paul.

As soon as I was positioned as he said, Grandpa Paul took the bucket and poured the water over my reddened hands.

"Aaahh! Oh, Grandpa, it stings and hurts!"

"I know, I know," Victoria, but we must get the heat out. I can see that your voice matches your beauty. It is a very strong voice. I see that your Grandpa Ed didn't tell me any tales about you."

Grandpa Paul shouted to be heard over my moans and groans.

Then, I heard the backdoor slam and footsteps running toward us.

"What's all that racket, Pa?! Shut that banshee up! Mama said that she had a little burn and whined to you about it. Well, let her go sit in the car while we eat if she gon' make all that noise!"

Daddy came to a stop beside us.

"Clyde, you may go back in the house, sit down, and not say another word for the rest of the time that you are in my house."

"But, Pa, I just, just," stammered Daddy.

"You just what, Clyde? Hmm? You want to explain how your work isn't done on the back twenty, and you left to go pester the Daniels to get Victoria? You want to stand here like a man and yell at a small child for being hurt by Betts' mean ways? No son, I don't think that you do, so turn around and walk yourself back into that house before I give you something to really yell about."

Grandpa Paul blue eyes almost glowing in his anger.

Daddy took one last mean look at me and stomped into the house. I glanced back as Daddy slammed the back door and through my anguished tears, I saw Betts snatch the window curtain closed.

When Grandpa Paul was through washing, cleaning, and bandaging my hands with strips of cloth from a sheet hanging on the wash line, he carried me into the back door to Betts and Daddy standing in the doorway between the kitchen and dining room. Daddy had his arms crossed with a smug look on his face. Betts looked like she was going to spit nails.

"Paul Roberts, did you threaten my son?"

"As you have already heard, Betts, I did."

Grandpa Paul's tone was dry as looked at Daddy.

"Well, don't you do it anymore, especially over a lying child," growled Betts.

"Lying child? What are you talking about, woman? You know what, never you mind. I don't want to know. We will discuss it later. Now, where is my dinner?"

Grandpa turned and changed the subject.

"On the table getting cold since you have been taking your sweet time babying that child outside. And why are her hands wrapped up? It was only hot possum grease, not a burning brand."

"That's what you say, Betts, but I saw and know better. I said that we will talk about this later. I am hungry and ready to eat."

Grandpa Paul put me down and with his hand on my back directed me into the dining room.

"Clyde, go get your mangy wife and brats out of my parlor so that they can eat," said Betts.

"Yes, ma'am," Daddy agreed.

He left through the dining room door where he had been staring at Grandpa Paul and me since we had passed him on the way into the room.

"Sit here by me, Victoria. I want to hear all about this singing and piano playing that you've been doing in Dallas."

I looked up in surprise beause I didn't know that any of my Roberts family knew about my singing or piano.

"Oh, Pa, we don't need to hear about that silly stuff," said Daddy.

He walked back in with Mama and my little brothers.

"Where is Ruth?" asked Grandpa Paul.

"She went to sleep in the front parlor," whispered Mama.

"I tell you what, Missy, if that child pisses on my divan, you will be asking your high and mighty Mama and Daddy for the money to replace it because I am not having any stanky mess in my house."

Betts stared hard at Mama's lowered head.

"Don't worry about it, Mama, I got the Daniels' by a rope," piped Daddy.

He glared at me.

I lowered my head and slid into the chair where Grandpa Paul had told me to sit.

I didn't get much of chance to tell Grandpa Paul about my singing and piano at dinner because Betts and Daddy kept the conversation, and no one else was able to get a word in otherwise. I looked around at the food and hoped that it would be something that I could eat because I knew that I could not eat that possum. I glanced at the naked possum, boiled chicken and potatoes, boiled eggs, creamed corn, turnip greens and cornbread. I thought that no one would notice that I only chose a little boiled chicken, greens and cornbread but that thought was too good to be true.

"So, Vicky, you don't like the food that's on your grandparent's table. I suppose that you think that you're too good to eat good country food."

I froze in place at Daddy's voice, and I lowered my fork without looking at him.

"Well, answer your father, girl," demanded Betts.

"Why don't you like my cooking? I bet you eat everything that ol' Chandra shoves down your gullet. I bet you and your silly mama want that food basket in the car. Well, your daddy's going to throw it away when we get done" she continued turning up her lips.

"Stop it Betts, Clyde. The child is fine eating what she has. She doesn't need the two of you causing her to have a bad stomach," said Grandpa Paul who had remained silent until now.

"Well, I am teaching her about respect, Pa. You know, that stuff that you keep reminding me that I don't have."

"Clyde, I want to see you outside in fifteen minutes ready to work. Maybe then I can think about you teaching your child about respect," said Grandpa Paul quietly.

Daddy paled at Grandpa's tone and sat back in his chair. I glanced at Mama to see what she thought of the whole thing and found her staring at me with hatred on her face. I again felt like someone had hit me, and I didn't understand. Why does my Mama hate me so much but want me to come with them for the rest of the summer? I lowered my head again and tried to finish what I had on my plate to avoid more trouble.

When Grandpa Paul had finished eating, he complimented and thanked Betts, excused himself, and beckoned Daddy outside with a tip of his head toward the door. Daddy noisily scooted his chair back, threw his napkin on his plate, and got up to follow Grandpa Paul.

Grandpa Paul stopped in the doorway and turned."

"Clyde, you may excuse yourself properly and meet me out front by the old well."

Daddy blanched at Grandpa Paul's direction, mumbled his excuses, and followed my grandfather out of the dining room.

"Alright, gal, you may clean the table and wash all of the dishes. We all work on this ranch," Betts spat at Mama.

Mama stood to start gathering dishes.

"Come, Vicky, let's clear the table, and I will wash while you dry."

"Oh no, ma'am, missy, you will not have my son talked to by his Pa. You will do it all while I talk to this dear granddaughter of mine."

Mama hesitated slightly but nodded her head and continued to gather the dishes.

Betts stood up and grabbed my collar.

"Come on, girl, I see you and I need to talk about how it's going to go for you."

As she was pulling my collar, I had no choice but to follow. I glanced back at Mama for help and found her head still down while picking up dishes. My little brothers had been quiet while at the table, but now seeing Betts drag me away, they began chasing each other loudly around Mama.

Betts dragged me down a hallway into the big bedroom in the back that belonged to she and Grandpa Paul. It was a very dark bedroom similar to the front living area of the house. The window curtains and furniture were a very dark almost black color. There seemed to be no light colors or even sunlight in the room. There was something white peeking out from under the bed on what I thought was Grandpa Paul's side of the bed, but I didn't have time to look as Betts dragged me all the way to a door on the rear wall of the bedroom and flung it open. It was a small closet lit on the inside with candles on small shelves in the corners and smelled like burning sage. On the walls of the closet, there were squares, circles, and x symbols marked in white. There was a small table with rocks and lines of salt directly in the middle with a large smooth black rock with a hole in the middle sitting on top. It looked like it was leaking white wax.

As I stood there in Betts' grip, I felt a cold numbing feeling enter my feet and spread until I was frozen in place. Betts quickly pulled her hand back from my arm and stood back. I could feel her whispering behind me, and it seemed as if the whispers began as a buzzing and then a loud roar of voices in my mind.

I was so frightened, but I remembered what the pastor at home in Dallas had said once.

"When you feel yourself being overcome, call on the Lord because He is always with you."

I heard myself choke out the words.

"God, you are my Father, and Jesus is my Lord and Savior. Help me, please!"

All of a sudden, I heard Betts hiss and the numbing feeling left my body. Then, I felt her shut the door loudly, and she jerked my arm behind my back.

"So, you think that you are something, huh, missy? I cowered your mother, and I will do the same to you and your sister. This family is mine, and no one, especially, a little piece of nothing like you is going to change that."

She dropped to her knees and leaned closer, and her breath was hot and smelled like the closet that she had just closed.

"Just because you look like Paul and his folks, don't make you nothing. He's mine, your Daddy's mine, your uncles are mine, and so are your brothers," she said coldly.

I could only stare at her fearfully because her eyes had turned red in her anger. She raised her hand as if to touch my face, but swung it and slapped me so hard that I fell to the hardwood floor. I tasted blood and grabbed at my swelling cheek with my bandaged hand, but Betts climbed on top of me, grabbed both of my hands, and threw her leg over me to keep me still.

"No you don't. Pain is part of this life and you will learn that, girl. My sons are everything to me, and I won't have you or that lazy Mama of yours making them look bad in front of anyone!"

She screamed into my face while squeezing my hands.

"Keep your eyes to the floor and your mouth shut, or you'll get worse than this!"

I felt the tears soaking my hair and the throw rug began to dig into my back from Betts' weight, but I didn't want to cry out because Betts was like a monster. I didn't want to be hurt anymore. She stared hard at me again, and I felt the buzzing in my head again. This time, I didn't say it aloud, but I closed my eyes and called again on my God in my mind. I tried to picture myself back with my aunts in Dallas when all of a sudden, I saw Aunt Mary's face as if she was there with me.

Then, I felt a peace and calm come into my small arms and legs. I opened my eyes to see a surprised look on Betts' face, and then she turned as if someone had touched her or spoken. There was no one behind her, and the door was closed. I waited fearfully and in pain from her grip on my hands and her full weight was settled across my stomach.

Finally, Betts raised herself to her knees then to her feet. She looked down at me shaking on the floor, "Get up and clean yourself with your grandpa's water basin on his side. Then take yourself back to that lazy Mama and get out of my house. I don't know who that was but you are never to come back in here or tell anyone about my special room."

I scrambled to my feet and ran to Grandpa Paul's basin. There wasn't any water, so I pumped some in clumsily with my arm as my hands were beyond painful. The water disappeared and I looked down to see that it was like Big Mama Chandra's bathroom sink. It had a drain. Not stopping to wonder at this being in the bedroom, I found the stopper, filled the basin, splashed water on my face, and turned around to find Betts staring at the corner by her side of the bed.

I hesitated not knowing whether to run out of the room or wait for Betts to say something else to me. I decided to run from the room when Betts leaned her head to the side as if she was listening to someone or something talking in the darkness of the corner. I didn't stop running when I got into the hallway but ran all the way into the kitchen where I heard Mama washing dishes and my little brothers playing.

Mama saw me run into the kitchen, she frowned, and turned all the way around with her mouth open as if to fuss at me for running. Tears were still streaming down my face, and I tried to wipe them and not hurt my throbbing cheek but it wasn't working because it made me cry harder.

"Go out into the backyard and play, boys," she told my brothers.

They had fallen silent when I ran into the kitchen, and now walked to the backdoor before running quickly outside to play. I walked over to Mama and tried to hug her around her waist but she pushed me away while turning back to the sink.

"That's what you get for trying to be better than you are. Your skin color doesn't mean anything here. Better get used to working and being treated like everybody else."

I looked at her in surprise and hurt.

"But, but, Mama..." I stammered.

"Don't you 'but Mama' me, Vicky, I'm not your Mama remember? You been acting like Charlotte and Mary is your "Mama", so let them act like your "Mama" and put up with you."

I turned to run outside to get away from all of the meanness in that house.

"Where are you going? You are not going outside to cry to Mr. Paul. You take those bandages off and finish these dishes while I go get Ruth before she pees herself."

I looked at her again.

"What about my hands? Grandpa Paul said don't take them off until tomorrow."

Mama grabbed my right wrist and snatched the bandage off of it. Some of the skin had blistered and broken so it stuck to the bandage when she pulled it. I bit my lip at the pain and tried not to cry out but as she turned to my left hand to snatch it off, I tucked it behind my back to avoid her reach.

"Give me that hand, Vicky," said Mama harshly.

I trembled in fear where I stood but I could not give her my other hand. Pain was making me crazy. I was becoming dizzy and faint from the pain and the heat of the kitchen.

"VICKY, GIVE ME THAT HAND!"

"What is all the hollering about, Tess?" asked Betts from behind me.

"Don't holler just get a switch and teach her a lesson about disobeying her real mama."

I could only watch as Mama lowered her head.

"Yes, ma'am."

Then she went through the back door leaving me with Betts.

"Well, well, not five minutes from teaching you a lesson, and now, I'm going to make sure that your foul Mama don't mess this one up."

As she spoke, I could hear the evil in her voice like nails on my tutors' chalkboard.

I glanced around when I heard the backdoor slam and saw Mama with a switch from the peach tree that I had seen on the side of the house when Grandpa Paul was fixing up my hands.

"Get on over here, gal, and give Miss Prissy what she needs," Betts demanded.

Mama kept her head down and began to walk toward me. I backed away from her until I felt the wooden worktable behind me.

"Come here, Vicky," growled Mama.

I stayed where I was, and this action angered Mama more, so she stalked forward, grabbed my arm and whipped me around to face the table. I cried out, and it was then that I saw Betts standing across the table looking excited at my pain. I felt the swoosh of air and the sting of the switch across the backs of my legs.

"No, no, raise her dress and give her a good switching, gal. Don't be lazy!"

I tried to cover my clothes with my injured hands, but Mama yanked my dress up and began hitting me with the switch with as much force as she could while Betts egged her on. My cries of pain went unheard, as Mama seemed to be possessed by a monster like Betts had been. All I could do was cry and scream because I couldn't understand what I had done for my Mama to treat me this way.

"What is the meaning of this?"

I heard Grandpa Paul yell with the slamming of the backdoor.

I lay on the kitchen floor in a ball of pain and tears. I looked up as he snatched the switch from Mama and pushed her away from me.

"She needs a lesson, Paul, and you got in her Mama's way. She was being disrespectful, and I know that you don't want that!"

"You hush your mouth, you spiteful old witch!" Grandpa Paul yelled back.

I felt his arms come around me, but the burn of the switch made me cry out more at his touch.

"Look what you have done, Tess! Look at what you have done to your own child! Betts, go get Marcos. He might have something to help her, and if he doesn't, I will send for Chandra."

"I'm not getting no one, and if you value your life, Paul Robert's, you will never mention Chandra Daniels' name in this house again," Betts declared.

Grandpa Paul raised himself to his full height.

"This child has done nothing to deserve your venom, Betts, and you will take yourself to your "room" and pray that she is not scarred from this evil."

His voice broke as if he wanted to cry with me, but he turned and said in anger to Mama and to Daddy who had just walked into the kitchen with Ruth.

"If you were going to mistreat the child, you should have left her where she was. This is my oldest grandchild, and I will not have her hurt because of your spite."

"What?! Pa! I wasn't even here! It's all Tess' fault, isn't it Tess?"

Daddy turned to Mama and gripped her arm. Mama looked down at the switch on the floor.

"Yes, Mr. Paul, it's my fault, this pregnancy is weighing on my mind that's all. I'm sure Vicky will be fine, it was just a little switching."

"THE CHILD IS DAMNED NEAR UNCONSCIOUS!"

"I am taking her to Marcos' myself since no one has moved. I will be there until I know that she is better. Then you can take her home, Clyde, but not after I have had a talk with you and your wife. Betts, I will deal with you later."

Hearing those words, I let my mind go blank from the pain and slipped into the blessed darkness.

I awoke to a burning pain in my hands and back, I knew I was lying on my stomach and when I tried to move, the pain shot through my body like lightning.

"Ow!"

It was all I could whisper as I was very thirsty, and I tried to swallow and started coughing.

"Aqui, mija, quieres agua?"

A mild male accented voice spoke softly to me in the dim light.

Then I felt a strong arm raise me gently and a cup of sweet water was placed to my lips. It felt so good in my dry throat that I wanted to drink it all.

"No, no mucho, es no bien a bebe mucha agua cuando tu eres enferma," whispered the voice.

"I'm sorry, I don't understand you."

"I am sorry, little one, I did not know that you did not speak Spanish as your grandfather and father. Only a little water to drink for you. It is not good to drink too much when you are sick. You have the fever. My name is Marcos, and your grandfather brought you to me because I bring many herbs from Mexico to heal my family when they are hurt or sick," replied Marcos.

"Your grandfather tells me that I am a better healer than your White doctors. On the ranch, they come to see me when they are sick. I take animals and food no mucho money like the White doctor likes to take. When su abuelo, I mean, grandfather, bring you to me, there were much for me to do for you. You need many cuts and the burns on your hands healed. You shed many tears into the dark. I make a special burning to the darkness to give you light while you sleep."

With this statement, he lit and opened the lamp that he was holding. The light was bright against the darkness that we were in before, and I squinted my bandaged hand around my eyes to see. I was lying on a cot in a small room that only held the cot, mirror, washstand, and the chair beside the cot on which Marco was sitting. I tried to get a good look at Marco but he was holding the light. I was starting to feel heavy and sleepy again. I wanted to ask more questions but my eyes wouldn't stay open and my tongue refused to work.

"Esta bien, mija. Sleep. No one bother you here," he said softly.

I drifted back into the familiar darkness.

The next time that I opened my eyes, I saw my Grandpa Paul sitting in the chair reading a book. I didn't feel the same pain that I had felt before or the same burning thirst. I was thirsty though.

"Grandpa?"

"Yes, child, I'm here."

He sat up and put his book down on the floor.

"Can I have some water?"

"Yes, child."

He raised a white polished cup to my lips.

I took a long drink and when I finished, Grandpa Paul covered and placed the cup on the floor near my hand.

"Nothing like good cool well water out of Marcos' special cup, is it?"

He smiled down at me, and I nodded.

"Where am I? Why am I here?"

I asked because I couldn't remember much except pain.

"Well, you're at Marcos' hacienda. Marcos works for me as a kind of doctor and all around helper for all of the ranch hands because most of them speak Spanish and don't trust our doctors. I was lost until I found Marcos looking for work with the Adams' and being turned down because they don't like Mexicans. He came here five years ago, and now, he does everything even picks up your Daddy's slack too. I brought you here to get you away from your grandmother and parents. Unfortunately, I can't let you go back to your aunts and Grandpa Ed and Chandra. I think that having you with them will make Clyde more responsible, and Tess less meek," he explained.

He paused and looked down at the floor.

"I'm sorry, sweetheart, that you got caught in the middle of all that nastiness last week, but I, " he began.

"Last week?" I interrupted him, "I've been here a week, Grandpa? What about Aunt Charlotte? Has she come to visit me, Aunt Mary, or Big Mama Chandra?"

"Quiet now, Victoria, I'm trying to explain, and you need to listen. Besides, you don't want to hurt yourself more."

I immediately hushed at his tone and settled back into the bed.

"Yes, your other folks have been to visit, and I told them that I sent you to see my sister, Alice, before you went back with your Aunt Charlotte. She's wanted to see you anyway so it wasn't too much of a stretch to say it. The reason that I told a fibber was to keep the mess down between your grandmothers. And believe me, Victoria, I have seen and felt what the bad feelings between Betts and Chandra can do. I couldn't just tell them that Betts had tried to break your spirit and hoodoo you or that you own mother tried to blacken your beautiful skin with a switch."

I looked up at my grandfather in surprise.

"Yes, honey, I know about your grandmother and what she does. I also know why Tess is the way that she is with you and why she did what she did. We can't help the way that they are but we have to accept them because they're family. All I can say is that if Marcos were not here, I probably would be hurt, crazy, or cold in the ground with all the mess that goes on here. Now, I don't have much belief in the same religion that you have been raised to believe in, but I respect that there is good and evil. I married Betts for reasons that you will understand when you get older, but she has kept me at her side reminding me of what a man owes his woman…and with that little room of hers."

I started trembling as the memories of what happened came flooding back to me and refused to look at my grandpa for fear that he would tell Betts that I said anything about her room.

Grandpa Paul looked at me then.

"One day, it will all be explained to you, Victoria, and maybe you will be the one to break the line."

I didn't know what he meant, but I felt scared just thinking about it.

4

I awoke suddenly with the feeling that I was being watched. I opened my eyes wider to the sunlight from the tiny window and raised my head to look around the room. My eyes met a pair of small dirty feet on the floor in the doorway, and I lifted my eyes up to the rest of the body to meet the eyes of the little Mexican boy, Juan, that had helped Grandpa Paul with the bucket. He put his finger to his lips and looked over his shoulder.

"I am not like my father; I speak English," he whispered.

I just continued to stare as he moved closer to the cot.

"Do not fear the old bruja. She likes it. This is my room, and my father had to do many things with it so that the darkness did not stay with you."

"The darkness?"

I felt the fear again and remembered the pain from Betts' grip.

"Ugh, estupido! Do you know how to listen?"

I shrank back onto the bed at his sudden change of mood, and when he saw this, he blushed.

"I am sorry, sometimes I forget to finish my words. My father tells me this is not good if I want to be like him and run su abuelo's ranch. I will try again, ok?"

I nodded my head to let him know that I understood, but he didn't notice, as he was looking over his shoulder again. When he turned around, he began again.

"Escucha, por favor, I mean, listen, please. Your grandmother is an old witch who does not like other women around her men. It does not matter if it is su abuelo, father, tios, hermanos, or primos. In English, is your uncles, brothers, or cousins. There is something very bad with her, and my father says that it is the curse of the dark line. That is a very, very bad thing. All the girls around her are sent away or go crazy. That is why no Mexicana works in the big house when su abuelo asks for help. They do not want to be cursed by the old bruja."

While Juan talked, I had been feeling the same cold, numbing fear that I felt while in front of Betts' small closet. I knew now that Betts was very bad, and all I wanted to do was run to the safety of my Aunt Charlotte.

Soon after Juan left, I looked around the room again as the shadows from the window began to spread into the room. I did not know that it was getting closer to night, and I began to tremble in my fear. I closed my eyes, but I could not make it go away.

"Do not be afraid here, mija," came Marcos' gentle voice.

I opened my eyes to see that he had lit the lamp and was carrying a tray with delicious smells. My stomach let out a small growl that startled us both in the silence that followed Marcos' entrance.

"Heh, heh, tienes hambre, si?"

He laughed.

I hoped that he was asking me was I hungry, so I nodded yes. He came forward into the room and placed the tray and lamp on the floor by the cot.

"Permiteme," he said while helping me to sit up against the wall.

After he had me settled, he picked up the tray and put it on my lap. There was roasted meat, beans, rice with tomatoes and onions, and something white that looked to be rolled up. It all looked and smelled so good that I wanted to attack it right away.

"I will check you hand so that you can eat, si? You don't look like I need help you today. You will not eat sopa and cold water like when you enferma and in the heat of darkness."

Marcos held out his hand towards my bandaged right hand.

I suddenly remembered my mama asking for my hand, and I lowered my head as tears came to my eyes.

"No, no, llore," Marcos crooned.

He gently took my small hand in his and gently unwrapped the bandage.

"Mida."

He showed me that my hand was healed with a small scar in the middle. Surprise must have shown on my face because he chuckled.

"You will have no scars when I am done, mija. Ahorita, how does it feel?"

"It's okay, sir", I whispered in awe as I flexed my hand.

I wanted to hug him, but I didn't want to spill all of that good food.

"Eat, now, before la comida is frio", si?"

He handed me a fork and placed a cloth on my chest. I bowed my head to pray, and Marcos stayed silent while I blessed my food.

"This very good that you talk to Dios, you need Him," he whispered as I finished.

I didn't know if he wanted to say something else as he had paused, but he just continued to look at me expectantly.

I decided then that food was more important than talking, so I turned my eyes back to the plate and was about to taste the meat.

"Do you like tortillas?"

"Tortillas, sir?" I asked.

He nodded his head to the white rolled up things.

"I don't know what they are, sir."

He took the roll and unrolled three white rounds.

"These are tortillas, and they like the biscuits that you eat with your food. It is what Mexicans eat with food sola we eat for the morning, day, and night. Is made with corn or flour. This corn. Eat."

He handed me a tortilla.

I took a small bite and found the taste different from biscuits or cornbread but it was still good.

"Let me show you how to eat it," Marcos offered.

He took some of the meat and rolled it up in the tortilla then handed it to me. I bit into it and closed my eyes at the tasty flavor.

"Bueno, si?" he asked.

"Bueno."

I nodded and smiled.

"Bien, Bien, I tell su abuelo that you learn quickly. Ahorita, you eat and I watch you eat, si?"

I barely heard him as I was already enjoying the food too much.

The food was very good and very welcome even though I had not known that I was that hungry. It was then that I realized as I ate my last filled tortilla that I had not thought once of what awaited me with my parents since I was better.

While I ate, I cast glances at Marcos to see what he looked like. His skin was just a shade darker than mine while his eyes and hair were a dark brown. He looked like one of the movie stars that my Aunt Mary had shown me in one of her magazines. He was handsome like my daddy, and there was something about him that made me keep staring at him. I felt like I had seen him before, but I knew that I had not. He caught me looking and smiled. I blushed and turned my attention back to my plate.

When the last bite was swallowed, Marcos took the plate and gave me some cool sweet water. Humming, he patted me on the head and left the room. I was thankful that he had placed the lamp on the chair beside my cot before he left. The light was very comforting, and I think that he knew that I needed it after everything that had happened. I fell asleep with the prayer to God and my Savior Jesus that the light would follow me into my dreams.

The sound of booted feet coming into the house woke me the next morning. They were very loud and heavy. My heart started racing because only one person that I knew walked like that. I had been hearing that walk since my aunts had been bringing me to the country for the summers. My Grandpa Ed! I raised myself up on my elbows and waited until his large frame filled the door.

"Grandpa Ed!"

I cried out and tears filled both of our eyes.

"Well little one, I can't let you go anywhere, can I?"

He came across the room and grabbed me in a big hug.

"Oh, Grandpa Ed, I don't want to go anywhere. Please, can I come home now? I promise that I'll be good for Aunt Charlotte and Aunt Mary. I'll help Miss Sadie in the house and everything. Just please don't make me go back with Mama and Daddy!"

I hiccupped into his shirt.

"Now, now, we have plenty of time to talk about all that. Let me look at you."

He pulled away to look me over.

He turned my head from side to side then he took my hands in his and turned them over to look at the tiny scars in my palms. It was when he drew back the covers that I saw his lips tighten, but he looked back into my face and gave me a small smile.

"I think that you'll be just right as rain after some of your Big Mama Chandra's biscuits. What do you think about that?"

"I would like some very much please."

I grinned from ear to ear because I just knew that this meant I could go back with him.

"I think that I'm going to let Marcos give you some of his good vittles first while I talk with your Grandpa Paul and your father. Then, we will get in the Oldsmobile and get you back with your Big Mama Chandra and aunts, okay?"

He nodded his head and got up to move toward the door.

I wasn't able to say a thing because just the mention that my Daddy was around made me want to shiver and cry for Grandpa Ed not to leave me. Grandpa Ed almost ran into Marcos with the food tray in his hurry to get to his talk with Grandpa Paul and Daddy.

"Whoa, senor, su nieta necesita comida, si? She need food to heal. Do not hurry, por favor, it be okay. I take good care of Miss Bictoria, okay?"

Marcos wiggled his eyebrows at me as he came towards the cot.

Even in my distress, I couldn't help but giggle. With his accent, the V in my name had turned to a B. My Grandpa Ed looked back at me with a small smile when he heard me giggle.

"Yes, Marcos, I owe you much, my friend, for taking care of Miss 'Bictoria'."

Grandpa Ed laughed then turned and left with the same booted footstep that had woken me.

"Mida, look what we have for desayuno, this word is breakfast in English. Say it."

He made the request while placing the tray on the floor.

"De-si-un-o," I said slowly.

Marcos laughed.

"It is okay but we try again later, okay?"

I nodded my head and looked toward the cloth-covered tray. The smells were making me really hungry.

"Now, you will need to limpia tus manos, eh, wash your hands, with this cloth and then you can eat. Would you like to go make water first?"

I shook my head, but I nodded toward the pee pot in the corner.

He chuckled.

"This okay, but now that you feeling better, you need go to the water room, si?"

I nodded again to let him know that I would and hoped that we could get back to the food. Talking about going to the bathroom was embarrassing.

"Here is wet cloth with jabon, uh um, soap."

He handed me the cloth.

I took it and rubbed my hands as clean as I could with the damp side and dried them with the dry corner.

After I was done, I handed the cloth back to Marcos who set it aside and handed me the tray. He whipped off the cloth and handed me a fork. I looked down at all of the food, and my mouth started to water. There were eggs scrambled with some kind of red squishy meat, smothered potatoes, tortillas, and my favorite, sliced cantaloupe! I looked up in surprise at seeing this, and Marcos just smiled.

"Su abuelo Paul knows more about you than tu piensas, si?"

I didn't know what to say to this, so I just nodded my head, picked up my fork, and went to town on that plate.

Marcos shook his head and smiled.

"You like mi hijo, Juan. He like comida too. It help you grow big and strong."

I heard that much in between swallows.

"Thank you for the food, sir, it is very good."

These were all the words I spared because I didn't want that good eating to get cold. Marcos just shook his head again and opened the small window to let in a little morning breeze before he sat in the chair beside me.

"I don't care what you want, Ed, Victoria is my daughter, and when she gets better, she's going home with me and Tess," came my Daddy's voice through the open window.

The food that I had been eating turned to rocks in my stomach, and the food in my mouth to ashes. I froze in place and heard a rushing in my ears.

"Ay Dios Mio!"

I heard Marcos say from a distance as I fell back onto the bed into the darkness.

When I awoke later, I heard angry whispers in the room with me. I barely raised my eyelids so that I could see who was there. Grandpa Ed was standing in the door as if he was trying to keep someone from coming inside the room.

"No, you and my daughter will not make the child suffer anymore. You had her less than one day and look what happened," he whispered in a stern tone.

"You have no idea what that brat did to her mother and mine," I heard my Daddy say.

"It couldn't have been something that deserved a switching like that on her legs. Chandra and I never whipped our children like that and neither will they do that to their own. Tess knows better even if you don't, Clyde," Grandpa Ed said angrily.

"Now wait a minute...," began Daddy.

"No, I won't wait another minute. She is seven years old, Clyde, still almost a baby. How could you let this happen?" asked Grandpa Ed.

"He wasn't there, Ed, that's what I've been explaining. Clyde was with me when Betts and Tess did their deeds. There is no need to take the child back to Charlotte yet. Marcos said that she is almost good as new, and I think that Clyde will take a stronger hand with his house, right Clyde?" said Grandpa Paul.

"Well, I'm her father, and I say that she can't go anywhere except home with me and Tess when she gets well. Go on back to the other side of the creek, Ed. We don't need you here," Daddy stepping up to Grandpa Ed.

I saw Grandpa Ed turn to check to see if I was awake, so I hurried and shut my eyes. He turned back satisfied that I was still sleeping.

"Look, Clyde," Grandpa Ed growled out, "I'm not going to disrespect your father by beating the snot out of you in front of him, but I'm going to let you know what respect is."

Then I saw Grandpa Ed reach out and grab Daddy by the throat, raise him from the floor, and shake him. Daddy couldn't do much while in Grandpa Ed's grip except pull and scratch at the hands around his throat.

"Alright, Ed, that's enough. Grandpa Paul put his hand on Grandpa Ed's arm.

Grandpa Ed dropped Daddy on the floor and stood over him.

"Next time, boy, watch what you say to a grown man."

I could see that Daddy's face was red and he was coughing and breathing hard to catch his breath.

"Get up, Clyde, and apologize to Ed," Grandpa Paul demanded with a frown at Daddy.

Daddy stood up and didn't say another word. He turned around and left.

"You should have done that to that boy when he started talking back, Paul."

Grandpa Paul chuckled.

"Now, how am I going to do that when Betts is around waiting on me to slip up?"

"You need to do it to her too," laughed Grandpa Ed.

Then he turned to check on me again.

Satisfied that I still slept, he twisted back to Grandpa Paul.

"C'mon, Paul, I think Marcos said that he made some fresh tortillas this morning. If I can't take Victoria home, I might as well eat something now because Chandra's not going to let me rest when I come back empty handed."

"Hot tortillas sound good to me, Ed. Chandra will be okay when she sees Victoria is just fine spending the rest of her time with her Mama and Daddy."

I didn't get to hear Grandpa Ed's answer as they were walking away. As I heard their footsteps fade to silence, I closed my eyes again to rest and think about what had just happened. My throat felt locked up as I tried to swallow the tears of disappointment at not going home with Grandpa Ed.

"Hello, muchacha."

I opened my eyes to see Juan's face above mine. I shrank back into the bed at his closeness.

"Do not speak because mi papa say not to bother you, pero, I wanted you to know. I heard sus abuelos talking outside, and the tall one says that he is to take you home soon. I think that this is good because mi papa is afraid of what the bruja will do if she comes here."

I didn't know what to say so I just nodded.

"Mi papa has talked to su abuelo Paul and told him to let you go with su otra abuelo for now," he whispered.

I frowned because I didn't know what the Mexican words meant. Juan saw my frown and rolled is eyes.

"Ugh! My father asked su abuelo Paul to let you go with you other abuelo."

My heart started to thump in excitement at the thought of going back with Grandpa Ed.

"What, what, did, did Grandpa Paul say?" I stuttered.

"He say that he will think about it. I have to go now before mi papa finds me. Adios," he said then ran out of the room.

I sat thinking about what Juan had told me and hoped that Grandpa Ed and Marcos could talk Grandpa Paul and Daddy into letting me go back to my aunts soon.

Later that afternoon, after Marcos had fed me some more good food, I felt stifled in the small room and wanted to get out of bed. I swung my legs over the bed to get up and felt a tightness in them that made me wince and glance down. I quietly gasped at all of the fading marks from the switch. Both of my legs were covered. I knew then why Grandpa Ed had been so angry this morning. I reached down to rub at one very long mark and my hand came away with something sticky.

"Is jugo made with cactus and aloe vera, mija."

I looked up startled to find that he had come into the room, and I hadn't heard him.

Marcos laughed at my expression.

"Is okay. I came to see if you want go outside for awhile."

I smiled.

"Yes, sir!"

Marcos laughed again and came over to the cot with my shirtwaist dress across his arm.

"You need ropas first."

He handed me the dress. I looked down at it and saw where it had several stitched places at the bottom in the front and all over the back.

"Lo siento, I am no good with needle and thread, pero, no holes, no?"

Marcos walked from the room, and turned at the door.

"There was dinero in pocket, and I leave it for you. Do not let su papa see it, si?"

Somehow, I knew what dinero was. I nodded and felt for the pocket Grandpa Ed had placed the money. It was comforting to know that it was still there. After Marcos had left the room, I took it out to count it. There were two five-dollar bills!

"Oh my," I murmured in awe feeling rich.

I smiled to myself because I already knew what I was going to do with the money. I hurried and pulled on my dress before Marcos came back to get me.

I was nearly bouncing in my excitement to go outside when Marcos came back to fetch me. He took me by the hand and led me out of the room into a large living area that had a large round table with six chairs off to the side in a smaller section. There were two doors on the right and one door on the left. I glanced into the door to the left and saw a basin and toilet like Big Mama Chandra's and Grandpa Ed's. One of the doors to the right was closed, and the other door looked like it led to the kitchen. The colors of the divan and chairs placed around the fireplace were shades of white, red, orange, and green. There were plants and herbs all along the back wall by the table. I could smell some of the same plants and herbs that Big Mama Chandra had in her greenhouse. I liked Marcos' house as much as I liked his food I thought smiling as he led me on the whitewashed porch and sat me in a large swing with red and orange cushions.

"There, now you sit and I clean mi casa, si?"

I smiled and nodded then turned my attention to his yard as he turned to go back into the house. The sun was shining and it made me so happy to be out of bed. I lifted my head up to enjoy the sunshine and a gentle breeze blew across my face. I giggled and lifted my hand into the moving air. I wanted to run with the breeze and chase it into the trees but I didn't want to upset Marcos, so I stayed put to just enjoy my time outside.

I must have drifted off because the sun had moved behind the house when I awoke. I was lying down on the swing, and I could hear Marcos moving around in the house. I knew he was cooking because I could smell supper, and it smelled good. I took the time to look around the yard and saw that it was just as neat and clean as the inside of Marcos' house. It had a large chicken wire fenced garden on the right and gravel driveway on the left. The entire yard was fenced with crooked crepe myrtle limbs. The gate looked like a bunch of the crepe myrtle limbs twisted into the square. It looked very strange to see a yard fenced that way but it still looked nice and neat.

I glanced over my shoulder then slid off the swing to walk out into the yard. I could see other smaller houses in the distance down the lane the closer I got to the fence. Marcos' house was at the end of the lane. There was a large circle of space in front of the fence where Marcos had a tractor, field wagon, and old Ford truck parked.

I walked over to the garden and looked around in it. There were tomatoes, okra, carrots, cucumbers, corn, watermelon, and cantaloupe. It looked like Aunt Charlotte's garden in Dallas. I could see smaller green tomatoes and some other small pointy green plants. I was curious because they looked like the banana peppers that Grandpa Ed liked with his supper. I leaned over the tomato plants and picked one of the small green vegetables. It was smooth and dark green. I thought that it might be some kind of cucumber, and I liked cucumbers a lot. I took a small bite, and found that it had seeds and a spicy peppery taste. The more I chewed, the spicier it became in my mouth.

Soon, I felt the burning in my mouth and throat. Water! I looked around for the water pump or well and found none. I ran around the side of the house where the driveway was and ran smack into Juan.

"Ow, cuidate!"

I tried to say that I was sorry but my tongue was stuck to the roof of my mouth burning.

"What is the matter with you? Why are you sweating? Does mi papa know that you are outside?"

I didn't wait to answer his questions, I got up and took off again to find water. I felt like all I had to do was open my mouth and I would breath out fire.

"Wait, muchacha, donde vas?"

Juan asked grabbing my arm trying to stop me.

I yanked loose and ran around the house and straight into a field of cotton. I looked around helplessly because there was no yard, only endless rows of cotton. Juan had caught up to me by then.

"What is it?" he asked breathlessly.

I held up the half-eaten green thing and he laughed.

"Ah, that is mi papa's new jalapeno pepper. He mixes them to make them caliente, er, hot. Come."

He grabbed my hand, ran around the house behind the garden, and showed me that the water pump was hidden there. He took his lunch bucket, rinsed it, and filled it for me to use. I dropped the jalapeno and grabbed up some of the cool water to splash onto my lips and mouth. The burning was still there, so I took the bucket, drank some water, then splashed the rest on my face.

"Que pasas, hijos?!What is it?"

I heard Marcos' exclamation.

"Papa, ella comiste un jalapeno," said Juan in Spanish.

"Well, Miss Bictoria, was it good?"

Marcos asked with a twinkle in his eye.

I swallowed and grinned at him.

"Yes, sir!"

We all laughed.

"Let us pick some for supper, okay, we have mucha gente tonight," Marcos said.

"Quien, papa, eh, who papa?"

"Senor Paul, his son, and wife will be coming," returned Marcos looking directly at me.

I froze at the thought that my Daddy and Mama would be coming to eat with us. It could only mean that Grandpa Ed couldn't talk Grandpa Paul into letting me go back with him. I knew that I couldn't stay at Marcos' forever, but it was like being safe until the storm passes. I didn't want to go back with Daddy and Mama, and I felt like the jalapeno was burning in the pit of my stomach again. I looked up at Marcos, and he winked at me.

"All be well, mija, espera, eh, wait, si?"

I nodded.

"Vamanos to get jalapenos," said Juan already on his way around the chicken wire to pick some jalapenos.

Marcos took my hand and we followed. I thought to myself as we began to pick the jalapenos that at least Betts wasn't coming.

My parents and Grandpa Paul came to the house shortly after Marcos rushed us all into the house to wash up for supper. Grandpa Paul came into the house giving me a big hug and asking if I had been a good girl. I hugged him back and nodded. I drew back and looked over his shoulder at Mama and Daddy. Mama was looking at me with a frown, and Daddy was looking at Juan and Marcos with his eyes squinted. I let go of Grandpa Paul to move so that I could see Marcos and Juan's faces. Marcos had a small smile on his face, and when he saw me looking toward him, he winked. I smiled at him and immediately felt a little better. I saw that Juan wasn't paying attention to anyone. His attention was on the delicious looking food on the table.

"Bienvendos, welcome, a mi casa, por favor tome asiento..." Marcos began.

"Marcos, speak in English, you know I don't like that Spanish mess," snapped Daddy.

"Clyde, this is Marcos' house, and you will respect that, you hear me," warned Grandpa Paul.

"Fine," Daddy snarled.

Marcos moved to the table and pointed to a chair.

"Sit here, Miss Bictoria."

I sat down, then he sat on my right and Juan on my left. I could see that my chair was smaller and had extra cushions that allowed me to be higher. My parents sat across from me with Mama next to Daddy and Grandpa Paul sat next to Marcos.

"Would you like ask Dios for His blessing, Senor Paul?"

"You can do it, Marcos. I don't think He would appreciate a blessing from me."

"I can do it, sir," I whispered.

Everyone, especially my parents, looked surprised. Marcos grinned.

"Pór favor, Miss Bictoria."

I bowed my head and prayed.

"God, please be with us, please bless this good food and the hands that made it. In Jesus' name, Amen."

"That was a mighty fine prayer, honey."

Grandpa Paul smiled at me.

I brightened at his praise.

"Well, I thought it was too short and could be better," spat Mama.

"Señora, la niña is only chiquíta, small, peró, she speaks to Díos well."

Marcos spoke with steel in his tone.

Mama's lips tightened, and she glared at Marcos.

"I'm hungry, can we eat?" asked Juan.

Grandpa Paul laughed.

"Yes, Juan, let's eat this food is making my stomach talk to me."

I couldn't wait to sink my teeth into the food. I could see roasted chicken, some other roasted meat, beans, rice with tomatoes and onions, and tortillas. There was also some kind of soup with green leaves floating in it. Marcos gave me a big bowl of the soup then squeezed lime into it. I picked up the spoon and tasted it. It was chicken broth and it was delicious. Marcos filled my plate with a little of everything while Juan filled his own plate.

Glancing around the table, I saw that Mama and Daddy had chosen the chicken, rice, and beans. Grandpa Paul had taken a bowl of the soup from Marcos and placed some chicken and rice in it. He reached for the tortillas.

"Marcos, I would swear that you have a woman hid in this house somewhere cooking all these tasty vittles."

Marcos chuckled.

"Nó, señor, mí mama teach me to cook because she say do not wait on a woman to fill your stomach."

"That's crazy. That's what women are for to cook, clean, and take care of a man's needs," snickered Daddy.

Silence greeted his statement. I lowered my head to my plate while I saw that Juan did the same.

Grandpa Paul cleared his throat.

"Fill your mouth with food, Clyde, so that we can enjoy ours in peace."

Daddy turned red and stuffed a big piece of chicken in his mouth and started to chew loudly with his mouth open. Mama turned back to her plate with a look of disgust at Daddy then she glanced back at him fearfully. I tried to keep eating but the tension in the air was making me sick. I started to breath heavily as my heart started racing. Marcos laid his hand on my knee under the table and patted it. I calmed a little bit but started to pick at my plate.

"You got all that food, now you're going to eat it all," snapped Mama.

"Señora Tess, is my fault. I put mucho on la plata for her. I will put it away for her breakfast, nó?"

Marco voice became even quieter.

"No, she needs to eat it now before it gets cold.

Her eyes were glinting with anger in the light from the lamps. I started to tremble and then the unthinkable happened, I wet myself. I could feel it going into the pretty cushion that I was sitting and onto the floor. My head fell in shame and tears began to fall.

"What the...?" asked Juan when he felt the wetness bounce onto his bare feet.

"I think Miss Bictoria is tired and needs her rest."

Marcos raised his voice to cover Juan's outburst.

I felt him quickly pull my chair back, pick me up, and take me to Juan's room.

"Oh míja, it be okay, do not be afraid."

Marcos reached for a dry cloth on the hook behind the door.

"Míra, I bring some warm water and soap for bath, si? No llorè, míja, cloth can clean," he paused, "su mama, well, her soul can be cleaned too because is very dark now. I think about this, and I talk to sú abúelo tambíen."

He left the room, and before he shut the door,

I heard Daddy voice.

"See, that's why she needs to be home with us. We ain't gonna treat her like she's a crippled over a few little scrapes."

My tears fell harder as I felt so alone in my misery. Why did my Mama and Daddy hate me so much? I couldn't understand it. Why? What did I do wrong? I fell onto my knees then and prayed to God to help me and send me back to my aunts and grandparents very soon.

5

I was surprised the next morning when Marcos came into the room, brought me a pair of Juan's clothes and told me that I could go play with Juan until dinner.

"He does not have to work at la cása grandè for sú abuèlo today," was all he said before handing me the clothes.

I got up and washed my face with the water from the pitcher then dressed in the denim dungarees and white tee shirt. I smoothed my hair back with a little water. I grabbed the two five dollar bills and shoved them into the back pocket. I walked into the front living area to find Juan already at the table.

"Búenos días, muchacha."

Juan's hands and mouth were full of stuffed tortilla.

"Good Morning."

I smiled at him then sat at the table. Marcos brought me a plate of beans and eggs scrambled with the red squishy meat.

Curious, I poked at the red squishy stuff.

"What is this?"

"Chorizo," said Juan and Marcos at the same time.

"What is chorizo?"

"Chorizo is stewed Mexican meat. You like sausage, sí?"

I nodded.

"Well, Mexicans like it jùntos con juévos, um eggs."

"I like it."

I took a big bite.

Marcos and Juan laughed then Marcos went back into the kitchen.

"Andale, I want to go look at the fields."

Juan pointed at my plate.

I thought he meant to hurry, so I started to stuff the food in my mouth. I took a big drink of the milk in the cup Marcos had sat out and started choking. Juan laughed and patted my back until I stopped.

"Okay, okay, hurry but do not kill yourself."

He chuckled.

I grinned back and noticed that Juan looked a lot like his father.

We finished eating, and Marcos came back with two small lunch buckets.

"Cùidaté, híjos, and regresârle aquí a la una, sí, Juan?"

Marcos handed us each a bucket.

"Sí, papa."

Marcos looked over at me and smiled.

"Míja, come back if you tired, okay?"

I smiled and nodded, itching to get outside.

"Vamanos!"

Juan yelled and ran through the door.

I followed and we ran around to the back of the house. Juan grabbed my hand when we came to the cotton field and showed me the trail that he had made through the plants. I walked carefully because I didn't want to get a sticker burr in my bare feet. Juan began pulling me as I had slowed down a little.

"Muchácha, we need to get to the other side of the field. Andalè!".

"I'm trying!"

I picked up my pace and soon we were out of the field and facing a large open meadow with a water tank and endless colors of wild flowers. I stopped and gently pulled loose from Juan's grip.

"It's so pretty. Is it my abúelo's?"

"Ah! You start to comprendé español! This is good. And yes, it is part of sú abúelo's land."

Juan smirked.

"Thank you, I didn't know."

I laughed when he rolled my eyes.

"It is good. Come, we can look around then eat by the water."

Juan nodded toward the field. I turned back to the meadow and saw that it was almost surrounded by large trees as if someone had planted them there. The area by the tank was covered in flowers with a few bushes on the right side and looked as if someone had cleared a part of it on the left. I felt the warmth of the sun on my head and raised my face to it. It felt so good.

We walked forward into the field, and I could still feel the coolness of the dew sticking to the wild flowers. I tried to be careful not to step on them because the whole place was so beautiful. Not Juan. He trampled on the flowers as if he were trying to stomp out a bug. I giggled and he looked back at me.

"What's funny?"

"You look like you're trying to stomp a bug."

I laughed aloud.

"Uh huh."

He looked sneaky like he was thinking something over in his mind. All of a sudden, he whipped around, dropped his bucket, and with a glint in his eye.

"Catch me if you can!"

And laughing, he took off across the field with his bare feet flying. I dropped my bucket and began to chase him. We ran all around the tank and across the field before I finally caught him.

As we stopped to catch our breath, Juan looked concerned.

"Are you okay?"

"Yes," I huffed.

"Good. I'm it!"

I took off running and laughing, he began to chase me. We had so much fun that morning that I didn't think once about what happened the night before or what would happen next. I just enjoyed playing and having fun. It was a time of being a child. Little did I know that it was about to end.

When Juan and I ran back around Marcos house after our playtime talking and laughing about our time, we came to a dead stop in front of my Daddy's big Chevy in the driveway. I immediately looked to the driver's side to see if he was there. It was empty. I looked toward the front porch to see if he was there, and it was empty except for the swing swaying in the breeze. My feet felt heavy. I didn't want to move when Juan looked back at me, grabbed my hand, and tried to pull me towards the door.

"Come. He has come for you."

Juan's voice reflected my sadness.

I began to shake my head and pull away from Juan's grip. I wanted to run away into the cotton and never come back, but I knew that I couldn't. It hurt to let Juan see my fear of my father, so I stopped pulling and let him guide me into the house. We walked into the house slowly letting our eyes adjust to the dimness of the inside of the house.

"It's about time you came back," Daddy sniped.

I looked toward the eating table and he and Mama were sitting eating dinner with Marcos.

"Senor Clyde, I told you that the children went to play behind the cotton and that they would return for their meal."

Marcos moved closer to us.

"It doesn't matter now. Tess and I are through with everyone taking their sweet time giving us our child. We are taking her home today. Right now."

Daddy's voice turned mean as he rose from the table.

I looked at how his face was so handsome and so ugly at the same time and felt the now familiar fear growing inside me.

"Senor Clyde, the children have not eaten. Permíteme, make food for la niña."

Marcos had smoothly given Daddy an order. Daddy was so caught up in the food on the table that he didn't even notice.

"I thought you said that they had eaten at the tank. That should be enough for now. We need to go because I need to get back to town. Tess and I have plans."

Daddy had a strange smile on his face.

"Está bíen, I put something in the bucket por la tardé, sí?"

Marcos persisted until Daddy shrugged his shoulders.

"Fine, be quick."

Marcos grabbed my hand and led me to the kitchen. I saw him beckon to Juan to follow us. I was shaking and didn't care where we went as long as it was away from Daddy and Mama.

"Escuchamé, Miss Bictoria, I have many things to tell you. I have some cream in this jar for your legs. Use it morning and night. Here, is múchas tortíllas. If you hungry, eat them. I do not know what is in sú pápa's head but is not good. I do not know where sú abueló is today, so I cannot keep you from him," Marcos said hurriedly.

Tears had begun to slide down my cheeks at the thought of leaving. I felt so alone even though Marcos and Juan were with me in the kitchen.

"Hurry up in there!"

Daddy's voice showed his impatience.

Marcos saw my tears and hugged me to him.

"No llore, no llore, it be fine soon. You strong, Miss Bictoria, remember this," he whispered.

I nodded unable to speak around my tears. Juan handed me a wet cloth.

"You must not let him see you cry. He is like la brúja and likes to see pain."

He watched while I wiped my face and tried to stop the tears.

"We are coming, Senor!"

I took a deep breath and was finally able to stop my tears. I wiped my face one last time with the cloth, gave it back to Juan, and turned to go when I remembered what I wanted to do with the money in my pocket.

"Mr. Marcos, I would like for you to have this for taking care of me."

I pulled out the fives.

Marcos looked down at the money in my hand in surprise and started shaking his head.

"No, no, this for you. You need it," he said firmly.

I shook my head and pushed the bills into his hand.

"Daddy or Mama will find it and take it. I want you to have it for you and Juan. You have been so nice to me, and I don't have anything to give you for taking care of me. I don't know what's going to happen to me, but I want you to have this please."

I had started to cry again. Marcos looked at me with tears in his eyes, took the money, and then crushed it in his fist. I drew back thinking he was angry with me, and when he saw this, he hugged me again.

"I will keep this for you, Miss Bictoria, and when all está bíen, come back and it be here, sí?"

He patted me on the back while he whispered in her hair.

Juan handed me the cloth to wipe my face again. I looked at him, and he had tears in his eyes too. He nodded at the cloth. I used it again and gave it back for good. Marcos handed me the bucket, which was a lot heavier than it had been with the few tortillas and pieces of homemade cheese that we had eaten at the tank. I thanked them again, straightened my back, and walked slowly into living room.

I saw Mama glance at me with the same strange smile on her face that Daddy had on his and became more afraid.

"It's about time. Look here, Marcos, we'll return these here Mexican duds when we get to the house. You need some other clothes, girl, you look just like one of them wetbacks."

Daddy laughed maliciously while looking straight at Marcos.

I didn't know what a wetback was, but from the tone of Daddy's voice, I knew that it was mean. My heart sank at the hurt his words might have caused Marcos. I looked back to see if it had, but Marcos and Juan's faces were in the shadows of the afternoon. Daddy grabbed my arm in a painful grip, but I didn't wince or say a word. He looked down at me in surprise that I had made no expression or cried out loud. I stared straight ahead waiting for him to pull me out of the house. His face tightened and so did his grip at my silence.

As we were leaving the house, I looked back and saw Marcos and Juan move to the door. Daddy pulled me across the yard, opened the back door of his Chevy, and pushed me into the car. I put my face to the window to see Marcos and Juan as Daddy started to back the car out of Marcos' driveway. They both smiled and waved at me, and I waved back and settled in the backseat before Daddy yelled at me again for waving.

Daddy drove all the way down the lane away from Marcos' house then turned down another dirt road that led to Grandpa Paul and Betts' house. My heart started thumping at the thought of going back to that house.

"We should stop by Mama's and let her see Vicky."

Daddy wickedly glanced into the backseat at me.

"Won't Mr. Paul be mad?"

Mama glanced at Daddy when she spoke.

Daddy frowned at Mama and leaned across and slapped her.

"I wasn't talking to you."

"I'm sorry, Clyde."

Mama's voice trembled and held her cheek.

"I was thinking out loud to myself. Are you too stupid to know the difference?"

Mama shook her head then lowered it.

"Mama can handle Pa, but we need to start on our plans."

Daddy glanced back at me again with an evil grin at me.

I shrank back into the seat afraid of what that meant.

We passed by my grandparents' house and kept down the same lane to a small unkempt house with my siblings outside running around in the dirt.

When Daddy drove the car into the yard, I could see a small dried up garden and chicken coop on the right side and an open space with nothing but small dirt piles on the left. My siblings crowded around Mama when we got out of the car. Daddy threw a nasty look at Mama.

"Control those brats and get into the house. Make sure you grab Vicky."

He dismissed us while walking into the house.

"Come on, Vicky, we have a surprise for you."

Mama bit out her words in a cruel voice while she followed Daddy into the house.

I liked surprises but I just knew that I wasn't going to like this one. I got out of the car and hugged my little sister, Ruth as Mama had left her and my brothers in the yard and followed Daddy in the house. I looked around to see if there was anybody to watch them, but no one was around. I realized then that Mama had left my small siblings alone to come get me. I felt bad for them, but I knew that I shouldn't take my time going inside the house. I didn't want another switching.

I walked across the yard and through the open door to find Mama and Daddy sitting at a dining table placed in the corner of a small living area with only a sofa against the inside wall. There was a doorway to the left to what looked like a kitchen and a doorway on the other side of the dining table. The walls were wood paneling, and the furniture was brown too. The whole room looked dark and dirty. The sunlight from the open door gave the only light to the room, and I could see Mama and Daddy were waiting anxiously for me to sit down.

"Come here, Vicky, we have to talk to you."

Daddy smiling. I walked over to the table and slid into a chair.

"Yes, sir?"

"It seems that because of what happened with Betts and your mother, Grandpa Paul doesn't want me around to work just now. He thinks that if I can't handle my house, I can't handle a ranch. I think that he's been listening to Marcos tell lies on me. The workers don't like me because I make them work. That's okay though, because I have a plan, heh, heh," he paused and chuckled to himself.

"So! I can't work, I can't eat, and neither can your Mama, brothers, or sister. What should we do about this Vicky?"

I didn't know if I should answer, so I just sat and waited. Daddy's face fell as if he were disappointed that I didn't reply.

"Oh, well, since you don't know, I'm going to tell you. I found you a job, Vicky! Yes, I know, I know, you are happy to help your family, right?"

I was shocked and confused. Who would let a little girl work for them? Daddy didn't wait for me to say anything. He started telling me all about how he had saw Ms. Sophie Adams in town and got to talking about good help and not hiring Mexicans. When he had told Ms. Sophie about Marcos and how he couldn't work a lot because of him, Ms. Sophie had offered him a job.

"And I told her that it wouldn't be right for Paul Roberts' son to be working for another farmer, but I had a daughter that needed to know about hard work and could pick her cotton. She was only too happy to bring you on, Vicky. So, you will clean the house and yard today. Oh, that includes the garden. Then you can eat that trash that Marcos gave you since I know your lazy Mama didn't make enough to feed you," he said in a hard voice.

"I want you on your pallet early because your Daddy is going to take you to Ms. Sophie early in the morning. Now, get the broom and get this house clean."

Mama smiled evilly and pointing at the straw broom by the kitchen door.

I got up and grabbed the broom to begin sweeping, turning when I heard Daddy.

"She'll get a dollar a week, and Ms. Sophie says that she will give me the money on Fridays."

I saw him rub his hands together and get up from the table. He reached over to caress Mama's face, but she flinched away from his touch. He frowned and grabbed her chin roughly. I stood there frozen in fear as he pulled her arm into a tight grip and yanked her through the other doorway and slammed the door. I heard muffled yelling from Daddy and Mama crying and begging. I trembled in fear as I tried to close my ears to Mama's cries and swept faster to make sounds to drown out the wickedness in that room.

I was outside picking the dried and ruined plants from the garden and watching my brothers and sister play when I saw Daddy come out of the house stretching. I tried to hide behind some dried stalks of corn but it didn't work.

"Here now, girl, you better hurry with these chores before sundown, you hear?"

"Yes, sir," I replied.

"Did you just back talk me, girl?"

He stalked closer. I didn't know what to say, so I stayed silent with my head down.

"I asked you a question, Vicky. You are not going to disobey me like you did your grandmother and mother, hear?"

He yelled and spit flew from his mouth. I kept my head down and didn't reply. Seeing me silent and fearful was enough. Daddy snickered.

"See, I'm teaching you how to obey a man, Vicky. Women are not to talk unless talked to. You have to learn your place like your sloppy Mama learned hers."

He then turned and walked to where my brothers were climbing the wild plum tree in the front yard and picked some of the green fruit.

"Tess, bring me the salt jar!"

He picked more of the green fruit.

"Vicky, we're going to take your brothers and Ruth down to Pa and Mama's house. You'll stay and finish your chores. Oh, and Vicky, if the schoolteacher passes by, don't speak, he might take you back to hell with him," Daddy laughed.

I felt the blood drain out of my face at Daddy's words. I didn't know whom the schoolteacher was but I would make sure not to say a word to him.

Mama soon came out of the house with a scarf around the neck of her housedress, carrying a small salt jar. She took Ruth by the hand and followed Daddy out of the yard without even looking my way. I was left all alone and the scary sounds of the woods behind the house seemed to be creeping closer with the shadows of the afternoon. I began to sing songs from church to keep my mind away from being afraid.

I heard my brothers' voices coming down the lane as I finished cleaning the yard. I breathed a sigh of relief as it was starting to get dark.

"Vicky, look what Betts gave us!"

I looked up to see Steven skipping to a stop beside me. He held out his hand and in it was a piece of wax paper with dewberry candy in the middle. I smiled at his excitement.

"That's good, Steven, are you going to eat it after supper?"

I asked knowing that he was.

"Yes, silly."

Steven giggled.

"Vicky, don't you be asking your brother for some of his treat."

Mama walked over to us and smiled at me. It wasn't a nice smile.

"She wasn't Mama, she was just asking me when I was going to eat it," said Steven.

"Well, she can't have any. It will keep her up tonight and she has to get up early in the morning."

Mama snickered at me.

"Tess, I'm hungry, go fix my plate and get these young'uns to their pallets."

Daddy walked up behind Mama.

Mama seemed to shrink at Daddy's voice, and then she walked across the yard and into the house.

"Come on, kids, let's eat."

Daddy grabbed Ruth and Clyde Jr.'s hands to take them in the house. I noticed that Ruth's eyes were red and she didn't have any wax paper in her hand like our brothers. Steven paused like he was going to say something but shrugged his shoulders and followed Daddy into the house.

I walked a little slower to enjoy the evening breeze and the colors of the sunset. I wasn't scared to be outside for some reason now, and I thought to myself that I didn't stop only to enjoy the outside. I was delaying going in the house with my parents.

"God, please help me. I won't be bad, and I'll help Aunt Charlotte and Mary with everything from now on. Please help me in Jesus' name. Amen."

I whispered my prayer to the sky, turned, and went inside the house.

The next morning, I was awakened with a stinging slap to the face. I looked up to see Daddy standing over me with his hand raised as if he would hit me again.

"I've been calling you and calling you, Vicky. Stop being lazy and get up. It's time to go to work," he said viciously.

He didn't even bother to lower his voice for my sleeping siblings. I nodded my head and tried not to let the tears in my eyes fall or rub my cheek. He lowered his hand and walked away. I got up from the pallet and looked around the back bedroom that Mama had pushed me into the night before with covers to make a pallet on the floor. I saw that it was still dark outside, and I hadn't heard the rooster crow. My brothers were still asleep on their bed. I turned around to see if Ruth was still asleep in the small cot by the door. I saw that she was up and staring at me with wide eyes.

"Ba, ba, Vick-ee," she mumbled around her thumb.

"It's okay. Go back to sleep before Mama wakes up," I whispered.

I put my finger to my lips and patted her on the head. She smiled and sat up to give me a hug. I hugged her warm little body and left the room trying not to let the tears fall. Mama and Daddy hadn't said anything about the clothes that Aunt Charlotte had sent with them for me, so I had worn what Marcos had given me to sleep. I figured that if Daddy wanted me to change, he would have given me my clothes. I smoothed my hair down and found a string to tie it. I still had no shoes.

I walked through the short hallway passing through Mama and Daddy's bedroom. I saw Mama tossing and turning but she remained sleeping. I quietly opened the door to see Daddy waiting by the back door.

"Well, girl, come on, we don't have all day. I need to get back so that I can get some rest."

I didn't want to anger him more so I sped up and my bare feet tripped on one of the uneven planks on the floor. I put my hands out to stop my fall but landed heavily on my stomach. My breath let out in a whoosh, and my chest locked up. I curled up in a little ball and grabbed my chest to catch my breath.

"What's this?! No, no, you're not getting out of work!"

I heard him come across the floor and felt him grab one of my elbows. He tore loose my arm from the other across my chest and began to drag me to the door. I tried to find a way to stand up while he was pulling me, but he was holding me tightly.

As we were going through the back door, I looked up to see my Mama standing in the door of their bedroom smiling.

On the way to the Adams', Daddy talked all about how much rest he would get and how he would teach Grandpa Paul a lesson. I just sat huddled in the backseat in pain, hungry, and trying not to cry.

"Oh, and you better not talk to nobody, and I mean nobody, while you're working at the Adams', hear?"

I nodded, but since it was still dark and he couldn't see me.

"DO. YOU. HEAR."

"Yes, sir," I quietly replied.

"That's more like it."

I tried to shrink back into the seat but I had already gone as far as it would allow. I closed my eyes and began to pray. I prayed for my parents, I prayed for the rest of my family, and I prayed that God would deliver me from it all.

We pulled into the lane that would take us to the Adams', and all I could think about was how close it was to my Grandpa Ed and Big Mama Chandra's land. I started thinking that maybe I could visit them while I was at Ms. Sophie's, but Daddy was already ahead of me.

"Don't even think about going to Ed and Chandra's to see them or your aunts. I've already told Ms. Sophie to keep you busy until I pick you up.

I couldn't see his face in the dark, but I could hear a smile in his voice like he was satisfied that he had made those plans.

The sun was starting to rise when Daddy parked the car in the front yard of a large ramshackle, white house with a small porch that had two steps. I saw a short, very round white woman with dark brown hair and flat, mean looking blue eyes come out of the house to stand on the porch. She was dusting her hands off with an apron that looked too small to cover the waist of her too short housedress.

"Clyde, now I told you that your girl has to work in the fields. You know I don't allow no Blacks or Mexicans in my house."

"Yes, ma'am, Ms. Sophie, I just wanted her to meet you and know who her boss lady was," Daddy replied silkily .

He got out of the car and smiled which made him more handsome. Ms. Sophie turned red and her whole face changed to smile back. She grinned and the fat under her chin looked like it grinned too.

"Well, I guess that's fine. Let me see this naughty child that Ms. Sophie needs to teach some manners."

Her voice turned singsong when she addressed Daddy.

"Vicky, get out of that car and bring your behind here."

Daddy turned towards my open window. I climbed out of the car and walked slowly to his side. I could see the surprise on Ms. Sophie's face and wondered at it. I didn't have to wonder long.

"Why, she don't look like you or Tess!"

Ms. Sophie looked shocked.

I could see the grin wiped from Daddy's face. Ms. Sophie started laughing.

"Clyde, you been cuckolded! That's a White man's child for sure!"

Daddy face tightened and he looked back at me and clenched his fists. I wanted to run away because I knew he wanted to hit me, or Ms. Sophie because she kept laughing and pointing. Soon, she got herself under control and cleared her throat when she noticed Daddy's face.

"Well, take her to the cotton field, that's where Bob has everybody working today."

She gave Daddy directions and tried to control her laughter.

Daddy grabbed my arm tightly and pulled me to the car. He pushed me into the back, got in, and slammed the door.

"Stupid bitch," he muttered, "don't she know who I am. She's seen my Pa, so she knows that you look like him."

He swung around to narrow his eyes at me.

"Don't you tell nobody about what that fat cow just said, hear?"

Frightened at his mean tone, I nodded and tried to slide into the corner without his notice.

After driving around the bumpy cornfield lanes, Daddy drove up to the cotton field. There was a wagon with a short, skinny White man with a balding head standing by it. He leaned into the car when Daddy pulled up to him. He had pale green eyes and a hooked nose. He also had a moustache stained with tobacco.

"Hey there, Clyde, I hear I gots me a new picker."

The little man spat tobacco on the ground.

"Yes, sir, Mr. Bob, right here. She might be a little slow starting, but she'll work hard for you."

Daddy got out to pull me from the car to stand in front of Mr. Bob. Mr. Bob's face changed.

"She's just a little girl, Clyde!"

"Oh, she'll be alright, sir. She's been real naughty and needs a lesson about hard work."

"Then take her back to your pa's and let him teach it. She looks like him anyway. I don't take on small children. They can't work fast enough or carry a heavy load."

Daddy looked upset before he began pleading.

"Sir, we need the money. I'm working hard for my pa and Tess is in the family way again. Please, let my baby work. She's the only big one that can help. The Daniels' won't help us either, and they're Tess's folks."

Mr. Bob looked like he would say no, but at the mention of my Grandpa Ed and Big Mama Chandra, he firmed his lips and nodded his head.

"Alright, if they won't help their own kin, I will. They some stingy, uppity Blacks anyway.".

He reached into the back of the wagon, and grabbed a huge burlap sack with a sash. He walked over and put it over my head.

"Go on, gal, the other workers will show you how to do it. I expect that sack to be emptied and filled three times before quitting time."

He issued his commands and pointed toward the cotton field.

I nodded and without looking back, I started walking to where he was pointing. The sun was already starting to get hot, but I held my face up to it and prayed another silent prayer to God to help me.

6

I found a path leading into the cotton field and walked all the way until it branched off to the left and right. I saw people bent over and moving at the end of the path on the right, so I walked that way. My sack dragged behind me, and I was about to pick it up when I heard a woman's voice.

"Would ya look at dat?! Da boss man done took on a lil girl!"

I turned at the voice, and a tall pretty black woman about my Aunt Charlotte's age stood two rows over with her own sack on her back.

"Wha's ya name, honey?"

She smiled at me with pearly white teeth.

"Vic, Victoria," I stammered.

"Well, Miss Vic, Victoria, people calls me Hope. Whatcha doin' out heah? Dis ain't no place for a chile."

"Stop bein' nosy, Hope."

A shorter heavier black man ordered as he walked up behind me.

I swung around at his voice to see him while Hope psshawed at him.

"Henry, ya take yo'self on down the fif' row. I cleared the thud and for'."

"Don' ya be tellin' me what ta do, woman."

Henry shook his head but already walked in the direction Hope pointed.

"Well, Miss Victoria, whatcha doin' heah?"

Hope persisted in her questions.

"My Daddy said that I have to work to help my family because he can't work for my grandpa right now."

I forgot all about Daddy's direction that I not speak to anyone.

"Why can' he pick cott'n?"

I shrugged my shoulders and looked away.

"Humph. Wait, what's ya granpappy's name?"

I became scared of telling her, so I said nothing.

"Okay, don' tell me, but I thank I knows 'cause only two Negra fellas in dis place wit' land."

"Ya pick cott'n afor'?"

"No, ma'am."

I shook my head.

"Okay, I'll hep ya," Hope smiled.

She took me by the hand and led me over to her row of cotton plants. She leaned over and snatched the balls of cotton from the stems until she had cleaned the plant. Then she stuffed it into my sack. I looked at her gloves and when she saw me looking at them.

"Ya gon' need some gloves for pick'n cott'n."

I just stared at her, and she looked at me with sympathy.

"Heah, les wrap ya lil hands wit' some pieces o' ya shirt."

She turned me around and tore a piece from the back of my shirt. Then she tore it in two long strips and wrapped my hands as much as she could before tying it off.

"Now, it's betta. Go on. Ya gotta pick 'til ya fill da sack."

She pointed to the end of the row where the path was to leave the field.

"Start on da row o'er der' and skip a row."

I walked over to where she pointed and began to pull the cotton.

Dinnertime came with the ringing of a bell. I looked over at Hope who took off her sack and walked toward the path out of the field. I did the same and followed her. We soon met up with Henry and about ten other workers coming out of their rows. I saw Mr. Bob at the wagon with a large covered barrel with a spout. Everyone got in line behind the wagon. I looked around and saw that the workers had empty cups and jars. I soon understood why everyone had empty vessels when the first worker held his jar under the spout to get the water from the barrel. I didn't have anything, so I just stood in the line. Hope looked back at me, and when she saw my empty hands, she frowned.

"Henry, ya still got dat cup ya made?"

Henry stood behind me.

"Shor' do, you wan' it?"

He pulled it out of his knapsack.

"Give it to da baby. She don' have nothin'," Hope said nodding at me.

"Oh, no, I don't want to take your cup, sir, you might need it."

I was so ashamed.

"It's okay, I got two."

Henry nodded and pushed the wooden cup at me.

I took it and turned around to wait my turn. I looked down at it and saw that it was polished with pretty figures in it. It reminded me of Marcos' special cup. I felt the tears and tried not to let them fall. I didn't want Hope or Henry to feel sorry for me. Soon, it was my turn at the water, and I held the cup under the barrel.

"Hey now, gal, your daddy said you not suppos' to eat but I'm gon' give you some of this water 'cause I don' want you to drop dead in this here heat."

Mr. Bob grinned and spat tobacco next to my feet.

I took the water and walked away looking down trying to hold back my tears. I was so hungry, and I had forgotten the few tortillas that I had left from Marcos rushing to leave in the morning so that I wouldn't get in trouble. All of the workers sat down at the end of the path and ate what they had brought from home. I didn't want to sit with them without my own food. I glanced their way but walked over to sit by my sack. I took a drink of the cool water and felt a little better, but my stomach was still empty. I drank a little more water and closed my ears to the sound of the other workers' eating and laughing.

"I 'eard what Mr. Bob say, and I don' reckon I likes ya daddy much."

Hope's voice sounded angry.

I opened my eyes to see a boiled egg in my face.

"Take it. It ain't much but it's betta den nothin'."

I took the boiled egg and whispered, "Thank you."

Hope waved away my thanks with the half-eaten boiled egg in her hand.

"Jus' eat it, and drank lots of dat watta."

She wagged her finger at me and walked away.

I began to peel the egg with shaking dirty hands and tried not to crush or drop it.

When I had it peeled, I bowed my head and prayed.

"Father God, thank you for blessing me with this food. I know that you touched Hope's heart to give it to me, and I thank you. Please Father God, help me get back to Aunt Charlotte and Aunt Mary. In Jesus' name, Amen."

I opened my eyes to see denim clad legs standing in front of me. I raised my eyes to meet Uncle P's big eyes widened in surprise.

"Miss Victoria! Whatcha doin' out heah in dis heat pick'n cott'n?"

Surprise showed on his face.

I took a bite of the egg and looked away from his gaze. I couldn't answer him while I chewed, and I tried to think of what I would say when I swallowed the bite. Nothing came to mind but the truth, and I knew that I couldn't tell him that. I felt him shift to sit down in front of me, but I kept my eyes on the ground in front him. He reached over and tilted my head up with his finger under my chin.

"Miss Victoria, what tis it? Ya can tell Unca' P. I won' hurt ya, and I won' let nobody else hurt ya."

His gentle words cut through me, and I began to cry. Not a soft whimpering cry, but a hard sob that I felt all the way to my soul. Uncle P grabbed me and put me on his shoulder like I was a little baby.

"I don't know what I did, Uncle P, Mama and Daddy are so mean to me. Everybody hurts me except for Grandpa Paul and my brothers and sister. I don't understand what I did for them to hurt me like that. I love my Mama and my Daddy but they hate me, Uncle P. I just want to go back to Aunt Charlotte and Aunt Mary so we can go home to Dallas. I'm only seven, and I feel like Mama and Daddy want me to be all grown up. Please, please, help me."

I sobbed into his shoulder and tried to hide my face. He held me back so that he could look at me. I felt that funny warm sensation going through my arms where he held me flow into all of my body. My sobs turned into hiccups, and I felt better but tired and sleepy. Then he put me back on his shoulder and stood. He grabbed my sack and walked to the end of the row where all of the workers had gathered when they heard my cries. Hope stepped forward and took the sack from Uncle P.

"Heah, I'll pick it wit' mine," I heard Henry say.

"Good, 'cos I'm goin' wit' P," came Hope's voice.

"Gimme ya sack, Hope," said a voice I didn't know.

"Imma take huh to the Daniels'."

Uncle P sounded determined.

I raised my head to protest.

"Please, Daddy said that I couldn't go there."

Uncle P frowned.

"We goin' to ya Big Mama Chandra. Now hush."

He placed his hand on my head to keep me on his shoulder and walked out of the cotton field toward my grandparents' land.

When Uncle P and Hope walked into the backyard, Big Mama Chandra was already there with her medicine basket.

"Lord, Lord! Mary told us that she would be coming today."

Big Mama Chandra ran over and tried to take me out of Uncle P's arms.

"Lemme put huh down where ya can tend to huh, Ms. Chandra," rumbled Uncle P.

Big Mama led the way into the house and told Uncle P to put me in bed in my room. Uncle P gently placed me in bed and moved back so that Big Mama could get to me.

First, she gave me a big hug, and only when Uncle P cleared his throat did she pull away and begin to look through her basket.

"Where is she?! Is she okay?"

I heard Aunt Charlotte while she rushed into the room.

Uncle P and Hope stepped back quickly because Aunt Charlotte made a beeline for the bed. Big Mama had to move as well because Aunt Charlotte picked me up out of the bed and hugged me so tight that I started to cough.

"Charlotte, put the child down so that she can breathe, and I can tend to her," commanded Big Mama.

Aunt Charlotte slowly put me down on the bed and moved back only enough to still hold my hand and look at Big Mama expectantly. Big Mama rolled her eyes and began to undress me.

Uncle P left the room muttering.

"Imma be outside, Ms. Chandra. I gots to find Mr. Ed and get ready for Mr. Clyde."

Hope moved backwards to the window and sat down on the floor as Aunt Charlotte had taken the only chair. I winced when I felt Big Mama touching my chest and stomach from my fall that morning. She frowned but said nothing. She took off the denim trousers and let out a small gasp at the fading whelps of the switch. Aunt Charlotte sat forward to see and let out a bigger gasp.

"Mama, Papa didn't say that they were that bad. How could Tess do this? She can't go back to them ever."

Tears pooled in her eyes.

I gave her hand a squeeze because I didn't want her to cry. She looked at me and smiled.

"She' righ', ma'am, I heard da boss man say huh daddy tol' 'im she couldn' eat, only wattah."

Big Mama Chandra hadn't noticed Hope until she spoke.

"Who are you?"

"I'm Hope. I comes from Lous'ana to work for da Adams' evr'y yeah. Dey not nice peoples but my pappy work fo 'em fo a long spell, so I does too."

"Well, Hope, bringing Victoria to us was a wonderful thing, but the Adams' maybe won't want you or P anymore after they find out you helped," warned Big Mama Chandra.

Hope shrugged.

"Righ' is righ'. I'd do it agin'."

Big Mama Chandra nodded too and told her to go find Ms. Sadie for a cold drink and some teacakes. I saw Hope's eyes brighten at the teacakes, and she left the room. Big Mama Chandra turned back to me and started grabbing jars and packets from her basket. She told Aunt Charlotte to go heat some water for her special cream and a cup of cold water for me. Aunt Charlotte left the room to do Big Mama's bidding.

"Victoria, I have to give you a posset to put you to sleep because my special cream with take all the scars and pains away but it hurts your stomach. I'll put more sun cream on you too because your skin is burned from the sun."

She paused when Aunt Charlotte walked back into the room. She took the cup of water that Aunt Charlotte gave her and emptied a packet of brown powder into it. She swirled it around for a minute then she raised me up to drink it. I made a face because it smelled like the chicken coop, but she pushed it to against my lips until I opened my mouth. It tasted as bad as it smelled, but I held my breath and swallowed.

"Ugh! Big Mama! That tastes so bad!"

"Uh, huh, it may taste bad now but you won't be complaining after while," she replied calmly.

I shuddered at the taste still in mouth and settled back on the bed. Aunt Charlotte grabbed my hand and started stroking it softly. I started feeling warmth spread through my body that was making me feel fuzzy. I smiled at the feeling and tried to turn my head to see Aunt Charlotte but she was now a colorful blur.

"She's feeling it, Mama."

Aunt Charlotte's whisper was loud in the room.

"A few more minutes and I can start. When I'm done, you can try to get a comb through those tangles," Big Mama Chandra murmured.

"Oh, Mama, how could they do this to her? I knew that it was crazy to let her go, but y'all talked me into it."

"Hush now, girl, they are her parents no matter what. Maybe with half the countryside knowing what happened, they will straighten up and fly right from now on," said Big Mama firmly.

I heard her pause, and I felt her hand on my forehead.

"She doesn't have fever, but I can sense there is something wrong deep within her soul. I wouldn't put it past that demon, Betts, to have hoodoo'd her own grandchild."

"Mama, we need to get Mary. She can clean it out before it gets too deep."

Aunt Charlotte sounded so far away. I felt like I was floating through the air, and I couldn't hear Big Mama's reply as I succumbed to her posset and drifted into the darkness.

All I can remember is the flashes of pain and the smell of Big Mama's sun cream. I would hear voices when I drifted in and out of a restless sleep. I heard myself cry out whenever anyone touched me. Whenever I awoke, Big Mama gave me more of her posset and wiped me down with cool wet cloths. I heard Aunt Charlotte and Aunt Mary praying to God for healing somewhere in the room. When the posset would start working, I gratefully gave in to the darkness so that I wouldn't have to feel the pain.

The sound of voices raised in anger woke me from a dreamless sleep. I looked around the room and saw that I was alone. I knew from the shadows from the window that it was very late afternoon. I saw that no light was on and became afraid of what would happen when the shadows turned into night. The voices sounded closer when I awoke, and I hoped that it was one of my grandparents or aunts so that they could turn on the light. I noticed then that the voices were louder like shouts, and I held myself still to listen.

"YOU WILL NOT GO IN THAT ROOM, TESS!"

It was the first time that I heard Aunt Charlotte yell.

"SHE IS MY DAUGHTER! AND I'M TAKING HER HOME!"

I began shaking at the violence in her voice. I was scared for Aunt Charlotte because Mama sounded like she did before she gave me the switchin'. I felt weak, but I got up and looked around for a hiding place. Seeing the slightly opened closet behind the door was like a miracle. I took a deep breath and dragged my sore little body to the door of the closet. I looked into the darkened space and shuddered at the darkness. I hated to go into the dark closet, but I knew that I had to hide from Mama. I heard footsteps and the voices getting closer to the door, so I threw myself to the floor of the closet and pulled the door closed. I could still see a little light from the crack at the bottom of the door. I scooted closer to the light and curled up into a ball to pray. I heard the room door slam open, and the light popped on. Three pairs of feet enter the room.

"Where is she?"

Mama sounded out of breath.

"As you can see, Tess, she's not here, so take your filthy husband and leave," Aunt Charlotte snapped.

I saw the covers being yanked up and Mama bending over looking under the bed. I scooted back a little so that she couldn't see me.

"I said that she's not here, Tess. You don't need her anyway. You mistreated her after less than two weeks! I would've run away from you too!"

I saw Mama's black work shoes turn quickly toward a pair of white walking shoes and start moving like they were tussling.

"Stop it, Tess!"

"YOU STOP IT, YOU STUPID COW! YOU CAN'T HAVE YOUR OWN BABIES, SO YOU STEAL MINE AND HIDE HER FROM ME! I'LL KILL YOU!"

I covered my mouth with my hands and inched closer to the crack. I felt like such a coward for staying hidden and letting Aunt Charlotte take the blame, but I couldn't bring myself to open the door.

Slap!

"Stop it, ma'am! I don' know ya', but I ain't gon' let ya' hert Miss Charlette, ya' heah?"

I heard Hope's voice as a pair of brown work boots rush toward the black work shoes. I guessed that Mama was like a monster again because she yelled at Hope.

"HOW DARE YOU LAY YOUR HANDS ON ME, YOU PIECE OF FILTHY FIELD TRASH! YOU'RE HELPING THEM KEEP MY DAUGHTER FROM ME! I KNOW IT! I'M CALLING THE LAW!

"Tess! Stop your madness, NOW!"

I heard Aunt Mary voice near the door.

I hadn't heard her footsteps with all of the shouting, but I saw a pair of moccasins walk into the room and stand beside the white walking shoes.

"NO, MARY! KEEP AWAY FROM ME WITH YOUR HOODOO STUFF!"

Mama screamed like she was hurt.

"Tess, you are with child. Do not let your child be filled with your evil. Let us help you."

Aunt Mary spoke to Mama very slow and soft.

"STAY AWAY FROM ME!"

I saw her black work shoes run from the room. I heard her footsteps echoing down the hallway. Then, I heard whispering before the brown work boots left the room as well.

I saw the white walking shoes come towards the door. I held my breath and waited. The door to the closet opened.

"Hurry, Victoria, come out of there."

Aunt Charlotte reached into the closet for me.

I scurried into her arms. She lifted me up and carried me over to the window.

"Listen, my love, Hope and your friend David are waiting outside under the window to help you into the fields. We have to get your mother and father to leave. Wait until you hear me, or your Aunt Mary call for you, okay?"

She hugged me tightly. Aunt Mary walked over and hugged us too. I returned the hugs praying that there would be no more trouble with Mama and Daddy. Aunt Charlotte opened the window and peered outside.

"Hope? David?"

"We's heah," I heard Hope say.

"Okay, Victoria, bend your head."

Aunt Charlotte gently letting me out of the window. I bent my head and Hope and David pulled me through.

After my feet were on the ground, Hope and David grabbed each of my hands, and we headed across the yard into the cornfield. Hope took us around into the field at the front where we could see the front of the house. She turned back to us.

"I wanna make shor' ya' folks don' hert nobody."

"Now, you wait just a minute, Ed. Vicky is our daughter, and we want her out here right now."

We all turned to look through the corn when we heard Daddy's voice across the field.

I saw him and Mama standing in the middle of the yard in front of Daddy's Chevy facing Grandpa Ed and Big Mama Chandra.

"Clyde, I already told you what happened. Do you not understand? I talked to your father after Victoria was brought here today. Your own father is ashamed of what you did to your own child. You put a seven-year-old child in the cotton field with nothing but the clothes on her back! No gloves, no water, no hat for the sun! ARE YOU OUT OF YOUR MIND?!"

Grandpa Ed's roar of anger echoed across the yard.

"We taught you better than this, Tess! How could you let this happen to your own baby?! What's wrong with you?"

Big Mama Chandra's voice sounded like she cried.

I saw Mama glance at Daddy and shrug her shoulders. Big Mama Chandra threw her hands in to the air. Aunt Mary came out of the door to stand beside Big Mama.

"Tess, let us help you. We can help you back over the line."

Aunt Mary pleaded with Mama.

"Oh, shush, Mary, you and your crazy ways."

"We are not leaving until we get our daughter, or we're calling the law," she sneered.

Grandpa Ed laughed out loud.

"Girl, go ahead and tell the Carson police that you beat your child so bad with a switch that she was in bed for a week. Or that your husband put your child out in the cotton field with no water or food. Go ahead. By the time they get through talking to me, you'll be in jail."

Mama drew her breath.

"You wouldn't, Pa?!"

"Yes, he would, Tess, to save that child from your cross over the line," Big Mama agreed.

Aunt Mary began walking toward Mama and Daddy.

"Clyde, you are a nasty little man, and if you don't change, bad things will happen to you, no matter what Betts does."

I was afraid for her to get too close to them, but Big Mama Chandra and Grandpa Ed weren't moving to stop her so I figured it was okay. When she reached them, she held her hand palm out toward them. There was something white wrapped around her hand. Daddy grabbed Mama's hand and backed away toward the car. I saw Big Mama Chandra wrap something around her hand and walk forward to stand beside Aunt Mary with her palm out too.

"Don't come any closer! Give us that silly girl and leave us alone!"

Daddy glanced around and shouted at Aunt Mary and Big Mama Chandra.

"No Clyde, let us help you across the line before it's too late."

Big Mama Chandra pleaded.

"NO!"

Daddy and Mama shouted at the same time.

They backed against the car door with no more room to spare. Aunt Mary moved to touch Mama's arm, and Daddy yanked her back against him.

"No one is touching my wife. She is mine, and I will do with her what I want."

Daddy sounded strange and his voice was gravelly.

"Now! Touch her, Mary!"

Before Aunt Mary could touch Mama, Daddy had somehow opened the door with one hand and shoved Mama into the car.

"NO!"

Aunt Mary ran forward with a scream.

Daddy launched himself into the car and locked before she and Big Mama reached it. He moved so fast that he seemed just a blur of motion.

Daddy started the car and hit the gas. There was a cloud of dust raised from the Chevy. Hope, David, and I covered our mouths and noses when the cloud drifted our way.

"Dis don' look gud," whispered Hope.

Daddy was driving in circles around the yard as if he were trying to hit something or someone. I saw Uncle P run from behind the house to grab Grandpa Ed from Daddy's path. Big Mama Chandra and Aunt Mary had run back to the porch to get out of his way. It was like he was possessed or something. He drove in circles a few more times, then he put the car in reverse as if he would back into the field where we were hiding. The sun went down, and we couldn't see well through the stalks of corn. Hope put her hand over her eyes.

"Lor' help us, he comin' dis way!"

She scooped me up quickly and moved out of his path.

"David!"

Hope reached for David.

"Here, I am."

He spoke from beside her.

I felt her breathe a sigh of relief at his answer when we saw the car back into the first row of corn where we had been.

Daddy rolled the car forward and stopped in the driveway as if he and Mama were leaving.

"Mary, quick erase the line!"

Big Mama Chandra's voice reflected her anxiety. She and Aunt Mary ran out into the yard where Daddy had driven the circles and waved their hands and kicked their feet on the wheel marks in the dirt. I heard Daddy laughing maliciously in the car.

"Go ahead! Erase the line if you can, but I'll be back to mark it again!"

He mocked them from the now opened car window.

Hope leaned forward to see, and I saw him leaning over Mama like she weren't there. I felt heat rising in my body. I felt so angry at my size, my age, my everything. I wanted to be a grown-up so that I could stand up to my own Daddy. Then I remembered to pray. I closed my eyes and prayed to myself.

"Please Father God, help us. Please take my Daddy away from here. Please don't let him hurt anyone. In Jesus' name, Amen."

"Clyde, you get on away from here. You and Tess will not get Victoria back until she can fend for herself and y'all have crossed back over the line. Tess, when you hear your blood calling, you are welcome to come home. We will help you."

Big Mama Chandra called out to Mama, but she stayed silent.

"She don't need y'all! She only needs me!"

Daddy rolled the window up and leaned back to his side. The car didn't move even though we all could hear the motor running. It was then that we saw the motions of Daddy hitting Mama right in front of Grandpa Ed, Big Mama Chandra, Aunt Mary, and Uncle P. It was the silence that made me want to cry. Not once could anyone hear Mama cry out against the pain or for help. The windows were closed but we could still hear the violence in the car. Everyone ran forward. Hope put me on the ground and told David to watch me even as she ran towards the car. Before anyone could make it to the car, Daddy sped off in another cloud of dust laughing.

"Oh Lord, Ed, what have we done?"

Big Mama Chandra asked the question in the silence as tears rolled down her cheeks.

Grandpa Ed went to her and hugged her in his arms.

"Nothing, Chandra, nothing. Tess chose Clyde, remember? Wouldn't hear of courtin' another boy when he started sniffin' around," Grandpa Ed reminded her gently.

Big Mama turned into his arms and cried. I had never seen Big Mama cry. I hung my head in shame because it was my parents causing her pain. Hope came back and with David's help, they carried me over to the middle of the yard where everyone was standing.

"Victoria! Have you been out here all this time?"

Big Mama sniffed and turned to us.

"Yes, ma'am."

"Where is Charlotte?"

Grandpa Ed asked and looked around the yard.

"She said she would call for me, but she's not here."

"Mama!"

We all looked around and Aunt Mary was leaning over Aunt Charlotte who was lying on the ground beside the cornfield.

"Charlotte!"

Big Mama screamed while running over to her. My heart felt like it a rock in my chest. I felt like I couldn't breathe. I became afraid and thought the worst. Aunt Charlotte was the only mother I had known whether she had given birth to me or not.

"Please David, help me over there."

I asked my question and tried not to cry.

"Victoria, I don't think that's a good idea. You might be in the way."

I could see that he tried to act all grown up, but I didn't have time for his mannish ways.

I snatched my hands away from his and dropped to the ground. I didn't care if I had to crawl inch by inch, I was getting to my Aunt Charlotte.

"Aw shoot, Victoria."

David gave in and helped me to my feet.

"Lean on me and we'll get there."

I nodded my head to let him know I understood. I felt the fear and tears rise up in my throat, but I knew that I couldn't give in to them. I began to pray silently for God to help Aunt Charlotte and to take away all of this evil.

As we moved closer, I could see that Aunt Charlotte moved and held Aunt Mary's hand. When she saw me, she held her other hand out to me. I felt a strength that I had never known enter my small body. I let go of David, and I ran the rest of the way to Aunt Charlotte's side on my own. I fell to my knees and grabbed her hand to my chest.

"Sweetheart, I'm going to be fine. It's just my leg, okay? I'm going to be fine. Big Mama's going to set it, and Ms. Sadie is going to wrap it real tight. I won't be able to walk for awhile, but I'm going to be fine," she rambled.

I stayed silent and squeezed her hand to my chest tighter. I breathed a sigh of relief that she would be okay, but the tears fell down my face at seeing her hurt. Then, I told myself that I would be strong for her, and that it was my turn to take care of her since she had been taking care of me. I stopped crying and wiped my tears away with my other hand.

"Alright, Ed, P, pick her up gently and take her to her room," Big Mama Chandra ordered.

I didn't want to let go of her hand, but I knew that Grandpa Ed and Uncle P needed to move her without me in the way. I was about to let go when Aunt Charlotte pulled me back to her.

"Why don't you and David go get some teacakes and sit in the kitchen for a spell?"

I nodded my head and slowly let go of her hand. Grandpa Ed and Uncle P lifted her while they tried not to hurt her more and toted her into the house. I felt weak after walking the distance to Aunt Charlotte and from the relief of knowing that she was alright. My legs dropped me to the ground and all of my feelings came out again. I began to cry silent tears at everything that had happened. Hope and David remained at my side and allowed me to cry it all out.

My crying fit soon passed and Hope cleared her throat.

"Ya' ready fa sum o' doz good ol' t'cakes, lil' miss?"

I wiped my cheeks with my arm and smiled up at her. David laughed.

"Victoria, you look like a mud duck with all that dirt on your face."

I laughed a little too because his face was covered in dust like mine.

"You too, David."

Hope giggled and grabbed both of our hands and headed toward the back yard.

"Le's git ya' wash'd up fore we all git in hot wat'r."

7

Ms. Sadie had teacakes and milk for David and me when we walked into the kitchen dripping with water.

"Now, now, you lil' ragamuffins, here's some cup towels. Wipe off and sit down at the table. I can't watch y'all long because I got to get in there to help Ms. Chandra. Don't leave this kitchen until somebody tells y'all to."

Ms. Sadie rushed around the kitchen gathering up supplies. Hope walked through the screen door before Ms. Sadie walked out.

"Good. Ms. Hope, can you keep these lil' uns busy in the house while we work on Ms. Charlotte?"

Hope sat down at the table and nodded.

"Why, I shor' can, Ms. Sadie."

Ms. Sadie smiled and walked towards Aunt Charlotte's room. I didn't want to think about Aunt Charlotte hurting and felt selfish that I had spent time playing around outside with Hope and David. I felt guilty that while I was having fun, Aunt Charlotte had been in pain from getting hit by my daddy's car. I felt the tears rise in my throat again, but I swallowed them back.

I bent my head and prayed.

"Please Father God, help Aunt Charlotte. Please heal her. And thank you for the teacakes and milk. In Jesus' name, Amen."

When I looked up, Hope and David looked at me with half-eaten cakes in their hands.

"Sorry, Victoria, didn't mean not to bless the food," David apologized quietly.

"It's alright. I did it for all of us."

"Ayyeeeeeeee!!!!"

A scream came from Aunt Charlotte's room.

I dropped the teacakes and was about to run from the table when Hope grabbed me in a tight grip.

"No, lil' ma'am. Let dem werk," she said firmly.

Tears fell down my cheeks because I knew Aunt Charlotte was suffering, and I couldn't do a thing about it. I sat back down slowly, but I couldn't eat. I tried to sip at the milk, but it tasted sour in my mouth as I listened to Aunt Charlotte's screams and moans.

All I wanted was to comfort her, and I wasn't allowed because I was too small and would be in the way. I felt so helpless, and the thought began to consume me that I needed to be a grownup. If I was a grownup, Mama, Daddy, or Betts couldn't hurt me no more. If I were a grownup, I would be like Big Mama Chandra and know how to heal and fix people. I lowered my head in despair and gave in to the here and now. I wasn't grownup, and I could do nothing but take what was given.

"Victoria, your aunt is asking for you."

Big Mama Chandra whispered in my ear and shook me awake.

I didn't realize that I had fallen asleep sitting at the table. I sat up and saw that David and Hope slept with their head in their arms at the table too. I quietly scooted out of my chair, and Big Mama guided me down the hallway to Aunt Charlotte's room. It was dark except for a single lamp lit in the corner. Ms. Sadie slept in a rocking chair beside the window, and Aunt Mary dozed on the chest at the end of the bed. I didn't see Grandpa Ed, so I figured that he slept in his and Big Mama's room.

Big Mama Chandra walked me up to the bed and sat me gently on the side of it. Aunt Charlotte rolled her head towards me and smiled. Her skin glistened with sweat, and her eyes shone with pain. Her left leg was wrapped up all the way from her thigh to her ankle, and she had a bandage around her head. But, she was the most beautiful to me at that moment because she was alive. I wanted to hug her, but I grabbed her hand and tried to keep the tears away.

"Hello, my sweet. Are you resting too?"

Her whispered was sweet music to my ears.

I nodded my head, and she smiled again.

"I'm sorry if you had to hear me hollerin'. I hope that I didn't scare you. I'm better now, but I won't be like I was before I was hurt. I'll walk a little funny, but it's alright. I'm still here."

"Hush, now, Charlotte. One of those doctors in Dallas might be able to fix your leg," Big Mama Chandra said from behind me.

"It's okay, Mama. Now, Victoria, we're going to have to stay here a little longer than we have before because I can't walk. I won't be able to travel back to Dallas just yet."

She sounded tired and out of breath.

"Please Aunt Charlotte don't say anymore. It's okay. I can help take care of you, and I can play with David. I prayed, and I know it's going to be alright."

I let the tears fall down my face this time.

"That's right, my lil' mirror, and we're going to keep Hope and P with us here on the homestead to help out Ms. Sadie and your Grandpa Ed. It's going to be a long road for your aunt to get better, and we're going to need lots of help."

I felt sad and happy, but I knew that everything would be okay. I felt sad that Aunt Charlotte couldn't walk yet, but I felt happy that Hope and P didn't have to work for the Adams'.

"Can I lie down with you, Aunt Charlotte?"

"How about we make you a trundle, and you can sleep beside her," suggested Big Mama Chandra.

I felt her move away from me to get the cot and covers from the closet across the hall.

Aunt Charlotte squeezed my hand.

"You cannot play outside the yard, Victoria. I don't know what your mama and daddy might do now or when they find out I'm down in the bed. Promise me."

"I promise."

I swallowed my tears and nodded.

"Here you go, dear."

Big Mama Chandra gestured toward the newly made cot beside Aunt Charlotte's bed. I got in and still holding on to Aunt Charlotte's hand fell quickly asleep.

The smell of coffee woke me the next morning. I opened my eyes and saw that Aunt Charlotte was still sleeping. She was not sweating as much as the night before. Her skin was almost as pale as mine, and her mouth was pinched in her sleep. I looked around the room expecting to see Aunt Mary or Ms. Sadie but didn't see anyone else. I got up from the cot as quiet as I could so that I wouldn't wake Aunt Charlotte. I walked down the hallway to make water and wash up before heading into the kitchen.

Big Mama Chandra and Grandpa Ed sat at the table drinking coffee and talking while Ms. Sadie cooked. They all looked up when I walked through the door.

"Good Morning, lil' mirror, did you sleep well?"

"Yes, ma'am."

I smothered a yawn and smiled.

"Sit down and get yourself some of these good ol' vittles."

Grandpa Ed motioned to the chair beside him.

Ms. Sadie put a plate down in front of me with crispy bacon, biscuits, and soft fried eggs just the way I liked. She went to the stove and scooped some grits into a small bowl and put that beside the plate. Everything smelled and looked good, but I wasn't hungry. I felt antsy like I needed to do something, but I didn't know what. I picked up the fork and tried to eat.

Aunt Mary came walking into the kitchen and covered her mouth on a yawn.

"Good morning, all. I just checked on Charlotte. She's still sleeping so I'm going to wash up before breakfast. Only melon and tea for me, Ms. Sadie. I'll be back in a jiffy."

Then she looked at me and paused like she had more to say but she shrugged her shoulders and mumbled, "Later" before walking out the door. Grandpa Ed laughed.

"That girl is something else."

Big Mama shook her head and smiled.

"Yes, she is."

Ms. Sadie loaded a tray and was halfway to the door when Big Mama stopped her.

"Not too much, Sadie. She might not eat too much with that posset still on her."

Ms. Sadie nodded her head and left through the doorway.

"Well, lil' miss, I want you to rest today too, okay? You've had a hard time since you left, and I don't want you under the weather too."

Big Mama tried to look stern while she scolded me.

I nodded and tried to eat some of the cold food.

"Just eat the grits, honey. The rest of that looks cold."

Grandpa Ed piped in before he buried his head in a big Bible.

I slid the plate away and pulled the bowl of grits closer. I took a bite and swallowed barely tasting the sweet buttery taste of the grits. I just wasn't in the mood and Big Mama could tell.

"Lil' Mirror, I want you to drink that milk, go have a wash, and head on back to your Aunt Charlotte's room," she fussed.

I picked up the cup of milk and drained it. I wiped my mouth with my napkin and asked to be excused.

"Yes, ma'am, you may. When you're done resting, maybe I can get me a story before supper."

Grandpa Ed chuckled at my hurry.

"Yes, sir!"

I promised him the story while I dashed out of the door.

I almost laughed in my happiness as my body and my soul felt so much better than it had just yesterday.

I tried to tiptoe past Aunt Charlotte's room, but she caught me before I could slip down the hallway to the washroom.

"Where are you going, Victoria?"

I turned around at the sound of her voice, and peeked past the doorjamb. She was sitting up in the bed with the tray of food across her lap.

"Yes, ma'am?"

I slowly inched into the room.

"Well, I see that Mama's posset and cream worked. You look better than a pork chop sandwich. Tee hee. Don't stand there being a little sneak, come give me a proper hug."

I giggled and ran into her open arms. I drew back a little so that I didn't turn over the tray, and when I saw that it was okay, I squeezed Aunt Charlotte as tight as I could.

"You know I love you, don't you, Victoria?"

She stroked my hair and trembled.

"Yes, ma'am, I love you too."

She gave me another squeeze and pulled away to lie back on the pillows.

"Now, where are you going?"

"Big Mama told me to wash and come back in here with you to rest."

"Ah, you are a little stinkpot."

She laughed and pinched my nose.

I laughed too.

"I guess I haven't had a wash off since Mr. Marcos' house."

Aunt Charlotte frowned.

"Mr. Marcos gave you a wash off?"

I shook my head and allayed her fears.

"I think he just wiped me off with cold water because he said I had a fever, and when I got well, he told me to use the water closet."

Aunt Charlotte looked off in the distance and spoke as if talking to herself.

"Hmm, a Mexican with a water closet. I guess."

Then she turned to me with a smile.

"Okay, well go on and wash real good. Then you can come back and take a nap with me."

I nodded and smiled then went to look for some clothes to put on after my wash off.

I spent the rest of the morning resting and napping on the cot beside Aunt Charlotte. Ms. Sadie brought us our dinner on trays.

"You get a tray too, lil' miss. I'm cleaning the kitchen floors today, so it's better that you stay in here."

I just took the tray and nodded.

"Say, yes, ma'am, please," Aunt Charlotte reminded me.

"Yes, ma'am."

I corrected my speech and rearranged myself on the cot.

Ms. Sadie just grinned at me and left. I looked down at the salmon croquettes, smothered potatoes, and biscuits and felt the need to push my face into the food. I hadn't eaten a lot at breakfast, so I was starving. I saw Aunt Charlotte bend her head to pray, and I did the same.

"Please God hear our prayers. We thank You for Your Mercy and Love. We thank You for our healing. We thank You for giving us Your Son, Jesus Christ. Please bless the food that we are about to eat and the hands that prepared it. In Your Son, Jesus Christ's Name, Amen.'

"Amen," I echoed and picked up my fork.

The first bite of the crispy croquette was delicious. I started to eat faster until Aunt Charlotte sighed.

"Victoria, please eat small bites like the lady that I raised you to be."

I swallowed the bite in my mouth.

"Yes, ma'am."

I began taking small bites and chewing slowly. Aunt Charlotte nodded and went back to nibbling and pushing her food around her plate. Ms. Sadie seemed to know when we were finished because she appeared in the doorway and took our trays.

Feeling full and sleepy, Aunt Charlotte and I laid down to take a nap. I reached out for her hand, and she turned to me and smiled taking my hand in hers. She gave it a gentle squeeze and closed her eyes to sleep. Holding her hand made me feel so loved and secure. I closed my eyes and fell asleep with the thought that I never wanted to be away from her again.

The next day, Aunt Charlotte was in a lot of pain, and Big Mama Chandra decided that I needed some fresh air.

"No, Mama, she can't go outside. What if Clyde is hanging around somewhere?"

Aunt Charlotte spoke while grinding her teeth against the pain.

"Hush, Charlotte, and take this posset. The girl needs some fresh air, and I could use the time to give you a bath and change your bed without her underfoot."

Aunt Charlotte nodded her head and drank the posset.

Big Mama winked at me.

"Go on. Wash your face and put on some clothes. Then, go sit on the porch in one of the rockers. Don't go any further, okay, little mirror?"

"Yes, ma'am," I agreed happily.

Then I kissed Aunt Charlotte and Big Mama Chandra's cheek and ran to do as Big Mama had said.

As I was putting on my clothes, I noticed that the scars on my legs had faded. I wasn't sore anywhere either. I wondered about this but didn't really care because I was going to get to go outside. I picked up my pace as soon as the last button on my dress was buttoned. I felt so happy and carefree at that moment. I knew everything would soon be right.

I sat on the porch Big Mama's rocking chair when Hope came around the side of the house.

"Hey dere, lil' un, whatcha doin' out heah?"

I loved her accent and smiled at her.

"My Big Mama said to sit out here to get some fresh air."

"Ah," was all she said.

She came up on the porch to sit in Grandpa Ed's chair beside me.

We rocked in silence for a while and just enjoyed the sunlight and sounds of the homestead. We could hear the chickens pecking and the hogs grunting and rooting for food. We heard the cattle mooing and field dogs barking. It was Hope who broke the silence.

"R, ya suppos' ta stay heah, 'o' can ya go out in da fiel'?"

"I can't go but in the front yard because Aunt Charlotte is scared Daddy is going to come again."

"Ah," she said again.

Then she got up and quickly went back around the house. I wondered why she left so suddenly. I thought maybe she had to get back to doing what she was before she sat with me.

I heard some noise coming from the field and saw David walk out of the cornfield. I smiled and waved, and he smiled and waved back at me.

"Would ya like ta play wit ya frens?"

Hope reappeared on the side of the porch.

I nodded.

"Yes, ma'am!"

"Ya Big Mama says dat ya can as long as I'm wit ya."

I laughed out loud in excitement.

"Thank you, oh, thank you, Hope!"

She laughed too and came up on the porch to take my hand. I grabbed her hand and almost ran off the porch to get to where David was waiting. He began laughing too as we got closer.

"Victoria! I'm so glad that you can still play with us."

David danced a little jig as we came to a stop beside him.

I was practically jumping in my happiness.

"Slow down, we gonna play lots of games today. Don't want you ta get tired too soon."

I stopped and raised my eyebrow.

"Don't you worry, I'm ready."

Hope laughed.

"I thank da lil' miss migh' out do ya, David!"

She grabbed my hand, David grabbed the other, and we ran into the corn to go find the other children to play.

After we spent the day playing, we returned to the house and met Ms. Sadie with a tray of ice-cold sun tea. She told me to make sure that I wash up for supper because Big Mama had invited some special guests then she went back inside the house. I froze and started shivering as the last time that I had heard guests invited to supper had been my parents and Grandpa Paul at Marcos'. Hope saw my reaction.

"I don' thank dat ya Big Mama wud ask ya Mama and Daddy ta dinnah."

I nodded but couldn't keep the thought that maybe she did trying to mend fences. I tried to tamp down the fear, but it was like an animal trying to break loose in my body. David took my hand and gave it a squeeze.

"Don't worry, Uncle P is your Grandpa Ed's foreman now, so he gets to eat with y'all to give your grandpa a report everyday."

I felt a little better when I heard that news because I knew that Uncle P wouldn't let Daddy hurt me again. I took a deep breath and straightened my spine. I would not be afraid. Ms. Sadie returned to get the tray and empty glasses.

"Come on, Miss Victoria, you have to get ready, and Hope, I'll need your help in the kitchen."

Hope nodded and stood up to go in the house. She turned around at the door.

"C'mon, lil' miss, ain't nuthin ta be scairt of heah," she said quietly.

David gave me a quick hug, and I stood and went inside with Hope.

When I had washed up and put on one of my blue day dresses that Aunt Charlotte hadn't sent with me to Mama and Daddy's, I went in to see Aunt Charlotte. She was propped up on the bed, and her leg was now propped up with a pillow.

"Why don't you look beautiful? Come let me do something with that hair."

I walked to the bed and turned to sit carefully on the side of the bed so that she could dress my hair. I didn't think she was well enough to do it, but I was not about to disobey my beloved aunt. Aunt Charlotte took loose my ponytail and brushed my hair to remove the tangles. Then she tied the blue ribbon that went with the dress around the crown of my head and left my hair to hang down my back.

She sat back on the bed and sighed.

"To have such beautiful hair, so straight and fine. Victoria, you should never cut your hair. It is a gift to have such hair in this family."

I stood up and turned around to face her.

"Yes, ma'am."

"Mama told me that y'all are eating supper with some good friends, so be on your best ladylike behavior," she said lying back on the bed.

"Can I help you with anything, Aunt Charlotte?"

"No, pumpkin, go sit in the living room and wait for your Big Mama."

She waved me away and picked up her Bible.

I wanted to stay and ask her to read to me from her Bible like she did in Dallas, but I left the room to follow her instructions.

I found the well-lit living room empty when I got there. I decided to sit on the divan and wait for Big Mama Chandra or Aunt Mary. I noticed that it had begun to get dark outside and all the curtains were still open. The beginning shadows of the night couldn't penetrate the lighting in the room, but I was afraid of the dark beyond the windows. As I began to shiver in fear, I heard Grandpa Ed's voice from the doorway.

"Well! I thought you'd never be out of bed, darlin'."

His eyes twinkled with a smile.

"Grandpa Ed!"

I launched myself at him.

He laughed when he caught me in his arms and twirled me around in a circle. He stopped and put me down but didn't release my hand.

"I'm glad to see that you're on the mend. You look good enough to eat," he teased.

I giggled.

"Thank you, Grandpa Ed."

He nodded and led me back over to the divan.

"Let me close those windows. I swear it gives me the heebie jeebies when all the lights are on and the windows are open."

He walked around the room closing the curtains. I breathed a sigh of relief when all the curtains had been closed.

Suddenly, there was a knock on the door. I jumped at the noise and began to feel the familiar fear.

"Victoria, I have a small surprise for you, so I want you to close your eyes."

I was afraid, but I closed my eyes anyway feeling a little safer that Grandpa Ed was with me. I heard Big Mama telling someone to come in and to follow her. Then, I heard lots of footsteps enter the room, and I felt someone sit down next to me.

"Open your eyes, Victoria," said Grandpa Ed.

I opened my eyes to see a set of familiar brown ones.

"Mr. Marcos!"

I cried and threw myself into his arms.

He laughed and gave me a big hug.

"Holá, Miss Bictoria! How you?"

He hugged me tightly.

"Good! I'm so happy to see you! Where's Juan?"

"He here. Míra."

Marcos motioned behind me.

I turned around and saw Juan smiling at me and tugging at the buttoned up collar of his shirt.

"Hello, múchacha."

He came across the room and stood beside Marcos.

I was so happy to see them both.

"My papa heard what your papa did to you, and he found sú abueló today in the fields and asked to come see you."

"And, I decided that a good dinner was better than a visit. Your Big Mama and I needed to return the favor of a good meal since Marcos took good care of you after...," Grandpa Ed paused.

There was awkward silence as everyone remembered why I was at Marcos'.

Grandpa Ed cleared his throat and continued.

"Any a ways, Marcos came all the way to the back twenty where I plowed to see about you. I told him you were better, but this stubborn Mexican wouldn't budge until I told him that he could visit."

Marcos nodded and grinned.

"Si."

"Alright, now, let's get on in to supper. Ms. Sadie been cooking up a storm," Big Mama said from the doorway.

Marcos looked at me closely, nodded, and stood up and followed Big Mama Chandra.

"Do not worry. He has been scared for you with your papa and mama."

Juan assured me quietly when he walked over to where I sat.

"Here," Juan said holding out his fist.

Thinking that I had left something at Marcos' house, I held out my hand. Juan placed the two five-dollar bills in my palm. I looked up frowning.

Juan gave a small smile.

"My papa has not been right since you left him this money. He wanted to bring it back to you. He took care of you because..."

"Juan!"

Marcos exclaimed from the door.

Then he said something in Spanish to Juan that I couldn't catch.

Juan nodded.

"Come on, muchacha, the food is getting cold."

He turned and followed Marcos down the hall. I stood there wondering what Juan was about to say, then gave up on thinking about it. I nodded to myself that Juan would tell me later and stood up to follow the delicious smells of food.

I enjoyed myself at supper that night. Marcos and Juan were good at storytelling even if Marcos sometimes forgot and spoke in Spanish. My grandparents, Aunt Mary, and Uncle P didn't seem to mind, especially, Aunt Mary. I saw her sneaking looks at Marcos, and I noticed he did the same to her. I smiled thinking that I would love for Marcos and Aunt Mary to fall in love and get married. Then, Marcos would be my uncle! I knew that he would be the best uncle ever. I had uncles but they were all off in the army. I decided that I would pray to God to help Aunt Mary and Marcos find love with each other. It would be like the fairytale in one of my books.

When supper was over, Marcos and Juan decided to leave early so that I could get some rest. I tried to argue, but a small yawn escaped my mouth and they won the argument.

Marcos leaned over and kissed my forehead.

"Buenos sueños, míja."

"Buen-os su-en-os," I replied.

Everyone laughed at my attempt, and Marcos gave me hug goodbye. Juan patted me on the head and followed his father out of the front door. Grandpa Ed and Uncle P moved to stand on the porch while they got in the old Ford pickup. Marcos gave a honk, and they both waved out of the open windows as they drove away. Uncle P said goodnight and walked into the fields to go home.

"Go on to the washroom and get ready for your bed."

Big Mama turned and she ushered me into the hallway. I turned and gave both of my grandparents and Aunt Mary a big hug.

"Thank y'all so much for letting Marcos and Juan come. They are my friends. I'm so happy."

I ran to the washroom to get ready for bed. I was so happy when I said my prayers and drifted off to sleep.

"You are nothing. Your Mama is nothing. You will cross the line one day, and I will have you then," screamed Betts.

Her face and body were twisted and deformed. She wasn't wearing any clothes and her whole body was a slick grey color. She was holding me in a painful grip with my arm pulled behind my back. I was in front of her closet again, and I couldn't move. Smoke was starting to inch from the inside and slowly drift across the floor to where I was standing. I tried to back away from it, but that only made Betts' laugh. It was an evil, cackling laugh that made me want to run. I could feel my heart beating faster as the fear and the smoke began to consume me. I didn't know what to do, and I was so frightened. I closed my eyes and screamed.

"Victoria! Victoria! Wake up! Victoria!"

I heard Aunt Charlotte's voice, but I couldn't open my eyes. Betts turned at the sound of her voice.

"She can't help you if she's dead!" she cackled.

"No! Please don't hurt Aunt Charlotte! No!" I yelled at her.

She pulled my arm again, and I felt the bone snap and pain like I had never known before in my short life. She laughed again in a deep, gravelly voice.

"Mary, she needs you! She's locked in some kind of evil dream! Victoria!"

"Victoria, call on Father God and His Son, Jesus. NOW!"

Aunt Mary voice cut through my dream clear and loud. When I heard her voice, I felt stronger.

"Father God, Help Me! Take away this evil! In Your Son, Jesus' Name!"

Betts screamed and let me go.

As soon as her touch was gone, I woke up in Aunt Charlotte's arms with Aunt Mary, Big Mama Chandra, and Grandpa Ed staring at me. They all looked out of breath and scared. When Aunt Charlotte saw that I was awake, she collapsed into sobs.

"Come here, Victoria."

Aunt Mary tried to take me from Aunt Charlotte.

"NO!"

Aunt Charlotte yelled and held onto me tighter.

"Charlotte, I need to cleanse her so that she can go back to sleep," explained Aunt Mary.

Aunt Charlotte nodded slightly and reluctantly released me to Aunt Mary. I saw that Aunt Mary had a silken white cloth around the palm of her hand. She rubbed this all over my face, head, and body. Then, she prayed silently. After her prayer, I felt sleepy.

I closed my eyes and began to drift to sleep. I heard Aunt Charlotte's quiet voice.

"Will she remember, Mary?"

"No, but she needs to so that she can gain the strength to fight it when it comes. If she doesn't learn to fight it, she'll give in to it," Aunt Mary said slowly.

I went to sleep wondering what "it" was.

Aunt Mary woke me early the next morning. I sat up in the cot to say good morning, but she shook her head and held her finger to her lips. She glanced at Aunt Charlotte who still slept, and I nodded. I slid quietly from the cot and followed her from the room. She led me into Big Mama's sunroom where she kept all of her special plants and herbs.

I loved this room. It had a unique earthy smell that made me want to breathe it in over and over again. At the back was a sitting area that had small baskets with cutting shears tied to each handle. I didn't pay much attention to the rest of the room because Aunt Mary led me to the settee and motioned for me to sit down, and she sat down beside me. I sat down curious to what Aunt Mary wanted that she had brought me all the way to the other side of the house away from the bedrooms.

"Victoria, I want you to tell me about your father's mother, Betts. I know that it may be hard, but I need to know everything that you saw and that she did when you were in that house."

I noticed that when she said Betts' name, she rubbed the white silk cloth wrapped around her right palm. I shook my head at Aunt Mary's request because I didn't want to talk about Betts or what happened while I was in the ranch house. Aunt Mary saw my refusal, and she reached out and put her hands on mine.

"Do not be afraid, Victoria. I'm want to help you. I fear that your grandmother has planted an evil seed in your soul that will be hard to remove. We must remove it now before it begins to grow. You are a beautiful, talented, and loving little girl. Those around you feel the goodness of your spirit. Don't let the evil take root within you," she whispered giving my hands a loving squeeze.

I knew what she was saying was the truth because I didn't feel quite like I did before I left with Mama and Daddy. I decided to tell Aunt Mary everything. I told her about what Daddy did to Mama on the porch the day that I left. Aunt Mary's nostrils flared, but she kept quiet. I told her everything up until Uncle P returned me to the homestead.

By the time that I finished, tears fell down both of our faces. Aunt Mary gathered me in her arms and held me tightly. I hugged her back and tried to stop crying.

When our tears dissolved into sniffles, we turned in surprise at Big Mama Chandra's quiet voice.

"Alright, Mary, you've heard what you need. Now, I will try to explain enough to her so that she can understand."

I looked up and saw that Big Mama's face was in shadow. I began to shiver. Aunt Mary gave me another hug and let Big Mama take her place on the settee.

"Ah, I guess, I better begin at the beginning," sighed Big Mama Chandra.

She paused and bowed her head as if she said a silent prayer, then she took both of my hands in hers. I sat silently on the settee waiting for her to begin.

"I know that you are only seven, Victoria, but you must use that special mind of yours to understand."

"Around a hundred years ago, four men headed from New York to Texas to find land and make their fortune. There were two Scottish brothers, a Frenchman, and a Jewish man. When they travelled through Virginia, the Frenchman and the Jewish man met and fell in love with two beautiful Cherokee Indian sisters selling their baskets and pottery in a general store. They courted them, married them, and brought them to Carson. The Frenchman became a wealthy farmer, and the Jewish man became a wealthy rancher."

"The Scottish brothers had continued on without their friends to try to settle bigger pieces of land. The brothers were greedy and foolish in their desires and had very little faith.

When they saw their friends again, they became jealous that the Frenchman and Jewish man were happily married and wealthy. They decided to make bigger fortunes and find better wives. They set up a cattle business in Carson with all the money that they had, but they didn't make very much money at first. Down on their luck, the Scots visited a local saloon where a drunken stranger told them that there was a voodoo woman who lived on the outskirts of town that could help them to become rich. They left quickly and didn't hear the stranger's warning about the woman. They travelled to her small shack and found a beautiful young Black woman sitting in a rocking chair on the porch.

When they approached the house, they were both struck by the need to have the woman, so they began to fight over which would have her. The younger Scot killed his brother in his sudden strength and madness while the beautiful woman watched from the porch with a evil smile on her beautiful face.

When the younger brother saw what he had done, he began to cry. The young woman left the porch and embraced him.

"Marree me, an ya can ha' me an' be welltee an' youn' fa evah," she whispered in his ear.

"Yes, anything!"

The young Scotsman agreed to her demands and tried to embrace the voodoo woman.

She yanked away from him and raised her hands to the sky.

"Dahk spirits! Dis man ha made a vow ta me! If he evah deny it, le' his chil'ren and dere chil'ren and dere chil'ren ta de end o' time be curse ta suffa de dahk line o' mis'ree an' pain. Let dem nevah see lastin' 'appiness ohr peace!"

The Scotsman barely heard her because he was filled with such longing and lust for the woman that carried her inside to claim his prize.

The next day, he awoke and came face to face with the evil that he had done. His brother's dead body was in bed with him, and the older Scot's face held an evil smile. The young Scot screamed in fear and stumbled from the house. The woman wasn't around, so he ran away from the small shack without looking back.

When he got back to town, he forgot all about his promise to the voodoo woman. He told all who asked that his brother returned to New York. Then, the young Scot's cattle business picked up and started to make him wealthy. He did so well that he built a ranch in the country. He married the local storeowner's daughter and brought her to the ranch.

Almost year later, the young Black woman showed up on his doorstep with a little girl with red hair telling him that she had come to take her place as his wife. The Scotsman ran her and the child off without thinking of the curse.

Soon after, while his young wife expected their first child, she fell ill. She and the child died in childbirth. His business went bad, he lost his ranch, and he got real sick. No one would help him because they knew that he had done something bad with the voodoo woman. He sought her out, but he found only an empty house. He looked all over town, but he could not find her. He searched high and low for weeks.

Finally, when he fell into despair, he returned to the voodoo woman's small shack in which he now lived, and there she sat on the porch. The Scotsman became enraged, and he wanted to kill her. He started forward to end it all, but his small daughter walked from behind her. He knew then that he had to accept his fate. He sold the cattle business for a good amount of money, and he bought a small farm in the nearby town of Rosedown. He and the voodoo woman had two more daughters and a son.

After awhile, the woman sent her daughters away to her family in Louisiana after she saw that the Scotsman adored them more than her son. No other women were allowed to be around her men. Against the Scotsman's wishes, she spoiled her son and made him evil.

When her daughters returned home as young women, she taught them all of her secrets and skills in voodoo, especially about the dark line. She also taught them to use those skills against other women if they felt threatened and on their men to hold them to their vows."

Big Mama paused again and looked down at the floor.

When she looked up at me, she looked like she would cry, but she started to speak again.

"You see, Victoria, the Scotsman and the voodoo woman were your grandmother, Betts' grandparents. Your great-great grandmother never removed the curse even after the Scotsman came back to her because she knew that he would leave her without it. Betts used the same voodoo to get your Grandpa Paul to marry her and hold him to her. And, it is in your grandmother's nature to bring others across the line until someone can break it," she finished quietly.

She stopped talking and looked me directly in my eyes.

"Mary has seen that your child will break the line, Victoria. Betts probably knows this too, so she'll try to cross you over the line to keep the power in future generations. You will have to be very strong from now on."

I nodded, but something about the story that Big Mama Chandra told me stuck in my mind.

"Big Mama Chandra? What happened to the Frenchman and the Jewish man?"

She chuckled a little and hugged me.

"Why, the Frenchman is your Grandpa Ed's grandfather, and the Jewish man is your Grandpa Paul's grandfather. He is from whom you get your white skin and blue eyes. You get your hair from Betts' father, the Scotsman, and your beautiful face from the Frenchman."

I nodded, and then my stomach growled. Big Mama grinned and looked at the window. She saw that it was bright sunlight outside.

"It's past time to fill that belly. Let's go find Ms. Sadie."

She took my hand and led me out of the room.

Later that day, I sat in the living room and thought about everything that Big Mama had told me. Now, that I knew more about Betts, I felt pity for her. I tried to pray, but every time, I closed my eyes and began my prayer, I forgot what to say. I decided to pray when I went to bed.

After about two weeks, Aunt Charlotte surprised us all by getting out of bed and walking with the crutches Grandpa Ed made her. She wobbled at first, but she soon got used to them.

"I wanted to surprise Victoria on her birthday," she said with a big smile.

I gaped in surprise because I forgot my own birthday. I ran to Aunt Charlotte, gave her a big hug, and tried not to knock her to the floor.

"Oh, thank you, Aunt Charlotte!"

I pulled back then hugged her again.

She laughed.

"And you know what else? We will be going home next week! Aunt Mary found someone to drive us back to Dallas!"

I whooped and ran to tell Hope and Ms. Sadie. Hope and Ms. Sadie laughed and jumped around with me when I told them that we were going back home to Dallas.

"I'm gonna miss ya, lil' miss," Hope said when we quieted down.

"So will I, Miss Victoria," said Ms. Sadie.

I hugged them both and tried not to cry.

"I'll be back one day."

They nodded and sent me back to Aunt Charlotte.

We left the next week in Aunt Charlotte's Oldsmobile driven by one of the field hands who knew how to drive and needed a ride back to Dallas. I sat in the back with Aunt Charlotte careful not to touch her leg.

As we left, Big Mama Chandra and Grandpa Ed stood in the yard and waved. Hope and David stood behind them waving too. I felt the tears rise up in my throat because I would miss my family and friends, but I was happy to be going back to Dallas being farther away from Mama and Daddy. I turned around and gave everyone a final wave before settling down to think about all that had happened that summer. I knew deep down that the things that happened had changed me. I wasn't the same happy, carefree little girl going back to Dallas, and that scared me.

8

"Freckle face, yella skin, na, na, na, na!"

The chant came from the group of girls around me. I covered my ears and tried to walk away, but one of the girls stepped in my way.

"Freckle face, yella skin, na, na, na, na!"

They crept closer and chanted louder.

"What is the meaning of this?"

I sighed when I heard Ms. Johnson's voice. The girls immediately quieted. No one said a word.

"Victoria, what happened?"

I shook my head knowing that I couldn't tell her what really happened.

"We were just playing, ma'am."

The tallest girl, Mia, stepped forward with a smile to convince Ms. Johnson.

"Yes, ma'am, we were just playin'."

Ms. Johnson looked like she didn't believe us, but she nodded anyway.

"Well, y'all get on home, now. I hear there's some folks catching sick around here."

She looked at me one more time, and then she turned around and left. All of the girls breathed a sigh of relief. Mia turned to me and made a spiteful face.

"Don't think you can be our friend just 'cause you didn't rat us out to Ms. Johnson."

I just looked at her, shrugged, and began walking home.

Mia had been mean to me ever since Aunt Charlotte enrolled me in Carver Middle School, and the other girls had followed her example. I hadn't wanted to go to school, but my aunts had insisted that I needed to be around other children my age.

Carver was a private school that wealthy Black people had put money together to build so that their children didn't have to be bussed all the way across town to the schools designated for Black children. It was within walking distance of Aunt Charlotte's house, and I hated it.

I hated the school with its musty hallways and dark lighting. I hated the food they served because it was always some kind of meat soaked in gravy with clumped rice or dry mashed potatoes. I hated the children because they all made fun of me, my clothes, my proper speech, anything so that they could laugh at me.

Most of all, I hated some of the teachers because they acted like the children. They made fun of the way that I spoke and my clothes too.

When I started, a few of them wouldn't call on me on purpose when I raised my hand. Soon, I just stopped raising my hand.

The only thing that I liked about Carver was Ms. Johnson, the music teacher. If I felt low from being ridiculed by either the teachers or students, I would run to her classroom before I went home. She would look up from her desk, smile, and nod her head at the piano. I would sit and begin playing and singing to whatever tune was on the stand.

Sometimes, I think Ms. Johnson left music there on purpose because she hummed or tapped her foot to the music. It was my solace to the misery that was Carver Middle School.

When I got home that afternoon, Aunt Charlotte and Aunt Mary waited for me at the door.

"Victoria, come in and shut the door."

Aunt Charlotte's voice brooked no disobedience because she turned and limped into the parlor without another word. Aunt Mary trailed behind her with a sympathetic glance in my direction. Scared at Aunt Charlotte's tone, I shut the door and followed them.

When I reached the doorway of the parlor, I took a moment to take a good look at my aunts. Both were still beautiful and shapely, but they had started to show small signs of getting older.

Aunt Charlotte looked older than she had before that fateful trip to see Big Mama Chandra and Grandpa Ed five years ago. Aunt Mary had not aged very much in her appearance, but her eyes seemed to have gotten darker and deeper. Now, as I looked at them, I regretted all of the mean things that I had said to them that morning before school.

"Victoria, there is an influenza sickness in Dallas. Your Aunt Mary and I don't want you to become ill, so we are sending you to Mama's and Daddy's until it passes," Aunt Charlotte said calmly.

Then, she coughed. She tried to cover it up by clearing her throat, but I wasn't fooled.

"Aunt Charlotte, are you sick?"

She smiled weakly.

"Just a bit. It's nothing for you to worry about. Now, I want you to keep up your studies while you're in the country, and I heard that the church that your grandfathers built has a piano. I'm sure they wouldn't mind if you practiced on it."

All I heard was that my beloved Aunt Charlotte was sick. I didn't want to leave her. I felt that I needed to stay and take care of her, but she thought ahead of me.

"Your Aunt Mary will stay with me to help me get better, so don't you worry."

Tears filled my eyes, and I crossed the room to kneel at her side.

"Please don't send me away, Aunt Charlotte. I won't sass back anymore, and I won't complain about Carver either."

She stroked the top of my head, and then she pushed me away.

"No, you have to go. I don't want you to get sick. You'll leave on the bus tomorrow morning. Your Big Mama will meet you at the bus depot in Carson."

My feelings were so hurt. I turned to Aunt Mary to see if she could help me change Aunt Charlotte's mind, but she gave me a sad smile and shook her head.

"Victoria, remember your faith and all that I have taught you. You must go, or you will fall sick too," she said gently.

I looked at her face and knew that Aunt Charlotte wasn't the only one ill. The knowledge filled me that my aunts sent me away not only to avoid the sickness, but also so that I wouldn't see them die if they became worse. My heart felt heavy. I didn't want to disobey my aunts, but I felt like a coward to leave them.

"Can I hug y'all?"

"It's not safe, but you can blow us lots of kisses."

Aunt Charlotte lips widened into a little grin. I knew that she tried to make me feel better. I smiled slightly and blew each of them kisses.

With heavy feet, I walked to my room and began to gather my things to put in the open suitcase that sat on my bed.

When I finished, I fell onto the bed and cried into my pillow so that my aunts wouldn't hear. I thought that I was being punished because it wasn't fair that what I wanted most was to be removed from Carver not to be sent away from my aunts too. When sleep came over me, thoughts that I returned to the place that had given me five years worth of nightmares made me shiver.

Big Mama waited for me when I finally arrived at the Carson bus depot. She gave me a big hug and kiss then chatted away while the driver found my suitcase. I gave her a tired smile and tried to keep up with everything that she said. She led me over to the shiny new Ford truck and motioned for me to get in the cab. She threw my suitcase in the back and climbed inside with me.

"Whew! We're so glad to have you, lil' mirror."

She seemed so excited that she almost bounced in her seat.

"You look so much more like me now than you did last year when me and your grandpa came to visit y'all in Dallas. You're just so beautiful and growing up shapely like your Big Mama."

She laughed out loud and started the truck.

She continued to ramble on about things that happened on the homestead since I was little. I just smiled and nodded to myself because she didn't need an answer. I perked up however when I heard my daddy's name.

"...and he's been acting a lot better since he returned from that Korean war. Your Grandpa Paul told us that he had been hit with shrapnel in his leg and that they almost had to cut it off. They saved it but he has a limp and his arm is all scarred up from cuts. Yeah, it was something else."

As she continued to try to tell me about everything on the ride home, my thoughts drifted back to how nasty my mama and daddy had been to me before when I visited them. I shivered at how mean they were, and I worried about what had happened to my little sister, Ruth. I felt guilt rise within me because I had only thought of her a few times during the five years since I had seen her. I prayed that Mama and Daddy hadn't been mean and nasty to her too.

When we drove down the lane, I noticed more field workers in the field. I wondered fleetingly if David was at the homestead with his aunt and uncle. I smiled when I remembered him and Uncle P. It was a good memory.

Big Mama parked the truck in the newly paved driveway, got out, and came on my side to help me, but I had already jumped out of the truck. I looked around the homestead and notice the improvements that had been made. The lane had been shortened to make the yard bigger. The windows had flowerboxes, and there were more flowers and plants around the porch. The driveway went all the way around the side of the house. It looked nice and peaceful.

I closed my eyes and took a deep breath of the country air. It made me feel a little better just being there. I opened my eyes and saw that Big Mama smiled at me. I returned her smile.

"Where's Grandpa Ed, Big Mama?"

She laughed and shook her head.

"He's in the house trying to polish off the big brunch that Ms. Sadie and Hope made for you."

I perked up at the mention that Hope remained at the homestead.

I followed Big Mama into the house and into the kitchen.

"Grandpa Ed! Hope! Ms. Sadie!"

Hope and Ms. Sadie turned around from their tasks and ran to give me a hug. We all laughed and danced around in the doorway.

"Well, my dear, I guess old Grandpa Ed will have to take a leftover hug," Grandpa Ed said stepping forward to claim his hug.

"Oh, Grandpa."

I giggled and hugged him tightly.

When I pulled back, I saw that Hope had a big belly. I was about to ask her a question, but I was interrupted.

"Ahem."

I heard a throat clear from the doorway.

We all turned around to see who it was.

"Andrew. Well, come on in and meet your niece," said Big Mama.

He stepped into the light, and I got a good look at my uncle.

He looked almost exactly like Grandpa Ed except his eyes were grey. He smiled and stepped forward to grab me in a big bear hug.

"I haven't seen you since you were no bigger than a thimble! Look at you now!"

"Andrew! Put the child down before you squeeze her to death!"

Big Mama fussed at my uncle, but a smile was in her voice.

Uncle Andrew laughed, gave me another squeeze, and put me down. I took a deep breath and smiled at him.

"You're my uncle?"

I grinned and teased Uncle Andrew. He laughed and stuck out his chest.

"Sure am. I've been away in the army since before you were born. I got to come home a couple of times, so I got to see you when you were a little mite. Now, I'm home for good, so I'll get to see you plenty."

His smile was contagious, and I returned it.

"Well, now that all the reunions are over, let's eat some of this meal before Ed and Andrew head to the field," said Big Mama.

I turned and noticed the spread of food on the table. There were bowls of cantaloupe and watermelon, platters of scrambled and over easy eggs, bacon, sausage, and biscuits. I also noticed some teacakes and lemon sticks. I breathed in the wonderful smells and moved toward the table.

"Let us say grace," said Uncle Andrew.

All of us stopped and bowed our heads.

"Father God, thank you for bringing us together on this day that you made. We thank you for Victoria's safe trip. Thank you for all the blessings that you have given us and have in store for us. We ask that you bless this food and the hands that prepared it. In Jesus' Name, Amen."

Uncle Andrew finished his prayer and crossed himself. We all said Amen and returned to moving toward the food. I thanked Uncle Andrew for his prayer.

"Aw, sweets, it's nothing. God saved me many a time while I was away. The least that I can do is thank Him and ask His grace."

I nodded and turned around to take the plate that Hope held for me. As I sat down and began to eat, I felt the love of my family. I realized that I missed being in the country. However, deep down, I knew I didn't want to remain here if Aunt Charlotte and Aunt Mary didn't get better. I closed my eyes and said a quick prayer for their healing.

The smell of coffee and biscuits woke me the next morning. The smells woke memories in my mind of my last visit to the country. I shuddered when the bad ones came forward with the good ones. I decided then and there that I would make more good ones this time. I smiled to myself at the promise and got out of bed to throw on some clothes. I went to the updated bathroom with its shiny brass fittings and washed up for breakfast.

As I followed the smells to the kitchen, I noticed that it was very early, because the sun had barely risen.

"Good morning, my dear, what are you doing up so early?"

Grandpa Ed spoke to me and took a sip of his steaming cup of coffee.

I smiled at him because he had his paper in front of his face just like I remembered.

"Good morning, Grandpa. I couldn't sleep with the smell of Big Mama Chandra's biscuits and your coffee."

Grandpa Ed chuckled.

"Well, c'mon and get you a couple of these biscuits before Andrew gets in here. I swear your uncle eats two trays of your grandmother's biscuits every morning."

I giggled, grabbed a saucer and biscuit, and sat down at the table.

"Grandpa, can I come with you this morning to the fields?"

I waited for his answer while I buttered my biscuit.

"Why, yes, you sure can. I'll be out a while today because I have to check the fence line on the back twenty. You'll need to check with your Big Mama Chandra first."

He took another sip of his coffee.

"It's okay. I don't think that she has anything for me to do with Ms. Sadie and Hope in the house."

"I heard my name?"

Big Mama Chandra came through the door. She stopped and gave me a small hug before going to the counter to cut more biscuits.

Grandpa Ed lowered his paper.

"Victoria would like to go with me today, and I said yes. She was thinking that you didn't have chores for her with Ms. Sadie and Hope with you."

Big Mama smiled.

"Yes, it's fine. We won't be doing much today but cooking. Now, tomorrow, I know that you're going to want to help in the garden."

I brightened up when she said garden because I loved to garden. I had actually taken over Aunt Charlotte's garden in Dallas.

"Yes, ma'am."

I nodded and happily chewed my biscuit.

"Big Mama? Why are your biscuits so good?"

She laughed softly and turned around from the counter.

"Because I make them with lots of patience and love. One day, I'll show you," she promised.

She twisted back around to put the pan in the oven. I nodded and grabbed another biscuit.

Before Big Mama Chandra would let me leave with Grandpa Ed, she slathered me with her special sun cream. I remembered it and the smell from five years ago. I crinkled my nose at the smell and allowed her to rub it on my exposed skin. Big Mama laughed.

"Since you're bigger, I know that you won't be rolling in the dirt to get rid of the smell."

I laughed too.

"No, ma'am, I won't. Aunt Charlotte will tan my hide if I got any of my clothes dirty."

At the mention of my aunt's name, Big Mama and I both got quiet.

"They'll be alright, Victoria. Just keep praying."

I nodded and went to find Grandpa Ed.

Grandpa Ed sat in his old Ford truck idling in the front driveway. I noticed that he had built sides onto the back like a wagon. He smiled and waved me into the cab of the truck with him.

"Can I ride on the back, Grandpa?"

He laughed and nodded. I jumped in the back and sat down behind the cab. Grandpa Ed laughed again and drove off into the fields. He made several stops to check with the groups of field hands who worked with the different crops before we made it to the back twenty.

We both got out and walked the fence line checking for holes. About halfway through, we found a large section that had been cut and reposted about twenty yards onto my grandparents' property. Grandpa Ed frowned and took out a notepad from his overalls pocket. He wrote something down then he made a drawing of the section. I was curious so I asked what was wrong.

"The Adams' keep trying to take land. They asked to buy a half acre, but I told them no. I guess they decided to take it. I'm marking the spot, so I can send P and David to put it back."

Hearing that Uncle P and David were around made me anxious to see them. They had been good to me last time I visited.

"Where are they now?"

"They're in the front twenty clearing the corn," Grandpa replied distractedly.

At his tone, I got quiet so that he could finish marking the fence line. I knew that he was upset, and I didn't want to bother him. I stayed quiet and tried to patiently wait for him to finish so that we could go find David and Uncle P.

It was almost dinnertime when we reached the front twenty, and I had almost run out of patience. I knew that Grandpa Ed had lost his with me because he kept clearing his throat when he thought I was about to open my mouth to speak.

When we drove up to the front twenty, I could see two men pulling up dried corn stalks and tossing them into the bed of the field wagon.

"Ho, there!"

Grandpa Ed waved and yelled out of the open window. I saw that one of the men was Uncle P as he turned around to return Grandpa's greeting.

"Ho, there!"

Uncle P waved at us.

I immediately became disappointed because I didn't see David anywhere. When Grandpa Ed parked the truck by the wagon, I could see the other man walking to join Uncle P who was heading toward the truck. No! It couldn't be! My mind screamed denial at me when my eyes took in the appearance of the other man. He was still slim but as tall as his Uncle P, and he still had a nice face only it was older.

David! I knew that it was him, and I ducked my head into the back of the truck. I became embarrassed that I didn't realize if I got older so would he. I still thought of him as that boy who had been my playmate and friend that awful summer. Now, he wasn't a boy. He was a man. I felt sad at the thought that I had lost my friend.

"Hey, Mista Ed. How you today?"

I heard Uncle P's voice approach the truck.

"Well, P, I was good until I saw the back twenty. The Adams' have decided if I don't sell to them, they'll just take it. I need you and David to go take it back. Just move the fence posts back in line with the rest."

Grandpa Ed gave his instructions with grim voice.

"The Adams' are something else, Mister Ed. I never saw such mean White people," said a new deep voice.

I guessed that it was David's.

"I have, son, any a ways, I got a surprise for y'all."

Grandpa Ed's tone lightened when he changed the subject.

"A surprise, sir?" asked David.

"Uh huh. I wonder why she hasn't come over to speak," I heard Grandpa Ed utter.

Footsteps approached the truck, and then I looked down at the open bed of the truck and saw Grandpa Ed, Uncle P, and David staring at me.

"Surprise?"

I smiled awkwardly, and I sat up and scooted off the tailgate. I stood up, dusted off the back of my jeans, and stared at the ground while I tried not to blush.

"Miss Victoria!"

Uncle P picked me up and swung me around in a tight hug. He laughed and turned with me still in his arms to face David.

"Lookee heah, David! Miss Victoria, done come back!"

David looked at me and smiled.

"Hey Victoria, how've you been doing?"

I blushed and squirmed in Uncle P's arms. He chuckled and put me down.

"Fine," I whispered and smiled shyly.

Uncle P laughed again and gave me long look.

"You so growed up now, Miss Victoria. So pretty and look at all that red har. You's the image ol' Mista Paul."

I smiled at him and moved closer to the back of the truck. David hadn't said very much, and I was a little disappointed.

Grandpa Ed turned and walked to the corn asking questions, and Uncle P followed. David and I stood in awkward silence.

"What are you doing here?"

David's question sounded abrupt and angry. I instantly became annoyed.

"I'm visiting," I replied with a roll of my eyes.

"Oh," was all he said.

We stood there silently until David gave a small sigh.

"I missed you when you left."

Tears rose in my throat and filled my eyes.

"I missed you too."

My throat felt thick with my feelings.

"I know that I'm a little too old to play like we used to, but can I still be your friend?"

"I'd like that," I whispered.

"Can I give you a hug too?"

He grinned at me, and I smiled back before going into his arms. It felt nice but different than when we hugged as children. I pulled back because I knew that our friendship had changed.

I shook my head in sadness.

"Well, I'll let you catch up to them, and just tell my grandpa that I'll wait in the truck."

David nodded and walked to the tractor where Grandpa Ed and Uncle P stood. I sat in the truck in regret of the time lost and tried to remember the games we played.

The next day, Big Mama Chandra said that she had to go into town for some supplies. I jumped at the chance to go so that I could get away from the memories that had swamped me on my return from seeing the older David. I put on one of my best sundresses that Aunt Charlotte helped me sew. It was fitted light green cotton with an empire waistline and full skirt. She had let me cut it a little above the ankle so that it wouldn't be so hot. I put on my bobby socks and white tennis shoes to finish off the outfit. I brushed my hair and used a white ribbon for a headband. I felt good and smiled at my reflection when I walked out of the room.

"My, my, don't ya look lov'ly!"

I grinned at Hope when I walked into the front room to wait for Big Mama.

She chuckled and fluffed the divan pillows. I remembered that I wanted to ask about her big belly.

"Hope, when is your baby coming?"

She laughed.

"Sometime in August. I'll be glad too 'cause he wearing me out."

I paused because I wanted to ask more questions but I didn't want to be nosy. Hope answered them for me.

"When ya lef ta Dallas, Henry ask'd to make a 'onest woman o' me. We got hitch'd dat ye'ah."

She came and sat next to me.

I smiled at her tone.

"I like Henry. I'm happy for you."

I gave her a hug. She hugged me then pulled back quickly.

"Now, don' get dirty."

"Are you ready, Lil' Mirror?"

I turned to answer, but my mouth fell open when I looked at Big Mama Chandra. She wore a beautiful blue full-skirted dress with a little matching jacket. She had on blue and white shoes, hat, and white gloves. I had never seen Big Mama dressed up like that.

"Cat got ya tongue, lil' miss?"

Hope laughed at my expression.

I nodded and stood up as Big Mama had rolled her eyes at my reaction and went out the door. I followed, shook my head, and thought that this summer had started off with lots of surprises.

Big Mama was well known in Carson businesses, and she was given the special privilege of going through the front instead of through the back like most Black folks. I noticed that we were stared at by most of the town folks while we walked up and down the sidewalks and crossed the streets. None of it seemed to affect Big Mama Chandra, and she seemed to just be focused on getting all the supplies that she needed. I noticed because most of the stares were aimed at me. Some of them curious and some smiling, but most were mean. I grew uncomfortable and anxious to get back to the homestead.

"Hola! Miss Bictoria! Ms. Shandra! How you are?"

I heard a familiar voice exclaim from behind us.

I turned, and Marcos walked swiftly towards us. I met him halfway and gave him a big hug.

"Míja, you have grown! Muy Boníta!"

When he released me, I saw that Juan stood behind him smiling.

"Well, muchácha, you have come back."

He had grown taller as well and looked as handsome as his father.

I smiled and nodded.

"Yes, for now. My aunts are sick, and I have to stay here until they get better."

"Ah, we pray for you tias," said Marcos solemnly.

Big Mama Chandra spoke to Marcos and Juan about their health and their garden. Thinking of the garden made me remember my first taste of jalapeno. Glancing at Juan, I saw that he smiled at me as if he thought about the same memory.

"They are hotter now," he said confirming that he thought of the same thing.

I giggled.

"We gotta get over to the feed store, so we'll see y'all later."

Big Mama Chandra waved at them and moved toward the truck.

Marcos and Juan said their goodbyes and went back towards the grocery.

Big Mama and I climbed into the new Ford truck and drove to the end of town to the feed store. There were barrels and bags of feed displayed along with different kinds of farming tools in front of the store. Big Mama turned to me.

"Stay in the truck. Do not get out and do not talk to anyone especially any White people."

Scared at her tone, I nodded.

"Yes, ma'am."

She nodded satisfied and got out to go into the store. This time, she went around to the back.

I sat and wondered what went on within the feed store. I saw several White people going into the front and some came out within few minutes. Most of them ignored me, but after a while, a couple of men came over and asked me for whom I waited. I looked forward and didn't say a word. They both shrugged and walked away.

Then, one of them turned.

"Wait a cott'n pickin' minute, Joe. That's Clyde's gal."

The man called Joe turned and squinted his eyes at me.

"Yep! That's her, Tex. Looks just like ol' Paul Roberts."

He grinned with a big gap in his yellowed teeth.

"Where's yo daddy, gal?"

I stayed silent.

"Didn't ya hear, gal?"

Tex raised his voice and moved closer.

I started to shake with fear because I hadn't ever been bothered by White people.

"Tex, Joe, y'all leave that poor girl alone," new voice ordered.

The men swung around to look at the newcomer.

"Aw, Billy, we was just funnin' with her."

The man named Tex whined to this "Billy" person.

"Leave. Now," the man called Billy said.

Joe looked like he would say something, but shrugged his shoulders and walked away.

"Are you alright, miss?"

I turned to look at him and looked straight into clear blue eyes in a handsome face that was filled with concern.

"I'm okay. Thank you, sir," I said shakily.

He chuckled.

"I'm not a sir. I'm just Billy. My father, Dr. Herbert, just bought the ranch next to your Grandpa Paul's, and those men work for my father. They're usually are okay, but they both have mean streaks."

I nodded and kept staring because he was a very handsome White boy. He was tall with light brown hair and clear blue eyes like mine. He had dimples and a nice smile.

"Who's here with you?"

His question snapped me out of my daze.

"Um, my Big, Big Mama," I stuttered.

He smiled at me again, and I blushed.

"Victoria Alicia Roberts! Didn't I tell you not to talk to anyone?"

Big Mama Chandra fussed with her hands on her hips from the other side of the truck.

I blushed again and looked over at the big burly man carrying bags of feed for Big Mama. I had been so caught up staring at Billy that I hadn't even heard them coming. I opened my mouth to tell her what happened, but Billy spoke first.

"It's my fault, ma'am. I saw a pretty girl sitting in the truck and wanted to speak to her. I apologize for my forwardness."

Billy flashed Big Mama Chandra a grin and walked around the truck to help the man.

"Well, she's still a girl and can't be speaking to boys just yet," Big Mama harrumphed.

Billy chuckled.

"Why ma'am, I'm only just a boy. I'll be fourteen on my birthday."

I glanced at him in surprise because he looked so much older. He saw that I looked his way and winked. I cast my eyes down and blushed. Big Mama harrumphed again and got in the truck. The big burly man shook his head frowning, and he retreated inside the store.

As Big Mama Chandra drove away fussing at me, I looked back to see Billy still stood on the sidewalk.

My appearance in town had gotten the local gossip mill stirred up, and soon Mama and Daddy found out that I was back in Carson. A few days after our trip to town, Big Mama Chandra and Grandpa Ed told me that Mama and Daddy would come to supper that night. I began to shiver in fear. I thought that the time away from them had made the fear go away, but it returned quickly when I knew that I would be within touching distance of them. I spent the rest of the time in my room praying for strength, courage, and protection from my own parents.

When I walked into the front room that night, Mama and Daddy were already seated on the divan. Daddy leaned forward on a cane, and Mama sat close to him. They both looked up when I entered the room, and I felt a weird sense that

I walked into the past. I shook my head to clear my crazy thoughts.

"Good evening," I greeted them politely.

"Vicky! How we have missed you!"

Daddy seemed happy to see me and struggled to stand up.

Mama helped him, and they crossed the room to give me hugs. I hugged them back awkwardly because their attitudes confused me.

"You've grown up so much, and you're so beautiful. You look just like your mother but with your Grandpa Paul's skin and eyes."

Daddy released me to return to the divan, and Mama followed him. I noticed that Daddy still did all the talking. I tried to shake that mean thought from my head, and I moved forward to sit on the cushioned stool by Big Mama Chandra's chair. We all sat there for a few minutes in tense silence, then Daddy cleared his throat.

"Vicky, your mother and I have spoken with your grandparents. We want to say that we're sorry for all that happened five years ago. It was ugly and mean. You're our daughter, and we love you. We'd like for you to visit us whenever you want.

Since I got home from the war, it's been rough on us. Your Grandpa Paul and grandmother, Betts, try to help us all they can, but it's hard for them too because they have the ranch to run."

He paused and looked down.

"Clyde Jr. and Steven try to help, but they have their studies. Watching my sons try to help me made me realize what I did to you. I'm sorry, Vicky. Please forgive us," he pleaded.

I didn't know what to say.

They were my parents, and I felt pity for them. They were having a rough time of it from what Daddy said.

I decided to do as God commanded and forgive them. I walked over to them and hugged them both. I thought Mama's hug felt a little forced, but I put it out of my mind.

"I love you both, and I forgive you."

I gave them a watery smile and tried to hold back my tears.

Daddy started to cry, and Mama comforted him. She didn't shed a tear.

"Well, now that's out of the way, let's eat some of those vittles I smell," Grandpa Ed suggested lightly.

"Yes, sir!"

Uncle Andrew, who had been sitting in the corner, agreed and jumped up to run to the dining room.

Everyone laughed. We all rose to follow him to the dining room. I hung back to help Daddy if he needed it. I saw him smile at Mama and nod his head. I smiled too thinking that all would be well now.

Supper went well because Uncle Andrew and Daddy swapped war stories until Big Mama called a halt to the really gross ones. They both laughed and gave their plates some attention. I felt silly that I had been so afraid to see my parents. I smiled and finished eating the delicious roasted chicken, sweet potatoes, greens, and cornbread. I was too full when Ms. Sadie brought out the lemon cake, and it was my favorite.

When I passed the cake to Mama, I saw her tighten her lips and lightly yank the cake from me. I glanced at her, but she smiled back at me. I relaxed and chided myself for being silly.

Supper ended, and the adults all went into the front room to have coffee. I stayed behind to help Ms. Sadie because Hope hadn't been well for the past two days. We stood in the kitchen while she washed, and I dried.

"I think your Mama and Daddy have turned a new leaf," said Ms. Sadie.

I smiled and nodded.

"Yes, ma'am."

When we finished the dishes, I was tired from being anxious all afternoon. I decided to go to bed. I went into the front room and said goodnight to everyone. I gave everyone a hug and kiss then went to my room. I undressed and said my prayers. I thanked God for everything especially for the change in my parents. When I drifted off to sleep, my mind wandered to the look on Mama's face when she yanked the cake from my hands.

The next morning was chaos. Big Mama Chandra received a telegram from one of Aunt Mary's clients that my aunts' conditions had worsened. Big Mama Chandra was hysterical when Grandpa Ed came from the field.

"You're going to have to get up there, Chandra. They need you," said Grandpa Ed firmly.

Big Mama Chandra nodded and sniffled.

"I know. I'll leave on the bus tomorrow."

I felt so useless. What could I do? They had sent me away, and now I felt like I could have helped them if I had stayed. Tears started to roll down my face at the thought of losing my beloved aunts. Big Mama saw my tears and tried to comfort me while she tried to stop her own tears.

"Victoria, you will have to mind yourself until I get back."

Big Mama Chandra fussed and gave me instructions while she packed later that night.

Scared and anxious for my aunts, I whispered "yes ma'am" and went to my room for a restless sleep.

The next morning, she left.

I stayed around the homestead for a week trying to help Ms. Sadie, but she lost patience and sent me to the garden. I worked on the garden during the mornings, but it was too well kept.

By the next week, I was at a loss at what I could do to help. There had been no word of my aunts from Big Mama Chandra.

My parents came to visit one afternoon a couple of weeks after Big Mama had left. They stayed to have supper and to talk with Grandpa Ed about his crops. It was then that the idea hit me. Since I couldn't help my aunts, or around the homestead, I could go help my parents. I presented the idea to them and Grandpa Ed over coffee, and my parents were overjoyed.

"Pack your clothes, then you can stay a while," Daddy said and sipped his coffee.

"A week is enough. I'll need her back before I get busy with the summer harvest."

Grandpa Ed frowned at Daddy and Mama with his firm demand.

Daddy shrugged his shoulders and nodded. When they got ready to leave, I grabbed my hurriedly packed suitcase and went with them.

When we arrived at Mama and Daddy's home, all of my siblings poured out of the small house. I saw that Clyde Jr., Steven, and Ruth had grown quite a bit. I guessed that the two small children tailing behind was my new brother, Will, and baby sister, Lacy. I gave them all a hug, but I held on to Ruth's hand when we walked into the house. I had missed her and wanted to talk to her.

"Put your suitcase in the back room, Victoria," said Daddy in a hard voice.

I turned around surprised at the difference in his tone. The smile on his face reminded me of the way he had smiled five years ago.

"After you put that up, go clean that kitchen."

Mama's voice and face looked hard and cruel. I stared at them both, and the fear rose within me. They had changed so quickly. My sisters and brothers crept outside when Mama and Daddy both laughed.

"Ha! Did you think that we would really ask you for forgiveness for teaching you lessons that you needed?"

Daddy sounded evil. I looked at Mama, and she was narrowed her eyes and turned up her lip. The tears came, but I refused to let them fall.

"I want to go back to Grandpa Ed's, please."

I whispered my request, Mama and Daddy just laughed.

"You'll go back when we want you to go back."

Daddy limped over and slapped me hard across the face. I took the hit, but I didn't fall because I was bigger. He frowned and raised his arm to slap me again. Mama stepped forward suddenly.

"Remember, she has to go to work day after tomorrow."

Daddy lowered his hand and nodded.

"Go on and clean that kitchen. Then, you can chase that hen down for dinner," Mama demanded with a vicious smile.

I felt betrayed and foolish that I believed my parents had changed. When I walked into the dirty kitchen, I prayed that God would deliver me from them again.

A couple of days later, Daddy drove me to the Adams' homestead again to pick cotton. This time, he threatened to beat Ruth if I talked to anyone. I felt sad because he had figured out how much I loved her. He also gave me a pair of old gloves, a wide brim straw hat, and a lunch pail with a cup. I looked inside the pail and saw there was only a large piece of day old cornbread. I sighed and thought that it was better than nothing. Then I smiled because thanks to Hope, I knew how to pick cotton.

When Mr. Bob saw me, he grinned and spat next to my foot.

"She's real grown up now. Yep, she can pick me lots of cotton. Don' think about running this time, gal. I reckon she gon' stay, Clyde?"

He turned to Daddy.

"Yes, sir!"

Daddy held his stomach and laughed out loud.

Mr. Bob chuckled and nodded before he threw a burlap sack at me.

"Fill that up twice before luncheon, gal."

I picked up the sack, stood up straight with my head held high, and walked into the field. That seemed to be the pattern for the next month. Daddy would drop me off, make small talk with Mr. Bob, and watch me walk into the cotton.

9

The whole month of July passed without any word from my aunts or my grandparents. I worked from sun up until sundown in the cotton fields. At first, my skin burned from the hot sun, but the burn went away when I turned a golden brown. I wore the white shirt and blue dungarees that Daddy gave me because he had taken my clothes to town and sold them to the seamstress. I didn't say a word because I didn't want him to hurt Ruth.

Every Friday, he was there to take all of my wages when Mr. Bob paid the workers. He'd take the money, rub his hands together, and tell me all about how he'd spend it. Mama was just as bad. She would take the little bit left over from Daddy and buy herself and my brothers treats. She never bought anything for my sisters or me. I still didn't say anything because Steven would take his and Will's treats and split them between all of the younger kids. When he offered me some, I told him to keep sharing with the little ones. I was too tired to enjoy anything anyway. I felt so weak, and I knew that it was because I didn't eat or sleep much.

Mama and Daddy didn't leave much for me to eat. I figured out how to take some seeds from the old garden and grow a tiny garden in the back of the house. Since, my parents made me clean and clear the backyard, I was able to keep it a secret. I ate the tomatoes and okra raw to keep the garden secret. But, when I felt my body become weaker, I couldn't tend the garden. I had to eat what I could. Sometimes, it was just leftover cornbread or biscuits. I'd say grace over it and eat it with some of the goat's milk that one of the field hands brought to me every morning. I wasn't full, and I was still hungry, but I would feel better.

Being hungry and weak, I felt like my mind started to play tricks on me. One Saturday, I sat by the open window in the front room of the house rocking my sister, Lacy, to sleep. Mama was in bed in her room, Daddy was gone, and all the other kids had gone to the creek to play. It was hot, and I had opened the front and back doors to try to get some air.

Suddenly, I saw a figure in a heavy black cape and tall black hat walk past the back door from behind the house. I sat up ready to see who had come to visit. Then, it came to me that there was nothing but woods behind the house. Fear came over me in the next moment. I couldn't hear any footsteps, but I waited for the figure to come to the front door. I felt my heart beating heavily in my chest. Without warning, the figure passed slowly by the window. I didn't see a head or face because the collar of the cape was turned up to meet the top hat.

My fear took over, and I lifted my still sleeping sister to my shoulder and ran to Mama.

"What's wrong with you? I should whip you for waking me."

She sat up and spat angrily at me when I burst into the room.

"Mama, someone passed by the window. It didn't look like a man, but it was dressed in black like one," I panted.

Mama laughed.

"Ah, you've just seen the school teacher. Did you speak to him?"

I shook my head still trembling in fear.

"Oh well, next time, say hello. He might take you with him. Now, go on back in there and rock that girl."

She waved me away and rearranged herself on the bed.

Curious and thinking that the schoolteacher could take me home, I hesitated by the bed.

"Take me with him?"

Mama opened one eye and looked at me nastily.

"Yes. To Hell where you should be."

I gasped and stepped back. I wanted to cry but didn't.

My sister was heavy, so I went back and sat down on the divan against the wall as far away from the window as I could get. Fear still travelled through my body, but I was more hurt by Mama's words. I loved my Mama even though she didn't love me. I closed my eyes and prayed.

"God, please help me. Please show me Your Loving Mercy. I don't understand. Is this how it's supposed to be? Am I being punished? Why does my Mama hate me so much? I love her, and I can't stop even when she's mean to me. Please take me away from this place. Please heal Aunt Charlotte and Aunt Mary. In Jesus' Name, Amen."

After I prayed, I felt a calm come over my mind, and I fell asleep hoping that the schoolteacher wouldn't come again.

The next day, when I looked at Mr. Bob's calendar by the water barrel, I saw that my birthday had passed. I shook my head sadly because I had forgotten my own birthday. I didn't even mind that Mama and Daddy had forgotten it because I knew that they didn't care. I did feel sad that my aunts or my Daniels family hadn't remembered. Then, I felt bad after that thought because I knew that something had to be wrong because Aunt Charlotte never missed my birthday. I immediately said a quick prayer for her and Aunt Mary's healing and went back to work.

It was after one grueling hot summer day in the fields later that week that I felt like God saw fit to give me a well-needed rest and bring my wretched situation to the light.

I had felt sick and hot all day. My body started to hurt more than the soreness of bending over cotton. My eyes were blurry, and my head felt like it was stuffed with the cotton from my sack. I looked down and saw that the ground was rising up to meet me. I heard footsteps and shouts as if from a distance.

"Miz Victoria! Miz Victoria!"

I heard Martin, the field hand who brought me the goat's milk everyday cry out.

"Here now, what's this?"

I heard Mr. Bob demand.

"I think she awful sick, Mistah Bob, suh," Martin cried.

"Well she can't be sick here. I don't want this pickin' ruined. Take her up to the front row and leave her for her Daddy to come get. He comes at sundown."

I heard Martin's concerned voice.

"Can I give huh water, Mr. Bob?"

"No! Just do what I said or you ain't gonna find no work here next year!"

After a few moments, I felt water being poured in my mouth, and I opened my lips and took a little more of the water.

I opened my eyes to Martin's worried face.

"Thank you, Mr. Martin. Now, can you help me up so I can finish my row?"

Mr. Martin looked so shocked that he leaned even closer to make sure that he had heard her right.

"No, miss, I'm takin' ya to Mistah Ed. He not far way."

He picked me up, and I tried to lift my head to protest. When I saw all of the other workers looking at me with pity, I closed my eyes in shame. The darkness was welcome to me for once.

Mr. Martin talked to me while he ran. He begged me to stay alive for all the people who loved me. I knew when he rounded the corner of the homestead because I could hear the familiar voices of some of the field hands ask what had happened. I heard them ask to help carry me, but Mr. Martin wouldn't let me go until he reached the shade of the porch, and then he bellowed for help. I heard Ms. Sadie's heavy footsteps run out of the door.

"What's all this?" she asked and drew a deep breath.

"Oh, my, Miss Victoria!"

Mr. Martin reassured Ms. Sadie quickly.

"No, Ms. Sadie, she ain't dead, but she close to it."

Ms. Sadie told Mr. Martin to take me to the back bedroom and yelled for Big Mama Chandra. I wanted to ask about my aunts, and when she got back from Dallas, but my mouth wouldn't work.

When Dr. Herbert arrived, I was barely awake, and I had the shivers. He examined me and told me all about how he had delivered me. I felt him tremble and opened my eyes.

"Hello Dr. Herbert. I'm glad to see you again," I whispered weakly.

I felt so horrible. He told me that I would be fine and that he needed to go talk to my grandparents. I tried to smile, and he returned it and touched my cheek. Then, he turned and left quickly.

"Well, I hoped that we would meet again in a better way," a voice whispered.

I tried to turn my head to look, but warm hands stayed my moving. I opened my eyes a little more, and I saw the boy from town, Billy. He smiled when he saw that I remembered him. I tried to smile back, but it hurt to move my jaw.

"I came with my father when I knew that it was you. Your grandmother said your name that day, and I remembered it," he said quietly.

He looked down and shook his head.

"I heard what your mother and father did to you. I'm sorry. I'll pray for you to get better. I have to go back to my mother's up north soon. But, I'll keep up with you through my father until I see you again."

Then, he leaned close and kissed my cheek. I was so shocked that even if I could have moved, I wouldn't have. He chuckled at the look on my face.

"Goodbye for now, Victoria Alicia Roberts."

I tried to say goodbye too, but he was already gone.

After Billy left, I closed my eyes and took small breaths. I was afraid to die, and I knew that death was near. It felt like a cold breath on my shivering body. I trembled in pain and tried to breathe, but I knew that I would fight to live because I knew that God had more for me to do. I would not give up. It was at that moment, I felt different. I opened my eyes and looked down. I saw myself lying there shivering on the bed, but I wasn't afraid. I turned and walked down the hallway to the kitchen looking for Billy.

"She has rheumatic fever. It's a sickness that we still don't know much about except that we have to wait and see. We have to keep her fever down, or it could destroy the mind of the Victoria that we know and love."

I heard Dr. Herbert's voice when I walked closer.

I stopped right outside of the kitchen door. The doctor had paused. Suddenly, I could easily see his thought that he still remembered the day that I was born and his joy at delivering such a beautiful baby. I also felt his sorrow and despair.

"I want to be truthful here. If the rheumatic fever is really bad, she could die. If she doesn't die, it could cripple her to not be able to care for herself now or in the future. Again, we don't know as much as we need to, but I can tell you that as long as I have been a doctor, I have only seen one patient survive and they were grown," he finished heavily.

At this news, tears fell down my grandparents' faces for what Dr. Herbert had told them. Then, Big Mama Chandra cleared her throat, handed the doctor a hot cup of coffee.

"Ok, so we have cried our tears, now tell me how to save my granddaughter."

The doctor looked up at her but didn't look surprised. I saw him smile slightly.

"She needs plenty of liquids, no solid foods, and plenty of rest. Some of your mama's possets might help, Chandra. They're better than what I can give her. Also, she can have visitors but only from a distance."

Grandpa Ed gave a quiet laugh.

"Have you seen the crowd outside my front door? Victoria has touched many a soul with hers, and I won't be able to keep them away. Are you telling me that this is catching?"

Dr. Herbert took a sip of the coffee.

"We don't think that it's contagious, but it is a fever, so like any other fever, keep people away from touching distance."

Then, Dr. Herbert gave Big Mama a squeeze on the shoulder, grabbed his hat from Ms. Sadie who waited just inside of the kitchen, and walked into the hallway.

When he passed by where I stood in the hall, he paused frowning in my direction. Then, with a shrug of his shoulders, he left.

"He didn't leave any medicines, Mr. Ed," said Ms. Sadie sniffling.

Grandpa Ed turned around from his place by the new icebox that he had just bought.

"He doesn't need to Sadie because he knows that Chandra will already have possets."

Ms. Sadie left the kitchen passing by me with a frown too. Grandpa Ed looked around the kitchen at Big Mama Chandra, and without a spoken word, they joined hands and prayed to God to heal me. As they said their prayer, I felt a strong tug, and the darkness claimed me.

A while later, I opened my eyes to see that Big Mama slept in the chair next to the bed. For the next three days, I was very ill, and had many nightmares of everything that had happened while I was with Mama and Daddy. At one point, I heard Grandpa Ed's raised voice outside of the room.

"She isn't going anywhere with y'all again. Y'all have done wrong by that girl, and one day, you'll pay for it."

I heard Daddy's laugh.

"Yeah, Ed, you sure are right."

I must have been cried out because I heard Big Mama shush and croon to me.

Soon after, the fever broke where I could stay awake, but I wasn't able to walk. I had to eat in bed, play in bed, and yell for someone to help me use the pee pot in the bed. I was ashamed and going slowly crazy from not being able to move around.

After about two weeks, I heard a familiar voice.

"Pumpkin, what have they done to you?"

I opened my eyes, and there was Aunt Charlotte. Slimmer than she had been but as beautiful as ever. She walked quickly to the bed and hugged me.

"Dr. Herbert said that you'll be ready to travel in a few weeks if you can walk. Your Aunt Mary stayed behind because she was backed up with appointments with her clients, but she sends her love."

I pulled back.

"What happened, Aunt Charlotte?"

"Well, your Aunt Mary and I had the influenza, and it became real bad. We didn't get better until Mama came. We stayed weak for a long time, and the doctor wouldn't let us leave because they didn't want us to take it anywhere else," she explained.

I nodded and reclined back on the bed.

"I'll let you get some rest while I settle into my room."

She smiled and caressed my forehead.

I smiled and closed my eyes. Aunt Charlotte was alive, and she had come to be with me. I slipped into the darkness with a smile on my face.

"Ugh! It hurts so bad! Please let me sit down!"

I cried as Big Mama Chandra and Aunt Charlotte tried to help me walk the next week.

I couldn't walk alone, yet. The pain was so bad that I'd rather slide my body around to avoid the pain. Dr. Herbert had told us that it would just take some time for my body to completely heal and that we should be grateful that I had survived the fever. We were grateful that I was alive, but I wanted to walk too. Big Mama Chandra also told me that Aunt Mary had "seen" that I would win this fight against the rheumatic fever but that it would have lasting effects on my future. I didn't know what she meant, and I didn't care as long as I could walk now.

One morning, I gave in to the pity. I began to cry. Big Mama Chandra walked in on my fit.

"What's wrong, child?"

I wiped my face on my nightgown and looked straight at Big Mama.

"I know that you, Grandpa Ed, Uncle Andrew, and Aunt Charlotte have kept me away from Mama and Daddy, Big Mama, and I want you to know that I love you for it. I just feel so helpless and useless." "

"Victoria, you are still ill, and your grandfather, uncle, aunt, and I want to make sure that you get back to good health."

"Big Mama, I know that what's wrong with me will come back again."

Big Mama gave me a strange look.

"Why do you say that, child?"

"Because, I've been seeing things, Big Mama, but it scares me so I don't talk about it with Aunt Charlotte," I replied.

I told her all about the schoolteacher and the day I fell sick.

"Do you believe me, Big Mama?"

I was frightened that she thought I was crazy.

"Yes, child, because your Big Mama gave this gift to you just like your Aunt Mary. It isn't something to be afraid of because it is a good thing. I'll teach you all about it before you go back home so that it won't scare you anymore. Then your Aunt Mary will help you learn."

She gave me a big hug and left the room humming.

Four weeks later, after much pain and hard work learning to walk again, Big Mama Chandra watched as Aunt Charlotte and I rode away on the bus. We waved out of the window at her, and she smiled and waved back. I saw her mouth, "Don't forget your lessons" before she got in the Ford to drive home. I smiled when I thought of my new gift and all that Big Mama had taught me.

10

"Mr. Brown, is there anything that we can do? Can we fight this?"

Aunt Charlotte sat on the edge of her chair in the lawyer's office.

Red Brown was one of the best White lawyers in Dallas. He was also a client of Aunt Mary's, and he had offered his services when he heard that Aunt Mary needed help.

"Well, Ms. Charlotte, since no papers were ever signed to transfer custody of the child, we can't really fight. We don't have a leg to stand on right now," he said sadly.

"How can this be? They mistreated her, starved her, and forced her to work picking cotton. There has got to be something we can do."

Mr. Brown pursed his lips.

"Isn't she about to turn seventeen this summer? Well, she only has another year before she's emancipated, and she looks like a big enough girl to tend to herself."

He paused to leer at me over his glasses.

Aunt Charlotte opened her mouth to argue, but I knew that it was a lost cause. My special "gift" had let me see that I would have to go back to Mama and Daddy. I reached over and took my aunt's hand.

"Aunt Charlotte, we don't have a choice. If I have to go back to Mama and Daddy, I will."

"See there! She wants to go back. She'll be fine. Now, I have another appointment, so if y'all don't mind."

Mr. Brown rose to dismiss us. We stood, thanked him for his time, and left.

Aunt Charlotte's feelings were hurt, but I didn't want trouble for her. She had been so good to me for so long. She had been the best of mothers, and I would never forget it.

Later that night, Aunt Charlotte gave me a list of activities for the week that we were going to do before I left. She stayed to talk with me about what I wanted to do after high school. I felt like Aunt Charlotte tried to spend as much time with me for her and for me. I smiled and realized that I would have good memories to think about no matter what happened with my parents.

The following Monday morning after tear-filled goodbyes with my aunts, I got on the bus bound for the country. The bus rolled into Carson that afternoon. I got off, took my suitcases from the driver, and saw no one to fetch me. I sat down on the bench to wait. I had just got up and gotten a cold soda from the bus clerk when a red Ford truck drove up next to the bench. My heart jumped because I thought it was Big Mama Chandra or Grandpa Ed.

"Well, fancy seeing you."

I knew that voice but couldn't think.

Sometimes, my "gift" didn't help me at all. I looked into the cab of the truck and saw a set of familiar clear blue eyes, but his face was shadowed.

"I see that you don't remember me, and it's not polite to talk to a young lady from a truck," he said opening the truck door.

I stayed quiet and waited for him to get out of the truck.

"Seems you're a mite prettier than the last time we talked, but then you were down sick in bed," the stranger teased.

I gasped when he stepped all the way out of the truck and shut the door. It was Billy! My mouth dropped open in surprise because I hadn't thought to ever see him again. My mind flooded with memories from five years ago. I thought of the day in town when he saved me from the mean White men, and I could never forget the night that he came to see me when I was very ill. That was the night that I got my first kiss from a boy who wasn't my family. I blushed and stood up from the bench to greet the boy that had been in my dreams for five years.

"Hello."

I ducked my head shyly as he approached. He grinned.

"How are you? What are you doing here? Are you waiting for someone?"

I laughed and felt better in his company.

"Okay, I'll try to answer you in order. I'm all right. I've come back to live with my parents, and I'm waiting for them to come get me."

He stopped smiling.

"Are you going to be okay with them now?"

I shrugged.

"Time will tell."

He nodded and started heading back to his truck.

"I can give you a ride home."

I knew that wasn't allowed, so I shook my head.

"Thank you, Billy, but I don't want any trouble with my parents on my first day back."

"You're right. Well, I can sit with you until they come. Let me park the Ford out back."

He hopped into the cab and drove away before I could tell him no. I shook my head and sat back down on the bench to see what would happen next.

Billy and I had caught up on each other lives when Daddy's old Chevy drove up to the bus depot. Daddy got out of the car with a frown. I noticed when he walked toward us that he had only a slight limp and didn't have his cane anymore. I became nervous because I knew from the look on his face that he didn't care for me talking to Billy.

"What're you doing, girl? I didn't expect for you to be carrying on with some strange boy. Didn't your aunts teach you better than that up in the big city? I'm not going to have no trouble out of you, am I?"

He finished fussing and grabbed my arm in a tight grip. I stood up without a word embarrassed at his scolding.

"Hello, Mr. Clyde. My name is Billy Herbert. I started talking to your daughter, and she tried to shoo me away before you came. I'm terribly sorry if I got her in trouble."

Billy held his hand out for Daddy to shake.

"Herbert? You the son Doc Herbert talks about all the time?"

Daddy looked skeptical at Billy's excuse and used his right hand to shake Billy's. He didn't let me go.

"Yes, sir, I came to live with him now that I'm finished with school. I lived in Maine with my mother and her family."

He looked at Daddy's grip on me and cleared his throat. I wanted to hide in shame.

"Get your suitcases, girl. Let's go home," Daddy demanded.

He let me go and went to get in the car. Billy lifted all three of my suitcases and loaded them in Daddy's trunk.

Then he whispered, "I'll see you soon," before he opened my car door and helped me get settled.

Daddy growled, struggled to crank the car, and drove away. I sat back and stayed quiet waiting on his punishment, but he didn't say a word.

When we got home, Daddy got out of the car and left me to get my suitcases. I opened the trunk and started to grab a suitcase when I heard a scream. I turned quickly to see what was going on and got knocked to the ground. I landed with a whoosh and immediately tried to rise. Something heavy lay on my legs, and I couldn't move.

"Victoria! I'm so happy that you've come home!"

I was confused and angry that I was still on the ground when I heard a male voice.

"Ruth, get off of her. She just got home. You're such a silly girl."

I sat up and saw that Ruth lay across my legs. She smiled at me when I looked at her.

"I'm glad to see you too, Ruth, but can I please get up to give you a proper hug?"

I pleaded and grinned at her.

She laughed and stood up, and then she held her hand out to help me stand. When I stood, I gave her a hug. She pulled back and offered to help me with my stuff. I nodded and turned around to face my younger brother, Steven, who stood back frowning at us. He hadn't grown very tall, but he was very handsome.

"Steven, may I have a hug?"

His frown turned to a smile, and he walked forward and gave me a hug.

"Hey, sis, I'm glad you're home too. Ruth and Lacy are driving me crazy."

He rolled his eyes, and Ruth punched him in the arm before grabbing a suitcase to head in the house.

I laughed and asked where Clyde Jr. and Will were. His frown returned, and he tipped his head in the direction of Grandpa Paul's ranch.

"They're down helping Grandpa Paul with the ranch. I didn't go because Betts caught me giving Ruth and Lacy some penny candy that she gave me. She gave me a switchin', so now, I tell Mama and Daddy that I'll help around here because I know that they don't like to do nothing. I don't want to be around her."

I gave him another hug for being brave and told him that I was proud of him. His chest puffed up, and he told me that he would get my other suitcases. I nodded and went into the house.

Mama lay on the bed when I walked into her bedroom to pass through to go to the back bedroom. I thought that she slept.

"So you think you're too good to speak to your own Mama? You come back here with big city airs thinking you're better than us country folks?"

She sat up and raised her voice with each word until she yelled.

I stared at her lying there looking like a mad woman for a moment.

"What are you looking at?!"

I smiled calmly.

"Hello, Mama, how are you? I thought you were asleep, and I didn't want to bother you. I just got here, but can I get you anything?"

My calm manner confused her, and I had known that it would. I patiently waited for her to speak.

"No, I don't want you to get me anything. You might have gotten something from your aunts to fix me with. Just leave me alone," she said and rolled over on the bed.

I smiled and went through to the back room to put away my things. As I unpacked, I thought about how much my "gift" might help me in my stay with my parents.

Later that day, Daddy walked into the front room and told us that we would be eating supper with Grandpa Paul and Betts. My stomach clenched at the thought of being in that house again with Betts. I closed my eyes and tried to bring forth anything to help me, but there was nothing. I wanted to be sick, fall down and hurt myself, anything to get out of going. Nothing happened and before I knew it, we all piled into the car for the short drive to the ranch.

When I got out of the car, I saw that there had been nothing done to stop the ranch house from aging. I couldn't help but compare it to Big Mama and Grandpa Ed's homestead. I thought about how Daddy would boast of Grandpa Paul's wealth and property. Looking at the ranch house, I didn't think that he had much to brag about anymore.

When I looked up, I saw that Betts stood in the doorway with her hands on her hips. She looked older and had gained pounds everywhere. She was a very big woman, and she filled the doorway. We all had to stop and wait for her to move, but it seemed like she had something to say to me first.

"Well, missy, I see that you're back where you belong. We ain't seen you in umpteen years."

She narrowed her eyes at me.

Out of the corner of my eye, I saw Steven step in front of Ruth and Lacy. I smiled at Betts.

"Hello, Betts, how are you? I'm sorry that you missed me, but my aunts wanted me to be real smart when I came home."

I saw that Steven and Ruth tried not to smile.

"Look here, gal, don't you be getting smart with me. It won't go well for you. You should remember that," Betts growled.

I looked back at Mama. She had her head down, and she trembled. I shook my head sadly at how meek she was with Betts. I turned around and met Betts' glare. I smiled at her again.

"I remember your lessons well, Betts, and I learned a few from Big Mama Chandra and Aunt Mary."

Betts' head snapped back, and she gasped.

"You can't come in my house, gal. You won't be bringing none of their hoodoo in here."

"What's this now? Why is everybody outside?"

I heard a voice say from inside the house.

Grandpa Paul stepped up behind Betts looking over her head.

"Victoria! Well, this is a mighty fine day! My oldest grandbaby is back home! Betts! Move your fat carcass out of the way, and let them come in the house. My word, you act like an old fishwife the older you get," Grandpa Paul fussed.

Betts threw him an evil look, turned, and moved further into the house. Grandpa Paul stepped forward and grabbed me in a big hug.

"Oo wee, it's good to see you, child! You've got your great-grandfather's red hair, but you look just like me! Clyde, you better get your shotgun ready, because with all this beauty around here, them ol' boys gone start coming 'round ready to court."

Grandpa Paul laughed and squeezed me in another hug.

"Yeah, I found one sniffin' today. I told him what for too," Daddy boasted.

I knew he lied, but I didn't say a word. I just shook my head and followed Grandpa Paul into the house.

When I crossed the doorway, I felt a moment of weakness. Steven whispered from behind me.

"Yeah, I feel like that too when I come here."

He gave me a little push, and I started forward again. Grandpa Paul waited in the front room. The room was still dark and chilly. I felt like the past rushed to greet me. The darkness in the corners remained alive and black. The sunlight looked weak as if it were afraid to come inside the room. I felt a hand grab mine gently, and I looked back and saw Ruth.

"I'm still afraid of this place, Victoria."

I nodded and agreed, "Me too."

Betts came to the door and said that supper was ready. Everyone turned to follow her to the dining room. I looked back and for a moment, I thought that I saw one of the shadows in the corner move. I shook my head to get that thought out of my mind and hurried to the dining room.

11

Two months later, Steven, Ruth, Lacy, and I celebrated my birthday while we fished at the creek. They sang happy birthday to me, and Steven brought out a batch of almost burned teacakes for us. I laughed and asked him where he got such a wonderful gift. He grinned and said that Mama had left them on the table with the back door open. He took them and blamed it on the raccoons. We all laughed and ate the teacakes while we tried to catch supper. I loved being with my brother and sisters. They made my life better living with Mama and Daddy.

For a moment, I thought about Clyde Jr. and Will. Since I had come back, Betts had told Daddy that they could stay with her to help. Daddy didn't want all those mouths to feed anyway, so he let them stay with her. They hadn't even come to see me. I wanted to tell Daddy that I had seen my brothers being turned mean and nasty by Betts, but I didn't want Daddy to think I was crazy or made up stories about his mother. I also figured since Daddy was mean and nasty, he wouldn't mind Clyde Jr. and Will being the same way. I felt selfish, but I kept quiet.

A week before my siblings started school, Mama and Daddy told me that I would start school as well. I frowned.

"Why do I have to go to school? I have a diploma from my tutors that I completed my studies."

Daddy looked like he would slap me.

"I don't care what kind of mess you got from those lace-shirted tutors. You're going to finish school here in Carson."

I wanted to argue, but I knew it would do no good. I had not liked school, so after I got sick and went back to Dallas, Aunt Charlotte had talked to the school board for home school. They had said as long as the tutors sign statements, they didn't care where I learned. It didn't make any sense for me to go back, but I said a "yes sir" and left the room. I hated everything about school, and I wanted to run away just thinking about going back.

When I stood at the bus stop the next week with my siblings, I thought about running away. I must have looked like I would because Steven and Ruth walked to my side and talked to me about little things until the old squeaky school bus came. I let them all climb on before I took a deep breath and got on the bus. I slowly moved to the open seat beside Ruth feeling like everyone was staring at me. I heard voices asking Steven and Lacy who I was, and they replied that I was their sister before going quiet.

"She too White to be their sister," I heard a voice say.

I gritted my teeth and stayed quiet. I wouldn't look anyone in the eye because I didn't want to answer questions that would give the kids something to make fun of me later. I sat there with my head up but my eyes down for the rest of the trip to Carson.

There was a line of buses when we arrived at the school. I noticed that there were many girls and boys that had light skin and eyes like me that got off the buses. I felt a little better, but I still didn't want to be there. Ruth took my hand and we got off the bus. She walked me around the gravel playground to the front of the building. The sign on the door read P.T. Smith. Ruth opened the door, and we went inside. The floors were freshly waxed, and it smelled like fresh paint.

There was a long hallway in front of us that also went to the left and right. I could see kids going though doors along each side.

"I have to go to class, Victoria. There's the office where you have to get your plan."

Ruth tipped her head toward a door to the left with 'Office' in black letters, gave me a hug, and ran down the hall. I felt like calling her back, but I knew she couldn't be late.

I looked at the office, squared my shoulders, and went inside. A skinny black woman with glasses sat behind a tall desk. She looked at me over the top of the glasses.

"Yes?"

I swallowed loudly and moved toward the desk.

"I'm Victoria Roberts, and I'm new today. I mean, I'm a new student."

She stayed silent for a moment, and then she broke out in a wide smile.

"Yes, I know who you are. You look a little like my cousin, Ed. Chandra told me that you might start this year. She was right, you are very different from your brothers and sisters."

I frowned at her.

"Cousin Ed? Chandra? You're a cousin?"

She rose with a nod.

"Yep. My mother and your grandfather were sister and brother. That makes us cousins too."

She walked forward and gave me a hug.

"My name is Cora. I'm glad to finally meet you, Victoria. I've heard a lot about you."

I didn't know what to say, so I stayed quiet.

"Now, let's get you to Ms. Addy. She is one of our best twelfth grade teachers," she said briskly moving back to her desk.

She handed me a tablet and pencil. She gave me directions to Ms. Addy's class, sat back at her desk, and bent her head back to her work. I left with a smile and a prayer that everything about school would be as nice as Cora.

October came, and I had begun to love school. Ms. Addy was actually Aunt Addy, David's aunt. She was so nice and very smart. Uncle P and David had told her about me, so she had special lessons just for me because I learned so fast. I like her a lot. Cousin Cora learned from Grandpa Ed that I played piano and sang. She then told the choir teacher, Miss Iris about me. Miss Iris made plans with Aunt Addy to let me go to her class everyday an hour before school ended to practice my music. She put me in the choir and let me be the piano player for the music class. I was so happy that I didn't mind that Mama and Daddy stayed in bed all day and made me clean and cook when I got home.

One day after choir practice, I missed the bus. I knew that I would to be in big trouble when I got home. I sat down and tried to figure out how I could get all the way from Carson to the country. I started to burst into tears when I heard the motor of a truck coming down the street. I gasped in surprise when I saw Billy in the cab. He smiled as he drove up next to me.

"Well, I guess this is going to be a habit," he said grinning.

I stood up and brushed off the back of my skirt.

"Schools out. What're you doing here?"

I smiled at his grin.

"I missed the bus back to the country. Daddy's going to give me a switchin' for this for sure."

Billy laughed.

"Now, we don't want that. Hey, I could give you a ride home if you want."

I shook my head because I knew I would get in trouble if I got a ride from Billy. Before I could say no, Billy took my arm and guided me into the truck. I turned to him speechless when he climbed into the driver's side. He looked at me and shrugged his shoulders.

"It's on my way home, so stop looking at me like that."

I scooted as close to the other door as I could to put some space between us. It made me nervous being this close to him, and it scared me to be catching a ride. I could only imagine the trouble that we could both get into if anyone saw us. I guessed that Billy didn't care because he cranked up the truck and started to drive.

Neither one of us said a word the whole way home until he stopped at Grandpa Paul's ranch's gate.

"I'm only letting you out here because I don't want to stir up trouble with your daddy."

He came around the truck and opened my door. I didn't know what to do, so I just stood there. Billy smiled and quietly said goodnight. I smiled back, turned, and started to walk down the lane. I looked back to see him standing there watching me walk home.

When I finally got home, Daddy and Mama were waited for me in the front room. I thought that they were angry because it was late. I stood there scared and trembled at the thought of a switchin' when Daddy gave me an evil smile.

"I'm so glad that you're here. I'm not even going to ask why you're late. I have a surprise for you, Vicky."

I flinched because whenever he called me Vicky in that way, it was bad.

"Your Grandpa Paul and I are not seeing eye to eye right now. My brothers are coming home from the army for a spell, and he wants them to work for him instead of me for a while. Something about me not getting along with the workers. Well, that means that I'm out of work for now, but that's okay because you're here to help, right, Vicky?"

I said 'yes sir' and waited for his 'surprise'.

"I was in town today, and I saw where Suzie Bell opened a sandwich shop for Blacks. She needs some help, and I told her that you would be perfect. Yes, indeed," he snickered rubbing his hands together.

I just stood there and stay silent. I didn't know what kind of mood he was in, and I didn't wasn't to test it. I looked over at Mama, and she was grinned at me.

"I can't wait to get me a new dress and shoes," she sneered.

"Yep, you're going to be paid and make tips, so you should be a gold mine."

Daddy cackled at his plans.

Since I didn't talk or sass back, they soon let me go to the kitchen to fix me a plate of the watery stew on the stove.

The job at Suzie's wasn't as bad as my parents wanted it to be for me. In fact, I liked the job a lot. Ms. Suzie was real nice, and she would let me make a sandwich to take home everyday. I'd pile on the meat and add extra bread so that it would be enough for me to eat for breakfast and take for lunch at school.

Billy came in a lot even though the shop was supposed to mainly be for Black people. He would sit at the counter and order a sandwich, soda, and pickle. Every night, he would wait outside to take me home.

We started to talk on our trips home, and I knew more about him now. He stayed with his mother because she was a Black Frenchwoman. Billy said her skin was like mine, but she had dark brown hair. He told me that while in medical school, Dr. Herbert had fell in love with his mother. He didn't know that she was Black, and he married her. When he found out later that she wasn't White, he left her and came back to his home, Carson. She had written him and told him of his son a year later. Billy said Dr. Herbert told his mother to never say that she was Black again so that Billy could grow up White. His mother made the promise but broke it when Billy was fourteen and told him everything. Billy said that it didn't matter to him, but for the sake of his father, he would keep up the lie. I thought that it was good that Billy played White. I wished that I could do the same thing, but everyone knew who my parents were. I felt better that he had told me his secret because I liked him a lot and didn't want to make any trouble with a White boy.

In late January, I walked happily down the street to go to work thinking how nice my life was when I felt heat fill my body. I stopped to take a breath, but it was hard because pain followed the heat. I fell down on the side of the road and tried to take deep breaths. The pain got worse, so I took smaller breaths. My whole body felt like it was being crushed and twisted. I looked around and saw that a few people stopped to stare. I tried to open my mouth to call for help, but the pain in my jaw was so bad that tears began to fall.

"It's Ms. Chandra's grandbaby! C'mon, she needs help, Timothy!"

I heard shouts, but I couldn't say anything.

I felt gentle hands lift me, and I cried out because it hurt. I wanted to say thank you, but the darkness came over me.

The church was decorated in white roses. The sunlight shone through the stained glass window to make the sanctuary a rose color. The aisle runner and the pews were covered in white. I turned to look out of the window. In the reflection, I saw myself in a long white wedding gown with long sleeves made of lace. The skirt was decorated with small white silk roses. My hair was dressed in curls and a flower garland was in my hair. I smiled at reflection and turned to look at the altar. I saw my pastor from Dallas, and I wanted to ask him how he got here. He smiled and waved me forward. There was a man in a suit in the shadow of the window. I couldn't see his face, and he moved towards the altar. He soon stood beside the pastor, but the light had followed him. I still couldn't see his face.

As I walked down the aisle, I saw that the pews were empty except for Big Mama Chandra. She cried and then smiled at me. When I looked closely at her face, her eyes were missing. There were deep dark holes where her beautiful eyes should be. I started to cry for her. The tears flowed down my face onto the beautiful gown, but I didn't care. I stopped in the middle of the aisle and fell to the floor sobbing. I didn't understand.

"Victoria! Victoria! Come back to us, please!"

I heard Aunt Charlotte voice, but I knew she wasn't real. She was back in Dallas. I had left her to come back to Mama and Daddy, and that thought made me cry more.

"Victoria! Wake up, please!"

Aunt Charlotte cried. I didn't want Aunt Charlotte to cry, but I didn't want to be back with Mama and Daddy.

"You have to do something, Dr. Herbert. She cries, but she doesn't wake up."

I heard Aunt Charlotte plead with the doctor.

"She has to choose to come out of the coma, Charlotte," he replied calmly.

Their voices got farther away, and then, I heard a familiar voice close to my ear.

"Please wake up, Victoria. I miss my friend. Please don't die."

I wanted to answer Billy, but I couldn't. I felt the comfort of the darkness, and I liked it. I let it surround me and take me away.

"Water, please."

The voice sounded unused and scratchy.

I felt the cool water wet my dry lips, and then down into my dry throat. I realized then it was my scratchy voice. I opened my eyes to see that Aunt Charlotte and Aunt Mary stood beside the bed. I blinked to make sure that they weren't a dream. They both looked tired. Their clothes were wrinkled, and their hair was messy. I didn't care because I was so happy to see them.

"Welcome back, ma'am."

Aunt Charlotte smile looked relieved.

I frowned in confusion.

"Dr. Herbert said that you've been in a coma. The rheumatic fever came back worse this time," Aunt Charlotte explained.

I was still confused, but I didn't want to talk about it anymore.

"Big Mama got sick too, didn't she?"

Aunt Charlotte looked at me in surprise. Aunt Mary smiled sadly.

"Yes, she did. I saw you and her become very ill, so we hurried to be with y'all."

"Is she alright?"

I asked my aunts the question, but I was afraid to hear what I already knew.

"She can't see. We hope she will get better, but the doctor says that she might not," Aunt Charlotte replied.

I felt the tears coming, but I wanted to be strong for Big Mama.

I swung my legs around to get up and felt the weakness still in them.

"Careful, Victoria. You are still weak," Aunt Charlotte warned.

I nodded and tried to stand. I made it, but my legs were shaky. Aunt Mary smiled and helped me put on a bed robe. Aunt Charlotte put on my shoes, and we all walked out of the room.

"I see you've come back to us, lil' mirror," Big Mama said before we entered her room.

She sat up in bed in a beautiful peach nightgown. Her eyes were covered with a white silk bandage. She gave a loud booming laugh.

"I was more worried about you than myself. I'll be fine. I won't be seeing nothing but visions for a while, but I'll be fine," she joked still chuckling.

I smiled and sat on the edge of her bed. She patted my hand and told me that she was proud of me. I didn't know what she meant, but I thanked her anyway. We sat with her while she talked about the homestead and the chores. My aunts offered to stay and help out, but Big Mama Chandra told them that Hope and Ms. Sadie would take care of things until she was better.

I asked how I got to the homestead. They told me that two of the field hands had been in town and saw me when I fell ill. They had brought me to the homestead because they hadn't known I lived with Mama and Daddy. Dr. Herbert was already out to the house tending to Big Mama Chandra when I was brought in unconscious.

I listened while they began to talk about other things, and I wanted to tell them all about my job and Billy. I had never kept secrets from my aunts, but something told me that I shouldn't tell them. It wasn't long after that I started feeling tired. I tried to hide it so that I could visit more with them, but Aunt Charlotte saw me and wouldn't hear it. She ushered me back to bed with the promise that I could visit Big Mama tomorrow. I grumbled a little bit, but I let her help me back to my room. I fell onto the bed in exhaustion. Aunt Charlotte smiled and said goodnight before she turned off the light.

For some reason, I wasn't that afraid of the dark anymore. While I lay there, I prayed to God to heal Big Mama, and I thanked Him for healing me. I also thanked Him for taking me away from Mama and Daddy's for a spell. I already knew that I would have to go back when I got better, but I decided to enjoy my freedom from hunger, chores, and my parents' spite. I fell asleep with a smile thinking about spending time with my aunts and my grandparents. Maybe, I'd get to spend some time with Billy too.

12

Eventually, I healed enough to go back to Mama and Daddy's house. They had raised a stink while was at the homestead. Uncle Andrew wouldn't let Daddy or Mama set foot in the front yard without pointing a gun their way. Daddy had threatened to have Grandpa Paul bring the sheriff, so to avoid any more trouble, I told my aunts, Uncle Andrew, and my grandparents that I felt good enough to go back with my parents. They all argued with me, but I held my ground. Aunt Mary finally talked them all into letting me go. Aunt Charlotte was upset, but she calmed down after she talked to Aunt Mary.

When Mama and Daddy came back with the sheriff, I was already ready to go. I got in the old Chevy and tried to fight the tears because I knew it would upset Daddy. I turned around and looked through the small back window to see everyone wave. I gave a small wave and turned around before Daddy got mad again.

Because I had missed so much school, I wasn't able to graduate with my class. Cora and Ms. Addy tried to talk to the principal, but he wouldn't change his mind. I had missed too much to graduate or go to summer school. He said that I would have to start my senior year over with everyone else. I cried because I felt that if I had graduated, I could move away from

Mama and Daddy and all of their demands. I had not "seen" this, which made me angry at my gift. Daddy and Mama were very happy that I wouldn't graduate. They laughed and said that I could work for the summer. I was to have two jobs, pick cotton during the week and Ms. Suzie's on the weekends. I hated picking cotton, and my parents knew it. I didn't say anything because I wanted to work at Ms. Suzie's. I hadn't seen Billy since I had been sick, and I hoped that he would come by Ms. Suzie's to see me.

"Did you hear, the doc's boy is seeing the Adams girl. She came home from school and went right after him. Dr. Herbert couldn't be happier," said a girl's voice from the table against the wall.

I had finished cutting the meat for the next day's sandwiches when I heard the girls talk. I turned quickly, and my heart sped up as I hoped that she talked about someone else. I saw a light skinned girl with freckles and dark hair talking to another darker skinned girl. I knew both of them from school, but I couldn't think of their names.

"He's so handsome. I wish he wasn't White, then I could have had a chance," said the darker girl.

"Lynn, you wouldn't have had a chance in a pig's eye," the other girl laughed.

Lynn looked sad, and then her face turned mean when she faced my way.

"At least, I didn't get led on like some people."

The other girl looked at me and gave me a kind smile. I looked away and busied myself cleaning up for the night.

Now, I caught a ride home from Ms. Addy who told me that she taught field hands from other farms to read at Cora's house. She didn't mind giving me a ride home because she said it was on her way. I hadn't seen Billy once since I came back to work at Ms. Suzie's.

I had made my sandwich and taken off my apron when the light skinned girl came up to me.

"Hi, I'm Nicole, and I know you're Victoria. I'm sorry about what my friend said. It wasn't nice," she said touching my arm.

I just nodded and tried to walk past her.

"Look, I know that you and that boy were friends, but he's White and even though you don't look it, you're Black. White boys only want to be friends with Black girls for one thing. When they don't get it, they go back to chasing White girls."

She started to walk with me towards the door. I rolled my eyes and stayed quiet. It hadn't been like that with Billy, but I wasn't going to tell Nicole all of my business. I turned around and said goodnight to Ms. Suzie, then I walked through the door to stop suddenly in surprise. Nicole, who had been talking non-stop bumped into me.

"What...?"

She paused and seeing what made me stop, gasped.

Billy waited outside beside his truck. He smiled from ear to ear.

"I asked Ms. Addy if I could drive you home, and she said it was okay if I dropped you at her house in an hour," he said.

He opened the door for me to slide in from his side.

I was so shocked that it was Nicole who spoke for me.

"What about the Adams girl? Victoria doesn't want to be played with, you know. It ain't gonna work either with you being White and all. Maybe you should stay with the Adams girl," she threw at him.

Billy laughed and looked at me.

"Well, I see you've made a nosey little friend. Hello, my name is Billy, what's yours?"

Nicole drew herself up to her full height, which wasn't taller than me.

"My name is Nicole, and I've heard the gossip about you and that girl."

When I saw her narrowed her eyes at Billy, I decided that I needed to talk to him myself.

"Nicole, thank you for trying to help, but I need to talk to Billy. We can talk on the ride home. Will you come by for a soda tomorrow?"

I gave her a big fake smile and hoped that she went for it. She smiled and whispered to be careful. She glared at Billy and turned and walked down the street. I looked over at Billy, and he waved toward the open truck door. I walked over and climbed in to scoot all the way to the other side.

Billy climbed in and started the drive towards the country.

"I went to see you at your Big Mama Chandra's with my father, but they said that you had went back to your parents. Are you okay?"

"Yes."

I knew that my answer was short, but I was hurt.

"Victoria, I wanted to tell you myself that my father found out that I was interested in you. He got so angry that he threatened to send me back to my mother. Now, he wants me to court Peggy Adams. He thinks that it would look good because Mr. Bob and Ms. Sophie own a lot of land. I told him no, but they keep coming to supper with us. I guess that's how the talk got out."

"Billy, you don't have to tell me anything. I know that we are just friends. It's okay," I murmured staring straight ahead.

"But it's not okay! I want to court you!"

I jumped in surprise at his shout. He pulled the truck to a stop and reached for me. I scooted over until I was pressed at the door. He slid over to where I trembled and pulled me gently into his arms.

"Victoria, I'm sorry. I know that if I start trying to court you, it will be trouble for everyone. Carson is still full of prejudice, and I can't take the chance that our families might get hurt or worse. My father likes you too, but he might lose his practice if we started courting. I love you, but it's not enough to be with you. Please understand."

I shook my head, and I know that he felt the movement because he tried to draw me closer. I couldn't talk because my chest hurt. My whole body felt numb from his words. I felt tears falling down my face, but I refused to wipe them.

"Just think about what I've said, and you'll know that I'm right. It would be different if you had been born somewhere else with no one knowing your parents are Black, but people do. People don't know about me, and I want to keep it that way. My father says that he's going to send me to medical school to be a doctor like him," he rambled.

He pulled away to restart the truck. I sat there silently feeling hurt and betrayed. I knew that Billy spoke the truth, but it was still hard for me because I had fallen in love with him. I had hoped that one day he would help me get away from Mama and Daddy. Now, I didn't know what I was going to do. I thought about his secret and telling everyone about it, but I knew that I wouldn't.

Nothing else was said until we got to Ms. Addy's. He got out and opened the door to let me out when David appeared in the yard.

"Victoria! I've missed you somethin' terrible!"

He walked through the gate to give me a hug. When he saw my tears, he immediately turned to Billy and grabbed him by the collar.

"What did you do to her!"

Billy yanked loose angrily.

"Nothing. I told her the truth. I'm sorry she took it bad."

I laid my hand on David's arm and pleaded.

"Please, David, take me home."

David looked at me with pity on his face and nodded. Billy turned to me with his hand outstretched.

"Can we still be friends?"

I looked back at him and knew that I could never be his friend again. It would hurt too much. I shook my head and smiled sadly.

"No, Billy. I hope that you do well in school and have a wonderful life with Peggy Adams."

I turned back around and headed for Ms. Addy's Chevy. I felt David follow behind me. Billy sped off without another word. I walked across the yard and got into the Chevy so that David could take me home. I could feel David's questions, but I wasn't in the mood to answer them.

Months passed, school started, and I still felt the rejection of Billy's choice. I still walked around in a funk when on Christmas Eve morning, Mama woke me up to clean the house and start cooking early. I must have moved slower than she wanted because she reached over and slapped me. I looked at her in surprise and rubbed my cheek. Usually, Daddy did the slapping and Mama smiled or laughed.

"Don't' look at me like that. You know you deserve more slapping moving around like you got all day. Now, get in there and get that food on cookin'," she hissed.

I nodded and walked into the kitchen. Daddy came through the back door.

"Good. I was afraid that lazy mama of yours couldn't get you going this morning. My sisters, Pearl and Hallie are back from California. Pa and Betts want us to go to the ranch house to celebrate."

Surprise must have been on my face because Daddy frowned.

"I know you probably heard that Betts don't like the girls. That ain't it at all. She wants them back so that she can teach them and make sure they know how to do things before they find husbands."

He waved away his explanation and walked through the door to the front room. I didn't say another word. I began to cook the roast, greens, red potatoes, and corn that Mama told me to make. I made sure not to burn anything because I didn't want to make a bad impression on my aunts.

"You are so beautiful, Victoria, short and shapely just like me," Aunt Pearl said.

"Pearl, she looks more like me."

Aunt Hallie tapped her hand and frowned.

"Y'all don't go putting that mess in her head, you hear," Betts huffed.

I smiled at her because I knew it irritated her and sat down at the dining room table. My aunts were pretty and funny. I liked them right away.

Actually, I looked like both of them too. They were short and shapely like Aunt Pearl said except their eyes and hair were light brown like Betts', although, they were also different from Betts. They had given all of the children candy and little trinkets from California. They had also brought dresses for Mama, Ruth, and me. They waved away our thanks and asked me about school. They asked if I was courtin', and I turned red. Aunt Pearl had laughed and said she would talk to me later. Aunt Hallie had frowned again and said she wanted to talk to me too. Everyone laughed except for Mama and Betts.

After dinner, we went outside because the day was warm for December, and we sat in the new shaded patio area that Grandpa Ed had made for Betts. I saw Juan and Marcos riding horses across the field and waved. They waved back and turned to go toward the back twenty. I turned around to see Daddy look at Marcos and Juan with narrowed eyes. He turned around and gave Grandpa Paul the same look.

"Pa, some cows are missing, and I think Marcos or Juan took 'em to town to sell."

Grandpa Paul whipped around and pinned Daddy with a glare.

"Clyde, you shut your mouth. Marcos would never steal from me. You're trying to start trouble."

"Pa, I'm just looking out for you. You been letting that Mexican take over the ranch for years. My brothers hurried back to their stations because of him. I'm telling you, he's stealing," Daddy persisted.

Grandpa Paul stood up to leave, and Betts grabbed his wrist to stop him.

"Is it too much trouble to believe your own son? What if they're stealing? You wouldn't know would you?"

Grandpa Paul looked down at her and smiled. I had never seen him smile like that.

"I do believe my own son. Marcos would never steal from his own father," he said with a malicious grin at Betts.

Betts, Mama, and Daddy gaped at Grandpa Paul.

Aunt Pearl whispered out loud.

"See, Hallie. I told you Marcos looked like Pa when he picked us up in town."

Aunt Hallie just nodded with her mouth open. All of us children were shocked, but we knew better than to say anything.

"Son?" asked Daddy.

"My son," declared Grandpa Paul.

He beamed with pride as he followed Marcos with his eyes.

"How did you get past the line?"

Betts voice sounded like a snarl. She trembled and looked like she was going to explode.

"I got my ways, Betts. When you started to chase men soon after we married, I went to Mexico with my father. I met a woman there who helped me back over your line. I stayed with her for a spell all the while telling you I fought in the army."

Slap!

Betts had sprung out of her chair and slapped Grandpa Paul. Grandpa Paul grabbed her hands and put them in his left hand and punched her face with his right. Betts crumpled to the ground out cold. My aunts and Mama screamed and ran over to her. Daddy lunged out of his chair at Grandpa Paul. Grandpa Paul ducked under Daddy's punch. Then he punched Daddy in the stomach and again in the face. He swung another punch across Daddy's face, and it knocked Daddy out cold like Betts. Mama screamed when she saw Daddy fall and ran to help him. Grandpa Paul turned around and saw the younger children crying while me, Clyde Jr., Steven, and Will were still in shock. His face softened, and he looked down at his bleeding knuckles. He turned back around and saw Betts sitting up rubbing her jaw. Daddy was still out cold.

Grandpa Paul looked ashamed but then he stood tall and pointed at Betts.

"Betts, you have made your own son attack his father. I give him a place to stay, pay his wages, and take care of his problems. He has shown me nothing but disrespect since you did your witchcraft on him. Maybe some distance is what he needs to earn his own way and learn respect."

He looked at us with tears in his eyes before he turned and walked away.

The following May, I walked across the stage to take my diploma from Mr. St. Francis, the principal of P.T. Smith while my family and friends cheered and clapped. I laughed and walked back to my seat to wait for my surprise gift to them. After all of the graduates had passed through, Mr. St. Francis introduced Miss Iris.

"Ladies and Gentlemen, we have a wonderful treat for you. One of the most talented students that I have ever known is going to play and sing for you. Miss Victoria Alicia Roberts," she announced.

She smiled at me and took her seat.

I heard gasps and murmurs from the audience when I rose and went to the piano that had been rolled onto the stage. I sat down and began to play my favorite song, *His Eye is on the Sparrow*. I closed my eyes to let myself go with the music and felt it all the way down to my soul.

When I finished the last note, I heard loud applause and cheering. I opened my eyes to see everyone on their feet. I stood and took a bow smiling in my joy. When I raised my head, I saw that Mama looked at me with hatred on her face.

About a month after graduation, Aunt Charlotte and Aunt Mary came to visit Mama and Daddy. They brought a basket of food and told the younger children to go have a picnic while they talked with Mama, Daddy, and me. Mama's face tightened, but she didn't say anything.

"Charlotte, you're looking lovely as ever. Mary, you can stay but don't try any of your hoodoo."

Daddy lit a cigarette and blew the smoke at Aunt Mary. She frowned and waved it away.

"I don't do hoodoo, Clyde, Betts does, but that's not why we're here."

"What do y'all want?"

Mama's lips tightened, and she trembled in her anger.

"We wanted to talk to y'all about Victoria's future. She is a very intelligent and talented young lady. She needs to go to college somewhere so that she can get a degree and have a career. We would like to pay for her to go to college," Aunt Charlotte finished looking at me.

I smiled because this was my chance to get away from Mama and Daddy. Daddy slid a sly look at Mama.

"Now, we know there ain't colored schools around here, and we know that she'll miss her family too much if she's off all alone. Anyway, she's our daughter, and we'll pay for her to go to school. As a matter of fact, Pa just got me a job at my aunt's new ranch right outside of Fort Worth in Littleton. Tess and I thought of sending Vicky to school after we moved."

I didn't like that smile, and I guess Aunt Charlotte didn't like it either because she raised her eyebrow.

"Why can't she go now? She's graduated, and I understand that she's been working. Did y'all save all of her money for her?"

Mama rolled her eyes.

"That's none of your business."

"Now, now, Tess, Charlotte is just concerned, right Charlotte?"

Daddy reached out and covered Mama's balled fist with his hand. Aunt Charlotte nodded slightly. Daddy turned to me.

"Vicky, if you stay with us until we get settled in Littleton, we promise that we'll pay for you to go to whatever school you want."

I felt torn. I wanted to stay to be with Steven, Lacy, and Ruth, but I wanted to be away from Mama and Daddy. Daddy had started to make and drink moonshine, and he became even meaner when he drank.

"Victoria, you're a young adult now. You can come with us and start to make your own way," Aunt Charlotte reminded me.

"Oh, hush, Charlotte! You think because you married a White man and he left you money that you can do whatever you want! I told you once that she is my daughter, not yours!"

Mama rose from the table as she yelled and pointed her finger at Aunt Charlotte.

"Tess, she doesn't need to stay here, and you know it! You're so jealous of your own daughter that you would make her stay with you so that she can't have a better life!"

Aunt Charlotte rose from the table too looking offended at Mama's attitude.

"I think you ladies have worn out your welcome. Vicky won't be going anywhere with y'all right now."

Daddy stood up and walked to open the door.

Aunt Mary gave me a sad smile, then she grasped Aunt Charlotte's arm. Aunt Charlotte looked at me with tears in her eyes.

"You know where I am, Victoria."

I said a quiet 'yes ma'am' and lowered my eyes before she saw the tears. I heard them leave, and all I wanted to do was run after them and beg them to take me with them.

"This is a really nice place. I think that I'm going to like it."

Steven looked around the land as we drove down the lane to the foreman's house on Aunt Alice's ranch.

I hadn't said anything to anyone when we had left the country. We had to wait two months before Aunt Alice called Grandpa Paul and told him that the house where we would be staying was finished. Since the ranch was brand new, a lot of the buildings were still being built. Daddy was to be the foreman so our house was completed after the ranch house.

The land was beautiful, and there were flat plains of grass combined with rugged little hills. I couldn't take joy in my love of the outdoors because Mama and Daddy had yet to tell me when I could go to school. Every time that I asked them, they would smile and tell me to wait until we got settled in Littleton. Mama slept all day while Daddy barely worked and stayed drunk. I was left to tend to my younger siblings, cook, clean, and wash. As we drove up to the foreman's house, I said a quick prayer that we would get settled soon.

"Hurry up, Vicky, we need to get back to the house so you can make supper."

Mama fussed at me all that morning, and when we walked out of the Lynn's grocery store. I struggled to hold all of the bags and hurry after her. One of the bags slipped from my hand, and I tried to catch it before it fell.

"Whoa, there! Here let me help," said a man's voice.

I couldn't see because of the brown paper bag in my face. Suddenly, a warm hand touched my arm.

"Let me have this one too."

The bag in my face was taken, and I came face to face with a handsome young Black man. He was tall and muscular with dark hair and eyes. His skin looked like warm chocolate, and he smiled while he held the two bags.

"Well, well, I'm glad that I came over to help," he murmured.

I smiled shyly and reached for the bags.

"Thank you, sir."

He started to say something when I heard Mama's shout.

"Vicky, hurry yourself on now. We got to have supper ready for your Daddy!"

Mama held the back door of the old Chevy open. The stranger shrugged his broad shoulders.

"We can't have your Daddy hungry."

He walked over to the car, and I followed.

"Excuse me, ma'am, I was just helping your daughter with her burden. My name is Harlan Sams," he said bowing his head to Mama.

Mama's face tightened.

"Thank you, young man, but we have to go."

Harlan placed the bags in the back seat, turned, and took mine to place beside the others. Mama walked around the car and got in the driver's side. Harlan closed the back door and opened mine.

Before I got in the car, he touched me on the arm and gave me a handsome smile.

"I would like to see you again, Vicky. Where do y'all live?"

I was surprised that he was so forward, but I wanted to see him again too.

"At the Four Winds ranch. My Daddy is the foreman."

"Vicky! Get in this car!"

I was so embarrassed at her shriek that I didn't even say goodbye. I slid into the car and felt the punishing pinch from Mama that I had taken too long. On the way home, I smiled thinking of when I'd see Harlan again.

Harlan found out where we lived and started to visit me. Luckily, it always seemed like he knew when Daddy was out on the range, or whenever Mama slept. We would take walks with Steven and my sisters because Clyde Jr. and Will had stayed with Betts and Grandpa Paul. I felt strange being alone with him, and it seemed like he was okay with my young chaperons.

Soon, word got out that Harlan visited me at the house. Daddy was so furious that he slapped me and locked me in the room that I shared with Ruth for two days. Steven and Ruth would sneak me water and food. Mama let me out the second day with an evil smirk. I knew then that I had to get away from my parents.

It turned out that Harlan told his family about me, and his parents went to Aunt Alice to ask about my character. She arranged a dinner at her large ranch house with his family so that they could meet me themselves. Harlan's parents, Ms. Dorothy and Mr. Jerry were very nice, and I smiled when they invited me to their ranch for a visit.

Later that night, Harlan asked Daddy for his permission to court me. Daddy had smiled at me spitefully and said no. Harlan looked surprised that Daddy had said no, but I wasn't. I was so used to Mama and Daddy's cruelty that I had learned to hide my feelings. Harlan tried again, but Daddy still said no. Soon, he gave up and went home with his parents.

The next week Lacy and I walked along the sidewalk in town on errands for Mama when I saw Harlan's silver Chevy convertible sitting in front of Nell's soda shop. I slowed down to see if I could catch a glimpse of him, and my heart stopped. There was Harlan with another girl. They were holding hands and drinking out of the same soda. I hurried and passed by so that they couldn't see me. Lacy was farther ahead, so she hadn't see them. I caught up with her, grabbed her hand, and hurried through the errands so that we could rush home.

When we got back home, I went into the woods at the back of the house and cried out my pain. Why? What was wrong with me that all the boys I liked ran to other girls? Would I never be able to have a boyfriend or husband? I asked myself those questions over and over until the tears stopped. My gift had not worked since I had cursed it. It stayed silent now when I needed it the most. I felt so abandoned by everyone and everything. Maybe I was supposed to stay with Mama and Daddy forever. That thought almost sent me into tears again.

Feeling hurt and wanting to get away from Littleton, I gave my parents an ultimatum to find the money for me to return to the country or send me to nursing school. Mama and Daddy laughed in my face and told me that there was no way that I was going anywhere because they could not and would not give me any money.

As I walked again to my favorite spot to shed tears of bitterness and disappointment, I thought about how much I had been through already: the stigma of being born multiracial in a pre-segregation era, the long days and nights watching my siblings and helping them with schoolwork, working in the cotton fields and at Ms. Suzie's to help feed and clothe my brother and sisters, and living through rheumatic fever. I was tired in body and mind, and I was only nineteen years old. I wiped my tears and prepared to face the people who had given me life and made it miserable, I prayed to God that He comfort me and put me on the path that He had for me. I prayed to God that He would provide a way for me to make my mark on the world and not to be stuck taking care of my family until I was too old to leave home.

After my prayer, I walked back to the house with a lighter step. I knew in my heart that God had heard my pleas and wondered when He would answer her prayer.

I sat with my back to the door in Nell's soda shop with Steven and Ruth on Valentine's Day, when the door opened. I felt the cold blast of air but didn't turn.

"Uh, oh," whispered Steven sitting up straighter.

Ruth elbowed him in the side.

"Hush."

I wasn't paying much attention to them. My thoughts were of Harlan around town with his girlfriend, Shirley. Steven had found out her name when he had talked to them at the soda shop a few months back. I sipped my soda, but I just wanted to go home and lie down.

"Hi, Victoria," said a familiar voice.

I looked up, and there was Harlan with a sheepish grin on his face. I looked back down at my soda.

"Hey."

"Can I sit with y'all?"

I was about to say no when Steven kicked me under the table.

"Sure," said Steven.

I gave him a glare and slid over for Harlan to sit down.

"Uh, Steven, Ruth, would y'all like another soda or a shake?"

Harlan pulled a dollar from his wallet.

"Sure," said Steven.

"Nope," Ruth grumbled.

She looked at Harlan like he was dirty.

Steven shook his head and grabbed Ruth's arm. He slid out of the booth and pulled Ruth behind him. He took the dollar from Harlan before going to the counter.

Harlan slid into their seat across from me.

"Vicky, I know that you're probably mad at me. What I did was stupid. I wanted to be your boyfriend so bad, and when your daddy said no, I was hurt. I didn't want to be around you if I couldn't make you my girlfriend. Shirley is a girl from school, and we used to court. She had heard about you and me and was jealous. She came by the ranch when she heard that I couldn't court you. I saw it as a chance to hurt you like your daddy hurt me. I'm sorry. Please forgive me. I'm going to your house tonight to ask your daddy again to court you."

Harlan looked as hurt as I did, and I felt pity for him.

My heart lightened a little when he told me what happened. I was still a little hurt and jealous at how easily he had left me for another girl. He smiled and reached for my hand. I smiled back and let him hold my hand.

When Steven and Ruth came back, we were laughing and talking. Ruth rolled her eyes, but Steven smiled.

"It's about time."

We all laughed, and they sat down with us.

Daddy gave Harlan permission to court me that night after supper. He told me later after Harlan had left that Aunt Alice had told him not to upset the Sams' by saying no again. He had no choice but to say yes. When he saw me smiling, he yanked me viciously up by the collar.

"Don't you be getting no ideas about marrying that boy. Remember your promise."

I could smell the alcohol on his drunken breath. I tried to pull at his hands but that only made him laugh more. I nodded because he tightened the collar of my blouse so that I couldn't answer. At my nod, he smiled and let me go. I fell to my knees gasping for breath. Mama smiled from her rocking chair and began to hum. Tears came to my eyes when it came to me again how much my parents mistreated me, and I knew that had to get away soon.

During the next few months, I forgot about the ugliness of my parents because Harlan made me blissfully happy. We took Steven, Ruth, and Lacy with us wherever we went. Harlan said that he liked my siblings because he was the youngest and had never had a chance to be a big brother. Ruth still hadn't warmed to him, and she would try to decline going with us except she didn't want to be at home with Mama and Daddy. I hoped that she would start to like Harlan because he had started to talk about the future, and how he would send me to school himself.

Early one morning in May, I sat on the front porch tired from making dresses all night for Ruth and Lacy's school program. Daddy was gone, and Mama in bed. I smiled, closed my eyes, and enjoyed the peace of the morning.

"There she is Mama. That's the girl that took Harlan away from me," said a girl's voice.

I opened my eyes to see an older Black woman with a younger pregnant woman who stood beside her and pointed at me. I must have dozed off because I hadn't heard them coming.

"Excuse me?"

I shook the fuzz of sleep off as I stood up. I looked at the girl again and gasped in surprise. It was Shirley, the girl that Harlan had courted! She was pregnant!

"Can I help you?"

"Yeah, you slut! You can let Harlan go, so he can come back to me and do right by me and his baby!"

Shirley snapped at me.

"Hush, girl. Let me talk to her," her mother fussed and Shirley became quiet.

"I'm Martha, miss. My girl says Harlan got her in the family way and started courtin' you. I'm sorry to tell you like this, but that's it. She said that he told her he'd do right by her if you let him go."

I stood there shocked. I couldn't believe it! Harlan had said nothing to me about a baby, and I wasn't going to let him go without a fight this time. I took a breath.

"Ma'am, if Harlan wants to go, he can go. He's a free man. He told me that your daughter was jealous of us. Maybe she made it up that Harlan's the father."

Shirley screeched.

"You stupid little witch! Harlan doesn't want you! He just wants what you have under that skirt!"

I raised my chin at her vulgarity.

"Get away from here! I'll talk to Harlan tonight, and we'll see who he wants!"

Martha shook her head and grabbed Shirley before she could run toward me.

"No, girl, let's go. I told you that coming here was wrong. We need to talk to Harlan."

She turned and pulled Shirley away down the lane while she screamed her hate at me. I let out the breath that I didn't know that I held. I turned and saw that Mama stood in the screen door with a smirk on her face. I sat down and closed my eyes to pray that what Shirley claimed wasn't true.

"She's lying! She tried her ways on me, but I didn't take it. I wanted you, Vicky! She just wants to make trouble! She's used goods anyway!"

Harlan vented his frustration later that night after I told him what happened with Shirley and her mama.

We sat on the porch, and the full moon cast light on our faces. I sighed in relief that Harlan had denied everything, but I still felt like he hid something from me.

"She said that you wanted what was under my skirt and then you'd leave me."

Harlan's eyes got bigger, and he looked like he wanted to yell at me. He took a deep breath.

"Vicky, I wanted to wait, but this is as good a time as any."

He reached in his pocket and pulled out a small gold and diamond ring. I could feel my heart beat faster when he went down on one knee.

"Vicky, will you do me the honor of becoming my wife?"

My throat closed up, and I felt the tears start to fall down my face.

"Vicky?" he prompted.

I squeezed out a yes through my tight throat, and Harlan jumped up with a holler. He slid the ring on my finger and gave me a kiss on the lips. It was our first kiss because he had only ever kissed me on my cheek or my forehead.

"Here now, what's all that racket?"

Daddy came through the door with a yell.

"Sir, Vicky said she'll marry me!"

Harlan moved back so Daddy could fit on the small porch. Daddy hissed and grabbed my arm.

"She meant to say no because she promised to stay with us until we're settled, right Vicky?"

Daddy gripped my arm painfully. Harlan frowned and took a step to cover the distance to where Daddy and I stood. He leaned down and looked at where Daddy had my arm.

"Sir, I would appreciate it if you'd take your hand off my future wife. Now," Harlan ordered softly.

Daddy tightened his grip then flung my arm away. "Fine, she can go, but she has to leave now. I don't want the lying little slut in my house another minute!"

He shouted the insult into Harlan's face. Harlan balled his fists, but I stayed him with my hand on his arm. I rubbed my bruised arm and nodded. Harlan started to speak, but I spoke up first.

"Alright, Daddy. I'll pack my things, and go to Aunt Alice's until we get married."

I held my head high while I moved past him into the house.

Mama stood just inside the door with a frown on her face and her hands on her hips. Ruth and Lacy looked like they would cry. I walked past them all to get to my room and opened drawers and the closet to collect my clothes and shoes. I put everything in pillowcases, and then Steven walked in and gave me a hug.

"Congratulations, sis. I wish you the best."

He gave me a sad smile.

I hugged him back tightly.

"I'll always be your big sister. Take care of Ruth and Lacy. I don't want Mama and Daddy to treat them like they did me."

Steven nodded and left the room.

I finished and looked around the room. I didn't see anything else, so I lifted the pillowcases and met Harlan on the porch. He took them and put them in his Chevy. I hugged Ruth and Lacy because they waited in the yard to say goodbye. When I pulled away from them, I heard Mama call them into the house. I turned around and saw that she shut the door without saying goodbye. I shrugged and told myself that I'd see them soon.

As Harlan drove me to Aunt Alice's, I didn't feel free like I thought I would. I looked over at Harlan and got this feeling that I had just traded one misery for another.

Epilogue

"Victoria. Wake up, sweetie. It's your wedding day," whispered a beloved voice.

I opened my eyes to see that Aunt Charlotte and Aunt Mary stood in the guest bedroom of Aunt Alice's ranch house. I let out a cry of joy and jumped off the bed to give them a hug. We all laughed and cried as we danced around in the room.

"We brought you something," Aunt Mary said with a secret smile.

Aunt Charlotte went outside the door and came back with the most beautiful white silk wedding gown. She hung it up on the door of the closet.

"First, let's get you bathed and dress your hair."

My aunts helped me get ready, and when the wedding dress was slipped over my head, they turned me to look at my reflection. I gasped when I saw that it was the wedding dress from the vision when I became very ill. The long sleeves were lace, the skirt was full and filled with tiny silk roses, and a flower garland was attached to the veil that Aunt Mary placed on my head. I felt strange that everything was the same as the vision. I turned to Aunt Mary to ask her about it, and she shook her head.

"I met Harlan. It isn't a mistake, Victoria. This is the path that you must take."

I wanted to cry at her tone, but I knew that she was always right. My gift told me nothing, so I would trust hers.

"Victoria, I want to give you something," said Aunt Alice walking though the door.

I loved Aunt Alice. She took me in that night when Daddy had put me out. She spent time with me and taught me all about ranching. She also told me about Grandpa Paul when they were children. Aunt Alice looked a lot like Grandpa Paul with her dark auburn hair, white skin, and blue eyes. I smiled at her when she came to stand in front of me. She held out a bunch of papers.

"Your Aunt Charlotte, Aunt Mary, and I have bought you and Harlan twenty acres on the other side of his parent's ranch. We've also put thirty thousand dollars in an account for you both to start up your own ranch and enough for you to go to college," she finished and smiled at Aunt Charlotte and Aunt Mary.

They moved to where Aunt Alice stood in front of me. I was speechless and shocked. My aunts had made it possible for Harlan and me to have a very good life. I started to cry, and then moved forward and hugged all of them.

"Thank you, oh, thank you so much! I love y'all so much!"

"Now, now, don't mess yourself up," Aunt Alice grumbled playfully.

Then she smiled and left the room. Aunt Mary turned back to me with a smile.

"It's up to you now, Victoria."

Then she left without looking back. Aunt Charlotte took my hand and gave it a squeeze.

"Your groom awaits!"

I laughed nervously and began to follow her as she left the room. I paused at the doorway and turned back to the room.

"Goodbye, Victoria Alicia Roberts," I whispered before turning back to let Aunt Charlotte lead me away.

I became Mrs. Harlan Sams a little after noon on the third of September. All I remembered was walking down the aisle on Grandpa Ed's arm and the nervous feeling while saying my vows. My aunts told me at the reception that I said my vows quickly, and everyone had laughed. Aunt Charlotte and Aunt Alice paid for the wedding because Mama and Daddy refused to pay or come to the ceremony. They didn't even let Steven, Ruth, or Lacy come either. I looked for them at the reception at Aunt Alice's ranch house, but they weren't there. I felt sad that they had missed my special day, but I felt relieved that my parents hadn't been there to embarrass me either.

Later that evening, when I changed into my honeymoon clothes, I heard voices outside of the window of Aunt Alice's guest bedroom.

"It's alright now. Don't worry. My mama said that we can be together after a little while of me being married. She wanted to make sure that Vicky and I married so that her Aunt Alice would settle some land on her."

I got closer to the window and saw that Harlan talked with Shirley. I covered my mouth so that they wouldn't hear me gasp. Tears filled my eyes because I knew then that Harlan had lied to me. They moved away from the window head together in deep conversation, and I fell to the floor in sobs.

"I saw that boy with a pregnant girl actin' all lovey dovey behind the house. I came to help you so stop your sniveling. Get up, girl, and I'll tell you how to keep your man," Betts' voice broke into my misery.

I turned around and saw that she had come into the room. I shook my head at her.

"I don't want to be married to him anymore."

Betts laugh mocked my heartbreak.

"It's too late for that. You don't want to embarrass your family, do you? You don't want to go back to your Mama and Daddy's, do you?"

I shook my head again.

"Now, wipe your face and listen. Tonight you will draw the line. After he takes you, let him sleep. Take the virgin blood from yourself and mix it with salt and sage. You can pack some from your aunt's kitchen. Sprinkle some on top of his forehead, at each door, and at each windowsill. He won't think about leaving you ever again. I had to entice your grandfather to my bed to draw the line when he was courtin' your Big Mama Chandra. He's still with me, isn't he?"

After Betts left the room, I got up and sat on the bed to think about what she said. At first, I was disgusted by what she said to do. Then, I decided that maybe she was right, and she did run her house. I wiped my face, fixed myself up, and went back to the reception. I saw Aunt Mary frown at me whenever I looked her way, but I didn't pay her any attention.

Soon after I returned, Harlan pulled me to the side and told me everything was ready to leave. I nodded and told him I'd meet him at the car. I went to the kitchen and grabbed the saltbox and a sprig of sage hanging in the window.

"Please don't, Victoria. You are already cursed by Betts' evil from when you were a child. She's bringing you across the line. If you do this, it will affect your life forever unless the line is broken."

Aunt Mary stood in the kitchen when I turned around from the window.

I shook my head, and my eyes filled with tears.

"I have to, Aunt Mary. I'm tired of being miserable and heartbroken. My "gift" won't work. God doesn't answer me. I feel so empty and useless, but this will make it all better."

Aunt Mary opened her mouth to argue, but I pushed past her and ran outside to meet my husband. I hugged the rest of my family goodbye, threw my bouquet, and slid into Harlan's decorated convertible. I saw Aunt Mary shake her head at me when I waved at everyone. I turned away quickly, and then I smiled at Harlan when he got into the car, and we rode away to begin our new life.

Victoria's Choice

Book 2

Prologue

"Look, darlin', there's our hotel, The Dallas Diamond. I've never been to this place. I thought it was only for the Whites, but your Aunt Charlotte told me that they started letting Black folk stay here too. She got us the bridal suite!"

Harlan hopped up and down in the car seat with excitement.

Victoria smiled at her husband's joy and fiddled again with the sage in her purse. Harlan returned the smile and drove into the entrance of the hotel.

"Hey, now, boy! You can't come this way! You need to go around back with the other colored folks!"

A short White man in a uniform with a funny hat on his head yelled and tried to wave Harlan to a stop. He almost ran in front of the car to make Harlan turn toward the back of the hotel.

Harlan frowned and kept driving right up to the front door and parked in front of the now angry White man. The man walked up to the car on Victoria's side and yanked the door open.

"Now, wait just a ..."

Harlan looked at the little man with fury and fumbled with the door handle.

"Oh, miss, I'm so sorry that I yelled at your boy. It's only that I saw him and didn't see you. The dim lighting, you see."

The man blushed and apologized for his rudeness.

Victoria didn't know what to say or do. She could feel Harlan's anger as he stared from her to the White man. She decided to act like her Aunt Charlotte. She looked at the nametag that identified the uniformed man as Johnny.

"Mr. Johnny, this is my husband, and we have a reservation under Sams. Please see to it that the car is parked and our bags are taken to our room. Thank you."

Victoria raised her chin and held her hand out to Johnny with authority to slide out of the car.

Johnny looked surprised at first then he frowned at Harlan.

"Yes, ma'am, well you'll have to take all that up with the manager. For now, you can go through the front, but your "husband" will have to go around to the back."

Johnny took Victoria by the arm and escorted her inside of the hotel without looking back at Harlan. Victoria tried to yank away and go back to her husband, but Johnny tightened his grip.

"Now, now, miss, it'll be alright. He can meet you in your room later if the manager lets you stay. We don't cotton to a White girl being with a Black man," Johnny whispered.

He nodded to a well-dressed White couple sitting in the beautiful marble and gold foyer. The woman turned and smiled kindly at Victoria. Victoria blushed and lowered her head.

Johnny took Victoria to the desk where an impeccably dressed White man stood looking down at some papers on the desk. Victoria looked more nervous when they approached the desk.

"Oui, Johnny, what are you doing away from your station?"

The manager spoke with a French accent. He hadn't yet lifted his head.

"Mister Sinclair, this girl came to stay at the hotel. She said that she's married to a Black man outside in the car. She said that she has a reservation."

Johnny had lowered his voice and leaned towards Mr. Sinclair.

"Oui, oui! Madame will stay! Go get the man!"

Mr. Sinclair narrowed his eyes at Johnny when his head snapped up. He waved his hand to dismiss Johnny.

Johnny looked confused, but he let go of Victoria and almost ran to get Harlan.

"Madame, my apologies for him. It is 1962, and yet there is so much Black and White problems."

Mr. Sinclair sighed.

"Now, a name please for your room, and I will send your bags up. Something to eat, perhaps?"

Curious at Mr. Sinclair's attitude, Victoria leaned closer to the desk.

"The name is Sams. Um, Sir, how did you know who I am?"

Mr. Sinclair chuckled.

"I do not know who you are. I only know that in France, all colours stay together."

Victoria smiled and nodded feeling relieved.

"Ah, such beauty. In France, you would be goddess to all men."

Mr. Sinclair gave a wide smile as Victoria blushed.

He turned and snapped his fingers and another uniformed man appeared. He whispered in his ear, and the man left. Hearing arguing coming through the doors, Victoria and Mr. Sinclair turned towards the noise. Victoria blushed again when the White couple also turned to see the commotion.

"She is my wife! I will not be treated this way!"

"And you shall not! Johnny, back to your post."

Mr. Sinclair came around the desk and shook Harlan's hand as he shooed Johnny away.

"Now, your wife and I have settled the matter. Please come."

Mr. Sinclair bowed and beckoned for Victoria and Harlan to follow.

Harlan looked at Victoria with anger and loathe on his face.

"I suppose you think that you're better than me because your skin is White? Well, you better get that out of your head because I'm not having it," he spat.

He looked as if he wanted to hit her.

Victoria shook her head and started to speak hurt by his tone, but Harlan stomped off behind Mr. Sinclair. Victoria lowered her head and slowly started to follow.

When she moved, her purse strap slipped and everything fell out onto the floor. Embarrassed, she dropped to her knees and grabbed for everything before someone noticed the sage and salt.

"Let me help you, child," the older White woman from the foyer said while bending toward Victoria.

Ashamed and still embarrassed, Victoria opened her mouth to say no, however, the woman already bent to help her pick up her items.

"It sounds like he is not worth what you are about to do, my dear. Leave him now, or it will only get worse."

Victoria glanced up in surprise.

"Do I know you, ma'am?"

The White woman shook her head and smiled.

"No, but I know you. My name is Linda, and I am a friend of your Aunt Mary's."

Victoria felt tears at hearing her Aunt Mary's name, but she swallowed them. What could anyone know of her pain? Betts knew, and now, Victoria would use her advice to make it all better.

"Thank you, Ms. Linda. But, everything will be better after tonight."

Victoria took her things from Ms. Linda's hands and turned around to follow a uniformed man waiting to take her to her room. She refused to look back.

1

As I stood in the kitchen watching the sunrise through the tiny window, I closed my eyes and thought about the choices that I had made. I felt the tears well up in my eyes and didn't try to stop them. The sunrise was so beautiful as it chased the darkness of night away. I wiped my tears and turned from the window because the bright light began to hurt my eyes. The dim light of the kitchen comforted me more than the sunlight. Embracing the shadows and darkness made me feel better these days. I smiled to myself when Harlan's favorite saying came to mind.

"Everyone is the same in the dark."

I woke before dawn to make sure that I had enough supplies to make breakfast. The last thing that I wanted to do was anger Harlan. My body ached from his attentions, and my heart hurt from my own stupidity. I shook my head to deny myself the thoughts that began to flood my mind.

I looked back at the freshly made biscuits on the counter and thought of my Big Mama Chandra. It was her recipe. I lifted my hand to smell the flour and baking powder. I could almost see her with her apron smiling at me as she put the pan in the oven. I smiled at the image and lowered my hand. No, I told myself again. I needed to quietly clean up the kitchen and try to go back to bed. My sons would be waking soon, and I wanted to enjoy being with them. After all, they were the only men in my life that had not rejected me.

I tiptoed down the hall and into our room. I slid the door shut so as not to wake Harlan. It wouldn't have mattered anyway. His snores were so loud that I could have slammed it, and he would have remained asleep. I climbed into bed and turned on my side away from the noise of my husband. Usually, I had to lie awake afraid that Harlan's snores would wake the children, but I closed my eyes and found the comfort of the darkness.

I walked down the aisle at my wedding. Everything was so beautiful, and all of my loved ones were there. I smiled at Aunt Charlotte and Aunt Alice standing at the altar with the preacher. They smiled at me, and through my veil, I could see the tears in their eyes. I turned my eyes to the altar and saw the man that would become my husband. The sunlight glistened in his light brown hair and blue eyes, and I fell in love all over again. I wanted to run but knew that wasn't proper, so I kept walking slowly until I stood beside him. I handed my bouquet to Aunt Charlotte and turned back to my love. He took my hands in his, and as one, we turned to the preacher. When we said our vows, I felt the warmth of love coming from him and my family.

"You may kiss the bride," the preacher said smiling at us.

I raised my face for him to lift my veil, but when the silk lifted, I cried out in anguish. Billy was not there anymore. Harlan had taken his place. He gripped my chin and kissed me roughly while I cried and screamed at the loss of Billy.

Harlan grabbed my arms and laughed.

"Forever and ever, Vicky!"

"NO!"

I tried to tear myself from his grip, but he was too strong. He dragged me away, and I screamed for help from my family. No one came to help me. Then, everything went black, and I saw Aunt Mary alone in a pool of light.

"I cannot help you now, Victoria. You will have to wait until you can make the choice that will pull you back over the line."

Tears fell from her face, and she faded into the light.

"Please, Aunt Mary! Don't go! Help me, please!"

I screamed and ran to her, but she was gone.

As I fell to the ground sobbing my heartache, I felt a tiny hand touch my cheek. I looked up to see a baby wrapped in a pink blanket lying on the ground next to me. She smiled and waved her arms. I wanted to pick her up but each time I tried, my arms caught air. I tried and tried again but I couldn't do it. I cried more tears and felt a stinging in my face. I wiped it away, but it kept stinging until it became painful. I screamed at the pain.

"Wake up, you lazy cow!"

I woke up to see a hand raised and realized that I had been having a bad dream. Harlan had slapped my face to awaken me. I grabbed my throbbing cheek and scooted away from him on the bed.

"I'm tired of you waking me up crying and screaming like some kind of crazy fool! I should hit you again just so you know I'm not having it!"

Harlan's breath was foul in his anger, and he moved closer to me with his hand still raised to strike me.

"Mama, Mama!"

Our four-year-old son, Mark, cried out and beat at the closed door.

"I have field duty for the next two weeks. You better get over all your problems by the time I get back. You hear me?"

Harlan gave me a look of disgust and turned to go into the tiny bathroom.

I breathed a sigh of relief when the door closed. I slowly got up and slid my housecoat on the way to the door. I stopped for a minute to wipe the tears from my face with my sleeve and put on a smile for my son.

"Good Morning, little one."

I opened the door and leaned over to give Mark a hug. I clung to his little body for a second too long, and Mark stiffened in my arms.

"What's wrong, Mama? Did Daddy hurt you again?"

I released him and smiled.

"No, honey, Mama just had a bad dream, and it scared Daddy."

He relaxed just a little and let me take his hand to lead him down the short hallway to his and William's, my baby boy's room. I smiled wider when I saw that William was standing in his crib waiting to be lifted to the floor. I walked over to the crib, kissed his smooth little chocolate cheeks, and felt to see if his cloth diaper was wet. I counted myself lucky because it was dry…this time.

I took him across the hall and stood him before the toilet. William grinned and shook his head. Mark came in behind me and crossed his arms.

"Go to potty, Willie!"

"No, Mark, let him go on his own, okay?"

"But Mama…"

Mark rolled his eyes at my light scolding. I frowned at him, and he lowered his head.

"Don't you "but Mama me", Mark Sams. William has to learn just like you did," I fussed.

Mark shrugged his shoulders and left the bathroom, and I sighed at his little adult ways.

"Mama, tee, tee," I heard William say from behind me.

I turned and saw that he went potty. Happy that he was learning, I picked him up before he finished. We both giggled, and I quickly put him back down. I grabbed a towel, cleaned him up, and made a mental note to clean the bathroom later.

The boys sat at the table playing blocks while I cooked breakfast when Harlan walked in dressed in his field clothes. I tried not to turn around because I knew that he would say something cruel.

"Hey, hey, boys! How's Daddy's little men, huh?"

"Dad-dee!"

William twisted to put the blocks down and hold his hands to Harlan.

"Good Morning, Daddy."

Mark barely glanced at Harlan and greeted him in his usual solemn tone.

"Mark, why are you always such a little downer, huh? You're just like your crazy Mama."

I heard a chair scrape and turned around to see that Mark stood by his chair with his little fists balled.

"My Mama is not crazy. She is different just like me."

When I saw Harlan began to frown, I walked over to Mark and grabbed his hand.

"Mark, you didn't wash your hands this morning. Go on and wash up, okay?"

I gave him a kiss on the head and a little push toward the bathroom.

He looked at me for a moment and nodded. I breathed a sigh of relief until I heard Harlan's voice.

"Next time that happens, I'm going to give that Mama's boy of yours a lesson."

I nodded and went back to the stove to get the food to the table. I placed the biscuits, the platter of bacon, eggs, and tomatoes on the table in front of Harlan. He immediately began to fix his own plate.

I decided to wait for Mark to return to the small dining area before I took my seat. He came back shuffling his feet, and I walked to him and guided him into the seat farthest from Harlan. Harlan looked up and narrowed his eyes at me because he saw what I had done. I gave him a big smile and sat down in Mark's usual spot. Harlan reached under the table and gave my wrist a sharp twist. Water came to my eyes, but I refused to cry out at the pain.

"Your food is getting cold, husband."

"Oh, it doesn't matter, it'll taste like slop anyway. I thought your old mammy taught you how to cook."

He chuckled to himself and reached for his fork.

I ignored his usual insult and picked up the half empty platter to feed the boys. Harlan took most of the food as usual, which always left me nibbling on toast. When I began placing food on Mark's plate, he shook his head.

"No, Mama, I just want a little. You and William have to eat."

I smiled at his earnest little expression.

"Well, I need you to grow big and strong so that you can take care of me when I'm old and wrinkled."

He shook his head again.

"No, Mama, you won't need me, and you're never going to be wrinkled."

He spoke so matter-of-fact while he stared at me in his usual adult way.

"Yeah, yeah, boy. You better eat that food. I work hard to put that food on this table, and you're going to eat it whether you like or not."

Harlan spat food crumbs in his anger and pointed his fork at Mark.

I saw that Mark had narrowed his eyes and opened his mouth to say something, but I broke in first.

"Guess what, boys, Aunt Charlotte sent y'all a box and probably a letter. After breakfast, we can sit down on the sofa and open it all together."

I tried to sound excited to change the mood at the table.

Mark lifted his face to mine and gave a small smile while William clapped and laughed.

"What's this? You didn't tell me that we got anything from that ol' stingy aunt of yours."

Harlan interrupted me with a sly look.

I lowered my head a bit because I knew that he liked for me to be cowered.

"It was addressed to the boys, so I didn't think that you'd want to see it. It's probably just toys and some candy."

I dismissed it with a wave.

"Well, if it isn't, I want to know first thing, you hear?" he demanded while giving my sore wrist another squeeze.

I winced but still didn't cry out like he wanted. He looked disappointed and went back to his plate.

We ate in silence until Harlan gave a big belch, broke wind, and left the table without a word. It was like a weight lifted when he left, and I placed my hands together and lowered my head.

"Father in Heaven, forgive us for asking Your blessing of our food after we have eaten. You know our hearts and our troubles. Thank You for all of Your blessings. Amen."

When I lifted my head, I saw Mark and William lifting theirs as well. My heart swelled with pride to know that my sons understood enough to know prayer.

After we married, Harlan had shown himself to be not quite as religious as he had pretended when we courted, among other things. At first, whenever I prayed or tried to pray in his presence, he made angry noises until I finished. As time went on, he would find ways to disturb me so much that I hid my prayers until he wasn't around me. I felt so ashamed, but I knew everything that happened between us was my fault.

Before I began those thought intruded, I let the boys play in their room while I cleared the table and washed the dishes. When I finished in the kitchen, I decided to do the cleaning and put on a roast for dinner. Since Harlan was going to be in the field for the next two weeks, I wanted to feed my boys well. I smiled again at the peace of no-Harlan and finished up my chores.

When the house smelled like Lysol, I went into Mark and William's room and lifted the covers from the large box in the corner. The boys had watched me cover it the day before but hadn't touched it. They started to jump happily around me when I led them to the living area where I placed the box from Aunt Charlotte on the small coffee table. I could feel their excitement because a box from my family was something special.

I promised myself not to open it until Harlan wasn't home. I raised my chin at the thought that I was being a disobedient wife, but I hoped God would make an exception for me every once in a while being married to Harlan.

"What is it, Mama?"

Mark looked curious and rubbed the sides of the large cardboard box.

William tried unsuccessfully to climb onto the table to stand beside the box.

"I don't know, honey, so let's open it and see."

I smiled and sat forward.

I grabbed William and held him to my lap. I reached over and drew Mark to my side. With the edge of my fingernail, I slit open the tape on each side. Mark and William got up to try to peek over the edge when I opened the flaps.

Right on top of a lot of newspaper stuffing were two letters. One was addressed to me from Aunt Charlotte, and the other was from Aunt Mary. I lifted them out like they were pieces of fragile glass.

For a moment, I lost myself to the living area, and my sons who started to try to turn over the box to see what else was in it. I hugged the letters to my chest and tried not to cry. It was hard, but I needed to focus on my children. I felt a familiar darkness began to creep into me, and I embraced it because it made me feel stronger and in control.

I sat up straighter, tucked the letters in my pocket, and shushed the boys. They immediately became quiet. I reached inside the box and began to pull out the newspapers.

"Oh my," I breathed when I saw what was under the stuffing.

"What is it, Mama?" Mark asked.

"Look, honey."

I pulled out a tiny train caboose.

"Mama! Mama! She sent us a train!"

Mark and William jumped around me when I pulled out all of the pieces to a miniature train set complete with tracks and a small motor. The detail on each piece looked exactly like the actual train. I had never seen anything like it before and had certainly never received such a gift from anyone. I smiled and jumped from the sofa to join my boys in their excitement.

Mark and I figured out how to put the train and tracks together while William stood by picking up the pieces until Mark yelled for him to stop.

"No, Willie! You gotta wait for us to get through with it!"

William's lip started to quiver, and I knew that the tears were about to let loose. I pulled him into my lap and gave his little body and squeeze.

"William, it's okay. You'll get to play too. Mama and Mark want to fix it just right, okay?"

William smiled and laid his little hand on my cheek. He looked at me for a moment then nodded his head. I smiled and gave him another squeeze before putting him down to finish helping Mark. Out of the corner of my eye, I thought I saw him narrow his eyes with a hateful glare at Mark, but I shook my head knowing that my two-year-old son wasn't capable of such a look.

When the set was complete, I attached the little motor and watched my boys' faces as I flipped the switch and the little train began its journey around the track.

"Whoop woo!" echoed William.

Mark rolled his eyes, but I could see that he enjoyed it too. I smiled at him and grabbed both of them in a big hug. Then, I laughed when they both squirmed loose to get back to watching the wonder of the train.

I watched them for a while until my mind turned to the letters from my aunts. I put my hand to my pocket to reassure myself that they were still there. My breathing picked up when I felt warmth coming from my pocket. I knew then that I needed some time away from my boys to open them.

"Mark, I'm going to my room for a little bit. Play nice with your brother until I come back to give y'all lunch, okay?"

Mark looked up from the train and gave me one of his adult stares.

"Are you okay, Mama?"

I felt the tears in my throat at his grown up concern. I swallowed and gave him a big smile.

"Yes, I am, silly. I'll be right back."

I turned and hurried into the hallway to get away from my son's awareness of my suffering.

2

When I entered my room, I closed the door and slumped against it. I fisted my hands over my mouth to silence the cries that I felt in my soul. I rubbed the letters in my pocket to give myself some comfort, but they weren't warm anymore.

The darkness began to creep into me, and again, I embraced it. I felt more in control when I dried my tears with my sleeve and reached for the letters. I decided to open Aunt Charlotte's first. A piece of paper fell out when I unfolded her letter. I ignored it because I was too anxious to read her words. Seeing her handwriting, an image of Aunt Charlotte sitting at her beautiful antique writing desk in one of her day dresses with her dark hair in a chignon came to mind. When I began reading it, I felt the familiar tremble of despair for my terrible choice.

"Dearest Victoria,
I pray that this letter finds you well. I have sent letters to you for a while now, and they have gone unanswered. I sent this package with a prayer that it would reach you and not anyone else. Mama said that you've written her a few letters and she's sent you a couple of packages. I'm very jealous because I don't hear from you. I miss you, Victoria. I had

hoped when you married that I would see you more often, especially when you were with child. It has been three long years since Harlan took you from Littleton when he enlisted in the service, and five years since your wedding. I won't ask anything of your business because whatever goes on in your marriage is your business not mine. I just want you to be happy.

Well, on to catching you up on family. If you don't already know, your Big Mama Chandra has gotten some of her sight back! She went to a hot spring in Colorado where your Uncle Andrew is living now, and she came back seeing shadows. Your Grandpa Ed is happy with that because he said that his legs couldn't take any more whacks from her cane. Your mother and father moved back home two years after you got married. I reckon you knew that part, but they also left Ruth, Lacy, and Steven with your Aunt Alice. Steven is your Aunt Alice's foreman, and Ruth and Lacy are going to come live with your Aunt Mary and me when they finish school! Mary and I are so excited because we haven't had much family coming to stay a spell since you.

How are my grandsons? Yes, I call them my grandsons to which your mother grumbles and gives me angry looks when we're all having Sunday dinner at Mama's. Mama says that I do it on purpose, and I reckon that I do because Tess won't ever talk about you.

Your Grandpa Paul has been sick lately. Dr. Herbert doesn't know what's wrong with him nor does his son, Dr. William.

My eyes widened at her words. Dr. William? Did she mean Billy? Billy is a doctor? My breathing sped up when I continued reading.

Speaking of Dr. William, he asks about you quite a bit. He says that he went to school with you, but since he's White, I know that's not true. Again, whatever happened is your business.

A tear fell onto the paper, and I wiped it away quickly to read her remaining words.

Well, I better close because I'm starting to feel an ache in my leg from sitting so long. I love you, Victoria. No matter how far apart we are, no matter how much times goes by, I love you. Please don't ever forget that I always just want you to be happy. I pray that these words reach you. Please give my grandsons a kiss and my love. I have sent you and the boys a little something to think of me.
  Love Always,
  Your Aunt Charlotte

My lungs felt tight, and my face felt hot while I tried to hold back the storm of tears that threatened to fall. Aunt Charlotte had been writing me, and I had never received the letters. I knew that Harlan didn't want me around my family after he lost all of our land and the money that my aunts had given me when we married. To keep letters from Aunt Charlotte denying me her love, it was too much. I began to feel the anger building, and I took deep calming breaths to tamp it down. I refused to give in and ruin the warmth of Aunt Charlotte's letter.

I picked up the paper that fell out of the letter and saw that it was a two hundred dollar check! I gasped in surprise at her generosity. The check trembled in my hand while my mind scrambled to the things that I could do with it. Then, I realized that Harlan had probably kept all the money that Aunt Charlotte had sent in her other letters. I tried again to take deep calming breaths because all I could see was red. The anger soon dissipated when a plan came to my mind of what I was going to do with the money. I smiled to myself and unfolded Aunt Mary's letter.

My dearest Victoria,

I know that you and your sons are doing well. We would like to see them, and I know that we will soon. I know that Harlan has been keeping our letters from you. I told your Aunt Charlotte to stop sending gifts, but she wouldn't listen. She misses you. We all miss you. I'm glad that you will be able to read this letter because I have some important things to tell you. Harlan can never see this letter so hide it when you are done.

Drawing the line was a choice that you made because you had been sent away to us at such a young age. You never saw your differences as a gift because of how you were treated. The events that happened to you when you were a child did not help you to make a good choice. I know about Dr. William, or as you called him, Billy. He was not the man for you then, so let it pass. What matters now is to bring you back across the line before it is too late. I can feel the darkness that has begun to control you. If not for your sons, you would be consumed.

You need to learn to love all of your gifts. It won't be easy because of the evil that has been planted in you since you were a child, but you must try, Victoria.

I have seen a vision of a baby girl wrapped in pink. This is backwards as life is death in dreams and visions. You will have another son soon. If you were with us when you have your children, the visions that you would have would show you how to break the line.

Know that I love you, and I am here to guide you, Victoria. Do not allow the darkness to consume you while you still have a chance. Your choice is coming.

Love,
Aunt Mary

I lowered the hand that I had raised to my mouth at her words that I would have a son. I allowed the tears to fall freely because I knew that Aunt Mary spoke the truth. I hadn't even thought about it until now, but I was late. I had not felt the familiar monthly pains for over a month. They had never been late in torturing me, so I knew that I was with child. I touched my stomach and closed my eyes to pray.

"Please Father in Heaven, I know that Aunt Mary has the gift of knowing. Please let this be the child that Aunt Mary's says will break this line of darkness and misery. If he is not, please take him now before he comes into this life of pain and despair. Amen"

I felt guilty for asking God to let me miscarriage, but I wanted to spare my sons and myself the grief of more suffering at the hands of my husband.

With the thought of my sons, I ran into the bathroom, washed and wiped my tear-stained face, and hurried into the living room. Mark looked up from the table where he and Willie sat eating peanut butter and crackers. He had even poured them a glass of milk. I smiled at him and felt pride rise within me.

"Well, look what we have here. Mark, you are such a wonderful big brother to fix William and yourself some vittles! I'm so proud of you."

I held out my arms, and he ran into them. I gave him a tight hug until he squirmed. I let him go to see Willie standing beside him with his arms raised. I chuckled and gave him a hug too.

"Alright boys, let's go outside and play hide-and-seek before supper, okay?"

Mark whooped and Willie clapped his hands. As we filed outside, I touched my stomach again.

Later that night, I picked up my aunts' letters and read them again. When I saw Billy's name, I felt a deep sorrow at the loss of his friendship and love. I thought about all the talks that we had when he drove me home from Ms. Suzie's. We had shared so much, and I wished that I could talk to him now. No. I shook my head at my foolishness. He was probably married with his own children by now. I shook my head again and climbed into bed because my body and mind were tired and sleep soon overcame me.

A few days later, Harlan came home and announced that he had been assigned overseas to Korea. He danced around the apartment saying he was lucky because a lot of his friends were going too. I smiled, and he accepted it as my joy for him, and I was happy. Now, I knew that my plans were going to happen sooner and with ease. He was so excited that he didn't even ask me about the box from Aunt Charlotte. I looked around at the boys, and Willie clapped and sang along with Harlan. Mark just watched silently until Harlan swung Willie up in his arms to dance. Willie whimpered at being handled so roughly.

"Daddy, please put Willie down. You might hurt him."

Harlan stopped dancing and narrowed his eyes at Mark. He lowered Willie slowly to the floor. I moved forward to protect my son, but Harlan saw me coming. He threw out his arm and knocked me to the floor. I let out a grunt, and Mark moved toward me with a cry. Harlan grabbed him and put him under his arm. Mark squirmed to get loose, and Harlan slapped his face. I got up as fast as I could and moved in front of Harlan. Willie screamed and ran to hide behind me.

"Harlan, put him down. You've already hit him. See, he isn't moving. He may really be hurt."

I pleaded silently for Mark to stay still.

"No, you stupid cow. This boy has too many of your ways. He's more like you than me. He probably thinks that he's better than me too because he's high yella. He needs lessons on how to talk to his elders, and I'm going to give it to him."

He pushed past me knocking Willie and me down. I tried to grab his leg, but he kicked me in the shoulder. Mark started to scream when Harlan walked into the bathroom and slammed the door. I stood up and ran to the door. I tried the knob, but it was locked. I pounded and screamed for Harlan to open the door, but I got nothing except my son's screams.

Whap! Whap! Whap!

Mark screamed louder with each strike. I yelled for him to be strong and a big boy. My heart cried out at his screams of pain. Finally, there was nothing but silence. I tried the door again, but Harlan opened it first.

"There. Now, he'll remember that whipping and never talk to me that way again."

He pushed past me, and I fell to my knees at the sight in the bathroom. Mark's pants were off, and his behind, legs, and back were covered in huge welts. Some were open and bleeding. He wasn't moving, and his breathing was slight. I turned and saw that Harlan had used his tough leather razor strap on my son. Numbness seeped into my limbs as I crawled across the bathroom floor to my child. I raised my hand to touch him, but I realized that I needed to remember what Big Mama Chandra would do. I stood up and grabbed some washcloths and two big towels. I wet the washcloths with cold water and wiped Mark's face. I wanted to turn him over to hold him in my arms, but I knew that I needed to clean the welts.

"Mama, Mawk, hurt."

William whimpered from the doorway, but I couldn't turn to him. I nodded because my throat was too tight to speak. I kept on wiping Mark's face and wounds until I felt a little movement. I shushed him and wrapped him in one of the big towels. I raised myself to my knees, and then I picked up my son. I rubbed my face to his and finally found my voice.

"William, come with Mama and take a nap."

He nodded and stuck his thumb in his mouth. I had only recently gotten William to stop sucking his thumb, but I was too worried about Mark to pull it out of his mouth.

When I walked into the boys' room, Harlan followed me.

"Just put him on the bed. He'll be fine. I want a sandwich and a beer to watch TV."

I swung around and felt the familiar darkness rising within me.

"Harlan, you will allow me to help our son. If you want to hurt me, fine, but you will not beat a child like this ever. Do you beat your daughter from Shirley like this? I doubt it, and I know that she talks back to you all the time. Know this, I will not have my children mistreated like I was. Fix your own sandwich. I'm going to take care of my son."

I turned my back on him and felt his anger. I waited for him to strike me, but he didn't. He picked up William who screamed at his touch. I turned back to him and reached for my child.

"I'll be in the living room waiting on my sandwich. In the meanwhile, Willie can keep me company. Isn't that right, little man?"

William kept squirming and screaming in his fear. I knew what Harlan was doing, but I needed to take care of Mark. I chose to handle the most important issue. I hushed William and reached in his crib for his favorite blanket.

"Here you go, my sweet. Take a nap with Daddy, and Mama will take care of Mark, okay?"

William grabbed the blanket and stuck his thumb back in his mouth. He nodded at me with tears in his eyes.

I narrowed my eyes at Harlan then turned back to Mark. I lurched in surprise to see his eyes open. He looked from me to William.

"It's okay, Mama. I just need a nap. Please take care of Willie."

Tears fell from my eyes at his courage. I nodded at him to let him know that I understood. I knew that he was in pain, but he wanted me to take care of William first. I wiped my tears away and turned to go into the kitchen. Harlan guffawed.

"Well, I guess the boy has some of me in him after all."

I hesitated for a second wanting to tell him that Mark was nothing like him, but I kept going. The sooner he had his sandwich and beer, the faster I could take care of my sons. I felt better knowing that Harlan would be shipped out soon.

A week after Christmas, Mark, William, and I dutifully waved goodbye to Harlan at the military airfield. He would be gone for a year before he could take leave to come home. I was elated, but I tried to hide my smile when I looked over at Shirley and her daughter Marianne. They were in tears and waved like Harlan wasn't coming back. I knew different.

Meanness like that could survive anything. I was about to turn back when I saw Marianne walk towards us with Shirley behind her.

When Shirley turned, I saw that she was pregnant. I held my gasp because I knew then why she was in tears. It all came together in my mind in an instant, and I knew the truth. All of the "field" assignments and weekends on duty were times that Harlan had been with Shirley. She was pregnant with his child as was I. I began to hope that something would happen to her baby, then immediately gave myself a shake at such an evil thought. I asked myself from where had it come, but I already knew that it had come from the darkness. I surrendered to it for a moment to give myself comfort, and then I looked straight into Shirley's hateful glare and rubbed my belly. Her eyes widened, and she almost tripped in her surprise. I wanted to giggle at her expression, but I held it in…barely.

Her daughter continued on her path unaware of her mother's plight. She walked up to me and gave me a hug. I stood there surprised for a moment until I lifted my arms to return it. She released me and stepped back, just as Shirley took her hand to pull her back with a frown.

"Hi, Ms. Vicky. My name is Marianne. I told my Mama that I wanted to meet you, but she said no. My Grandma Martha told me to do it today when Mama wasn't looking, but she caught me anyway. Can I visit and play with my brothers, please? My grandma said that I'm the big sister, and I should know them. Can I please come?"

I looked at the little skinny, dark skinned girl who looked like a perfect combination of her parents. There was no maliciousness in her spirit or on her face. She looked to be honest in her desire to know her half-brothers. It took me all of two seconds to make up my mind.

"It is very nice to meet you, Marianne. This is your brother, Mark, and this is William. We're going on a trip soon, but you can visit us before we leave, okay?"

I smiled into her surprised expression.

"Really?" she asked.

She began to jump up and down in her excitement. Shirley tapped her shoulder, and she stopped. She moved closer to my sons and hugged them.

"I can't wait to visit. Daddy bought me a bicycle and games for Christmas, so I can bring them with me."

She was so excited that she didn't see her brothers stiffen in surprise or her mother's smug expression.

"Marianne, you don't have to bring anything with you. The boys have plenty of toys and games. They even have a tiny train with a little city and tracks that lets the train circle the city. I'm sure that you will have plenty of good play time."

I returned Shirley's smug look. Her face held surprise that my children would have such an extravagance. I wanted to curse Harlan for forsaking his sons of bicycles and games.

Marianne grabbed her brothers' hands and began to jump up and down again. Shirley once again tapped her shoulder and reminded her that they had to get back to Littleton. Marianne turned to me with a smile.

"Thank you so much, Ms. Vicky! See y'all soon!"

Then she turned and followed her mother off of the platform.

I turned back to the airplane that took off with my husband and narrowed my eyes in anger. When the plane rose in the air, the annoyance fell away from me. I smiled, grabbed my sons' hands, and started towards the big Chevy car that Harlan had purchased with my money after we married. I thought about Marianne and her excitement of seeing her brothers. I sighed at how some things come to pass. God only knew what surprises life had in store for us next.

Later that afternoon, I sat at the dining table with an envelope and a blank sheet of paper. The boys were down for a nap, so I decided to start bringing my plans to life. I picked up the pen and held it over the paper. I glanced over at the check that Aunt Charlotte had sent me and smiled. It was time to stop being a doormat and stand up for myself. It was time to go home.

3

One month after Harlan left, I locked up the small house on the Ft. Green army base, packed my sons and as much luggage in the Chevy that I could fit, and headed towards Carson. It was cold and icy, but I was determined to follow my plans. I bundled the boys under the car blanket and headed down the highway. I kept up a stream of conversation with them about the country and all of our loved ones. They didn't join in, so I told them to take a nap until we got to Aunt Alice's. I wanted to see her, Steven, and my sisters before we went home.

When I wrote Aunt Alice of my plans, she sent me another two hundred dollars. I was grateful that she still wanted to help me after Harlan had swindled away all of the land and money that she and Aunt Charlotte gifted to us. I almost started to cry again at the events since the wedding, but I took a deep breath and kept driving toward home.

"Well, well, look at my nephews! They're the picture of your brothers! Come here and give your old Aunt Alice a hug, boys!"

Aunt Alice held out her arms, and William launched himself into them. Aunt Alice laughed, squeezed him, and gently put him down. She turned around to do the same with Mark. Mark stared at Aunt Alice for a moment before giving her a hug. Aunt Alice frowned and looked at me. I shook my head and mouthed, "Later". She nodded and turned to lead us into the warmth of the ranch house.

"Steven is out on the range, and your sisters are still at school. I'm going to tell Dee to start cooking up a big homecoming supper for y'all," Aunt Alice said.

She spoke over her shoulder while she walked back toward the kitchen. Suddenly, she turned around halfway down the hall.

"This is your home, Victoria. Never forget that. Now, the guest room that you were in before is empty, and when I knew you were going to come, I moved a crib and a trundle in there. Cedric, my houseman, will put your suitcases in there for now. Go on have a seat in the front room. I'll be back in a jiffy."

She turned around and walked on down the hall. My heart ached at her generosity. A few tears escaped my eyes before I could stop them.

"Mama, why are you crying? Don't you like Aunt Alice?"

Mark looked up at me with curiosity.

I smiled down into his beloved face.

"Yes, I love Aunt Alice, and you will too. I'm just so happy. These are happy tears."

I gave him another watery smile, but he didn't look convinced. I decided to make us comfortable in the front room.

I turned to the left and walked down the finished oak planked hallway to the front room. While we strolled to the front room, I glanced at all of the photos and whatnots that lined the walls. There were pictures of everyone in the family. I stopped and almost gasped at all of the pictures of Harlan and me on our wedding day. I looked so happy in my beautiful dress. I glanced away when the memories began to flood into my mind.

I turned and guided the boys into the bright, sunny front room. There was a large picture window that looked out onto the front lawn. The fireplace roared, and the beautiful carved pine mantle had a warm shine. The divans and chairs were reds and browns, but it didn't make the room dark. Towards the back of the room, I could see Aunt Alice's office with its carved oak desk and matching chair.

My mouth began to water at the smells that wafted from the kitchen. The boys and I had finished the sandwiches that I made for the trip all while ago. I looked over at Aunt Alice's grandfather clock to see that it was almost luncheon.

"Willie, don't touch that! You might break it!"

Mark moved to where Willie had grabbed a wooden gun from the small cabinet by the fireplace. He was about to snatch it from his hand when Aunt Alice came through the open doorway leading to the dining room.

"It's okay, son. I bought those for you and your brother."

Aunt Alice walked over to Mark and handed him another wooden gun from the cabinet. She also took down a small metal box.

"These guns are very special because if you load them just right, you can hit a few squirrels right in the kisser."

Aunt Alice chuckled while she opened the box and showed the boys how to load the guns with large rubber bands. Mark's face lit up when she explained that he and Willie could go with Cedric and play in the backyard. He looked at me and his face fell.

"I can't leave Mama, she needs me."

Aunt Alice gave me a look, and I called Mark to me.

"Mark, Cedric is a nice man. He knew me before you were born. You'll have a good time with him and William. I'll stay here with Aunt Alice for a spell. She wants to talk to me about what good boys I have, okay?"

I hugged him and tickled him a little to which he giggled. He looked into my eyes and nodded.

"Alright, here's Cedric now. Have a good time and stay warm."

I grinned and nudged Mark towards where Cedric stood.

"I'll take good care of the little mites, Miss, I mean, Ms. Victoria."

Cedric smiled at me before he pulled his own wooden gun from his pocket.

"Now, which one of you varmints wants to shoot us up some squirrels."

Cedric spoke with a bad cowboy twang and struck a gunslinger pose.

Mark and William jumped up and down and yelled that they did. We all laughed as Cedric led them outside to play.

"Mark is a special child, Victoria. He thinks of you and William before himself. Tell me how this came to be."

Aunt Alice waited for our laughter to die down before she turned to inquire about my unusually smart son. She took a seat in the biggest chair in the room next to the fireplace. It was a rocking chair but cushioned all over with a stool to match. I took the smaller matching rocking chair across from it.

I began to speak when Dee, the house hand brought us cups of hot tea. I thanked him and took a sip. It was minty and good. I knew that it was Aunt Alice's special mix. I waited until Aunt Alice sampled hers before I started again. She took a long swallow and waved her hand at me to start. Drawing in a deep breath, I decided to tell her the truth.

"Well, Aunt Alice, I guess, Mark is the way that he is because of Harlan. I married a monster and didn't know it. Wait, I take it back. I didn't want to know it. I made a terrible choice, and now my sons, especially Mark, pays the price."

I took another sip of the tea, and it felt like a hot rock going down my throat. Aunt Alice said nothing. She just waited for me to continue.

"From the time that he was born, Mark has never liked his father. I can't explain it, but it's like he knows something isn't right with Harlan. The bad thing is that Harlan can tell that Mark sees his meanness, and he tries his best to break him. I try to head Harlan off when I can, but he uses William to make me choose which of my sons that I can help. Mark sees this too, and he always makes me choose William. He never thinks about himself."

Aunt Alice reached into her bosom and handed me a handkerchief. I looked at it and realized that my face was wet with tears. I took it and covered my whole face while I sobbed my despair. I felt Aunt Alice's arms come around me, but I wanted no comfort. I jerked away from her.

"I'm sorry, Aunt Alice, but I deserve to hurt and to feel all of it. It's my fault that my sons and I are going through this. I don't deserve compassion!"

I threw myself out of the chair and onto my knees.

"Victoria Alicia Sams! You'll not become a sniveling weakling on me!"

Aunt Alice grabbed my shoulders and shook me. I looked up at her in surprise at her strength.

"If you don't like your situation, change it. You are the grandchild of a Roberts! You have strength that you have not even touched yet. Do not give into this selfish pity."

She grabbed my chin and pulled my head up to look into her face. I looked into her faded blue eyes and felt her desire to give me her strength. I felt the darkness in me shrink in the face of her determination. When my tears stopped, she released my chin and sat back down in her chair.

"Come here, girl."

She beckoned me to her with a regal wave of her hand.

I stood up, walked to her, and laid my head on my aunt's lap like a child. She began to stroke my hair.

"You know, Victoria, I was like you once. I was ridiculed and made fun of because my father was a White man who turned his back on his family for the love of a Black woman. When your Grandpa Paul and I came along and we didn't look Black, your great-grandfather only wanted to teach us about White people. He didn't want us to know much about our Black side. He did us a great disservice, especially me. I didn't know where I belonged. We weren't allowed to go to White schools because our mother was Black. The Black children hated us because our skin was too White. Our father wouldn't accept our differences or the rejection we received, so he sent us away to his uncle in Maine. Since we looked White, our uncle made us pass for White so that we could attend school. Your Grandpa Paul hated it, but I didn't because I wanted to be accepted. Our uncle sent your grandfather back to Carson, and our mother taught him herself. I didn't go back until after finishing school."

Aunt Alice paused. When I looked up at her face, I saw that she wasn't in the room with me - she was in the past. I stayed quiet because I knew that she told me her story for a reason.

Aunt Alice stopped stroking my hair and looked down at me.

"Victoria, I had to leave Carson to find myself. I came to Littleton where no one knew my parents. I lived as a White woman for a long time until I saw that I wasn't accepting my mother's heritage. In rejecting her, I denied myself. I became very wealthy living a lie, and no one, not even the White people would gainsay me when they found out that I had Black in me. When you were born, I told your Grandpa Paul that you were special. I hoped that you would learn faster than I did to love your differences, but your parents messed that up."

Aunt Alice put her hand to my cheek.

"I know that Charlotte and Mary tried their best with you, but you needed to learn to accept yourself, Victoria. When you do that, you'll find your joy. Don't become old and bitter wishing that you had made different choices in the past. Learn from those and to live for today."

She looked into my eyes, and then she gave my cheek a little pat.

"Now, that's enough of the sad stuff. Let's go find those nephews of mine and have some fun until luncheon."

Later that evening, I hesitated before I walked into the dining room. I could hear Steven's deep voice while he told

Aunt Alice about the cattle, and Lacy's as she told Ruth about her history lesson.

I felt odd hearing their voices after being away so long. I wished that Aunt Alice hadn't fed the boys early, so that I didn't have to go in there alone. Oh, well, I took a deep breath and thought about what Aunt Alice had told me that morning. I straightened my back and took the last few steps into the dining room.

"Victoria! Vicky! Sis!"

I heard the excitement in my siblings' voices as they almost knocked over their chairs in their haste to get to me. Steven had grown taller and his legs longer, so he hugged me first. Ruth scooted under my arm, and Lacy inched under Steven to grab my waist. I tried to hug them all and found myself laughing along with Aunt Alice who scolded Lacy about wrinkling her new dress.

"I'm sorry, Auntie, but I've missed Vicky so much. Steven and Ruth were hogging her all up," Lacy said turning an innocent look on Aunt Alice.

"Yes, yes, well, let's all sit down and have a nice supper. Y'all have plenty of time to visit with Victoria in the front room before bedtime."

Aunt Alice waved her hand at our seats, and we all sat down.

"I got to see my nephews today, Victoria. Cedric brought them to the backfield to see the cattle. After Cedric told me who they were, I grabbed them up in a big hug. Think about it. I'm an uncle."

Steven stuck his chest out and beamed around the table.

"And we're aunts. I'm going to stay home to play with them all day. I'm so excited that you're home, Victoria. I have lots to tell you," Ruth gushed.

"I'm happy to be here too, but the boys and I have to get to Carson in a few days."

I kept my eyes on my plate when I made the announcement. It got quiet, so I glanced up to see everyone frowned at me. Aunt Alice broke the silence.

"There is no hurry, Victoria. You and the boys may stay as long as you like. Now, let's finish all this food before Dee skins us alive."

We all turned our attentions to the delicious food that Dee cooked. There was a garlic roast, baked chicken, turnip greens with small pieces of turnips, rice and gravy, squash, and cornbread. I hadn't eaten food like that in a long while. Harlan didn't like country cooking, so I didn't cook it much anymore. I shook off those thoughts and loaded my plate with a little of everything.

After supper, we filed into the front room. The fireplace crackled and burned bright. The entire room looked warm and inviting. I sat in the small rocking chair by the fire, and Aunt Alice sat across from me. Steven sat in one of the large cushioned chairs by the door while Lacy and Ruth took cushions from the divans and made themselves comfortable on the rug in front of the fireplace.

"So, Vicky, what is it like living on an army base?"

I glanced at Aunt Alice before I answered Lacy's question.

"It's fine. Harlan is away a lot so most times, it's just me and the boys."

My answer didn't seem to satisfy Lacy, and she opened her mouth to ask another question, but Ruth beat her to it.

"If Harlan is away a lot, why don't you come home more?"

I reached over and smoothed her hair down to give myself time to answer. My throat felt tight with unshed tears for all the time that I missed with my sisters and Steven.

"It's not that easy, Ruth, to get away to come home. When you have your own family, you'll understand."

I looked over at Aunt Alice for support, but she stayed silent. Ruth yanked away from me and stood up.

"You left me behind, Victoria. Again. Didn't you once think of what would happen to me, to us, when you left? Well, if I won't be able to visit my family, then, I don't want to get married...ever!"

Her face crumpled, and she ran out of the room with a sob.

I stood up to follow, but Lacy stopped me.

"No, Vicky, I'll go. I've been doing it."

She turned and left the room too. I saw her wipe tears away as she left.

"What did I say wrong?"

I looked from Aunt Alice to Steven and sat back down. I let the tears fall as I reeled from Ruth and Lacy's actions.

Steven came over to me and knelt beside the chair. He took my hand and looked into my eyes. I saw tears gathering in his.

"Sis, when you left, Ruth became Mama's and Daddy's slave. When I took over Daddy's duties for Aunt Alice, he got drunk more and more and turned meaner. Mama got a job because I could only work after school, so she started working for Harlan's parents in their house. It was the only job that she could get, and they tried to work her real hard. Mama got to where she didn't want to do much work, so when Ms. Dorothy saw Daddy in town one day, she told him that she was about to let Mama go. He beat her and made her start taking Ruth to help with the work. She missed a lot of school. Ruth hated it because they talked about how Harlan treated you in front of her. They laughed about it. Mama didn't care about the names they called you, but Ruth did. Whenever, Ruth talked back to them, Mama whipped her right there in the house where they could see. I didn't know it was happening, Victoria. I didn't know until Lacy saw the sores and welts, and Ruth broke down and told her. I tried to stop it, but Daddy wouldn't listen to me. He just didn't care as long as the money hit his hand every week.

Finally, I came to Aunt Alice about it. She put a stop to Ruth working there. She put enough money in Daddy's hand and made him go back to Carson. I tried, sis, I tried to do what you told me and protect them. If I had known about the beatings, I would have come to Aunt Alice sooner."

Steven lowered his head and shook with sobs at his pain of not being able to protect Ruth. I turned my head to his suffering because it was too much to bear. My little brother had tried to stem the flow of our parents' neglect and abuse of Ruth. The darkness in my soul whispered that he should have done the same thing for me, but I ignored it.

"Steven, gather yourself and go make sure your sisters are okay for the night," Aunt Alice said gruffly

Steven wiped his sleeve across his face, gave Aunt Alice and me a quick hug, and left the room.

"Victoria, I know now that you rushed into that wedding with that little jerk Harlan because of what you went through with your Mama and Daddy. I suspected it when you came here that night with all your things in your hand and fear in your heart. I wish you had let me know before you went through it."

Aunt Alice sighed, and I could see just how much she had aged.

"Well, things happen, good or bad. We can't think of what's behind us. We have to always look ahead. It's late. I'm sure you want to get some rest before those boys hit the floor running in the morning."

She got up and patted me on the arm before heading to her room.

I turned my head to watch the flames dance in the fireplace. I thought I would feel warm this close to them, but I wasn't. I rubbed my arms and closed my eyes while I tried to find the darkness so that it could give me comfort. Nothing. I shook my head at my wayward thoughts and went to find the oblivion of sleep. Maybe tomorrow, I would find the courage to tell them that I was going to have another baby.

I followed the uniformed man up the stairs. He looked back at me a few times as we climbed higher.

"We're almost there ma'am," he said with a big smile.

I blushed and nodded. I looked around at the beautiful gold and beige walls with the antique tables placed just right. I could see gold numbers on the carved wooden doors that we

passed. I had been paying such attention to the hallway that I hadn't noticed that the man stopped. I felt his hand on my arm to stop me.

"Here we are, ma'am. Mr. Sinclair ordered some food and wine for you and your husband that will be up soon."

He pointed at a door with no number. I thanked him and moved forward to open the door. The handle felt cold when I touched it, and I drew back from it. I knew that I had to open it, so I took a deep breath and turned the knob. The door slid open quietly, and I hesitated while peered into the dark room.

"Get in there and draw that line!"

I felt a hard push from behind, and I cried out and stumbled forward. I looked back to see Betts stood where the uniformed man had been. I gasped at her yellow eyes and her sharp and pointed teeth. She had an evil grin on her face.

"Everyone thought that the line would break with your child. They just didn't know how weak you were."

She cackled and spat a steaming yellow glob at my feet.

"You want to keep hold of that man, don't ya? Get to it!"

She cackled again and slammed the door.

With the light from the hallway gone, the room was pitch black.

"Hello? Harlan, are you there?"

I trembled and waited on a reply.

"Yes, I'm here, my love."

I sighed in relief at hearing his voice in the darkness.

"Can you turn on the light, please?"

I stood up and turned towards his voice when I asked for the light.

The light blinded me for a moment when Harlan flipped the switch. When I could see, I gasped and stepped back towards the door. Harlan sat on the bed with blood, sage, and salt smeared atop his head. I looked around the room and felt the scream stifled in my throat. More of the blood mixture was smeared on the walls and windows. I tried to take another step towards the door and felt my foot slip in something. I looked down to see the carpet covered in blood. I opened my mouth to scream when I felt claws grab me from behind. I turned to see Betts smiling at me.

"You're mine now!"

She snatched her claws away from me, and I sank to my knees. Sobs racked my body at my choice.

"Mama! Mama! Wake up, please! Please, Mama!"

I felt a pull on my shoulder as if someone shook me. I opened my eyes to see the dim light of dawn creep through the curtains. I turned my head when I heard heavy breathing near my ear. Mark stood by the bed with a tear-stained face, and William sat up in his crib whimpering.

"Are you alright, Mama? You were crying."

Mark looked worried and moved closer to the bed. I calmed myself from the dream that wasn't just a dream. I sat up and hugged my son. I smiled at William, and he relaxed.

"I'm fine, Mark. I just had a bad dream. I'm alright now."

I waved it off and hoped that he would let it go. He pulled back in my arms and gave me a long look. I stayed still until he made up his mind. After a few moments, he nodded.

"Okay."

I put Mark and William back to bed before I got back under the covers. I knew that I wasn't going to be able to sleep after that dream, so I began to go over the rest of my plans in my mind. However, every time that I tried to put my thoughts together, I couldn't stop thinking about the dream. I tossed and turned to get away from it, but it didn't work because there was no running from the choice that I made.

4

Over the next few days, I tried to enjoy my family. Everyone spoiled the boys. Mark's eyes held a light that I hadn't seen before, and his laughter came freely when he played. I felt the guilt gnaw at me that I allowed my despair to cloud my son's childhood. I prayed that the time with our family would give us strength when we had to return to the Ft. Green…to Harlan.

Ruth came to me and shared all that she had been through the day after we arrived. I cried for her, and I cried for myself that we had been through so much pain and suffering at the hands of those who were supposed to love and protect us. As we hugged and wept, I decided to share the events of my childhood with Ruth. I knew that she may have heard about some of it, but I wanted to give her some comfort that she was not alone in her mistreatment. She couldn't believe that Mama and Daddy had done that to me while a small child, but she accepted it as why I wanted to leave everything behind.

"Victoria, is your life with Harlan as bad as Ms. Dorothy brags about?"

Ruth looked at me with such sympathy that my tears doubled. I wanted to answer her and tell her everything. Instead, I reached for the comfort of the darkness. I took a deep breath and wiped my tears. I summoned a smile to hide the weight of my heartache.

"No, it's not that bad. Being married is a good thing. I love Harlan. It's just that sometimes husbands want what they want, and the wives have to give it. I have Harlan that's all that matters."

I smiled and swallowed the lump in my throat at the lie that I told my sister. She nodded and gave a watery smile before she hugged me and ran off to find Mark and William to play.

The boys and I stayed with Aunt Alice and my siblings for the rest of the week. Aunt Alice kept me busy going over her books and around the ranch. I actually enjoyed myself because she praised my work, and I liked it. It had been so long since someone had praised me that I wanted to cry. I just smiled and made sure that I kept doing well.

The day before we left, Harlan's parents, Ms. Dorothy and Mr. Jerry, came by the ranch while Aunt Alice and Steven were out on the range. Almost finished with the work on Aunt Alice's books, I glanced up in surprise when Cedric popped his head into the office.

"Ms. Victoria? There's a gentleman and lady asking for you. I've seen them before in town, but I don't know their names. The little ones and me were in the front playing when they came up. Mark grabbed Willie and ran away when they got out of the car."

He had a slight frown on his ageless face. At that moment, I wanted to ask him how old he was because he had been with Aunt Alice forever, but I didn't because it dawned on my that he had said that Mark had run from the visitors.

"Okay, Cedric, show them into the visiting room. I'll see about the company, and you find Mark and Willie."

I didn't know who could frighten my son so, but I was going to see for myself.

Cedric nodded and left to do as I asked.

I stood up and smoothed my new wool day dress that Aunt Alice had bought and had altered for my tiny waist. It was a soft red color with a fitted bodice and full skirt. She had surprised me even further with a pair of black flats made to fit my small feet. I felt lovely and loved. I looked into the small mirror next to the door to smooth any strands into my usual bun. I saw a young woman with pale peach colored skin and dark auburn hair with red and blonde streaks. Blue eyes, a prominent straight nose, and full lips fell into place under a regal forehead. In disgust, I rubbed my hand across my face as if I could erase it. I shook my head at my vanity and turned to go through the rear door of Aunt Alice's office to see about the visitors. I stopped into the kitchen to tell Dee that we had company and to bring the refreshments, but he already worked on it. I gave him a little wave before I turned to go down the hallway into the visiting room. My steps faltered when I heard familiar voices.

"Why is she here? Harlan would have a fit if he knew that she had brought her lazy tail to Littleton. She probably came to beg for money again for that nursing school mess. Harlan said that he had spent so much already for her to be a nurse, but she was too lazy to do the work. Humph. She's the reason why our boy had to join the army! And did you see those boys? They were filthy and ran away from us like little animals, especially that oldest one. What is his name again? Matthew, Martin, Mack, oh, I don't care. He's too much like her for me. Crazy and lazy. Ha! That rhymes! Did you hear that, Jerry? That rhymes, crazy and lazy!"

Ms. Dorothy laughed out loud at her own cleverness. She talked non-stop until she had to laugh at her own joke. I fisted my hands at the lies that she spouted to Mr. Jerry. Harlan made sure that I'd never go to nursing school when he'd wasted away all of our money. I took a deep breath and said a prayer for wisdom. When I felt calm, I entered the room.

"Well, hello, Mama Dorothy and Big Papa Jerry. How are y'all doing?"

I breezed into the room and dutifully hugged and kissed both of them before taking a seat in the carved oak chair across from them. I sat up straight and looked at them down my nose. Ms. Dorothy narrowed her eyes at my regal pose.

"We're good, Vicky. I was just telling Jerry what a wonderful surprise it was that you and the boys came down from Ft. Green. I suppose Harlan told you to come stay with us while he's away, and we'll be so glad to have you and our grandsons for a spell."

Ms. Dorothy gave me a very toothy smile that almost made me giggle because one of her front teeth wasn't there.

When I looked closely at Ms. Dorothy, I saw where Harlan had gotten his dark skin. I glanced at Mr. Jerry, and nodded to myself confirming that's where Harlan had gotten his handsome looks.

"Harlan doesn't know that we came to visit my family. We leave in the morning for Carson, so please don't put yourselves out to get anything ready for us to stay."

I smiled at her surprised expression. She narrowed her eyes at me again and opened her mouth to speak, but Mr. Jerry squeezed her hand.

"That is good, my dear. I'm sure that Harlan wouldn't want his beautiful wife stuck on an army base with so many men around and only two little boys for company. It'll be better for you to be in Carson with your family where they can help you."

Even though he spoke mildly, I didn't like that Mr. Jerry mentioned men like that. I was not one to be unfaithful to my husband. After all, I did what I needed to keep him with me.

Before I could answer, Dee came in with a tray filled with cups of tea, glasses of water, and sweet treats. I thanked him and waited for him to serve us. He handed me a cup of tea and touched my hand. I looked up to see him eye Ms. Dorothy and Mr. Jerry. He shook his head a little and moved back to stand at the door. I smiled into my teacup and took a sip of my tea. Ms. Dorothy shot him a nasty look before she turned back to me.

"Vicky, it's fine and good that you leave. We don't want to have any trouble between you and Shirley. She's been out to the house to complain that you've been to town several times with the boys. Some people are starting to call her names."

Ms. Dorothy spoke in a stern tone like it was my fault that Shirley had made the choice to keep up mess in my marriage. I couldn't believe that they would choose that whore over their daughter-in-law. I stared at her in disbelief. She treated me to a very smug smile and took a long drink of her water.

"Well, if that hussy would find another man, an unmarried man, to fool around with, she wouldn't have to worry about being called names," Aunt Alice boomed as she walked into the room.

Ms. Dorothy and Mr. Jerry jumped in surprise when Aunt Alice leaned over them with her hands on her slight hips.

"Why, Alice, you scared me to pieces!"

Ms. Dorothy patted her chest and gave Aunt Alice an innocent look. Mr. Jerry nodded and let out a loud breath before he sat back on the settee and crossing his leg.

"Oh, Dorothy Sams, don't you give me that! You're here to cower my niece and stir in the mess. Don't you know, when you stir in mess, it stinks? Sometimes, woman, you need to mind your own business."

Aunt Alice wagged her finger in Ms. Dorothy's face, and then took a seat in the matching oak chair next to me. Ms. Dorothy sniffed with her nose in the air while Mr. Jerry took a quick sip of his tea. I tried to hide my laugh behind a teacake.

"Y'all need to tell that girl to go on about her business. Harlan isn't going to marry her. He's using her for what she gives so freely. Vicky is his wife, and that needs to be respected. Now, I'm glad that y'all came to visit, but looking at my niece's face, you've worn out your welcome."

Aunt Alice stood to her full height which wasn't much, but she had a larger than life way about her, so the Sams' quickly said their goodbyes and left.

"Watch them, Dee. Make sure that they don't say not one word to my nephews."

Aunt Alice and Dee exchanged a look before Dee glanced at me and followed the Sams'.

Aunt Alice took hold of my shoulders and raised me into her arms for a quick hug.

"Don't you mind those two old sourpusses. I watched them both grow up. I had hope for Jerry until Dorothy stuck her claws in him."

Aunt Alice shook her head and released me.

"Don't you let what they said about that girl make you do something silly, you hear? She'll soon see that all her sneaky ways aren't getting her anywhere."

"Yes, ma'am."

I nodded, and Aunt Alice looked me up and down.

"Harlan's a fool anyways if he doesn't value what's in front of him. You look just beautiful in that getup. I ordered you a few more like it and some with a slim skirt. Even having those young'un's didn't change that Coca Cola bottle figure of yours."

Aunt Alice admired her handiwork and chuckled.

"If my nephew-in-law don't get it together, somebody might be tempted to steal you away."

I laughed with Aunt Alice because I knew that it was crazy to think that any man would want me with children in tow. And, I wasn't the kind of woman to run off with another man. I had already gone through too much to keep the one that I had.

Saturday morning, my sons and I said a tearful goodbye to Aunt Alice, Steven, Lacy, and Ruth. I hadn't thought that they would become so attached to my family, but it gladdened my heart that they had felt so much love in so little time. I swallowed the tears threatening to rise with the knowledge that they had been deprived because of me. No, I scolded myself. I wouldn't think about that right now. We had a long trip to Carson, so I had plenty of time to think of my stupidity. I allowed the darkness in for a moment to mask my pain. Steven, my sisters, and Cedric went back to their chores while Aunt Alice stood by the open car door with a slight frown on her face. I walked to her and hugged her slight frame. She hesitated before she returned the hug. She pulled me back and looked into my eyes. Her forehead creased with a bigger frown. I stood still until she nodded and released me.

"Dee packed you a trip box with lots of food and treats. It should take you all day to get to Carson. Don't drive too fast, you hear?"

Aunt Alice turned to give Mark and William a hug and kiss. I realized at that moment Aunt Alice knew what I had done but would not come right out and accuse me of it. I opened my mouth to ask her then closed it because it was a talk that I didn't want to have. I watched while Aunt Alice settled the boys into the car with their new toys. Mark grabbed her hand and held it to his chest.

"I love you, Aunt Alice. Thank you for everything. I won't forget you ever."

His expression was so earnest and sincere that Aunt Alice's eyes began to tear. She took their joined hands and put them to her cheek.

"Well, thank you, Mark. I won't forget you either."

She cleared her throat loudly and dropped their hands.

"Now, don't you boys mess with your mama while she's driving, you hear?"

Mark and William nodded and waved until she shut the passenger door. Aunt Alice turned to me with a slight smile.

"Be careful, and send me a letter or two sometimes so that I know that my nephews are doing well."

I said a quiet "yes, ma'am" and got in behind the steering wheel. I took a moment to pray for safe travel and waved again at Aunt Alice before starting the car to go down the graveled lane. I slowed and honked the loud horn twice in farewell. I looked into the rear mirror to see that she had already gone into the house. I realized then that I never got to tell her about the baby.

The closer that we got to Carson, the more nervous I became. I hadn't seen my family in almost six years, and I felt ashamed. The darkness shifted to give me comfort, and I closed my eyes to let it.

The sound of a car horn brought my eyes open abruptly. In allowing the darkness to comfort me, I had let the car drift into the other lane. I quickly turned the wheel to move the car out of the way.

My actions had once again put my sons in harm's way. I felt myself begin to tremble and knew that I needed to stop the car. I found a wide roadside spot and pulled the car to a stop. I turned my head to make sure that the boys were all right and smiled a little because they had slept through it all. I said a quick prayer to God that He had kept us safe. It was almost dark, and we still had a ways to go. I got out and reached into the back seat for the food box. I took a drink of water out of the jug and said another prayer of thanks that Aunt Alice had provided us food and water to get to Carson.

After a few moments by the roadside, I began to feel better. The cold air helped to settle my nerves. I closed my eyes and leaned against the trunk. The trees rustled with the night wind, and I smelled the faint odor of pine. I threw my arms out and turned slowly with my eyes closed while my mind found peace in the surroundings. My arms dropped when I heard another car coming. I felt silly in that moment, almost like a child. I huffed out a breath and returned to my sleeping children to get back on the road to Carson.

I could hear my heartbeat when I turned off of the highway onto the lane to my grandparents' homestead.

"Mama, are you okay? You're breathing funny."

Mark put his hand on mine, and I smiled at him.

"Yes, my love. I'm fine. Just a bit shaky because I've been driving so long, but I'll be fine."

I couldn't tell my son that fear rode high in my veins, so I acted as if nothing was wrong. We continued down the lane until I drove the car around the paved driveway. When we slowed to a stop, memories of my last visits here flooded my mind. I shook them off quickly. I didn't need anything more to increase my fear. I looked up and saw the screen door open.

"They're here! They're here! Thank you, Jesus! They're finally here!"

Ms. Sadie stood at the open door almost jumping in her excitement.

"Calm yourself, Sadie. You might scare her all the way back to that army base," Big Mama Chandra scolded.

She lifted her cane and pushed through the door.

I opened the door and got out on shaky legs. I could feel Mark wake William, and they slid out of the car behind me.

"Ms. Victoria is heah?"

I heard a familiar voice behind Big Mama Chandra that made me relax just a bit.

"Yes, she is, Hope."

Satisfaction rang out in Big Mama's tone.

"She's going to run up here any second and give her old blind Big Mama a big hug. I just know it."

I felt the tears start to flow, but I didn't care. I ran the few steps up the porch and grabbed Big Mama in a tight hug. I felt her hot tears splash on my arms as she hugged me back. I could hear Ms. Sadie and Hope introduce themselves to Mark and William behind me. All I could think of was how good it was to be held in my Big Mama's arms. She laughed suddenly and pulled back.

"Look at us, Victoria! We're a wet mess!"

She laughed again, and I did too.

"Hope. Sadie. It's cold out here. Bring my great-grandsons inside so that I can grab them up too."

Big Mama moved back inside the house. Ms. Sadie walked over to give me a hug before she turned toward Mark and William.

"I got some hot chocolate and tea cakes for you fellas. How's that sound?"

The boys hoorayed and followed Ms. Sadie inside the house. Mark lingered at the door for my approval as usual.

"I'm coming, sweetheart."

I smiled, and he allowed Ms. Sadie to take his hand.

I started to shiver in the cold and turned to Hope, who stood beside me.

"Hello, darlin'. It's been a mighty long spell."

She smiled and pulled me into a tight hug. I hugged her back because I had missed my friend. When she pulled back, my throat tightened with unshed tears. She nodded and slid her hand down to hold mine. She squeezed it before pulled at me to go inside where Big Mama Chandra waited.

"Now, where are my great-grandsons? I can see one but not the other."

Hope and I walked into the front room where Big Mama sat in her large stuffed chair. I frowned at her statement because both boys stood in front of Big Mama with half-eaten teacakes in their hands. Then, I remembered that her sight wasn't good, so I shrugged it away. Mark looked back at me, and I nodded with a big smile.

"Here I am, Big Mama. My name is Mark, and this is William. I'm sorry that you can't see us, but we're here."

Big Mama laughed and held out her arms. Mark smiled and walked into her hug. William hung back a little until I gave him a little nudge. Big Mama release Mark and held her arms out for William. William touched her outstretched hand lightly, and Big Mama took hold of it and pulled him into a hug. Her face changed a bit, and she froze for a moment. She drew back from William swiftly and narrowed her eyes. He squirmed and started to whine until she let him go. I wanted to ask her what all that was about, but William ran to me and clung to my leg with a whimper. I patted his head and made soothing noises as Mark ran over and stood in front of us. I saw his fists balled and knew that he was about to voice a protest because he thought William had been mistreated.

Ms. Sadie saw Mark's reaction, walked forward, and knelt her ample self down in front of Mark.

"It's okay, little man. Your Big Mama was just checking your brother for a spot to get some sugar."

She tickled William under the neck, and he giggled.

"See. I think I found a spot right there. How about we go find us some more teacakes? Hope made them this morning. They're almost as good as mine, tee hee."

She held out her hands, and my boys allowed her to lead them into the kitchen with the promise of more treats.

Hope smiled at Ms. Sadie's back and then walked over to Big Mama.

"Ms. Chandra. Can I help you with anything?"

"No, Hope. I want to chat with Victoria while the children are having their treat."

Big Mama Chandra waved her away and beckoned to the chair opposite hers. Hope smiled and waved at me as she left the room. I sat in the chair to join my Big Mama Chandra. We sat in silence for a few moments until she broke it.

"So, you're with child again. I felt him when we hugged. Mary was right. I don't know whether to rejoice or cry. Well, we'll see. We'll see. Mary's visions are not always steady, especially since she aged. Heh, heh."

She seemed talk to herself because she had answered her own questions. I stayed silent and waited.

"Your Grandpa Ed should be here soon. I know that he'll be glad to see you. Those boys will probably be out in the field with him in the morning. Just you wait. With all the attention that they'll get, you might not see them much while you're here."

She paused and looked at the darkened windows like she could see through them. And still, I waited. Big Mama didn't keep me waiting long.

"Before those boys come looking for you, I want to get some things out of the way. We forgive you for not talking much to us all these years. So stop thinking that we're not going to take you in if you need us to. Family is family. Now, about William. Has he been around Betts? He has a darkness in him like hers."

I jerked my head in her direction and was ready with a hot denial of anything wrong with my son.

"No, don't get angry with me. I felt it, but it's only a little bit now. We can bind it so that he can learn the right way. Don't worry. God is still in control."

I trembled as she spoke. In the distance, I could hear the loud motor of a truck coming closer. I thought about everything that Big Mama Chandra spoke of, and I trembled again until the darkness shifted within me to give me comfort.

5

Dinner that night was loud and boisterous with Grandpa Ed playing with the boys at the table. Big Mama Chandra kept scolding him to let them go to bed, but Grandpa Ed just laughed at her. He winked at me before he tickled Mark into a fit of giggles and pretended to arm-wrestle William. Hope and Ms. Sadie tried hard not to laugh at his antics, but I could see their smiles behind their napkins. I wasn't in much of a mood to laugh after the talk with Big Mama, but I put up a false face and grinned like there was no tomorrow. I felt Big Mama Chandra's cloudy gaze on me every once in a while, but she stayed silent.

After dinner, I put the boys down because they were falling asleep in their desserts. I hugged and kissed them before they drifted off to sleep. Ms. Sadie had given us the room that Aunt Charlotte stayed in when I was a girl. She'd found a crib and placed it in the corner for William while Mark had my old trundle. I stopped at the door and looked around the room. Nothing much had changed except the curtains. I felt the memories start to unfold in my mind again. I sighed when one particular memory lingered. It was the memory of Billy giving me my first kiss. I raised my hand to my cheek and smiled. The memory faded, and I sighed with regret. No. He had rejected me. There was nothing I should regret. I frowned and snapped the light off and joined the adults in the living room for tea.

"How are my grandsons, my dear?"

Grandpa Ed's eyes twinkled while he sipped his tea.

I smiled and took a seat next to Hope on the large divan before I replied. Everyone had a cup of tea and a teacake, but I shook my head when Ms. Sadie offered me the last teacake. Seeing that I declined it, Grandpa Ed swiped it from the tray when Ms. Sadie sat it on the coffee table. I smother a giggle and turned to face Grandpa Ed's rocker.

"They're out for the night, Grandpa. Thank you for wearing them out tonight."

"Oh, honey, he enjoyed it as much as they did. I bet he's already made plans to get them up early and sweep them off to the fields."

Big Mama turned her gaze on Grandpa Ed with a slight frown.

"Well, I thought I'd take them and show them the land, yes. I'm sure Victoria would appreciate some time to herself."

"That would be so good, Mr. Ed. Then, we could have us a good catch up talk."

Hope grabbed my hand and gave it a squeeze.

"She can also get some rest. Having two young'uns and being with child isn't easy."

I gasped at the casual way that Big Mama Chandra announced my pregnancy.

Grandpa Ed stood up so fast that he almost dropped his cup. Hope giggled and squeezed my hand again. When I glanced her way, I saw that she looked at Grandpa Ed's hand. I pursed my lips because he'd held on to that teacake.

"You mean to tell us that we're going to have a baby?"

My grandfather sat back down and gave a big boom of a laugh.

"Ed! Hush your mouth! You going to wake those boys!"

Big Mama Chandra frowned and tried to tap him with her cane. Grandpa Ed scooted away from where Big Mama tried to tap him and laughed again but not as loud.

"Alright, alright, Chandra. Put your cane down. I'll hush," he said and waved his hands in surrender.

"You better or I'm going to get you later."

She pointed her cane in his general direction and jabbed it to make her point.

"Well, I'm excited too, Ms. Chandra. We haven't had a baby in the house since my boy Bernie."

Hope beamed at me and patted my hand. I immediately felt bad for not asking about her son. I opened my mouth to ask her, but she shook her head at me. I shrugged because I figured she'd tell me later.

Ms. Sadie picked up all the dishes and said goodnight. Hope asked if we needed anything else to which my grandparents and I said no. She smiled at me, then turned and followed Ms. Sadie out of the room.

"I think it's time for us to find our beds too, old man. You gotta get out early in the morning."

Big Mama rose from her chair when Grandpa Ed nodded and got up as well. They both gave me a hug and kiss before going to their room. I was left alone in the living room with only my thoughts. I sighed and realized that I didn't want to be alone with those.

I turned the lamp off and stood in the dark for a moment to let my eyes adjust. In the quiet, I heard someone whisper my name. I turned around towards the door, but no one was there. I walked to the window and opened the curtain, but I still didn't see anyone. I shrugged and waved it off as my imagination. I left the room to join my boys in slumber.

Grandpa Ed came early to take Mark and William to the fields the next day. I awakened when he walked into the room with overalls just like his in their sizes. I shook my head at this generosity and motioned at their play clothes. He frowned and shook his head while he shoved the overalls at me. I went along the overalls because I didn't want to make him mad at me. He helped me to get them ready.

Mark and William left with him eagerly giving me sloppy wet kisses in their hurry to go with their great-grandfather. I waved at them from the front porch when Grandpa Ed sat them in the front seat before he drove into the cornfields.

I turned to open the door to the house when I felt sick to my stomach. I ran to the edge of the porch and heaved everything in my stomach. I tried to suck in the cold air to help calm my belly, but it only made the heaves worse. Hope came from nowhere with a glass of lemon wedges and wet cloth. I gladly accepted the cloth to wipe my mouth, but I shook my head at the lemons. She pushed them my way anyway.

"Lemons help ta settle yor belly a bit betta than cracka's."

Hope grabbed one out of the glass and put it in my hand. I bit into the tangy fruit and felt a slight calming in my belly. I nodded at her. Then, it struck me that Hope had spoken with her accent.

"Hope, where was your accent last night? You spoke very well then, and now I can hear it."

I threw the wedge in my hand into the yard before reaching for another one.

"Well, Ms. Victoria. Ms. Chandra and Mr. Andrew helped me to speak well when my boy was a baby. I didn't want him to learn bad speech from me. I wanted him to be smart, and you know what? He is. Why even now, him and Henry are out in Colorado with Mr. Andrew to help him to build his ranch. Bernie goes to a real good school that has Whites and Blacks."

Hope beamed with pride. I smiled at her and wanted to ask her how she felt with her child so far away, but I just sucked on the lemon. I also realized that I was cold and hungry.

"Let's go get something to eat, Hope. I'm starved."

She laughed when I grabbed her arm and rushed inside out of the winter sunshine.

Ms. Sadie had breakfast ready when Hope and I made our way into the kitchen. I could smell the bacon, sausage, and ham. My stomach growled but immediately flipped when I took one look at the over easy eggs in the pan. I grabbed another lemon wedge from the glass that Hope placed on the table. Ms. Sadie snatched the lemon from my hand and handed me a cracker. Hope frowned at her. Ms. Sadie turned an innocent look on Hope and returned to flip hot cakes. I didn't care what I used as long as it worked. I took a nibble of the cracker, and it helped to calm my sickness. I frowned at the cracker when it came to me that I had not been sick while with Mark or William. Hope saw my frown and patted my hand.

"Don't ya worry, Ms. Victoria. It'll go away soon. Are ya gonna stay 'til the baby comes? Ya should, ya know. Ya don' need ta be by yorself wit just them boys."

She nodded and wagged her finger at me. I stared at her in wonder because her speech sounded almost the same as when I met her. I laughed and grabbed her finger.

"Yes, Hope. I had thought to stay until well after the baby is born. Harlan won't be home for a year, and it's past time that I enjoyed someone's company."

"Well, I'm as happy as a singin' lark. Now, I'm gonna' make ya some lemon water to keep by ya bed for that thick spit."

She narrowed her eyes at Ms. Sadie and went out the back door. Ms. Sadie rolled her eyes and flipped the ham slices.

I looked over at the counter and saw heaps and piles of food. I knew that it was too much for just Big Mama Chandra, Hope, Ms. Sadie, and myself. Ms. Sadie had packed an all day lunch box for Grandpa Ed and the boys. I walked over and picked up a slice of bacon.

"Ms. Sadie, I know that I'm having a baby, but this is too much to fit in there with him."

She laughed and tweaked my nose. Waving her spatula in the air, she shooed me away from the bacon.

"Don't you worry about that, ma'am. Now, I've got to finish the biscuits and sausage."

I moved away and sat at the table more curious than ever knowing that someone was coming. I hope that it was somebody that I wanted to see. The right side of my nose started itching. I raised my hand to scratch it when I heard a car horn blow in the yard. I glanced back at Ms. Sadie, but she just gave me a sly smile. I stayed seated at the table. I was curious but not that curious.

When the car doors slammed, I tensed and waited for the visitors to knock. Instead, I heard the front door open and a familiar voice call out.

"Hello? Hello? Mama, Hope, Ms. Sadie? We're here!"

I stood on trembling legs when I heard Big Mama Chandra answer from her bedroom. My feet started walking that way like they had a mind of their own. I stopped in the short hallway across from Big Mama and Grandpa Ed's room. My body started to tremble, and I felt the tears gather in my eyes.

"Oh, Mama, it's so good to see you. We drove most of the night to get here because Mary wanted to be here early. I don't know why, but she did. Oh, it's so nice and warm in here. Are they here? Did she really come? How long is she staying? Mary wouldn't tell me a thing."

Aunt Charlotte rambled on like she was nervous. I let the tears fall at having her so close. I moved closer to the door until I could see Aunt Charlotte and Aunt Mary standing beside Big Mama's rocking chair. Aunt Mary turned her head and saw me in the door. She winked and smiled.

"Charlotte. I already told you that they came. That's enough. Now, let's go in the kitchen and get some of that good smelling food."

Aunt Mary moved behind Aunt Charlotte and turned her toward the door where I stood. Aunt Charlotte froze when she saw me. Fear gripped me in that moment that maybe I had lost my beloved aunt's love, but it went away when she smiled and held out her arms to me. I ran into them, and we almost fell on Big Mama while we hugged and cried.

"Oh, my wonderful girl! You're here! You're here! I'm so glad to see you and hug you. You're still so beautiful."

I laughed because I knew that she said that because she was my aunt, and she had missed me.

"Charlotte! Let the girl breathe!"

Big Mama waved her arms in our direction while she chastised Aunt Charlotte. Aunt Mary laughed behind her hand then cleared her throat.

"Yes, Charlotte. I would like to hug her also."

Aunt Mary touched Aunt Charlotte on the shoulder and gently pushed her away from me. She picked up my hands and spread my arms wide as she looked at me. A little frown creased her brow before she dropped my hands quickly and gave me a hasty hug. She stepped back and almost stumbled over Big Mama Chandra's rocking chair in a rush.

Aunt Charlotte frowned at Aunt Mary for a moment then shook her head and moved forward to grab my elbow. She started walking us to the door.

"Where are my grandsons? I want to see them. I have waited so long to give them a hug and kiss."

I smiled at her excitement and told her that they were in the fields with Grandpa Ed.

"Well, I guess that you will just have to keep me occupied with a long chat until they get here."

Aunt Charlotte granted me with a gentle smile, but I wasn't fooled. I had seen those smiles plenty enough growing up in her house. That smile meant, we're going to have a long talk and no buts about it. I nodded and led her into the kitchen where she said her hellos to Ms. Sadie and Hope, who had returned to the kitchen with a jug of water with lemon slices at the bottom. Aunt Charlotte looked at it with a question, but I jumped in because I wasn't ready to talk about the baby.

"Ms. Sadie cooked up a whole mess of food, Aunt Charlotte. I hope that you and Aunt Mary are hungry," I said with a grin toward Ms. Sadie.

Aunt Charlotte waved her hand at the counter.

"I have missed Ms. Sadie's cooking, but I'm getting much too old to eat a lot."

She chuckled and rubbed her still slender waistline. I laughed as well because Aunt Charlotte looked almost the same as she had at my wedding except for a few gray hairs.

"I don't care what I eat anymore. I'm not vain like Charlotte," said Aunt Mary from behind us.

I hadn't even heard her enter the kitchen. Aunt Charlotte laughed and plopped down at the table.

"Well, Ms. Sadie, I'm going to have some of everything. If you don't mind fixing my plate after you take Mama her tray, that is. I don't trust myself with all that food."

"I can fix it for you, Aunt Charlotte."

Excited to do something for my aunt, I moved toward the cabinet for a plate.

"No, Victoria, let Ms. Sadie fix the plates for us. Just sit down, please," Aunt Mary said in a hard voice.

I stopped and turned to her, and Aunt Charlotte narrowed her eyes at her tone. Even Ms. Sadie and Hope stopped what they were doing.

Aunt Mary glanced at Aunt Charlotte and nodded her head towards me. Aunt Charlotte lowered her gaze with a guilty look in my direction.

I felt hurt at the way that they were acted, but I just sat down in the chair at the end of the table. I couldn't meet their eyes because I felt the tears about to fall. A wave of nausea hit me, so I put my hand to my stomach and rubbed. I felt someone place a plate on the table in front of me, but my stomach was too upset. I wanted to get up and leave the table because I knew that something was wrong. I felt the darkness creep close to comfort me, and I let it.

"No! Victoria, you mustn't let it in. Bind it back where it came from," I heard Aunt Mary say from a distance.

I heard chairs scrape and voices cry out in horror. I smiled to myself and slipped all the way into the blackness that rose to greet me.

"Will she be all right, Mary?"

I could hear the pleading sound in Aunt Charlotte's voice as if Aunt Mary could make me all right. I played possum because I didn't want to talk to them yet after how they treated me in the kitchen.

"Yes, but it is in her very deep. Betts did her evil in such a way that I didn't even know it was that bad. It calls to the child in her womb, and it will have him. She has no choice now but to answer the darkness of the line because she has accepted it. Mama and I will try to help her when the time comes."

I heard Aunt Charlotte ask another question, but I didn't hear Aunt Mary's answer because their voices faded when they moved away.

I wanted to cry at her words. I wanted to scream and wail at the unfairness of it all. Why me? Why? When would I be able to have love and goodness instead of "the line this or the line that"? Why must I sacrifice my children's well being to something that started long before I was born? Why me? I stayed silent to hear an answer, but all I heard was the faint echo of evil laughter.

6

With my aunts home, time seemed to fly by. The boys loved going to the fields with Grandpa Ed, and I loved spending time with Aunt Charlotte. Aunt Charlotte loved that I was pregnant. She spoiled me with clothes, shoes, and food, whatever I wanted. She even bought a brand new crib that saddened Big Mama Chandra for some reason. Aunt Mary told Aunt Charlotte to keep it out of the house, but she refused. Aunt Charlotte complained that it was too expensive to sit outside, so she had it put into the corner of our room opposite William's.

Mark and William were excited about their new sibling. Mark took extra care and tried to wait on me hand and foot. William tried to mimic his brother's actions that caused everyone to laugh at his efforts. It was a happy time for us until Aunt Charlotte brought up Harlan.

"Victoria. Does Harlan know that you're having a baby?"

We were sitting on the front porch enjoying a cold ice-tea in the late afternoon heat. I almost dropped my glass at the mention of my husband's name. I had tried to forget about him over the past four months. I stroked my large stomach before I answered her.

"Yes, Aunt Charlotte. I sent him a letter before we left Ft. Green. I sent a few more since we've been here, but I haven't heard back from him. It's probably just the slow army mail service."

I hated lying to my aunt, but it was for the best. I had sent him one letter before we came to Carson, but none since I'd received his nasty response.

Aunt Charlotte made sympathetic noises and patted my hand. The baby gave a hard kick that made me gasp and Aunt Charlotte laugh in delight.

"I think my grandson or granddaughter likes my touch."

I laughed along with her and rubbed my belly until the baby calmed.

Aunt Charlotte started to take me to see Dr. Herbert at his new office in town as my time came to an end. It surprised me that Dr. Herbert had married. His wife, Ms. Constance, worked the front office and was very nice to me. She was very beautiful with an ageless face and had a lisp in her speech. It dawned on me one day that Ms. Constance was Billy's mother because she shared some of his features except for his eyes. Whenever she talked with Aunt Charlotte about fashions and the like, I listened for any news of Billy.

After a few visits, Dr. Herbert revealed to Aunt Charlotte that his son, Dr. William, had gone back East to learn a special skill for doctoring.

"He's a good boy, my son is. William plans to carry on the practice with a surgery."

Dr. Herbert sounded so full of pride, and Aunt Charlotte listened with patience when he talked on and on about Billy's accomplishments. I was happy that Billy was doing well and jealous at the same time. I wondered about his wife and if they had children. I shook my head at those thoughts. It was none of my business anyway.

One afternoon, when we left Dr. Herbert's office, a familiar voice snapped.

"Well, well, if it isn't my lazy slut of a daughter. Charlotte, what are you doing out of your castle?"

We turned around to see Mama and Daddy walk down the sidewalk. Mama was carrying bags while Daddy licked a cigarette to seal it.

"Tess, Clyde. How are y'all? Tess, still the jacket that Clyde steps on to avoid the mud, I see."

Aunt Charlotte greeted my parents in a nasty tone that I had never heard her use. I stared at her in awe.

"Charlotte, still a bourgeois bitch, I see."

Daddy spit at Aunt Charlotte's feet. Aunt Charlotte looked like she wanted to swing her cane at Daddy. Daddy smirked and took a good look at me.

"Knocked up and in the country. What happened? Did you cuckold that little jerk that you married? He and I should talk. Sent you to the country, huh? Must be real bad then if he let you come all this way, or is he slinking around somewhere?"

Daddy laughed and nudged Mama to laugh at his jokes too.

"Hello, Mama, Daddy. I pray that y'all are well. I'm staying with Big Mama Chandra and Grandpa Ed because Harlan is in Korea. Harlan and his folks didn't want me to be alone with your grandsons having the baby. They thought that I'd be more comfortable with my family. I…"

I stopped because Aunt Charlotte pinched me on the back of my arm. I glanced her way, but she shook her head.

"Tess, Clyde, while it's always a pleasure to see y'all, we have to get going. Y'all have a nice day!"

Aunt Charlotte sounded almost cheerful as she limped away pulling me behind her.

When we got into the car, she turned to me and fussed.

"Victoria, please do not feel that you need to share your all of your business especially with your parents. Remember that not everyone will treat your business like you do."

She tsk'ed and cranked the car before driving us home. I thought about her advice as we neared the homestead and knew that she was right.

"Mama, your belly looks like you swallowed one of Grandpa's watermelons," Mark giggled as he rubbed my belly.

I laughed and leaned over to hug him. As I released him, I heard a voice whisper my name. I looked around and didn't see anyone on the porch with us. Mark didn't look like he heard anything, so I ignored the sound. It was probably the wind.

I looked up to see a large Black car come rolling slowly down the lane. I put my hand on Mark's shoulder to keep him still as the car pulled to a stop.

"There's my oldest grandchild! I told you she'd be outside, didn't I, Marcos? She's just like her Grandpa Paul, a nature child."

My Grandpa Paul climbed carefully out of the car and made his way around the car. I walked down the porch steps with a smile on my face and my arms wide open.

"Grandpa Paul! Marcos! It's so wonderful to see y'all!"

I gave Grandpa Paul a tight hug and wondered at his weight loss. He let go of me and grinned at my huge belly.

"I see that I'm going to have another great-grandson! That husband of yours don't waste time, huh?"

He slapped his knee and guffawed. He turned his attention to Mark while I gave Marcos a hug. He tensed for a moment before releasing me. The smile that he gave me looked forced. Marcos turned to watch Grandpa Paul and Mark.

"Hello, there, little mister. I'm your Grandpa Paul. Do you think that I can shake your hand? Your Grandpa Ed has been filling my ears with everything that you young'uns been up to, so I made your Uncle Marcos bring me across the creek."

He held out his hand to Mark. Mark smiled and shook Grandpa Paul's hand. Grandpa Paul laughed and looked back at Marcos.

"Come on over here, son, and meet your great nephew."

Marcos walked over and knelt down in front of Mark. Mark looked at him for a moment before giving Marcos a hug. Marcos looked as surprised as Grandpa Paul and me.

"Your name is Marcos. My name is Mark. I like you. You look just like my Strongman toy. Do you have special powers too?"

Mark looked at Marcos with wonder.

Marcos cleared his throat and sent me a questioning glance. I giggled and shrugged.

Grandpa Paul stepped forward and helped Marcos out of his predicament.

Grandpa Paul chuckled.

"Where's your Grandpa Ed, little mister?"

"He forgot the lunch box today, so we had to come back to get it. He's in the house with Willie."

Mark smiled and pointed inside the house.

"Ah, well, Marcos, you can go on back to the house if you want. Juan is working the ranch, and I'm going to stay here and spend some time with Victoria and my great-grandsons."

Grandpa Paul took a seat on the porch to wait for Grandpa Ed and William.

"Uncle Marcos, can you stay too? You can go with us to the field. Grandpa Ed lets us ride horses and feed the cows. I like driving the tractor," Mark rambled as he grabbed Marcos' hand and tried to pull him to the porch.

Marcos laughed and allowed Mark to lead him to sit in the other rocker on the porch.

"Sí, little one. I stay. You may call me tío. I tell you stories of you mama when she your age, okay?"

Marcos winked at me, and I relaxed. I told myself that his earlier behavior was because we hadn't seen each other in so long.

"Paul? I thought I heard your voice," said Grandpa Ed.

He struggled through the door trying to carry William and the lunch box.

Grandpa Paul laughed and got up to help Grandpa Ed with the lunch box.

"I thought I'd invite myself along with you and the boys this morning, Ed. I'm a little jealous, and I felt it's time that I got to spend some time with them too."

Grandpa Ed laughed and nodded at Marcos.

"Well, hello, mi amigo! Glad to see you too. This old badger dragged you over here, huh? How's everything at the hacienda?"

Marcos stood and gave Grandpa Ed a hug before he replied.

"Everything good. Juan does all the work, and I take care of Señor Paul."

I looked from Grandpa Paul to Marcos with questions on my tongue, but Mark interrupted with his introduction of William.

"Tío, this is my brother, Willie. He's little."

Mark puffed his chest out like he wasn't little too. Marcos chuckled and bent to shake William's hand. The moment that he touched William, he drew back quickly. Grandpa Paul stepped forward and began talking to William to cover Marcos' reaction, but I noticed. Marcos had acted just like Big Mama Chandra when meeting William. A trickle of fear ran down my spine.

"All right, let's pile into the truck and get to the back twenty while we still have some time. Since we got Marcos with us, do you boys want to ride in the back of the truck?"

Grandpa Ed's eyes twinkled when he turned toward Mark and William.

They whooped their agreement and let Marcos put them in the bed of the truck before he climbed in with them. I reminded them to be good and be careful and received a dutiful "yes ma'am". I waved them off thinking that Marcos looked to be sitting as far away from William as he could get.

"Victoria."

"Yes, ma'am," I turned to see what Aunt Charlotte needed but no one was there.

Thinking that she had called me from inside the front room, I walked into the house and stood in the front room door. No one was in the front room. I felt goose bumps rising on my arms until I heard the voice call my name again from outside. I breathed a sigh of relief and went back outside. There was a

Black woman dressed in an old-fashioned black dress turning to go into the cornfield at the edge of the yard. I raised my hand to my brow to shade my eyes from the noonday sun and took a step toward her. I looked down at that moment and knew that I missed the steps! I tried to turn to protect my belly but I fell hard off of the porch onto my side. The breath whooshed out of me, and I cried out at the pain. I tried to sit up and ask the woman for help but when I looked back at the cornfield, no one was there.

"Help me, please! Aunt Charlotte! Hope! Anyone! Help!"

Tears fell down my face when I tried again to sit up. Pain lanced through my stomach, and I gasped at it. I felt the rush of liquid as my birth water broke.

"No!"

I sobbed and grabbed my belly as if I could stop the coming labor.

"Victoria! What happened? Oh, never mind! Hope! Mary! Come quick! Victoria has fallen off the porch!"

Aunt Charlotte's limp disappeared as she almost dived off the porch to get to me.

"It's okay, honey. It's okay. Calm yourself, Victoria, please."

Aunt Charlotte held my hand and pleaded with me.

Aunt Mary and Hope came running from the house with Ms. Sadie and Big Mama Chandra on their heels. My eyes met Aunt Mary's for a moment, and she looked from me to the spot where the woman had been. She shook her head sadly and hurried down the steps.

"We have to get her inside. Ms. Sadie, strip the bed and put old sheets on it. Get the hot water ready. Bring some ice and my ointment. Bring the purple tea too and send for Dr. Herbert," Big Mama Chandra commanded and turned back into the house.

Hope and my aunts got me inside the house and placed me on the newly made bed. The pain was coming in waves as I fell back onto the covers. I decided that it would be so wonderful to slip into the darkness at that moment, but Aunt Mary grabbed my chin and opened my eyes wide.

"No, Victoria. You will not give in to it. Stay with us. I know that it hurts, but you have to stay here."

She stared at me until I nodded. She smiled and released my chin to stroke my brow.

"Aaah!"

I felt like something ripped my body in two. I forgot all about my promise to Aunt Mary and slipped into the relief of darkness.

"She's in here, Dr. Herbert. She fell off of the porch, and she hasn't woken since. She grabs her belly when she has a pain, so we know that they are getting close, about ten minutes apart now. We didn't know what else to do."

I smelled Aunt Charlotte's light perfume and another more masculine smell. It was a clean, outdoors odor, and very pleasant - kind of familiar too.

"It's fine, Ms. St. Francis. I'll take good care of her," a deep male voice promised.

"Oh, thank you! Thank you! If you need us, we'll be right outside the door."

I heard the door shut quietly as Aunt Charlotte left the room.

"Well, Victoria. It's been a long time."

I felt a hand on my face, as my eyes were lifted open. I shook with recognition as the face of the boy, no, the man that I loved, smiled at me.

"Billy!"

I breathed and the darkness swallowed me again.

I sat at the piano in the Baptist church that my aunt used to take me to when I was little. The pastor finished his sermon and told the congregation, "God is always on the Throne. No matter where you go, no matter what you do, no matter who you are, God is always on the Throne. He will deliver you from all pain, sorrow, affliction, despair, or whatever troubles that you have. He will deliver you. Never forget the lesson of the prodigal son because you can always come back to God."

"Aaah!"

The labor pains yanked me out of the darkness.

Billy sat down on the bed and gripped my hand as I panted in pain.

"Victoria, you're going to have the baby today. I've examined you and you're in labor too early. It seems your baby will be a May flower instead of June bug."

He attempted a smile at his joke then hesitated when his eyes misted.

"I promise you that I will do all that I can to save your child."

He squeezed my hand at my tearful nod.

The door opened, and my aunts and Hope rushed into the room. I glanced their way before turning over in the bed to try to grab the pain. Billy attempted to turn me over towards him.

"Victoria, don't fight the pain."

I barely heard him because another pain gathered to attack me, and I arched off of the bed.

"Dr. William, please, do something!" Aunt Charlotte sobbed.

I heard Aunt Mary praying from somewhere in the room.

"I'm trying, ma'am. Victoria. Listen to me. Calm your breathing. Yes, that's it. Breathe slowly. When the pain lessens, turn towards me."

Billy motioned to Aunt Charlotte and Hope to help keep me still. I hurt so bad that I didn't care anymore. Billy moved his hands up and down my body before lingering on my stomach. I saw a pained look cross his face before he turned his head and whispered something to Aunt Charlotte and Hope. Aunt Mary moved to stand beside Billy. She looked from him to me and nodded. She turned towards Billy and began to pull him towards the door.

"Ma'am!" "Mary!" "Ms. Mary!"

I heard Aunt Charlotte, Hope, and Billy cry out at once.

"Dr. William needs to leave the room, so that we can wipe Victoria down. Dr. William, we will let you back in just give us a moment," Aunt Mary commanded.

"Ma'am, Victoria needs me, and I mean to take care of her."

I could see the mulish look on Billy's face as he yanked his arm from Aunt Mary's grip. Aunt Mary turned to grab him again, but Aunt Charlotte put herself between them.

"Mary, do you know what you are doing?"

Aunt Charlotte put her hands on Aunt Mary's shoulders and looked into her eyes. Aunt Mary nodded. Aunt Charlotte exhaled and attempted a smile at Billy.

"Dr. William, Victoria is moving around quite a bit in her suffering. Please allow us to wipe her off with some cool rags and put her in another gown. It's so hot in here. Why don't you go to the kitchen for a cold glass of ice-tea? We'll call you in a moment."

While Aunt Charlotte had been pleading with Billy, she maneuvered him out of the door and locked it before he could stop her. Billy banged on the door until I heard Big Mama's Chandra's voice in the hallway.

Aunt Mary moved to my side and pried my right hand away from my chest. She began wrapping it with a strip of white silk. She did so with my other hand and placed them both over my heart. Aunt Mary handed strips to Aunt Charlotte and Hope before wrapping her hands as well.

"Now, Victoria, listen to me. Your time is close. You cannot drape yourself in the shadows for comfort. You must pray and trust in your faith in God. He can protect you."

Aunt Mary started rubbing my belly with her silk wrapped hands. I tried to pray, but something that she said stuck in my mind.

"My baby will be all right, Aunt Mary?"

I stopped the movement of her hands and tried to look into her eyes, but she avoided my gaze.

Out of the corner of my eye, I could see Aunt Charlotte letting Billy back into the room as Big Mama followed. He rushed to my side and picked up my wrist. He frowned at the white strips but said nothing when he saw that my aunts and Hope had similar wrappings.

"No!"

I arched my back at the pain. I tried to calm my breathing but the pain worsened.

Billy lifted the sheet that Aunt Charlotte had placed over me. I almost felt embarrassed…almost. If letting Billy see my lower body stopped the pain, so be it.

"Alright, Victoria. You need to push."

Billy raised his gaze from the sheet to give me that order. I became angry that he would order me about after leaving me for some White trash. We could have been together instead of me marrying Harlan. Harlan. He wasn't much of a husband or father, always wanting to hit us or call us names. Billy and I should have run away, but he had been too scared of the stupid White people. I raised myself to my elbows and pushed down with all my strength. When I could push no more, I fell back onto the bed. Aunt Charlotte rushed to my side.

"Victoria, that is not enough. Push. Now."

Billy's voice sounded angry. How dare he get angry with me? I'm the one in pain. What gave him the right to be angry?

"Again, Victoria!"

Billy nodded at Aunt Charlotte who sat down behind me on the bed and helped me to rise.

"Come, Victoria! Let's have a baby!"

Aunt Charlotte sounded so cheerful. I felt a surge of anger at her. Why was she so darned happy? Didn't she know having babies hurts? I felt the pressure of my child then, and I did push. Needing to do it again, I strained and pushed again.

"Good. Now, one more, Victoria. One more good push."

Billy sounded like he wanted to laugh. That made me angry again. What was he laughing about? What kind of doctor was he to laugh at a woman giving birth? Oh, well, he said one more. I glared at Billy while I pushed until I felt the urge leave as my child entered the world with a loud cry.

"You have a son, Victoria! A son!"

Billy held him up for me to see before passing him to Hope.

I blinked as tears of relief and joy filled my eyes. Aunt Charlotte dropped me back to the bed in her haste to get to my baby. I heard Big Mama and Aunt Mary whispering as Billy finished his work on me. A wave of embarrassment hit me as he lowered the sheet. He saw my blush and chuckled.

"You didn't seem too embarrassed as you fussed at me and your aunt just a while ago."

"What?"

I frowned at him while keeping an eye on the clean up of my baby.

"While you were in labor just now. You talked to yourself about your husband, your aunt, and me. It was interesting to say the least."

Billy's smile turned to a frown as he turned to clean himself up with the towels that Hope held.

Aunt Mary filled my line of vision as she brought my son and placed him in my arms. I hugged him to me and kissed his rosebud lips. He opened his eyes and I gasped.

"Victoria, are you all right?"

Billy rushed back to my bedside.

I could only nod because I couldn't find my voice. I looked up at his beloved face and smiled. I held my son out for him to take. Billy glanced at me with a question in his eyes before taking my son. He looked at him and blinked in surprise.

"Why, he has blue eyes and red hair just like you!"

Billy rubbed his finger against the baby's cheek before turning back to hand him to me.

"What is his name, Victoria? You must name him now," Aunt Mary demanded as she moved closer to the bed.

"His name is Victor like mine is Victoria," I announced with pride.

Aunt Charlotte clapped her hands and sat on the bed to ooh and aah over her new grandson. Hope guided Big Mama Chandra from the room on the promise that she could hold the baby later. Billy left but promised that he'd return in the morning to check on Victor and me. Aunt Mary stroked Victor with her silk wrapped hands before volunteering to keep Mark and William busy for the evening. I felt weary all of a sudden, and as Aunt Charlotte propped herself in the rocker by the new crib, I took a well-needed nap.

7

Over the few months, Victor grew at such a rate that Dr. Herbert asked if he could send some samples of his blood to a colleague for study. I just laughed and shook my head reminding him that he had told me I was the same way. Victor's progress was amazing for a baby born so early. Billy told me that many babies have problems when they come early, but not Victor. There was something about his joy at everything around him. He was a happy baby. He loved to eat, and cried very little.

Everywhere we went, everyone wanted to hold him. Well, everyone who knew that he wasn't a White man's love child. Sometimes, White and Black people in Carson would stare at Aunt Charlotte and me whenever we took Victor to the doctor or carried him about while we shopped. The whispers soon got back to Aunt Charlotte that people believed my husband had sent me away because he found out I carried a White man's child. I laughed off the rumors, but they still hurt my feelings. I started to wonder if that was how Mama and Daddy were treated before they sent me away to Aunt Charlotte.

Billy visited the homestead often. He told us that he needed to check on Victor, but he spent most of his time with both of us. He met Mark and William when they came from the field with Grandpa Ed early one day. He smiled when he found that I had named my son William. I rolled my eyes and told him that it was pure coincidence. He didn't believe me.

I tried to discourage his visits because I felt guilty keeping him away from his other patients and his family. I brought it up to him, and he gave me a strange look before laughing. He was still laughing when he left that evening.

"Victoria, is there something that you should tell me?"

Aunt Charlotte asked me one morning as Billy played with the boys in the yard. He held Victor as if he were his own.

"About?"

I knew what she meant but decided to play stupid.

"Don't play coy with me, young lady. I know when a man is smitten, and that man's nose is so wide open, I could drive your grandfather's tractor through it."

I laughed at the image from her words, but immediately quieted when she turned a fierce frown on me.

"Do not encourage him. He is a man, and you are still a married woman. The gossips have enough to talk about with Victor's looks."

"Aunt Charlotte, I have not given him any reason to keep coming. When I reminded him of his work and his family, he laughed at me. I think that he is just crazy about Victor because he's so healthy and handsome for an early baby."

I nodded at my wisdom and sat back with a smile watching the man that I loved play with my sons. Billy caught my eye and waved. I returned it with a guilty glance at Aunt Charlotte.

She narrowed her eyes, harrumphed, and took a sip of her coffee.

The Thursday before Labor Day, Aunt Charlotte and I pulled up to the house to find the sheriff's car parked in the driveway.

"Oh no, I wonder what's wrong?" she murmured as she came to an abrupt stop.

I felt a sliver of fear run down my spine as we climbed out of the car. I grabbed Victor from his basket in the backseat and held him close to my chest.

Aunt Charlotte limped up the steps and almost ran into the sheriff coming out of the screen door.

"Whoa, there, ma'am. Where's the fire?"

The tall White man chuckled and grabbed Aunt Charlotte's elbow.

Aunt Charlotte gave the sheriff a cold glare and took her elbow out of his grasp.

"There is no fire, sir. I am just a bit anxious as to why the sheriff is at my mother's home."

The sheriff looked over at me and nodded with his eyes twinkling.

"It's not for me to say, ma'am. I'm only the delivery man today."

He tipped his hat to us and left.

"Well, that was strange. Victoria, cover the baby's head. There is a slight breeze. Let's find out what he came to deliver."

Aunt Charlotte turned and walked into the house. For some reason, I wanted to take my time going in the house. I got the feeling that something wasn't right.

I opened the door and walked into the front room. I almost dropped Victor in my shock.

"Hello, darlin'. I've been waiting for you to get back. It's been so long since I've seen my wife and children. Come on over here and give me a proper hello."

Harlan sat on the divan in his uniform with his arm in a sling. A buzzing started in my head as I stared at my husband. I felt Aunt Charlotte take Victor from my arms, and I wanted to snatch him back. Harlan narrowed his eyes at Aunt Charlotte before turning to me with a phony smile.

"Well, well. I guess she's in shock. It has been almost a year. Stay there, darlin'. I'll come to you."

He got up and walked to stand in front of me. I stood mesmerized by the evil glee in his face as he took me in his arms and hugged me tight. Then, he bent me over his arm for a sloppy, wet kiss. When he stood me back up, I resisted the urge to wipe my mouth. He turned to my family sitting around the room while keeping an arm around me. He ignored Victor all together.

"Thank y'all so much for taking care of my family while I was away fighting for my country. You know, just doing my duty. I'll send some funds back after we get home. We'll leave on Monday evening, so Victoria and my boys can have this holiday with their family."

Harlan smiled another greasy smile at everyone and gave my arm a hard squeeze.

"Victoria and her children are family and always welcome here, Harlan," Big Mama said from her chair.

I sneaked a glance and saw that Hope, Aunt Mary, Ms. Sadie, and Aunt Charlotte frowned at Harlan. I lowered my head to hide my smile. Harlan hadn't fooled my family with his slick words and slimy smiles.

Aunt Charlotte walked forward and handed Harlan the baby. Harlan held Victor away from his body as Victor squirmed.

"This is your new son, Victor. He's three months old now. Beautiful, isn't he?"

Aunt Charlotte smiled at Harlan and patted Victor's back.

Harlan cleared his throat and looked at all of the women in the room. He held Victor up to his face and gave him a peck on the cheek. Victor smiled at Harlan then spit up his lunch all over Harlan's uniform. I snatched Victor from Harlan as he jumped and yelled for a towel. He turned to me when Ms. Sadie handed him a cup towel.

"Why didn't you tell me that he had just eaten, you stupid cow? Now, you're going to have to clean my uniform," Harlan growled and tried to wipe the stain.

Aunt Charlotte moved forward with her cane lifted to hit Harlan but Aunt Mary stopped her. Harlan didn't even care about their reactions to showing his usual ornery self. He walked back to the divan and sat down.

"Mama and Daddy said that he probably wasn't mine anyway, and look at him. He looks just like a White man's baby."

He flung his statement at me without care that my family listened.

"I believe that we raised my granddaughter to have more respect for herself than what you are speaking of, son, and a good man does not berate his wife in front of others, especially her family. I will not stand for it in my house, so if you cannot treat you wife, my granddaughter, with respect, I will be happy to teach you some in the front yard."

Everyone turned to the doorway as Grandpa Ed walked through it. His fists were balled, and he looked fit to be tied.

Harlan sputtered his outrage and stood up from the divan. Grandpa Ed's long legs covered the space between them in seconds. He got right in Harlan's face, and no one said a word.

"Yes, I know what kind of man you are. I pegged you for a little shit at the wedding, but I didn't dare interfere if you made Victoria happy. You didn't, though, did you? You wasted away her money and tried to belittle who we raised her to be. Well, I'm only too happy to give you some lessons now, boy."

I had seen Grandpa Ed that angry once before…with Daddy.

Harlan puffed his chest out and sneered at Grandpa Ed.

"What're you going to do, old man? Nothing. You think you can talk to me like this and get away with it? Well, think again."

He jabbed Grandpa Ed's chest with his uninjured arm.

Grandpa Ed snarled in his throat before grabbing Harlan's finger and twisting his whole arm behind his back. Harlan howled and went to one knee. I took a step forward, but Aunt Charlotte clutched my arm.

"Grandpa! Please don't hurt him! I don't want you to go to jail!"

Mark ran in and tapped Grandpa Ed on the leg.

Grandpa Ed looked down at Mark and let Harlan go with a little push. Mark hugged his leg and gave him a big smile. Grandpa Ed lifted him into his arms and walked outside without another word. I looked through the window and saw them get into the field truck and leave. As the truck passed the cornfield, I saw a figure in black watching the house. I inched closer to see who it was, but nothing was there anymore.

Harlan picked himself off the floor and threw an angry glance at the door.

"Well, I can see that my family isn't welcome, so we'll leave now. Victoria, get packed."

I was about to tell him no when I felt Victor gurgle loudly and go stiff. I looked at his face, and it turned blue. I opened his mouth quickly to see a pool of blood.

"Aunt Charlotte, call Billy! Hurry! Something's wrong with Victor!"

I hugged him to my chest and felt him struggling to breathe. Blood dripped from his mouth down my chest, but I didn't care. All my attentions focused on my baby. I closed my eyes and began to bounce him in my arms. I could hear commotion all around me as everyone rushed to help. I felt a calm come over me and began singing "Jesus Love Me" while I rubbed my son's back. Aunt Charlotte talked nonstop and pushed me into the car to drive us to Carson. I held Victor to my heart and kissed his soft, auburn curls.

The car stopped with a jerk. Someone tried to lift Victor from my arms. I cried out and held on to his little body.

"Victoria, it's me. Billy. Let me help Victor, please," he sobbed and tried again to take him from me.

I let him go because I knew Billy would save him. I opened my eyes to see him lift Victor's limp body and run into the hospital. Aunt Charlotte and Harlan helped to pull me from the car before we followed Billy. I didn't rush because I knew that Billy would save Victor. He wouldn't let anything happen to him.

A nurse directed us to sit down beside a door with a small window in it. I sat in a chair close to it. Harlan and Aunt Charlotte chose seats on either side of me. I smiled at Harlan and told him that I knew about Shirley and the baby that was his. His face went ashen at my calm acceptance of his second love child. I giggled and sat back. Aunt Charlotte gave me a strange look before reaching over to hold my hand. Soon, Aunt Mary and Hope arrived with Big Mama to wait for Billy to tell us when Victor could come home.

I don't know how much time passed before we heard a loud cry of pain. I knew that it wasn't Victor, so I turned and gave Harlan another smile.

"It shouldn't be long now. Billy is a very good doctor. He delivered him, you know."

I nodded and smiled at my husband again.

Harlan looked across me at Aunt Charlotte who squeezed my hand. I could hear Aunt Mary and Hope's whispered prayers.

The door opened, and Dr. Herbert and Ms. Constance stepped through it. Their faces were grim, and they looked like they had been crying. I stood up and smiled.

"Hello, Dr. Herbert. Can I take Victor home now?"

Dr. Herbert took my hands and looked into my eyes. I wished that he would hurry up and tell me yes. I wanted to hold my baby.

"I'm sorry, Victoria. Victor's lungs didn't grow as fast as the rest of him did. There was nothing we could do. He's gone."

He dropped my hands and stepped back pulling a sobbing Ms. Constance into his arms.

My chest started hurting as his words sank into my mind. I heard a keening wail and fell to the floor. I shook off the hands that tried to hold me. I hugged my arms around the spot where I had last held my son. I felt my mind snap. I looked up at Dr. Herbert and smiled.

"You're lying. Billy wouldn't let my son die. He loves him. I know he does. Where is he? Where is Billy?"

I stood up and turned around. Everyone was crying except for Harlan. I narrowed my eyes at him and felt the anger building. I walked slowly toward him.

"Why are you here? It's your fault Victor got sick. You made him sick with your meanness. He even threw up on you. If you hadn't come, Victor wouldn't be sick!"

I started beating Harlan's chest until Aunt Charlotte and Hope pulled me away. Aunt Charlotte spun me around and looked into my face. I didn't want to see her sympathy or her sorrow. It wasn't true what Dr. Herbert said.

"It's not true! Where is my baby?"

I screamed and knocked Dr. Herbert and Ms. Constance aside and snatched the door open and ran into the hallway calling my son's name. I felt Dr. Herbert trying to catch hold of me, but I yanked away and rounded the corner. Billy sat on the floor with his head on his knees.

"Billy! There you are! Where is Victor?"

I knelt beside him as he lifted his head. I saw anguish and sorrow on his face. He glanced toward the room across from him.

I stood up and walked with heavy legs into the room. I heard voices from a distance, but I ignored them and walked toward the bed. I barely noticed the blood stained cloths lying on the floor as I pulled the sheet back. My beautiful baby boy was on his side with his eyes closed. He looked like he was sleeping. I reached down and picked him up. I held him to my chest and hoped to feel his chest heave with breath, but I knew that he was gone from me. The pain that I had felt before was nothing compared to what I felt at that moment.

"No, no, no, no, no," I sobbed over and over while I rocked Victor's small body.

"Why? Why? Why?"

I screamed, but there was nothing but silence. I felt a small sting on my arm. I felt the darkness rising and for once in a long while, it didn't give me comfort.

Victor's funeral was held the Tuesday after Labor Day. Aunt Charlotte arranged everything. She had to because I wouldn't. To arrange my baby's services meant that I accepted he was dead.

Big Mama Chandra said that I went a little crazy after leaving the hospital. She said that I wouldn't let them throw away Victor's clothes that he had on that day or my bloody blouse. She said that I kept talking to him and holding my arms as if I he was there. I wanted to tell her that I remembered those things and that I wasn't crazy, but I didn't care what they thought.

Dr. Herbert came by the house a few times after the funeral. He looked into my eyes, ears, and mouth. He listened to my heart and had me breathe in and out. I didn't feel any of it. I didn't want to feel anything. The horrible pain of that day had become a deep ache in my heart. Dr. Herbert told Harlan not to give up on having other children. I wanted to hit him. How dare he suggest we try to replace Victor? Tears pricked my eyes and I rubbed my chest where he used to sleep. I yelled at Dr. Herbert and Harlan to get out and leave me alone.

After a few weeks, Aunt Mary came into my room to tell me that she and Aunt Charlotte had to go back to Dallas for a few days. Nettie, the woman whose family took care of their house had fallen ill. Aunt Charlotte wanted to check on her and take care of some of her affairs while she was there. I turned my head back to the window. I didn't care what they did. I wanted to feel my baby in my arms. I felt Aunt Mary grip my chin and forced my gaze back to hers.

"Victoria. I do not know how it feels to lose a child, but you are sinking too deep into your sorrow. Victor is gone, and there is nothing that you can do about it. There was nothing you could do to stop his passing. Stop blaming yourself. You heard Dr. Herbert. There was no way anyone could know what was wrong with Victor. Accept his loss and know that he walks with God. We never know God's plan, but we must accept it."

I saw the sheen of tears in her eyes as she released my chin.

"No, Aunt Mary. It's my fault. I should never have come home. I heard someone calling my name ever since we arrived. The day that Victor was born, I saw a woman dressed in black by the cornfield in front of the house. I fell down and almost lost him then. On the day that he died, she was there again."

I felt tears coursing down my cheeks. I wiped my face and saw Aunt Mary's face pale.

"Victoria. How did you answer her when she called?"

I thought her question was strange, but I answered it.

"A few times, I said nothing. Before I went into labor, I think I said, "yes ma'am" because I thought it was Aunt Charlotte."

Aunt Mary shook her head sadly and caressed my face.

"Victoria, never answer anyone unless you know for sure who called you. There are spirits that walk among us that sometimes attached themselves to the pure of heart. They thrive on the pure life force until they join them in death. When a woman is pregnant with a pure soul, they call out to her. If she answers yes, that opens the connection."

My heart broke again knowing that I had caused my child's death.

My breath released on a sob, and I clung to Aunt Mary and cried my pain.

The next few days, I tried to spend time with Mark and William. Grandpa Ed talked them into staying with me instead of going with him to the fields. I hadn't seen them in a while and being with them gave me some comfort. I felt Mark's gaze on me several times. I saw the concern on his small face, and I felt the tears rising. I swallowed them down and made a show of playing Cowboys and Indians.

I was sitting on the porch rocking Victor when I saw the woman in black standing at the edge of the cornfield. I stood up and left the porch to reach her before she turned away.

"Hello?" I yelled. "Who are you?"

I ran faster when I saw her turn to walk back into the corn.

"Please, wait," I yelled again and came closer to the spot where she was.

I saw her stop, so I slowed my pace. I could hear my own loud breathing from running. She stood there with her back turned. I reached out and touched her shoulder to turn her towards me and gasped. It was my face! The woman smiled, and I could see the dark holes where her eyes should have been. I took a step back, and she took a step forward. She laughed a cackling laugh as she lifted Victor from my arms.

"He's mine now, girl!"

I screamed and shouted for help but no one came. She walked into the corn and disappeared. I tried to run after her but tripped and fell to the ground. I screamed and cried but silence was my answer. It was then that I saw a baby wrapped in a blue blanket. I peered into the blanket but couldn't see the baby's face. He raised his tiny hand and touched my face. I felt the ache of sorrow recede at his touch. I smiled and tried to pick him up but he faded away.

"Victoria, I'm glad to see that you're enjoying the last of our good weather."

I sat up from lying back in the rocker on the porch to see Billy standing in front of me. I shook myself to cast off the horrible dream. I looked around for Billy's truck because I hadn't heard him drive up. He gave a quiet laugh.

"Marcos gave me a ride. He says that I have been walking too long, and I need to settle my spirit."

I didn't know what he meant, and I didn't care. Billy hadn't saved my son. He had let him die. I didn't want to see him.

"Go away, Billy."

I waved him away.

"I can't, Victoria. I need to say what's on my mind first. If after you want to kick me off your grandparents land, I'll start running, but please hear what I have to say."

I narrowed my eyes at him. I remembered a time when I loved him. I looked at his handsome face and felt nothing. His skin and hair was a shade darker than it had been when we were young. His face was still handsome with the high cheekbones, straight regal nose, full lower lip, and dimples, but he looked tired and older than his twenty-eight years.

My silence was all he needed to climb the steps and sit down in the other rocker. Neither of us said a word for a while. I wondered if I made a mistake letting him vent his spleen, then he spoke.

"When the nurse told me that your aunt had phoned an emergency call, my heart stopped because I knew something was wrong with you or one of the boys. It was sheer torture waiting for the car to arrive, and when I saw all of the blood on your chest from his mouth, my stomach heaved. I'm a doctor, and yet, I felt sick at seeing that blood. You looked so helpless as you sat there rocking him. I knew then that I would be strong for you.

When you passed him to me with so much trust in your eyes, I vowed to myself that I would save him. The moment that I laid him on that bed, I did everything that I was trained to do and more. My father and two of the best nurses that Carson General Hospital has, also worked to save your son.

When he took his last breath, I took him in my arms and held him to my chest. I kissed his little hand and felt the life leave his body. I didn't know I was crying until the nurse wiped my face. When my father saw that he was gone, he tried to take him from me. I cried out and placed him on the bed myself. I took a cloth and wet it in the sink. I cleaned him up and made sure all the blood was gone. I turned him on his side and covered him up. I felt myself moving into the hallway. I ran into the wall and slid down. My mother tried to comfort me, but I wouldn't let her. I stayed there devastated by his death until you came, Victoria."

At the mention of my name, I turned my head and looked at Billy. He stared straight ahead locked inside his memory of that horrible day.

"Your grief, your anguish, it brought me out of my own. I wanted to take you in my arms and share your pain, but your husband was there. He stood at your side even though you didn't know it. I saw, and I felt jealousy and anger grip my heart. He didn't know that beautiful boy. I did. I wanted to tear him apart with my bare hands, but I left instead. I walked out of that hospital, and I haven't been back since."

I wiped the tears from my eyes realizing that Billy had loved Victor more than I had known. The anger that I had been holding onto faded as I heard Billy's sobs. When his final words sunk in, I stood and knelt beside the rocker he occupied.

"No, Billy. Victor is gone, and you know as well as I do that there was nothing that we could have done to save him. He was just too wonderful for us to keep. God took him where he belonged, with Him and Jesus. I have to believe that to stay sane. We won't ever forget him, and you can't stop being a doctor because you couldn't save him. What about the people that you can save? Think about them."

I put my hand to his cheek. He turned his face into it before falling into my arms. I allowed him to grieve until his sobs became hiccups. I giggled and stepped away from him.

"Feel better?"

I arched my eyebrow at his sniffles.

Billy laughed and nodded. He reached out and caressed my cheek. Embarrassed, I took a quick step back.

"Where is your husband, Victoria?"

Billy cocked his head to the side.

"He went back to Littleton with his parents after the funeral," I replied. "Where is your wife?"

I felt jealousy rising and put my hands on my hips.

"Victoria, haven't your figured it out by now that I'm not married? Every time that you ask me that, don't I laugh?"

He drew me into his arms.

"I can't think about marrying anyone else. You were right about what you said when you were in labor. We should have run away together, but I was a coward. I love you, Victoria. I love Mark and William. We can be a family. You said yourself that Harlan's not much of a husband. Leave him, and we can be together."

Billy crushed me to his chest, and I squirmed to get free. I opened mouth to tell him to let me go when a sharp pain sent the breath from my body with a whoosh.

"Aah!"

I arched my back as another pain rolled through me.

"Victoria! What is it?"

Billy sounded frantic as he lowered me to the porch and began feeling my arms and legs for what hurt.

"Victoria! Dr. William! What is going on here?"

Aunt Charlotte and Aunt Mary pulled to a stop in the yard and climbed out of the car. Billy answered her without turning.

"I don't know, ma'am. She starting hollering with pain, and I laid her on the porch to see what it was."

"Well, take her in the house, and put her on her bed."

I barely heard the rest of what they said as I fell gratefully into the darkness.

8

A white-hot spear of pain lifted me to consciousness. I cried out and felt hands trying to hold me down while someone poured a liquid between my lips. I swallowed it and felt some of the pain receding. I opened my eyes to see Big Mama leaning over me. I took a heavy breath to speak, but she shook her head.

"No, Victoria. Don't speak. Let the tea work."

Her lips widened into a small smile.

"We had to almost hogtie Dr. William to get him to leave your side. He's been here everyday from sun up to sundown for three days. Dr. Herbert and Constance tried to take him away, but he wouldn't leave as long as you were in bad shape."

She turned her head and nodded.

I heard the creak of a chair, and Aunt Mary moved forward into my line of sight. She looked very tired. She wobbled a little before catching herself. She sat at the foot of the bed and gave me a direct look.

"Victoria, Mama and I have been fighting for you for the past three nights. The line is wrapped around your spirit. I don't know how it became so strong, so fast. You need to fight for yourself."

She hesitated and looked at her silk wrapped hands.

"Tell us what happened with Dr. William. Mama and I know some but not all. Keep nothing in the dark."

I blinked in surprise that Aunt Mary had brought up my relationship with Billy.

"I know the pain has abated, Victoria. You must tell us what happened between you and Dr. William."

She waved her hand and moved back into the shadows. I heard someone moving closer and turned my head to see Aunt Charlotte sitting down in the chair beside the bed where Big Mama had been. She held my hand in hers and gave me a watery smile.

"Please, my darling girl. Speak your mind."

She squeezed my hand and gently wiped my brow. I nodded and turned my head away in shame.

Tears gathered and fell as I started to speak.

"Billy and I…"

I stopped because just saying those words brought a shadow of the pain back. I gulped and started again.

"When I came to live with Mama and Daddy for good, we became good friends. We loved each other but couldn't be together because he was White, and I wasn't. I had hoped that he wouldn't care and would love me enough to take me away from Mama and Daddy's, but he didn't. They were so mean and hateful to me, Aunt Charlotte, and Billy was so good to me."

I wiped my face with the sheet as the memories came back. No one said a word while I gathered myself. I took a deep breath and continued.

"One day, I found out that he was seeing another girl. He told me that Dr. Herbert made him do it because people had started talking about seeing us together. He begged me to understand and told me that he loved me. He chose the White people over me, but I couldn't hate him. It wasn't his fault that I was born deformed. No, please don't try to say I'm not because I am."

I shook my head at Aunt Charlotte when she tried to interrupt me.

"Let her get it out, Charlotte. She has to," whispered Big Mama Chandra

She put her hand on Aunt Charlotte's shoulder. Aunt Charlotte's mouth opened on a sob then closed it again. She nodded for me to keep talking. I squeezed her hand and attempted a smile.

"I didn't see Billy much after that talk. I made up my mind to be a nurse when y'all came to talk to Mama and Daddy about my schooling. Then Harlan came along, and he reminded me of Billy except he gave up on me when Daddy told him that we couldn't court. He started seeing that slut, Shirley. I asked Mama and Daddy to let me go to away to school. They laughed at me and told me that it wasn't going to happen. I cried and prayed. I begged God to help me, but nothing happened."

I broke into sobs. I couldn't go on anymore. I didn't want them to know what I had done because I had been weak and stupid.

Aunt Charlotte moved to comfort me, but Aunt Mary's hard tone stayed her.

"No, Charlotte, she must tell us everything."

I shook my head over and over asking them to go away, but Big Mama scooted Aunt Charlotte aside and grabbed my face between her hands.

"Victoria Alicia Sams. You will do as I say right now."

Her tone brooked no disobedience. She wiped my tears with her apron and waved her hand for me to continue.

"At the reception, I found out how stupid I had been. That's when Betts found me. She gave me something to hope for, and I took it. I knew it was wrong, but I didn't care. Aunt Mary tried to stop me, but I wouldn't listen. I did what Betts told me to do. And ever since that night, I've been in my own Hell. Coming back here and having Billy around made me feel better. I saw how he was with my sons, with Victor, and I fell in love with him all over again.

When he came the other day, he was still hurt over Victor's passing. I tried to help him heal his heart, and he offered to take me and the boys away to be a family. I remember feeling like someone stabbed me with a butcher knife."

I sighed and covered my face with the sheet.

There was nothing but silence when I finished. I felt embarrassed that my family now knew my shame. I wanted to shrivel up and die.

Aunt Mary spoke first.

"Victoria, you are bound to Harlan. Not only by marriage and children, but also when you drew the line. Even if you divorced Harlan, you can't be with another man until that line is broken. The pain that you felt is part of that. I'm sorry, but the choices that you made seven years ago are going to affect you for a long time.

"Don't you think that I know that, Aunt Mary!" I yelled with all the bitterness in my soul.

"What is going on in there? Victoria, I'm here! Ms. Chandra, please let me in. I need to see that she is okay!"

I heard the doorknob shaking as Billy tried to get to me.

Aunt Charlotte turned to me with a stern look.

"Victoria, you have to discourage Dr. William. You have to let him find someone else to love and start his own family."

I bit my lip and more tears spilled down my cheeks. I knew that Aunt Charlotte was right. I couldn't make Billy pay for my mistakes. I nodded at her, and she limped to the door and opened it. Billy gave her a ferocious frown before rushing to kneel at my bedside. He grabbed my hand and held it to his chest. He had on the same clothes from the day that I collapsed. His face was unshaven, and his eyes were blurry. He had never been more handsome to me than in that moment of his concern for me. I closed my eyes and stored this memory for another day.

"Are you all right, Victoria? Are you still in pain? They wouldn't let me see to you."

He threw an angry glance back at Big Mama and my aunts.

I attempted a smile when he turned back to me. I steeled myself to lie to him. Looking into those clear blue eyes filled with love for me, made it harder. I swallowed the tears threatening to surface.

"Yes, I'm fine. I guess bringing up the day that Victor died was too much for me. I'll be all right. Big Mama Chandra gave me some of her special tea, so I'll be right as rain soon."

Billy breathed a sigh of relief and reached into the black bag that he had sat on the floor.

"Well, I think that I'll see for myself. Ladies, I need a moment with Victoria," he demanded.

Aunt Charlotte opened her mouth to protest, but Big Mama Chandra stopped her.

"Yes, Dr. William. We'll be right outside. Victoria, remember, tomatoes spoil if you try to keep them too long."

I wanted to pretend that I didn't know what she was talking about, but I gave a quiet, "yes, ma'am", and they filed out of the door.

When the door closed, Billy took his stethoscope out and listened to my heart and lungs. He asked me questions about the pain and shined a light in my eyes. I took my time answering because I wanted to delay what I had to do. When Billy put away all of his medical supplies, he turned to me and smiled.

"Well, I think that you are on the mend. It's strange how sudden and bad that pain hit you. After four days of being in bed, you look absolutely beautiful."

He reached out and caressed my cheek. I closed my eyes and allowed his touch for a moment before snatching my face away. I felt the pain building and knew that I needed to hurry. I looked back at Billy to see a hurt look on his face. I gathered my courage and smiled. He relaxed a little and returned the smile.

"Billy. I'm glad that you came to see me. I wanted to tell you how much I appreciate your friendship. You've been such a good friend to my family, and I won't forget everything that you did for me and for my son."

I hesitated and took a peek at Billy from under my eyelashes. He looked confused. I took a deep breath and continued my lies.

"Harlan wants us to come home now. He misses us like crazy, and I miss him too. So do the boys. Aunt Charlotte and Aunt Mary are going to take us back with them in a few days. I don't know when I'll see you again, but I hope that you have a wonderful life."

I stopped then because the lump in my throat felt too big for me to say anything else.

Billy looked at me in disbelief. He opened his mouth and closed it. He shook his head and leaned away from me. I stayed quiet hoping that I had done enough damage.

In a quick move, Billy grabbed my arms and yanked me up to his face. His grip hurt, but I remained quiet because I knew that I had hurt him more.

"You are lying. Why are you doing this? Don't punish me for being a coward when I was a boy. We're together now. We can run away from here – with the boys. I love Mark and William. They should have been mine, Victor too. You should be my wife, not his!"

I shook my head no. He narrowed his eyes at me and tightened his grip. His eyes had a distant look as he held me still.

After a few moments of staring, Billy went from shaking me to hugging me and telling me his plans of running away. I felt fear creeping up my back, but I ignored it. Billy tightened his grip again, and when I whimpered, he came to himself and dropped me back on the bed. I rubbed my arms as he got up from the chair and walked to the door. He turned the knob but looked back at me before opening the door.

"I know that you're lying, Victoria. Harlan has no more love for you than you do for him. I'm going to respect your "wishes", though. Don't give me that swill about "have a good life". I don't want to hear it, but I'll pray for you to have one."

His last words ended in sobs as he opened the door and left.

I barely heard Big Mama Chandra and my aunts come back in the room. I turned over and sobbed my misery into the already soaked sheet.

Seeing to Mark and William kept me busy for the next few weeks because Grandpa Ed was busy with the fall harvest. An early Norther came though, so everyone was busy. I decided to stay out of the way because I wasn't much good to anyone, so I bundled the boys up and took them on long walks around land. I felt like I hadn't spent enough time with them over the past year. They had grown, especially Mark. I was in awe at how tall he'd gotten. William had also grown a little, but there was something about him that sent a shiver down my spine.

I watched them as they ran ahead of me playing and saw William trying to strike Mark with rocks. I caught up with them and chastised William and grabbed his hand to make him drop the rocks. I was so busy trying to dust off his hand that I almost didn't see the malevolent glare on his face aimed at Mark. I ignored the familiar shiver coursing down my spine. I stepped back still holding his hand and walked forward keeping him at my side. I told myself that he was only three. He would grow out of it.

Big Mama surprised us all Thanksgiving day when she announced that Mama and Daddy would be joining us for dinner. Aunt Charlotte and I gasped while Aunt Mary frowned at Big Mama. Ms. Sadie crossed herself and disappeared into the kitchen. Hope gave a nervous giggle before she mentioned that Ms. Sadie needed her help and almost ran out of the front room. Grandpa Ed grabbed Mark and William from the divan muttering something about making corn dolls for the field children.

"Mama, why would you do that without telling us?"
Aunt Charlotte broke the tense silence.

"Charlotte St. Francis. I do believe that this house is still mine, and Tess is my daughter too. I don't have to tell you a cotton pickin' thing."

Big Mama turned her cloudy gaze to me.

"I'm sorry, Victoria, if it makes you uncomfortable. They are your parents, and I figured this would be a good time to hash out the bad blood. Well, that and good food makes for good company."

She chuckled.

"Mama, Victoria has been through enough this year. Please don't do this," Aunt Charlotte pleaded.

Big Mama Chandra whipped around and grabbed Aunt Charlotte by her elegantly clad shoulders.

"Charlotte, Victoria is grown woman with children. She will learn how to handle Tess and Clyde, or she will forever be a weakling. Think about how you raised her. She has the strength."

She turned that cloudy gaze on me.

"She just needs to learn to use it and not that other."

I jerked my eyes away from hers and met Aunt Mary's. She smiled and tapped a finger to her heart. I nodded and turned to Aunt Charlotte.

"It's going to be all right, Aunt Charlotte."

I waited until Big Mama moved away then walked to Aunt Charlotte and gave her a hug. She stared at me in disbelief then limped to the divan. She arranged the full skirt of her dress and clasped her hands together in her lap. She looked like a beautiful queen holding court.

"How long before they get here, Mama?" Aunt Mary asked as she rolled her eyes at Aunt Charlotte.

"They should be here any minute. Now, remember, your sister probably made a pie or something. I've already told Sadie to take it to the kitchen and leave it. If she asks, we'll remind her of all the food on the dining room table."

Big Mama cast her eyes at each of us until we nodded.

"Good, because I hear that raggedy truck of Clyde's coming up the lane."

After we ate our fill of all the delicious food, Ms. Sadie announced that she and Hope would bring the dessert table into the front room. I groaned at the mention of more food. I hadn't eaten much because of the tension between me and my parents, but what I had managed to get down was plenty.

Everyone got up from the table and started making their way to the front room. Mark and William jumped up and ran noisily out of the room.

Grandpa Ed laughed and followed behind them. My aunts and Big Mama grinned at each other and kept up a stream of talking as they walked into the hallway. I turned to go into the kitchen to ask if Hope and Ms. Sadie needed my help. I didn't notice that Mama was behind me until I turned around. I bumped into her and grabbed hold of her arms to steady us both.

"Watch it, girl! You've always been so clumsy!"

She jerked loose from my grip, and I stepped back into the kitchen. As she pretended to straighten herself, she looked over my head at Hope and Ms. Sadie.

"I didn't see the corn pudding or pumpkin pie that I made on the table. I want it on the dessert tray."

She narrowed her eyes at them before glaring at me.

"I suppose we should talk, Victoria. I feel it's my motherly duty to help you and those boys. Let's go to Mama's sunroom while everyone enjoys their dessert in peace."

Her voice sounded oily just like Harlan's when he pretended to be nice.

I opened my mouth to tell her no, but she put her arm around my shoulders and steered me into Big Mama's sunroom. I tried to yank away, but her grip was too strong. She pushed me onto the settee and sat down beside me. She covered my hands with hers and squeezed them hard. I felt the anger begin to build at her high-handed treatment. I arched my eyebrow and sneered at her.

"What's wrong, Mama? You need to get away from Daddy? Yes, I can understand that. It's funny. I married a man almost exactly like him. I wonder if I'll turn into you soon... "

I leaned close to her face and yanked my hands from hers. "…a resentful, bitter doormat."

Slap!

I felt the sting of her slap, and it made me angry. I was not a child anymore.

Slap!

I drew satisfaction from the surprised look on my mother's face as she held the cheek that I hit. She narrowed her eyes and raised her hand like she wanted to hit me again. I gave her a look filled with annoyance. She slowly lowered her hand.

"Now, what did you want, Mama? I want to get back to my sons. You know, your grandsons? The beautiful boys that you have ignored since you got here?"

Mama's look turned vicious. She opened her mouth to speak but closed it again. I saw her sizing me up to deliver one of her insults and jumped up from the settee ready to leave. She stood up and grabbed my arm. I turned cautiously to face her.

"I knew sending you away to Charlotte and Mary wouldn't do any good. You just keep coming back."

She had a crazy look in her eye, and I didn't want any part of it. I tried yanking my arm from her grip, but it was too strong. She smiled and drew me closer.

"I know what you did on your wedding night."

She flicked my arm away and laughed at the surprised look on my face.

"Did you really think that man would stay with a little nobody like you? Ha! I bet he couldn't wait to run back to that other gal."

She laughed even louder when she saw the tears forming in my eyes.

Seeing her having fun at my expense made me see red. I became so angry that I wanted to hit her again. I felt the heat of violence rising in me, and I knew that I had to get away from my own mother. I turned toward the door and started walking.

"Oh no, you don't."

She rushed ahead of me and stood in my way.

"Mama, please move. I want to leave. Now."

I glared at her with teeth clenched and fists balled. I stood ready to break God's commandment to "honor thy mother".

"Not until I have my say. You think you're smart running back to your family now. No, you deserve everything you get, even more. You don't deserve to live."

Mama's eyes held an evil glow as she finished her vicious speech.

I almost lost my breath at her harsh words. I felt tired all of a sudden. My heart and soul felt such sadness that the unshed tears began to fall. It was time for me to know why my own parents couldn't stand the sight of me.

"Mama, why do you hate me so much? What did I do to you, to Daddy?"

I reached to take her hand, but she drew back. All of her mirth died in that moment. She looked as tired as I felt. Mama walked back and sat down on the settee. She seemed not to notice me anymore.

"You should never have been born. I tried everything. Dried mustard, Black root tea, salt and baking soda hot water bottles. Everything. But nothing worked. You still came," she said with disgust in her tone.

My feet felt like lead as I made myself walk to the chair beside the settee. My heart hammered in my chest at my mother's words. I opened my mouth to ask why, but she started talking again.

"I had walked over the creek to see the new graveyard that my daddy and Clyde's daddy had donated to the church. Mama had told me not to go anywhere by myself because one of the field hands had brought word that a White drifter was making threats with Mr. Bob about our land. I thought it was hogwash, so I took off across the creek on my own. When I neared the bend where all the trees hang low, I heard a noise behind me. I looked, but no one was there. I kept going until heard a rush of footsteps behind me, then I felt a pain in the back of my head. I remember falling, but that's all."

Mama hesitated and looked down at her clenched hands. I didn't make a sound because of the fear that began building inside me. I wanted to yell at her to stop, but she took a deep breath continued.

"I woke up in a field covered in wild flowers, and Betts stood over me frowning.

"What you been doing, gal?" she asked.

I told her what happened, but she looked at me like she didn't believe me.

"Well, somebody did beat the hell out of you. C'mon, I have some herbs, and I'll check you out."

Clyde and I were going to be married in a couple of months, so I went with her hoping that she'd take me to him. My body hurt, but mostly my head and face. When we got to the Roberts' ranch, Betts took care of me. Clyde came, and I told him what happened. He looked strange and left the room. It was later when Betts came back and told me that they didn't believe that someone beat me and just left me there. They believed that someone had taken what wasn't theirs. I knew that it wasn't true. I just knew it, but Clyde and Betts, well, they didn't. Mr. Paul told my mama and daddy what happened, and they came for me. I was glad because Clyde told me that he didn't want to marry me anymore. He said that I was soiled goods. He told Betts and Mr. Paul that he was going to join the army. Betts didn't want that, so she sent me a package the next day with a letter."

Again, Mama paused like she lived that day over again.

Tess,

I know that what happened to you was bad, and Clyde only made it worse. I know you still love him, and I can help you get him to come back to you. I sent you a package with some special herbs. Tell Clyde that you want to say goodbye and fix him some tomato dumplings. Prick your finger, and then mix the herbs and blood with the dumplings. Make sure that you only give him the dumplings, and he will be yours forever.

Betts.

"Mary tried to warn me. She knew that I was up to something, so did Mama. They tried to tell me to let Clyde go, but I loved him too much. I did just what Betts said to do, and Clyde became different. He loved me and hated me at the same time. I didn't understand what I had done. Then, he wanted to get married right away. Mama and Daddy tried to tell us not to rush, but we didn't care. I was so happy when he loved me that I didn't think about when he hated me. We got married two weeks later. It was three weeks after the attack. Two months later, I knew that I was pregnant. I thought it was too soon for it to be Clyde's baby."

She blinked, stopped talking, and turned to me. I sat with a look of horror at what she had revealed to me. She smiled an evil smile.

"I tried to get rid of you, but I couldn't. You came a little late, so I knew then that you were Clyde's. But Clyde took one look at you and thought different. He believed that you weren't his. I tried to change his mind so many times, but I gave up a long time ago trying to convince him. He's forgiven me for what happened, and I'm happy with that. Everyday that you take a breath, is a day that hurts my marriage. You're just a leftover from a very bad thing that we want to forget."

She cocked her head to the side and narrowed her eyes.

"You know, sending you to Charlotte and Mary was the best thing that we could do for you, but you just kept coming back."

She shook her head chuckling to herself and got up from the settee. She studied my devastated face.

"Maybe one day I'll be able to look at you without disgust, but not today."

I looked at her as she smiled, fluffed her dark curls, and left the sunroom with her head held high. I wiped my tears and chided myself. I had opened a Pandora's box that afternoon. I prayed that "hope" for me and my parents was still in it.

9

After I dried my tears and straightened myself up, I rejoined the family in the front room. I realized that only a half hour had passed while Mama and I had been in the sunroom. I glanced in her direction to see her giving me a look filled with malicious glee. I frowned at her and sat beside Aunt Charlotte on the divan next to the window. I saw Mark and William playing with the wooden cars that Grandpa Ed had whittled for them. They were making motor noises with their mouths. I smiled at their carefree fun.

"Well, my dear, where have you been?"

Aunt Charlotte patted my knee and sipped her tea.

"I went for a walk to make a little room for some dessert," I replied looking straight at Mama.

She dipped her head with a sneer.

Grandpa Ed chuckled and dug his fork into his dessert plate.

"Well, I guess, I'll take me a walk after this here plate is empty."

Everyone laughed except Mama and Daddy. Mama narrowed her eyes at the dessert cart.

"Where are my dishes? I thought I told that simpleton woman to put my corn pudding and pumpkin pie on that tray. Mama, doesn't your help know how to follow orders?"

Mama threw an innocent look at Big Mama and stirred her freshly poured tea.

"Tess, I know that you haven't been around polite company in a while, but you will act like you have been in my house, you hear?"

Big Mama Chandra slowly placed her teacup on the coffee table beside her before turning her cloudy gaze on Mama.

Mama spluttered and coughed on the sip of tea that she had taken before Big Mama Chandra's dressing down. Aunt Charlotte and Aunt Mary hid their smiles by taking sips of their own tea.

It was unfortunate that Hope walked into the room at that moment.

"Ms. Chandra, I'm gonna be in my room writin' a letta to my boy. Do y'all need anythin' more?"

"Yes, you lazy cow, I need you to bring my corn pudding and pumpkin pie out here. Now! And when I tell you to do something, you better do it!"

Everyone turned in shock at Mama as she yelled at Hope. Big Mama opened her mouth to speak, but Hope beat her to it.

"Excuse me, ma'am. I work for Ms. Chandra and Mr. Ed, sometimes for Miss Mary, Ms. Charlotte, and Ms. Victoria. I don't work for you or yor' rott'n husband who pinched my bottom when y'all got heah. Getcha own house right a'for ya try ta tell me somethin'!"

Then, everyone turned to stare in shock at Daddy as Hope walked off in a huff. Mama opened her mouth and closed it. Then she opened it and closed it again.

"Oh, Tess, stop that. You look like a fish out of water. You know that Clyde has a roaming eyes," Aunt Mary said and frowned at Daddy.

"Mary, you shut your mouth. That witch lied to make me look bad. Clyde loves me and only me."

Mama patted Daddy's knee and sat back on the divan opposite Aunt Charlotte and me.

She rolled her eyes at Mark and William when they kept making their loud motor noises.

"Oh, Tess, nobody has to make you look bad. You do that all on your own."

Grandpa Ed sat his plate on the table with a clang as he delivered those hot words.

"Tess, I think you should gather your things and leave. This is supposed to be a day of thanksgiving and family, but right now, I'll be thankful for you and Clyde to leave," Big Mama said with a fierce frown in Mama's direction.

"Fine, we'll go to Mr. Paul and Betts. They're more like a mama and daddy than y'all are."

Mama patted Daddy's knee again before sending a mean glare at Grandpa Ed and Big Mama Chandra.

"Tess! How could you say such a thing to Mama and Daddy? Are you that far gone?"

Aunt Charlotte fussed and sat up looking ready to do battle.

"Oh shut up, Charlotte! You make me so sick with all your high and mighty airs. We're leaving, so get off your soapbox."

Mama stood up so quickly her teacup and saucer hit the floor.

"Shut up that racket! Can't you hear grown folks talking?" Daddy shouted and stood up over my boys.

For a moment, there was silence. Then, when I opened my mouth to give Daddy what for, William looked up at Daddy with an evil grin before making an even louder "vroom, vroom" sound. Daddy narrowed his eyes at William, and before anyone could move, he snatched William from the floor and began spanking him. I screamed and ran forward as did Aunt Mary and Aunt Charlotte.

"ENOUGH!" Grandpa Ed roared.

He pushed Clyde away from my screaming son and picked him up. He handed William to me when I reached for him. I grabbed Mark's hand and moved toward the door. I turned to berate Daddy for his crude actions when I saw Grandpa Ed slap Mama and grab Daddy by the collar.

"For the rest of your days, Clyde, don't you ever lay a single finger on my great-grandchildren. Now, take you miserable hide out of my house, and don't forget this disrespectful wife of yours either."

Grandpa Ed let go of Daddy and gave him a little push toward the door. I met Mama's eyes, and I almost felt pity for her until she looked at me with such dislike that I stepped back out of their way. I bumped into something and turned to see Uncle P and David in the doorway with grim looks on their faces.

"Well, looks like we came at a bad time," David said.

He gave the boys and me a puzzled glance before sending a fierce frown Mama and Daddy's way.

"David! P! It's good to have y'all back! Let's get y'all a plate fixed, and we can talk."

Grandpa Ed rubbed his hands in excitement.

"Now, Ed, let them settle in before you start talking about the homestead," Big Mama fussed lightly.

Daddy looked at David and Uncle P with hate and dislike before sharing a glance with Mama.

"So, we see blood ain't thicker than water over here. Let's go, Tess."

Mama nodded her head and threw me another malicious glance.

Mama snatched her dishes out of Ms. Sadie's hands when she tried to hand them to her while she put on her coat. Then, without saying goodbye or looking back, Mama and Daddy got in their old raggedy Ford truck and left. I breathed a sigh of relief as the tension in the room left with my parents.

"Miz Victoria! It'z so good ta see ya! And you brung us some lil' mites too!" Uncle P laughed and grabbed me up in big hug.

"It's good to see you too, Uncle P. This is Mark and William," I grinned as I introduced my sons.

Mark cocked his head in his usual assessing way before holding his hands out to Uncle P. Uncle P smiled down at him and picked him up in his arms. Mark smiled back and hugged Uncle P's neck. I glanced at David and saw he looked confused. I shrugged my shoulders when I saw the question in his eyes and patted William on the back as he hiccupped on my shoulder.

"Well, it's good to see everyone. Aunt Addy sends her love. Uncle P and I are a tad bit hungry and tired from that bus ride, though," said David.

Grandpa Ed laughed and gave David a thump on the back that almost knocked him down.

"I couldn't have said it better myself. You know, I think I have a little more room for some of Chandra's chocolate chess pie."

Grandpa Ed put his arm around David's shoulders and nodded at Uncle P. They turned and headed down the hallway when Mark leaned over Uncle P's arm and said, "I'll be fine, Mama, please take care of Willie until I get back."

Tears pooled into my eyes, but I smiled at my little blessing and nodded. Satisfied, Mark looked up at Uncle P and began telling him all about his new racecar.

"Victoria, maybe you should go lie down with William and have a nap," Aunt Charlotte said from beside me.

"Yes ma'am," I replied and almost ran down the hallway to get to my room.

I walked through the open door of our room and laid a limp William down into his crib. He smiled up at me before turning on his side to sleep. I stood there humming until I knew that he slept soundly. I looked down at his silky dark hair and smooth chocolate skin and felt my heart swell. I knew then that I would kill my daddy if he laid another hand on my son. I sighed and turned away to lie down when the weariness hit me. I told myself that would just lie down for a while. My body had other plans, and I slipped into the waiting darkness.

"Victoria, wake up."

I opened my eyes to see Aunt Mary sitting beside me on the bed. I smiled at her and sat up in the bed with a yawn.

"I'm sorry, Aunt Mary. I just felt so tired after all of the commotion this morning. Is it very late?

Aunt Mary leaned forward and gave me a tight hug. Surprised, I hesitated before hugging her back. Then, I laughed lightly and returned her hug. When she pulled back, I saw the serious look on her face, and I became afraid. I glanced at the crib to see William still asleep. Then, I remembered Mark.

"What is it, Aunt Mary? Is it Mark? Please tell me."

I moved to get out off the bed, but she stayed me with her hand.

"No, Victoria, Mark is fine. I had a vision, and I need to talk to you."

Puzzled at her solemn behavior, I sat back and nodded. My heart started a slow thumping because I knew that she was going to tell me something bad.

"Victoria, it's time for you to return to Harlan. I know that you have a troubled marriage, but you know that it's the price of your decision. In order to break the line that you have crossed, you have to go home."

She paused and caressed my face. I felt the tears building because I did not want to go back to the base house.

"Aunt Mary, you don't know what it's like with Harlan. Why are you telling me this?"

My anguish echoed through my words.

Aunt Mary grasped my hands and looked me straight in the eye.

"Victoria, if you don't return, your life will be nothing but suffering. You have a choice to make soon, and Harlan is a part of that choice."

I turned from her and took my hands from hers. I didn't want to leave. My chest hurt as my mind wandered to Harlan's abuse of me and my sons. I felt the darkness rising, and I closed my eyes to embrace it.

"Victoria! No! You must stop letting the dark line comfort you!"

My eyes popped open, and I turned my head to stare at Aunt Mary.

"Why? Is it so bad to let it give me strength? I pray and pray and pray, but I still get no peace, no joy. Sometimes, I feel that God doesn't even hear me anymore."

Aunt Mary leaned forward and hugged me. I tried to break away, but she held me tighter. I relaxed and accepted her affection. I felt her nod when she released me.

"Victoria, listen to me. The more that you let the darkness in, the more it steals a piece of your soul. Do you not shy away from the brightness of light now? When you accepted Jesus, you accepted the light of all things good. You will miss your blessings if you turn from Him now. Yes, there are blessings in store for you and your children, but you won't receive them if you succumb to the darkness. Learn to fight it, endure the pain and suffering, and find your strength in that."

Aunt Mary lifted her white silk wrapped right hand and rubbed my forehead. I frowned because I hadn't even noticed that she had wrapped it while she spoke to me. She closed her eyes, and I saw her lips moving in prayer. I closed my eyes and allowed her to minister to my soul.

When she completed her actions, Aunt Mary took a small vial from her dress pocket. She dabbed a drop onto her finger then smeared it across my forehead. I shivered as the oil touched my skin. It went from cold to hot in a few moments. I felt a little dizzy when she pulled her hand away. Aunt Mary's face became fuzzy as I laid back down and fell into a deep dreamless sleep.

"Did you tell her, Mary?"

I heard Aunt Charlotte ask in the distance.

"Yes, Charlotte, I have told her what she needed to know. I have placed a blessing on her to get her through returning to Harlan. It is battling the darkness that has been growing inside her." Aunt Mary sighed.

"I know that you don't want her to leave us, but she has to so that she can break the bond of Betts' voodoo."

"Alright, Mary, I trust your discernment. It's just that she is the daughter of my heart, and I want her to be happy. She has been through so much pain and heartache." Aunt Charlotte's voice broke.

I felt Aunt Mary move from the bed and make soothing noises to Aunt Charlotte. I knew that Aunt Mary was comforting Aunt Charlotte as she always did when Aunt Charlotte was upset. I tried to wake to tell Aunt Charlotte that I'd be fine and not to cry, but I didn't know myself if that was true.

The next afternoon when all the family lounged in the front room, I announced to the family that it was time that Mark, William, and I went home. Everyone was surprised except Aunt Charlotte, Aunt Mary, and Big Mama Chandra. Grandpa Ed protested that the boys were just getting to know how to tend the homestead. Hope and Ms. Sadie argued that I should stay through winter, but I stayed firm in my decision. Mark frowned at me and ran to stand by Grandpa Ed. William looked confused and popped his thumb in his mouth. I looked at my sons and knew that I made the right decision. I wanted to go back to Harlan if it would help to release us from our misery. Tears came to my eyes when I saw the reactions of my family. Aunt Charlotte saw them and came to stand beside me.

"Alright, alright. I think it's hard enough for Victoria to leave us, but Harlan is her husband. She cannot forsake the vow that she made to him."

Aunt Charlotte looked at each face in the front room as she spoke. Grandpa Ed, Hope, Ms. Sadie, and Mark all looked guilty before shifting their eyes away from hers.

"Now, I'm going to go with her and help her settle into the house. P says that the weather will be good for the next few days, so we'll go back on Sunday."

She turned to me and put her arm around me.

"Is that day fine with you, my sweet?"

She gave me a squeeze, and I smiled back and nodded unable to speak.

"Well, that settles it. Mama, I'm going to need some of your special tea. My leg has been bothering me lately. The doctors might have helped it to hurt more with that last surgery to stop my limp."

Aunt Charlotte made a face, and everyone relaxed and laughed.

"Why, I just made some this morning in case your Pa's elbow started bothering him from lifting that fork to his mouth so many times yesterday," Big Mama harrumphed.

Everyone laughed again because Grandpa Ed rubbed his elbow and waggled his eyebrows. I laughed too, but I wasn't really in the mood. I looked outside and felt the need to be out there.

"I think that I'm going to take a walk around the land. It's too nice of a day to be outside," I said trying to sound cheerful.

"Yay! I want to go too, Mama," Mark said and ran toward the coat rack.

"Me too, Mama," William said following Mark.

"Well, do you want me to go with you, my dear? We could take the field truck to the back twenty and walk the land from there."

Grandpa Ed smiled as the boys agreed jumping up and down.

"Thank you, Grandpa Ed, but I think that we'll just walk from here? We won't go too far."

I smiled and walked over to give him a hug. He hugged me back and whispered in my ear.

"This homestead will always be here for you. The root of family is love."

I nodded and stepped back. He gave me one of his special smiles, and tears gathered in my eyes. I nodded again before turning to grab my coat to join my boys at the door.

I opened the door, and the boys ran outside.

"Don't stay out there too long, lil' mirror. Remember it gets dark faster now."

I turned around surprised at her words. I felt strange for a moment because Big Mama Chandra hadn't called me her lil' mirror in a long time. I swallowed the lump in my throat, said a quick "yes ma'am", and followed my boys outside.

My boys and I walked through the cornfield at the edge of the yard. I let them run ahead of me so that I could think about Aunt Mary's vision. I remember when I was a child how she would tell me that one day, I would have a "special choice" to make. Well, I had been making choices all this time--most of them bad. What was this special choice? Had it already come and gone? How will I know it? Why was Harlan a part of it? I shook my head as I racked my mind for answers. Aunt Mary also told me that my child would "break the line". Which child was it? Mark? He was a special little boy, but that didn't mean that it was him. Was it William? William was special too but not like Mark. Ugh! Why, why, why? A headache began building strength as I sought answers to questions that didn't have any.

"Mama! Mama! Look what I found!"

I looked up to see Mark holding something shiny. I hurried forward to see his discovery. It was a silver dollar. I laughed as he jumped up and down.

"I'm rich! I'm rich! Now, I can buy you a big house here with Grandpa Ed, and we can stay forever!"

I felt a huge swell of love and pride for his generosity and selflessness. I looked into his loving face and saw mine reflected in his features. His innocent face was just a shade darker than mine, and his eyes a golden brown that twinkled with enthusiasm. My heart broke knowing that I had to crush his feelings.

"Mark, it's a wonderful thing that you have found, but honey, it's not enough to buy a house. We also need to ask Grandpa Ed if this money belongs to anyone. That is the honest thing to do, okay? If no one comes for it by Sunday, you can keep it. Then, when we get home, I'll take you to the store so that you can buy you something. Mark, we have to go back home on Sunday—we have to." I pulled him to me and hugged him as his bottom lip began to quiver.

"Why do we have to go back, Mama? Daddy is mean to us. I don't want to go back. Don't you like it here with Grandpa Ed and Big Mama? I know that they like us here," he sobbed on my shoulder.

Before I could answer Mark, I saw William creeping closer out of the corner of my eye. He held something in his hand too. My eyes widened when I saw what it was, and I yanked away from Mark.

"William! Where did you get that kitten?"

I moved toward him slowly because the tiny orange kitten looked limp in his hand.

"Ober dere," he mumbled and held out his hand.

I drew back horrified when I saw that the kitten's neck was at a crooked angle. Mark gasped when he took a step forward and saw it too.

"William, was it like this when you found it?"

I held my breath and waited for an answer.

"No, Mama, he moobed a lot."

He frowned and shook the kitten.

"No! Stop! Put it down!"

William looked like he was going to cry at my raised voice, but his face changed and he shook his head at me. He looked just like Harlan at his meanest.

"No! I want it!"

William gave me another vicious glance before running off with the dead kitten in his hand.

"No! Willie! Come back!"

Mark threw me a helpless look before taking off after William.

I ran after them and quickly caught up with them when William stumped over a cornstalk. I tried not to gag at the thought of that poor kitten's body being abused more when William landed on it.

I grabbed William by the arms and yanked him off the ground. Mark stood by me panting from the chase. I didn't want him to see what I was about to do.

"Mark, I want you to see if you can find the other kittens. Don't go to far, okay?"

He looked from me to William, and I could see the indecision on his face. He looked like he was going to protest my demands, but he nodded and ran back the way we had come.

I turned my attention back to William. He started to whimper in my grasp. I increased the pressure until he dropped the kitten. I looked at its poor mangled body and felt anger rise within me. I grabbed the fallen cornstalk and began whipping my son with it. I ignored his cries because I knew that he needed punishment. All I could think of was the cruelty that he had shown to that poor kitten.

"Mama! Please stop! You're being just like Daddy!"

I heard Mark cry out and threw himself in front of William.

I paused with my hand in the air. I thought about whipping Mark too for yelling at me and stopping William's punishment, but I lowered my hand. I looked down and saw both of my sons crying and whimpering in the face of my rage. I dropped the cornstalk and fell to my knees. I gathered them to me and rocked them back and forth while we all sobbed. When my boys had quieted, I pulled myself together to face them. I held them away from me in a loose embrace and took a deep breath.

"I am sorry for losing my temper, but I am not sorry for giving you a whipping, Willie. I know that you're little, but what you did was wrong—very wrong. You are never ever to take a life that is not yours to take. Do you understand?"

I gave him a stern look in the eye. Willie hiccupped and nodded. I looked at Mark, and he nodded too. Satisfied, I turned toward the end of the cornrow where I saw the field wheelbarrow. I knew that there had to be a hoe somewhere nearby.

"Now, Mark run down to that wheelbarrow and see if there is hoe somewhere. We need to bury this little fella. Did you find the rest of the kittens?"

"Yes, ma'am, there's about four more deep in the cornfield under a pile of stalks. I didn't see the mama. Will she come looking for him?" Mark asked fearfully.

"I would if I were her. We'll leave the rest of the kittens where they are so that she can find them. Now, go on and find the hoe. We'll bury him and say a few words over his little grave, okay?"

Mark nodded and ran off to do as I bid. I glanced at Willie and saw him narrow his eyes at Mark. I didn't understand what was wrong with him, but I knew sooner or later, I'd find out.

After we buried the kitten, I asked God to forgive Willie for what he did and to receive the kitten's soul in Heaven. Mark said a quiet "Amen" while Willie stayed silent. I shook my head thinking that he was probably thinking about God's forgiveness. At least, that's what I told myself.

10

I decided to finish our walk around the land before night fell. I enticed the boys into a race across the empty wheat fields to lighten our moods. They jumped up and down excited at racing their mother. When I yelled go, they took off while I jogged behind them. We had almost crossed the wheat fields when I saw Uncle P and David bumping down the dirt track in the field truck. They stopped beside some bales of hay and got out of the truck.

"Well, if it ain't, Miz Victoria, and the lil' mites," Uncle P said and gave me a big bear hug.

I laughed and re-introduced Uncle P and David to Mark and William who stood watching Uncle P with excitement. Uncle P knelt and reached out his hand to Mark who immediately took it. Uncle P held on to his hand, and Mark watched with wide eyes as Uncle P gave him his special handshake. When Uncle P released Mark's hand, Mark smiled at him before looking at his hand. Willie ran up to Uncle P then and held out his hand. Uncle P took it and frowned as he held on to Willie's hand. I watched closely at the pained look that crossed Uncle P's face. I stepped forward to move Willie away, but Uncle P glanced at me and shook his head. I looked at

David who had a frown on his face as well. Uncle P's face cleared, and he released Willie's hand.

"Well, now, have ya boys played on da bales?"

Uncle P stood up and nodded toward the hay bales.

"Yes sir," Mark said.

Willie just shook his head.

"Les go, den," Uncle P waved his hand and walked toward the bales giving David a pointed look.

Mark looked back at me before grabbing William's hand and following Uncle P.

"They're good lookin' boys, Victoria. Mark looks just like you, and William looks like a handful," David said watching the boys play with Uncle P.

"Thank you, David. They're both a handful sometimes."

I turned and saw that he watched Uncle P and my sons with a frown on his face. I was about to ask him about it when he spoke.

"Uncle P sensed something in your youngest. Is he all right?"

He turned to me with concern on his face. I shook my head not wanting to tell David that I worried about William as well.

He sighed in relief and smiled at me.

"So, someone snatched you up and put the shackles on you, huh?"

David chuckled at his own joke. I felt my face pale at his words. Shackled was a good word for how I felt. David turned and started walking across the field, so he didn't notice my reaction.

"Let's take a walk while your boys are playing, Victoria," David said turning to me with a smile.

I hesitated before joining him. David's pace slowed as he stepped over the plowed field.

"How have you been, Victoria?"

David stopped to pick up a clump of dried wheat. He took out a piece of straw and started chewing on it. I took the time to think of what to say.

"I'm fine. Everything is fine," I said with a shrug and kept walking.

David put his hand on my arm, and I paused and turned around to him.

"Victoria, we've been friends since we were kids. You know that you can tell me anything. I know you too well to know that everything's hunkie dorie. What's wrong?"

I looked at the sincere concern on his face and felt the need to unburden my mind. Tears welled up in my eyes, and I began to tell David my troubles. I told him everything from Harlan's abuse of Mark and me to my frustration of not being able to leave him. David hugged me and allowed my storm of torment until my sobs turned into hiccups. David sighed and pushed me away to arm's length. He sighed again as he brushed a tear from my cheek.

"Victoria, you are a very beautiful woman. You need to find someone who truly cares for you and your sons. This, this, Harlan, he needs a swift kick in the pants for what he has done. I wish I knew where to find him. Me and Uncle P would enjoy pounding him into the ground."

David fisted his hand and pounded it into the other as if it were Harlan. I knew what he said was true, but there was nothing that anyone could do about it.

"David, thank you for that. I know you're right, but Harlan is my husband and the father of my children. Nothing can change that right now. Anyway, I know that no other man would accept me and my boys, so there's no need for wishful thinking. By the way, how have you been doing?"

I didn't want to talk about me anymore. I already felt like a broken record. I shook off my despair to concentrate on David.

After he stopped looking at me with doubt on his face, David began smiling.

"Well, I got myself a wife around the time that you went to Littleton. Her name is Grace, and she is a beautiful handful."

David laughed, and I saw the true joy on his face. I squashed the twinge of jealousy that crossed my mind.

"She keeps me in line and on my toes. I love her something fierce. I can never thank her enough for the gift of my son, Eddie. I named him after your Grandpa Ed. He's eight now and just a mite smaller than your oldest boy. Real smart too. He asks a lot of questions and drives me and his mama up the wall, but he's a good boy. It made us a little nervous when they integrated the schools here, so I was more than happy to go with your Uncle Andrew to Colorado to help him on his ranch. The schools there aren't so bad with Whites and Blacks living together on the ranches."

David paused looking to the west as if he could see his family. Again, I felt that twinge of jealousy.

"It wasn't long after we moved to Colorado that Aunt Addy got sick. Uncle P heard about a healing hot spring not too far away from Andrew's ranch. He brought Aunt Addy to Colorado, and she's a little better now."

My heart hurt for Aunt Addy's illness. She had been so good to me when I was a girl. I shook away the nostalgia and focused on what David was saying.

"Uncle P and I came for a spell because your Grandpa Ed sent us a letter that the Adams' new son-in-law, Ray, has been moving the fence line. Uncle P and Grace made all the arrangements to get us here on the first thing smokin'. We know how dirty the Adams are. They think all Black people should be workers and never the bosses. Your Grandpa Ed has done too much for our family for us to forget. We owe him a debt that can never be repaid, so we came to help."

David turned and glared in the direction of the Adams' land. I felt guilty because I hadn't even known that Grandpa Ed had problems with the Adams.

At that moment, Uncle P brought the boys back over to me. I noticed that he was very careful not to touch William.

"Well, Miz Victoria, here's ya boys, all tuckered out."

I smiled and thanked him. He held out his arms, and I walked into his embrace. I felt the familiar warmth that was part of Uncle P flowing from him into me.

"Hang on ta God, Miz Victoria. Hang on. He'll always be there when ya call 'im," he whispered in my ear.

I swallowed the tears and nodded before taking my boys' hands to walk them back to the house.

On Sunday morning, after tearful goodbyes and promises to keep in touch, Aunt Charlotte packed the boys and I into her car and took us back to Ft. Green. She kept up a steady stream of chatter until she saw that I wasn't participating. We rode in silence for a long while until Aunt Charlotte stopped at a diner outside of Dallas for a late lunch.

"Okay, y'all, let's have a quick bite since we already ate the food in the box that Ms. Sadie packed," she said pulling into a parking spot.

I nodded and got out of the car. I opened the back door for the boys. They ran around the car to Aunt Charlotte who took their hands and walked into the diner. My back and legs ached, so I followed a little slower. I opened the door to drop my jaw in shock.

"You go on round back, girl. We serve your kind at the back door. You're not allowed to sit in here with these good White folks. Now, take them pickaninnies on to the back to get something to eat. You're standing in that White lady's way," said a fat White waitress that reminded me of Ms. Sophie.

She wagged her finger in Aunt Charlotte's face.

I saw the other White people stop eating to gawk at Aunt Charlotte as her spine straightened. In shock, I could only stand there as she let the White woman have it.

"How dare you speak to me that way? This is 1968, and there is no segregation any longer. Is this town so small that you haven't heard that? Oh well, my daughter, grandsons, and I will find a seat on our own, thank you. I will have a coffee, the children will have vanilla malts, and my daughter will have a Coca Cola."

With those words, Aunt Charlotte sailed past the open mouthed waitress to sit in a booth right in the middle of the diner. I saw the waitress give the White man behind the counter a nod and knew there was about to be trouble. Forgetting my aches and pains, I walked quickly to the booth were Aunt Charlotte sat and catching her eye, nodded toward the White man on the phone.

"Aunt Charlotte, let's go, please. Now is not the time to make a stand. Think of my boys if something happens to us here. Please, let's just go."

I didn't notice that the White waitress had followed me to the table.

"Daughter, huh? I'll bet you got some poor piece of White trash to knock you up."

She turned to me and sneered.

"So, you're one of them White Blacks that I heard about. Humph, I guess you think that you're better than us like this uppity stupid bitch sitting there. And those are your brats?"

She snarled and shoved her fat body closer to me. I saw that she had a steak knife in her hand, and I stepped back. She held it up and started waving it at us.

"Now, if y'all don't want to get cut up, y'all better get the hell out of here."

I refused to turn my back on her, so I stepped back until I could feel Mark's shoulder. William started to whine. I heard Aunt Charlotte gasp and felt her get out of the booth. I took a quick glance around the diner and saw that no one got up to stop the waitress.

"You call me stupid, but you're the stupid one. You can be arrested for hurting us. I should call the police, but I won't. This place isn't worthy of my money. Come on, Victoria, let's leave this dump."

I saw Aunt Charlotte grab William and Mark's hands and began to leave the diner.

I kept my eyes on the White woman and the White man behind the counter while I backed up toward the door. I almost backed into Aunt Charlotte when she paused and turned to face the diner.

"Here's some information for you poor uneducated folks. The word "stupid" implies that I am not intelligent, and the word "bitch" suggests that I am a female dog. Well, if the phrase applies to anyone, it is that woman there. For, I haven't been attacked by an unintelligent female dog until today. To stand and do nothing when a crime is being committed is to become a part of the crime itself. Y'all have a nice day."

Aunt Charlotte gave everyone a big smile before narrowing her eyes at the red-faced waitress. She motioned for me to open the door, and we left. I glanced back to see several people getting up from half-eaten plates of food and smiled when I saw the waitress spluttering and trying to explain herself. Aunt Charlotte honked her horn, and I hurried to get into the car.

Further down the road, we found a more welcoming drive-in to get food. It smelled and looked a lot better than what I had seen on the plates of that diner. I glanced at Aunt Charlotte to see her still fuming over the actions of the White waitress. I glanced back at the boys to make sure that they were busy with their food before broaching the issue with Aunt Charlotte.

"Aunt Charlotte, I know that you're upset by what happened at that nasty place, but you of all people know that the fight for Black people's rights didn't end with the Civil Rights Movement. I know that it's a struggle to bring about the changes even at Ft. Green."

Aunt Charlotte gave me a sad smile and nodded. My heart hurt for her.

"Victoria, don't you think that I know that. Why do you think that I spend so much time away from my own home? I am a wealthy Black woman living in a White neighborhood. My fight began long before the Civil Rights Movement. I married your Uncle Jake in California in secret because Whites and Blacks weren't supposed to marry back then. I was blessed that he didn't have any family left, or I wouldn't have received all of his money. As it was, the lawyer that made his Will tried to denounce our marriage to keep my husband's money. I vowed then that no one, and I mean no one, would make the color of my skin an issue."

She paused and rubbed my arm.

"When your mother and father became embarrassed to have you with them, I came forward to take you. I looked at your beautiful face and didn't see a Black baby with White features, I saw a baby that needed love and acceptance. I knew that you would be able to bridge gaps that I could not. That's what I need you to do, Victoria. I need you not to be afraid to help close those gaps. It can be done. The world is a swirl of color, and we need to stop separating them."

Aunt Charlotte squeezed my arm before starting the car to get back on the road.

I sat and thought about what she said. I felt overwhelmed at her request. How could I make such changes in the world? I couldn't even make the right choices for myself.

We arrived at Fort Green right before the sun set. Aunt Charlotte had insisted on stopping at the local grocer and buying enough food to last a month. I protested, but she remained stubborn.

"You haven't been home in a year, Victoria. Harlan could be out in the field, and you could walk into a house with bare cabinets. So, stop complaining about how I spend my money," she fussed.

I hushed up and let her buy the groceries and special treats for the boys.

I directed Aunt Charlotte to the base house and felt her surprise.

"This is it? Why, it's tinier than the garden shed behind my house in Dallas!"

I felt my face began to burn in embarrassment because the house was small. I got out of the car and ran to the door fumbling with the keys.

"Victoria, I'm sorry. I guess I just expected something else," Aunt Charlotte said from behind me.

I nodded unable to speak around the lump in my throat.

"Do you mind if I stay the night? I don't think that I can make the drive back to Dallas tonight."

I knew that she asked to spend the night to make me feel better, but it only made me tense up more thinking of Harlan's reaction if he was home. I didn't want to respond until I found out if Harlan was home. I finally got the key in the lock and turned the knob. I pushed the door open to feel a cold blast of air. I shivered and reached for the light switch.

"My God! It looks as if no one has been here since the summer!"

Aunt Charlotte moved past me into the tiny front room. She made a complete circle before turning to me with a frown.

"Victoria, where is your husband?"

I couldn't answer her because shock kept me rooted in the doorway. I told myself that maybe he left the windows open to air the house out for us, but the house smelled and looked like no one had been there for a while. I walked on leaden feet and closed all of the windows in the house before turning on the furnace. My shock must have shown on my face because Aunt Charlotte directed Mark and William while they unpacked the car.

I sat on the sofa and stared at the blank television screen. I couldn't believe that Harlan had practically abandoned the house leaving the windows open. All of our possessions were in the house. What if someone had cut the screens and stolen everything? I became furious. We may not have much, but we treasured what we had. At least, the boys and I did. How dare he? I wrapped my arms around my stomach and began rocking back and forth.

"Here, drink this. I brought some of Mama's tea back with me. It's not for shock, but it'll help you. The boys are in their room playing."

Aunt Charlotte pried one of my hands away from my body and placed the hot mug of tea in it. I took a sip and closed my eyes at the smell. It made me want to run back to Carson, to my loving family. I took another sip and felt a little better. I eyed Aunt Charlotte over the rim.

"Aunt Charlotte, I can't thank you enough. I'm glad that you're here," I said giving her a hug.

Aunt Charlotte laughed and got up from the sofa.

"Now, I think I'll fry us up some of that summer sausage that we got at the store and make some sandwiches."

I put the mug on the coffee table and shook my head.

"Aunt Charlotte, I'm fine now. You go ahead and sit down. You've been driving all day. I'll make the sandwiches."

Aunt Charlotte chuckled.

"Yes ma'am. I'll just go visit with my grandsons."

I smiled and made my way into the kitchen.

After making up the sofa for Aunt Charlotte and bidding her goodnight, I checked on the boys before seeking my bed. I felt an ache deep in my bones that gave me a slight limp. I frowned at the soreness and went into the bathroom to find some aspirin. I grimaced as I opened the squeaky medicine cabinet hoping that the noise hadn't woken anyone. Something dropped into the sink, but I ignored it because the pain began to increase. I found the aspirin, popped two in my mouth, and cupped my hand under the faucet to get some water to swallow the pills.

I gasped and backed away from the sink. The aspirin went down dry, and I started to choke. I swallowed again, and they struggled down my throat. I crept forward and stared into the sink. A pair of black women's panties sat under the faucet.

My breathing became harsh in the silence of the tiny bathroom. I turned around and opened the towel cabinet. There was another pair! I ripped the towels out of the cabinet to find more, but there was only a large piece of paper lying at the bottom of the cabinet. I picked it up and almost dropped it in my shock.

TAHOMA   COUNTY   CERTIFICATE   OF MATRIMONY
IN THE COUNTY OF TAHOMA

MARRIAGE RITES WERE SPOKEN BETWEEN
SHIRLEY HORN AND HARLAN SAMS
ON THIS DAY, OCTOBER 21, 1968

My breath whooshed out of my body, but I continued to read the marriage certificate for Shirley and Harlan. I couldn't believe my eyes! Harlan had married Shirley while he was still married to me! I shook my head and dropped the certificate to the floor. I felt my body start shivering as a cold numbness came over me. How dare he violate our vows? I fisted my hands and hit the wall uncaring that Aunt Charlotte and the boys were asleep.

"Victoria! What is it? What's happening?" Aunt Charlotte whispered loudly from the hallway.

I felt laughter bubble up and spill out of my lips. What's happening? Ha! I laughed louder and louder until I fell to the bedroom floor bent over in my madness. Betts had trapped me good with her lies. I laughed harder at my foolishness.

"Victoria! I'm coming in!"

"Yes, please come in, Aunt Charlotte. Come in and witness my fall into insanity. You know, I think I'll take a walk," I said trying to catch my breath.

I heard the door open, and I heard Aunt Charlotte gasp. She walked to me and tried to help me up from the floor. I shook her off and narrowed my eyes at her.

"I want to stay here on the floor so that Harlan can keep walking all over me. Here I am turning down a wonderful man while Harlan runs off with his whore!"

Tears streamed from my eyes as more laughter shook my body.

Slap!

I felt the sting of Aunt Charlotte's hand on my cheek. I stopped laughing and looked at her in surprise. Aunt Charlotte had never slapped me in the face.

"Now that you've stopped that awful laughing, tell me what's happened to put you in such a state."

Still looking at her in surprise, I got up and picked up the certificate from the bathroom floor. I handed it to her and watched as Aunt Charlotte's eyes widened.

"Oh my God, he didn't? Well, I guess he did because it's right here in my hand. I don't blame your crazy spell. This is madness," Aunt Charlotte whispered.

I stood there and waited—for what I didn't know. I felt a moment of dizziness and closed my eyes.

I saw Harlan and Shirley standing in front of a White man in a black robe. He held a Bible in his hands. When he closed the Bible, he motioned to Harlan who took Shirley in his arms and kissed her.

My eyes popped open from the vision. I smothered my surprise at my "gift" returning to give me a glimpse of what happened.

"Are you okay, Victoria? I need to know that you won't fall into that crazy spell because I have a solution for some of your troubles with Harlan. It may not be too right, but it might be helpful."

I nodded and turned my attention to what Aunt Charlotte had to say. I could concentrate on what the return of my "gift" meant later.

"Okay, what Harlan has done is a crime. You now have proof of that crime. I'll take the certificate back with me so that Harlan can't destroy it. This may be your chance to make your situation better. Use his crime as a bargaining chip and make your demands. Demand that he leave Shirley alone. Make him respect you, and if he doesn't, threaten to expose him for the bigamist that he is."

I could feel my mouth dropping at Aunt Charlotte's advice. My aunt had a devious mind, and I hadn't even known it. Her plan was genius. I felt myself nodding in agreement.

Aunt Charlotte smiled and patted me on the shoulder.

"Now, I need to get some sleep if I'm going to leave early in the morning. Your Aunt Mary is supposed to be coming into Dallas on the bus tomorrow, and I'm supposed to be there early. You know your Aunt Mary, she doesn't like to be late."

Aunt Charlotte kissed me goodnight and left me planning for when Harlan finally came home.

11

The next morning, Harlan unlocked the door to stare at us in surprise. Aunt Charlotte and the boys were sitting at the table eating while I made my plate. Aunt Charlotte shot me a mischievous look before waving her fork at Harlan.

"Well, hello there, Harlan. How are you doing? Can you shut the door? It's still getting warm in here from all that cold. Boys, wipe your mouths and greet your father."

Mark glanced at me and wiped his mouth.

"Hi, Daddy," he whispered.

"Daddee!"

William threw his napkin in his plate and held out his arms to Harlan.

Harlan recovered from his surprise and narrowed his eyes at Aunt Charlotte.

"Charlotte, this is quite the surprise. What are you doing in my house?"

I gasped at his rudeness, but Aunt Charlotte chuckled.

"Well, I brought your wife and children home last night and stayed because it was so late. I'll be leaving right after breakfast," Aunt Charlotte explained.

Harlan came closer to the table and glared at me.

"I hope that you didn't put all this on credit at the store. We ain't rich, and you can't be acting like we are just because Charlotte's here."

I opened my mouth to tell him otherwise, but Aunt Charlotte cleared her throat and stood up from the table a few inches from Harlan.

"Victoria did not buy the groceries, I did. She whined about me doing it, but I wasn't having her come back here to nothing. It turns out that I was right. So, if you want to gripe at someone, here I am."

Harlan stepped back with a frown on his face.

"Fine then. That should be enough to last until I get back from the field."

I sent Harlan a pointed glance, but he ignored me. He walked to William and gave him a hug and a loud kiss. He turned his back on Mark, threw me an angry look, and went into the room slamming the door behind him. Willie turned around and gave Mark a smug look. Mark smiled at Willie and went back to eating. I frowned at Willie until he sat back down.

Aunt Charlotte sighed and shook her head.

"I need to get on the road. On the other hand, I feel that I need to stay for a while after that little interlude."

I understood her concern, but I knew that I needed to confront Harlan on my own. I put my plate of cold food on the counter and walked to her to give her a hug.

"I love you, Aunt Charlotte, and I'm glad that you came. I don't think that it would be a good idea for you stay. I need to change my husband's attitude by myself. Now, don't forget that you have to pick up Aunt Mary," I whispered.

Aunt Charlotte drew back from me and cocked her head.

"How did I raise such a beautiful and intelligent woman? Oh, that's right, because you take after me!"

We both laughed until I heard something thrown at my bedroom door. Aunt Charlotte frowned, and I let out an exasperated breath.

"Well, I'm going to get going. Mark. William. Come give me a hug and some sugar."

Mark and William ran into Aunt Charlotte's waiting arms. She closed her eyes and hugged them tightly before sending them back to the table. I could see the tears shining in her eyes, and I could feel them in mine. She grabbed her purse and small overnight bag then walked to the door. She opened the door and looked back at me. She dropped the bag and came back to give me a hug.

"Don't forget what I said. Make your life better," she whispered and pressed something into my hand.

I nodded, and she stepped back. Aunt Charlotte turned, grabbed her bag, and walked through the door without looking back.

I watched through the tiny front room window as she got in her car and left. I released the breath that I had been holding while I tried not to cry and opened my hand. I laughed out loud at the folded money in my palm. I knew that it was a substantial amount, but I decided to wait until I was alone to count it.

I turned around and saw Mark and William beginning to play with their food. I decided to let them watch cartoons. I needed to clean up the kitchen and pay a visit to my husband, so I turned on the television. As soon as Mark and William saw that cartoons were on, they ran over and sat on the rug in front of the television. I smiled and fussed at their nearness to the small screen.

"Not too close, boys. You'll hurt your eyes. Now, I have to clean up and go talk to your daddy, so behave yourselves."

They both nodded barely paying me attention as they watched the large cartoon dog run after the cat.

I made sure that they were absorbed into the cartoon before I started cleaning up the kitchen. As I scraped the food into the trashcan, I began thinking of what I was going to say to Harlan.

Before long, the dishes were done, and the kitchen cleaned. I took out some pork chops and wiped a few crumbs off the counter. Looking around and seeing that there was nothing left to clean, I took a deep breath and headed to the bedroom.

I heard Harlan talking when I approached the door. I almost put my hand on the knob to open it thinking that he was talking in his sleep again when I heard my name.

"Yeah, she came back yesterday. No, no, no, it looks like she's here to stay. Well, I'm sorry, baby, I can't leave her just now. She's still hurting over the baby dying, and she still thinks we're married. I think she went a little crazy, but as soon as she gets better, I'll bring you back home. I need to be here to work anyway. Aw, don't be mad at me. I told you that everything's going to be all right."

I stood there feeling my anger building listening to Harlan reassure his whore that he had divorced me and that I wouldn't accept it. When he got off the phone, I opened the door. He jumped off the bed in surprise. I almost laughed at his flabbergasted expression…almost.

"So, when did we get divorced? Please let me know so that I can take my children and get away from your viciousness."

I stepped into the room and closed the door. I crossed the room and stood at the end of the bed with my hands on my hips.

Harlan regained his composure and sneered at me.

"Eavesdropping now, Vicky? Well, you know what they say, "Eavesdroppers never hear any good". Did you enjoy my conversation?"

My anger increased at his smug tone. I felt like tearing his face into shreds with my long nails. Instead, I took a deep breath and smiled at him. The smile on my husband's face disappeared.

"Well, let's see. Let me tell you what I know. You just told Shirley that we're divorced which I know we're not. You also told her that you and she will be together soon, which I know you won't. She thinks that I've gone crazy because of Victor's death, which I know I haven't. So to answer your question, yes, I enjoyed your conversation very much."

Harlan shook his head and chuckled. He got up slowly from the bed and came to stand in front of me. He towered over my short frame, but I refused to back away.

"I guess being around your family made you forget who wears the pants in this house. I didn't think that I'd have to teach you a lesson so soon, but it looks like you need it."

Harlan raised his hand, and I laughed in his face.

"Hit me if you want to. I'll be only too happy to send you to jail for a long time. I hear I can get a real divorce for two dollars if you're put behind bars. Now, go ahead. Hit me."

Harlan lowered his hand and frowned at me.

"Jail? What are you talking about, Vicky? No one can put me in jail for punishing my wife."

I laughed at him again. He took a step back and looked at me as if I were a mad woman. Maybe I was. My body felt lighter with each defiant word that I spoke.

"Oh, I know that the law won't do anything about you hitting me or Mark."

I paused and narrowed my eyes at him.

He nodded his head and took a step closer to me. Before he could raise his hand to me, I pushed him hard in the chest. Harlan fell backward onto the floor. I had taken him by surprise with that push, and I decided that I liked him at my feet. He struggled to get up in the small space. I kicked him hard in the groin when he rolled towards me. He hollered and grabbed himself. I felt the violence growing and wanted to do him more harm. I closed my eyes to his thrashing and moaning.

A man with a white lab coat stood in front of me asking questions. He handed me a stack of papers to fill out before walking out of the room.

I opened my eyes and frown in confusion at my vision. I looked down at Harlan writhing on the floor and put my foot on his chest. He tried to throw me off, but I increased the pressure.

"Hush, husband! Now, I want you to listen and listen well. I know that you married Shirley while you're still married to me. That's a crime, you know."

I paused and tapped my finger on my chin. I glanced down and saw that I had his full attention.

"Wasn't there a man in the newspaper for that last year? They put him in jail for a long, long time. Putting you in jail would give me great satisfaction, however, it wouldn't do me any good. You see, in your hatefulness and jealousy, you didn't let me get a job or go to school. In fact, until I do one or both of those things, I'm going to need your money, which you are going to give without complaint. You aren't going to walk around angry and mean anymore. You're going to be a decent husband and a good father to our children."

Harlan tried again to remove my foot from his chest, but I leaned forward adding more of my weight. He grunted and stopped moving. A wave of weariness rushed through me, and I finished my demands.

"Harlan Sams, if you cross me or think about hurting me or the boys in any way, I will turn you in for the bigamist that you are. Try me."

I took my foot off of his chest, and he breathed a sigh of relief. He raised himself to a sitting position at the end of the bed.

When Harlan looked up at me, his face held an expression of grudging respect. He nodded his acceptance and bowed his head. I bowed my head slightly and walked to the door. His next words made me pause with my hand on the knob.

"What about Shirley? What am I supposed to do about her and my children?"

I turned around and narrowed my eyes at him.

"Shirley is now a part of your past. Let her go. As far as your children go, you will take care of them. They didn't ask to have a sorry set of parents like you and that whore mother of theirs. Those children are my children's siblings, and they will grow up having something to do with one another."

I stared at Harlan until he nodded again in agreement. I knew he only agreed to keep himself out of jail, but I nodded back and left to pry my boys away from the television.

A few weeks passed and Harlan stayed on his best behavior. He went to his post everyday, came home, and spent time with the boys. I began to see the man that I thought I had married. My heart began to thaw a little when he played with Mark and William. Mark wasn't as solemn as usual, and I felt less tense when Harlan was home. I refused to think about when Shirley would try to entice Harlan back to her. I just enjoyed the moments that we spent as a family.

One day, the boys and I passed the small chapel at the edge of the large base. I slowed the car because the doors were open, and I cold see the stained glass cross reflecting the sunlight.

"Mama, what's that?" Mark asked sitting up in the backseat.

"It's the chapel, honey."

"Can we stop and go in it? The door is open."

"I guess it's okay. Let me pull the car into a parking place," I said giving in easily.

Something called to me in that chapel, and I wanted to find out what it was.

It was a cold January day, so I made sure the boys' coats and hats were fixed before we climbed out of the car and walked up the steps. I could feel my heart thumping harder the closer that we came to the door. When we stepped inside, I paused to let our eyes adjust to the dim interior. The chapel was beautiful. I saw that someone had recently shined the light oak pews and intricate woodwork in the paneling. There were steps leading up to a carved oak podium behind an altar table at the front of the chapel. There was a stand of lit candles on the right under a painting of a shining cross. The entire chapel was covered in a rich red carpet and smelled like sweet honey. I squeezed the boys' hands and took a step toward the altar.

"Mama, what's that?"

I turned in the direction Mark pointed and saw an upright piano. I dropped my sons' hands and walked to the instrument. My fingers tingled as I reached towards it. I looked around to see if anyone had seen my madness, but no one was in the chapel except my boys and me. I shrugged and sat down on the bench. I could feel my hands shaking as I lifted the lid off the keys. I felt Mark and William move to stand beside me, but I wasn't paying them any attention. I placed my hands to the piano keys and let the music fill my soul.

I began playing one of Aunt Charlotte's favorite songs, "Ode to Joy". While lost in the music, I felt a warmth take over my spirit. I sensed that something had changed within me. The line was broken! It had to be! I laughed out loud as the last notes from the piano faded into silence. I opened my eyes feeling a happiness that I had never felt in my life.

"Mama, why you cry?" William asked touching my tears.

I laughed and kissed his little hand.

"I cry because I'm happy, little one. I'm happy at last."

I stood up and grabbed both of my sons into a tight hug. I chuckled when they squirmed and tried to get away.

"Alright, alright. Let's go home, and I'll tell y'all about music's healing power."

I tickled them both until they laughed, then I got up from the piano to walk out of the chapel. With each step, my heart felt lighter.

Later that day, I collected the mail and found a letter from Aunt Mary. My heart raced because I knew that she had seen me "breaking the line" in the chapel in one of her visions. I waited until the boys were down for their afternoon nap before I tore open the letter to read the good news. I felt light-headed in my excitement until I read her first words.

Victoria,

By the time you read this letter, you will have made the mistake of believing the line is broken. I hate to be the bearer of bad news, but you must understand that you don't have the power to release yourself from this curse. It will be a child born of your body that will break the line. You must have patience, Victoria. A choice will soon be given to you, and you will have to decide whether to take it or miss your chance. Stay in prayer.

We love you and pray blessings on your family.
Love,
Aunt Mary

I covered my mouth on the sob that threatened to escape. I felt crushed by Aunt Mary's letter. She had to be wrong even Big Mama Chandra said that sometimes Aunt Mary's visions could be wrong. I sensed the lightness in my spirit when I sang and played the piano in the chapel. She had to be wrong! I crumpled the letter and threw it in the corner. Aunt Mary was wrong. She had to be, but in my heart, I knew that she wasn't.

Time passed quickly after that day. Harlan was discharged from the army and got a job in construction near the base. We moved to Jackson, the nearest city to his job. We had three more children, twin girls, Leah and Gia, and another son named Grayson. It took Harlan six years to make up his mind about me working. I finally got a job working part time in a factory making clothes for Georgia's, a department store chain in Oklahoma.

After a while, I began to have bouts of sickness like when I was a young girl, but they didn't last long. I didn't tell my doctors about it because it went away with a little aspirin and a hot bath.

Anyway, I didn't have time to dwell on my aches and pains because my children kept me busy, when I wasn't working. It seemed like I was always at the school about William. He got into trouble more than Mark and the twins together. Harlan's job kept him on the road, so I had to handle William's discipline. I tried everything before I figured that only a whipping would work. It didn't.

I kept in touch with my family by letters and by phone. I tried not to let them know how depressed I was about my life.

Whenever Aunt Charlotte called, I let all of the children talk to her first so that she wouldn't be able to talk to me long with the long distance charges. I avoided talking to Aunt Mary because she had lied to me. I felt like I'd never be freed because each child that I gave birth to only bound me to Harlan more. I began to feel anger toward my own children for not saving me from my past mistake.

The day before Grayson's fourth birthday in January, Harlan came home excited because he had gotten a promotion at work.

"This is it, Vicky! It's more money, a truck for me, and a house!"

Harlan grabbed me and started dancing around. I broke loose and stared at him.

"A house? Here is Jackson?"

Harlan rolled his eyes and said, "Haven't you been listening? We're moving to Dallas!"

I began to feel his excitement. Dallas! I would be closer to Aunt Charlotte! I took the arm that he held out and began dancing a jig with him. Then, it hit me.

"What about the kids' school? I've heard bad things about the schools in Dallas."

Harlan rolled his eyes again and put his hand on my shoulders.

"Vicky, we won't be living in the bad neighborhoods. We're buying the house from the company in the new suburbs. Anyway, we can always send them to private school," Harlan explained with patience.

"Now, smooth that frown away and let's celebrate."

I smiled and tried my best to act happy for his promotion. A sinking feeling settled in my stomach, and I knew that it had to be something bad.

Harlan and I decided to wait until the children got out of school for the summer before packing and moving to Dallas. I called Aunt Charlotte and gave her the news. She was ecstatic and made plans to come over as soon as we were settled. I laughed at her excitement and hung up the phone.

I still felt the butterflies in my stomach, so the next day, I went to the pharmacy to get something to get rid of them. It was a beautiful day, so I parked the car on the town square and walked over to the pharmacy. I bought some bubbling tablets that I could put in water to help my stomach. As I left the store, I looked up and saw a Baptist church across the street. I felt my feet moving toward it before I knew it. I opened the door and breathed a sigh of relief at the cool interior. When my eyes had adjusted to the dim light, I looked around and saw that the church looked a little shabby. The pews were crooked, the carpet was well worn, and water stains showed throughout the paneling. I crept forward to the first pew and sat my weary body down.

I saw something move out of the corner of my right eye. When I turned my head, there was nothing there but a beautiful grand piano. I gasped and almost ran to it. I plopped down on the bench and ran my hands lovingly over the keys. Before I knew it, I felt my fingers playing the music and heard myself singing, "Amazing Grace". It felt so good to feel the music wind its way through my spirit.

When I finished playing, I heard someone clapping. Embarrassed to be caught playing without asking, I stood up quickly.

"No, no, don't be afraid. I was in the office when I heard your beautiful voice. You play very well too."

I turned to see a tall Black man standing in the shadows. I squinted my eyes and tried to get a better look. He chuckled and moved forward into the brighter light. I gasped.

"Pastor James?"

"Yes, do I know you, child?"

"Pastor James! It's me, Victoria! You were my pastor in Dallas when I stayed with Aunt Charlotte and Aunt Mary!"

I hurried over to stand in front of him. His faded brown eyes widened in recognition, and he pulled me into a hug.

"Little Sister Victoria. It's good to see you, child. It's been a long time," he said as he loosened his hold to look me in the eye.

"You don't look well. How have you been?"

Pastor James' concern almost made me break down and tell him everything, but I shook my head.

"Oh, I'm fine, just a little tired. How have you been, and what are doing in Jackson?"

Pastor James clicked his tongue and gave me a skeptical glance. Then, he shrugged his shoulders and sat down. He motioned for me to sit down, and I sat down beside him.

"Well, my dear, my son is stationed at Ft. Green. I've been here to be close to him since my wife passed."

"Pastor James, I'm so sorry. Ms. Violet was always very good to me."

Pastor James waved away my condolences.

"There should be no grief in death, Sister Victoria, only joy. Besides, whenever someone plays her piano, I feel her spirit."

I frowned thinking that the loss of his wife had made Pastor James a little insane. Joy in death? Yes, definitely not all there.

"Pastor, I don't understand."

"Victoria, the sorrow that we feel when a loved one passes is for their presence leaving our life. When we have God in our hearts, we share that love with our loved ones. Our joy is in the knowledge that love is everlasting, so our loved ones are always with us. Yes, we miss them, but they are the lucky ones because they are with our Savior while we remain here waiting to join them."

I thought about Victor, and the sorrow that I felt losing him. It remained a deep ache in my soul. I knew that Pastor James spoke the truth, and I promised myself to think about it when I got home.

"Sister Victoria, our pianist fell ill last week and cannot play during service anymore. Would you mind sharing your

God-given talent with my congregation? It would only be on first and third Sundays for a little while. Bring your family too. I'd like to meet them."

"I'd love to, Pastor, but we're moving in a few months. I'd hate to start then leave you in a bind."

Pastor James laughed.

"That's just fine. If you play for us during that time, I'm sure that we can find someone before you leave."

I smiled and agreed. I hugged Pastor James and promised to come back on first Sunday.

A few months later, I returned to the church to say goodbye to Pastor James. We were all packed and ready to leave the next morning, but I wanted to see Pastor James before we left. I found him in the church praying before the altar. I grimaced when the pew squeaked as I sat down. Pastor James turned quickly then relaxed when he saw me.

"Hello, Sister Victoria. How are you and your family? I just prayed for your safe travels."

Tears sprang into my eyes when I saw how slow Pastor James rose from the altar. I hadn't realized until that moment that Pastor James was quite old. I let the tears fall because I sensed that this would be the last time that I saw him.

"Now, now, what's this? There's no need to let the dam loose. You're going to be fine."

Pastor James handed me a handkerchief and patted me on the back.

"Thank you, Pastor," I sniffled.

He chuckled and sat down beside me.

"Victoria, I know that you struggle with yourself. It's in your face every time you walk in here. Let me tell you that you're not alone. There are many people who fight Satan's temptations everyday. I know because I'm one of them."

I stared at him in disbelief.

"Yes, I do, child. Now, close your mouth before a fly gets in there while I explain. We are all born in sin. The paths that we choose as we grow are influenced by how many good and how many bad people we accept into our lives. I said accept because it is our choice to let either one in depending on our earthly wants and desires. There are some people that never let in the good, and they turn out to do very bad things. That doesn't mean that they can't change. The same goes for the good people. Good people can make mistakes just like bad people. The important thing is not to hate a mistake but to accept the lesson learned from it. Your light in Christ is not gone, my sister. It is only dimmed."

Pastor James stood up and began walking toward the altar again. I took a step to follow him until he held up his hand without turning.

"I'm not going to say goodbye, Sister Victoria, but see you later."

I felt the tears began to run down my face again. Pastor James gave me a smile from over his shoulder.

"Remember, Sister Victoria, Jesus can fix anything. You just have to trust and believe."

I nodded and walked out praying that I would be able to find a way to make my light shine brighter. And soon.

12

Once we got settled into our new home on the outskirts of the Dallas city limits, Harlan's parents, Ms. Dorothy and Mr. Jerry came to visit. Harlan complained that Mr. Jerry reprimanded him several times during their visit. It seemed that Harlan couldn't do anything right. Mr. Jerry brought it up several times that Harlan needed to pay more attention to his wife and children. I didn't pay it much attention until Mr. Jerry came to speak to me the morning that they left.

"Victoria, my dear, I want to thank you for your wonderful hospitality and to tell you how well my grandchildren behaved – well, except for William. Anyway, I feel like I should apologize for any wrong opinions that we may have made through these years. You have done right by Harlan, and he should appreciate it."

Mr. Jerry smiled, patted me on the shoulder, and joined Ms. Dorothy at the car.

I tried to erase the frown that creased my forehead at his roundabout apology. I didn't understand why Mr. Jerry felt that he needed to apologize for his and Ms. Dorothy's behavior towards me all these years. I shook my head in wonderment and waved goodbye as they drove away. Ms. Dorothy didn't wave and shot me a very nasty look before turning around in the seat. I sighed because it seemed that Mr. Jerry was the only one who wanted to say sorry.

A month after my in-laws' visit, Aunt Charlotte and Aunt Mary showed up on my doorstep. I stood shocked because Aunt Charlotte had said that they wouldn't be coming to visit until next month. I had agreed thinking that would be enough time for me to prepare my mind and pray about my relationship with Aunt Mary.

Aunt Charlotte gave me a big hug and smiled while she held up two shopping bags. I narrowed my eyes at her as she breezed into the house oohing and aahing over the décor. Aunt Mary didn't follow her into the house. She stayed outside waiting for me to invite her. I met her eyes for a moment and stifled the urge to shut the door in her face, but I nodded and waved her inside. She didn't try to hug me, and I certainly didn't attempt it either.

"Well, Victoria, this is a very nice house. I am so glad that Harlan came to his senses and left the military. This is the kind of house that you should have been in all along. Well, that's neither here or there. We're so glad to see you, aren't we, Mary? I'm so happy that you'll be this close to us, but we won't come visit unless we're invited..." Aunt Charlotte paused awkwardly.

I wanted to laugh at the look on her face, but I didn't. Instead, I glanced at the shopping bags and raised my eyebrow in question. Aunt Charlotte recovered her poise and laughed.

"I thought that we could have a tea. I brought some goodies and that Earl Grey tea that you used to like so much. By the by, are the children at school?"

"All of them except for Grayson. He's down for his nap. Harlan found a private school for the other children. It even has a van that picks them up and drops them off. I'm overjoyed at that because I didn't want them going to a public school in Dallas after the stories that I heard about how rough they had become."

I shuddered just thinking about it.

"Well, we're glad as well. Let's put this food together, then, we can have a long chat. Hopefully, the children will be here before we leave," Aunt Charlotte said.

I nodded and led her into the kitchen. Aunt Mary had been silent since she walked into the house. She could stay that way for all I cared. I didn't want to hear any more of her lies.

After tea, I showed my aunts to the gazebo in the large backyard. It was my special place to go when the children were gone or asleep. I could see the admiring look on Aunt Charlotte's face, and I flushed with pride.

"Victoria, this is nice. I like it, and I know that you do too. You always were an outside child," she said.

I smiled as the memory of running around her gardens crossed my mind. Then, the smile vanished as the memory of trying to grow my own garden to have food at my parents' chased the good memory away. I frowned and looked away to find Aunt Mary staring at me. I quickly turned back to Aunt Charlotte and suggested that we take seats.

As soon as we sat down, Aunt Charlotte turned to me and frowned.

"Victoria, you must stop this nonsense of ignoring your Aunt Mary. I'm tired of being in the middle trying to fix what's broken. Both of you need to talk about whatever this mess is before it's too late. I didn't raise you to be so stubborn and shut out your family. We have been worried about you because we love you, Victoria. We took you in and raised you as our own out of love, not obligation or duty. Whatever problems you face were created by your own hand, not ours. Don't stand alone when you have family that will stand with you."

I opened my mouth to argue and suddenly felt ashamed. Aunt Charlotte was right. I had let the anger and misery of my life cloud the love of my family. I looked at Aunt Mary and saw the crow's feet and gray streaks showing her age. I could feel the tears forming. I got up and walked to Aunt Mary. I picked up her hands and raised them to my cheek.

"Please forgive me, Aunt Mary, and you too, Aunt Charlotte. I just felt so disappointed and hurt. I'm so sorry if I made y'all feel that I didn't appreciate everything that y'all have done for me and my children. I love y'all."

I laid my head in Aunt Mary's lap and cried my anguish. I felt her stroke my braid until my tears slowed.

"Ah, Victoria, I know your difficulties. I have not only seen it, but also felt it. Your life is a little better now, I think. Has Harlan been treating you and the children well?"

Aunt Mary raised my face to look into my eyes. I nodded, and she smiled.

"Well, maybe it's like Mama said. The older I get, the more my visions change."

Aunt Mary frowned as if she didn't believe what she had just said.

Aunt Charlotte cleared her throat. Aunt Mary and I turned to see that she was standing at the edge of the gazebo steps looking at a newly awakened Grayson. I heard her breath hitch while she walked to him and knelt before him.

"Hello, little one, my name is Granny Charlotte. Would you like a treat?"

Grayson rubbed the sleep from his eyes and nodded. Aunt Charlotte hugged his little body and laughed. Grayson gave his "Granny Charlotte" a shy smiled and let her lead him into the house.

Aunt Mary chuckled and patted my hand.

"It seems that Charlotte has worked her magic on another of your children, Victoria."

I laughed lightly and stood up to sit in the chair beside her. My laughter died when I saw the love in her face. I felt so guilty for blaming her for my mistake.

"Aunt Mary, I am sorry for treating you badly. I never thanked you for the blessing that you put on me to keep the darkness at bay. If you hadn't, I wouldn't have been able to make it to the grand old age of thirty-three."

My attempt at humor failed because Aunt Mary looked into the distance and sighed.

"Victoria, you have always been a dutiful child, and then a dutiful wife. Your bright spirit and loving nature was dampened by Betts' evil, but you have done well. The line has to be broken, or you will never find your joy. I still believe that you will have a child that will break the dark line. "

I tried to smile and accept her words, but having lived all these years waiting on nothing gave me a bitter taste in my mouth. Besides, I was too old to be having more children. I nodded just to agree and avoided her gaze. At that moment, Aunt Charlotte came back with Grayson. I stood up grateful to get away from Aunt Mary's empty promises. I walked to my aunt and son and saw that Grayson had a mouth and hand full of teacakes.

"Well, look at you, my little man. I see Aunt Charlotte has stuffed you like a little turkey!"

I laughed and opened my mouth for the teacake that Grayson tried to stuff in my mouth. I looked up as I chewed his offering to see Aunt Charlotte nod her head at Aunt Mary. I glanced over my shoulder at Aunt Mary who was slowly getting up from her chair. I felt sympathy for her in that moment until the bitterness crept back into my heart. I viciously tamped it down because I was determined that I wouldn't harbor any ill will toward her anymore.

"Victoria, let's go back in the house for a spell. It's getting a bit warm, and I just made some ice tea," Aunt Charlotte offered.

I smiled and took Grayson's hand to follow her inside the house. I turned back to Aunt Mary to ask if she needed help but found her looking at the neighbor's house. She frowned and walked to the fence.

"You should stay right there, lady. Some of those weasels' fence is on my property. I don't want to have to shoot you where you stand," growled a mean voice from the other side of the fence.

I gasped at the threat of violence to my aunt and joined her at the fence. Angry, I put my hands on my hips and straightened my spine.

"Who are you to threaten my aunt? And, who are you implying is a weasel. I see no weasels, but I do hear one. Stand up, you coward."

I heard a chuckle before a tall, fair skinned Black man stood up from behind the fence. He had on white paint spattered overalls with a paintbrush raised in his hand. He also had a mean sneer on his ugly face. I grabbed Aunt Mary's arm and backed away from the evil that I felt coming from his body. He laughed.

"Yeah, back away now, witch. Weasel, huh? Better watch how you call grown men names, girl," he growled.

I raised my chin and sneered back.

"I don't know who you are, sir, but you need to mind your business on that side of the fence. This side of the fence belongs to my husband and me."

"You don't know nothing except to sit at home and have babies by that bastard husband of yours. I've told him once already to move this fence. He doesn't want me to have to tell him again."

The man turned away without another word.

Aunt Mary's hand shook, and she grabbed my arm to pull me toward the house.

"Victoria, that man is very bad. I felt like I stood before Betts just now. Please stay away from him."

She shuddered and looked back at the fence.

I felt panic rising, but I shook my head to push it away. I narrowed my eyes at the fence.

"I haven't met that man before now, Aunt Mary. I'll ask Harlan when he gets home."

Aunt Mary nodded and let me take her elbow to go inside the house.

True to their word, my aunts stayed to see the children when they came home from school. Aunt Charlotte brought in more shopping bags of treats and presents for them. It felt like Christmas with the ripping of wrapping paper and squeals of glee. I smiled at my children's joy until I saw Mark's arm. There were deep scratches across his forearm, and his hand looked swollen. I waited until my aunts had left before I questioned him. I grasped his arm and lifted it up to the light ignoring his struggles to get loose.

"Mark Sams, what is this? It looks like a wild animal attacked you."

"It's nothing, Mama. I fell on the way to the bus. I'm okay."

I looked into his eyes and saw that my oldest and most responsible child lied to my face. I felt the anger building, and a tendril of darkness snake its way around my mind. I allowed it in to give me strength to deal with whatever my son hid from me.

William and the twins stopped playing with their new toys to watch Mark and me. I glanced their way and saw worry on the girls' face and wicked delight on William's. I frowned at him and decided to deal with Mark in private.

"William, take your sisters and Grayson out to the backyard to play."

William looked like he wanted to argue, but stopped at the look on my face.

"C'mon, Leah and Gia. Let's see if we can find some bugs to put in the ant hill."

I shook my head at my son's fascination with torturing things. I promised myself that I would address that with William later. Right now, I needed to focus on Mark.

As soon as the other children were outside with the door shut, I turned to Mark and guided him to the sofa. I put my arm around his shoulders and looked him in the eyes.

"Son, please tell me the truth. Did you hurt yourself, or did someone hurt you?"

Mark's bottom lip trembled, but he bit it and turned his head. I put my finger under his chin and turned his gaze back to mine.

"Mark. Please don't keep secrets that can hurt you. I'm your mother, and I don't want anyone hurting my baby..."

Mark yanked loose and stood up to leave before I finished. I almost gave in to my anger at his disobedience, but I took a deep breath and tried again.

"Don't you dare walk out while I'm talking to you, Mark Sams. I will give you the whipping of your life. Now, I want to know who is hurting my child."

I got up to stand in front of Mark. I realized then that my son had his father's height and stood a good six inches over me. Mark's face crumpled at my rage, and my heart melted to see my strong son cry.

"Mama, there's this teacher, Ms. James. She's always mean to me, and she lets the other kids call me "red" or "high yella". I try to ignore everything like you told me to do, but she started talking about you today. She said that you're lazy and think that you're better than Black people because you're skin is White. She said that Daddy only married you because he couldn't get a real White woman, and that's why he's spending time with other Black women now. Ms. James kept calling you names until I stood up and told her to please be quiet. The whole class started calling me a dummy and retarded, and she just laughed, Mama. She just laughed," sobbed Mark.

I hugged and comforted my son until his sobs turned to sniffles. He hadn't mentioned the scratches, so I waited until he caught his breath. When he didn't speak, I nudged him to look into my eyes.

"Mark, what happened to your arm?"

He avoided my eyes for a moment before mumbling something and turning away to look wistfully at his siblings playing outdoors. I sighed and asked him again louder.

"Mark, what happened to your arm?"

"Ms. James decided to paddle me in front of everyone for talking back. When she tried to pull me to her desk, I snatched my arm out of her hand. She grabbed for me again, and I ran towards the door. One of the kids tripped me, and I fell. Ms. James hit my hand with the paddle when I tried to get up. She yanked my arm and yelled at me that I was a coward just like you. I tried to get away from her, Mama, but she was like some kind of monster. She told the class that I needed to learn my place as a little bastard, then she squeezed my arm until it hurt and pushed me back to my desk letting her nails dig into my skin."

I barely heard the rest of what Mark said because I was locked in the memories of how Betts and Mama treated me that awful day so long ago. I knew Mark's pain and anguish, and for a moment, I wanted to kill this Ms. James. I felt the darkness turn over like an awakened beast at my rage. I closed my eyes and did something that I hadn't done in a long while – I embraced the darkness.

The next day, I took Mark to school myself. He had complained and whined about being a stool pigeon, but I wasn't about to allow such treatment of my child. I also wanted to know what this Ms. James had against me.

When we arrived, I took a good long look around the immaculate campus of Founders Street Private School. The lawns were beautiful in the September morning, and the windows sparkled with a fresh shine. The picture the school presented on the outside was clean and prestigious. It was the inside that I worried about now.

Mark led the way inside hesitantly as if he didn't want me to enter the school. I nodded encouragement at him to continue to the school office. We followed a hallway lined with classrooms until we rounded a corner and stood before a large glass door marked "Office". Mark stood back, and I opened the door and approached the vacant chest high desk. There were two Black women and one White man behind a partition drinking coffee. I waited for them to acknowledge me, but they were too busy laughing and talking. I glanced at Mark to see that he looked ready to run away. I took his uninjured hand and gave it a reassuring squeeze. I turned back to the little social gathering by the coffee pot to see that they still hadn't noticed me. I decided enough was enough.

"Hello? Excuse me? Can anyone help me?"

The trio glanced in my direction and frowned. One of the Black women waved her hand dismissively at me, and they struck up the conversation again.

"Mama, let's just go. It's always like this. They told me to "be a man" the last time I was here," Mark whispered.

I turned back to him in surprise. He had not told me that he'd said something about this to anyone in charge.

"What do you mean, "the last time I was here", Mark? You mean to tell me that you told on Ms. James, and no one helped you?"

Mark's gaze dropped from mine, and he started scuffing his shoe on the rug. I heard a muffled, "yes ma'am".

I swung around and narrowed my eyes at the social club of three. I lifted my fisted hand and began beating on the counter. They jumped in surprise, and one of the Black women ran to the desk with a frown directed at Mark.

"What are you doing out of class, young man? It seems Ms. James is right about your behavior," she said clicking her tongue.

I smothered the urge to strangle her. I knew that she deliberately ignored me.

"Excuse me, ma'am. My name is Victoria Sams, and this is my son. I am here to talk to the principal about Ms. James and her treatment of him."

The Black woman sent me a chilling glance and beckoned the younger slimmer Black woman forward.

"Verna, this here is the Sams woman. You know, the one Rita told us about," she said in a loud whisper.

The woman called Verna covered her mouth in a loud guffaw before covering it. I frowned at them because I didn't know a Rita nor did I care. I was tired of their games.

"I would like to speak to the principal now, please," I said angrily.

Their eyes widened before narrowing at my tone. The older, fatter Black woman gave me a fake smile.

"Principal Wells is not seeing visitors today. You can come back tomorrow."

She turned around and walked back behind the partition leaving me with Verna. I narrowed my own eyes at her and decided to bluff my way into the principal's office.

"If I don't get to see Mr. Wells today, I am going to the police to report this abuse of my son by this Ms. James."

Verna looked down her nose and lifted her lip in disgust. I returned her glare with an icy scowl. We stared at each other for several seconds before she lowered her gaze.

"Fine. I'll see if he is busy. Don't say that I didn't warn you," she huffed and went into the principal's office.

I smiled at Mark's look of awe and waited for her to come show us into the office. We waited for another ten minutes before Verna came back and motioned for us to enter the office. The White man that had been at the coffee pot sat behind a large cluttered desk. He had a file sitting on top of it, and I could see that it had Mark's name on it. The White man's head was down, and he didn't lift it when we entered the room. He also didn't ask us to sit.

"Alright, you threatened your way in here. Now, what do you want, Victoria. I am a busy man," he growled.

Puzzlement creased my brow in a frown because he had called me by my first name. I knew that I had never met him.

"Do I know you, sir?"

The principal did lift his head at my question, and I was struck by the hatred that I saw in his gaze. I knew in that instance that I had never met this man before in my life.

"No, but I know all about you. I know that you're a mixed Black who thinks she's White. Seeing you now, I agree that you could pass for it except for the fact that you married a Black man the color of my shoes. I also know that you blackmailed your husband to stay with you and keep having babies to make him feel guilty," Principal Wells sneered.

I sat in shock at his vicious attack in front of my son. I gathered the rising darkness around me like a cloak and raised my eyebrow as I sat down in the chair across from him.

"Mr. Wells, whatever you think that you know about me, you are mistaken. I don't know who or what has spread these malicious lies about me, but they are wrong and so are you for speaking to me in this fashion. Contrary to your opinion, I have never attempted to pass as White because my own mother is "as black as your shoes". Is that how you put it? Yes, I think that it was. That is neither here nor there. I came today to speak with you about my son's teacher, Ms. James. She paddled his hand and viciously scratched his arm while ridiculing him in front of the class."

I held up Mark's wrapped hand and peeled back the bandages to show Mr. Wells the scratches. He paled a bit when he saw the depth of the scratches.

"Now, my husband has paid a year of tuition for four of our children to attend this private school, and we do not appreciate this Ms. James abusing Mark. I would like to speak to her. Now."

Mark winced at my tone because I used the same one on him the night before our visit to the school.

Mr. Wells also winced and went to the door to tell Verna to bring Ms. James. He returned to his seat and held up his hands.

"I don't want to hear anymore until Ms. James arrives, Victoria."

I laughed nastily.

"Mr. Wells, I hadn't planned on speaking again until Ms. James had arrived. Also, since we've never met, and I am the mother of one of your students, you will show me the respect of calling me, Mrs. Sams or Ms. Sams, not Victoria. I'd hate for all the other tuition paying parents to find out how disrespectful their children's principal is to other parents. Do you understand?"

Mr. Wells jerked his head in a nod.

There was knock on the door, and he barked for whomever it was to enter. I turned my head to see a tall Black woman with smooth brown skin and black hair stride into the room. There was something familiar about her. Mark flinched away as she brushed past him.

"Ah, Ms. James. This is Mrs. Sams, Mark's mother. She has stated that you disciplined Mark yesterday in the extreme. Please clear this up for me," Mr. Wells requested.

Ms. James whipped her head around at me then Mark.

I saw hatred in her gaze as she took a step towards us. Again, Mark flinched. I raised my eyebrow in question.

"Mark is a little weakling. Now, I can see why. He hides behind his mama's skirts. I'll bet he's a dirty, lowdown liar just like his Daddy. Damn right, I taught him a lesson."

I stood to my full height at her malevolent words. Mr. Wells sat back in his chair with him mouth open in surprise. Ms. James smiled in satisfaction as if she knew her words at hurt me. What she didn't know was that I didn't care about what she said about Harlan, but I wasn't going to let her get away with cowering my son.

"Ms. James, you seem to know a lot about my family. Do I know you because I would remember your nasty attitude?"

She looked like she wanted to hit me, instead she delivered a shocking blow.

"Oh yes, I know you. My sister has three children by your "husband" and has been hoping that you'd let him go all these years that they've been married."

She paused and cocked her head to the side.

"How does it feel to be an adulteress with three bastards?"

I stepped back in the face of her revelation. Shirley's sister was my son's teacher! I shook my head in denial.

Mr. Wells cleared his throat.

"In the face of this new information, Ms. James consider yourself terminated immediately. I cannot allow you to corrupt a student's learning or abuse a student because of your family ties of hatred. This is absolutely unacceptable."

Ms. James swung around on Mr. Wells and laughed.

"You think I care about this job? Ha! I've done more than my sister could have ever done."

She looked back at me and left the office laughing maniacally.

Mr. Wells apologized for his behavior and that of his staff. He offered to mentor Mark for the rest of the year and through the summer. I delayed agreeing to his offer by saying I needed to talk it over with Harlan. Mr. Wells accepted my answer and took Mark to class. He whispered to me that he had to watch the class while Verna and Ms. Dee, the other Black woman found another teacher. I nodded and hugged Mark before walking to my car.

On the way home, I shed a few tears before shrugging off Rita James' accusations. Shirley had made her bed just like I did, and now we had to lie in it. I frowned when one of her statements ran across my mind. "My sister has three children by your "husband". Harlan only had two children that I knew of by Shirley. Well, it seems that he had broken his promise after all. All that time on the road for work was probably a shield to hide his cheating. I bet he was with her right now. Despair and heartbreak returned to open wounds that I thought were closed forever. I pulled over to the side of the road and began to sob and wail.

"When would I be able to break free from this misery? God. Help me. Please. What is wrong with me that I have to fight so hard to be happy? Will I ever receive any joy?"

I cried until I had no more tears to cry. Then, on the edge of madness, I calmed myself, cranked the car, and drove home to prepare dinner for my children.

Epilogue

"Victoria, what we need is a fertile female that is willing to raise the implant as her own," Dr. Michaels said.

The doctor paused to wait for Victoria's reply. He prayed for a "yes" because she was the perfect candidate for the experiment.

"I will have to discuss this again with my husband, Doctor. We already have five mouths to feed."

"Oh, well, if you must, discuss it with him, by all means, do so. However, also inform him that we will give you a lump sum of $25,000 and a generous monthly stipend after the implant is born."

Victoria took a deep breath to steady herself after hearing the amount of the lump sum. All she could think of was that the money would deliver her family from the money troubles that they had acquired since moving to Dallas. Her other thought was that Mark would be attending one of the worst high schools in Dallas next year, and she could not put him in that kind of danger every day.

Since placing the boys in public school to save money, both of her boys had already been in scuffles. Her heart sank at the knowledge of what could happen to Mark in that awful high school.

Dr. Michaels knew that the offer was substantial enough that Victoria would give in, and he knew from her heritage that she would not make the decision without consulting her husband, Harlan. From what the doctor knew of Harlan, he would jump at the amount of money that was offered.

"Alright, Dr. Michaels, when do you want me to let you know our decision?"

"Call the office number that we gave you on your first visit and leave your name, the secretary will contact you and schedule the vitamin therapy," stated Dr. Michaels as he took Victoria's elbow and guided her to the door.

The doctor paused before turning the knob.

"Victoria, this experiment is top secret. No one, and I mean no one, can know what takes place here."

Victoria nodded with wide eyes at Dr. Michaels' tone. Satisfied, the doctor opened the door, and Victoria slipped out with a polite wave.

"Have a good weekend, Dr. Michaels."

"You too, Victoria."

As Victoria left the office, Dr. Michaels smiled to himself and walked toward the lab calling his secretary, Jane, to his side.

"Bring me Victoria's file, please. I want to look over the psychological exam and ancestry profile."

Jane retrieved the file and handed it to the doctor.

Dr. Michaels sat back in his chair and rubbed his hands together. He laughed to himself thinking of his genius plan.

Victoria stepped out of the building into the dimmed sunlight of the early Spring afternoon. For a moment, she felt like the sun went from dim to bright. She laughed lightly at her imagination and began walking to the bus stop. She smiled to herself thinking that all of her prayers were about to be answered.

Joy

Book 3

Prologue

"Nurse!"

Victoria felt the urge to push and trembled in fear as she felt the icy breath of Death creep closer.

"Nurse!"

She began to grow angry at her unanswered pleas for help. The darkness nudged her to close her eyes and embrace it, but every time she tried, it slipped beyond her mind. In frustration, Victoria reached for it again. She closed her eyes against the physical pain to let in the darkness for comfort.

"Oh!"

Her eyes popped open when a light shock passed through her body. The darkness shrank like a wounded animal in protest at the intrusion, and the pain increased its intensity with a whoosh through Victoria's body.

"Nurse!"

"Yes, yes, Mrs. Sams. What is it?"

The Black nurse poked her head into the room rolling her eyes to whoever stood behind her. Victoria's anger grew in her chest and began to burn at the nurse's behavior. She took a deep, halting breath against the pain and the nurse's stupidity.

"The baby is coming. I feel it."

The nurse rolled her eyes and came further into the room.

"Mrs. Sams, you have a while to go. The doctor said so. Now, if you're still worried because you're too old to be having babies, just don't think about it."

She nodded with a vague smile while inching toward the door. Victoria's fingers itched to throw the bedpan at her, but she took another deep breath and tried again.

"Nurse Waters, I AM worried about this labor, but I also have had enough babies to know when a baby is coming!"

As Victoria spat out her last few words, she knew that her voice bordered on hysteria, and from the look on Nurse Waters' face, she did too.

"I'll go call the doctor and see if he can get you something to calm down."

Nurse Waters turned and rushed from the room just as Victoria gave in to her anger and threw the metal bedpan at the door.

Tears of frustration and pain began building in Victoria's eyes, and she swiped at them blindly. She felt hopeless and afraid that she would die in childbirth and leave her beloved children behind with Harlan. Oh, why had she agreed to this? Just when she thought life was going to get better with the money from the implant, everything had turned bad all at once.

After Dr. Michaels' first good test, Harlan had changed and become bitter. The more swollen that Victoria became; the more Harlan seemed to hate her. Victoria gave a pain-filled and bitter laugh. Harlan was bitter about everything except the money. Victoria had worried that he would tell someone the secret, but he assured both her and Dr. Michaels that he could care less about the implant as long as the money kept coming. Well, Victoria couldn't really fault Harlan. After all, she had felt the same way at first. Then, the implant kicked and began to move and grow under her heart. The feeling had been different from her other children – lighter and filled with more love. There was something special about it...

"Ahhh!!"

Victoria's meanderings disappeared in a wisp of smoke as the pain came rushing back.

"Nurse! Nurse!"

Victoria screamed because the pains were so close. She felt dizzy and that Death had come for her.

"Mrs. Sams! Are you okay?"

Victoria raised her head to see the tall White nurse race into the room with concern on her manly face. Victoria squinted her eyes and tried to remember her name. Maya, Mina, May! Nurse May!

"Nurse May, please help me! The baby is coming! Now!"

Nurse May ran toward the bed and lifted the covers. She gave a surprised cry, ripped the covers off the bed, and started yelling for help while kicking at the brakes. Nurse Waters and another young Black nurse came running down the hallway. Nurse May gave the other nurse orders to find Dr. Michaels and told Nurse Waters to help her move Victoria to the delivery room. Nurse Waters looked about to protest but seeing Nurse May moving the bed by herself, she grabbed the other end and started pushing.

Victoria, in her pain, felt relieved and hoped with a mother's love that the implant would live even if she didn't. As the bed flew down the hall, Victoria raised her self to relieve some of the pressure and felt the implant expel itself from her body. The bed barely made it into the delivery room before she heard the loud cry of her newborn baby. Nurse May grabbed a hospital gown from the rack, turned, and scooped the baby from the bed. Breathless, Victoria fell back to the bed and waited nervously for a peek at her new baby.

Dr. Michaels came rushing through the doors at that moment and looked around at Victoria and the baby in surprise. He walked to Nurse May and took the squalling infant into his arms. With a glance at the clock, he noted the time of birth.

"11:11am."

Looking down at the tiny body convulsing in anger, Dr. Michaels began to chuckle. He opened the makeshift blanket, checked the baby's condition, and tried to shush the baby's cries by humming a little ditty. As he crooned, the baby stopped crying and gave him a wide-eyed stare. Dr. Michaels stood captivated by the baby's brownish red hair, dark brown eyes, and peach colored skin. He shook his head gently as if waking from a trance while chiding himself at his whimsy. He walked the few steps to Victoria's bed and handed her the baby.

"Victoria, you have given birth to a beautiful baby girl. She is healthy as far as I can see. We need to run some tests on her, and then you may see her again when you get out of surgery. What will you name her?"

Victoria nodded before she took a deep breath and looked down at the baby girl in her arms. Her eyes began to fill with tears when they met the unblinking stare of her new daughter. The baby reached her tiny hand and touched Victoria's face. A shot of electricity zoomed through Victoria's skin similar to the shock she'd felt during labor. She gasped and almost dropped the baby when she remembered her visions of this moment.

"Are you alright, Victoria?"

Dr. Michaels stepped forward in concern.

Victoria hiccupped and threw the doctor a watery smile.

"I'm just fine, Dr. Michaels. I'm just fine."

"Well, what is her name?"

"Valora. Her name is Valora Elise Sams."

1

I opened the mailbox and took out the stack of letters. My left hand had been itching, so I knew that most of them were bills because Harlan hadn't brought his check home in a few weeks. In fact, Harlan hadn't been home in a few weeks. I blew out a breath of frustration into the late winter morning before those thoughts started and turned to go back in the house.

"Oh!"

I grabbed at my left leg feeling a sharp pain that shot through it. I stopped to rub the pain away and shook my head at myself for moving so fast. Since my youngest daughter's birth, I felt every ache and pain in my bones. I made my way to the rocking chair on the porch and lowered my aching body into it. Dr. Michaels had warned me that the hormones and pills might affect me one day, but I didn't think that it would be so soon after Valora's birth. I closed my eyes for a moment to rest my tired body and felt a cool wind brush against my skin. I sighed at the comfort of nature and opened my eyes to allow my "gift" to take over my mind.

Memories of the past year flooded my mind. Valora's birth, Harlan's distance, Ruth and Lacy's visits, Aunt Charlotte taking the twins and Grayson to her home last summer to allow me to heal after Valora's birth. I appreciated Aunt Charlotte so much more because I knew that she spent time with all of the children to give me time to myself. Leah and Gia loved visiting Aunt Charlotte because she showered gifts on them and spoiled them. I didn't think that it was too good to spoil them because they were getting headstrong and willful when they returned. I didn't want to hurt Aunt Charlotte's feelings, so I didn't say anything. I just made sure that I reminded Leah and Gia that I was their mother and punished them for their stubbornness.

I frowned thinking about how William and Gia had reacted to Valora. Both of them had avoided her unless a guest was visiting then Gia would dote on her. Not William. He never wanted to hold or touch Valora and always shot hateful looks at her, so I never left him alone with her. The looks that I had seen Gia and William giving the baby made me want to keep Valora locked away from her own siblings.

Mark, Leah, and Grayson had shown no such hostility or indifference to Valora. They seemed to genuinely love their baby sister, but sometimes I could see Gia influencing Leah to ignore Valora or give her angry glares. I knew that I should have put a stop to it earlier, but I had enough problems trying to feed and take care of my children.

I felt my frown grow deeper at Harlan's desertion of his family obligations. Harlan. My anger rose when his face came to mind. He always made excuses for not coming home, and when he was home, he was getting ready to leave again. He had acted like that since Valora was born. I didn't mind, though, because the house was at peace when Harlan was gone. I just missed his paychecks, but not much. Dr. Michaels had begun sending the checks for Valora with just my name on them, so I cashed them and used them to take care of all of my babies.

I sighed at the glorious feeling of freedom in the peace that Valora's birth brought to my heart and soul. I closed my eyes again and brought her tiny face to mind. Valora wasn't just beautiful - she was enchanting. Another sigh escaped my lips. It wouldn't be long before my beautiful little pumpkin awakened from her nap ready to eat, and I didn't like for her to awake alone. Maybe tomorrow my right hand would itch and bring some much-needed money.

Feeling the cold set in, I inched my body out of the chair. I stood and mentally queried my body to find that I could move with just a little pain. I sent a quick prayer up to Father God to thank Him for the blessing and made my way into the house.

"Victoria, she is such a delight. You should take her down to the television station for that baby contest."

I smiled at Aunt Charlotte and sipped my tea without answering her. She made that statement every time she visited. I watched with a smile as she lovingly stroked Valora's face and hair. Valora gurgled and smiled at Aunt Charlotte causing her to laugh.

"You are such a charmer. Yes, you are. You remind me so much of your mother when she first came to me. All the neighbors were fascinated. Yes, they were."

Valora seemed to hang on every word that Aunt Charlotte said. She even nodded when Aunt Charlotte finished speaking. Aunt Charlotte chuckled and nuzzled Valora's neck. Valora gave a loud gurgle of glee. Aunt Charlotte laughed and gave her a quick kiss on the cheek before placing her in the brand new playpen that she had just brought.

"Aunt Charlotte, you really shouldn't spend so much on the children. I don't want my siblings or other cousins to feel badly toward you."

She turned away from watching Valora biting her new toy cat to frown at me.

"Victoria Alicia Sams, I will do whatever I wish with my resources. Do you understand? I did not raise your siblings – I raised you. I am sure that they know by now that I love them too. I helped Ruth and Lacy with their weddings, and I helped Stephen buy a house for his family. What I do for you and my grandchildren is my business. Do you hear?'

Ashamed at Aunt Charlotte's chastising, I nodded and mumbled an apology.

"I didn't raise you to be a coward either. When a lady is wrong, she admits it for all to hear and moves past it. That way when she is right, she is respected more because everyone knows that she is smart enough to admit when she's wrong."

I looked up from my teacup to see Aunt Charlotte smiling at me. I felt the shame slipping from my face and smiled back at her.

"Yes ma'am. I apologize, Aunt Charlotte. I didn't want anyone thinking bad things about you. You are my mother in spirit, and I would never want anyone to hurt you by word or deed."

Aunt Charlotte just shook her head and picked up her teacup.

"Your Aunt Mary sends her love. She wanted to come with me, but Mama called her to come home - for what, I don't know."

"Mum, mum, mum, mum, mum!"

We both turned in surprise at Valora's little voice coming from the playpen. She saw us looking at her and smiled before turning back to the toys around her. Aunt Charlotte and I looked at each other and laughed.

"Has she been trying to talk?" Aunt Charlotte asked sipping her tea.

"A little here and there. Harlan picked her up and said "Daddy" a lot in her face the last time he was home, but she wouldn't say a word. Whenever Mark comes home, he sings to her, and she makes little noises and moves her mouth with him. I'm getting worried because she's almost a year and hasn't begun walking or talking. She stands up, but nothing else."

"Oh, Victoria. Don't rush her. Soon, she'll be talking up a storm and running around so much that you can't catch her."

Aunt Charlotte waved away my concern with a pat of my hand.

I nodded and wondered to myself if Aunt Charlotte was right. Dr. Michaels had said she was doing well at her last checkup, so I put the worry out of my mind.

After Aunt Charlotte's visit, I put Valora down for her nap and grabbed the laundry to put on the line. The early afternoon sun had dried the backyard from the rain the day before, but I still stayed on the worn footpath to the clothesline at the back of the yard. I cast a quick glance at the neighbor's fence to see if there was any movement. I didn't like the neighbor, Ellis Carter or his wife, Orna. Ellis had kept up a feud with Harlan since we moved into the house, and Orna was just as bad. I told Harlan that there was something about them, but he wouldn't pay me any attention. I could feel the evil pouring off of both of them and their house. Something wasn't right about them, and I didn't want it to hurt my family. I said a quick prayer to God to put His Hand on the situation and hurried to hang out the clothes.

"Well, well, the slovenly slut graces us with her presence."

I turned quickly at the malicious tone to see Ellis Carter leaning on the fence. I grabbed the clothespin that I had dropped in my surprise and turned my back on him.

"You know, you shouldn't turn your back on people. That's rude. But I guess I shouldn't expect manners from a stupid cow. Where's your coward husband? Has he left you all alone again? That's what cheaters do, you know. They leave a dumb broad like you tied down to them with a passel of brats while they sample all the other goodies."

I closed my ears to his taunts and kept hanging the clothes. I could hear Ellis moving along the fence, and I picked up the pace.

Whoosh!

I felt a rush of air pass my head and heard the crash of glass on the tree behind me. Shards of glass flew into my leg and ankle. Pain shot through my body. I looked down to see blood leaking from a large piece of glass protruding from my right leg. I refused to cry out because I knew Ellis was watching. I glanced up to see him smiling at my distress. I growled and grabbed at a large rock beside the gazebo.

"Go ahead and throw it. It'll be the last thing you do, witch," he snarled.

It was then that I saw him rubbing the barrel of a shotgun. Fear at leaving my children motherless with Harlan made me drop the rock and reach for a towel from the basket to staunch the blood on my leg. My instincts wanted to pull out the glass, but I knew that I would lose more blood if I did. I wrapped the wounds as best as I could before limping my way into the house trying to drown out the sound of Ellis' maniacal laughter.

I made my way into the bathroom and ran a tub of warm water while reaching for the first aid kit under the sink. I stripped off my housedress and lowered myself into the tub. The pain made me want to cry out, but I didn't want to wake Valora. I let out small hisses of breath and watched the water turn red. I raised myself to the side of the tub and left my legs in the water. Grabbing a towel to bite to mask my cries, I began picking out the smaller pieces of glass. I felt dizzy looking at the largest piece sticking out of my flesh. The pain was unbearable pulling the smaller shards from my leg. I prayed to God for healing and guidance because my hands began to shake.

When I felt the shivers take over my body, I knew it was time to call for help. With trembling hands, I reached for another towel and wrapped myself in it. I climbed out of the tub trying not to slip and fall because I knew that if I did, all would be lost. I limped into the hallway feeling the blood running down my leg. I refused to look down at my leg because deep down I knew that I would faint.

I struggled the few steps to the master bedroom. I felt my consciousness began to slip when I grabbed the doorknob. I shook my head viciously berating myself for the weakness. I pushed the door open and collapsed to the floor in agony at another searing pain flooding my leg. Hearing my harsh breathing in the silence, I began to drag myself to the bedside phone. Relief poured through my body when I reached the bed and felt the cord in my fingers. I pulled the phone down and dialed the operator.

"West Bell Operator, how can I help you?"

"Please help me. The neighbor threw a glass or something at me and hit a tree. The glass got in my leg. Blood is everywhere. I need help," I whispered heavily into the phone.

"Let me connect you with emergency services."

Before I could protest to just send someone, she transferred me to another ringing phone line.

"Emergency services, how can we help you?" a deep-voiced man asked.

"Please help me. My name is Victoria Sams, and I'm hurt very badly. There's blood everywhere. I need help," I cried.

"Okay, ma'am, calm down. What is your address?"

I gave him the address while trying to hold back my sobs.

"Someone is on the way to you. Don't move anymore. Just stay where you are for now. Is there anyone there with you?"

"Just my baby, Valora, and she's still sleeping. My other children are at school, but they should be home in a couple of hours."

Thinking of my children finding me like this made me want to give into hysteria. The man on the phone must have felt it because he began asking me questions about the kids and how they were doing in school. I appreciated his effort to get my mind off the pain and began telling him about the children.

"Well, my oldest son, Mark, he's a very smart and respectful young man. He plays football and works for a rancher outside of Dallas. He worries about us, and he takes his role as "man of the house" very serious when my husband isn't home which is almost always."

"He sounds like a son to be proud of."

My heart swelled with pride at his comment.

"Yes, he is. I have two more sons, William and Grayson. William could be a good boy if he wanted to, but he's a lot like his father. Grayson just started school last fall, and he is already ahead of children in his grade. He's a lot like Mark in looks and respecting his elders. I also have twins, Leah and Gia. They're not identical. Gia is the oldest and very willful, but Leah is sweet and caring when Gia's not around to influence her," I rambled to the man.

"Tell me about the baby," he asked.

I shook my head and bit my lip at the increasing pain. I began to see stars until I heard the man calling my name.

"Mrs. Sams! Victoria! Don't go to sleep! Hello!"

"Yes, I'm here," I sobbed.

"Help is almost there. Just hold on for a few minutes," he pleaded.

I nodded even as I heard the ambulance siren. Someone knocked on the door, but I couldn't rise to answer it. There was a loud boom, and I heard people calling my name. Valora must have woken up at the sound because I heard her crying.

"I have to get to my baby," I mumbled while trying to rise.

I felt someone touch my arm, and I opened my eyes to see Billy's face. I smiled at him and told him that I was ready to leave Harlan. I tried to raise my arms to him, but they wouldn't move.

"She's in shock. She's lost a lot of blood. Someone get the baby. Maybe that will help her. Let's get this leg iced and wrapped before we move her," I heard Billy say to someone behind him.

I just smiled and knew that Billy was going to make everything right.

"Where have you been, Billy? I've missed you. I asked Big Mama Chandra about you, but all she told me was that you left Carson," I rambled until I felt someone grab my leg.

"Ah! Please don't let them hurt me, Billy!" I cried.

"Ma'am, my name isn't Billy. My name is Rick, and I'm an emergency medic. You're in shock. We're taking you to the hospital, okay?"

I nodded my head and tears of foolishness and pain fell down my face.

Rick looked at me with sympathy before nodding to someone behind him. The other man brought a hiccupping Valora to me and sat her beside me while they worked. Valora stood up and gurgled in my face. I closed my eyes when her tiny hand caressed my cheek.

"I'm here with you, Mama," I heard a soft voice say.

My mind became sharper and I didn't feel as weak as before.

I looked up in surprise thinking that the other children were home, but there was no one in the room except Rick and the other two medics. I turned around to see Valora staring intently at me. Goosebumps skittered across my skin at her direct gaze.

"Alright, Mrs. Sams, we've got your leg in a tourniquet to keep the blood loss down while we get you to the hospital. Do you have anyone that can take the baby? She won't be allowed to stay with you at the hospital," Rick explained.

"No. There's no one here, but I can call my aunt to meet us there," I replied.

"Okay, make it quick because we can still save your leg," he said handing me the phone.

I made the quick call to a horrified Aunt Charlotte who agreed to meet us at the hospital. Rick and the other two medics put me on the stretcher, grabbed Valora and her bag, and carried me out of the house. Rick was kind enough to leave a note for my children and lock the door before they loaded me into the ambulance. Some of the neighbors had come out into the street to be nosy. I almost laughed at the look on their faces until I saw the gleeful smirk on the faces of Ellis and Orna Carter.

2

A sharp, drawing pain awoke me from a deep sleep. I took a deep breath to ease the burning ache. I tried to swallow but my throat felt like cotton. Coughs erupted from my throat.

"Here, my sweet. Have a sip of water," Aunt Charlotte whispered.

I glanced her way to see her holding a cup with a straw to my lips. I tried to take a long draw from the straw, but Aunt Charlotte snatched it away.

"No, Victoria. You can't have too much water right now. It's not good for you. Wait a while and you can have some more," she said with concern.

I felt too weak to argue, so I just nodded. I looked around the room and saw that I was in a private hospital room with a large window shuttered against the winter sun. I sat up quickly at the thought of being away from my children.

"How long have I been here? Where are the children?"

Aunt Charlotte gave me a small smile and pushed me back down to the bed.

"They are at my home with your Aunt Mary. She was on her way home when you called me yesterday. You were in surgery when I got here, and the young medics had Valora in their department doting on her every whim. They verified all of my familial credentials before they would allow me to touch her. I didn't know whether to laugh or call their superior. I kept her here with me until you were out of surgery, then I rounded up the other children and took them to my house. I didn't take them to school today because I knew that they wouldn't be able to concentrate." She hesitated before continuing.

"Victoria, the doctor said that you would have died if the medics hadn't come when they did. The large piece of glass had nicked a vein, and you lost a lot of blood. They had to give you several transfusions before they got the bleeding stopped. Your leg will be fine with time, but it left a long scar that I might have to call a specialist to look at when you're better. You were blessed, Victoria."

Aunt Charlotte's voice had risen with her accounting. I could see her swallow her ire, and she assumed her usual regal posture.

"How did this happen? You will tell me everything, Victoria. Everything."

I felt so very tired from the aching pain in my leg. I wanted to go back to sleep, but Aunt Charlotte deserved an explanation. I took a deep breath and almost cried out trying to move my leg and get comfortable to tell Aunt Charlotte what Ellis Carter had done. I beckoned for another sip of water, and Aunt Charlotte complied raising a skeptical eyebrow at my delay. I cleared my throat and began.

"After you left, I went into the backyard to hang up the wash. I was almost finished when Ellis Carter came pestering me across the fence. He called Harlan and me nasty names, but I ignored him. I thought he would leave me alone, but he kept at it. When I still didn't give him the response that he wanted, he threw something glass at me, but it hit the tree next to the gazebo and broke. The glass hit me in the leg. I wanted to throw a rock at him, but he had a pistol in his hand. He threatened to shoot me if I threw the rock, so I put the rock down and ran into the house to take care of the cuts. I tried, Aunt Charlotte, I tried to fix myself, but the big piece was too deep and bleeding like a stuck pig. I called for help, and that's pretty much it," I recounted with a shrug.

I looked over at the incredulous look on Aunt Charlotte's face.

"Do you mean to tell me that the neighbor next door that's telling any and everybody that will listen that he saw you fall on the broken liquor bottle that fell out of your hand, did this to you?"

I gave Aunt Charlotte a disbelieving stare.

"What?" I uttered in my shock.

"Ellis Carter told police when they went to question him that you were drinking spirits and dropped the bottle, on the same rock that you later picked up to threaten him with because he offered his help, that you slipped in your drunkenness and fell in the glass. He told them that he's seen you drunk before when your husband leaves you for other women. He also told them that he wanted to help you move the fence off of his property because Harlan won't do it," Aunt Charlotte finished with a frown.

I could only stare at her as she repeated the lies that Ellis had told to everyone to get out of trouble.

"Aunt Charlotte, you don't believe him, do you?"

Aunt Charlotte's frown softened, and she took my hand.

"No, my sweet girl. Your Aunt Charlotte may have been born at night, but not last night. I can smell the evil in that man even without your Aunt Mary telling me that he is a lying piece of scum."

She chuckled at the look on my face before patting my hand.

"Your Aunt Mary and I know that Harlan's desertion doesn't drive you to the bottle. Just the duty of caring for your beloved children keeps you from it. Ellis Carter doesn't know that he is digging his own grave because there are too many people to attest to his nastiness and your godliness."

A tear escaped at Aunt Charlotte's faith in me. I swiped at it and grew angry at Ellis' intended deception.

Before I could ask Aunt Charlotte what to do, there was a loud knock on the door. Aunt Charlotte limped to the door and opened it. She stepped back quickly when Harlan burst through the door and rushed to my bedside. He drew me into his arms and started rocking back and forth.

"Victoria, my love! I came home this morning to a house covered in blood and thought the worst had happened! Ms. Drury from next door told me that you had an accident and was in the hospital! I called around until one of the desk nurses told me that you were here! What happened?"

He drew away from me and waited for me to explain. Aunt Charlotte limped to the other side of the bed and frowned at Harlan. I frowned at his so-called worry too.

"Harlan, while you were away doing God knows what, your wife and children were in danger. Whatever feud that you and your neighbor, Ellis Carter, have going on has transferred to your wife and children. Ellis Carter threw something glass at Victoria, but he missed and hit the tree. The shards flew into Victoria and almost severed vital arteries in her leg. We are blessed that she is alive and her leg isn't damaged," Aunt Charlotte fussed.

Harlan looked to me for affirmation, and I nodded. His face grew even darker in his anger. Anger that he turned toward me.

"I told you to stay away from Ellis, Victoria. He is a very bad man. He could have killed you. What did you do to him to make him attack you?"

Harlan's voice had become louder in his rising anger. He dropped me to the bed, stood up, and leaned over me like he would strike me right in front of Aunt Charlotte.

"Harlan Sams, you will remove yourself from this room that I paid for my niece to have! You will also cease blaming Victoria for your mess! If you want to be angry at anyone, it's Ellis Carter!"

Aunt Charlotte moved slowly around the bed with her cane raised to strike Harlan. I tried to move myself to get between them, but the pain was too excruciating.

"Harlan, Aunt Charlotte, please! This is what Ellis Carter wants! He wants us to be angry at each other and cause trouble! We can't let him win!" I pleaded.

Harlan backed away, and Aunt Charlotte lowered her cane. Both of them nodded a silent and reluctant truce. I breathed a heavy sigh of relief.

As soon as everyone calmed down, a knock at the door startled us in the awkward silence. Harlan moved first and opened the door. A White man in a rumpled suite walked in with Dr. Michaels behind him. Dr. Michaels greeted Harlan before pushing past the White man to get to me. He nodded to Aunt Charlotte and placed his bag on the bed beside me.

"Victoria, I came as soon as I heard. I'm going to look you over and make sure that you're going to be fine. Officer Jackson is waiting to take your statement of what happened," Dr. Michaels explained.

He looked from me to Aunt Charlotte to Harlan while he took various medical instruments from his bag.

"I'll need a bit of privacy with Victoria, and then I'll leave so you all can come back to sit with her," Dr. Michaels commanded.

I nodded at Aunt Charlotte who turned with a gracious smile to Harlan and the officer. She grabbed both of their elbows and chatting about nothing efficiently escorted them from the room.

Dr. Michaels chuckled at Aunt Charlotte's competent manner.

"I should hire her to handle my clients and investors."

I was so tired that I could only give him a weak smile. He frowned and began his examination. When he uncovered my leg, I turned away so that I didn't have to see the stitches and scars. He gently poked and prodded until he was satisfied.

"I'd say that you'll heal nicely as long as you don't overdo anything when you are home, Victoria. I am concerned with the blood loss because of your past history of anemia and fevers, but that is something that we'll have to watch, okay? Now, tell me about Valora. How is she doing?"

Dr. Michaels wiped his hands on a cloth soaked with alcohol before turning back to hear my answer. I gave him another weak smile and the report that he wanted. I told him about how Valora continued to surprise me with her abilities. What I didn't tell him was that I suspected that her abilities included my "gift". I wasn't sure yet, but I had a strong feeling that she had a "gift" more special than mine.

Before long, Aunt Charlotte poked her head back in to tell us that Officer Jackson was getting impatient. Dr. Michaels told her that they could return, and he left with a reminder to visit him in a couple of weeks.

The interview with the stern-faced Officer Jackson felt more like an interrogation. He questioned every action that I took and almost called me a liar several times. I could see Aunt Charlotte and Harlan growing angry at Officer Jackson's high-handed manner, but I kept my patience and answered all of his questions.

"Well, Mrs. Sams, right now, it's a "he said, she said" kind of thing. If Mr. Carter is as bad as y'all say he is, then y'all should stay away from him. He says that y'all are the bad ones, so I gave him the same warning. You Blacks need sort this out because we can't waste valuable time doing it for you," he said in a deep Southern drawl standing up to leave.

"I beg your pardon!" Aunt Charlotte and I exclaimed at the same time.

Harlan growled and took a step toward Officer Jackson. A quick hand on the officer's holster made Harlan back off.

"Now, now, I can see that maybe Mr. Carter may have been right. He understands his place. Y'all probably need a few lessons to understand yours, huh?"

He pointed at Aunt Charlotte and almost spit.

"You with your high and mighty airs acting like your niece and her old man are angels. No matter how much money or fancy educations you got, you're still a bunch of niggers," he sneered.

Aunt Charlotte grabbed Harlan's arm before he could take another step. My head fell back to the bed in frustration that justice would not be served to Ellis because of this racist bigot. I felt a refreshing wash of anger and strength go through my body. I raised my head and looked into the smug and superior smile of Officer Jackson.

"Thank you so much for coming by the hospital to take my statement, Officer Jackson. I'm sure that there is a car waiting somewhere that needs a parking ticket. My fancy education will be put to good use when I write your superiors a letter describing your rude and disrespectful attitude. I'm not worried about your assessment of the situation because God will fix everything – including you. Please remember that what goes around, always comes back around in a nasty way. I will pray for you that when it does, you will have a loved one like my aunt to be there for you. Please leave and have a good day."

I narrowed my eyes at his astonished expression at my dressing down of his attitude. He threw me a hateful glance before stomping out of the room.

Aunt Charlotte laughed and patted my hand.

"Well, well, my dear. I couldn't have said it any better."

I looked up to see Harlan glaring at me. Tired and in pain, I returned his glare.

"What now?" I growled.

"That White man is probably going to send the WCC after us now."

Aunt Charlotte waved away his concern of the White Citizen's Council.

"No, he won't say a word to anyone because he's going to be too caught up in Victoria's "what goes around" curse. Now, why don't you go get something to eat and head on home? Victoria is tired, and I'm sure the nurses need to get her ready for supper."

Aunt Charlotte smiled sweetly at Harlan dismissing him from my room.

Harlan narrowed his eyes at me then Aunt Charlotte before leaving the room.

All of a sudden, I felt tired and sick to my stomach. Aunt Charlotte called a nurse to give me some pain medicine. I swallowed the large pills and allowed Aunt Charlotte to fluff my pillows while I waited for the pain to subside.

"The nurse said that you could go home in a couple of days if you don't set up infection. I think that Harlan should remodel the house and backyard to make sure that nasty man can't bother you all. Maybe you could live somewhere temporary for a while," Aunt Charlotte suggested.

I chuckled at her hopeful look. I knew what she was up to, and I was going to allow it.

"I think that's an excellent idea, Aunt Charlotte, except, I would rather move. Harlan isn't going to want to, but he's not home enough to care. There are some very nice apartments a few blocks from the house that we could sign a short lease while the house is remodeled."

Aunt Charlotte frowned at me for a moment, and I watched the wheels turning in her mind. Her face brightened with an idea, and I knew it was going to involve a lot of maneuvering.

"I know! You could live in the apartments while I remodeled my house in Littleton. Aunt Alice is there and still strong as an ox, and my house isn't that far from her ranch. You could still keep the house in Dallas, but you'd be away from the horrible Ellis Carter. With you all gone, he might forget about this stupid feud."

Aunt Charlotte waved her cane in her enthusiasm. I could only watch her in awe as she continued to expand on her plans for the children and me. Harlan's name was mentioned in passing a few times. I wondered what he'd think of it, and then as sleep came over me, I shrugged, because I really didn't care.

Later that night, I felt something cold touch my forehead. I opened my eyes to see a young White woman in a long flowing nightgown. I smiled at her gentle expression and opened my mouth to say hello. She shook her head with her finger on her lips and sat down on the side of the bed. I nodded and kept silent. The young woman tapped her finger to her head and leaned towards me. When I heard her voice in my mind, I almost jumped from the bed.

"Hello, Victoria. Don't be afraid. I am not here to hurt you. I've been watching over you since you came here. You are very strong. I can feel your strength even across the rift."

She smiled at me again, and I made my body relax from the fear riding through it. I opened my mouth to speak, but she shook her head and tapped her head again.

Frustrated at wanting to talk to her, I frowned.

Her tinkling laugh filled my mind.

"You have the "gifts", and you must learn to use all of them. I know that you can hear me and that means you can talk to me the same way. Just try."

I felt my face scrunching up trying to think back to her. Her laugh again filled my head.

"Don't think about it. It's just like talking to yourself," she explained.

"Like this?" I asked speaking in my head.

She clapped her hands and bounced up and down. I tried to move my leg so that she didn't bump it, but she became still again.

"Yes, now, we can have a real talk. I haven't had a real talk with anyone in so long," she sighed.

"I'm sorry. I have never spoken to anyone like this. Do you have "gifts" like mine? Is that why we can speak like this?" I asked.

A sad look came over her face, and she shook her head.

"No, something happened to me, and now, this is the only way that I can speak. Enough about that. I try not to think about that. How did you get hurt?" she asked briskly

"We live next to a very evil man. I've never understood why he doesn't like us and goes out of his way to cause us trouble. He always seems to vent his hate at me. I tried so hard to think of something that I may have done to make him dislike me, but I come up with nothing."

I finished explaining and realized that I didn't know the young woman's name.

"By the way, what is your name?"

She looked sad again for a moment, and then she smiled and said, "Liza."

I smiled and reached out to her, but she flinched away from my touch. I figured that she didn't like people touching her, so I shrugged and pulled my hand back to my lap. Liza smiled at me again.

"Tell me what's on your heart, Victoria," she suggested.

I smiled back and began telling her about the past year. I didn't think we would have time for everything, so I tried to cut it short.

"Well, almost a year ago, I gave birth to a beautiful baby girl. I already had five children, but the chance came along to have another. To tell you the truth, my friend Susan, knew of a doctor who needed smart women to have special babies. I passed all of the tests and took all of the medicines. The doctor told me that it only took me one try to get pregnant with the "implant". There were other women, but I never knew if they had "implants" too. At first, I treated it like a duty or job, but when I felt the tiny feet kicking and moving, I felt a mother's love. Something was so right with it all except my husband became angry and resented me for having the "implant" in my body. It wasn't his baby, and he reminded me of that over and over again. I didn't care how he felt because as the baby grew, I began to feel different. I felt less depressed and angry about my situation. I felt warm and light. There was darkness in me, you see, and I couldn't get it out of my heart. I prayed and prayed, but it wasn't until I got pregnant that it began to go away. I haven't felt it since the night she was born. My husband is still distant, but I don't care anymore because I feel peace in my soul. I haven't felt this way in a long time."

My words drifted off when I realized what I had told Liza. I had broken the contract with Dr. Michaels by revealing his work. I wished the words back, but they were already said. I glanced at Liza to see her looking at me with a pleasant expression on her face.

"Feel better?" she asked.

I nodded my head relieved that she didn't ask about the "implants".

"Victoria, there is a reason why your daughter was created. She had to be a part of you because she needs you as you will need her. Your strength is hers and hers is yours. I know that you only told me a little of your story, but one day you will tell it all. There will be so many more hardships, but you will always have love. Don't forget that, Victoria. You will always have love."

Liza had moved closer to me while she spoke. A shiver went through me from a rush of cold air. I shifted a little under the covers thinking that there must be a draft in the room. Liza cocked her head to the side and looked at the door. I followed her glance to see the door creeping open.

"Mrs. Sams? Are you okay? I came to check on you. Do you need something for the pain?" a young Black nurse asked. She hesitated and frowned at the open door. She rubbed her arms and turned back to me.

I opened my mouth to tell her that I didn't need anything for the pain and not to be angry with Liza, but when I turned to see Liza's reaction, she wasn't there. My heart began to beat faster when I looked at the indention where she had sat speaking with me. I heard the nurse's voice asking me questions, but she sounded far away as the events of the past few days took their toll on me. I closed my eyes and drifted into a dreamless sleep.

3

The next few days were filled with me being discharged from the hospital, being fussed over by my aunts and children, and moving into the apartment that Aunt Charlotte had leased for us. She said Harlan hadn't put up much of a fight about moving his family to a temporary home while the builders that Aunt Charlotte hired made alterations to our house. I felt guilty at all of the money that Aunt Charlotte spent on us, but I didn't dare bring it up to her again. Anyway, it was nice to have someone's loving attentions beside my children's.

Aunt Mary came to visit once we settled into the two-story apartment. She grabbed Valora from the playpen the moment that she came through door and held her while whispering in Valora's ear the entire time that she visited. I cast a puzzled look in Aunt Charlotte's direction, but she just shrugged and sipped her tea.

The children came home while my aunts were still visiting, so they spent time with them before Aunt Charlotte ushered a reluctant Aunt Mary out of the door with a promise to me that they'd come back soon. I wondered at Aunt Mary's fascination with Valora, but I dismissed it to another heart that the little imp had stolen.

Later in the week, Harlan came home and announced that we would move to Aunt Charlotte's house in Littleton for a spell because the remodel on our Dallas house had hit a snag. Someone had burned down the fence, and the fire had spread to the roof. The fire department put out the fire, but the damage meant that the builders would have to fix the roof first. I shivered while listening to Harlan telling me the details.

Deep down, I knew that Ellis Carter had set that fire, but I didn't want to give voice to it. It didn't matter that we weren't there. That evil man would be trouble to us anywhere. I said a quick prayer for peace from his evil and got up to cook supper.

I heard the phone ringing through the haze of my afternoon nap. I rushed to answer it before it woke Valora. I grimaced as the healing scar on my leg pulled in my hurry.

"Hello?"

"Lil' mirror? Is that you? You sound just like you did when you were a little girl. Heh, heh. How are you and my great-grands doing? And why do you sound so out of breath?"

Big Mama Chandra's voice was a balm to my frayed nerves. I smiled and drew a deep breath before I answered her.

"Big Mama Chandra! I'm so glad to hear from you! We're doing just fine. I rushed to get the phone because I didn't want to wake your newest great-grand. How is everything in Carson?"

I heard the hesitation in my grandmother's voice before she answered my inquiry.

"Well, me and your Grandpa Ed are doing fair to middlin'. Sadie is under the weather, but Hope takes care of the house now. It was hard to get that ol' Sadie to sit herself down, so we made a deal that she could do anything from a chair. She didn't like it, but I know she appreciates it now. You know they're about to officially call our little countryside community Allsville. It seemed to me that they should have been calling it that this whole time, but you know how those politician folks are."

I smiled and sat down on the stool next to the phone. Big Mama Chandra could talk up a storm until she ran out of steam, so I started thinking of what I would cook for dinner. It took only a moment for me to figure on meatloaf when something that Big Mama Chandra said caught my attention.

"I wanted to make sure that you knew about it. He's been real sick and that ol' Betts won't let nobody see him including your Grandpa Ed. I just hope she ain't doing any of that hoodoo on him. He looks real bad. She had the sheriff go and throw Marcos from the house, so nobody really knows what's going on over there."

"Wait, Big Mama. Who's real sick and what do you mean Betts threw Marcos out of the house?"

I felt the hairs rise on my arm waiting for Big Mama to answer me.

"Hey now, girl! Haven't you been listening? Your Grandpa Paul is sick, and Betts is doing what she wants to do now. Marcos is the only one to stand in her way, but she had the sheriff go over there and put him out of the house. He's lucky that Paul deeded him his house and land, or she would have put him off that too."

My stomach took a dive hearing that my grandfather was at the mercy of Betts. I gripped the phone tighter as an image of Grandpa Paul lying still in the bed rushed through my mind. I took a deep breath to stave off the hysteria building in my veins.

"Isn't there something that we can do, Big Mama? I mean, what about my aunts and uncles? Can't they go check on him? Please, there must be something."

"I don't know, child. I guess we'll just have to pray about it, and God will make a way," Big Mama Chandra answered.

I nodded my head not thinking that she couldn't see me. I swallowed the knot that had formed in my throat and said my goodbyes to my Big Mama promising that I'd bring the children to see her soon. I stood there for a few more moments thinking about Grandpa Paul and how he had saved me from

Betts when I was a small child. I couldn't let that old witch keep up her evil. I got down on my knees and prayed.

"Father God, I know that it has been sometime since I laid my burdens at Your Feet. I want to thank You for all the blessings that You have poured upon my family and me. You have always been there for me even when I have turned from You, Father. I know that I have done wrong, and I ask Your forgiveness in Jesus' Holy Name. I've come to You now on my knees to ask You to protect my grandfather, Paul, from the evil that lives in his house. I ask You to please put Your Mighty Hands of Protection around my family and keep us from all hurts, harm, and danger. I pray for Your Guidance and Wisdom in all that I do. In Your Son, Jesus' Name, Amen."

I opened my eyes and felt the wetness of tears on my face. I allowed myself one quiet sob before rising to go check on the blessing of my baby girl.

Saturday dawned with the kids wanting to get their chores done early because our neighbor and my good friend, Sarah was going to visit. Sarah always brought treats and everything to make the kids' favorite food, spaghetti and meatballs. I was grateful for the company because I hadn't been able to keep my mind off of my conversation with Big Mama Chandra.

When a knock sounded at the door, all of the kids ran for the door. I laughed when Susan bounded through the door and began to hug them. I frowned when I noticed that William hung back from any affection with narrowed eyes and balled fists. I opened my mouth to scold him when Susan pulled him into a reluctant hug.

"Well, you little mites are a sight for sore eyes! Here, take this bag of goodies to the kitchen and split them between yourselves. Mark, make sure that everyone gets an equal share," Susan said handing a large brown paper bag to Mark.

Mark smiled and grabbed the bag while motioning with his head for the little ones to follow him. William followed at a slower pace pushing Grayson ahead of him.

"William! Stop pushing your brother!"

I folded my arms and frowned at him until he went through the swinging door. I turned when I heard Susan chuckling behind me.

"Victoria, that boy just doesn't know when he has it good, huh? I would have tore his tush up a long time ago," Susan said moving forward to hug me.

I gave her a small smile and returned her embrace feeling inadequate next to her well-dressed self.

"Sometimes, I think that Harlan leaves his spirit in William when he goes on the road."

Susan chuckled again, handed me the grocery bag, and went to sit down on the divan next to Valora's playpen. I watched as she settled her ample body and bent over to pick up a sleeping Valora. I started to stop her but found that I couldn't. Susan had lost two babies since I met her at Dr. Michaels' office two years past. She had dropped out of his program because she said that the heartbreak was too much. I felt sorry for her but with her tough attitude, Susan wouldn't accept any kind of pity.

With her dark brown hair and smooth light brown skin, Susan looked like one of my sisters except she had a proper British accent and a more voluptuous body. Harlan had slavered over her when she first came to the house, but Susan had quickly put him in his place. I smiled in memory of Harlan's set down.

"She has gotten so big, Victoria! What do you feed her?" Susan asked while she rocked and kissed Valora.

I shook my head at my meanderings and swelled with pride at the praise.

"She's naturally fed from me and homemade baby food, and I give her the vitamins that Dr. Michaels told me to give her. Sometimes, she'll reach out and grab at table food. It tickles the kids to see her shoving the food in her mouth, but they know not to give her too much solid food."

Valora opened her eyes and smiled at Susan. Susan cooed at her and pulled out a butter cookie from her purse. Valora almost went cross-eyed trying to pull the cookie to her mouth. I laughed when she became fussy trying to reach it. Susan stood her up and put the cookie in her hand. She laughed too when Valora gave her a smile before putting the cookie in her mouth.

"She is wonderful, Victoria. Absolutely wonderful. I can see she's very smart. I guess her other half is a genius," Susan said in a lowered tone.

"I don't know. Dr. Michaels said that the whole thing is a secret, so I can only assume that he is because Valora is becoming more advanced in her speech. She listens to music like she understands it. Sometimes, that's the only thing that will quiet her or put her to sleep."

"How about I take Valora and Grayson home with me for a little while this afternoon? You can get some rest let the older kids spoil you," Susan suggested.

I smiled and nodded knowing that Susan just wanted to spend some time with the little ones.

Susan patted Valora on the back and gave her another cookie seeing that Valora had gnawed and eaten the first one. I walked to the basket by the door to get a clean wash towel to clean Valora up when I saw William skulking in the hallway.

"William! What are you doing? Why aren't you in the kitchen with everyone else?"

William narrowed his eyes at me and crept back to the kitchen. I followed him into the kitchen and saw that the other children were almost finished with their juice and snack cakes. They looked up when I walked in to the room.

"Mama!" Grayson said launching himself at me.

I laughed and leaned down to give him a hug. He had grown so much that he didn't even look like a six-year old. I squeezed him and pulled back to see William's balled fists and anger on his face. I opened my mouth to give him a dressing down when Mark asked if he could go finish his homework in their room. I said yes and frowned at William again.

"Y'all behave, you hear?" I said directing my gaze at William.

Mark, Grayson, and the girls said yes ma'am and ran from the kitchen. William followed at a slower pace almost stomping his feet. I rolled my eyes at his behavior and reminded myself to talk to Harlan about William when he returned home. I went back to check on Susan and Valora.

"Do you know that you're a special baby, huh? Yes, I think that you do, Valora."

I smiled hearing Susan talking to Valora as I returned to the room.

"I think she does sometimes," I said handing Susan the towel.

Susan laughed and squeezed Valora in a hug. Valora giggled and touched Susan's face.

"William, no!!"

My heart plummeted when I heard Mark's distressed yell. I ran into their room to see the screen off of the window. I looked at Mark hanging out of the window and pulled his sobbing body back into the room thinking that William had tried to push him out of the window. Mark took off running out of the door, and my fears escalated. I looked out of the window and screamed. Grayson lay sprawled on the concrete at a crooked angle with blood pooling on the screen under his little body.

"Victoria! What is it, luv?" Susan asked anxiously.

"My baby, my baby!" I cried.

I rushed from the room and ran down the first floor flight of stairs. I couldn't breath from the sobs erupting from my body. All I could think about was Victor. I couldn't do anything to save him, and he had died. I felt a numbness entering my body at the memory of holding his lifeless body. I couldn't lose another child. I just couldn't.

I burst through the safety door and ran to kneel beside a sobbing Mark. He muttered incoherent words at Grayson about not protecting him and not to die. I brushed him aside and knelt to feel for a pulse. Breathing a sigh of relief when I felt the slight beat signaling that Grayson still lived, I picked his head up and put it in my lap. I felt more in control and turned to give Mark orders.

"Mark, one of the neighbors probably called the ambulance but go call again just in case. Now, stop blaming yourself. William did this not you. We'll figure it all out after Grayson is better. Go get me the blanket off of the divan and my purse on the counter."

Mark nodded and ran into the glass safety door. He caught himself and opened the door passing Susan holding Valora with Gia and Leah behind her.

Susan took long strides to get to me and held out her hand to the girls to stop about a yard away from the edge of the screen. Seeing Grayson's chest move, she took a deep relieved breath.

"I called the ambulance, so they should be here soon. Don't worry, Victoria, I'm sure he'll be right as rain. I'll take the kids with me to my apartment. What else can I do?"

An older Black woman rushed up to us before I could respond to Susan and shook her head.

"Poor thing. You shouldn't have moved him. That could kill him, you know."

I narrowed my eyes at her. Anger rushed through my veins and I wanted to strike out at someone. Besides, she looked like Betts. I gave her an evil smile.

"You can mind your own business, old biddy. He's my son, and I'm not going to let him lie on the ground like this!"

She huffed and walked away from us.

Susan frowned at the old woman, then turned to me and asked again to help.

I smiled my thanks and shook my head. I didn't want to break down in front of my girls. They were already in tears and hugging each other. I sought to relieve them.

"It's okay, girls. Grayson is going to be just fine."

Out of the corner of my eye, I saw Mark dragging William out of the safety door. I wanted to rail against William and his inner evil, but I knew that I needed to concentrate on Grayson.

I tried to gather my rising hysteria when the loud sirens of the ambulance rounded the corner. The big white van came to an abrupt stop almost running up on the curb. Two White medics, one taller than the other, jumped out of the back and ran to us.

"Ma'am, please gently place his head back down. Yes, that's it. Now, please stand here and hold his hand while we see how we can help. My name is Tim. What's his name?"

Tim patted me on the back when I reluctantly rose to give him access to Grayson. I didn't want to let him go, but I knew that I had to let them help my baby.

"His name is Grayson. He fell out of the second story window. I checked his pulse like I learned from an old friend a long time ago. He's still alive. I need him to be alive, but there's so much blood," I rambled.

The other medic gave me a sympathetic look. He glanced at Susan and the girls.

"Yes, ma'am. He's alive, and we mean to keep him that way. My name is Milton, and I promise we'll do our best for Grayson. Why don't the ladies go get you a change of clothes for you to change when we get you to the hospital?"

Susan nodded and moved to take his advice. I looked around and saw the courtyard begin filling with curious bystanders. I felt a twinge of resentment at seeing them flooding out of nowhere when none of them came out to help before the ambulance arrived. I opened my mouth to spew my feelings at them when Tim ran to the ambulance.

"What is it? What's wrong?" I asked feeling panic flood my veins.

Tim shook his head and opened the back door to get the stretcher.

"Nothing, ma'am. We just need to get Grayson to the hospital. He needs more attention than we are trained for right now. He's doing okay, but he's not waking up," Tim said.

The numbness crept in, and I wanted to lie down beside my baby.

The screech of tires brought me out of my trance. I looked up to see a news crew getting out and running towards us. I heard Tim curse under his breath and tell Milton to hurry up with bandaging Grayson's head.

"Excuse me, ma'am. What happened here?"

The young White male reporter stuck a microphone in my face and waited for a reply. I shook my head and rose when the medics picked up the stretcher. Not taking my response for an answer, the reporter tried again.

"Ma'am, what happened here? Did the little boy fall or was he pushed? Did you do it? Are you his mother?"

My mouth fell open in awe at his inappropriate and uncouth questions. Tim shoved the microphone away from my face and grabbed my arm pulling me with them to the ambulance.

I heard Susan addressing the reporter in her proper and direct way.

"How dare you ask a mother those questions while her baby is injured! I'll give you what you want. Her name is Victoria, and his name is Grayson. That's all you're getting from me. Nosey bastard."

I felt the hysterical laughter building at Susan's response, but I stifled it when she handed me a small bag. Tim helped me into the back of the ambulance, and Milton hit the glass door for the driver - who I hadn't noticed – to drive. I grabbed Grayson's little hand and held on to it saying a prayer to God to heal him of his injury. I moved to the rear window to wave to my children when I saw Mark punch William's smug face. I smiled and turned around to see to Grayson.

Tim and Milton worked on Grayson until we arrived at the hospital where we met more news crews. I didn't care about anything except Grayson. I followed the stretcher through the pristine hospital corridors until a Black nurse caught my arm and tried to direct me to the waiting area. I yanked my arm loose from her grasp and pleaded with her to let me be with my son. The memory of not being with Victor when he died made me panic. I pushed past the nurse and ran down the hallway. Memories swamped me of that day while I ran through hallways calling for my son.

"Grayson! Grayson!"

Strong arms grabbed me from behind before I felt the sting of a needle in my shoulder. Everything slipped away, and I reluctantly surrendered to the darkness.

4

"Victoria."

I heard a familiar voice calling me from the darkness. I cringed at the soreness of my body and opened my eyes. The breath rushed from me with a gasp.

"Hello, Victoria. It has been a long time," Dr. William "Billy" Herbert said.

I gaped at the man that I had loved all of my life. My mouth fell open in shock, and I closed my eyes to the dizziness. This had to be a dream, I told myself until I felt his fingers grasp my chin.

"No, Victoria, you cannot go back to sleep. Your son is calling for you. Quite loudly, I might add," he said with humor.

I opened my eyes to the beloved blue eyes that had haunted my dreams for ten years. I felt the tears building, and I closed my eyes to them. Memories of the last time that I saw Billy brought guilt and heartache. I attempted to shake off those feelings and concentrate on what he had said.

"Grayson? How is he? Can I see him?"

I raised myself up with the aim of getting to my son and away from Billy. He chuckled and pushed me back down to the bed.

"He's going to be fine. They called me in to assess his head injury in case he needed surgery, but it's just a small fracture that will heal quickly because of his youth. No internal bleeding or swelling. He's going to have headaches for a long time, but aspirin should take care of those. He's a very lucky little boy."

I breathed a sigh of relief.

"No, he's blessed. When can I see him?"

I wanted to hold my son to see for myself. Billy chuckled again.

"I'll take you to him in a few minutes. The nurses told me that they had to sedate you because you were in shock. Our strongest orderly, Able, almost couldn't hold you down."

I flushed with embarrassment. Memories of my mad dash to be with Grayson kept the blood in my face. I turned my head away from Billy's smiling face and muttered an apology.

He laughed out loud.

"Well, well, I can still make you blush."

I glanced back at him and knew that he enjoyed my discomfort. I narrowed my eyes at him.

"I'd like to see my son now."

Billy held up his hands in surrender.

"Alright, alright. You'll need to take a shower first, I think. The nurses removed your blood stained clothing, but they didn't bathe the blood off of you. Do you want me to help you or should I call a nurse?"

My mouth fell open in shock.

Billy chuckled at my face and sighed in regret.

"I guess it's the nurse, then. You know, Victoria, I am a doctor, and I have seen you in all your glory before now."

I blushed again at the memory and felt the pull of sorrow of Victor's life and death.

He must have felt it too because his mirth immediately sobered.

"I'm sorry, Victoria, that was in bad taste."

I swallowed the rising tears and waved away his concern.

"It's okay. It was a long time ago, and I'm okay."

Billy looked skeptical but said nothing else. Then he cleared his throat.

"Well, I'll call in the nurse so that you can get to your son," he said turning away.

"Billy?"

He turned back with his brow raised.

"Call me William now. It's been a long time since anyone called me Billy."

I nodded and laughed.

"That's going to be hard for me because my son has the same name. Oh, well, I'm sure that I'll know who's who. Anyway, I'm glad to see you."

His face lit up with a smile, and he turned to leave the room.

I waited for the pain of the dark line to punish me for feeling pleasure at Billy's, I mean William's, return to my life, but nothing happened. I moved a little and waited. Still nothing. Feeling optimistic, I threw off the covers and made my way to the room shower wondering what other surprises God had in store for me.

"Mama! Mama!"

Grayson, surrounded by three nurses, held out his hands for me to get a hug. I walked quickly to the bed and hugged his little body. I pulled back from him to look him over for myself. His head was covered in a big white bandage, and he had tiny bandages on different places on his skin. He looked pitiful and beautiful to me at the same time. I kissed his forehead and hugged him again. He squirmed from my embrace.

"Mama, all the nurses are so nice, and a doctor gave me a fishing pole! Can I stay here forever, Mama?"

The nurses and I laughed at his request. Relieved that my son was alive and mending, I sat on the side of the bed with a sigh.

"Grayson, I know it's nice, but you can't stay. Remember your brothers and sisters? We have to go back home to them, okay?"

Grayson's lip trembled, and he looked away.

"I don't wanna go back home. Willie is mean to me."

I looked up to see the nurses frowning at me. I returned their frown and waved my hand at them to leave. They didn't move, but the oldest of them stepped forward.

"Ms. Sams, the policeman outside said that we had to stay in here with Grayson. He said that we shouldn't leave him alone with you."

I opened my mouth in shock at her statement. I started to lambast her, but I didn't want to upset Grayson. I lowered my tone to address her.

"What? What policeman?"

My heart thumped waiting for them to respond.

The nurse didn't have a chance to answer because the door opened. I almost gasped when Officer Jackson walked in to the room. His face twisted in a sneer when he looked at me.

"Well, well, if it isn't Ms. High and Mighty. I'll take over the watch, ladies. Thank you," Officer Jackson said smoothly.

The nurses looked from me to Officer Jackson before nodding and taking their leave. I moved closer to protect my son.

"So, here we are again. I'm sure that you'll be more cooperative this time seeing as how you could lose the little brat to social services pending my investigation," he said nastily.

I straightened my backbone to his threats. Grayson whimpered and hid behind me. Anger at Officer Jackson's behavior swept through my body.

"Hello, Officer Jackson. As much as it is pleasure to see you, I don't think your presence is needed. Please remove yourself from my son's room," I demanded.

Officer Jackson gave a humorless laugh at my attitude and moved to place his taller frame over me. I refused to back down at his intimidation. He smirked and stepped closer.

"You know, you aren't a half bad looking Blackie," he whispered in my face.

His hot and foul breath made me cough, so I took the chance to scoot further away from him. I felt Grayson's little hand circle my back. I would not allow this man to continue to treat us this way. I shot Officer Jackson a look of disgust.

"Please leave, Officer Jackson. You are disgusting and uncouth."

My demand seemed to enrage him, and I could see his hand rising to strike me. I pushed Grayson all the way behind me and prepared to defend myself.

"What is going on here?"

I breathed a sigh of relief seeing William stride through the door and place himself between Officer Jackson and me. William's stance forced Officer Jackson to take several steps back. Anger radiated off of William, and he looked ready to throw a right hook at the startled policeman.

"I know that I didn't just see you raise your hand to hit a woman, officer. You bullied yourself in here to question Ms. Sams when I told you to wait. You'll need to leave. Now," William said through clenched teeth.

Officer Jackson recovered his slimy attitude with a smile and put his hands up in a defensive manner.

"Hey, there, Doc. Look this Black woman is being difficult in an active investigation. I only meant to shake her a little. You know that's what you have to do with these Black folks. They only understand violence," Officer Jackson stated with a reptilian smile.

William's drew himself up to his full height several inches taller than the idiotic policeman.

"Are you serious, man? I'll need your name and badge number because I'm going to inform your superiors about your attitude. It is definitely not "protect and serve"," William growled.

Officer Jackson's smiling face dissolved into a fierce frown directed at William.

"Okay, Doc. Whatever you say. I'll wait on Ms. Sams to get out of here, then she's going to answer my questions," Officer Jackson bit out and turned to leave.

"Oh, and officer?"

William turned to stand protectively in front of Grayson and me. Officer Jackson turned his head and paused.

"I'm Black too," William stated with a gleeful smile.

I looked at William in shock hearing him admit that he was Black. I glanced to see a look of disbelief on Officer Jackson's face before he glared at William and stomped out of the room.

William turned back to us with a concerned look on his face.

"Are you okay, Victoria?"

William took his stethoscope out of his pocket and moved to examine me. I shook myself from my shock and put up a hand to stop him.

"No, William. I'm fine, but thank you for coming in when you did. Officer Jackson has been a pain in my behind since the issues with our neighbor. I don't know why he hates us so much," I whispered.

William nodded and put his medical instrument back in his pocket. He smiled and stepped to the other side of the bed to speak to Grayson.

"Hello, little man. How are you this evening? Did you show your mother your new fishing pole?"

Grayson smiled shyly at William and nodded. He pulled the small fishing pole from the bedside table and waved it towards William. William chuckled and ran his hand through Grayson's silky brown curls. I smiled at William's show of affection and relaxed from the previous tense moments. Questions immediately came to mind about William's presence. I cocked my head to the side and let loose.

"William, how have you been?"

William raised his head and looked into my eyes. The intense look made me squirm in discomfort. I handed Grayson the crayons and coloring book on the bedside table before rising to go stare out of the window. I heard William's quiet laugh from behind me. He walked to the window and stood beside me.

"After I left Carson, I went away to a special school in North Carolina to become a brain surgeon. When I graduated from the program, I stayed there because there was a huge need for good surgeons. I became well known for assessing head injuries without invasive surgery. It wasn't too long before my parents came to live nearby. My father enjoyed having a smaller practice and sometimes working with my wife and me until…"

William paused at my hitch of breath at the mention of his wife. Jealousy wove itself through my heart thinking about the man I love with another woman. I realized in an instant that I wasn't being fair. I had sent him away because of my twisted bond with Harlan. I pasted a fake smile on my face and turned to look at William. The intense gaze returned to William's face. The smile died from my lips. His handsomeness hadn't faded in the time since I'd seen him last. In fact, the years had made his patrician face even more handsome.

"Victoria, does it bother you that I married? Have you thought about me at all?"

Not trusting my voice to answer William's questions, I shook my head. William moved closer and put his hand on mine. I felt paralyzed by his direct gaze.

"Liar. I never took you to be a coward, Victoria," he whispered.

Feeling uncomfortable with his nearness, I backed up a step and broke the spell that he had over me. I ran my hand over my face and glanced at Grayson coloring in his book. I looked back at William and decided to tell him the truth.

"A long time ago, I made a stupid mistake because I hadn't gotten over my feelings for you, William. My bond with Harlan was inescapable when you and I saw each other again in Carson. I sent you away because I knew that you deserved better than a woman with another man's children in tow. I hope that your life with your wife makes you happy."

William moved forward and hugged me.

"Victoria, I feel like I have had a good life even with the stupid mistakes that I have made as well."

I returned his embrace until I heard Grayson's little voice.

"Mama, that's how Daddy hugs his friend."

I jumped back from William's arms to stare at Grayson. William turned in surprise too.

"Daddy's friend? Who's Daddy's friend?"

My heart started beating faster because I felt like I already knew the answer, but I needed Grayson to affirm it. Embarrassment crept into my face knowing that William would hear it too.

"When Daddy took me to see Mam-maw and Pop-paw, we went to a little house. A fat lady came out and brought me candy. Daddy went in the house with her. I ate all the candy and wanted some more, so I went to the house. I opened the door, and Daddy was hugging the lady a lot. He saw me and told me that she was his friend."

Grayson shrugged his shoulders and returned to coloring in his book.

I stepped forward with more questions on my tongue when I felt William's hand grab my arm. I swung around to see him shake his head.

"No, Victoria. Do not question your son. You should question your husband."

Anger directed at William's interference made me lash out at him. I threw his hand off of my arm.

"You know nothing about this, William. It's not any of your business. I'm not any of your business. Remember that you made your choice a long time ago, and I made mine. You're married, and so am I. Now, I'm sure that there are other patients for you to see."

I turned back towards the window so that he wouldn't see my tears. I heard him sigh before he gently laid a hand on my shoulder.

"Victoria, to move forward, we have to reconcile and let go of the past."

I stayed quiet and unwilling to face him again.

William sighed when I didn't respond.

"I will respect your wishes as long as you respect my professional opinion. You will not press Grayson with any more questions due to his head injury. Do you understand?"

I jerked my head yes and waited for him to leave. He squeezed my shoulder and left the room. I glanced back at Grayson to see him sleeping. I sat down in the chair next to the bed and allowed myself to sink into the depths self-pity.

5

William didn't return for the rest of Grayson's hospital stay. He sent one of his colleagues - a White doctor names Dr. Jones - whose bedside manner was not as pleasant. I regretted my harsh words but felt that it was for the best. He had a wife and probably children, and it wouldn't do him or me any good to pick up our association. I tried to put him out of my mind.

"So, Dr. Jones, can he go home today?"

I waited anxiously for the doctor to say that Grayson could go home. I knew that Aunt Charlotte, Aunt Mary, and Susan couldn't keep babysitting my other children for too much longer. Aunt Charlotte had traded places with me several times so that I could feed Valora and take her to her checkup with Dr. Michaels. I broached the subject of weaning her, but Dr. Michaels argued against it saying that she needed to be two. It was an inconvenience, but I agreed to his opinion.

I rolled my eyes at Dr. Jones' slow assessment of Grayson and hoped that he would hurry up. Before he put away his stethoscope, the door opened to an irate Harlan.

"Daddy!"

Grayson held up his arms to Harlan in his excitement.

Harlan narrowed his eyes at Dr. Jones and me and moved to embrace our son.

"Hey, there, buddy. How're you doing?"

He pulled Grayson to arm's length. Dr. Jones cleared his throat and held out his hand to Harlan. Harlan looked the doctor's hand with contempt and refused to take it. Dr. Jones dropped his hand with a frown.

"Sir, I assume that you are the boy's father. I'm Dr. Jones, and I'm in the middle of examining him for discharge. Would you mind stepping back, please?"

Harlan rose to his full height and looked down at the doctor and me.

"What happened to him, doc? I get home, and the neighbors are telling me that he fell out of our apartment."

He raised his lip in derision and stepped towards me. Grayson whimpered at Harlan's movement.

"What were you doing, you lazy cow, that you let my son fall out of a window?"

Anger began building in me at Harlan's behavior in front of Grayson and the doctor. I took a step toward him and poked a finger into his chest. Dr. Jones and Grayson faded into the background.

"You must be out of your mind speaking to me like that, Harlan. Instead of blaming me, you should be pointing the finger at yourself for being gone all of the time. You leave like the devil is chasing you from your wife and children. Remember us? Or did you forget that you are married with children while you're "hugging" your "friend"?"

Harlan looked shocked and glanced at Grayson with tightened lips. All I could see was red at his reaction confirming my suspicions. I balled my fists and forcibly lowered them to my sides to avoid hitting Harlan in front of the doctor and our son.

"You disgust me with all of you faulting and blaming, Harlan. If you were home to see about your own children, you would know that William is out of control. He did this to Grayson! If you weren't gone so much, you would know when something happens to your wife or your children!"

My voice rose while I spewed my hurt and anger at Harlan. Suddenly, I felt sick and very tired. I felt a rush of air like a door opening or closing, but when I looked around, the door remained shut. I plopped down on the foot of the bed and held out my hands to my son. Grayson crawled out of the covers and into my arms. I held him while he cried tears that I refused to shed at Harlan's betrayal. Dr. Jones cleared his throat.

"Well, I think that Grayson is well enough to go home today. I'll prescribe some headache powder for him at discharge. Don't give him too much just when he has a headache. Watch him closely for the next week or so for extreme tiredness and vomiting, okay?"

I hugged Grayson to me and nodded at Dr. Jones. He smiled for the first time since he started caring for Grayson. He patted me on the shoulder and left the room with a reminder to bring Grayson for a checkup at his private practice in two weeks. I looked up to see Harlan frowning. I returned his frown and put a now sleeping Grayson back under the covers. I went to the closet to get the clothes that Aunt Charlotte brought to the hospital for him. Harlan stopped me with his hand on my arm.

"Vicky, I'm sorry that you found out this way. I wanted to tell you when Ellis hurt you, but I couldn't. Do you want a divorce?"

I stood looking down at the bag of clothes thinking that this was my chance to be free. My heart hurt at Harlan's betrayal, but it wasn't as bad as I thought it would feel. I wanted to ask him questions about his affair, but something told me that I didn't want to know. I raised my gaze to Harlan's and smiled.

"Yes, Harlan, I want a divorce. You can have the Dallas house, and the kids and I will move to Littleton and be with Aunt Alice for awhile."

Harlan frowned at my easy compliance and shook his head. A mean smile crossed his face before he replaced it with false sympathy and concern.

"No, this isn't right. A divorce isn't right. What about my children? I don't want to lose them. How about I take the boys and you take the girls?"

My mouth fell open in astonishment at his suggestion and malice. He knew that I wanted my freedom from him, and I had walked into his fake offer of divorce like an idiot. Harlan knew that I'd never give up any of my children. I put my hands on my hips and leaned towards him.

"You're such a piece of work, Harlan Sams. You think that you're the only smart one in this marriage? Well, you're wrong. You have committed adultery more than once, and I can get a divorce..." my voice trailed off at the sudden cries of my son.

"No, no, please don't go!"

I pushed past Harlan and ran to the bed thinking that he had heard us arguing, but Grayson remained sleeping only stuck in a nightmare. I dropped the bag and picked him up in my arms. I hummed and smoothed his brow to awaken him from his troubled sleep.

When his eyes opened, they were filled with tears. I rocked him and waited for him to tell me about the nightmare. I glanced at Harlan to see that he stood closer to the bed. Grayson hiccupped and pulled back in my arms to look in my face.

"Mama, please help Aunt Alice. She doesn't wanna go away, but the man with wings took her. Please help her, Mama," he pleaded burying his face in my lap.

My breath hitched, and I looked at Harlan in terror. Fear and numbness clawed their way into my heart as I rubbed Grayson's head and reached for the phone at the same time. My hand missed it in my shock, and the phone fell to the ground.

Harlan bent to pick it up, and through a veil of tears, I saw Aunt Alice behind him smiling at me. Heartbreak slammed into me when she waved at me and turned towards the door. She disappeared right before Aunt Charlotte burst through the door with the news that Aunt Alice had fallen sick that morning and wasn't expected to live. I could hear her asking me why I cried, and Harlan's response of what Grayson had said. Pain and sorrow filled me to the core as sobs of mourning shook my body at the loss of my beloved Aunt Alice.

"It was a lovely service, Ms. Victoria. Your Aunt Alice would be proud," said Joan, the old houseman, Cedric's wife.

I smiled and nodded to her. I placed my forgotten cup of Aunt Alice's special hot tea on the tray that Joan held. She frowned at seeing it untouched but said nothing. I turned back to my post at the large picture window in Aunt Alice's living room. It was a chilly late February day, but the ranch house was warm. I could hear members of my family and the community milling around consoling each other, but I refused to join them. Half of them had only come to be nosy, and the other half had come to feel important around Aunt Alice's many wealthy and prestigious friends. I giggled thinking what Aunt Alice would say to them.

"Victoria, girl. There are some peacocks in this crowd of busybodies."

I giggled again a little louder.

"Ms. Victoria? Are you okay?"

I turned to see Cedric's concerned face and a fresh cup of Aunt Alice's tea pushed into my hand. I tried to smile but seeing Cedric's familiar face made me think of Aunt Alice. Tears gathered and fell before I could stop them. Cedric drew a handkerchief from his pocket and handed it to me. I nodded gratefully and dried my eyes.

"You know, Ms. Victoria, your auntie wouldn't have wanted you to cry for her. She always said that she had lived through enough things in all her years. The doctor said it was all those things that weakened her heart," Cedric whispered.

I nodded again and thanked him. Before he moved away, I stopped him.

"Cedric? Aunt Alice didn't suffer did she?"

Cedric smiled sadly and shook his head. I breathed a sigh of relief and turned back to the window while taking a sip of the tea. I stood fascinated by the drops of rain that look like the sky cried for my aunt too.

"Victoria?"

I turned at the sound of my mother's voice. Tess Roberts had aged into a handsome woman, but the loose black silk dress that she wore disguised the curves that I had inherited from her. I waited for her to launch into her usual tirade, but she didn't. I was even more surprised when she stepped forward and embraced me. I stood stiffly in her arms unused to affection from my mother. I instantly became suspicious and pulled away from her. Tears ran unchecked down her cheeks.

"Victoria, I don't know how to begin. Saying that I'm sorry for everything is not enough. I can't believe that I mistreated you and drove you away for all these years," she sobbed.

I stood stunned at her words. I decided to take her to the parlor because other mourners began to notice Tess' distress. I put my arm around her shoulders and escorted her to the settee in the parlor. I took the chair adjacent to it. I looked around the room while my mother gathered herself together. Aunt Alice had redone the room in white and russet orange colors. The look was pleasing and attractive. Hearing Tess' sobs abate, I turned back to her.

"Tess, why are you apologizing now? It's been so many years, and I have forgiven you and Clyde. Don't I send you pictures of your grandchildren?"

Actually, Aunt Charlotte and Aunt Mary convinced me to forgive my parents to pave a way for me to "break the line". It took awhile, but there weren't any bad feelings toward my parents and their actions any longer.

"Yes, and I have appreciated seeing them grow. I didn't know how much I appreciated the pictures until I held your little one today. She is so wonderful, Victoria. It's like she knew who I was, and she wrapped her little hands around my neck in a hug. I couldn't do anything but squeeze her little body. It brought such delight to my heart, and she put her hand on my face and laughed. She laughed, and I had to laugh too!"

I felt my eyes widen at Tess' reaction to Valora. I had never seen my mother without a nasty smile or grimace on her face, and she looked like she had really enjoyed herself! A strange feeling came over me, and I wanted to find Aunt Mary.

"Victoria, do you accept my apology? I don't want there to be bad feelings between us anymore. You are my daughter, and I want to have a relationship with you."

Tess put her hand on mine and squeezed it gently. I looked in her eyes and saw no anger, malice, or hate. Tears gathered in my eyes, and I moved to the settee to hug my mother. All the pain of the past dissolved in our tears.

Most of the guests left before a long black Chrysler stopped in the driveway. Valora wiggled in my arms while I stood in the hallway waiting for Cedric to open the door. I let out a loud gasp when my Grandpa Paul shuffled through the door with an irate Betts behind him.

"Cedric! It's been a long time! How are you, man? I tried to get here for my sister's service, but this old bat kept stopping to puke," he boomed and motioned at Betts.

My feet wouldn't move in my shock. My grandfather looked like he had aged a hundred or more years! Grandpa Ed was the same age, and he remained a robust, hard-working man. Grandpa Paul's skin looked papery, his posture bent, and all of his glorious auburn hair had disappeared.

I couldn't believe that he was in such frail condition. Fear for my grandfather's life skittered across my nerves. I glanced at Betts and saw that she had not aged well either. She was still fat, and her back was hunched. She looked like the demon Betts of my nightmares. I shook my head thinking that her evil ways had done her in finally. It was sad that they had taken their toll on Grandpa Paul as well.

Cedric escorted my grandparents down the hallway to the living room. I stayed in the shadows rocking Valora until she pulled away and tried to get down. I scowled at her because she had never acted like that, and I didn't want her getting in the way. She started to push at me harder to get down, and I raised my hand to spank her leg.

"No, Victoria. You must let her down to do what she feels."

I swung around to see Aunt Mary standing behind me. I started to explain why I didn't want Valora crawling around during Aunt Alice's funeral reception when Aunt Mary stepped forward and plucked Valora from my grasp. She placed her on the floor beside my leg and walked back towards the dining room.

Valora cooed at me and began taking halting steps down the hallway. I covered my mouth in surprise and walked slowly behind her ready to pick her up if she fell. She walked until she reached the steps to go into the hallway leading to the living room. I picked her up thinking that she had walked enough when she wiggled to get down again. I set her down on the top step and knelt down in front of her.

"What is it, Valora? Why are you walking now? What does Aunt Mary think that you need to do?" I wondered aloud knowing that she didn't understand.

She babbled and smiled at me. I couldn't help but return the smile. She put her little hand on my cheek, and I covered it with mine. I jumped and almost fell back when I heard a soft voice in my mind.

"Mama, it's okay. I need to walk now. I have to do this for you. It has to be done."

Valora kept her hand on my cheek and gurgled. Shock kept me still. My eleven month-old daughter could talk like an adult in my mind. I closed my eyes at the craziness of it and opened them to see her gazing at me intently.

I could only nod my head at my imagination. I waited for her to speak again, but she just smiled again and turned her chubby legs towards the living room. I followed at a slower pace shaking my head at the strangeness of my life.

I could hear Grandpa Paul's voice before we appeared on the top step leading into the large living area.

"Well, lookee there! Ms. Valora is using those hams to get around now," chuckled Cedric.

He came forward from serving Grandpa Paul a cup of tea and picked Valora up in his arms. She giggled at Cedric, and he tickled her neck. She laughed and squirmed in his arms. Cedric released her to stand on the floor. I walked down the three steps in dread because Betts turned her attention to us.

"What was that Cedric? Valora? Who's that?" Grandpa Paul asked.

I strode to the divan and knelt beside him.

"Grandpa? It's me, Victoria, and Valora is my daughter."

Tears gathered in Grandpa Paul's eyes, and he leaned down to embrace me. I heard Betts harrumph behind me, and I released my grandfather to narrow my eyes at her.

"Don't you be squintin' your eyes at me, missy! I'm still your grandma, and I'll still beat your butt!"

All voices stopped, and everyone remaining at the reception turned at Betts' threat.

I dismissed her threat with a wave of my hand.

"Oh, Betts, it'll take more than you to do any of that."

Everyone went back to their conversations and food seeing that it wasn't going to be any confrontations or disputes.

She opened her mouth to spew more of her venom but released a long hiss. Then she cackled.

"I guess somebody got them some backbone, huh, girl? I guess you've got some of my blood in you after all."

I glared at her and turned back to Grandpa Paul. Valora gibbered at him and placed her hand on his knee. I sat her in his lap and held on to her. Grandpa Paul leaned down and kissed Valora's little cheek.

"Well, I do say. This little one is something else, Victoria. She's like a breath of fresh air. Look at those ham-hocks, Cedric!"

Cedric stood by smiling at Valora charming her great-grandfather.

"Yes, sir. She sure is something else," Cedric agreed.

I smiled with pride at the praise heaped upon Valora until I saw Betts' narrowed eyes focused on her. Her light brown gaze had a glow when she turned it to me. I wasn't afraid, though, because her gaze was filled with fear. I'd never seen Betts fear anything, and yet, she seemed to be afraid of Valora. My heart started thumping at what it could mean. Valora looked at Betts from Grandpa Paul's lap and reached her little hand out to her. Betts shuddered and jerked away from Valora's touch.

"Get that thing away from me, now. I never want it to touch me," she snarled at me.

Offended by her calling Valora a thing, I stood up and stepped toward her. Then, I felt Valora's tiny hand touch my leg. I glanced down to see her blow a raspberry at Betts and laugh. Astonishment crossed Betts face, and she heaved her bulk off of the divan and fled the room. I leaned down to take Valora from Grandpa Paul before he got tired, but he shook his head.

"You know, my dear, I feel like I just got my second wind."

I glanced at Cedric, and we broke into laughter.

Having settled the children in the guest rooms for the night, I heard a noise when I rounded the corner of Aunt Alice's darkened living room. I stopped and peered into the darkness but saw nothing. I shrugged my shoulders and started toward the room that Harlan, Valora, and myself had taken upon our arrival. My steps faltered when I heard the noise again. It sounded like the creak of the outside screen door in Aunt Alice's office. I frowned and crept through the living room to see who had invaded my beloved aunt's office when I heard a familiar voice.

"Jenny, we should be sleeping. We have to get home tomorrow," Stephen whispered.

I wondered what Stephen and his wife, Jenny, were doing on the office patio so late at night. After all, they had their own room for them and their two sons. Jenny had seen to that, I thought wryly.

"Stephen, stop being such a weakling. If your Aunt Alice left it all to us, we only need to go home to pack up and sell the house to move here. She loved you the most, I know she did," Jenny whispered.

I felt guilty for eavesdropping, but not that guilty. I knew that if Aunt Charlotte or Aunt Mary hadn't left before nightfall, I'd surely get a good scolding for listening to someone else's conversation. That is, if they had caught me. I turned my attention back to my brother and his wife.

"Look, Jenny, Aunt Alice took care of all of us. She didn't have any children, but she has more than me to leave stuff to. Why don't we wait for the lawyer to tell us, sweetheart?" Stephen pleaded.

"No, we won't wait because they'll probably feel sorry for that brood mare sister of yours - the White one. I know you told me that she looks like your grandfather's side of the family, but I think something else is going on there. What if she's your Aunt Alice's long lost daughter, and she gets everything? I saw her acting funny with your grandmother, Betts. Something is going on there. I know it. You need to know these things, Stephen. We could use them to our advantage," Jenny huffed.

My fingers itched to slap Jenny for her stupidity. When she walked into the house three days before, her head had been so high that I was surprised that she could see where she was going. Ruth and Lacy stayed away from her. Now, I knew why. I felt pity for Stephen for marrying such a greedy, conniving woman.

Stephen sighed loudly.

"Jenny, every family has problems. It's the way that families solve them that makes them weak or strong. My family is no different. No, we will not go looking for trouble, and you will never speak like that about my sister, Victoria. She has been through enough. Now, we're leaving early in the morning so that I can clock in for at least a half day's work."

I heard more movement, so I turned to make my escape running into a sniggering Betts.

"What have we here? An eavesdropping little witch? Yes, that's what you are. Who were you listening to, I wonder? Shall we let'em know what you were doing?"

I composed myself and raised an eyebrow at her questions.

"And what were you doing, grandmother? I'd say that you were up to the same thing. I must have inherited the trait from you," I stated in a low voice.

Betts cackled quietly and moved closer. I shrank back a little from the heaviness in the air around her. I knew that she did it on purpose, so I straightened my back and stood to my full height. The heaviness slipped from me like water from a duck. The look on Betts' wrinkled face switched from malevolent to shock. She grabbed at her throat and took a step back.

"What have you done, girl?"

"I don't know what you mean, Betts."

I shrugged and took a step toward her. This time, she shrank away from me. Betts tried to recover her composure and took a tiny step forward.

"Whatever you did, it don't matter, you hear? It don't matter because you're still married to Harlan which means you haven't crossed back over the line," she whispered harshly.

I shook my head and turned to walk away. I heard Betts hiss and felt a rush of air behind me. The light snapped on in the living room, and I blinked at the brightness.

"Ms. Betts! What is wrong with you? Are you about to hit my wife?" Harlan asked. He stood holding a fussing Valora.

I turned to see Betts' claw-like hand lifted to strike me, and I quickly moved away from her. Harlan came down the steps into the living room, and Betts stepped back toward the darkness of Aunt Alice's office. I felt a calm replace my anger and fear towards my grandmother. I walked to Harlan and took Valora from his arms. I turned and fixed my face with an innocent expression.

"Betts? Would you like to hold your great-granddaughter?"

Valora had stopped fussing and held out her chubby little hand to Betts. Betts hissed and almost ran from the room. I smiled and let out the breath that I had been holding. Stephen and Jenny walked in at that moment.

"What are y'all doing up, Vicky?" Stephen asked while looking guilty.

I rubbed Valora's back and shrugged my shoulder.

"Nothing much, and y'all?"

Jenny narrowed her eyes at us before stomping from the room. Stephen made his excuses and went after her. I shook my head and turned to go to bed.

"What was all that about with your grandmother?" Harlan asked.

He threw a fearful glance over his shoulder.

I waited for him to walk ahead of me to turn on the hallway light. I turned around to snap the living room light off when I saw Aunt Alice standing in her office smiling sadly. I returned her smile before answering Harlan's question.

"Freedom."

6

I got up early the next morning and found my way to the kitchen. Dee stood at the stove stirring a large pot. He glanced at me with a frown and kept stirring the pot. My nose told me that it was Dee's delicious oatmeal, but I didn't have an appetite. I poured a cup of tea and sat on a stool at the woodblock counter to watch Dee. He had been with Aunt Alice for as long as I could remember. Aunt Alice had flaunted convention and kept a Mexican cook. Sometimes, he reminded me of my Uncle Marcos, just not as handsome and no accent.

"He's a mean old goat, but he can cook up some vittles anywhere," Aunt Alice used to say with a laugh.

She always said it within earshot of Dee who would cross his large arms and put a scowl on his face. Aunt Alice would laugh at his intimidation stance and give Dee a whopping pat on the back. Dee would grimace and return to his duties. I smiled at the memory and took a sip of my tea.

"Ms. Victoria, I'm sorry about Ms. Alice. She was a great lady."

I looked up to see Dee holding a kitchen towel in my face. I touched my face and realized that I had shed tears at the memories of Aunt Alice. I took the towel and wiped my face.

"Thank you, Dee. She loved you, you know, in her own way."

Dee nodded and returned to the stove.

"You should go sit in the new rocker that she put on the porch. She bought it a few weeks ago for you and your young'uns."

I looked up in surprise at Dee's back. I swallowed back the threatening tide of tears and chuckled.

"I think I will go sit outside for awhile this morning before those young'uns hit the floor running."

Dee had moved to placing bacon in a skillet and waved his hand at me.

I picked up my tea and walked through the dining room to Aunt Alice's office. I grabbed the lap blanket from the back of her chair and opened the patio door. I gasped when I saw the beautiful light colored oak two-seater cushioned rocker with matching ottoman. I allowed the tears to flow at Aunt Alice's generosity. I swiped at my face with the blanket and chided myself for sniveling. Aunt Alice would have had a fit if she had seen me crying over a chair. I laughed quietly and sat down sinking into the deep cushions. I breathed a sigh of contentment and put my feet on the ottoman. I put my teacup on the small table beside the chair and covered myself with the blanket.

Another sigh of contentment escaped my lips when I looked out over Aunt Alice's beautiful ranch. Aunt Alice had chosen her land well and made her home a paradise. My mind wandered to Stephen and Jenny's conversation last night. Stephen had worked hard for Aunt Alice for many years, but she had to find another ranch foreman when he went college in Bouton. He didn't return after he married Jenny, and I don't think that he kept in touch with Aunt Alice very much afterwards. At least, as far as I had known. I shook those thoughts out of my head and allowed the peace of the morning to lull me to sleep.

"Grayson, don't throw the driveway rocks at your sisters. Gia and Leah, go get your bags to put in the car," I yelled from the porch.

Gia looked about to argue, but Leah took her hand and ran in the house. I rolled my eyes at her stubbornness and took a step to round up Grayson. I worried because since his head injury, he had become more unruly. I said a quick prayer that he didn't start acting like William.

William. Frustration at him made me grind my teeth. Harlan had given him a beating before we came to Littleton, but I felt that it wasn't enough. I wanted to take him to a doctor to see what was wrong with his mind, but Harlan forbade it saying that William would grow out of it. I said another quick prayer that he would.

I saw dust from a vehicle coming up the lane to Aunt Alice's ranch. I held my hand over my eyes to shade them from the late winter sun so that I could see who it was. I couldn't tell, but I knew that they were coming to fast and reckless. Panic filled my heart seeing Grayson playing in the circular driveway.

"Grayson, why don't you come play on the porch?" I asked trying to keep my tone calm.

Grayson looked up and shook his head. Anger at his disobedience made me step down another step.

"Grayson David Sams! Come here right now, or I'm going to tear your behind up, young man!"

Grayson stood up and ran to me just as the raggedy looking brown car rounded the driveway and screeched to a stop where he had stood a moment ago. Relief rushed through me to be replaced by a mother's fury. I stepped off the last step and waited with balled fists for whomever it was to get out of the car. When the door opened, my fury escalated.

"Where's Harlan?" Shirley demanded.

I ignored her and snickered at her appearance. Shirley's face had pockmarks all over it, and her hair was grey and scarce. The old faded housedress that she wore looked dirty and hung shapeless on her tall frame.

"Well, bitch, where is he?" she demanded again.

Her use of such a vulgar word in front of Grayson rekindled my anger. I felt him quivering beside me. I leaned down and gave him a kiss on his bandaged head.

"Grayson, please go find your Daddy and tell him to come here. Then, tell Cedric to bring me the shotgun."

I heard Shirley laugh behind me.

"You're just a mewling bad of hot air. A shotgun?"

She laughed again and settled herself next to her car. I narrowed my eyes at her boldness.

"How dare you invade my beloved aunts home, you whore! You almost hit my son in your madness! I'm going to enjoy pumping your old musty body with holes!"

I wanted to rip the smug smile from her face in my rage. I took another step toward her and felt someone grip my arm. I glanced back to see Harlan's grim face shaking his head at me. At me! In my fury, I yanked my arm from his and turned on him. I heard Shirley guffawing behind me.

"Yeah, Harlan, you better get your "wife" before I tear her to shreds."

Shirley launched herself at me, and I planted my feet to defend myself. Harlan stepped forward and put his hands out to keep us apart.

"No! You will not do this today! Shirley, what are you doing here? Never mind, I don't want to know. You shouldn't have come," he said frowning at Shirley.

Shirley looked taken aback at Harlan's response. Her eyes widened in pretend innocence. She ran into his open arm and began crying.

"Oh Harlan! I'm not feeling well, and I wanted to come get you to come see the children. Marianne is leaving to go to nursing school soon, and she misses you. Simon and Mac are running wild while you cater to her," she raised her head and pointed at me.

Harlan pushed Shirley away and shook his head.

"No, Shirley, I stay away because of your games and because you married Walter Sparks to spite me. Vicky has nothing to do with this."

Harlan stepped closer to me, and Shirley became enraged. She threw herself at Harlan and began scratching his face. I grabbed what little hair that she had left with my right hand and slapped her face with my left. She howled and kicked me in the leg. Excruciating pain shot through my body, but I refused to release her hair. I felt my thumb pop when she twisted in my grasp.

"Vicky, let go!"

I let go of her hair with relief. He picked up a fighting Shirley and began walking to the car. Cedric rushed out of the house with Dee, Mark, William, and Grayson on his tail. Cedric raised the shotgun and pointed it towards Shirley.

"Mr. Harlan, we ain't gonna let no one come here and hurt Ms. Victoria. Now, please get that heffa off this property."

Dee and Mark came and stood protectively in front of me. Grayson grabbed my hand. I jerked at the pain in my thumb. I looked over at Harlan trying to shove Shirley in the car. She heaved against him and screamed her hatred at me.

"It's all your fault, you little nobody! You came here with your high and mighty ways and wealthy family and stole Harlan from me! He didn't want you. He wanted me! I bet you had to hoodoo him to keep him all this time! 'Cause you know that no one else wants your needy ass! I hate you, you stupid cow! I hate you!"

I glanced behind me to see the rest of my family standing on the porch watching the horrible scene. I grew angry that Harlan's whore had the gall to embarrass me. I stepped forward with a snarl. My tone lowered, and Shirley stopped her struggles to hear me.

"You are still so stupid to think that I need Harlan. Look around you, Shirley. If Harlan wants to go, he can go. In fact, he can get a divorce today and come back to you if he wants to. I doubt he will though since you look like a swamp thing."

I heard my Grayson and the girls cry out at the mention of Harlan leaving, but I held my ground. It was past time that Shirley understood how much good her whoring ways had done her with Harlan. I glanced at Harlan to see his mouth open in shock. He dropped his arms from trying to push Shirley into the car and came to stand in front of me.

"I don't want a divorce, Vicky, and I'm not going to let you divorce me either," he said in a low voice.

I knew he meant it, so I nodded and smiled for my children's sake. My hope that he'd take the chance to be with his whore and leave me alone died a quick death. He turned around to Shirley and shooed her with his hand.

"Go on home, Shirley. Tell my children that I'll visit them another day. Give them my love and tell Marianne that I'm proud of her."

Shirley spit in our direction. It didn't come close to where we stood, but her meaning was clear. For a moment, I thought she'd come back to attack us more, but Cedric waved the shotgun in her direction.

"Harlan Sams, you can keep all that to yourself. I'm not telling my children nothing. You think that you can toy with me and drop me like a hot potato? Well, think again," she said angrily.

She got in the car and threw a can out of the window at Harlan before starting the jalopy and driving away in a cloud of dust.

Everyone breathed a sigh of relief and turned to go in the house from the cold. Cedric picked up Grayson, and Dee promised all of the children hot sweet milk and cookies. They cheered and raced into the house. I put my hand on Harlan's arm, and he paused and looked back at me.

"Harlan, why are you staying when you and I both know that our marriage is over? You can finally be with Shirley."

I rubbed my arms from the cold and felt the soreness in my leg and thumb from the fight with Shirley. A mysterious and mean smile crossed Harlan's face before he answered me.

"Shirley has nothing for me. Besides, I stay for my kids, Vicky. I don't want another man to be over them or hurt them. Don't you read the news about stepfathers abusing their stepchildren? Well, that's not going to happen to mine. After all, you're such a great judge of men, right?"

Harlan's hateful words stunned me. I couldn't believe the poison that had just dripped from his mouth. He laughed at my expression.

"Oh yeah, I'm also staying for my half of the big money from Valora when she turns a year old next month, and just in case your Aunt Alice left you anything. Now, let's get the kids and leave this place. It makes me feel strange."

He turned and almost skipped up the steps into the house. I shuddered at Harlan's evil duplicity and followed him.

As soon as we got back to the apartment in Dallas, Harlan disappeared with the excuse that he had to go check on the house. I sighed at his blatant ignorance and directed the children to unpacking. Except for Grayson. I kept Valora and him with me and told Mark to unpack Grayson's clothes. I didn't trust William anywhere near Grayson. I knew that I'd have to do something about him soon, but I wanted to wait until we had moved out of the apartment.

The thought of moving made me think about moving to Aunt Charlotte's house in Littleton. My heart felt heavy thinking about living in Littleton and knowing that Aunt Alice wouldn't be there. It was probably for the best that we just moved back into the Dallas house once it was finished. I felt pretty sure that Ellis and Orna Carter would leave us alone after the glass incident. I leaned down and rubbed the scar. Aunt Charlotte had called in a specialist for the scar, and he told us to wait for it to heal completely which would take about a year for all of the tissues to mend together. I didn't mind because I didn't care if anyone thought it was repulsive. I wasn't looking for another man in my life – especially one like Harlan.

The next day while the kids were at school, a heavy knock sounded at the door. I stood up from feeding Valora in her highchair at the kitchen table, and ran to open the door thinking that Susan had come for a visit. I barely opened the door before it swung wide to admit Officer Jackson. He strode through the door and kicked it shut with his foot. I backed away from the vicious look on his face. He sneered at my retreat and stalked closer. I realized that he liked my fear and stopped to confront him.

"Officer Jackson, you will remove yourself from my home right now. My husband I can come to the police station for the business about my son."

He laughed viciously and then abruptly stopped. He narrowed his eyes at me.

"I guess it's just me and you now, huh? I don't hear all that "high and mighty" tone in your voice now, huh?"

My mouth went dry when I thought of the things that this evil man could do to Valora and me. I prayed for safety and wisdom. All of a sudden, I felt calm and collected. My heart stopped racing, and I thought of a plan. I smiled at Officer Jackson and gestured toward the couch.

"Officer Jackson, I apologize if I have used a "high and mighty" tone with you. Please come and sit down so that we can talk," I said keeping my eyes lowered.

He laughed and swaggered to sit in the large recliner. I waited for him to sit down and smiled again.

"Do you mind if I get us some coffee and tea cakes from the kitchen? They're fresh baked this morning."

Officer Jackson relaxed against the sofa and spread his arms along the back.

"Yeah, yeah, go ahead. I could use a couple of those Black people cookies," he said.

He waved me toward the kitchen and turned to look at my shelf of whatnots. I forced myself to walk slow and steady into the swinging door. Valora looked up and grinned with her arms out to me. I shook my head and kissed her little hands. My own shook so bad that I almost dropped the lid to the cookie jar. I grabbed several teacakes and handed Valora one to keep her quiet.

If Officer Jackson found out that she was home with me, there's no telling what he would do. Valora giggled and hummed as she nibbled the large cookie. Seeing that my daughter was all right, I turned and picked up the rotary phone on the wall. I dialed zero and peeked through the door to see Officer Jackson tossing around one of the tiny crystal vases that Aunt Charlotte had given me two Christmas' past.

"West Bell Operator, how can I help you?"

"Please, there's a bad man in my apartment. He means to hurt me and my baby," I whispered.

I intentionally didn't tell the operator that a bad policeman was in my home. I knew that I'd never get help.

"Okay, ma'am, I'm contacting the police now. What is your address?"

I gave her the address and begged her to hurry. Another peek into the living room showed an annoyed Officer Jackson looking towards the kitchen. I started to hang up the phone when I heard the operator speaking.

"Ma'am, would you like for me to stay on the phone until the police arrive?"

Fear of discovery made me drop the phone on the counter and reach for the coffee pot. I grabbed the plate of teacakes and met Officer Jackson at the door with a smile.

"I'm so sorry to keep you waiting, Officer, but I couldn't find the tray. May I place these down on the coffee table and get a couple of coffee cups for us?"

I gestured toward the living area without getting closer to him. His body odor reeked, and I wanted to gag. He shot me a superior smile and reached around to pinch my bottom. I cringed at his disgusting and disrespectful touch but straightened my face when he leaned back to look at me.

"Sure, I like having you wait on me, gal. You don't look half bad doing it. Go get me a cup, so I can watch you fix me up, huh?" he breathed.

Trying not to vomit, I hurried and placed the plate and coffee pot on the coffee table while he resumed his seat. I attempted another smile and almost ran into the kitchen. With dismay, I saw that Valora had demolished the teacake and stood in her high chair waving her arms at me. I took her down and debated about trying to slip into the master bedroom and lock the door. I decided against making Officer Jackson angry with my child in the apartment, so I opened a cabinet and let her play with the towels.

"What's taking so long to get me a cup, slut?"

Panic rushed through me at his yell, and I said a prayer that the police would come soon. I grabbed Harlan's favorite coffee cup from the drying rack and rushed through the door. The phone fell off the counter and stuck in the door. I ignored it and prayed that Valora wouldn't come through the crack.

"Here you go, Officer," I replied.

I placed the cup in front of him and poured out the steaming black liquid. Thankful that I had made myself a fresh pot of coffee, I smiled at the vile policeman.

"Cream, sugar, or both?"

"I like mine Black," he sneered.

He gave me a nasty smile and picked up the cup. I knew what he meant, but I ignored it and sat down in the chair across the long length of the coffee table. I waited for his next move. Adrenaline pumped through my veins because I felt that I would need to fight the short muscular policeman for my life. I sat poised on the edge of the chair to run. He smacked his lips and sat his cup down before raising his malevolent gaze to me.

"It seems like you have two choices here, gal. You can do what I say, or you can go to jail for hurting your little brat. After all, the word of a cop goes a long way, and it won't matter how many fancy pants lawyers you get. You'll rot in jail until I say it's time for you to get out," he jeered.

I opened my eyes wide to look innocent then lowered them quickly.

"Officer Jackson, please don't do this. I haven't done anything to you. Why are you doing this?"

I heard him laugh and peeked at him through my auburn lashes.

"Look, here, gal. When all that civil rights nonsense happened, I gladly beat, pummeled, arrested, set dogs on, and killed your kind. Y'all need to learn your place. That's what most of the force thinks anyway. When you called yourself putting me down in that hospital, you opened up a can of worms. Your old man knew it, but you sat there with your hoity-toity ways overlooking the way things are supposed to go. Blacks are animals, and you should remember that while I'm teaching you this lesson," he snarled.

He picked up his cup of coffee again and took a sip. I raised my chin at his immoral and racist statements. All of a sudden, I didn't care that the police hadn't arrived. I couldn't let this fool get away with calling Black people animals. I stood up and pointed a finger into his flabbergasted face.

"Officer Jackson, your name should be jackass because that is what you are. How dare you boast about beating and murdering Black people? You are the animal. When Black people ruled the lands of Egypt and Babylon, White people roamed the earth like cattle. It was White people who convinced Black kings and queens that they were nothing more than vermin when for centuries before, Black royalty had captured White people as slaves, but that doesn't matter now. Everyone is equal because we're all God's children. There are smart people of all colors, and I'm proud to carry all of them in my veins. You are an uneducated fool, and I want you to leave my home. Now!"

He slammed his cup down and stood up to rush me. In my anger, I picked up the coffee pot and threw it at him. The lid opened on impact and splashed the hot liquid all over his chest. He roared in pain and anger and took a step towards me.

"Open up, Jackson! We know that you're in there! Open the door, or we're coming in!

I breathed a sigh of relief at the sound of policeman on the other side of the door, but it was short lived because Officer Jackson grabbed me by the throat and squeezed.

"So, you think that you're smart, huh? Well, they won't do you any good if you're already dead when they get in here," he growled in my face.

I clawed at his grip, but he only squeezed harder. I could hear the police demanding entry, but they sounded so far away. I knew that I couldn't let him win. I raised my knee and kicked him in the groin. He let go of my neck and dropped to the floor holding himself. I kicked him in the face for good measure and hopped over him to open the door. Policemen rushed into the apartment. A tall Black man in a suit came in after them and took me by the arms. I struggled against his grip, and he tightened his grasp.

"Mrs. Sams, are you all right? It's okay. The operator patched us in to your conversation. I'm Wade Earl, one of the police captains. Are you hurt?"

I nodded my head and broke into sobs. He drew me into his arms and patted me on the back. I scolded myself for being weak and pulled away.

"I have to go get my baby. She's in the kitchen," I sniffed.

Mr. Earl chuckled and motioned his head behind me.

"Is that her?"

I turned to see Valora giggling and hugging a laughing White uniformed older policeman. I smiled at them, but it died away when I had to move for the other three officers to escort Officer Jackson out of the door.

"This isn't over, slut," he growled.

Mr. Earl stepped forward and laughed in Officer Jackson's face.

"Oh, yes, it is Tim. You stalked and attacked this woman after you were suspended for falsifying your police reports. We don't even need her statement because the operator heard everything. I'm just grateful that we arrived in time. Now, get him out of here, boys."

The policemen snickered at Officer Jackson's look of shock and pushed him through the door into a hallway of bystanders. Mr. Earl shut the door and turned to smile at me.

"You were very brave, Mrs. Sams. I'm glad that we got here when we did. We have been watching Jackson's actions for some time. He's going to jail for the rest of his life. Do you want us to take you to the hospital to get checked out?"

I whispered no, and then felt my legs go numb. I almost fell, but Mr. Earl caught me and guided me to the divan. I looked around at the mess from the fight with Officer Jackson. The White officer holding Valora came forward and handed her to me. The urge to wail and scream built within my body, but Valora put her head on my chest and hugged me with her little arms. Calm and peace filled my spirit. I pulled my beloved daughter closer and bent to kiss her.

The White officer patted Valora's head and pointed to the mess.

"Mrs. Sams, if it wouldn't be too much bother, may we help you clean this up before we leave?"

I smiled at his kind offer and nodded. I hummed and rocked Valora finding love in her embrace to forget the horror of the afternoon.

7

"I still don't understand why you didn't look through the peephole to see who it was. This neighborhood isn't as nice as it used to be when these apartments were new," Aunt Charlotte scolded.

I took a sip of my tea and smiled into my cup. Ever since Aunt Charlotte had found out about Officer Jackson's invasion the day after it happened, she had ranted and raved about my actions and Harlan's absence. It had been two months, and Aunt Charlotte still wouldn't let it go.

"You handled yourself well, but you shouldn't have had to face all that nastiness alone. I'm furious with Harlan for not being here to protect you. Where is that scoundrel anyway?"

Aunt Charlotte patted my knee and looked around as if Harlan would walk out of the walls. I remained silent because I knew that she would keep fussing if I told her that he hadn't been home but four times in the last month. Nodding and an occasional "yes ma'am" seemed to satisfy her anyway. I took another sip of my tea and allowed my mind to wander while Aunt Charlotte continued her tirade.

The commotion of that day was something that I wanted to forget, but my nightmares kept reminding me. Officer Jackson was in jail for fraud, abuse of power, discriminatory actions of a peace officer, and assault. Not many people knew exactly what happened because Captain Earl had tried to keep the press out of it for my sake. At least, that's what he told me. Deep down, I knew that it was because the police department didn't want to be on trial with Officer Jackson. I shuddered at the memories of that day and decided to interrupt Aunt Charlotte with her favorite topic.

"Aunt Charlotte, I want to thank you for giving Valora such an extravagant first birthday party. The neighborhood children loved the tiny carnival that you organized. My mind was so crazy from everything that I wouldn't have been able to plan a menu."

Aunt Charlotte smiled and patted her neat bobbed hairstyle.

"Oh, it was nothing, sweetheart. I wanted to do it for my little precious angel. By the way, is she up yet? I want to see her before I leave."

"I'll go check on her. She should have been up by now," I said rising from the divan.

I walked into the master bedroom and over to Valora's large crib expecting to see her asleep. My heart skipped a beat seeing the crib was empty. I walked around the crib thinking that she had tried to climb out and fell. Valora wasn't anywhere around the crib. I began to panic when I heard a giggle. I breathed a sigh of relief and forced my body to relax.

"Valora? Come here, pumpkin pie," I called playfully.

I heard another giggle near the closet. I neared the closet and flung open the door. Valora squealed and threw herself at my legs. I laughed and picked her up. She snuggled into my arms and let out a sigh.

"Ma-ma, lub you," her tiny voice said.

Surprised and delighted at her speech, I lifted her in my arms and twirled in a circle in my excitement. She squealed again and hugged my neck. I laughed and hugged her.

"Victoria, what is all this?" Aunt Charlotte asked from the doorway.

"Oh, Aunt Charlotte, Valora climbed out of her crib and hid in the closet. I found her, and she said, "Mama, love you!"

I danced around again with Valora on my hip. Aunt Charlotte laughed and came forward to pluck Valora from my arms. I held on for a moment because I didn't want the good feeling to pass. Aunt Charlotte frowned at my reluctance and shrugged off my arms. She turned to walk from the room nuzzling Valora's neck.

"Did you just make your Mama happy, little girl, huh? Is that what you did? Can you say it again for Auntie?"

Valora blew a raspberry, and Aunt Charlotte and I laughed before returning to the living room.

Harlan returned the next week and told me that the Dallas house was ready. Fear entered my heart about our problems with Ellis and Orna Carter until Harlan told me that they were getting ready to move out of their house. I sighed in relief and began the process of packing up the apartment. Harlan left again the next day leaving me with the difficult job of packing up six kids and a fully furnished apartment. I thought about asking my aunts for help, but I didn't want to hear Aunt Charlotte harping about Harlan again.

At the end of the next week, I had worked hard to get almost everything in the apartment packed. I left the living room for last because of all my delicate whatnots. I put Valora down for her morning nap and began the process of wrapping and packing the whatnots. I jumped and almost dropped a souvenir teacup hearing a heavy knock on the door. I finished wrapping the whatnot and placed it in the packing box. Another knock sounded before I reached the door. I sighed at the impatient knock and rose on my tiptoes to look through the peephole.

A distinguished looking White man stood at the door with an irritated look on his face. Fear of another Officer Jackson incident made me wary to open the door all the way. I put the chain on the door and opened it a crack. The irritation slipped from the man's face to be replaced with a friendly smile.

"Yes? Can I help you?" I asked quietly.

"Mrs. Victoria Alicia Sams?" he inquired.

"Yes, that's me. Can I help you?"

"Mrs. Sams, my name is Peter Honeywell, and I am an attorney with Booker and Worthy. Actually, I was your Aunt Alice's attorney. May I come in and speak with you?" he said flashing his pearly white teeth at me.

Hearing Aunt Alice's name brought heaviness to my heart. I slid the chain off the door and opened it wider for Mr. Honeywell to enter the apartment. I closed the door and moved a box from the divan for him to sit. He thanked me and sat down with his briefcase on his lap. He motioned for me to take the chair next to him and opened the case. He took out several papers and an envelope. It was when Mr. Honeywell lifted his gaze to mine that I was struck by the sympathy in his green eyes.

"Mrs. Sams, I want to let you know what a pleasure it was to work with and for your Aunt Alice. She was a shrewd businesswoman, but she was also very generous. I'm very sorry for your loss. She will be missed," he stated.

My throat went tight, and I lowered my gaze to swallow back the tears. Mr. Honeywell remained quiet for a few moments, and then he cleared his throat. He slipped a pair of tortoiseshell glasses on his nose and picked up a sheaf of papers.

"Now, Mrs. Sams, I have full disclosure of the events that happened when you married Mr. Sams. Your Aunt Alice was actually quite vocal about the situation. You were deeded a piece of land and gifted money to start a ranch and go to nursing school, but your husband misappropriated the funds and lost the land. Am I right?"

Feeling anger that this man knew about my stupidity, I jerked my head in confirmation. Mr. Honeywell nodded too and went back to reading from his papers.

"Your Aunt Alice actually bought the land back and put it in trust for your children. She also left enough money to cover the yearly taxes until your youngest child turns twenty-five. At such time, any or all of the children can divide the land and live on it, but none can sell it to anyone but another sibling.

Also, you will receive a monthly stipend to supplement the income received from employment as a nurse's aid. If the children choose to further their education, monies will be provided at the completion of said education. If they drop out of school, the money will revert to a charitable trust."

I snapped my mouth shut when Mr. Harwell finished reading Aunt Alice's wishes. Aunt Alice had provided for my children and me even though I had made the mistake of allowing Harlan to do away with her first gift. Wait, income from employment as a nurse's aid? I frowned and leaned towards Mr. Honeywell.

"Mr. Honeywell? I understand everything that you just explained except for the nurse's aid part. I'm not a nurse's aid. I don't have any skills at all except for cooking and cleaning. I'm just a housewife. You must be mistaken."

Mr. Honeywell chuckled and shook his head.

"No, Mrs. Sams, I'm not. You Aunt Alice's instructions were to enroll you in nursing school and monitor your progress until completion. She had hopes that you would still be a nurse, but she realized after your last child's birth that you wouldn't be able to work full-time for some years."

Stunned, I sat back with a thump and hit my head on the back of the chair. Mr. Honeywell rose to assist me, but I waved him back into his seat. I rubbed my head and tried not to stare at him with my mouth open.

Mr. Honeywell laughed out loud at my expression. His laugh must have woken Valora because she awoke with a yell. I excused myself to fetch my daughter and walked on legs that felt like rubber to the master bedroom. I picked up a humming and clapping Valora and returned to the living room.

Mr. Honeywell's expression turned to astonishment. He placed his papers on top of a box on the coffee table and rose to his feet. Valora waved at him and wiggled to get down. I placed her on the floor, and she walked to Mr. Honeywell and raised her arms. I stepped forward to explain that my baby girl didn't mean any harm when Mr. Honeywell reached down and drew Valora into his arms. He stared at her a moment, and then he turned his gaze to mine with a strange smile on his face.

"Mrs. Sams, I'm sorry if I am acting strange. Your daughter looks like the child that my wife and I lost a few months ago," he whispered.

Tears filled my eyes at Mr. Honeywell's loss. I stood still while Valora worked her special "gift" on him. I smiled when Mr. Honeywell sighed in contentment and put Valora down. She laughed and started shuffling around the coffee table to play with the newspaper that I had out for packing. Mr. Honeywell cleared his throat to get my attention.

"So, Mrs. Sams, I just need you to sign these documents to accept your inheritance, and I'll be out of your way. One more thing, in compliance with your aunt's wishes, your husband cannot know about this," he stated returning to his efficient manners.

I hadn't planned on telling Harlan anything, but nodded my assurance for Mr. Honeywell. He nodded and began putting some of the papers back in the briefcase. Remembering the conversation between Stephen and Jenny, I became curious about the rest of Aunt Alice's estate.

"Mr. Honeywell, what happens to the ranch now?"

Mr. Honeywell pulled a pen from inside his suit pocket and held it out to me.

"The ranch has been gifted to the houseman, Cedric and the cook, Dee. Your Aunt didn't want them displaced in the event of her death. They will be responsible for all incomes and debts that they incur during the ranch operations. The remainder of your aunts financial estate has been divided among other family members, employees, friends, and some charities."

I stepped forward and took the pen fixing my signature to the documents. Satisfied, Mr. Honeywell closed his briefcase and stood up to leave. I followed him to the door thinking that Aunt Alice had done well in the division of her estate. She had been a fair woman in life, and she remained so in death. I looked up and mouthed a silent "thank you". As if he heard me, Mr. Harwell turned around and held out the envelope in his hand.

"This is for you. Your aunt left it with us to give to you."

Curious, I took the letter and slipped it into my dress pocket. Mr. Honeywell glanced at a giggling Valora and smiled.

"Take care of her, Mrs. Sams. I have a feeling that she is going to be a very special person."

I looked at my daughter creating a mess and laughed.

"She already is, Mr. Honeywell. She already is."

Later that night, I opened the letter from Aunt Alice. I put my hand to my mouth in shock at her words. An image of her writing at her antique mahogany desk came to my mind.

Victoria,

By the time that you read this letter, I'll be gone to that big ranch in the sky with The Lord. I haven't felt like myself in a long while, so I know that it's almost time. I can't complain because I have lived a good life and on my own terms. Now, that's something that I can't say for a lot of folks, including my younger brother, Paul. I had hoped that he would break away from Betts' cursed ways before I left this world, but I guess these things take time. Anyway, what matters is that you break away from her curses, Victoria. Yes, I know about your wedding night. When Dee found the box of salt and all his sage missing, I knew what you had done. Why you did it? I guess I'll never know, but you need to figure it out, gal. You can't let other people give you the strength that you need. You have to find it inside of yourself and use it to carve a place in this world for yourself and those young'uns. I've left y'all a little something to help you find your way. Don't you tell that old lying wretch of a husband about it either. I wish that I could have horsewhipped

him just one time, but I never got the chance. He's a
slick one, but you have to jump in a barrel of grease
to be slicker than a Roberts. You have royal and
strong blood running through your veins, Victoria,
and don't let anyone convince you otherwise. Hold
your head up high no matter what the situation and
teach those young'uns to do the same.
Don't cry for me, gal, I don't want anyone's pity. You
just remember that it's not how many years that you
live, it's how you live in the years that the Good Lord
gives you. I love you, Victoria Alicia Roberts-Sams.
Your dear Aunt Alice

I dropped Aunt Alice's letter and buried my face in my
pillow to stifle my sobs of grief. She had known all along what
I had done to keep Harlan, and she hadn't judged me for it. I
jumped when I felt Valora's little hand on my arm trying to
give me comfort.

"Mama? Otay?"

I raised my face to see her standing my bed with that
intense look in her eyes. I dredged up a smile and pulled her
into the bed to lie beside me. She nestled against me and laid
her hand over my heart. My sorrows melted at her touch, and I
hummed her favorite song, "Jesus loves me" until I knew that
she slept. I thought about the scolding that Aunt Alice
would've given me and vowed not to sink into sadness again. I
snuggled against my sleeping beauty and drifted into a
welcomed slumber.

8

The move back into the Dallas house didn't take very long. The children were excited to be moving home, so they worked hard to help me unpack and get the house in order. Looking through the curtains, I breathed a sigh of relief because Ellis and Orna's house looked deserted and quiet. I more felt peaceful and content than I had in a long while.

About a month after we returned to the house, Harlan's parents came to visit. I didn't mind so much because Mr. Jerry redirected all of Ms. Dorothy's insults and complaints into loud compliments. He didn't seem to mind insulting and scolding Harlan, though.

"Now, what could have been so important that you were gone so long away from your wife and children, boy? I mean, every time I call, Vicky has some excuse why you're not home. A God-fearing man always takes care of home and family, son. You seem to be slacking."

Mr. Jerry sat back with his coffee mug after wagging his finger in Harlan's face. Ms. Dorothy frowned at me and patted Harlan's knee.

"Well, Jerry, a man has to have a good God-fearing woman supporting everything that he does, don't you think, Vicky? Harlan works so much to provide all this for you, and

I'm sure that you're grateful. After all, it's not like you can't work," she sniffed with her nose in the air.

Mr. Jerry turned a fierce scowl on his wife. She shrank back from him and sipped her tea. Harlan looked like he wanted to run away – again. I stood up and picked up the tray and went to the kitchen to get more tea and coffee. Harlan followed me into the kitchen.

"Why didn't you tell me that my parents were coming to visit? I would have come home sooner," he whined.

I rounded on him with narrowed eyes. I filled the teapot with leaves and hot water. I picked up the percolator and waved it in his direction.

"Harlan, if you had been home more then two days this month, I would have told you."

My breath released in a heavy sigh. The urge to be free from Harlan made plea with him. I softened my tone.

"You're never home anyway, Harlan. I can't remember when you spent more than two whole days here with us. Why won't you let go? You obviously have another woman. This would be so much easier on both of us if you just gave me a divorce."

Harlan's face twisted. He grabbed me by my shoulders and pulled me into his arms. I held still not wanting him to touch me more. He chuckled and whispered in my ear.

"Oh Vicky, I can't let you go. You're my safety net. You're still decent looking and shapely even after having all those kids. If my new woman ever makes me unhappy, I can always come home to you, Vicky."

Disgusted at his touch and his selfish immoral attitude, I pushed the forgotten coffee pot in my hand into his stomach. He jumped back at the heat and laughed.

"Now, now, Vicky, you don't want to harm me with my parents in the other room, do you? Imagine what my mother would say?"

He waggled his eyebrows and leaned an elbow on the counter to watch me. I narrowed my eyes at him and turned my back on him to pour the coffee into the serving carafe effectively ignoring him until he returned to the living room.

Glancing at the sink, I saw the bottle of floor cleaner. I thought about pouring it in the coffee pot but cast the thought from my mind. I closed my eyes and said a quick prayer.

"Please Father, help me to be away from this demon disguised as my husband."

I opened my eyes and finished gathering the drink tray. I shook my head at myself because I had begun to feel guilty about keeping the secret of Aunt Alice's Will from Harlan, but not anymore. I would need all the help that I could get when God blessed me with my freedom. I picked up the tray and took a deep breath to suffer through the rest of the visit with Mr. Jerry and Ms. Dorothy.

Later that evening, I washed and dried the dishes while trying to come up with a plan to escape Harlan's clutches. I discarded mostly all of the ideas due to the fact that Harlan would probably come after me and find a way to take my children. I wiped my hands on a dishtowel and closed my eyes to use my "gift". I tried not to use it too much for fear of Harlan or the kids finding out about it. It wasn't that I was ashamed of it. On the contrary, I took pride in being blessed with such a talent. It was the thought that Harlan would use it against me that limited my use of the visions.

I leaned against the counter and allowed my mind to go blank. A burning and intense pain shot through my head with an image of Grandpa Ed. My eyes opened with a snap. My chest heaved with a deep breath like I had been holding it. I bent over with my hands on my knees at the memory of the pain. Hot, burning pain crawled down my spine. I clenched my fists to my head and applied pressure to make it stop.

Once the pain calmed, I rushed to the phone in the living room and called Big Mama Chandra. The phone just rang and rang, so I hung up and tried again. No answer. Frustrated and worried, I called Aunt Charlotte. I cringed when I saw how late it was, but I needed to know if Grandpa Ed was okay.

"St. Francis residence," Aunt Mary's voice sounded strained.

"Aunt Mary? I'm sorry for calling so late, but I just had a vision of Grandpa Ed. I called but no one answered. Have y'all heard from them today?"

I heard a small sob come from Aunt Mary, and my heart plummeted to my feet. I slid to the floor still holding the phone. A buzzing like a swarm of bees started in my head.

"Victoria! Victoria!"

I heard Aunt Charlotte's voice like it came from far away. I realized that I still held the phone. I shook my head to stop the buzzing and answered Aunt Charlotte.

"Yes ma'am? Oh, Aunt Charlotte, please tell me that Grandpa Ed is all right!"

I heard Aunt Charlotte take a deep breath and feared the worst.

"Your grandfather had an accident before nightfall. He fell and hit his head getting off a tractor. He hasn't woken up yet, and the doctors think he won't," she finished with a sob.

Tears ran down my face unchecked. I wanted to cry out at the injustice of it. I had just lost Aunt Alice! I prayed a selfish prayer to God not to take Grandpa Ed too. Aunt Charlotte rushed me off the phone to travel to Carson in the dark to be with Big Mama Chandra. I wanted to go with her, but I knew that I couldn't leave my children.

I put the phone on the cradle and went to the kitchen sink to wash the tears from my face.

Grandpa Ed had been more like a father to me than my own. I knew that he had other grandchildren besides me, but I always felt closer to him. The tears started again at the thought that I might lose him. He had to wake up. He just had to. Then it came to me. William! William was a special head doctor. Maybe he could help him. I reached into the spice cabinet and drew down my recipe box. I rummaged through it until I found the card with his name on it that Dr. Jones had given me when he started caring for Grayson. My shaky legs carried me back to the phone. I said a quick prayer that he would be on duty or have an answering service before I dialed the number.

"Grace General Hospital, how can I direct your call?"

"Yes, can I have Dr. William Herbert, please?"

"Just one moment, ma'am," she replied.

A second later the phone began ringing. I gripped the phone tighter waiting for William to pick up the line.

"This is Dr. Herbert," he answered in his deep voice.

I almost cried out in my joy that he was on call.

"William?"

My voice shook nervously.

"Victoria? Are you okay? Is something wrong with the children?"

William's sincere concern for my children and me made me burst into tears. I muffled the sobs by biting my fist, but it took several more moments before I could speak.

"William, I'm so sorry for calling you and for calling this late. The children and I are fine. It's Grandpa Ed. He fell off of his tractor and hit his head. Aunt Charlotte said that he won't wake up and that the doctors in Carson don't think that he will. I thought about what you said about head injuries, and I found your card in my recipe box. I didn't know what else to do, William," I rambled into the phone.

"Well, I'm glad that you called me, Victoria. I've been thinking about you especially since I heard about what that nasty policeman did. I wanted to break his neck, but he was already in jail," William said grimly.

I almost smiled at his protectiveness, but all thoughts were on Grandpa Ed. I guess William's were as well because he began asking me questions about my grandfather's condition. I told him as much as I could from Aunt Charlotte's report. I heard a noise in the hallway and peeked out to see if the kids were awake. I didn't see anything, and the only noise that I could hear was Harlan sawing logs. I rolled my eyes and hoped that he didn't wake up the kids. I turned my attention to what William was saying.

"Alright, Victoria, I can't get down to Carson tonight, but I'm going to call a med school buddy at the Carson hospital to see if your grandfather is stable enough to transport to Tharkin to the bigger hospital there. I'm not on call tomorrow, so I can get to Tharkin early in the morning to assess his injury myself. I can't make any promises, but I'll do my best, Victoria."

"That's all I can ask, William. I am so grateful that you're willing to do this for my family," I sniffled.

William gave a quiet chuckle.

"What would be good for your Grandpa Ed is to see you and your children when he wakes up, Victoria. Are you going to Carson?"

I felt goose bumps rise on my arms at his suggestion. Something told me that William didn't just ask if I was going to Carson for my grandfather's sake. I realized that I wanted to go to Carson or Tharkin or wherever as long as my Grandpa Ed would be all right.

"Tomorrow is Friday, so we could make it down there after the kids get out of school. You'll call me tomorrow to let me know how he's doing, right?"

"Of course. As soon as I assess him and speak with the treating doctors, I'll call you," William promised.

I breathed a sigh of relief and said goodbye. Feeling exhausted and knowing that I needed rest for the long trip to Carson, I flicked off the kitchen light and stepped into the hallway right into my son, William.

"William! You startled me! What are you doing out of bed?"

I patted my chest to calm my speeding heartbeat. I allowed my eyes to adjust to the dim hallway night-light and looked at my son. His face held a mulish expression.

"Who were you talking to, Mama?"

I stepped back and frowned at William. His tone was just a little too belligerent for me. I put my hands on my hips and leaned toward him. I didn't have to look up at him like I did Mark because we were the same height.

"Were you eavesdropping, William? That is very rude. Well, for your information, Grandpa Ed is hurt and I was talking to a doctor that can help him. We'll be going to Carson tomorrow after y'all get out of school."

I saw him narrow his eyes and open his mouth to ask another question, but I beat him to it.

"Now, let's go to bed because we need to rest up for the trip tomorrow."

I put my arm on his shoulders and tried to turn him around toward the bedrooms. He jerked loose and rounded on me. Surprised at his behavior, I raised my hand to slap him. William stepped out of my range. Anger started building at his actions. I wanted to call for Harlan, but I could still hear him snoring. I glanced around for a belt but saw nothing to punish William. I swung around and stepped closer ready to slap my son into next Sunday.

"I don't want to go to Carson. I hate your family. They don't like me, and you don't say anything. I know it's because I don't look like the other kids," he all but yelled in my face.

Sympathy started inching its way in front of my anger, and I reached out to hug my unhappy son. He yanked away from me with tears in his eyes.

"Why did I have to be born Black? Why couldn't I be the one who looks like you do? Why did you have to marry Daddy with all his Black skin and evil ways, Mama? Why?"

William threw himself in the chair and lowered his head in quiet sobs. I wanted to console him, but I figured that hugging him would only make him angrier. I stood still knowing that I couldn't answer his questions because I didn't trust myself not to tell him the truth. That in marrying Harlan, I had been able to get away from the abuse of my parents. In binding Harlan to me, I had ensured that I wouldn't be rejected again by someone that I thought I loved. I watched as his sobs turned to hiccups.

"William, you're wrong. My family loves you. Maybe when you are older, everything will make sense, okay? You're only thirteen, and things are happening to you right now that cause you to feel strange. It won't be long know that you'll be able to figure it out," I promised.

William narrowed his eyes in a skeptical look and without another word, stomped from the room.

I rubbed my arms at the chill that came over me and went to find the peace of sleep.

As soon as Harlan showed up in the kitchen for breakfast, I told him about Grandpa Ed. He paused and rubbed his hands in glee.

"Well, well, the old buzzard is gonna croak. I sure hope he leaves you some of that land down there. I could rent it out to a farmer and make a lot of dough."

My eyes widened at his callous attitude. I put down the butcher knife for fear of stabbing him in the back at his indifference and greed. Feeling the violence creeping in my nature proved that I needed to get away from Harlan. Permanently.

"How could you say that? Did you say that about your own grandparents before they died? You are such an ass, Harlan Sams. Remember what I told Officer Jackson. What goes around comes around," I growled.

Harlan narrowed his eyes and took a long swig of his coffee. He smacked loudly and picked up his fork.

"You think so, huh? We'll see, but I doubt it because if it hasn't come around on me in all these years, it's not going to," he laughed.

Valora's tiny voice made us both jump.

"No, Dad-dee, no."

We both turned to see her standing in the open doorway to the dining room holding her stuffed lion and frowning at Harlan. She walked to him and shook her head. Harlan leaned down and picked her up to place on his knee. I worried for a moment that her night diaper would leak on his starched pants, but I smiled maliciously hoping that it would.

"Hey there, little Mama! How's Daddy's girl this morning?"

Valora raised her hand to Harlan's face, and he went still. Harlan grimaced and shuddered. Valora grinned and let go.

"Dad-dee, no," she whispered and slid off his lap.

Harlan stared at Valora with a confused frown on his face. Valora walked to me and hugged my legs. I laughed and picked her up. She giggled when I tickled her, and I sat her in her highchair with a buttered biscuit. I looked up to see Harlan still staring at my daughter.

"Children recognize evil when they see it, Harlan."

I snickered when he blinked and hurriedly rose from the table. He grabbed his bag without another word and left.

"Ba, Dad-dee!"

Valora waved at the closed door with the remainder of her biscuit. I laughed again and grabbed my plate to have breakfast with my little angel.

As the day worn on, I kept myself busy packing weekend bags for all of us, playing with Valora, and cooking some food for the travel basket. My frayed nerves made my hands shake as I fried the chicken and rolled biscuits. I almost dropped the platter of chicken when the phone rang. With my heart racing, I hurried to the living room to answer it.

"Hello?"

"Victoria, it's William. I'm sorry that I haven't called before now, but I needed to assist with your grandfather's surgery."

"Surgery?"

I trembled as all kinds of thoughts went through my mind.

"Victoria, calm down and let me explain. Your grandfather's head injury was worse than the doctors in Carson thought. When my buddy and I reassessed him this morning, there was increased swelling on his frontal lobe. We had to get the swelling down, and surgery was the only option. I won't go into all the details, but it took a while for us to locate the bleeding and stop it. We're keeping him in a medical sleep or coma until all the swelling goes down."

Needing the comfort of my daughter, I picked her up from her playpen and hugged her little body before I responded to William.

"Is he going to be all right now, William?"

William hesitated and my heart picked up speed waiting for him to answer.

"We don't know at this point, Victoria. He's a strong man for his age, but the injury that he sustained is very bad. I'm going to stay here until late Sunday just in case."

I relaxed a little knowing that Grandpa Ed was closer to being out of the woods. I felt even better knowing that William was there to help. Glancing at the clock, I thanked William and told him that we would be in Carson late that night.

Once I hung up the phone, I put Valora down for her afternoon nap and waited for the children to come home to begin our journey to Carson.

9

I barely heard the noise and exuberance of my children during the trip to Carson. My mind was on Grandpa Ed and Big Mama Chandra. My heart went out to her because I knew how much she loved Grandpa Ed. I said a quick prayer to God for her comfort and peace.

We arrived at the homestead late that evening. The house looked deserted when we pulled up to the steps in the old Oldsmobile station wagon. There was still a little daylight left, so I told Mark and William to unload the bags. William looked as if he would argue, but Mark grabbed his arm and pulled him to go the trunk. Grayson open the back door and climbed out of the car with Valora in tow. Gia and Leah got out on the other side and walked around to stand beside me. I picked up Valora and climbed the porch steps with a frown. There should be somebody home to welcome us, I thought to myself. I raised my hand to knock on the screen door when the door opened to a surprised Hope.

"Ms. Victoria! I thought I heard a car in the driveway. Ms. Charlotte told us that you would probably be coming tomorrow, but that's okay you're here now. I was just fixing Ms. Sadie a plate. Come on in," she said.

Hope opened the screen door and beckoned to us to follow her inside the house.

"The house is a little full with Ms. Charlotte, Ms. Mary, and Mr. Andrew and his family, but thanks to the storage rooms that Mr. Ed built last summer, we can fit everybody in the house. I made your old room up for you, and the girls can sleep in my room with me. We can make pallets for your boys in the storage rooms because they're empty now."

Hope waved her hands at the children and opened her mouth to say something else when Valora caught her eye. She blinked and cocked her head to the side. Valora giggled and held out her hand to Hope. Hope visibly shivered and smiled at Valora. She reached out her hands, and Valora went to her. Hope chuckled.

"Ms. Victoria, this is the prettiest little thing that I've ever seen. Full of joy, too. I like friendly babies, and I always wanted a little girl," she sighed.

Valora laid her head on Hope's shoulder and hugged her with her little arms. Hope squeezed her and then handed her back to me.

"Enough of that, or I'll forget what I was doing. Okay, now your aunts are with Ms. Chandra at the hospital in Tharkin, but they should be on their way back by now since it's getting dark. I cooked up a mess of food, are y'all hungry?"

I smiled at her offer and shook my head.

"I cooked up a mess of food today too for the trip. We stopped in Haysfield and had dinner."

Hope looked from me to the kids.

"Well, I should have known that you'd feed the young'uns early. If you're sure that y'all ain't hungry, I'm going to finish fixing Ms. Sadie's plate and eat with her in the kitchen. Y'all are family, so y'all know to make yourself comfortable."

Hope smiled and almost skipped from the room. I laughed at her easy-going attitude. She hadn't changed a bit just the accent had disappeared. I let out the breath that I hadn't known that I was holding. Family. It made me think about what

William had said last night. I glanced around at his usual stubborn expression and prayed for him to come to a better understanding.

"Come on, kids. Let's sit down in the parlor and wait for Big Mama Chandra and the aunts," I whispered.

Since the sun had gone down, the big windows in the parlor were dark. Grayson whimpered and moved closer to me. I remembered how I felt about those darkened windows when I was a girl, so I gave Valora to Mark and closed all of the curtains. I turned around and found a seat on the large sofa on the other side of the room. I patted the seat, and Grayson came and sat with me. Holding Valora, Mark found a chair next to the sofa while William and the twins sat on the divan by the windows. I saw that my children looked as nervous as I felt, so I smiled at them and began to tell them a story.

"Y'all know when I was a young girl, I loved to come to the homestead. There was always something to do or eat," I laughed.

Mark, Grayson, and Gia giggled with me while Leah narrowed her eyes and thrust up her chin. William's frown turned to a glower. I ignored their looks and kept talking.

"I know that we've visited a few times since we've been in Dallas, but it always feels comfortable when I come home. I never get tired of walking the land or helping in Ms. Sadie in the kitchen. That's where I learned to cook. If it wasn't for Big Mama and Ms. Sadie, we'd be eating a lot of burnt up food!"

I laughed louder and tickled Grayson. Everyone except William laughed and relaxed against the backs of their seats.

"What's all this ruckus in my house?"

I stood up feeling guilty when Big Mama Chandra, escorted by Aunt Charlotte and Aunt Mary shuffled into the house. I opened my mouth to explain our laughter and ask about Grandpa Ed, but Big Mama Chandra chuckled.

"It's all right, child. I know what you had to do, and your Grandpa Ed is still out like a light. Now, where's all the hugs and kisses that I need from my great-grands?"

I relaxed at the news and nodded to the children. Leah and Grayson jumped up and raced to hug Big Mama Chandra. Mark got up and handed me a sleepy Valora before running over to join his siblings. Gia shuffled her feet like she didn't want to hug Big Mama Chandra. William didn't move, and I tamped down my anger because I knew my aunts were watching. I didn't want them to know the extent of the trouble that I had with William.

Big Mama Chandra and the aunts laughed and reached down to hug the other children. Big Mama Chandra made a pained noise and moved to her large easy chair. She lowered herself slowly and motioned for the children to come closer. Grayson elbowed himself in front of Leah and Gia to which they objected. Big Mama Chandra shushed them and put her hands on Grayson's shoulders.

"Buster Brown, is that you? You seem a little different than when these old eyes saw you last."

Grayson giggled, but Big Mama Chandra turned her blind gaze to me with a puzzled frown.

I case a questioning look of my own to my aunts because I thought that they had already told Big Mama Chandra of Grayson's head injury. Aunt Charlotte glanced at Big Mama and shook her head. I wondered at her secrecy, but I complied.

"He's grown a little bit this last year, Big Mama. That's all. He's going to graduate from kindergarten at the end of the month," I said.

Big Mama Chandra grinned and hugged Grayson again. She put her hand to his face and closed her eyes. Grayson giggled and jumped up and down. Big Mama Chandra opened her eyes and smiled. She lifted her eyes toward Gia and Leah, and then turned toward Grayson.

"Buster Brown, let Big Mama tell you something. A gentleman always lets a lady go first unless there's something bad going on, okay. I know that you're smaller than them, but Big Mama wants you to be a gentleman, all right?"

Grayson bent his head to the side and nodded as if in a trance. He moved back and all but pushed his sisters to stand in front of Big Mama. She chuckled and tried to pull the twins into each of her arms. Leah went willingly, but Gia turned her nose up in disdain and stepped back.

"Gia Sams! Don't be rude!"

Big Mama Chandra held up her hand to keep me from scolding her more. I snapped my mouth shut and sat back on the sofa to let her handle Gia. She let go of Leah and grabbed an arrogant Gia. Gia looked surprised at Big Mama Chandra's grip. Big Mama Chandra put her hand to Gia's face, and Gia began to struggle. Big Mama Chandra frowned and abruptly released Gia. Gia fell to the floor with a cry. Leah would have dropped to the floor beside her, but Big Mama Chandra put a hand out to stop her.

Gia stood up and rounded on Big Mama Chandra.

"I hate you! You smell bad, and you make me sick!"

I remained silent, but my hand itched to smack my daughter for her insolence with my grandmother. Aunt Charlotte and Aunt Mary gasped at Gia's nasty words. Aunt Charlotte stepped forward, but Aunt Mary beat her to it. She took hold of Gia's shoulders and shook her a little. When she spoke, I shivered because I had never heard Aunt Mary use that tone on anyone.

"You ungrateful and hateful little girl. Your great-grandmother is worried sick about your Great-Grandpa Ed, and here you are spewing meanness at her. I know that your mother taught you better than that. Now, you will apologize."

Gia stubbornly kept her mouth closed. Again, my hand itched to slap her. Aunt Mary shook her head and lowered her voice. I had to lean forward to hear her.

"There is a darkness in you, Gia, just like your great-grandmother, Betts. Your spirit is filled with envy, jealousy, hate, and vanity. You won't ever find happiness until you learn to love yourself and your family."

Gia narrowed her tear-filled eyes at Aunt Mary and said nothing. Big Mama Chandra let out a big sigh.

"Gia, go sit on the sofa beside that ol' ornery brother of yours," Big Mama Chandra commanded.

Sniffling and shooting hateful glances at Big Mama Chandra, Gia wiped her eyes and stomped over to sit beside William. Her gaze caught mine, and I frowned at her. She lowered her gaze to her hands.

Leah had stood quiet during all of her sister's drama. She took a step to go sit with Gia when Big Mama Chandra stopped her.

"Leah, you don't have to follow your sister in everything. Make your own place, okay? Big Mama loves you," she said while pulling Leah into a hug.

Leah stood stiffly at first then she melted against Big Mama Chandra. Glancing at Gia's angry face, I knew that Leah would hear about it later. I shook my head and patted Valora on the back. She slept and hadn't woken during Gia's dramatics. Big Mama Chandra hugged Mark and told him that she was proud of him for being such a good young man. Mark beamed from the praise. Big Mama chuckled and opened her purse. I thought she would give him a few coins, but she handed him four five-dollar bills. I gaped at the money thinking that Big Mama Chandra couldn't see how much money that she handed Mark.

"Big Mama Chandra! That's too much! Mark, give that back to your great-grandmother," I demanded.

Mark promptly handed the money back, but Big Mama pushed it back at him. She turned to me.

"Excuse me? First, I need you to change your tone to one of respect. No wonder that gal is the way she is. Second, if I want to give my great-grandson twenty dollars, I will, do you hear?"

Thoroughly chastised, I said a quiet yes ma'am and nodded to Mark. He hugged Big Mama and thanked her before returning to his seat. Aunt Charlotte cleared her throat in the awkward silence.

"I'm sure everyone is exhausted from all the happenings today. Why don't we all find our beds, yes?"

I started to agree, but Grayson piped up first.

"Big Mama Chandra? You didn't hug my little sister."

Big Mama Chandra laughed.

"Buster Brown, I don't want to disturb your little sister. Her light is a little dim tonight. I'll hold her first thing in the morning, okay?"

Satisfied, Grayson nodded and ran to help her up out of the chair. She rose from the chair and made a big deal of grabbing and holding Grayson's outstretched hand. Grayson giggled and hugged Big Mama Chandra again. She returned his embrace and shuffled from the room with a chattering Grayson by her side.

Aunt Charlotte walked over to me and picked up Valora from my shoulder. She hugged her little body and waited for me to rise. I got up and hugged Aunt Charlotte before taking Valora back. Aunt Mary came and patted me on the back. She kissed Valora and left the room. Aunt Charlotte swung around with a frown at Gia and William. They both cowered under her scrutiny.

"It's obvious that you two need some time to think about your actions tonight. I'm going to speak with your mother about your discipline while you're here and when you go home. It is unacceptable how you've acted during this difficult time. I am very disappointed in both of you," she said angrily.

Aunt Charlotte stood for a moment frowning at my son and daughter. Then, she shook her head and left. I looked at Mark and Leah standing silently waiting for my direction. The events of the day caught up with me all of a sudden, and my legs felt weak. I signaled Mark to get Valora, and I held on the arm of the sofa for a moment. I waved away the concerned look on Mark's face.

"I'm just tired. Let's all go to bed and say our prayers that tomorrow is a better day."

Mark nodded and turned around to his siblings.

"Come on, y'all. I think we've been enough trouble to Mama today. Let's go to bed."

I smiled at his calm commanding manner. He waited with a frown until William and Gia followed Leah from the room. I smiled and silently thanked God for blessing me with such a wonderful oldest child. I sighed heavily into the stillness and glanced around the room. Memories of another wonderful son rushed in, and I felt tears form in my eyes as an image of Victor's little face came to my mind. I put my hand over my heart and bent my head to say a prayer for his little soul.

"Victoria."

I raised my head to see who had called me and saw no one. Knowing whom it was, I went to the window and opened the curtain. The woman in black stood at the edge of the sprouting cornfield. I felt no fear at her presence anymore. I saw her bow her head and turn to disappear into the night. I dropped the curtain and went to find my bed.

The smell of bacon and biscuits awakened me the next morning. I looked over at Valora still sleeping heavily and sprawled across the bed. I smiled at her carefree slumber and rose from the bed.

After washing up, I checked on Valora again before I made my way to the kitchen. Hope and Aunt Charlotte were busy making piles of food. Hope, chewing a piece of bacon, waved a dough-encrusted hand and turned back to the counter.

Aunt Charlotte came to give me a peck on the cheek. She had deep circles under her eyes. I felt a moment of discomfort that my children's behavior had caused them.

"Good Morning, my dear. I hope that you slept well. I couldn't sleep worrying about Pa. I kept having these bad dreams, but it's not seven o'clock yet, so I can't tell anyone. Where are the children?'

I frowned at her mention of bad dreams. My thoughts turned to the woman in black, but I shrugged them away. Grandpa Ed was a grown man, and I remembered that Aunt Mary said that she only took babies. Aunt Charlotte placed a cup of coffee in front of me, and my thoughts turned back to her.

"Aunt Charlotte, you look tired. Why don't I help Hope this morning?"

An argument looked to be on her tongue, so I dangled her favorite distraction in her face.

"Valora may be awake, and I know that Big Mama Chandra would want to spend time with her before we go to the hospital. Can you get her, please?"

Any argument that Aunt Charlotte was about to utter, died a quick death at the mention of Valora. She smiled and left the room without another word. I got up to help Hope at the counter with a chuckle. Hope joined me in my mirth.

"That was some fine maneuvering, Miss. I couldn't think of anything to sit her down. She looked so tired when she came in this morning."

I nodded and washed my hands.

"I know. Aunt Charlotte does so much for everyone that she doesn't think about herself enough," I sighed.

Hope and I finished preparing the stacks of hotcakes, sausage, bacon, eggs, smothered potatoes, and biscuits. Uncle Andrew made his appearance as I placed the last platter on the table. He grabbed me up in one of his bear hugs. I laughed and wiggled to get down. He grinned and put me back on the floor. He held me at arm's length and looked me over a bit.

"Well, if it isn't one of my favorite nieces! It's been so long! You're all grown up with a passel of young'uns I hear! How long are you staying?"

"We'll be here until Sunday because the children have to go back to school. It's the end of the school year, and I don't want them to miss anything, Uncle Andrew. How is your family?"

I saw several emotions cross my uncle's face before he put his customary grin back in place.

"Well, your Aunt Retta is good, and your cousins are all doing well working on the ranch with me. Percy and Rich came with me. Star and Winter stayed with their husbands to take care of things until we get back," he explained.

I smiled and nodded happy that my cousins were doing well. I wondered at the emotions that I saw on my uncle's face, but forgot about it because Aunt Charlotte carrying Valora with Big Mama Chandra trailing behind her came into the kitchen. Uncle Andrew guffawed and grabbed at Valora, but she had seen me.

"Mama, Mama, eat!"

Everyone laughed, and Valora held out her hands to me. Aunt Charlotte kissed her little hands and shook her head.

"No, Valora, honey, I'm going to feed you in here this morning so that your mother can feed your siblings and cousins in the dining room."

Valora looked from Aunt Charlotte to me and held out her hands again. Big Mama Chandra laughed. Hope looked up from pouring coffee.

"Ms. Charlotte, I can feed the children. I wanted to spend a little time with Mark and William anyway."

"Charlotte, stop being selfish and give that baby to her mama."

Aunt Charlotte huffed and handed Valora to me. Valora gave me a wet kiss on the jaw and giggled. Uncle Andrew helped Big Mama Chandra to her seat and sat down on her left. I took the right side with Valora on my lap. Aunt Charlotte sat next to me and Aunt Mary came through the door to sit in the empty chair. Hope grabbed a large tray heaped with more food and left. Uncle Andrew grasped Big Mama Chandra's hand and bowed his head.

"Dear Heavenly Father, we thank You for the blessing of being together as a family. We ask that You place Your Healing Hands on my earthly father, Ed, and bless him to come home safely to us. We thank You for traveling grace as we go back and forth to Tharkin and our homes when this crisis is done. Thank You for the bounty of this table and for the hands that prepared it. In Your Son, Jesus' Name, Amen."

I raised my head to see Big Mama Chandra cover her face in sobs. Shocked to have ever seen Big Mama Chandra cry, I watched while my aunts and uncle surrounded her to give her comfort. I leaned over to put my arm around her when the phone rang. I put Valora down on the floor to get up to answer it. Hope arrived in the hallway at the same time, but I waved her back to the dining room.

"Hello? Daniels residence?"

"Victoria? It's me, William. I'm sorry to call so early, but I think that y'all better get up here. Now."

William's tone sounded grim, and my heart started beating at what it could mean.

"Okay, I'll get my family together, and we'll be there shortly," I whispered.

"Please hurry, Victoria, just hurry," William said and disconnected the phone.

I turned around to see Aunt Mary standing in the kitchen doorway. Tears ran down her eyes, and I knew that something was wrong. She turned halfway around into the kitchen.

"Mama, Charlotte, Andrew, we need to get to the hospital now. Victoria, bring Valora, and ask Hope to watch the other children."

I nodded and picked up Valora who had waddled out of the kitchen to stand by me. Trying to control my emotions, I walked into the dining room and smiled at the children and my cousins.

"Hey y'all, we're going to go on to the hospital to see Grandpa Ed. Mark, I'm leaving you in charge with Ms. Hope, all right? William, Leah, Gia, Grayson, y'all better listen to your brother. Percy and Rich, I'm sure that the field hands need some direction while Grandpa Ed is in the hospital."

My cousins and Mark knew that something wasn't quite right, but they didn't say anything. Percy and Rich nodded and grabbed some biscuits and bacon. They got up and left towards the front of the house. Hope rose from the table and hugged me.

"No mattah what hap'ns, lil' Miss, be strong."

I pulled back and looked at Hope in surprise at the return of her accent. She laughed softly and sat back down.

"Alrigh', young'uns, let's eat our vittles and find som'thin ta do."

Leah and Grayson giggled at her accent while William and Gia kept eating in silence. I ignored them because I didn't have time to set them straight. I rushed to my room and put Valora down to play with her alphabet toy. I threw open the suitcase and pulled out an outfit for her and a quarter sleeved high waist dress for me. The orange dress was comfortable and easy to clean if Valora got me dirty. I pulled it on and brushed my shoulder length auburn locks into a bun. I slipped on some casual canvas shoes and turned to dress Valora. Her dress and bloomers were orange and almost matched my dress. I slipped some white socks over her feet adding her baby moccasins to complete her dress. I brushed her curly hair into an Afro and put a headband on it.

Grabbing my wallet and Valora's bag, I hurried into to meet the rest of my family in the living room. Aunt Charlotte nodded her approval in my dress and reached to take Valora's bag. Aunt Mary walked Big Mama Chandra out to Aunt Charlotte's Cadillac. I heard Uncle Andrew on the porch giving Percy and Rich orders on taking care of the back forty.

Aunt Charlotte and I followed Aunt Mary and Big Mama Chandra to the car and got in the back. Uncle Andrew got in the driver's seat and made his way down the lane to get on the highway toward Tharkin. I snuggled against Valora and said a prayer that all the grieving and sadness was for nothing, and Grandpa Ed would be awake and well when we got there. However, seeing the woman in black standing in the cornfield, proved what I already knew.

10

Once we got to the hospital, a nurse took us in an elevator up to a waiting room on the top floor. Aunt Mary and Big Mama didn't say anything, but Aunt Charlotte let loose.

"Why are we in here? I want to see my Pa. I don't want to be in here. Mama, tell them to take us to Pa," she demanded.

Aunt Mary went over to her and put her arms around Aunt Charlotte.

"Charlotte, we need to wait for the doctor."

Aunt Charlotte snatched away from Aunt Mary and turned to look out of the window. Aunt Mary shrugged and returned to sit next to Big Mama Chandra. I sat on the small uncomfortable loveseat next to them. Uncle Andrew came over and put his hands out to hold Valora. She went to him with a little smile. He chuckled softly and hugged her. He took her to the window to stand beside Aunt Charlotte. Aunt Charlotte moved closer to kiss the hand that Valora held out to her. She turned to ask me something when the door opened. William's tall frame strode into the small room. Everyone stood to attention except Big Mama Chandra. He walked to her, knelt, and picked up her hand.

"Mrs. Daniels, your husband took a turn for the worse this morning. He's developed a blood infection that refuses to be treated. We've tried everything, but it's taken its toll on his healing. I'm so sorry, but there's nothing else that we can do for him except make him comfortable."

I put my hand to my mouth to stifle my cry of sadness. Big Mama Chandra squeezed William's hand in comfort while the unchecked tears ran down her face.

"Thank you, Dr. William. I know that you've done your best. I also know that you are here because of your love of our family. Thank you. Now, can we see him?"

Big Mama Chandra's voice broke on her request.

William glanced at me but returned his attention to my grandmother. I saw Uncle Andrew holding Valora and with an arm around a weeping Aunt Charlotte. Aunt Mary sat back down and tried to comfort Big Mama Chandra. William cleared his throat.

"I have cleared your visits with the treating physicians. He is in the surgery observation room. When you are ready, just knock on the glass door right out side of this room."

William bowed his head to me and left the room. I ran and caught up with him in the hallway.

"William, please, is there nothing else that can be done? I just lost my aunt, I don't want to lose my Grandpa Ed, too."

I could barely see William through my haze of tears. William made a sound and pulled me into his arms. His compassion broke the dam, and I sobbed my grief into his warm embrace. I knew that it wasn't appropriate, but I didn't care.

"Victoria Alicia Sams! Have you lost your marbles?"

I broke free from William's arms and turned to see a furious Aunt Charlotte. William stepped in front of me.

"Ms. St. Francis, please don't blame Victoria. I only wished to give her some comfort in this difficult time."

Aunt Charlotte's anger melted in the face of William's sympathetic manner. She jerked her head in a nod.

"I apologize, Dr. William. My grief is affecting my behavior," she whispered.

William walked forward and put his hand on her arm.

"Ms. St. Francis, please know that if there was anything else to be done, I would do it."

Aunt Charlotte looked up at William and smiled.

"Yes, I know. When the accident happened, I called for the best specialist for head injuries. Every doctor that I called recommended you."

She glanced at me and her eyebrow lifted.

"It was to my surprise that you were already here before I could make the call to request your presence."

William stepped back and stuck a finger in his collar to loosen it. I lowered my head to hide my reddened face. Aunt Charlotte waved her hand at our embarrassment.

"Dr. William, we would like to see my father now."

William said yes ma'am and walked down the hallway to knock on the glass door. The door slid open. William beckoned for us to follow. Aunt Charlotte moved back toward the waiting room and waved her arm. Aunt Mary and Uncle Andrew came through the doorway supporting a sobbing Big Mama Chandra. I strode forward and plucked Valora from Uncle Andrew so that he could help with Big Mama Chandra. Valora hugged me around the neck with her little arms as we our loved ones through the glass door. A solemn White nurse behind the desk stood up to escort us to Grandpa Ed until she saw Valora.

"I'm sorry, ma'am, but no babies allowed."

I began to object when William touched my arm. He leaned over the nurse intimidating her with a frown.

"Nurse Wood, a man is dying. I'm sure that seeing all of his family would be his last wishes."

The nurse pursed her lips but nodded. She turned without another word and walked into a short hallway that led to a large room with a long wall of windows. I could see another nurse's station beyond it. I glanced back at the beds and saw my Grandpa Ed in the occupied bed. My breath caught at the huge bandage wrapped around his head and all of the tubes and machines around him. His body was swollen with his skin an ashy gray. I felt a deep sorrow at not being able to see the Grandpa Ed that I had known all my life in the pitiful looking man on the bed. Valora whimpered, and I patted her back to comfort us both. Big Mama Chandra moved to the bed and sat in the chair beside it. She covered Grandpa Ed's hand with her own.

"I know that you can hear me, Ed. I'm not going to fuss at you for leaving me, and I know that you'd tell me to stop all this silly crying. We've had many a good year and a blessed life. Thank you, Ed Daniels for being the love of my life and a good man."

Big Mama Chandra broke into more sobs and leaned forward to put her head on their joined hands. My heart ached for her. I knew the pain of losing the love of your life, and I wished in that moment that Big Mama Chandra didn't have to know the same pain. I glanced at William to see him staring at me. I frowned at him before turning to see Uncle Andrew and Aunt Mary hug and kiss Grandpa Ed from the other side of the bed. Aunt Charlotte waited until they had moved and with visibly shaky legs stepped to the bed. She stared at her father for a moment and shook her head. She began plucking at the tube covering his body.

"No, my father is not dying. He is not dying. He can't die. He's a strong man and still tends to his fields. Pa, you have to get up now! You have to wake up and come home!"

I stood in shock watching my aunt try to pull the medical apparatus from my grandfather while she yelled at him. William and Uncle Andrew rushed to the bed and grabbed Aunt Charlotte. She struggled against them and kept yelling.

"No, no, no! You will not let my father die. He can't! He can't, do you hear me? I'm wealthy and can pay you anything! Help him! He can't die!"

Several nurses from the nurse's station ran into the room. William gave one orders to bring something, and the others ran to help subdue an insanely strong Aunt Charlotte. I held on to Valora and moved to a corner out of the way. I watched Aunt Mary crouch protectively over Big Mama Chandra while they watched Aunt Charlotte's hysterical behavior. The nurse that William gave orders came back with a syringe. William nodded to her and she dived forward to inject Aunt Charlotte. Aunt Charlotte resisted for a few more moments before collapsing against Uncle Andrew.

Everyone breathed a sigh of relief, and the nurses returned to their station. Uncle Andrew placed Aunt Charlotte in the wheelchair that William held.

"She always was dramatic."

Everyone's mouth dropped at Grandpa Ed's gravelly whisper. Big Mama Chandra cried out and clenched his hand. William moved to the bed pulling his stethoscope from his neck. Grandpa Ed raised a shaking hand in his direction. William stopped with a confused look on his face.

"No, son. I don't need it. You're a good man like your father. He must be proud, the old goat. Tell him that I said that."

Tears formed in William's eyes, and he nodded.

Grandpa Ed pointed to Aunt Charlotte.

"Chandra, Mary, take care of Charlotte. She so busy taking care of everybody else that she never lived her life."

He coughed and shuddered.

"Thank you, Chandra, for loving me even at my worst. God blessed my life, and I won't complain that He wants me to come home now. Don't you cry another tear, Chandra Daniels."

Big Mama Chandra nodded and wiped her face with her handkerchief. She sniffled and raised a composed face for my grandfather to see. He nodded his approval and glanced at Uncle Andrew.

"Andrew, I know that you have the ranch in Colorado to see after, but I need you to come home or send one of your boys to check on the homestead."

Uncle Andrew bobbed his head up and down, and then grabbing the handles of Aunt Charlotte's wheelchair left the room. Aunt Mary touched her head to Grandpa Ed's and whispered something in his ear. Grandpa Ed gave a slight nod. Aunt Mary touched a white silk wrapped hand to his forehead.

Grandpa Ed whispered a thank you to her. Aunt Mary smiled sadly and left the room with a strange glance in my direction.

Hugging Valora to me, I approached the bed on leaden feet. Grandpa Ed turned his eyes in my direction.

"Well, hello, my dear. Is this my beautiful great-granddaughter that I've heard so much about?"

Unable to speak around the lump in my throat, I nodded. He smiled and motioned for me to come closer. I moved to the side of the bed and shifted Valora to my hip. Valora reached out and touched Grandpa Ed's hand before I could stop her. Grandpa Ed held on to her hand and tears began to run down his face. His breath hitched, and his body shuddered. Concerned, I turned to William, but William just shook his head. I turned back to my grandfather. He opened his eyes wider and smiled sadly.

"Victoria, I used to hold you hand like this and lead you into the pasture to watch the cows. You would get so tickled when you fed them that I had to keep a strong hold on you. My great-granddaughter is as enthralling as her mother. I hoped to teach her the same things, but you'll have to do it now. Teach her how you were taught and never forget our connection to the land, Victoria. Never forget..." he broke off in a coughing fit.

Big Mama sat up and wiped the spittle from his mouth. Grandpa Ed recovered and released Valora's hand to grab mine. His touch burned hot with fever.

"You'll sing at my home going, my dear. "Amazing Grace" is what I want to hear from my seat beside the Lord."

He smiled again at Valora before turning his glazing eyes to the corner.

"Ma, Pa, I'm ready now," he breathed and closed his eyes.

Panic filled me at that moment, and I knew how Aunt Charlotte felt. I watched in pained horror when his chest slowed its rising. I started to sink to the floor in my grief when I felt William lift me into his arms. He bent his head to my ear.

"No, Victoria. Allow your grandmother these moments alone with him. You can grieve with your aunts and uncle," he whispered.

I started to fight him but realized that he was right. Big Mama Chandra leaned forward and put her head on his chest. Embarrassment flooded through my sorrow to witness the private moment. I nodded to William and accepted his assistance from the room. He took a willing Valora from my arms, and I followed him from the room.

Once in the waiting room, William directed me to the loveseat and sat beside me still holding Valora. The warmth from his body soothed my nerves but I refused to acknowledge him. I watched as Valora leaned forward and snuggled against William. He sighed at her embrace and leaned back against the loveseat while patting her back. I started to take her until I saw that she had fallen asleep in his arms. William shot me a tired smile and lowered his head to kiss Valora's dark auburn curls. I wondered if he was this good with his own children. Thinking of his children made me think of his wife. In respect to her, I tried to put a little distance between us on the tiny sofa.

Numb from my intense sadness, I watched the rest of my family in silence. Aunt Charlotte remained in her medically induced unconsciousness. Uncle Andrew paced and Aunt Mary sat silently watching the door. I felt like I should do more than just sit like a bump on a log, but I didn't know what to do. I sighed and sat back until Big Mama Chandra came through the door led by a nurse. She looked much smaller than her usual statuesque self and as if years had been added to her face. No trace of tears could be found. She stopped in the middle of the room.

"He's gone home. We'll respect his wishes and not turn into a bunch of blathering idiots. Mary, call Mack & Taylor funeral home and tell them to come get him. Let them know that I'll come around tomorrow and work out all the details. Andrew, we need to get home and take his best suit to the cleaners. The funeral will be a week from today to allow all the family to come out of the woodwork."

My mouth gaped open at Big Mama Chandra's businesslike tone. William nudged me with his elbow. I glanced at him to see a slight frown on his face. He motioned with his head at Big Mama Chandra. I shrugged at his silent question. I knew that he wondered why she didn't wail and cry at her husband's death. I certainly wanted to sink into my sorrow, but we Daniels' were made of stronger stuff. We would carry the pain and memories in our hearts for the rest of our lives, but we wouldn't let it break us.

Later that afternoon, I sat in the rocking chair on the porch mulling over the day. My emotions felt like they'd been on one of those Ferris wheel rides. Once we got home, Big Mama Chandra had broken down again and retreated to her room. Uncle Andrew and I broke the news to everyone else. Mark took it the worst and ran from the house with my cousin Percy chasing after him. I thought to chastise him when they returned but hugged him instead. Afterwards, Hope took all the children for ice cream at the new general store in Allsville.

Aunt Charlotte recovered from her "issues" and helped Aunt Mary complete Big Mama Chandra's directions. They both suffered in silence at the passing of their father. Sympathy for them radiated from my gaze so much that Aunt Charlotte refused to look at me and wouldn't let me help.

Since there seemed to be nothing for me to do, I put Valora down for her nap and found a quiet place on the porch. As I looked out over the cornfield, resentment at the woman in Black filled me. I narrowed my eyes and shook my fist at the young cornstalks. Why? He wasn't a pure innocent babe! Why did you take him? I railed silently. Nothing but silence answered me.

"Victoria."

I opened my eyes to see William standing in front of me in his shirtsleeves and Levi's. I sat up and grimaced at the soreness from napping in the rocker. William put his arm on me to keep me from rising.

"No, don't get up. I'm only going to be here for a few minutes. I'm on my way back to Dallas. I just wanted to come by and check on y'all before I leave."

Memories of the last time that he woke me on this porch made me blush. I looked away from his blue-eyed scrutiny.

"Thank you for everything, William. I know that my family's grief isn't easy for you either. My grandfather held you and your father in high regard. Anyway, we're going to be fine. Big Mama Chandra is suffering in her loss, but I know that she's going to be okay. You're the doctor, so you know that's it's going to take some time. Grandpa Ed was such an important piece of our family puzzle," I muttered to the floor.

My head popped up when I heard William step closer, and I became wary. William laughed softly at my look.

"Victoria, I was glad to be here for your family...and for you. You only have to call me."

I squirmed a little at his lowered voice. He's married, girl! Get a hold of yourself! I yelled silently at myself. I took a deep breath to get a grip but it came out as a sigh when William squatted next to my chair. His gaze paralyzed me. His lips turned up in a small smile.

"One day, Victoria, you're not going to be able to ignore your feelings. I need to clear the air about some things, but not now. Call me when you're ready."

I almost jumped when he broke eye contact. I swallowed and patted my chest. William grinned at my reaction, and I wanted to kick him. He held his hands up as if in surrender.

"Alright, alright, another time. Anyway, I'm going back to Dallas to fetch my parents for the services. Are you returning to get your husband?"

My eyes narrowed at him for bringing up Harlan. Anger rushed through me at the thought of that disrespectful lout anywhere near my Grandpa Ed. I pursed my lips and shook my head.

"No, Harlan is on the road. He didn't think Grandpa Ed was that serious to stay home."

William's head snapped back in surprise. I glared at him just waiting on him to say something bad, but he remained silent. Then he looked towards the house.

"Where is Valora? I'd like to see her before I leave."

It was my turn to look surprised at his request. I gaped at him until he reached over and pushed my mouth shut with his finger. A tiny shock tingled where he touched me. He laughed again. I frowned at his mirth and shushed him in case he disturbed my grandmother or Valora.

"Hush up, William. Valora is down for her nap, and Big Mama Chandra might be sleeping too."

William looked put out at my words and then shrugged.

"That's alright, I'll see her when I return."

I stared at him in confusion until he waved goodbye, got in his car, and left while passing Hope and the children returning from their outing.

Shooing all the children inside, Hope came back to sit in the other rocker. She turned a secretive smile on me.

"Well, some things never change, huh, Ms. Victoria."

I glanced at her smug face and rolled my eyes. We both laughed, and it relieved some of the sadness of the day.

"I guess they don't Hope. Now, do you know where Big Mama Chandra put all my piano music? I have a promise to keep to my Grandpa Ed."

11

I didn't see much of William at my grandfather's services, but I did see his parents. Dr. Herbert looked older and walked with a distinct limp. Mrs. Herbert had aged but carried it well. They both expressed their sympathies and gave their compliments of my singing and piano performance after the service. I had thanked them and prayed that Grandpa Ed felt the same. An awkward moment came when Mrs. Herbert caught me staring at William when he ran to get the car in the rain. She looked at me with a strange smile and nodded. I frowned and return the nod before walking away to take Valora from a harassed looking Aunt Charlotte. I didn't think about the moment again.

Life settled into its normal pattern after Grandpa Ed's death. The children and I returned to Dallas, and Big Mama Chandra assured me during our now weekly calls that life on the homestead was just fine. Sometimes, I knew that she kept up the happy façade to placate me because I knew that she missed Grandpa Ed.

She also told me that my mother had taken Grandpa Ed's death very hard. Guilt rose within me because I hadn't really thought about Tess and her grief of losing her father. I prayed that she had mended fences in her new more genial attitude before Grandpa Ed's accident. I also felt guilty because

I had gotten to say goodbye as his granddaughter over his daughter. When I expressed this to Big Mama Chandra, she shrugged it with some vague comment about life choices.

Two months after my Grandpa Ed's passing, the phone rang and easily woke me from my restless sleep. I hurried to pick it up before it rang again and disturbed the children.

"Hello?"

My voice sounded weak and tired, so I cleared my throat.

"Vicky! Where's Harlan? Oh my God! Where's my son? Hurry and put him on the phone, you lazy fool!"

A hysterical Ms. Dorothy screeched demands in my ear. I sat up and rubbed the sleep from my eyes. Hearing the hysteria in her voice, I sought to remain calm.

"Ms. Dorothy, Harlan isn't here. What is it? What's wrong?"

I heard nothing but a click and dial tone. I frowned at the receiver and hung up the phone. Ms. Dorothy had always been a woman that needed lots of attentions. I shrugged and got up to get some warm milk with honey to soothe my nerves.

Finished with my "pick-me-up", I washed the used dishes and snapped off the light. I took a step towards my room when the phone rang again. Puzzled at the late night calls, I picked up the phone.

"Hello?"

"Vicky! It's Jerry!"

Ms. Dorothy's terror was reflected in her screams. Hearing Harlan's father's name, my heart dropped. My mouth went dry even though I had just finished a drink.

"Ms. Dorothy, please calm down. What's wrong?"

She didn't obviously didn't hear me because her voice got even louder.

"It's Jerry! His nose started bleeding this morning, and it hasn't stopped! He's crying out in pain and holding his head. I've tried everything, but nothing works!"

All of a sudden, I remembered that Big Mama Chandra had to stop one of the field children's nosebleeds so that they could get him to Carson General Hospital. It had taken awhile to get him to town, and he almost didn't make it. Hearing Mr. Jerry's moans and groans, I shuddered and tried again to keep Ms. Dorothy calm.

"Ms. Dorothy, you need to get him to the doctor. Call an ambulance, please."

"Oh, you don't know nothing! I've got to get the bleeding stopped! I need Harlan!"

The dial tone signaled that she hung up on me again. My hands shook at her hysteria. I prayed for patience and guidance, and then I dialed the Sams' Littleton home number. The phone just rang and rang. I hung up and tried again. I disconnected the call when no one answered. I let out a worried sigh praying that Ms. Dorothy called the ambulance. I looked into the darkened living room at the front door with narrowed eyes. Where are you, Harlan Sams?

A knock at the front door woke me from my light sleep early the next morning. A quick glance at the clock confirmed that it was a little after five o'clock. Nothing good comes this early, I groaned and got up to put on my robe. I said a prayer that the knock hadn't woken the children. I hurried into the living room and peeked through the side window. A Black policeman stood on the porch. My heart started to beat faster with memories of Officer Jackson. I flipped the curtain down and slid the security chain on the door before opening it.

"Yes?"

The policeman's face looked grim.

"I'm looking for a Mrs. Sams?"

Puzzled, a slight frown touched my forehead, and I reached up to smooth it away.

"I'm Mrs. Sams, officer. Is something wrong?"

His look turned to sympathy.

"Mrs. Sams, your husband, a Mr. Harlan Sams was involved in an altercation. He suffered two stab wounds to the abdomen and is in Grace General Hospital."

Feeling numb at the officer's news, I thanked him and moved to shut the door. Something told me not to just yet.

"Officer? Can you tell me what happened?"

The policeman hesitated, but seeing my confusion, he straightened his shoulders and nodded.

"Reports indicate that your husband attended a party last night and got into a fight over the woman that your husband has been seeing. I believe the man's name is Ellis something or other."

Anger and rage washed through my shock. Harlan had been in a fight over one of his whores while I had to deal with his mother's hysterics? And if the Ellis that he fought with was Ellis Carter, he knew better. For a brief moment, I reveled in the pain that his injury might cause him, but I snapped back from the madness to smile at the policeman.

"Thank you so much, Officer. I need to take care of my children."

The officer tipped his hat and turned to leave. I shut the door and leaned against it. Harlan needed a swift kick in the pants for his stupidity. I wanted out of this farce of a marriage now more than ever. I covered my face with shaky hands at the embarrassment that other people knew about my so-called husband's adultery. I didn't care that they might be strangers because it was still humiliating. I wanted to sink into misery, but the anger kept me from it.

The phone rang, and I pulled my tired body from the door to answer it.

"Hello?"

I grimaced at my harsh tone and hoped that whoever was on the other end didn't take offense.

"Is this the Harlan Sams residence?"

I frowned hearing the woman's professional tone. What now? I asked myself.

"Yes, it is," I answered.

"Ma'am, my name is Molly Yearly, and I'm the charge nurse at Littleton Country Hospital. I'm sorry to tell you that a Mr. Jerry Sams passed away last night. His wife is being held for observation because we don't yet know the nature of Mr. Sams' death. Again, I'm very sorry."

I almost fell where I stood hearing Nurse Yearly's impersonal delivery of Mr. Jerry's death. I managed to pull the phone to the small bench by the kitchen door and dropped on to it.

"Nurse Yearly, what do you mean that Ms. Dorothy is being held for observation?"

I could hear the impatient sigh of the nurse at my questions. She started to speak slowly as if I couldn't understand her.

"Mrs. Sams has been admitted so that we can watch her for a day or so because Mr. Sams came in with blood coming from various orifices but primarily from his nose. He had severe head and chest pains, and we do not know the cause of his symptoms."

I frowned at the phone and started to give the nurse a dressing down, but I glimpsed into the hallway and saw Mark standing by his bedroom door. I thanked the nurse and hung up the phone.

"Mama, what's wrong? I heard a knock and then the phone," Mark asked.

He looked frightened and nervous as he came to stand in front of me. I decided in that moment that I would lie to my son and the rest of the children when they awoke. I didn't want them to know that Harlan was a cruel and lecherous husband who abandoned his family for the wiles of whoring women. I chose to break the news of their grandfather's death.

I motioned for him to sit beside me on the bench.

"Mark, it was just a salesman at the door, but the phone call was about your Grandpa Jerry."

Mark sat up and looked into my face. Tears began to well up in his eyes.

"Is he okay?" he asked hopefully.

I shook my head and put my arm around him when his shoulders started to shake in his grief. I knew that Mr. Jerry had tried his best for a while to be a good grandfather to the children to try to make up for Harlan's shortcomings. I had respected him for his actions and because he had treated me like a daughter. He didn't deserve to die as he did, and I grew angrier with Harlan for not being there for his father. As I p I allowed myself to cry for his soul and for the man that he had been.

Later that day after informing all the children of Mr. Jerry's death and Ms. Dorothy's confinement, I called Aunt Charlotte over to watch the children so that I could run some errands. She expressed sympathy when I told her about Mr. Jerry and asked if Harlan knew about his father. I avoided her gaze and shrugged. Seeing my discomfort, she asked if I needed her to go to Littleton to help. I shook my head.

"Aunt Charlotte, I'm not rushing off to Littleton. From what the nurse said, it'll be a while before they know what killed Mr. Jerry, and Ms. Dorothy is probably not getting out anytime soon. She was crazy last night, and when she wakes up and realizes Mr. Jerry is gone, they might keep her in the hospital."

Aunt Charlotte cocked her head to the side and nodded in agreement.

"Well, if you need to get out there, I'm more than happy to go with you. I know that Dorothy can be a bit of a handful from Aunt Alice's telling."

I laughed and the memory of Aunt Alice letting loose on Ms. Dorothy rose to my mind. I sobered and felt the ache of loss. Aunt Charlotte saw the pain and cleared her throat. Valora took that moment to pull on Aunt Charlotte's skirt. Aunt Charlotte laughed and shooed me out of the house. She smiled and told me to take my time.

On the way to Grace General Hospital, I felt guilty at deceiving Aunt Charlotte by telling her that I needed to run errands. She hadn't said a word when I opened the bedroom door in the fitted blue eyelet dress that she bought me. Paired with the white-heeled sandals, I knew that I looked nice. My skin glowed from the summer sun and the red highlights in my hair shone bright. I felt beautiful and strong. Aunt Charlotte had always told me not to get into a fight looking like a sad sack, and Harlan was about to get his due. I squelched the desire to laugh out loud and got out of the car.

When I introduced myself and asked for Harlan at the busy front desk, a young candy striper looked up the information and told me that Harlan had been moved from the surgery recovery room to a private room on the same floor. She offered to have me escorted by another candy striper, but I declined. I didn't want anyone to see or hear the conversation between my husband and me. I made my way to the surgical floor and rounded the corner to the private rooms. I almost lost my nerve halfway to the room and turned to go to the waiting area by the nurse's station. Keeping my head down to avoid anyone's eyes, I ran smack dab into someone. I lifted my head to see William's surprised face. He grasped my shoulders to steady me.

"Victoria, what are you doing here? Is everything okay?"

I took a moment to compose myself to cover my own surprise. I hadn't see William since Grandpa Ed's funeral. He looked more handsome than ever. I felt my mouth widen in a big smile until I remembered my purpose.

"William, what a nice surprise. I hope that you've been well."

William smiled and squeezed my shoulders. I lifted an eyebrow at him, and he dropped his hands with a guilty look.

"Yes, I've been very well. How is your family?"

"Oh, we're doing fair to middling, I suppose," I lied smoothly.

A slight frown creased William's brow.

"What are you doing here, Victoria?"

Lifting my eyebrow again at his forwardness, I remained quiet. William looked displeased at my silence, but he said nothing. I sighed inwardly. I didn't have time to deal with William. Harlan had to be dealt with first. I dismissed him with a smile.

"It was nice seeing you, William. Please tell your parents hello for me."

I moved quickly down the hallway leaving a fuming William behind me. At the end of the hallway, I glanced back to see him shrug and walk into one of the rooms. I blew out a relieved breath and proceeded to find Harlan's room. I took deep breaths to calm my speeding pulse and opened the door to find a very large and dark skinned Black woman sitting by the bed. I thought she was a nurse until she stood and narrowed eyes that were filled with jealousy. She pointed at me and bared her yellowing teeth like an animal.

"You bitch, how dare you come here?"

Taken aback by her attitude, I walked further into the room and shut the door.

"Excuse me? Who the hell are you?"

The unattractive Black woman rose from her chair and strode around the bed. I stood my ground when she moved closer. She looked me up and down and lifted her lip in a sneer.

"Harlan said that you were booshie."

I stared at her butchery of the word bourgeois. Stupid and ugly, I thought. I returned her sneer.

"Well, he didn't tell me that he had a new uneducated whore that looked like an ugly, Black sow. Now, I'm going to have to ask you to leave before I have you escorted out of here."

Her eyes widened in surprise at my verbal attack. She stepped back and put her hand Harlan's bed.

"I'm Lila, and Harlan is my man. Why don't you just leave him alone? He doesn't want you. Even his mama, Ms. Dorothy said that he'd be better off without you."

I absorbed the shock that Ms. Dorothy had condoned Harlan's adultery with this woman and schooled my expression not to show any emotion. I looked her up and down and then did so to myself. Thankful that I had dressed up, I rounded on her with an evil smile.

"Sweetheart, do you really think that Harlan is going to leave all these curves for one big one? It's like comparing a rib-eye steak to ground round, honey, and you are definitely round."

I surprised myself at the sarcasm dripping from my tone. Lila's expression turned thunderous, but she didn't move away from Harlan's bed. I wanted her out of the way so that I could do what I needed to do. I lost what little patience that I had.

"Lilly, Lila, Laura, whatever your name is, you are going to leave this room. Now!"

Her lips twisted, and she shook her head. I took a step toward her.

"Vicky?"

We both turned to see Harlan open his eyes and grimace at the movement. Lila rushed to the bed and grabbed his hand.

"I'm here, baby," she crooned.

I rolled my eyes at the smug look that she threw over her shoulder. Harlan pulled his hand from hers and shook his head.

"Who are you?"

Harlan sounded confused at Lila's presence. I pursed my lips because I almost believed his charade. I stepped to the other side of the bed.

"Harlan Sams, you need to stop fooling and send your whore to wait outside. I need to speak with you," I stated while fondling one of the IV tubes.

His eyes widened at my unspoken threat. He turned to Lila and waved his hand toward the door.

"Lila, go on home. There's nothing for you here," he whispered.

Lila squeezed his hand and started to cry. I rolled my eyes again at the crocodile tears. I wanted to yell and scream at her, but I refused to lose my dignity.

"Go on home, Lila. I don't want to see you anymore."

Harlan cleared his throat and waved his hand again at the door. Lila's tears turned to sobs as she lumbered towards the door. She spun and shot a hateful glance at me before leaving the room. Harlan sighed and rolled his head towards me with an apologetic glance.

"Vicky, it's not my fault that she was here. I broke it off with her when her cousin came into the house. He started the fight, I promise."

I knew that Harlan lied through his teeth, but I didn't care. I leaned forward and put a finger on his chest.

"Harlan Sams, this is the last straw. There are no excuses that you could give for this. I'm tired of being your patsy, and it stops today."

I surprised myself that my voice sounded so cool and calm. Harlan's eyes narrowed, and he tried to grab my hand. I snatched it from his chest and stood smiling down at him. He shifted and moaned in pain. I grinned at his discomfort.

"Well, now, I suppose that hurts. I hope it hurts a lot because I want you to feel all of the pain that you've put me through all these years."

Tears of pain escaped from the corner of Harlan's eyes. I almost felt sorry for him – almost.

"Aw, don't feel bad. I'm going to let you come home and recover because it wouldn't look right for me to send my wounded husband away right after his father's passing," I said maliciously.

The moment that the words left my mouth, I regretted them. Harlan went still in shock. His whole body started trembling, his eyes went blank and rolled. I ran to the door and called for a nurse. William and two nurses came running down the hall and into the room. I shrank into the corner while they worked on my husband and prayed to God that Harlan would be all right. I wanted my freedom but not this way.

12

"Vicky, where are my slippers? I want to go sit on the gazebo before Mama and Aunt Julia get here," Harlan yelled.

Tired and frustrated from cleaning and cooking for Harlan's mother and aunt's visit, I returned his yell.

"Find them yourself! It's been four months since you got out of the hospital! You're not an invalid!"

I heard him muttering angrily from my seat in William's room, but he proceeded to find his own slippers. I rolled my eyes and went back to cleaning my unruly son's room. Mark and Grayson's room hadn't needed cleaning, but William's and the twins' rooms were pathetic. I made a mental note to punish them when they came home from school.

"Victoria, this baby is just wonderful! I want to take her home and just spoil her rotten," said Harlan's Aunt Julia.

"Thank you, Ms. Julia, you're too kind."

She chuckled.

"Honey, call me Aunt Julia. You've been my niece for fifteen years. There's no need to stand on ceremony with family."

She frowned at Ms. Dorothy who scowled back. I wanted to laugh at someone giving Ms. Dorothy a dose of her own medicine. Mr. Jerry's death hadn't changed her disposition much except she was even more of a busybody in our marriage.

Valora stopped playing with her shape toys to toddle up to Aunt Julia.

"Hi," she said with a giggle.

Aunt Julia laughed and picked her up to sit on her lap.

"She's so smart! I'm telling you, I might have to steal her and take her back to Littleton."

I beamed at her praise of Valora and took a sip of my herbal tea. Aunt Charlotte had brought it from Uncle Marcos in Allsville on her last trip. It lessened some of my aches and pains, so I drank it all the time now. Ms. Dorothy's fake cough interrupted my wayward thoughts.

"Vicky, you need to clean that child's nose. A good mother wouldn't bring a sick child around company," Ms. Dorothy sniffed.

Aunt Julia glared at Ms. Dorothy before snatching Ms. Dorothy's napkin and cleaning the tiny bit of snot from Valora's nose. Ms. Dorothy gasped in outrage when Aunt Julia returned the napkin to her lap. I didn't know whether to laugh or keep quiet, so I sipped more of my tea. Harlan shoved a teacake in his mouth and looked towards the door.

"Julia, that was uncalled for. You'll apologize to me right now," Ms. Dorothy snarled.

"I will not Dotty. You are such a sourpuss that you can't enjoy your own grandchildren. Well, that's okay, because I don't have any and will be more than happy to take yours."

Aunt Julia held Valora up and tickled her. Valora laughed a full belly laugh and slobbered. Aunt Julia shifted so that it got on Ms. Dorothy. Ms. Dorothy's expression became furious, and she got up and stomped from the room wiping the drool from her wool skirt. Aunt Julia laughed, handed Valora a teacake, and went out the back door whistling. I glanced at Harlan to see him biting his napkin to hold back his humor. I followed Aunt Julia through the back door and faked a coughing fit to cover my own laughter.

I paused by the back door and watched Aunt Julia pointing out plants to Valora. Aunt Julia's gold headscarf sparkled in the October sun. Her skin was a milk chocolate color, and she was very short and slim. She reminded me of my mother when I met her that morning except Tess had more height. For a moment, I wondered why she had left California to live with Ms. Dorothy after Mr. Jerry's death. She seemed to be well off just like Aunt Charlotte. Seeing Aunt Julia motion for me to join them, I shrugged away the concern because it wasn't any of my business.

"Lil' mirror."

I turned around at Big Mama Chandra's soft whisper. She stood by the counter in the kitchen rolling biscuits. I smiled at the familiar sight of her baking powder covered apron. She returned the smile and looked down at the biscuit dough.

"Lil' mirror, when you were a little girl, I used to make these biscuits and give you the extra dough to play with on the table. I can still see your little nose peeking over the counter at everything that I did. Your Aunt Charlotte used to pitch a fit at you getting dirty with flour until I shooed her away. You'd get so tickled pink trying to make those little dirty biscuits that I couldn't do anything but laugh."

Big Mama Chandra started laughing until it turned into a bad cough. I became afraid when she wouldn't stop. Blood began pouring from her mouth with each chest heave. I tried to stand up and help her, but something held me down to the chair. I turned my head towards the door and screamed for help, but no one came. Helpless, I looked back at Big Mama Chandra. All the blood had disappeared, and she had on a long dazzling white gown. She moved forward and kissed my forehead. Her lips were cold as ice, and I shivered. She smiled and stepped back into a bright pool of light.

"Victoria, the Light of the Lord shines within all of us. It's how you accept and reflect that Light that defines your destiny. You are a special woman, and Valora is too. Hold her close and teach her well. It's time to let your Light shine, my lil' mirror."

I reached out to her, but she shook her head and looked up into the light.

"I'm coming, Ed, I'm coming."

I shook my head and screamed for her not to go. She grinned and the light went dark. My heart ached, and I dropped to the floor sobbing my pain.

"Mama, okay?"

Valora's soft hand touched my cheek and woke me from my nightmare. I picked her up and tucked her into my arm under the covers. I kissed her hand and patted her back while wiping my tears on the covers. Harlan's loud snoring and snorting startled me. I rolled my eyes in exaggeration and made Valora giggle. Slowly, I began to relax from the heartache of the dream, but my mind struggled against the strands of lingering dread.

"Mama's okay, now," I whispered into Valora's dark locks.

I continued to pat my beloved daughter's back until we both drifted to sleep.

The next day was the day before New Years Eve at the dawn of nineteen seventy-nine. The sky had let loose with a flurry of snow that morning, so all the children were dancing and playing in it before it melted. Well, all of them except William. He had gone with Harlan to the store. Ever since Harlan had been at home healing, William stuck to him like glue. I hadn't complained because William actually smiled a bit from time to time. He wasn't as ornery either.

After a morning of holiday cooking, I heard a knock on the door. Curious as to whom it was on such a cold, wet day, I hurried to open it. A distraught Aunt Mary stood on the doorstep. Concern washed through me because I glanced over her head to see that she had driven Aunt Charlotte's Cadillac to see me. Aunt Mary didn't drive as far as I knew. Fear for Aunt Charlotte, made my heart pound. I ushered Aunt Mary into the house to a chair and threw a blanket over her knees. She tried to smile her thanks but burst into tears. Her outburst brought tears to my eyes. I hadn't seen Aunt Mary cry since Grandpa

Ed's passing. My heart clenched. I knelt painfully beside her and gripped her hand.

"Aunt Mary, please tell me what's wrong!"

Aunt Mary shook her head and folded over in sobs. I felt so helpless because I didn't know what caused her such grief. Thoughts of Aunt Charlotte went through my head, and I shifted to kneel in front of Aunt Mary to grab her shoulders and look in her face.

"Aunt Mary, you have to tell me what's wrong," I said firmly.

Aunt Mary hiccupped and nodded. She took a deep breath and her next words broke my heart.

"Mama passed away this morning. She had been sick and didn't tell anyone. The doctor had to come over and sedate Charlotte. I didn't know what else to do," she whispered.

I fell back on my feet as the devastation of her statement worked its way through my body. I trembled and rubbed my arms when a deep coldness from the shock came over me. I stared at Aunt Mary in disbelief, but seeing the confirmation in her face, I surrendered to my heartache. I leaned forward and embraced Aunt Mary with a tortured cry. I recalled my dream of the previous night and knew that it hadn't been a dream at all. Big Mama Chandra had come to say goodbye to me. My beautiful, intuitive grandmother had surrendered her soul to be with her beloved husband.

"Victoria, I'm so sorry for your loss."

I turned to see William standing behind me holding Valora. I felt my mouth twist at how much Valora favored William. Valora also looked too comfortable in William's arm. I moved to take her, but William swung her away. I held my hands to Valora, and she giggled before snuggling into William's shoulder. Not wanting to loudly demand my daughter back during Big Mama Chandra's funeral reception, I frowned at William.

"William, I'm sure that you have more to do than cater to my daughter. Where's your family?"

William chuckled.

"Valora is no problem for me, Victoria. I found her with a harassed Mark. He was only too happy to let me take her off his hands for a little while. I didn't see your husband. Is he here?"

I narrowed my eyes at William's innocent expression.

"He left right after the funeral with Gia, Leah, and William. They hitched a ride with his Aunt Julia. The rest of us will drive back tomorrow."

I snapped my mouth shut at revealing my business to William. He snorted at my mean glare. Valora tried to snort too. William chuckled and bounced her on his shoulder.

"See, she knows that she's so safe with me that she follows my example."

I rolled my eyes and tried not to smile at his antics. Glancing into the living room of the homestead, I saw many of my Daniels' and Roberts' relatives including my aunts, Pearl and Hallie, who stood in the dining room with their families. I remembered that Big Mama Chandra had told me that Grandpa Paul had settled some land on them not far from Mama and Daddy's house. Aunt Hallie saw me looking and waved. I waved back. I glanced over William's other shoulder and saw Aunt Charlotte's grief-stricken face. William swung around in concern. Aunt Charlotte smiled sadly in his direction.

"Aunt Charlotte? Can I get you something? Are you all right?"

I worried about Aunt Charlotte because she hadn't been herself since Big Mama Chandra had passed. My mother and Aunt Mary had taken it just a bit better, but not Aunt Charlotte. She had eaten very little and slept even less. Not even Valora's little "gift" had broken her sorrow.

"Dr. William, I'm so glad that you could attend Mama's services. She counted you as part of the family."

William tipped his head.

"Thank you, Ms. St. Francis. I'll be around in Carson until tomorrow while my parents check on the ranch and visit old friends. If you need me, just call the Avalon hotel. Now, if you'll excuse me, I'm going to see if my father can guess Valora's age."

William sauntered away to the sound of a rare laugh from Aunt Charlotte since my grandmother's death.

"Are you all right, Aunt Charlotte?"

Tears slid from her eyes as she nodded. I leaned forward to hug her, but she stepped away with a frown.

"No, Victoria, Mama would have a fit if I wallowed in my tears and wails. It's going to take me some time, but I'll be fine. Now, you can help me by being the good hostess that I raised you to be, okay?"

Speechless at Aunt Charlotte's sudden stoic attitude, I felt my head bob before my feet moved to do her bidding. I glanced up and sent Big Mama Chandra a grateful smile.

Valora turned two on St. Patrick's Day a few months after Big Mama Chandra's passing with as much pomp and circumstance that we could give her. Aunt Charlotte, Aunt Mary, and Aunt Julia came to help us celebrate the occasion. I had decided not to have an extravagant party because I didn't think that she'd remember it, and Harlan wasn't working as much since his injury.

Aunt Charlotte had offered to foot the bill, but I'd declined because I didn't want to be a burden. She had understood and only bought a small mountain of presents for the birthday girl. Aunt Charlotte explained after the party that William had contributed most of the presents including a brand new pink big wheel. I told Aunt Charlotte to return the expensive gift, but she refused. I sent William a thank you note to the hospital using Aunt Charlotte's address as the return.

Earlier in the week, Dr. Michaels had kept Valora overnight for some tests. I stayed anxious the whole time. When I picked her up the next day, I informed Dr. Michael's that there would be no more overnight tests. Dr. Michaels was so delighted with her progress that he readily agreed. I wanted to ask him why he seemed so pleased but knew that I couldn't.

About a month after Valora's birthday, Harlan came home and announced that he had been transferred to Tyson and that we had to move.

"What? Why do we have to move because you got transferred? Where is Tyson, anyway? What about the children's school?"

I became angry at each question that I spilled from my lips. Harlan held up his hand. I put my hands on my hips and waited.

"We have to move because they're going to put someone else here. Tyson is not far from Littleton, so I thought we could just move into your Aunt Charlotte's house there. The schools are good in Littleton, you know. It's my alma mater. Besides, we'll be closer to Mama and Aunt Julia."

I gave him a skeptical look, then twisted around to look at the house that had been our home for several years. I sighed because I knew that there was nothing to do but move. At least, Aunt Julia would be around to soften the edges of Ms. Dorothy.

The move to Littleton took about three months because I refused to remove the children during the school year. Harlan had been angry at first, but he soon saw the wisdom of waiting. I didn't really give him a choice.

Aunt Charlotte's house was beautiful and part of a new suburb on the outskirts of Littleton. Aunt Charlotte had told me that I would love it when she gave us permission to move into it. She hadn't liked that we'd be moving an hour away, but she understood that we needed to move.

Once we unpacked and settled, the children began spending time at Aunt Julia's house a few houses down the lane. I didn't mind because she genuinely seemed to love having them around her. Unlike Ms. Dorothy, Aunt Julia didn't mind getting dirty teaching the children how to fish, hunt, and garden.

Actually, Ms. Dorothy spent most of her time and energy on Shirley's children. She gloated about it often when she came to Sunday dinner. Sometimes, I just wanted to smack that smug look from her face as she bragged and boasted about Harlan's bastards, but I'd paste on a smile and ignore her to talk to Aunt Julia.

Fall came rushing in with the change of color. Valora and I began exploring local farmer's markets with Aunt Julia. It was one of those trips that I got a horrific surprise.

"Well, well, if it isn't that slut that blamed me for the little cut on her leg."

Aunt Julia and I turned at the malicious voice to see Ellis Carter standing behind us with a big bucket of pecans. I stepped back from the evil that I felt coming off of his body in waves. Aunt Julia frowned at my reaction and pulled on Valora's hand to bring her closer to her. She narrowed her eyes at Ellis.

"Ellis Carter, we haven't seen you at church in a month of Sundays. That must be the reason for all that devil in you. How's Orna's teaching job doing?"

I tried to keep my expression bland at the shock that Aunt Julia knew Ellis and Orna. My mouth went dry to think that Orna was a teacher at my children's school. I bit the inside of my jaw to keep the questions from spilling out of my mouth.

Ellis Carter smirked and took a step towards Aunt Julia.

"I've been working at my new job in Tyson. Someone helped me get it to keep me quiet," he snapped.

He sent a vicious glance at me then sneered.

"I hear that your nephew goes on the road a lot. Must be something or someone mighty important to keep him away from home."

I felt the blood rising in my face at his blatant attack on my marriage. I opened my mouth to speak, but Aunt Julia beat me to it.

"Ellis Carter! If I didn't know any better, I'd think that you had a problem with my nephew and his wife. I hope that isn't the case because I'd hate for you to get hurt messing with my family."

Aunt Julia dropped Valora's hand to reach inside her purse. A shiny black pistol appeared in her hand. She kept it close where others in the market couldn't see it. Ellis' eyes narrowed, and he patted his bulging pocket in silent warning.

Aunt Julia cackled.

"I guess we're at a standstill, then. Just remember what I said, Ellis. Have a blessed day."

Aunt Julia grabbed a whimpering Valora's hand and nudged my arm to walk away from Ellis. As soon as we rounded the corner, I stopped to stare at her.

"Aunt Julia, how do you know Ellis and where did you get that pistol?"

Aunt Julia glanced around to see if anyone had heard me before responding. She scowled at me.

"Victoria, what have you and Harlan done to Ellis Carter? He's a mean piece of work."

I glared at Aunt Julia for blaming Harlan and me for Ellis' evil ways towards us.

"We've done nothing. At least, I haven't done anything to that horrible man."

I raised my pants leg to show her the ugly scar. I twisted it so that she could see its length.

"See this, Ellis did that when we lived next to him in Dallas. I'm just glad that they moved finally moved away."

Aunt Julia looked stricken for a moment like I had hit her. I flicked my pants leg down because a few people passed by us. I lowered my gaze to hide my embarrassment. Aunt Julia cleared her throat.

"Victoria, you and Harlan better be on your guard from now. Ellis and Orna are pure evil, but that's not the half of it."

She paused to pick Valora up and hug her protectively. Dread filled my stomach. I touched my hand to my throat as fear welled up in it. Aunt Julia turned a wary look on me.

"Ellis and Orna are your right side neighbors."

I counted myself blessed to not run into Ellis or Orna after Aunt Julia's revelation of their nearness. Although, I worried about Gia and Leah because began coming home with bad grades and stories of how mean Ms. Orna Carter was to them. A call to the school principal, Mr. Jeffries informed me that their previous teacher, Ms. Clark, had become very ill all of a sudden, so Orna had been assigned some of her students - which included Gia and Leah. I requested that they be transferred, but Mr. Jeffries denied it because he said there were no spaces in the other classes. After I told him of Orna's actions, he stated that he'd take care of the issue. I didn't feel confident that he would, so I prayed that it wouldn't be another situation like Mark's with Rita James at Founders Street Private School.

"Mama, do you know where my piglets are? I put them in the pen next to the fence, but it's empty."

I turned from the sink to see Mark dressed in his future rancher jacket and muck boots. I chided myself for forgetting his swine auction. I wiped my hands on a towel and smiled.

"Did those little monsters get out again? I swear they're more trouble than a bunch o' young'uns," I laughed while looking up into my handsome son's grinning face.

Mark guffawed and shook his head at my attempt at a country twang.

"Go on, son, get the rest of your things together. I'll go get the piggies."

"Yes, ma'am," he nodded.

I put on my plaid lumberjack coat, grabbed the slop bucket, and went to find the little piglets. I hoped that when they heard the slosh of the slop bucket, they'd come running. I made it to their mama's pen and poured some of the smelly mix into her bin. I glanced around to hear the piglets' hungry squeals, but there was only silence.

Letting out a big breath of frost into the cold air, I moved to the fence to see any hoof prints in the wet grass. I walked around the fence until I came to a trickle of blood leading to Ellis' side of the fence. Thinking that Ellis had stolen a piglet and harmed it, I lengthened my step and strode to the fence. Halfway there, I fell in a freshly dug pile of dirt. I took a moment to catch my breath, and then tried to plant my hand in the soft dirt for leverage to stand. It was my horror to feel the little feet of a piglet. I gasped and began to use my aching hands to uncover the seven dead and mutilated bodies of the piglets. I felt the tears running down my face at their maimed little corpses. Maniacal laughter filled the morning air. I swung around to see Ellis standing at the fence.

"Oh, poor little piggies, and they cried 'wee, wee, wee, to go home'," he mocked.

Nauseous at his display of evil, I twisted my head and threw up in the dirt.

"Mama? Are you all right?"

Mark rushed to my side to help me up, but his hands dropped with an alarm cry when he saw his piglets. He swung around with balled his fists and took a step toward Ellis.

"What are you going to do, sissy boy? Come on, I dare you," Ellis taunted.

Mark took another step before turning at my distressed cry. Ellis only laughed harder and went inside his house. I caught Mark's arm to lead him into the back door. I sat him down at the kitchen table and called the sheriff. The irritated operator said that she'd send a deputy right away. Relieved, I turned around to see Mark break into sobs. My heart ached for his loss. I wanted to comfort him, but I picked up the phone and called Aunt Julia. She hurried over in her housedress and coat. After a thorough explanation, she examined the piglets herself. She returned to the house with a grim look on her face.

"Mark, you hush now. I'll buy you another sow to have some babies. Right now, I want you to get your brother and sisters ready to go to my house," she commanded.

Mark said a quiet yes ma'am and left to do her bidding. Aunt Julia sat down heavily at the table.

"I'm too old for Ellis' nonsense."

I poured her a cup of coffee while murmuring my agreement. The front door opened to an irate Ms. Dorothy and Harlan.

"What nonsense?"

Harlan asked the question as he all but pushed his mother into the kitchen.

Aunt Julia and I looked at them in surprise. Harlan dropped his head with a guilty look. Ms. Dorothy swung around on me in anger.

"What have you done, gal? Orna Carter called me to tell me that the oldest boy killed some of her livestock in spite. She said that you're blaming it on Ellis. You're going to apologize to those good people and give that good for nothing son of yours a beating."

I narrowed my eyes at the stupid drivel dripping from Ms. Dorothy's mouth. I glanced at Harlan to see that he remained quiet. Rage of more than ten years of ridicule and humiliation filled me.

"Ms. Dorothy, you are such a vindictive, hateful woman. You can't see beyond your own busybody nose. Don't you know the saying? Blood is thicker than water, but I guess it's the opposite in your case. Why did you come? I don't owe you an explanation, so get the hell out of my house. One day, you'll wish that you had treated my children better."

Tears of anger ran down my cheeks. I swiped at them before turning to my wayward husband.

"Harlan, Ellis made some accusations about you being off cheating again. Is that how he got the job to move here? Did he use your lying adulterous ways against you?"

Harlan's mouth tightened in silence. I stepped towards him and slapped his face.

"Answer me!"

Aunt Julia pulled me back before Harlan recovered from my blow. Ms. Dorothy put her arm around Harlan and hissed like an old alley cat in my direction.

"How dare you touch my son! You've always thought that you're better than us because your family had money. What good is money if you can't keep your man at home? Lila was right about you! I'm so glad that Harlan has a woman that can take care of him now, and I have a new grandbaby girl that I can be love."

Aunt Julie gasped while I struggled with my shock of Harlan's lies and deceit. A baby? He'd had a baby with Lila? I stared in fury as Harlan's face filled with anger towards his mother. She turned an innocent look on him. He snarled in her direction.

"Mama, enough, now go home."

Ms. Dorothy's eyes watered at Harlan's harsh tone. She removed her arm from his shoulders to leave. She turned at the doorway.

"Now, maybe you can let my son go, Vicky."

I wanted to give in to the hysterical laughter building in my chest; however, I wanted to give her a "thought" for later.

"Ms. Dorothy, I let Harlan go a year ago, but he wouldn't give me a divorce."

Ms. Dorothy's gaze swung to a grim-faced Harlan for confirmation. He nodded. Ms. Dorothy lifted her nose and pushed past a confused Mark and William. I wanted to comfort my sons in their shock, so I moved toward them. Aunt Julia stopped me with a hand on my arm.

"Are y'all ready, boys? Where's Grayson and your sisters? Oh, there they are behind you. Wait, I only see Gia and Leah. Where's the baby?"

Mark nodded and mumbled, "Valora's asleep."

Aunt Julia sighed and bobbed her head.

"That's all right. Let her sleep. She's a sound sleeper anyway. Okay, let's go to my house for some chocolate chess pie and hot chocolate, okay? Your Mama and Daddy need to talk for a while."

The children allowed Aunt Julie to shuffle them out of the door. Harlan stared at me in the awkward silence. He opened his mouth to say something when a rock flew through the back window. Harlan's face twisted in anger, and he ran out of the back door. I followed him to see what happened. My steps faltered when I saw Ellis tossing a rock up and down in his hand. A large white bucket sat on the ground next to him. He snickered.

"Well, the rooster comes home to his clucking hen, finally. Did you have a good time with my wife's cousin? I had a good time here with your lazy wife."

Harlan clenched his fists and stepped closer to the fence. My heart pounded in fear. I knew that Ellis carried a gun from when he patted his pocket at the market. Oh, why hadn't the sheriff or deputy arrived? I tried to slide unnoticed toward the safety of the house. Wifely duty made me call out to Harlan.

"Harlan, remember that we need to be at Aunt Julia's for dinner later. You haven't said hello to Valora since you came home. Let's go see if she's awake," I rambled.

Harlan didn't turn or answer me. Ellis laughed at my unsuccessful attempts to get Harlan away from him.

"Nah, he doesn't want to do any of that, right, old man? You want to play with the big boys, don't ya?"

Harlan scowled at Ellis.

"You've been a pain in my ass for too long, Ellis Carter. What did I ever do to you, you coward? What's your problem?"

Ellis' laughter died. He looked over at me.

"You and your uppity wife are my problem. What kind of woman accepts the way that you treat her? She's a stupid cow having baby after baby knowing that you're a cheat. When you decided to cheat with my wife's cousin, your problems with me got real, you jive turkey," he snapped.

As Ellis spoke, he started bending toward the white bucket. I stepped forward to tell Harlan to ignore him when Harlan pulled a pistol from his coat and started firing at Ellis. I fell to the ground and covered my ears. With horrified eyes, I saw Ellis' body jerk as each bullet entered to create blooming mushrooms of dark blood on his overalls. Harlan emptied the pistol into Ellis. I glanced at his face from my position on the ground. Harlan sneered as Ellis thrashed around on the ground.

"I'm not your problem now, you bastard. Should have minded your own business."

He turned and went back into the house without another word. Shock held me paralyzed while I watched Ellis struggling for breath.

"Please, help me," he gurgled.

The sight of Ellis fighting for his life mobilized me to get up and run around the side of the house. I slipped but regained my balance as I crossed Ellis and Orna's yard to get to their backyard gate. I slammed it open and hurried to Ellis' side. I fell to my knees beside him. They sank into the cold ground wet with Ellis's blood. He coughed up more blood when I turned him to put his head on my lap. Blindly, I tried to put my hands over his wounds to staunch the blood. Ellis looked into my eyes, and I saw regret and fear in their depths. I thought that I heard sirens in the distance and prayed that they arrived in time.

Ellis' body trembled violently, so I leaned closer to cover him with my jacket. He gasped and tried to lift his hand to my face. My panic became terror when his hand dropped to his side, and his eyes lost the light of life. Screaming for help, I bent over Ellis' lifeless body and allowed my sobs to fill the silence.

Epilogue

"Mama? Can we go for a walk before we leave?"

Victoria turned from the packing boxes to smile at Valora. She had grown so much over the past three years. Dr. Michaels was so excited at Valora's progress that he hadn't put up much of a fuss at Victoria's decision to move to Carson.

"You'll need to keep me updated with her progress in this journal. I'll arrange for you to visit a nearby specialist so that I can get the fluid and tissue samples that I need," he had said mildly.

Victoria had taken the journal and promised to keep in touch with Dr. Michaels. As she looked over Valora, a rush of pride ran through her. Valora's striking looks and personality affected everyone around her. Very few could resist her open friendly nature. Victoria lifted an eyebrow at the shadow of her own curvy figure in her small daughter. She is going to look more like me that Gia and Leah, she said to herself.

"Yes, pumpkin. We can walk down the lane for a while."

Valora whooped before running to get her shoes. Victoria laughed at her daughter's excitement. Yes, definitely like me, she thought. Valora loved the outdoors and wanted to know everything about the plants, trees, and animals. She had a way with animals that matched Mark and Grayson's. Victoria shook her head. Those three are more like me than Gia, Leah, and William put together. At least Harlan wasn't around anymore to influence the children. Harlan. If it weren't for his uncontrollable rage, they wouldn't be moving. Victoria sighed heavily at her inward thoughts before the last few years intruded on her walk with her baby girl.

Valora chattered away on the walk down the graveled lane. Victoria laughed at her exuberance and patiently answered her questions. I'm glad that I kept her home these last two weeks, she thought.

As soon as the move was confirmed, Victoria had taken Valora out of the Littleton kindergarten school. The teacher had taken a dislike to Valora and saw fit to paddle her once without verifying the word of another child. Furious at the idiotic teacher's actions, Victoria had lodged a complaint with the principal. The problem was that Victoria had been filing complaints with the Littleton school district for all the children over the past three years since Ellis' death, Harlan's trial, and Orna Carter's accusations that Victoria had something to do with it all. Her teacher friends had rallied around her and conveniently forgotten their duties as educators.

Now, Victoria intended to give her children a fresh start. After all, it was nineteen eighty-two not nineteen sixty.

Victoria sighed as she came to a stop and turned her gaze up into the darkened canopy of trees covering the lane. A bright beam of light came through the darkness to shine on them. Victoria's throat felt tight with unshed tears. Thank you, Big Mama Chandra, she mouthed.

"Are you okay, Mama?"

Victoria looked down into Valora's upturned face and nodded.

"The Light of The Lord is within all of us. It's how you reflect that Light that defines your character. Always remember that, Valora, always remember that."

THE LEGACY

Book 4

Prologue

"Mama, look!"

Victoria glanced up to see a car speed down the lane. She moved Valora to the side of the dirt road and continued to walk on the rough path. The car slowed to a stop beside them.

"Victoria! I hoped to get here before you left!"

Victoria's mouth dropped open in shock to see William hop out of the sporty Oldsmobile. She placed a hand over her heart to stop its runaway beat. William took note of her hand placement and smiled. Victoria frowned and dropped her hand. William chuckled softly and stepped toward where Victoria and Valora stood. Victoria stifled the urge to step away and lowered her face in shame at William's friendly manner.

William had tried to help during the ordeal with Harlan, but not wanting to stir up trouble, Victoria bade him to stay away. Since then, Aunt Charlotte had told her that William and his family returned to live on Dr. Herbert's ranch in Carson. Now, Victoria was on her way back to Carson as well. Her heart skipped another beat as thoughts of peace and happiness with William flooded her mind.

Victoria shook her head slightly to rid herself of those wayward and silly thoughts. She raised a puzzled gaze to William's handsome face.

"William, what are you doing here?"

William smiled down at Valora before turning his twinkling blue-eyed gaze to Victoria.

"My mother spoke with yours about a job for you at my practice in Carson. Is it true? Are you moving back to Carson?"

Speechless at Tess' interference, Victoria nodded. William's smiled widened before he glanced at Valora with pride. He knelt down beside her.

"Well, hello, little one. I haven't seen you since you were knee high to a grasshopper."

Valora giggled and touched William's cheek. He looked startled for a moment and then his laughter filled the silence. He took Valora's hand from his cheek and kissed it. He turned back to Victoria.

"May I give you and this beautiful little lady a lift somewhere?"

Victoria shook her head.

"No, we aren't far from the house, but thank you anyway."

William shook his head and grinned. He strode over to the shiny Chrysler sedan and opened the passenger car door. He made a grand bow to which Valora giggled. Victoria's lips pulled into a reluctant little smile.

"No ma'am, I'm not taking no for an answer anymore."

1

I stood next to a distraught Tess as the well-dressed funeral director signaled for the young Mexican man to turn the crank to lower my grandfather to his final resting place. I felt the tears roll down my face mimicking the rain that dripped down the umbrella, but I couldn't wipe them away while I held Valora's hand. I peeked at the dull and dark clouds for a moment and felt the reflection of my mood.

It wasn't as if I hadn't prepared myself for Grandpa Paul's death because he had been frail and sick for some time. Marcos and Juan tended to him until the end, and they had got us as ready as they could for his departure from this world. I guess that I hadn't been ready for it. I closed my eyes for a moment to remember his dynamic presence and his piercing blue gaze. I prayed for Grandpa Paul's soul and that he had come to accept Jesus as His Savior. Then, memories almost engulfed my mind and my heart began to ache in earnest. I felt a tug on my hand. I looked down into Valora's concerned face. Memories of Grandpa Paul's reaction to her presence made me smile at my small daughter.

"Mama, are you okay?"

Unable to speak, I nodded my head and squeezed her plump little hand. I turned back to hear the funeral director dismiss the family for the final burial rites.

"Our sympathies to the Roberts family at this time of loss. However, if you all would care to join the family at the Roberts' ranch house for the luncheon prepared by the Unity Christian Church's ladies mission, please do so now."

Everyone seemed to breathe a sigh of relief to be dismissed from the rain and muddy cemetery. When Tess turned to Clyde to comfort him, I nodded to Mark to gather the other children to our old Plymouth car. I returned my gaze to my grandfather's open grave and silently said another goodbye. I felt Valora's warm shock of comfort and squeezed her hand again. I released a heavy sigh and began to slowly move away from the gravesite. When I turned to go to the car, I saw Betts hand the funeral director an envelope. She had a coy smile on her face and batted her eyelashes in the director's handsome face. The director's face looked disgusted at Betts' attempts at flirtation. A similar disgust rose within me at her disrespect of Grandpa Paul. Anger filled my body, and I felt the words of hatred and anger on my tongue ready to unleash on Betts. I took a step toward them and felt rooted to the ground. I looked down to see my feet had sunk into the mud. Valora giggled at my predicament, and I felt a release of the negative emotions while I joined her in a small giggle. I waved to Mark to come help me. He immediately jogged over to see what was wrong.

"Are you okay, Mama?"

I pointed to my sunken feet. Mark looked down and shook his head. Then he raised it with a big smile on his face. I was glad to see him smile because Grandpa Paul's death had been hard on him.

"No problem, Mama. I'll have to pick you up to get you out of that muck. Valora, run tell Grayson to dig out a towel in the trunk for Mama, okay?"

Valora looked at Mark with all the hero worship of a little sister and ran to do his bidding. Mark moved toward me with his arms out, but he stopped and looked behind me. His face lit up with a smile. Curious, I tried to turn to see what caused his reaction, and a warm hand settled on my shoulder. I knew that hand.

"Victoria, you're going to break your neck."

William's soft laugh echoed through the dreary afternoon silence of the cemetery as he moved within my line of vision. He wore a dark and well-tailored suit, and my heart skipped a beat at his handsomeness. I glanced at Mark to see if he noticed my reaction to William's presence, but he already walked towards the car. I saw him grab Valora when she looked about to run over to where William and I stood. Mark whispered in her ear, and she nodded and waved to us. I waved back and lowered the umbrella from the now dry sky. I fidgeted with the snap to delay looking at William. He cleared his throat loudly, and I turned my gaze at him. He looked serious, but I saw him smother a smile. Suspicious, I narrowed my eyes at him. He threw me a look of innocence.

"May I assist you out of your quandary, Victoria? I wouldn't want that mud to dry and have to chip you out with a chisel."

I glanced down at my feet that sunk even more into the wet ground. I shook my head at the loss of my good black heels. I took a deep breath and looked up in time to see William step closer with his arms out to me. Before I could react, he swooped me up into his arms and strode towards the car. Surprised, I attempted to push against his strength, but he squeezed me tighter. Embarrassed and self-conscious, I pushed again.

"Careful, Victoria. I'm slipping a little too. I wouldn't want us both to go down in this muck. You're too prideful to say yes, so I'm answering for you."

"Put me down now, William. I'm out of danger of sinking into the mud, and my children are watching. I don't want them to get the wrong idea."

William glanced at the children and back to me.

"It's nineteen eighty-two, and the children know that I'm a good family friend. Besides, I'm also your employer, and

I can't have you miss work on the account of hurting yourself in the mud."

He smirked at me, and I narrowed my eyes at him again. William squeezed me to him and smiled wide at the children as we approached the car. I turned to see Mark, Leah, Grayson, and Valora smile at William while Willie and Gia's faces looked pinched and angry. I pasted a thankful smile to my face when William put me down next to the open car door. Mark handed me a towel. I turned to William and began wiping my feet.

"Thank you so much, Dr. William. I was in quite a situation. Now, I'm sure that you want to catch up with your mother and father at the ranch house. Children, say thank you to Dr. William for his ..."

"How dare you act so coarse and whorish at your grandfather's funeral, gal!"

All of us turned to see that Betts had followed William's steps across the graveyard. Dressed in all black, she looked like a red-eyed vulture that had swooped from the sky to lean on the silver capped cane. I felt the children's distressed murmur at her venomous words. William stepped backwards to stand in front of the children. Betts saw his movement and sneered. When I heard Valora whimper, I felt anger rush through my veins. Enough was enough.

"How dare you come over here with your filth, Grandmother? You've been a nuisance since I came home. Why can't you leave me alone - especially today?"

Betts' eyes widened at my behavior, but her face darkened with evil.

"Well, well, lookee here. I guess you think you're ready for me, gal? No, you're not and don't think you ever will be neither. You may have done a little something with that ol' ainty of yours, but it don't matter. Ya hear me? It's too deep!"

She began to cackle and shook her head. She turned to William.

"You think you're all high and mighty, don't ya, boy? You know, I heard that you're a widower. I guess that leaves the door wide open for Vicky, huh? Think you can save her with that little brat? It won't happen! I'll see to that!"

She cackled again and spat in the mud. I looked back at William and the children to see anger and confusion on their faces. Except for Willie and Gia. They looked pleased at Betts' outburst. I frowned at them and turned back to Betts. She stared at Willie and Gia with pride. I felt my fists ball in anger, and I took a step toward Betts. Valora's small hand slipped into mine and stopped me. Again, I felt the anger and hate leave my body. Betts frowned at Valora and backed away. I smiled at her retreat and squeezed Valora's hand while I looked at Betts.

"Betts, today we laid Grandpa Paul to rest. In respect of him, I am not going to fight with you or allow you to criticize Dr. William in any way. Now, we're going up to the house to be with the family. I'd suggest that you do that same."

Betts' face twisted, and her glowing eyes were all that could be seen. She shifted her body and narrowed her eyes. I knew that she meant to spill her hatred, so I turned my back to her. I looked up to see pride on William's face before I gave Valora a little push towards the open car door. She turned to give me a wide snaggle-toothed grin. William let out a loud boom of laughter at her smile. All of the tension began to leave my body.

"Watch it, gal. Your life isn't going to be the bed of roses that you think now. Remember that the bed that you make is the one that you have to lie in."

The ugliness of Betts' words hung in the air for a moment. Goosebumps skittered across my skin but I shook them off. I decided to dismiss Betts' parting shot as the envy of an old bitter woman. I pasted a smile on my face, nodded to William, and got in the car to drive over to the ranch house. It wasn't until I tried to sleep later that night that her words returned to haunt my dreams.

"Willie! Willie! Come here, right now!"

I stomped through the tall grass on the side of the small, dilapidated farmhouse to find my stubborn second oldest child. Willie became more disobedient as he got older. I couldn't whip him these days without all of the children chasing him down for me. I shook my head in wonder at his behavior, but I needed him to come out of hiding now. There was something important that I needed to tell him.

"Willie! William Sams! You come here, right now!"

Mark stuck his head out of the kitchen window.

"Mama, do you want me to find him? You don't look so good."

I smiled at my handsome oldest son. His deep concerned voice and creased forehead made me want to hug him. I waved a hand at him and shook my head no.

"No, Mark, I'll find him. I'm fine. It's just a little hot today."

He didn't look convinced, but being the opposite of his brother, he nodded his obedience and ducked back inside the window. I turned and shaded my hand to my forehead against the hot sun. Memories of another summer began to unfold in my mind. The heat of the cotton fields. Big Mama Chandra. Grandpa Ed. I felt my throat thicken with tears. Suddenly, the tall grass seemed to grow around me and I felt stifled. I walked forward a few steps and Willie appeared at the corner of the house. I hadn't heard his approach so his sudden presence startled me.

"Willie! You scared the daylights out of me!"

Willie stood there with a mulish look on his face that caused my anger to rise. I stepped closer and shook my finger in his face. He didn't back away.

"When I call you, you better answer me or come running! Do you hear me, son?"

He didn't say a word. He just stood there in sullen silence. I took a deep breath and tried to calm my nerves. I glanced up to see Mark glare at Willie with his arms crossed. I frowned at his protective stance but his focus was on Willie. I mentally shrugged away his concern and turned to face Willie.

"Willie, the Holly's just called and said that you can work for them if you still want to work. They bought the piece of the ranch that Betts just sold, so they're going to need extra help bailing hay. Since Mark is already working as their evening and Saturday foreman, they'll give you a ride too."

I smiled at my handsome dark-skinned son and hoped that he'd be excited to earn some extra money. Willie stared hard at me for a moment, and when he saw me began to frown, his face brightened into a small smile.

"That's good, Mama. I'm real glad. Now, I can help you just like Mark, right? Maybe I can work more hours when summer comes and we can move away from this dump. I'll work harder than Mark, you'll see."

I stared at my son as he uttered those words. Something within me felt like they were wrong and that I should figure it out for my son's sake, but I'd spent enough time looking for him. I still had cows to milk. I murmured my approval with a tight smile and turned towards the shed.

Later that night, I kept the window open to cool off the house after I cooked on the old wood stove. I cast my eyes into the darkened kitchen and felt my disappointment rise again. The cooking stove wasn't working, and the refrigerator was on its last legs. I swung my aching body into the bed and let my thoughts drift.

When I decided to come home, Tess told me that she'd found the ideal house for the children and me. She wouldn't tell me much about it except that it would do well for us. Because our relationship had come so far, I'd trusted that it was a decent house for us to start over after Harlan's mess.

When we arrived at the old rundown farm, I wanted to cry out at my stupidity. I realized that Tess thought that any house was fine as long as it wasn't in Littleton. I confronted her, and it set off a round of arguments that I hadn't had the energy. I prayed to God and He gave me peace and lightness that maybe I could make the old farm a home for my babies. In fact, I became determined to make it happen. We left our belongings at Big Mama Chandra's and Grandpa Ed's, rolled up our sleeves, and got to work.

The previous tenants had gutted the house, and the land around it was filled with trash, weeds and tall grass. It'd taken a week to clear enough of the weeds to see the large yard and put down gravel. I put all of the children to work sprinkling seven-dust around the edges of the property for snakes and other critters. I opened an account at the hardware store and bought planks and wood to fix the holes in the floor and walls. Mark rebuilt the animal shed and made Willie help him cut down a chopping block. Leah and Gia painted the inside walls and helped me to decorate. Grayson kept Valora busy teaching her how to dig for grubs and worms and climb the yard trees. It took us a month to make the house our home, but we did it together. We just didn't know that later the foundation that we built as a family would begin to crack.

"Victoria?"

I heard William's whisper before I felt the coolness gently wipe across my skin. I followed it to get more and murmured in protest when it went away.

"Victoria, open your eyes now. I'll let Valora smooth the cloth on you again if you do. She's very good at it for a little stinker."

I heard Valora's soft giggle, and I tried to lift my arm out to my pumpkin. Pain skittered through my arm and I gasped as it wound its way through the rest of my body. Valora uttered a little sound of dismay.

"Victoria. You must open your eyes and comfort Valora and the other children. They need you to wake up now. Now, Victoria."

I felt my brow crease at William's hard tone, but his words made my heartache for my babies. I raised my eyelids slowly and saw blurry forms around me. I heard and felt William's sigh of relief.

"Very good, Victoria. Now, I'm going to shine this light in your eyes for a bit. No, don't back away. There, now that's not so bad, is it?"

I tried to shake my head when he removed the light from my eyes, but the movement sent more pain through my body. I felt stifled and cold. Very cold.

"Victoria, you have a fever and your hands and joints are swollen. I need to take some blood back to the hospital to see what's going on with you. It's not like the episodes that you've had before is it?"

My eyes adjusted to the room, and I could see that William knelt beside the bed. Valora sat in bed beside me while Mark, Grayson, Leah, and Gia stood behind William. All of them looked worried. I glanced back to William and shook my head. He nodded and twisted to look at Mark.

"Mark. Son, why don't you take your brother and sisters outside for a spell? I've got to talk to your mama."

Mark immediately moved to do William's bidding. He held his hands out to Valora, and she shook her head. Grayson wouldn't move either. Leah and Gia had already gone through the curtain that separated my room from the living room. William smothered a smile at Valora and Grayson's refusal to leave me. Mark stood with an exasperated look on his face. Then, he pressed his lips together and put his hands on his hips.

"Valora, Grayson, Mama needs to talk to Dr. William. Come with me now or I'm going to whip your butts!"

He held his arms out for Valora again, and she almost jumped into them. Grayson looked at Mark's face and ran from the room. William coughed to cover his laugh as Mark walked toward the curtain. Curious, I stopped him with a weak voice that didn't sound like mine at all.

"Mark? What happened?"

Mark turned with Valora on his hip and one hand on the curtain.

"You're usually up early to wake me and Willie for breakfast before our ride gets here. The Holly's honking woke me up, and when I came through, you were still in bed trembling. I put my hand on your forehead, and you felt really hot. I touched your hand to wake you, but you wouldn't wake up for nothing. I called Dr. William because I didn't know what to do."

Mark's voice deepened, and he turned his head but not before I saw the sheen of tears. He cleared his throat and attempted a smile. Valora put her hand to his cheek. Mark closed his eyes and took a deep breath. When he collected himself, he glanced back at William, then at me and smiled.

"You're in good hands now. We'll be outside. In fact, I think I'll teach my little sister how to play basketball today. How about that Valora? Want to learn how to play a game?"

Mark went through the curtain while he talked to Valora about what they would do. I turned back to William to see concern on his face. I let my eye ask the question that my voice wouldn't. William understood and nodded.

"I don't know for certain what's wrong with you, Victoria. I have a suspicion, but I'll have to take some blood and run several tests to be sure. I don't think it's life-threatening right now, though."

I nodded weakly and let him take the blood. When he finished he turned back to me. He gently picked up my aching hand and leaned forward. I closed my eyes at the comfort of his body heat.

"Victoria, why didn't you tell me about this house? I could have helped you build a new one. Why do you have to be so stubborn? I want to help you so much that I can't sleep at night. I don't want you living like this when there's better things for us, I mean you."

William glanced down at his slip of the tongue, and my heart jumped at his admission. I took a deep breath and squeezed his hand weakly. He raised his head and smiled.

"Well then, it's something to see about, oui?"

2

"Mama!"

I heard Mark's shout from outside and tried to rush through the house to see what was wrong. I couldn't move as fast as I wanted to because my body still ached from my sick spell.

"Mama! Are you home?"

"Yes, boy! I'm coming as fast at these legs can carry me! What the blazes is going on out there?"

Finally, I got to the door to see my oldest son standing on the porch in his graduation cap and gown. I glanced to see Tom Holly, Mark's best friend, wave from his father's Buick. I turned back to Mark to see that his smile lit up the cloudy afternoon, and I felt my lips echo his grin. Several emotions swept through me at the evidence that one of my chicks were about to leave the nest. I swallowed the tightness in my throat and stepped forward to hug my son.

"Is it that time already, Mark? I didn't know that y'all picked up your graduation packages today."

"Yes, ma'am. I didn't know either until they called my name. I know that we hadn't paid yet, so it kind of surprised me to get it today. Would you look at it, Mama?"

Mark pulled away from my embrace and stepped back to preen in the reflection of the front window. I had a hunch how the package got paid for and who did it, but I didn't dwell on it. I just took the time to wonder when had my beloved son grown into such a handsome and responsible man.

Smooth skin and a light five o'clock shadow met my gaze. Mark had received the majority of his looks from me with the high forehead and patrician features. His light complexion glowed with health. His tall frame had changed from slim to strong with working outdoors all of the time. The knowledge that Mark never used that strength against others was just another feather in his cap. My oldest son had a gentleness about him that made me wary that someone would take advantage of him when he left home. I felt the frown touch my brow at that thought and dismissed it with shake of my head. God would protect him because I made sure that Mark always knew that, but worry still sat in my heart.

"I'm going to take it off now, Mama, and get ready to clear the patch behind the animal shed before it rains. Tim said that I could have a few chickens and a calf."

I shook myself again from my troubled thoughts, smiled, and nodded at Mark. A small frown crossed his face, and I knew that he felt the change in my attitude.

"Mama, are you okay? I know that Dr. William told you to stay in bed for a while, but you've been up doing a lot. Maybe, you should listen to him. He is a doctor."

"Mark Sams! I am just fine. Don't you patronize me, young man. Now, I'm going to let you go take that cap and gown off and hang it up in my room closet. I don't want it getting dirty before your big day. Willie is at track practice, so why don't you wait for Grayson to help clear the patch? The school bus should be here soon. He can do his lesson after y'all finish. Oh, and watch out for Valora. You know she'll be trying to help."

I rambled to a stop because Mark said 'yes ma'am' and started into the house through the twins' room to get to his. When he closed the door, I let out a breath that I hadn't realized that I'd been holding. Mark had always been intuitive, and I didn't want him to feel obligated to stay home after graduation. Memories of what my parents did to me at his age surfaced. I glanced at the darkening sky and the swirling, swaying tall grass and felt the disappointment in my life rise within me. I viciously tamped down those feelings and swore that I would never do that to one of my children. I turned away from the sky with the prayer that the school bus would hurry before the storm arrived. The sound of the phone ringing and the rising wind sent me pushed me through the living room door. I tried to calm my breathing before I picked up the antique black phone.

"Hello?"

"Yes, may I speak with Mrs. Sams?"

I sat down with a frown at the woman's abrupt tone. I responded with coolness.

"This is she. Whom may I ask is calling?"

"This is Ms. Danvers, one of the English teacher, from Carson High School. I'm sorry to disturb your day. Actually, I didn't think that you'd be home from what Gia told me. I know that you have a busy schedule, however, we need to talk about Gia's work and behavior."

I felt my frown deepen at the mention of my headstrong daughter. Gia became more difficult with each day. Each day was a struggle to have patience with her without cutting a switch to tan her behind. I sighed and relaxed a bit that the call wasn't anything more serious than a schoolteacher.

"It's okay, Ms. Danvers. How might I assist you?"

"Gia's grades in my class and a few of her other classes are failing. I know that you all came from a smaller school district and things may have been different. It's just that Gia has been disrespectful and defiant to staff and students. I believe that the transfer affected her attitude toward her education. I also have Leah in another class, and she is an absolute treasure."

I heard the change in Ms. Danvers tone when she spoke of Leah and I smiled. Leah was friendly and fun loving. She had always been the opposite of Gia except when Gia influenced Leah. I understood Mrs. Danvers confusion because they were twins, but I couldn't explain it myself. I turned my attention back to the phone when I heard Ms. Danvers continue to speak.

"I'd like to have a conference with you and Gia, Mrs. Sams. I can gather together all of Gia's work and reports from her other teachers so that we can put together a plan to help her. I don't want her to fall behind or fail because it might cause her behavior to worsen. If you can schedule some time away from your patients this week that would be wonderful."

Confusion hit me when Ms. Danvers mentioned patients.

"I'm sorry. What did you say about patients, Ms. Danvers?"

"I said if you can schedule some time away from nursing your patients this week that would be wonderful. Gia told us that you always stay very busy nursing patients at Dr. Herbert's office. I assured her that you would make time for her and her adopted younger siblings."

Ms. Danvers voice sounded impatient as if she talked to one of her students. I ignored it to focus on what she said. I raised my voice a bit because the wind started to howl like a pack of wolves.

"Ms. Danvers, I don't nurse patients at Dr. Herbert's office. I'm one of the medical secretaries, and I don't have any adopted children."

There was a pause on the other end of the phone.

"Gia distinctly told everyone that you were a nurse and that her father died on an oil rig in the gulf when she was a baby. That's why you adopted so many children because you and your husband weren't able to have more before his death. I assure you that I understand, however, it may have been just a bit overboard to adopt so many as a single parent."

Now, I paused to take in Ms. Danvers' revelation. My daughter lied, and it was a big lie. I didn't understand why she'd do that. Well, maybe, I understood about not telling everyone about what Harlan did or where he was. I just didn't understand why she'd tell such a story that could easily be proven wrong. I felt anger rise at Gia's selfish need for attention. My hands began to shake so much that I almost dropped the phone. I tried to focus to get Ms. Danvers off the phone.

"Ms. Danvers, I don't know why my daughter would tell you those things. Gia told you and everyone else a pack of lies. I'm not a nurse, I have no adopted children, and Gia's father is alive and well. I can also assure you that I make time for ALL of my children. Actually, I work half days to be home when they arrive from school. As to Gia's grades and behavior, I am happy to meet with you this week, and her behavior will be corrected by tomorrow."

I heard Ms. Danvers began to sputter, but I didn't have time to gauge her reaction because I heard the sound of the school bus. I knew that I needed to deal with Gia, but I knew that we had to deal with the storm first. I said a polite but firm goodbye to Ms. Danvers, got up, and called Mark to me. He came running through my room's curtain.

"Yes, ma'am?"

His concerned voice soothed my frayed nerves. I nodded to the breaking storm outside the window.

"You and Grayson don't have time to clear the patch before that storm gets here. It looks like a pretty bad one's brewing, and I hope it's just bluster and not a tornado."

Just the word tornado caused my heart to beat heavily. I'd only been in one tornado in my life. It'd been when the children and I lived on the Blocks' ranch after Harlan went to prison. God only knows how we all lived through that nightmare, but we did. I glanced at Mark and saw the same memory on his face. I reached over and patted his back just as Valora ran through the door to hug around my legs. I felt her small body tremble and knew that she was afraid. Grayson and Leah came through the door with the same fear on their faces. I looked behind them to see Gia, but she wasn't there. With the thought that she delayed outside in stubbornness, I shrugged and decided to address the other children. I gently pulled Valora off my legs and sat down in the nearest chair to pull her in my lap. I snuggled Valora for a moment to feel her energy but it wasn't a comfort as usual. I looked up at my babies and put on a big smile to hide my own fear.

"Okay, I know the sky looks scary, but this area doesn't get too many really bad storms. Now, Mark, you and Grayson run outside and put the wood post on the shed to lock the animals inside for the time being. Leah, you and Gia, gather all the dogs and cats and put them on the back porch and double latch the screen to keep them in too. After all of y'all are done, we'll sit down and eat dinner."

Mark took a step to towards the door, but Grayson's deepening voice stopped him.

"Wait, Mark. Mama, Gia's not with us. She got off the bus at Betts' house. We asked her why and told her to get back on, but she wouldn't listen."

I sat in stunned silence as the tight look on Leah's face confirmed what Grayson said. Mark looked just as shocked and started to frown.

"Mama, do you want me to take the car and go get her?"

I shook my head in awe at Gia's open defiance. I couldn't worry about her with the storm coming. I'd deal with her later.

"No, I'm sure that she'll be fine on the ranch. Now, y'all go do what I said, okay?"

Everyone left the room except Valora. I could feel her special love and energy return. She turned around and snuggled into my lap. I knew that I should put her down because she had started to get bigger. I allowed myself one more squeeze of her firm little body and sat up to put her on the floor.

I stood and walked into the kitchen with Valora on my heels. I stirred the oxtail stew and made some hot water cornbread. Valora helped me with all of the ingredients and kept up a steady stream of chatter. The other children made it into the house just as the thunder boomed. I glanced out of the kitchen window to see that the afternoon darkened like nightfall. The wind and rain beat at the old glass and it began to shake. Valora grabbed onto my legs again when another clap of thunder sounded. In fact, I looked up at the kitchen door to see that Mark, Grayson, and Leah stood there for my comfort as well. I wanted to tell them that they were too old to be frightened but the words wouldn't form. I smiled instead and beckoned them to their plates of food. Relief brightened their faces until the glass from the kitchen window broke against the wind. The backdoor flew open and the cats and dogs ran inside the house. Mark ran forward to shut the door but struggled and called out for Grayson's help. I pushed Valora into the boys' room with Leah and stepped forward to help Mark and Grayson. By the flickering light of the kitchen, my dread increased with the sight of a funnel cloud on the horizon in the window. Mark saw it too and pushed harder to shut the door. The faint sound of a freight train filled the now silent kitchen. Determined to save my children, I spoke and moved quickly. I turned to a frightened Mark.

"Mark, take your brother and sisters to the inside hall closet between your rooms. I'll be there in a minute."

Mark looked like he would object but knew my hard tone meant to obey. He grabbed Grayson and Leah, picked up Valora, and looked back at me once before heading to the closet. I ran into my room, pulled my Bible from my nightstand, and took the storm kit from under my bed. The freight train sounded closer, so I hitched up my housedress and ran to get to my babies. Mark stood outside the closet to protect his siblings. I felt pride even though I didn't have time for it. I handed him the storm kit and pushed him into the closet to take his place. I opened the Bible and pointed it toward the North.

"Hear, O Lord, when I cry with my voice: have mercy also upon me, and answer me. When thou saidst, Seek ye my face; my heart said unto thee, Thy Face, Lord, will I seek. Hide not thy face far from me; put not thy servant away in anger: thou hast been my help; leave me not, neither forsake me, O God of my salvation. When my father and mother forsake me, then the Lord will take me up. Teach me thy way, O Lord, and lead me in a plain path, because of mine enemies. Deliver me not over unto the will of mine enemies: for false witnesses are risen up against me, and such as breathe out cruelty. I had fainted unless I had believed to see the goodness of the Lord in the land of the living. Wait on the Lord: be of good courage, and he shall strengthen thine heart: wait, I say on the Lord."

I closed my eyes and shut my Bible to pray. I felt the children pull at me as I heard the windows shatter. I raised my voice.

"Father God, where you say there are two or more, you are there. Please protect us, Father! Please keep us safe in this storm! Please give us what we need from it and let the rest pass beyond us! We love you, Father, and ask that You wrap Your Hands around us until Your Will be done! In Our Lord and Savior, Jesus' Holy Name, Amen."

For a moment, after my prayer, I felt the house lift and reached back to hug my children. Tears fell from my eyes that this was to be our end. Their cries echoed in my heart, and I closed my eyes. I bowed my head and whispered my prayer again. The noise of the old house creaking with the violence of the winds became so loud that I wanted to cover my ears, but I refused to let go of my babies. I whispered my prayer again and pushed my children behind me until I knew that they would be safe in the closet. In that moment, I only cared that they lived through this nightmare. I kept my eyes closed until I felt the hard rush of the wind and felt something hard hit me in the head. The only thought as the darkness rushed to greet me was that my children would live.

"Victoria, where would you like to go today?"

I turned and saw that William stood beside his sporty Ford Mustang with the door open. He looked so handsome in the sunlight with happiness in his smile. I couldn't help but return it. William held his hand out to me, and I reached out to take it. William tightened his grip and pulled me to him. I fell against his chest and felt the rumble of his laughter. I looked up into his face and saw the sly look that he tried to hide. I frowned at him for just a bit before a smile began to tug at my lips. I placed my hands on his chest and pushed, but William wrapped his hands around my back and pulled me even closer. I raised my face to see William's beloved face so close to mine that I could smell the peppermint on his breath. My heart began a slow beat as he lowered his head. I closed my eyes and felt the beat echo in my head while I waited for the touch of his lips. Suddenly, I felt a tug on my skirt and looked down to see Valora smiling up at us. William saw her too and picked her up in his arms.

"Well, I guess we'll have to continue that conversation at home tonight when this little lady is sleep."

Valora smiled at us and placed her hands on both of our faces. I absorbed her usual zing of energy and returned her smile. She put her head on William's shoulder and pointed behind me.

"Look, Daddy, it's a rainbow."

"Well, yes, it is, sweetheart. God made it just for you. You are a special gift and one day, you'll share it with the world."

I turned to see the rainbow, but William tucked me into his arm and gave me a little push toward the open car door.

"Our family picnic awaits, madam!"

Valora giggled and William put her down on the soft grass. She giggled again before her eyes rolled into the back of her head. I screamed and reached for her but she fell onto the ground beside the open car door. My stomach clenched. I turned to pick her up and hit my head on the door. I heard William yell my name, but the intense pain in my head made me close my eyes and surrender to the darkness.

"Mama? Mama? You have to wake up, please! Valora is hurt and I need your help! Mama, please, wake up."

Mark's voice sounded like he stood in a tunnel. I reluctantly opened my eyes and saw that he leaned over me. Mark sighed in relief and sat back. He wiped his eyes with his sleeve. I felt wetness on my face but the pounding in my head forced me to close my eyes again.

"Mama, you have to help me. Valora won't wake up, and I don't know what to do. The storm is over, but it's wet everywhere with the holes in the roof. Please, Mama, please!"

Mark's voice sounded far away again, but I heard the plea in it. I strained against the pain of the hammer in my head and opened my eyes. I queried the rest of my body to find just a few aches but nothing broken. I tried to move my head to find that I lay on top of the closet door. I looked up to see the holes in the roof that Mark mentioned that dripped water. I glanced at Mark to see him twist around to shake something behind him. I now heard Grayson and Leah's sobs in the background. I held out my hand to Mark's back and gently touched it. He swung around and almost fell over on me. The relief in my oldest son's face was enough for me to know that I needed to move quickly. I chose to work on the most important first.

"Mark, where is Valora?

I grimaced at the pain in my head and the sound of my weak voice.

"She's right here, Mama. I wrapped her in a dry blanket from the top of the closet. She won't wake up."

Mark's voice ended on a sob, and I knew that my usually levelheaded son was at the end of his rope. I slowly raised myself to a sitting position and shoved the pain violently away. Mark shifted for me to see Valora's pale face and still body wrapped in the soft blue blanket. Memories of Victor's pale face and motionless little body threatened my sanity, but I refused to allow them. I inched toward my baby girl and placed my hand on her neck to feel the weak pulse. I let out a small sigh of relief and leaned closer to feel her body for any broken bones like William had taught me at his practice.

William. The dream, or was it a nightmare? What if it was a vision? I shook my head again and thrust those thoughts away. My baby needed me.

I noticed a few scratches and a trail of blood in her beautiful hair. I finished my rudimentary exam to find no breaks that I could see or feel, but I knew that something was wrong. Valora was such a vibrant and sturdy child. I glanced around at the frightened faces of Grayson, Leah, and Mark and sought to reassure them.

"Remember the other bad storm? This one was just like that one, and we are still here. God has a purpose for us and will not take us from this earth until we fulfill it. God has a purpose for Valora too, and she will be fine. Just keep praying for her and all of us, okay?"

Mark nodded, but Grayson and Leah still looked unsure and scared. My heart felt for them, and I realized that I'd used a gentle tone to comfort my children. I needed them to understand that we had come through the storm alive and together for a reason. God protected us from the true devastation that could have been. I cleared my throat and decided to get busy fixing our problems in my usual brisk voice.

"Now, Mark, I need you to go all around the house to check the damage and see what can be fixed before it gets dark. Leah, I see that the storm kit flew over there in your brothers' room. Please bring that to me. Grayson, please go see if there are any dry clothes in the chest in my room for Valora."

The children seemed to need the direction because they hopped up and ran to do what I asked. I scooted closer to Valora and saw that her skin wasn't as pale as when I first saw it. I struggled and pulled her closer into my lap. I leaned against the edge of the closet door and held Valora close to my body. I kissed the top of her head and felt the song build in my heart.

"When you walk, through a storm, hold your head up high; and don't be afraid, of the dark; for at the end, of the day, there's a golden sky; and a sweet, silvery, song, of the night; walk on, through the wind, walk on, through the rain; though, your dreams be tossed, and blown away; walk on, walk on, with hope in your heart, and you'll never walk alone, you'll never walk, alone."

"You sing pretty, Mama."

The whisper came from my little pumpkin. I looked down to see Valora's direct gaze and soft smile. I stroked hair from her face and returned her smile. Tears of joy and relief fell down my face. Valora snuggled closer to me, and I almost gasped at the electricity that came from her little self. The pain in my head ran from the energy like a wounded animal. The power in her touch made me want to get up and fix everything myself. I chucked and offered up a silent prayer to God while I hugged the miracle in my arms.

3

After the storm blew over, the children and I worked to restore as much as we could to make the house livable for the night. We gathered in the living room because it weathered the storm better than the rest of the house. I talked and encouraged Mark, Leah, and Grayson while we ate a makeshift dinner of cold summer sausage and the crackers that survived in the storm kit. Regrettably, the oxtail stew and hot water cornbread hadn't survived the storm.

Valora didn't eaten much before she drifted back to sleep. I smiled at my sleeping beauty and touched her face to reassure myself that she slept naturally. I sighed in relief that it was a natural slumber. The angry whispers of Mark and Leah drew my attention back to them.

"We need to go see about her! I'm worried, Mark! Don't you care?"

"I don't care! She knew what she was doing! Shut up about it, Leah!"

I knew that they talked about Gia, but I didn't say anything to stop their bickering. My heart wanted to grab up all the children and head over to Tess' to make sure that my hardheaded child was fine, but I couldn't make myself get up to do it. I worried about Willie too but not as much because somehow I knew that the storm didn't hit Carson as bad as the countryside.

I sighed. Gia. Gia had chosen her path, and I didn't have the strength right now to deal with her. Besides, my other children were still frightened, and Valora slept soundly. I would not disturb this peace for Gia's bitterness. I cleared my throat to stop Mark and Leah from fighting. They immediately turned to me, and I smiled at the eagerness in their faces.

"Hey, y'all, we've been through enough today. Tomorrow is going to be a busy day, so we'd better get some rest. Mark, you and Grayson, can make a pallet on the floor. Leah, let's pull out the sofa bed for you and Valora. I'll sleep in the recliner."

Mark looked like he would protest, but I shook my head firmly. He nodded and moved to help Grayson with the pallet. When everyone slept, I whispered a prayer.

"Thank you, Father, for bringing us through the storm safely. I pray that Gia and Willie are safe, as well as, the rest of the family, friends, and community that were in the storm. Bless us and keep us. In Your Son, Jesus' Name, Amen."

Before I closed my eyes to find Mr. Sandman, I saw Big Mama Chandra smiling in the corner. I smiled and nodded to her. She hadn't visited in a long time, but I wasn't afraid. Her presence brought me comfort. Big Mama Chandra had a soft glow around a beautiful soft blue empire-waist gown. Her eyes were filled with love. She held her hand out and I felt a soft caress on my cheek. I touched the spot and felt the wetness from the tears as they fell.

My smile widened, and I whispered, "I love you and miss you so much."

Big Mama Chandra nodded and smiled before she glanced at Valora. Her face held a look of pride and love. She held out her hand again towards Valora, and I glanced over to see my baby smile in her sleep and turned over to let out a loud snore. I felt Big Mama Chandra's chuckle and looked back to see her smiling face fade into the darkness.

"See you later, Big Mama Chandra."

Surprised, I turned to where Mark sat on the pallet. I relit the candle and cast its glow in my son's direction. Mark's face looked wet, and he wiped his nose on his sleeve. I wanted to ask so many questions, but I also wanted to give my son some time to gather himself. I didn't have to wait long.

"I know what you're going to ask me, Mama, and I didn't want you to think I was crazy. I also didn't want you to worry because I remembered how you saw the black spirit before Victor ..."

Mark paused at the name of his beloved baby brother. At the mention of Victor's name, my heart twisted slightly, but I swallowed the tears that threatened and focused on Mark's ability. I could see him struggle to continue, but I had to allow him to tell me in his own way. I saw him take a deep breath, and he began again.

"It started when Daddy killed Mr. Ellis. Every time I looked outside, Mr. Ellis stood by the fence. I was so scared. That's why I wouldn't let Grayson or Valora play alone in the backyard. You fussed at me for messing up the front yard by building them that tree house in the mulberry tree, but I couldn't tell you that he was still there with that evil look on his face, Mama. I just couldn't. After we moved, I began to have dreams about Big Mama Chandra and Grandpa Ed. It's funny because I wasn't afraid of them at all. They'd tell me stuff that would happen or stuff to do, and I'd do it. Sometimes, they come to check on us, just like Big Mama Chandra did now, but most of the time, they're in Heaven. Since I turned eighteen, I haven't seen them much, so I'm really glad to see Big Mama Chandra tonight."

I stared at Mark for a brief moment because his revelation shook me to my core. I'd seen Ellis in the backyard of Aunt Charlotte's house as well, and if I'd known Mark had seen him, we'd have moved much sooner. Guilt rode through my body because I had fussed at him and almost whipped him for building that tree house in the front yard. Mark had only been protecting his younger siblings. The tears I'd held back began to slide from my eyes. My son's ability almost paralleled my own, and I'd been blind to it. I closed my eyes and took a shaky breath. There were things that I needed to explain.

"Mark, I'm so sorry that you haven't been able to talk to me about your gift. I would never have thought that you were crazy or that anything was wrong with you because I have a similar gift. They are special gifts that only a few people have in the world. Sometimes, we can see evil and good spirits, and there are times that we can feel the evil and good in people. There are also times that the gifts don't work, and that's when we have to figure out things with our own common sense. The only thing is to remember not to share it with just anyone. They might think you're crazy or take advantage of you."

I paused to let it sink in and wait for Mark's questions. When he remained silent, I glanced at the other children to make sure that they still slept before I continued.

"I'm glad that Big Mama Chandra and Grandpa Ed guided and helped you along the way. They loved you very much, son. You are becoming a wise young man, and I'm sure that they wanted to be there in spirit if not in body."

Mark nodded and shifted to return to lie on the pallet. I smiled at my oldest son's easy acceptance of his unusual gift.

"Goodnight, son."

"Goodnight, Mama. I'm staying home from school tomorrow to help get the house together, okay?"

The knowledge that he'd probably get off the bus down the road and walk home to help with the house made me agree to his request.

"All right, but you better not miss any tests for graduation, Mark Sams."

A quiet snore answered me, and I smiled. I blew out the candle and relaxed against the old recliner. Exhausted from the eventful day, I closed my eyes to find sleep too.

Mark and I started outside the next morning after the other children left for school to move all of the broken limbs and rubbish to the burn barrels. The outside of the house withstood quite a bit of the storm, so we decided to work on the inside in the afternoon. We were ready to take a break to eat the leftover summer sausage and crackers when Williams' sporty Ford car came to an abrupt stop in the graveled drive. Relief that he survived the storm flooded my body and made me dizzy. I looked down and saw how dirty and disheveled I was. I dropped the limb that I carried and dried to smooth wayward hairs back into my headscarf. William's door flew open, and he almost ran to where I stood. I glanced around to see that Mark still worked in the back of the house and couldn't see William yet. When I turned back, William stood only a hair's breadth from me. I almost took a step back...almost.

"Victoria, I've been so worried about you and the children. I wanted to come last night, but the creek flooded one side of the road and a tree fell across the other. I would have cut the tree myself, but Juan and his sons cleared it this morning so that they could check on the back crops. I came as soon as I could get across the road. Are you all okay?"

I nodded and tried to fix myself with my hand. William stopped my fidgeting with a caress to my face. I dropped my hand and stared at him.

"I'm such a mess, William."

William leaned in closer as he spoke. I could see the dark blue flecks in his deep blue eyes.

"You are beautiful to me, Victoria."

I almost became lost in those eyes until I remembered Mark. I looked back guiltily to see him wheel a pile of limbs to the burn barrels on the other side of the house. He didn't even notice us because he was so absorbed in his task. I turned back to William to see him close the distance and pull me into his arms. I gladly absorbed his heat and nearness. I raised my arms to his back and placed my head on his chest. He held me tighter at my acquiescence.

"I couldn't sleep last night while I thought of you and the children. I wanted to tear down that tree with my bare hands to get to you, Victoria. My heart couldn't bear it if anything happened to you."

William's whispered words soothed my soul and his arms felt like Heaven. I stood there while he stroked his warm hands down my back. All thoughts of embarrassment flew out of the window.

"I couldn't sleep either because I worried about you too, William. My heart was so heavy with fear for you."

William squeezed me tighter at my admission. I smiled and raised my head to find his lowered with his gaze on my lips. An unfamiliar feeling of heat swept through me, and my eyes drifted shut with it. For a moment, I thought that I dreamt or suffered from delusions from my head wound, but it was real. William's hand tilted my chin up to him before I felt his firm yet soft lips touch mine. I could hear nothing but the pound of my heart as he shifted to hold me closer and deepened the kiss. Years of longing swept by in the wonder of our first kiss, and I didn't want it to end. In that moment, I finally felt happy and whole. William slowly broke the kiss to look down into my face. His smile lit up the dreary day.

"Well, that was certainly something that should be examined thoroughly, Ms. Sams," he whispered in his Dr. William voice.

I leaned back in his arms and chuckled. I patted his chest and gave him a coy smile.

"Why, Dr. William, I think that you are on to something. Perhaps, I should make an appointment, hmm?"

William threw back his head and guffawed.

"Dr. William, Mama? What's so funny?"

At Mark's voice, William dropped his arms, and I stepped away quickly. I tamped down my body's reaction to the loss of William's arms and tried to gather myself to turn a smile on my son. William frowned at me and walked towards Mark to give him a hug. Mark returned the hug and looked over at me with a knowing smile. I raised my eyebrow to let him know his place. Mark covered his mouth with his hand, cleared his throat, and turned back to William. William put his arm around Mark and began to walk towards the porch.

"Mark, your mother and I were just having a talk. I think that we should let someone come help you with the house. You and your mother need to rest. Would you mind if I had someone come to work with you?"

I opened my mouth to object to William's highhanded manner, but Mark's answer stopped me in my stubbornness.

"That would be great, Dr. William. Then, I could finish with the shed repair and clear the rest of the patch behind the animal shed. It would have been a lot for Mama and me to do today."

"Well, that's it then. I'll see if Juan can send some of the workers from your great-grandfather's ranch," William said with a smug glance at me.

Mark nodded and started to run back around the house, but William stopped him.

"Oh, by the way, Mark, I brought some of my mother's chicken casserole for you and your mother to eat for lunch. Can you get it from my car?"

Mark's face brightened at the mention of Ms. Constance's chicken casserole, and he ran to Williams' car. I turned and narrowed my eyes at William. He shrugged his shoulders and gave me an innocent look. I tried to remain stern but couldn't. I shook my head at myself. William was too handsome for his own good…and mine.

As Mark returned with the basket of food, William stopped him with a hand on his arm.

"Mark, I'd like to speak to you and the other children tonight. Would you all come to the ranch for dinner, please? We eat around six thirty."

Mark looked from William to me, and then looked back to William. I felt like I knew why William wanted to speak to my children. I didn't want to think more into his request than a simple dinner invitation, so I stayed quiet. Mark looked past William for a moment before he broke into a big grin.

"Sure, Dr. William. We'd be glad to come to the ranch. I hope that Ms. Constance chases your cook out to make her special French food. It's too bad I'm too young, or I'd have to steal her away from Dr. Herbert."

Mark's eyes twinkled and his smile was so infectious that William and I burst into laughter.

All of the children got off the bus in the afternoon. I narrowed my eyes at Gia and Willie, but they avoided my glare and ran into the house. Mark walked up with the last of the tree limbs in his hand and shook his head at his brother and sister.

"You'll need to be harder on them when I leave, Mama. Willie still has a mean streak, and Gia is just plain ugly inside and out. Sometimes, I just want to choke her when she spits her venom at Grayson and Valora."

I stayed silent because I knew exactly how Mark felt. I knew that I should have chastised him, but I couldn't. I looked up just in time to catch Valora when she ran and threw herself at me.

"Mama, Grayson got hurt."

Grayson and Leah weren't far behind her, and I gasped when I saw Grayson's face. My youngest son's eye was black and swollen. His lower lip cracked and scabbed with dried blood. That same lip quivered and one look into his eyes showed unshed tears. I pushed Valora toward Mark and grabbed Grayson closer. He collapsed into my arms with a sob. I held him to me while I tried to get a hold of my questions and my anger. I waited until the sobs turned to hiccups.

"Grayson, tell me what happened?"

Grayson hiccupped one more time and pulled away from me. He glanced at Mark who stepped forward to stand beside me. I saw Grayson nod at Mark, take a deep breath, and swipe at his tears with his sleeve. Out of the corner of my eye, I saw Mark return Grayson's nod. Understanding of the brotherly bond between Mark and Grayson ignited a spark of pride in my heart before my concern overrode it. Grayson took another deep breath and looked back at me.

"We were waiting to get on the bus at school. Tim Adams started pushing Leah and Valora around and called them names. I told him to leave them alone, but he wouldn't.

Willie hadn't gotten to the bus stop yet, so I got in Tim Adams' face and told him to leave my sisters alone. Some of the other kids started to egg Tim on and yell, 'Fight! Fight!' Leah yelled back at them to be quiet and leave us alone. They didn't pay her any attention, and one of the Clements boys grabbed her. I ran over to push him off of her, but somebody tripped me. Tim Adams jumped on me and started to punch me. I hit him back too, Mama, but he was too big to get him off of me. The bus driver, Mr. Lowe, came and pulled him off me."

As Grayson spoke, red mist filled my vision. I felt my body shake in my anger, and something uncoil within my mind. My eleven-year old son had put himself in danger to protect his sisters. I couldn't feel pride in his deed because he'd gotten hurt in the process. Anger at the Adams' and their grandson flooded my senses. Anger at the Clements did too because they were distant kin to the Roberts side of the family. Finally, anger at Gia and Willie rolled across my mind. How dare they let this happen? Willie wasn't as tall as Mark, but he was strong and the other kids never messed with him. I tried to control my thoughts so that I could figure out what I needed to do. Mark stepped forward before I could say anything and put his hand on Grayson's shoulder.

"I'm proud of you, little brother. You did a good thing for our sisters. I'll take care of Tim Adams and Rory Clements. They're a couple of bullies just because they're White and have money. They don't even ride the same bus, so they shouldn't have been there. Matter of fact, Willie should have been there, and I'll talk to him too. Now, let's go get you cleaned up and we'll go out back to finish clearing the patch."

Grayson stood up a little straighter and nodded. He turned to go, but turned around to give me a tight hug before he ran inside the house. Mark smiled and winked in my direction before following his little brother into the house. I stood there in wonder at my oldest son until I felt a little hand creep into mine. I looked down into Valora's beloved face. My eyes roved over her face while I looked for any sign of the injury from the storm. When I saw none, I smiled at her and turned to

Leah who stood a short distance away. I almost gasped because the look on Leah's face spoke of her inner pain.

"Mama, Grayson helped us. I don't like it when the kids call me names, but there's nothing that I can do. Sometimes, I wish that I could go away from here and back to Littleton where I was happy. Why did you have to bring us here to this stupid country bunk place?"

Leah's words ended on a sob, and she ran into the house. Valora's hand tightened in mine at Leah's outburst. I knew that Leah's feelings were hurt, but I'd have to deal with them later. I knew Mark would take care of the situation with Grayson, but I'd call the school tomorrow anyway. I sighed and squeezed Valora's hand.

"Come on, Pumpkin Pie. I need to finish with the house so that we don't all have to crowd into the living room tonight, and I need to find everyone something to wear for dinner at Dr. William's house."

Valora giggled and followed me into the house.

"Ms. Constance, that was a delicious meal. Thank you so much for having us."

Ms. Constance smiled regally and lowered her well-dressed slim body into a russet colored embroidered armchair. William assisted the elderly Dr. Herbert into the living room and sat him gently into an armchair similar to Ms. Constance's next to the fireplace. The night was a bit chilly, so the fire was welcome. William handed his mother a glass of sherry from the tray on the mantle, but when Dr. Herbert beckoned for one, William turned the tray and gave him the glass of water. Dr. Herbert harrumphed at William and stared at the mantle longingly.

I giggled and herded all of the children onto the matching long sofa while I sat on the loveseat. William's sly grin at the seating arrangement made me beckon Valora to sit next to me. I smirked at William when his smile died a quick death. I hugged Valora to me and turned to Ms. Constance to start a conversation, but the frown on her face kept my lips closed. I sat silent until Valora left my side to go to Dr. Herbert's chair. She placed her hand on his arm.

"Dr. Herbert, how are you doing today?"

Dr. Herbert and William chuckled. I sat lost for words at her mature question. Dr. Herbert squeezed Valora's hand and leaned toward her.

"Well, I'm fair to middlin', little lady. I heard you got a little bump on your head during the storm. How are you feeling?"

I could see Valora's eyes twinkle from where I sat.

"Well, I'm fair to middlin' too, Dr. Herbert."

Everyone laughed except Willie. I shot him a frown, and he cast his gaze to the floor. I turned to see William walk over and pick up Valora like she was a doll. Valora put her arms around William's neck and gave him a big wet kiss on the cheek. William chuckled and kissed Valora's cheek. She giggled and patted him on his face.

"Dr. William, why is your face so scratchy?"

William laughed and rubbed his face with his hand.

"It's because I spent all day taking care of my patients that I couldn't groom properly before you all got here. I promise that it won't ever happen again."

Valora patted his face again and nodded.

The room fell silent until William cleared his throat. He looked nervous which wasn't like his usual confident self at all. He turned toward my children and walked over to sit on the shiny mahogany coffee table in front of the long sofa with Valora in his lap. I heard Ms. Constance's little noise of complaint, but William seemed not to hear it. His attention was on my children. My heartbeat faster at what he would say to them. I saw him take a deep breath.

"Children, I know that you have known me all of your lives in a way – some of you more than others. As you know, I'm a doctor, and most people say that I'm a good man. I'm also not White like most people believe. I'm just like your mother except I have a White father, but that doesn't matter. The color of someone's skin doesn't matter. What matters is how someone feels about someone else. I have deep feelings for your mother and for you all. I would like to ask your permission to court your mother."

I heard Ms. Constance's soft gasp, and Dr. Herbert's guffaw of 'It's about time, son.' My mouth dropped open because it was not what I expected William to say or do. I thought he would tell them something about helping us whenever we needed it, or anything but what he just asked. My head spun at his proclamation and intentions.

The entire room went silent for a few moments before Mark stood up and held out his hand to William. William put Valora down and stood up to shake Mark's hand. Mark glanced at me and smiled. I still sat stunned at this insane turn of events. Mark looked back at William and nodded.

"Dr. William, I know that your intentions towards our mother are good and honorable. As her oldest child, I am more than pleased to give you permission to court Mama. It's not going to be easy because our mama can be kind of stubborn, but I know that she's a great catch."

"Well said, young man, but I don't agree. William, how could you do this to your father and I?

Everyone turned around to see that Ms. Constance stood furious in all of her aging beauty.

"Oh, sit down, Constance. You cannot be outraged when you've been filling the boy's head with ideas of settling down. You just didn't bet on the fact that the girl he's had his nose open for all these years would finally be free for him."

I heard some snickers come from the children at Dr. Herbert's outburst, and I silenced them with a raised eyebrow. William stood with an amused look on his face at his father's words. He glanced at me, and I motioned at the children. He nodded his understanding and turned back to them.

"Mark, I'll bet there's some strawberry candies in my study that you and your brothers and sisters would like to have. Would you like to take them in there and give them some? There's also a new telescope to look at the stars in the window. That should be fun, too."

Mark understood William's suggestion and pulled his reluctant siblings out of the room, past an irate Ms. Constance, and disappeared through the branded oak door. William strode to the door and shut it before he turned to his mother with anger.

"Mother, what in the world is wrong with you?"

4

Ms. Constance slowly lifted her slim body from her chair and turned toward her angry son. I saw her ball her elegant hands into fists before she unleashed her vitriol.

"William Herbert. You will never speak to me in such a tone. I understand that you may feel upset with me, but you will get over it. I thought at one time that you and Victoria would make a good pair. It was when I watched you barely mourn for Maggie that I began to see this love that you carry for this woman as insanity. She is not the woman for you, William!"

Ms. Constance's accent became more pronounced as she finished. Her words felt like needles across my skin. I swallowed to keep the tears away. I glanced at William's face to see fury and sadness. He took a step toward his mother, but Dr. Herbert's quiet voice stopped him.

"Constance, you are wrong, darling. I thought like you did once, but when I saw how happy our son is compared to what he shared with Maggie, I knew that Victoria was the one. She is a good woman from a good family. Settle yourself before you lose your son."

Dr. Herbert hadn't looked up from his gaze at the bright burning fire. William stood still and stared at his mother with a plea in his eyes. Ms. Constance's lips firmed and she turned toward me. I shrank back into the loveseat because in all the years that I'd known Ms. Constance, I'd never seen her beautiful face marred in such anger.

"Victoria, please get your children and leave my house now. If my son wishes to disrespect my wishes by courting you, he will not do it here. Please understand that it isn't your fault that you bore such an evil man six children. You have nothing to offer my son, and I cannot stand by and watch him lose the respect of this community or his reputation because he fancies you."

"Mother!"

"Constance!"

Dr. Herbert and William spoke at the same time. Through the sheen of tears, I could see their appalled expressions at her "explanation" of what was wrong with William's love for me. I blinked back the tears and rose with all of the dignity that I could muster in that moment. William rushed to my side, but I put up a hand to stop his advance. He ignored me and stepped towards me to put his arm around me. I tried to slide away but he held firm. He opened his mouth to speak, however, Dr. Herbert beat him to it again.

"Constance, you know what we had to do in the sixties to be together and raise our son. We both made sacrifices, but I will not allow you to cause our son to distance himself from us because of your old French aristocratic ways. Besides, this is my house, and I will be the one to put someone out if I see fit. Now, if you want to leave, fine. Go ahead, but remember, it was your choice. Just like it's our son's choice."

Dr. Herbert rose slowly on his cane to face Ms. Constance's shocked face. Hurt and disbelief at his words crossed her face. I saw the shine of tears pop into her eyes, and I felt William's arm tighten around me. I felt sorry for Ms. Constance in that moment because I couldn't imagine treating someone the way that she treated me only to find herself out on that limb alone. I wanted to go to her and tell her that I'd obey her wishes and never see William again, but my heart clenched at the thought. Love and happiness stood in the doorway for me finally, and I refused to let anyone close that door.

William cleared his throat loudly in the awkward silence.

"Mother, I love you, but I'm not getting any younger."

I heard Dr. Herbert's 'you can say that again', and tried not to giggle at his attempt at humor. William cleared his throat and tried again.

"What I'm trying to say, Mother, is that I didn't have a long life or children with Maggie for a reason. It didn't mean that I didn't love her in my own way, but she wasn't for me. I couldn't connect with her because you made me feel obligated to marry her. Since she died of the flu, I know that you've thrown women in my path that suited your standards. None have been able to even interest me because my heart has been with Victoria for a long time, Mother. I don't want to cause a rift between us, but you have to let me make my own choice to be happy."

William left my side to go to his mother when she dropped into her chair with a sob. I sat back down on the loveseat and swiped at the tears on my cheeks. I glanced at William and Ms. Constance to see that he knelt with one of his hands in hers while he consoled her with the other. The room filled with her sobs for a few moments until she seemed to collect herself. She smiled a watery smile at William and Dr. Herbert who had moved to her side during her storm. The smile stayed on her face, but her eyes remained dull and distant when she held out her hand for me to join them. I looked at William who looked so happy that his mother changed her mind and reluctantly moved to take her hand. The men backed away as she stood holding my hand. Her dark brown eyes narrowed a bit before she smiled wide and pulled me to her in a French embrace. She air-kissed both of my cheeks and laughed. I felt like I'd been kissed by a snake, but I stepped away and gave her a smile as fake as her own. William and Dr. Herbert both laughed when we hugged each other. William grabbed my hand and pulled me to his side to face his parents.

"Well, Mother, Father, I'm glad that we could work through that as a family. Now, if you all will excuse us, I'd like to sit with my sweetheart for a spell."

We all laughed because William spoke with a twang and wiggled his eyebrows. He pulled me to the loveseat and put his arm around me. Dr. Herbert nodded and turned to Ms. Constance.

"C'mon, Constance. I need to rest these old bones."

Ms. Constance pursed her lips at us like she wanted to say something, but she shook her head and took Dr. Herbert's offered arm to leave the room. Once the door shut, I turned to William to ask him some questions, but he stared at me intently. He caressed my face gently and smiled. I closed my eyes at his touch and snuggled closer to his heat. He chuckled and whispered into my hair.

"Yes, Victoria, I meant every word. And no, I wouldn't have married Maggie if you hadn't turned me away that day. She was the daughter of one of my mother's close friends from France, so we were already friends. Yes, I loved her in my own way, but it was nothing close to what I feel for you. Yes, I mourned her passing because we had been friends and because I felt sad that I couldn't love her like she wanted. And I believe your last question is why do I still want to be with you and you have six children by another man?"

My eyes popped open when William began to answer all the questions that I'd wanted to ask him. I felt pity for his wife, sadness for him, and weak at the thought that he'd loved me all those years. When he didn't answer the last question, I turned to look at him again and found his lips close to mine. Those full lips curved into a knowing smile. I forced myself to switch my gaze to the glowing blue of his eyes.

"Victoria, I want to be with you because I love you and your children including Leah and William who I know aren't fond of me. I've waited a long time to feel this complete. I've always wanted a big family because I was always jealous of yours. Now, I have everything that I want."

At his last words, my heart melted and I lifted my chin to accept his offer of love. The binding kiss felt like our first and I knew it would always be so. I got so lost in his embrace that I almost didn't hear the knock on the door. William pulled away and turned with a breathless, 'Come in'. I smiled that I could affect him as he did me. He glanced around and saw my impish grin. He chuckled and looked back at the door where Mark stood.

"Excuse me, Dr. William, but Valora is asking for Mama."

William chuckled and stood. I rose beside him and Valora burst into the room past Mark. She saw William first and took a flying leap. William caught her and spun around twice. Mark laughed at the carefree moment while I smiled and prayed that it would last.

The next few weeks passed by with a breathless blur. I couldn't remember being so happy. There were times that I'd think of Betts' evil and curses, but I'd just look around at how much William's love lightened our lives and laugh to myself. I lived in the light now, and I refused to allow any darkness into our lives. My ignorance and blindness to Betts' evil influence would cost me dearly.

"Mama! Mama! Look what we found!"

I looked up from writing my weekly letters to see Grayson and Valora rush past the window towards the front of the house. I raised myself slowly from the antique writing desk that was another of William's gifts. I slid my hand across its mahogany top and smiled at the memory of his generosity. Mark, Grayson, Leah, and Valora helped William to surprise me. William did a wonderful job of including the children whenever he could. Well, he tried to with four of the children. Gia and Willie ignored him even as they accepted his gifts. I frowned at their rudeness and made a note to address that as soon as possible. Bright sunshine greeted me when I opened the front room door. I held my hand over my eyes until they'd adjusted to the light. The sight that greeted me caused me to cover my mouth to hide the laugh that threatened to escape.

Grayson and Valora, covered in grass, dirt, and hay, held five squirming and mewling kittens while the mother, a large silver cat, pawed at their legs. The sight was so hilarious with the excitement on my children's faces while they held the kittens away from their mother and scolded her for trying to get her babies back. I uncovered my mouth and allowed my laughter free rein. Grayson and Valora glanced at each other and nodded. I already knew what they wanted, so I calmed my mirth into a smile and waited. Grayson spoke up first.

"We found them behind the cow shed, Mama. They tumbled out of the bed that their mama made in the hay. She came back while we played with them and let us play with her too. Can we keep them, please? We'll take care of them. We promise. Please, Mama, please?"

I looked at their hopeful little faces and hid my grin. I gave them a mock frown. I tried not to laugh when the mother cat jumped up and grabbed one of the little kittens that Valora held. A small tug of war began until the silver cat clawed Valora's hand and Valora let her have the kitten with a hiss in the mother cat's direction. I decided to intervene on the poor mother's behalf.

"Grayson and Valora Sams. Y'all give that mama cat her babies back. Mamas don't like for people to mess with their babies. She's probably scared that y'all will hurt them. Why don't you put the kittens back in their bed? They're probably tired and hungry from playing with y'all. I will let you help the mama cat take care of them until they get big enough, okay?"

Grayson and Valora looked crestfallen, but said a low 'yes, ma'am'. They walked toward the back of the house slowly with the silver mama cat protectively following. Grayson turned and gave me a toothy smile.

"Mama, after we help them grow up some, can we keep them? They'll need us to show them how to do stuff when the mama cat is gone."

I smiled at my son's logic. Even after his fall, Grayson remained very smart and intuitive. Valora stepped up beside her brother and gave me a big smile too. I laughed at their enthusiasm and cajoling ways. I couldn't help but give in to them.

"I guess it would be helpful to the kittens to be around people. Go ahead and put them back. Y'all can visit with them later."

Grayson and Valora yelled their excitement and ran to put the kittens back. I turned to go back in the house and caught Willie's evil grin in the window. The memory of a long dead kitten surfaced in my mind. A slow chill slid up my spine as I glanced to where Grayson and Valora disappeared with the kittens. It wasn't going to be helpful for those kittens to be around some people.

We spent the last two weeks of school in preparation for Mark's graduation. The trepidation and sadness that crossed my heart from time to time outweighed the happiness on my oldest son's face every time that he received a card in the mail. He'd offer me half of what he received, but I smiled, shook my head, and encouraged him to open a bank account. William also took up a lot of time with Mark, and I appreciated it more than William would ever know. One night after dinner, I tried to tell him just how much.

"William, I don't want you to take this the wrong way, but I really appreciate how much time that you spend with Mark and the other children. I know that it's not easy with Gia and Willie, but you keep at it. You are a true blessing."

William looked around the steak restaurant in Tharkin and leaned close. I saw the twinkle of his eyes and giggled at his impish grin.

"Well, Ms. Victoria, I believe that I appreciate you appreciating me."

I smothered a giggle and took the hand that he'd placed on the table. William squeezed it, and we returned to our dinner.

A few days before school let out, I dragged the rocking chair to a sunny spot on the porch and sat to enjoy the beautiful day. I looked across the highway to see the tall, green Johnson grass sway in the light breeze and felt glad that William only wanted me to work three days a week. I smiled at his reason that he couldn't have me around too much because his mother, who still worked at the clinic, wouldn't be able to do anything without being nosy. I chuckled because he'd been right. Ms. Constance never let us have a moment alone when I worked. She walked around with narrowed eyes and disapproval written all over her face and in her voice when she addressed William or me.

I sighed into the late afternoon at her resistance. I tried to understand Ms. Constance's position, but I couldn't. As a mother, I wanted the best for my children but not at the expense of their happiness. William always told me that he was happier now than he'd been in his entire life. It bothered me a little that Ms. Constance wanted to take that away from her own son. I sighed again and the sound of the school bus creak to a stop redirected my attentions.

I stood up slowly because I didn't want to aggravate the soreness that hid behind my bones. I hid the grimace of pain behind my smile as Valora ran to hug my legs. At her touch, all thoughts of pain receded into the back of my mind. I chuckled and squeezed her sturdy body. She let out a small sigh then raised a serious face to mine. The sadness reflected in the liquid brown of her eyes caught my breath. My heart twisted at what could be wrong with my normally exuberant daughter. I put both hands on her shoulders and she bowed her head. Her small body began to shake under my own trembling hands. When the sob broke, I grabbed her to my side and held her close. I glanced up to see that Grayson, Leah, Gia, and Willie approached the porch as if afraid of Valora's tears. Surprised, I saw that Willie's hand was wrapped in a bloody rag, Grayson had another black eye, and Leah's shirt looked torn. A quick glance at Gia confirmed my thought that she'd avoided any scuffle. I frowned in her direction and Gia's face twisted into a hateful frown. I bit my lip because the Good Lord knows that if I didn't have Valora in my arms, I would have slapped that frown into next week. I stared at Gia over Valora's head until she lowered her eyes to the ground. Satisfied that Gia was cowered, I returned my attention to Valora and the other children.

"I don't want any tales or exaggerations, just facts. Now, one at a time, tell me what happened. Willie, you go first so that you can go soak that hand."

Willie's head shot up in surprise. He looked skeptical that I'd let him tell his story first. For a moment, I thought that his shocked look indicated that I didn't care about him or his hand. I shrugged away the thought as foolishness and nodded for him to begin.

"Valora got to the bus stop first. I guess something happened to her at school because she was crying. Rory Clements' little brother John started to make fun of her and call her a "cry baby". Grayson walked up at the same time as Tim Adams and Rory. I wasn't far behind Grayson, but I stopped to talk to Terry Harper about last week's state track meet. I heard Grayson ask Rory to tell his brother to leave Valora alone, but he didn't. Tim and Rory started to push Grayson and call him a "wimp". I told Terry that I'd see him later, but he followed me. I yelled at Tim and Rory to leave Grayson alone and go home, but they ignored me and Tim punched Grayson in the eye. I ran, grabbed Tim, and pushed him down. Mama, I didn't want to fight, I promise! Rory grabbed my arms and tried to hold me until Tim got up to hit me, but Terry threw him off of me. Tim got up and tried to hit me. I ducked and hit him in the jaw. Terry grabbed Rory and told him to take his brother and Tim home. Well, Leah and Gia walked up and saw what happened. It was almost over until Leah heard John yell at Valora that everything was her fault. Leah grabbed him and pushed him toward Rory. Rory got mad because John stumbled and almost fell. He broke loose from Terry and ran toward Leah. Mama, Leah did good! She waited until Rory was almost to her, then she moved and he fell. He grabbed her shirt, but she shook him off of her. Before Tim could get up, the buses came and they ran off toward their bus stop."

I stared at Willie for a few moments because I just couldn't wrap my mind around the fact that almost all of my children had participated in a fight. One look at them told me that Willie's story was close to the truth, but I nodded to Leah to begin. Leah's beautiful but chubby face had white tear tracks, so I knew that she'd shed tears over what happened. At least, that's what I thought until she began her story.

"I'm so sorry, Mama. I'm glad that Rory hurt himself! I know that you told us that young ladies don't fight, and to never give anyone our class. It was so hard, though! Those boys always mess with us especially Tim Adams. I couldn't help it when I heard that boy call Valora names! She's so little and she doesn't do anything to anyone. I'm sorry, Mama. Willie is partly right except Rory and Tim called me names too while they ran for their bus. They also said that they'd bring more help and get us tomorrow. I don't want to go to school tomorrow, Mama. They're gonna call me fat, ugly, and other nasty names in front of my friends! I just know it!"

My heart ached for Leah because I knew that she struggled with her weight and her confidence. I always tried to tell her that no matter what other people said, she had a beauty within that most people only dreamed to have. I frowned again at Gia because I knew that she put Leah down to keep her influence over her. I made a mental note to give Gia a dressing down later and to take Leah out for a mother-daughter day. For right now, I tried to give as much love and support as possible.

"Leah, I understand and it's okay that you defended your little sister. Sometimes, circumstances cause us to resort to physical violence. It is even more so when it comes to someone hurting our loved ones. You did fine, sweetheart."

A cool breeze wafted across my face and made me aware that tears flowed down my face. I took a deep breath and squeezed Valora for my own comfort. I felt her body begin to lose its tension and melt into mine. I glanced back at Leah and saw a look of resentment cross her face. I didn't know what that look was about, so I decided to end the reports with a question to Grayson.

"Grayson, do you have anything to add to your brother and sister's explanation?"

Grayson pursed his lips and shook his head. He didn't say another word to anyone before he turned to go around the house. I didn't chastise him because I knew that he went to find comfort in his cats, Plato and Aristotle. I turned back to the other children.

"Willie and Leah, I'll handle the Adams and Clements boys. Y'all don't worry about it anymore. Now, Willie, I need you to cut down the weeds that have grown up on the side of the house. Gia and Leah, make sure that y'all clean up the living room and kitchen. Oh, and you'll need to clean your room too. I went in there today and I couldn't even get all the way through the room without almost falling."

Willie and Leah nodded before they left to do as I instructed. Gia sent me a hateful and bitter glance that almost made me jump off the porch to grab the sharpening leather to lay it on her behind. I glared at her and took a small step in her direction. Fear quickly replaced the bitterness. She turned quickly and ran around the side of the house. When I heard the backdoor slam, I sighed. I looked down at a downtrodden Valora and hugged her to me again. She lifted her arms and returned the hug. I pulled her away from me and held her at a distance. Her eyes were dull, and her light dimmed. Anger began to push its way into my mind at who or what caused my beautiful baby girl to feel so bad. I bent a little closer to her, lifted her chin with my finger, and found a gentle smile for her.

"Pumpkin? Is my smiling pumpkin in there? I know she is in there. My pumpkin doesn't like to keep quiet. She likes to ask questions, read comic books, and play adventure games with her brother. She's smart and loved by a lot of people no matter what anyone says. Won't she come out, please?"

As I spoke, I could see a spark flare in Valora's eyes. The dark sadness began to lighten. I could feel her special energy build through my hands on her shoulders. I felt my smile widen.

"I think I see my pumpkin pie now. Yes, there she is!"

I laughed when Valora giggled. My forehead wrinkled in a small frown because even though my daughter giggled, her head remained bowed. When I felt that Valora's sadness disappeared in the face of my love and reinforcement of that love, I decided to find out what happened. I raised her head again with my hand under her chin.

"Valora? Can you tell Mama what happened, please?"

Valora tried to avoid my eyes, but I firmly held her chin and drew her face closer to mine. I placed my hands on her each side of her face and gently kissed her forehead. When I pulled back, tears shone in her eyes. I wanted to comfort her again, but I also wanted her to tell me what happened. I took a deep breath to stem my impatience and allowed her to begin. Valora hiccupped and gulped.

"Today, the principal Mr. Monts came to sit in our class. Almost everyone was bad, but my table was good. Mr. Monts said that Ms. Wilters should reward us for good behavior. She smiled and said that she would. Then, Mr. Monts looked at me and said that I was a very pretty girl. He asked me questions about school, you, my brothers and sisters, and Ms. Wilters. I remembered what you said, Mama, and I said "yes sir" and 'thank you'. Mr. Monts told Ms. Wilters that I was very smart and needed to be tested. Ms. Wilters smiled and said that she would. I looked at her, Mama, and she didn't look nice at me."

A vision of the slim, dark-skinned young woman with the unhappy demeanor filled my mind. I stayed quiet so that Valora could finish, but a premonition of what happened already encouraged the anger that burned within me. Valora's voice dropped when she continued.

"After Mr. Monts left, Ms. Wilters started being mean to me. She snatched my papers from me when I turned them in at her desk. She put me in the corner when I dropped my pencil and got up to get it when it rolled under the table. She said that

I did it on purpose to make noise. She told the teacher's aide, Ms. Pilar, not to answer my question on what to color the dogs and cats on my paper because I was "smart enough to do it myself". Then, I wanted to show the shiny rock that I found when we dug the trench for the hogs at "show and tell". Ms. Wilters told us to get in line, but when I went to get in line, she told me to get to the end. I thought it was okay since whoever went last had the most time, but when it was my turn, she said that "show and tell" was over. I asked her if I could show my rock, and she took it and put it in the trash. I asked her for it, and she laughed and told the class that I wanted trash. They laughed and called me "trash girl". Ms. Pilar told them to stop, then Ms. Wilters told them to hush. I didn't cry, Mama. I didn't cry until Ms. Wilters grabbed me afterschool when I went to get on the bus. She told me that my skin doesn't make me prettier or smarter. She told me that I needed to learn how poor country folks should act. She was so mean to me, Mama. She was so mean!"

Valora collapsed against me in tears, and I knelt on my sore knee to wrap my arms around her sob-wracked body. Anger washed through me at Ms. Wilters, and I felt the echo of my own cries at my parents' mistreatment. Red mist filled my vision, and my hands clenched to feel Ms. Wilters' throat between them. I wanted to ensure that my baby girl was okay before I began to plan how to deal with such ignorance. I waited for Valora's storm to end and when she went limp, I gently guided her to the queen bed that she shared with me. I undressed her and pulled off her shoes. I placed a light cover over her and smiled when I saw that she'd drifted quickly to sleep. I turned and felt the smile slip into a frown of anger. I sat at my writing desk and wrote down everything that the children told me. When I looked down at the furrowed page, I felt lightheaded from the hot course of anger that sang within my blood. My children would not become victims to my horrible choices.

5

I chose to make a personal visit to the schools the next day instead of telephone calls. I was in no mood to be put off, and I knew that a phone call would allow Ms. Wilters and the other staff the chance to dismiss my concerns. I didn't care if it was the last days of school. Someone would answer for my children's distress. I called William's office and told the head nurse, Arta, that I would be in after I'd taken care of some business. Arta sounded as if she wanted to ask what that business was, but my tone left no room for discussion.

Aunt Charlotte's words of dressing for battle came to mind when I hung up with Arta. Carefully, I dressed in my peach and beige striped dress pants and beige blouse with a ruffled collar. I added a light peach sweater and William's latest gift, a string of pearls with matching earrings. To complete my outfit, I searched high and low for my low off-white Easter pumps. I brushed my hair and rolled it into a bun. I applied a light foundation and blush before I selected a clear gloss for my lips. One look in the mirror told me that I was more than ready to fight for my children with class and dignity. I lifted my chin and nodded to my reflection. When I turned, for a moment, I thought that my reflection lingered in the full-length mirror. I turned back to see nothing unusual and chided myself for being so fanciful. I had fish to fry.

I drove the old blue Plymouth up to the red brick primary school building. As I got out, I saw my cousin Juan walking out of the church across the road. I waved to him, and he ran across the street with a big smile on his face.

"Holà, chica! Comò estás, prima?"

"Bíen, bíen!"

Juan threw back his handsome head and laughed. I knew that he would find humor in my pronunciation. His laughter cooled some of the hot anger in my veins. I smiled when he calmed his mirth.

"How is my uncle?"

A shadow of concern crossed Juan's face.

"He is okay. He misses his father. I miss him too, sometimes. Your abuela is still a witch. She wants to sell land to a gringo from Tharkin, but your aunt, Hallie, won't let her. I think she will do it anyways, but we will see, huh?"

I frowned at the thought of Betts selling away the land that Grandpa Paul worked his whole life to keep. I saw that it worried Juan and knew that it worried Marcos as well.

Juan turned around to see his wife, Lucy, exit the church. He beckoned her to where we stood. I wanted to ask them why they were at the church but figured that it was none of my business. Besides, I had enough to do. Lucy approached with a wary look on her face. I wondered again what was wrong.

"Holà, Señora Bictoria. How are you and all of your niños?"

I cocked my head to the side a bit at her belligerent tone when she mentioned my children. I glanced to see a slight frown on Juan's face as well. I didn't want to offend my cousin's wife, so I gave Lucy a big toothy smile.

"Hello, Lucy. I'm fine and the children are well. How are all of your little ones? I'm sure they keep you busy."

Juan chuckled but silenced it when Lucy narrowed her eyes at him. Lucy turned back to me, and her eyes widened with innocence.

"Yes, the niños keep me ocupado. I'm glad that you are well."

Lucy's tone didn't sound like she was glad that I was well. I looked over her head at Juan, who had moved behind his wife. He shrugged his shoulders and rolled his eyes in answer to my silent question. I nodded and glanced back at Lucy to see anger spark in her brown eyes.

"Señora Bictoria, por qué te fijas en mi esposo? Quieres, sì?"

"Lucìa!"

I didn't understand Lucy's words, but from the thunderous look on Juan's face, I knew it couldn't be good. He grabbed her arm and squeezed. Lucy flinched. She looked scared of my cousin. In that moment, Harlan's viciousness crossed my mind. Before I knew it, I stepped forward and placed my hand on Juan's grip. He looked like he would yell at me. I silently pleaded with him for a moment. He released her and stepped back. I nodded and took a slow breath.

"Juan, what did Lucy say?"

Juan shook his head. I persisted.

"Juan, what did your wife say to me?"

Juan looked about to argue, but he saw that I wouldn't give up easily.

"She asked why you looked at me. She asked did you want me. She is jealous."

I gasped at Lucy's assumption. It was ridiculous, but in the back of my mind, memories of Juan's visits to the old homestead to fix things surfaced. Since he stayed late, I would fix him a plate to take home or he would eat with us. I quickly understood why Lucy had come to that conclusion. I stepped forward and lightly placed my hands on her shoulders. She flinched under my touch and tried to back away. I held on gently but firmly. I glanced at Juan disgusted expression and returned my gaze to Lucy.

"Juan, you may need to translate if she doesn't understand me, okay?"

Juan nodded.

"Lucy, I am sorry that you thought I wanted Juan. I do not because it would not be right. First, he is my cousin, and second, he is married with children. Please understand that it is only family love, and nothing else."

I didn't move while until Juan finished his translation. Lucy's face lifted in understanding and crumpled in tears. My heart ached for her, and I hugged her to me. Juan crooned to her and patted her back. I narrowed my eyes at him.

"Juan, you didn't tell her that we are cousins? You are lucky that she didn't poison you while she was jealous."

Juan chuckled and patted Lucy's backside.

"She knew better. I am too handsome for my own good."

Lucy pulled away from me and swatted at Juan. I rolled my eyes at him. Lucy's face looked lighter and happier now that she knew I wasn't after her husband. Out of the corner of my eye, I saw the children burst out of the door for recess. Now was the time to act.

"Well, I'm happy to have seen you both, but I must go speak with Valora's teacher. Tell my uncle that I said hello, Juan."

Juan opened his mouth to ask something but shut it quickly and nodded. He grabbed Lucy's hand and kissed it while he turned to go to their Chevy sedan. I waved at them with a smile, then turned with the anger reignited in my blood.

"Ms. Sams, it's so nice of you to come speak with me, however, a phone call would have sufficed."

"It's Mrs. Sams."

There was a slight hesitation in Ms. Wilters' step when I corrected her, but she kept going. I walked behind the teacher while she talked and led me to her classroom.

When I'd entered the office and told them what happened, Mrs. Peet, one of Aunt Charlotte's friends and the school secretary, took down some notes for the principal and called Ms. Wilters to the office. Ms. Wilters' dark-skinned face held surprise and impatience when she saw me. Mrs. Peet directed her to take me to the classroom and that she'd send the principal when he finished his phone call. I stared at the elegant up do on the back of Ms. Wilters head and narrowed my eyes. This woman had hurt my baby's feelings. 'An eye for an eye' kept going through my mind.

"Please have a seat. Well, the only chair that I have is really mine, but I'm sure that you can, um, fit, I mean, sit in one of the students' chairs."

I glanced at the tiny chairs and turned an incredulous look on Ms. Wilters. I knew that she'd meant to refer to my lush curves.

"Surely, you wouldn't expect any parent to sit in those small chairs. How about I sit in your chair and you can fit, I mean, sit on a desk? Or the floor, or you may stand, I give not one care."

Ms. Wilters' eyes widened at my hard tone, and she dropped the mask of congeniality that she'd worn. She shook her head and walked behind her desk to sit in her chair. She narrowed her eyes as she steepled her hands and placed her bony chin on top of them.

"I guess the gloves are off, Ms. Sams? No, you may not have my chair. You may sit where you like or stand."

I gave Ms. Wilters an unpleasant smile to acknowledge her nastiness and stepped closer to the desk to lean over her. Her chin dipped as if she wanted to lower her head, but she firmed her lips and glared at me.

"What would you like to talk about, Ms. Sams? Why are you here?"

"It's MRS. Sams, and I really don't have anything to 'talk' to you about, Ms. Wilters. I'm here to caution you to leave Valora's bright spirit alone. She is a very smart and talented little girl. I won't allow your bitter perceptions to cloud her internal and external beauty. Do you understand?"

Ms. Wilters backed away from the violence of my quiet tone. I looked down and saw that I'd fisted my hands and leaned closer to the hateful woman until I almost lay across the desk. I tried to temper my anger and backed away just a bit. I liked the fear in Ms. Wilters' eyes. She narrowed her eyes at me and let the devil inside of her loose.

"Caution me? Huh! You think that because you look White that you can tell me what to do! I've heard about you, Victoria Sams. You're nothing but a poor, piece of trash with too many mouths to feed! Your daughter isn't special or bright! She's a freak and no better than any of the other dumb Black kids that I teach!"

I stepped back with a hand on my chest as Ms. Wilters vented her spleen. There was something ugly deep inside of Ms. Wilters, and I was not going to allow it to affect my child. I took three large steps and surprised Ms. Wilters and myself. I grabbed her up do viciously and shoved my face into hers. The fear on her face awakened a sliver of darkness within me.

"As for my child, I will request her removal from your class. I thought that as a Black woman and educator, you would ensure that the Black children that you taught would be nurtured and on a level playing field as the White children. I see that I made a mistake. I should have listened to my cousin when she told me that you were distant and reluctant to teach the Black children. Don't you know that they already suffer so much in this world by being born Black? How could you not want them to have the same privilege as the people on the other side of the tracks? You are a complete bitch, Ms. Wilters, and you should not be allowed to teach any children."

I yanked my hand away from the trembling dark-skinned woman and stepped away. I made a point to pull an embroidered handkerchief from my purse and wiped my hand slowly while I stared at Ms. Wilters. She stood up and pointed to me with a shaky finger.

"Get out of here, now. I should call the police, but you just proved a point. Your skin may be white, but you act like all those other ignorant Black mothers. Go on! Get out!"

I stared at the stupidity that dripped off Ms. Wilters' tongue. I opened my mouth to blast her.

"What is the meaning of this, Ms. Wilters? Why are you yelling at Ms. Sams? The whole school can hear you."

Surprised, Ms. Wilters and I turned to see the tall White principal, Mr. Monts, in the doorway with Ms. Wilters' class and several teachers behind him. I glanced back to see Ms. Wilters touch her neck and drop into her chair. I bit my lip to hold back the smirk that threatened my lips.

Mr. Monts turned around and spoke to the teachers behind him. I saw Valora's frightened little face peek past Mr. Monts leg. I smiled, waved, and blew her a kiss. She smiled and backed away when Mr. Monts closed the door. The only sound in the room was the sound of his muted footsteps on the carpet. The principal's eyes looked like pieces of grey flint behind the glare of his glasses. He looked from me to Ms. Wilters who looked like a frightened deer in the front of headlights.

"I would like an explanation, please."

Ms. Wilters couldn't seem to find her voice for a few moments. Mr. Monts and I waited until she cleared her throat several times before she could finally speak. My mouth dropped open when she did.

"This woman came in here to insult and assault me, sir. You know how these people can be. She didn't tell me what she wanted. She just attacked me."

Mr. Monts' eyebrows shot up at Ms. Wilters' incredulous statement. He looked at me and turned back to Ms. Wilters. I narrowed my eyes at the smug look on her face. Mr. Monts stepped closer to Ms. Wilters' desk.

"Ms. Wilters, you cannot be serious. Mrs. Sams has a reputation for being a very fair parent. I cannot believe you. You must be mistaken. Now, none of us have time for this nonsense. Explain yourself."

Ms. Wilters' jaw dropped at Mr. Monts' refusal to believe her tale. His tone was hard and sharp. I almost felt sorry for her, but she'd hurt my baby. My heart wouldn't allow the pity into it.

Mr. Monts expressed a sound of impatience at Ms. Wilters' continued silence. He turned to me with a grim smile.

"Mrs. Sams, since Ms. Wilters cannot find her voice, can you explain to me what is going on here?"

I glanced at Ms. Wilters' sunken posture and nervous fidgeting. She seemed defeated. The small space of darkness within my heart wanted her broken. I looked back at Mr. Monts.

"My daughter, Valora, came home to tell me that she had been insulted and mistreated by Ms. Wilters and some of the students in the class at Ms. Wilters' direction. My daughter is usually very happy and full of life, but when she came home yesterday, her sadness was too much for us to take, Mr. Monts. I will not have my daughter's light dimmed by anyone – especially a teacher."

Mr. Monts looked confused and skeptical.

"I don't understand, Mrs. Sams, and I want to very badly. Are you saying that one of my teachers behaved in such an abominable way towards a child? I'm sorry, Mrs. Sams. I can't believe it."

I narrowed my eyes at the tall White man. I felt my hands fist at his disbelief and lifted my chin.

"Forgive me, sir, if you can't bring yourself to believe that you have one Black teacher on staff that hates herself so much that she is bitter to the Black children in her class and ingratiating to the White children. Forgive me if I have seen and have heard her categorize these innocent children and their parents to fit her notions. Forgive me, sir, if I don't really care if you believe me or not, but you will understand and believe this much. I want my daughter removed from this woman's class immediately. I don't care that school is almost out for the summer. She is envious of my daughter because you took notice of her, sir, and she took out her jealousy and spite on a six-year old child. No one, and I mean, no one, is going to make my child feel inferior."

Mr. Monts' eyebrows were lifted so high on his forehead when I finished that they almost disappeared into his hairline. I stood there in the silence and waited. Mr. Monts had known the minute that I mentioned that he'd taken notice of Valora that I spoke the truth. He bowed his head to me and turned to Ms. Wilters with a fierce frown.

"Ms. Wilters, I now understand what has transpired. I did wonder why I didn't have a recommendation for gifted and talented testing on my desk for Valora Sams today while I had all of the children that you selected – all of the White children. I will not have this kind of behavior on my staff. Since it is the last days of school, I will have Ms. Spacy conduct your class for the time being because as of right now, you and I need to have a private conversation about your conduct. Now, please collect your things. I will escort you to my office."

Ms. Wilters looked like she wanted to cry, but she took a shaky breath, stood up, and grabbed her coffee mug and purse. She glided past me with her head held high, but I saw the glance of anger and hate that she sent my way before she schooled her features. Mr. Monts took her elbow and nodded. He started towards the door and stopped. He turned around and smiled.

"I apologize if this situation has inconvenienced you in any way, Mrs. Sams. Valora can stay in Ms. Sheffield's class. I will also make sure that she is tested before the end of the day today. Please rest assured that nothing like this will happen here again. If you'll give me a few minutes, I'll come back and escort you to your car."

I nodded my acceptance, and he bowed his head. He ushered Ms. Wilters out of the room and spoke to someone in the hall. The door closed and I breathed a sigh of relief. I glanced at my watch to see that it was barely nine o'clock. I still needed to get to the middle and high schools to address the Clements and Adams' fight with my children. I said a prayer that the bit of darkness that lingered with my tension wouldn't present itself in my next meetings.

"Mama?"

I turned to see that a young White teacher held my smiling pumpkin by the hand in the open doorway. I strode towards them with a smile and my arms open. Valora ran the few steps to me and hugged me tightly. I closed my eyes for a moment and absorbed her gentle warmth. I waited for the darkness to retreat as my tension eased, but it wouldn't. The combination of it and Valora's special gifts made me sick to my stomach. I pulled away and smiled at my striking daughter.

"I'm happy to see you, pumpkin. How is your day?"

I glanced at the teacher who stepped up to take Valora's hand. She extended her other hand to me. Her smile looked genuine and open.

"Hello, Mrs. Sams, I'm Ms. Sheffield. Mr. Monts told me that Valora would be in my class until school is out. She is a wonderful little girl. I wish that I'd had her when you all moved here, but that is neither here nor there now. I'll take good care of her while she's with me."

I nodded at the eager young woman. She looked no older than Mark or Willie. With a glance at my watch, I leaned down and kissed Valora's forehead. She giggled and touched my hand.

"I love you, Mama."

Tears sprang in my eyes, and I tried to cover them with an eye roll and chuckle.

"Of course, you do, Pumpkin Pie! I love you, too. Now, Mama has to go. I'll be at the bus stop when you get off the small school bus, okay?"

Ms. Sheffield saw my distress and smiled her understanding. She looked down at Valora and tugged on her hand.

"C'mon, little miss. I'm sure that Ms. Lina is being overwhelmed with my class."

Valora gave Ms. Sheffield a questioning look.

"What does overwhelmed mean, Ms. Sheffield?"

Ms. Sheffield laughed and pulled Valora from the class while she explained the word. I smiled, glanced at my watch, and almost ran from the room. I shook my head at myself. 'The best laid plans…'

6

I arrived at William's practice after a very unproductive meeting with the middle and high school principals. They seemed not to care that the Clements and Adams boys were bullies. Their nonchalant attitudes got the best of me, and I'd ended up promising retribution if they continued to allow my children to be hurt. I didn't think it had done any good because both principals were more concerned about if Grayson and Willie were going to play football the next year.

Ms. Constance and Nora, the young White nurse, were behind my desk whispering and laughing when I made my way into the door. They immediately stopped, and I knew that they had been talking about me. With difficulty, I tried to bury my anger. I smiled widely at them both while I walked to my desk.

"Good Morning, Ms. Constance, Nora. I trust that it's been quiet today?"

Ms. Constance frowned at my greeting and glanced at the clock. She smiled and handed me my time card.

"Yes, it has been quiet until now. It is almost eleven. I thought that your message said that you'd been in around nine. You'll have to make up that time this afternoon."

I turned sharply and glared at Ms. Constance. I saw Nora's smirk from the corner of my eye. Oh, how I couldn't stand Nora. She wanted William so bad that she probably could taste it. It didn't help that Ms. Constance egged her on either. I took a step toward Ms. Constance to give her a piece of my mind when William appeared in the examination room hallway.

"Victoria, is everything all right? Arta said that you needed some time off this morning."

I heard Ms. Constance say something under her breath and Nora's giggle. I whipped around on them both. I forgot all about William as all of the anger that I'd tried to hide spilled off my lips.

"Did you say something Ms. Constance? No? I didn't think so. You're not woman enough to say it to my face. You just vent your spleen to this bird-brained nurse. You don't know enough about my children or me to know why I took off this morning. You think that you're so bourgeois when you're...?"

"Victoria!"

I turned towards William's shout and saw him through the veil of my tears. He made a noise of sympathy. I felt him grasp my elbow and pull me down the hallway. I tried to wipe my tears away and saw that we were in his office. He shut the door and locked it. I stood there and waited. He turned and closed the gap to gather me in his arms. I tried to hold myself stiff, but his love seeped into my body. I collapsed into tears and explained everything that happened that morning. He held me until I hiccupped. He patted my back and led me to the sofa. I sat down and expected him to sit beside me, but he walked over to his desk and picked up the phone. When I heard him speak, I stared at him in shock because I'd never heard William use that tone.

"Mr. Gibson? Yes, this is Dr. Herbert. No, I'm his son. Actually, it doesn't matter. I want to know what's going on with the Sams boys. I hear that the Clements and Adams boys have it in for them. Yes, I know school is about to be out. I will be attending the graduation services tonight. Right. I see. Well, I'm a friend of the family, and I do have their mother's permission to talk to you. Uh huh. Okay, so you've known about the fights and have done nothing? It is your job to do something. I don't care if you have their mothers on staff. They are trouble. No, I don't understand. Please explain it."

William looked like he would explode while he listened to the high school principal, Mr. Gibson's explanation.

"So you mean to tell me that because the Clements and Adams are White and the Sams boys are Black, that it's okay? This isn't the old days of Black persecution, Mr. Gibson. Black children and White children are entitled to the same rights and privileges – including a safe schoolyard. What do you mean that I should understand because I'm White? Mr. Gibson, it is obvious that no one told you about me, but I will enlighten you. Never judge a book by its cover. With that being said, if you don't address this matter now and before the next school year begins, I will have the NAACP so far up your craw, you won't be able to breathe. Do you understand me, Mr. Gibson?"

William's voice rose as he threatened Mr. Gibson. I stayed silent in awe of William's authoritative manner.

"Excellent. Thank you, Mr. Gibson. I'll look forward to following up with your inquiry into this matter. Have a good day."

William disconnected the call and shuddered with revulsion on his face. He looked at me grimly.

"I feel like I need to take a bath after talking to that slimy fool."

I couldn't help but burst into laughter at William's disgusted look. He burst into laughter too and came to sit down beside me. He picked up my hand and caressed it. My laughter died a quick death when he leaned closer and kissed me softly. He pulled back and I laid my head on his shoulder. We sat like that for a while until William cleared his throat.

"So, is that why you went off on my mother and Nurse Nora?"

I hesitated to tell William about Ms. Constance and Nora's scheming, so I nodded. He chuckled and squeezed my hand.

"They probably needed it. They've been thick as thieves lately, and I don't like their gossiping in the office. I'll talk to Mother, okay?"

I was glad that William couldn't see me roll my eyes at the idea of him telling his mother to stop her meddling ways. I just nodded again. William cleared his throat and got up from the small sofa in his office. He turned and pulled me up in front of him. He looked at me from head to toe and smiled.

"You are a beauty, Victoria. Maybe Mother is jealous to have such beauty around her to remind her of her age. Yes, that's it."

As he spoke, William wiggled his eyebrows, and I laughed at his shenanigans. He chuckled and spun me around towards the door.

"Alright, woman, we have a practice to run and a graduation to attend tonight. Let's get to work. Oh, and don't worry coming in late this morning or making it up. I'm the boss, not my mother."

I smiled and blew him a kiss from the doorway. I closed the door with a laugh on my tongue because William pretended to catch the kiss from the air and hold it to his chest. I turned and walked down the hallway with a lighter step and a lighter heart.

"Mark Daniel Sams."

Mark sedately walked with his head held high to the small platform to receive his diploma from the Carson school superintendent to the cheers of Daniels, Sams, and Roberts' clans. Tears of joy slipped from my eyes, and I felt Valora's small hand try to wipe them away. I kissed her hand and hugged her to me for comfort. I glanced at William to see him look at Mark with pride. I looked around him at old Dr. Herbert and Ms. Constance. I couldn't help but chuckle to myself at the seating arrangement that Aunt Charlotte orchestrated when she saw William's intent to sit with us. She'd taken one look at his determination and Ms. Constance's reluctance and knew what to do. Oh, how I'd loved my Aunt Charlotte.

After the graduation, everyone joined the graduates on the field. We easily found my tall son in the sea of burnt orange caps and gowns. Mark ran to us and hugged the family in his happiness. He shook Dr. Herbert and Ms. Constance's hands. I saw several of my Daniels and Roberts cousins had attended the ceremony as well. I looked at Aunt Charlotte and Aunt Mary and silently asked them for help. They nodded and turned to direct everyone to Cousin Anabelle's barbeque joint. I turned to see William and Mark in deep conversation. Mark laughed at something William said, then William shook Mark's hand. Mark looked down at it. William leaned in and whispered something to Mark. Mark looked up at William in adoration and gave him a bear hug. Everyone in the vicinity laughed except Ms. Constance. I felt Aunt Charlotte and Aunt Mary come to stand on each side of me.

"Maybe I was wrong about Dr. William, Victoria. He seems determined to be in your life. Are you going to let him, I wonder?"

I kept my gaze on Mark and William. I shifted slightly to the right so that Aunt Charlotte could hear me.

"I love him, Aunt Charlotte. I tried to leave him alone, but he doesn't want me to. Ms. Constance does though."

Aunt Charlotte chuckled and shook the grass off of her cane.

"Constance has forgotten that she carries more than a drop of Black blood. Dr. Herbert shouldn't have made her pass all those years. Now, the chickens are coming home to roost. That boy isn't going to forget even if she has."

I nodded and smiled widely at William when he waved his goodbye. We'd already discussed that he'd take his parents home and return to Cousin Anabelle's joint for Mark's party.

"Victoria, now is the time for you to live. There will be paths that you can't take if you want to stay happy. Remember that your life is yours."

I glanced at Aunt Mary's serene face and shrugged. Aunt Charlotte leaned back and frowned at Aunt Mary.

"Oh, Mary. Now is not the time for your cryptic visions and prophecies. The girl is happy. The kids are happy. Well, all the kids except Willie and Gia. I'll always wonder about those two. Oh well, they can't all be angels. We'd better get going. I'm sure Anabelle is going to charge us double if she has to keep the meat on the grill."

I laughed at Aunt Charlotte's no-nonsense ways. She reminded me so much of Big Mama Chandra. I sighed. Big Mama Chandra would be so proud of Mark. Somehow, I knew that she was.

Since the children would be out of school for the summer, I asked William if it'd be okay for me to work a regular schedule. He brought up his mother's nosiness and me being a distraction to him again as reasons for me not to work a regular schedule. When I explained that we would work around it, William gave in but grudgingly. I found his reluctance strange, so I told him that I'd stay with my old schedule. William's easy acceptance of my change of mind made me suspicious, especially since I knew that from Arta that Nora had begun to wear shorter nursing skirts when I wasn't scheduled to work. Jealousy took root within the darkness that lingered in my heart. My mind started to show me visions of William and Nora kissing or in his office alone. It was when I had a vision of them at the altar that I decided to go to work on one of my usual days off.

"Victoria? What are you doing here today? You're not scheduled to work."

I tried not to let my confidence slip at Ms. Constance's shocked face.

"Oh, I thought I'd come in and catch up on some of the work from yesterday. William said that I could come in early from time to time. Is that a problem?"

Ms. Constance gathered her composure and answered with elegant cool.

"I'm sure that when William said early, he meant at an earlier time not an earlier day. Wait, I thought that you told me you'd finished the patient records for billing yesterday."

I shrugged nonchalantly while looking towards the examination hallway for William or Nora.

"I guess that I forgot a few. I don't want the billing to be late, so I'll just make sure that they're all done today."

Determined, I walked to my small corner desk and sat down. I saw Ms. Constance narrow her eyes at me, but I ignored her. I glanced again at the hallway and at the clock. William should be in his office or in the records room. Since both were down the hallway, I decided to find him for myself. I stood up and Ms. Constance did too.

"Where are you going, Victoria?"

I frowned at her nervous attitude. Something wasn't right.

"I'm going to the records room, Ms. Constance. You know, where we keep the records."

Ms. Constance fidgeted with the elegant scarf around her neck and slowly sat back down in her chair. She looked down at the papers on her desk and waved her hand with a quiet 'Fine'.

I nodded and walked down the hallway to the second door on the left that said, RECORDS. I put my hand on the door, and I pushed it open a little to make the noise. I peeked down the hallway to see if Ms. Constance could see me. When I knew that she didn't, I tiptoed down to William's office. It was cracked open, and I could see Nora's bare legs crossed on the sofa. Anger and rage filled my blood. Betrayal joined them. I forced myself to stay quiet and still to listen.

"Nora, have I answered all of your questions?"

"Oh, yes, Dr. William. It's just that I don't want to disappoint you."

Nora's voice sounded breathless like she tried to sound like a vixen. I rolled my eyes and clenched my fists. I waited for William's response.

"Nora, if you keep doing your job, you won't disappoint me. Now, I'm sure that some of our appointments have arrived."

Suddenly, the door swung open and William looked surprised to see me standing there. Embarrassed at being caught eavesdropping, I glared at William. I saw Nora get up to stand behind him with malicious grin.

"Victoria! I thought you didn't work today."

I narrowed my eyes at William and Nora's hand that crept into his elbow. William shifted to open the door more, and Nora's hand fell to her side. My hands itched to strangle her and her overexposed body. I took a small step into the doorway, but William saw my fury and blocked me.

"It's not what you think, sweetheart."

His murmured words only enflamed my anger more. Before I could unleash my rage, William turned to Nora with a brisk, businesslike tone.

"Nora, please go set up the patient rooms and tell Arta to go ahead and assess any patients that are already here."

Nora looked crestfallen for a moment and didn't move. My patience wore thin but my dignity held strong.

"I believe that Dr. William gave you directions, Nora. I'm sure that you don't want to disappoint him."

William's eyes widened at my words and tone because he now knew how much I'd heard. Nora sniffed and stuck her nose in the air. William and I shifted sideways so that she could leave. She threw me an ugly look before went down the short hallway to the first patient room. I stared at her back and wanted to slam her to the ground. I took a step toward her, but William grasped my arm.

"No, Victoria. Come in and I will explain."

I spun around on him with tearful anger.

"I will not allow you to lie to me, William. Is this why you didn't want me here every day? Is it because you want to see that slut your mother wants for you to be with in tight and revealing clothes? How could you do this to me, William?

How could you do this even after I told you about Harlan and his women?"

I'd whispered my pain, but it felt like I'd yelled it because William's face was pale. I saw him glance over my head and knew that we had an audience. I didn't care. The ache in my heart was too great. I didn't give him time to speak. I turned around with my head held high and walked down the hallway. William called my name, but I refused to answer. Ms. Constance stopped me with a hand on my arm before I could go out of the door.

"Victoria, can't you see that you hurt yourself. My son is a single man with no children. This had to happen for you to see that it will never work between you. He's ashamed of you. He takes you out of town to court you because he can't be seen with you. He needs to find a woman that can give him children and help him build his practice."

I wanted to slap Ms. Constance for digging the knife deeper into my heart.

"That's enough, Mother. Leave her alone. As a matter of fact, leave us alone."

I heard William's voice, but I didn't want to be around him or in the practice. I grabbed my purse and ran out the door. I ran down the sidewalk and across the street blindly. The screech or tires and the honk of a horn slowed my flight of despair. I motioned my apology to the driver and moved out of his way. A broken heart wasn't worth my life. I continued down the sidewalk and chided myself for putting too much stock in the love and fidelity of a man. I thought back to the first time that William had hurt me. I'd hidden within myself from the pain of his rejection. Then, Harlan came along and hurt me more times than I could count. I reckon the only men who hadn't hurt me were my sons. I sighed when the rejected voice inside of me said, 'there's still time for them to hurt you too.' A cynical laugh escaped my lips. Yeah, there was still time.

When I thought that the practice had closed for the day, I left my stool at Mr. Ned's burger place. I walked slowly around the city square until I came to my old Plymouth. I got in and put the key slowly into the ignition. It coughed a few times, but it started loudly. I made a mental note to have it checked for problems when I came to town again. A memory of William's offer to buy me a new station wagon came to mind and I viciously shook it away. I needed to stop thinking about William. The pain of his betrayal sat heavy in my heart while I drove down the highway with the windows down and the wind whipping auburn strands of hair in my face.

I'd barely driven past the new Allsville sign when the Plymouth coughed and slowed to a stop. I let it rest for a spell, and then I tried to start it. The old car coughed and spewed steam but didn't start. I slammed my fists against the steering wheel in frustration. I just wanted to get home, cook dinner, and go to bed. That wasn't too much to ask for, was it? I exhaled a big breath and got out of the car. I shaded my hand to the sun and realized that I could probably make it home walking before sundown. With that thought, I let up the windows on the Plymouth, grabbed my purse, and locked it. I shook my head at someone stealing the troublesome car. My luck wasn't that good. I turned and started to walk down the side of the road.

Halfway down the highway, I said a prayer of thanks that I'd worn my flats instead of heels. Whew! I laughed to myself. I'd dodged a big bullet with that one. Although, as I came across several vulture ridden animal corpses, I wished that I'd worn boots and carried a gun. The vultures flew above like I was some kind of prey. I picked up a long limb and broke it for a walking stick. Ha! Those buzzards didn't stand a chance.

Five minutes after I'd passed another smelly polecat corpse, I heard a car coming down the highway. I moved a little further off the road and waited for it to pass. It was my surprise when the car slowed to a stop beside me. I glanced to see that it was William in his parents' Buick. Anger flared, and I turned to keep walking.

"Victoria!"

I ignored William's shout and kept going. I heard the gravel crunch under tires, and the car door slam. When I heard his footsteps come closer, I turned and held up my hand to stop him.

"What do you want, William? Do you want to feed me some lies to make yourself feel better? Or have you come to say that you're sorry? Well, you are sorry! You are a sorry excuse for a man if you couldn't tell me that you didn't want to be with me anymore! I deserved that much, William! I deserved that much!"

I held my hand to my chest and let him see the tears fall. I wanted him to see how much that he'd hurt me even if he didn't care anymore. William stepped closer and grabbed my shoulders. I tried to shake him off but he held firm.

"Victoria Alicia Sams! You are going to hear me out! NOTHING HAPPENED!"

I jumped at William's roar. He looked angry and frustrated. I stopped moving and waited. William saw that I stopped fighting him and let out a pent up breath. He hugged me to him. I wanted to melt into his arms, but the pain held me at bay.

"I apologize for yelling at you, Victoria. It's just that you are so stubborn that you wouldn't listen. I waited for you to come back and when you didn't, I told Mother to close the practice for the day because I wanted to find you and explain. She didn't like it, but I reminded her that I am a grown man. I told her that she was wrong about us. She doesn't understand and she doesn't want to, Victoria. That is why she said those nasty things to you."

I nodded, and William began to rub my back.

"Nora came into the office dressed provocatively too many times. I asked Mother to address it because it didn't look right in front of my patients. She said that she did, but Nora kept dressing the same way. Well, she dressed that way when you weren't around the office. When I walked in this morning and saw her skirt up to here and blouse down to there, I decided to speak to her. I warned her that if she wore those clothes again, I'd have to write her up for it. We hadn't been in the office very long before I opened the door and you were there. Why were you there, anyway, Victoria?"

William's explanation seemed believable but Ms. Constance's words stuck in my mind. I shook my head and tried to pull away. William allowed me the distance of an arm's length. He kept his hands on my shoulders. I looked into his eyes and found my voice.

"I believe you, William, but Nora is still there. Your mother isn't going to leave us in peace. I came today because I was jealous and because you acted like you didn't want me around every day."

William nodded and began to smile.

"You were jealous? How could you be jealous when I've told you that I love you? As for not wanting you around every day, I didn't want you to work too hard or be away from the children too much. They need you, and the time that you spend with them is more important. I'll always be here. They're going to grow up and leave the nest."

William's smile widened into an infectious grin. I wanted to let go of all the anger, jealousy, and pain, but it seemed stuck inside of me with Ms. Constance's words. I shook my head. My heart ached when William's grin faded into a look of hurt.

"Maybe it's you that doesn't want to be with me anymore, Victoria. Maybe you don't trust me to love you. Is that it?"

The look of rejection on William's face pulled at my harsh emotions like a string releasing from a knot. I stepped back into his arms and hugged his tall muscular body. The sob that William let go told me how wrong his mother and I had been. This man loved me with all of his heart, and I vowed to return that love. William lifted his arms and returned my embrace. I felt his chest rumble with laughter, and I joined him. I looked to the sky to give thanks and saw the black wings of a vulture circling to cast a shadow on our embrace.

7

A knock sounded on the door. I hurried to open it thinking that it was William coming to get us for the community picnic. I swung it open to find my Aunt Hallie bent over in tears. Alarmed that something had happened to Clyde or one of my cousins, I reached to pull her into my arms. She shook her head and took a few deep breaths. I waited with dread in the pit of my stomach.

"Victoria. It's Mama. She's had a stroke and they don't know if she'll live!"

I felt my eyes buck at Aunt Hallie's announcement. She fell into the house in broken sobs. I was taken aback for a moment. Betts had a stroke? I could hardly believe it. I always figured that her evil ways would keep her alive forever. I bit my lip to keep from uttering those words to Aunt Hallie in her distressed state. I guided her to the large armchair and sat on the coffee table across from it. Aunt Hallie's smooth light caramel skin looked dry and ashy from her tears. I leaned back and grabbed the box of tissues to offer her one. She snatched one from the box and glared at me.

"What's wrong with you, girl? I just told you that your grandmother is in the hospital barely alive. I'd think after all that she did for you, you'd be a little more upset."

In shock, I stared at Aunt Hallie's vehemence. Betts hadn't done a thing but ruin my life. I frowned at Aunt Hallie. Usually, I would let her attitude slide, but I wanted to know what she meant.

"I may not be upset like you, but I am concerned, Aunt Hallie. What do you mean, all that Betts has done for me?"

Aunt Hallie narrowed her eyes. In that moment, she looked like her mother.

"You know that she's been giving that oldest gal of yours money and teaching her everything that you refused to teach her. Why, I was over there the other day when Betts showed her how to make her special sage candles."

Numbness settled into my body at the mention of Gia learning Betts' ways. No, Aunt Hallie had to be wrong. I dropped Gia off at Tess and Clyde's on my way to William's practice. I shook my head at her.

"You must be mistaken, Aunt Hallie. I guess it doesn't matter right now. Thank you for coming to tell me about Betts. The children and I were waiting on Dr. William to pick us up for the community Juneteenth picnic. I'll be up to see Betts as soon as we leave the picnic."

Aunt Hallie turned an incredulous look at me.

"You mean to tell me that a picnic is more important that your grandmother's life? I am appalled at your behavior, Victoria. Maybe you're just in shock. Yes, maybe that's it. Well, I've got to get back to the house in case Pearl or Clyde calls. Oh, by the way, I think that your Dr. William is the attending doctor with Mama."

It was my turn to look at Aunt Hallie with disbelief. Surely, William would have come by to tell me since he knew that the phone lines were being fixed. I waved at Aunt Hallie as she drove away and turned back into the house. In a daze, I walked through the house to the back porch. It smelled like dirt and dogs. I put my finger under my nose and opened the door.

A pile of unburnt trash greeted me. Willie. He acted like he had no time for chores since Mark left for truck driving school. I turned my head away from the trash and looked across the gravel packed yard. Grayson and Valora were bent over pulling sour-weed. I frowned because I knew that they'd get their shorts and shirts dirty.

"Grayson! Valora! Get out of those weeds! Y'all are going to be filthy before the picnic!"

Grayson handed Valora a bunch of the edible sour-tasting weed and they ran over to me. Valora covered her nose when she passed the trash. Grayson stopped beside it.

"Mama, do you want me to burn the trash? Willie left already, and I know how you don't like it to sit. I'm big enough now to set the fire and watch it."

I smiled at Grayson's offer. He became more like Mark every day. I noted the resemblance between Grayson and Valora. No one could tell that they had any difference in them. No one would ever know if I had my way. I hugged Valora to me and shook my head at Grayson.

"I don't know, son. I know that you've grown a lot, but I don't want you to get burned. Remember what happened to the Howard's boy. He set the trash on fire and himself too. He almost died. I don't want that to happen to you."

Grayson's helpful demeanor fell at my caution. He stuck out a determined chin.

"Mama, you have to let me help around here. Valora too. Willie is always at his friends and Gia at Grandma Tess'. Leah helps sometimes, but she's started to follow Gia. Valora is six and I'm thirteen. We're big enough to help you, Mama. Please?"

I looked at my son's face and knew that he spoke the truth. Willie, Gia, and Leah had practically abandoned us. I realized that I'd spent so much time being happy with William that I hadn't paid attention to the growing rift in my family. A strange guilt blossomed in my heart, but I refused to acknowledge it. I sighed in agreement.

"Alright, Grayson. You can burn the trash."

Grayson whooped in his excitement. Valora and I laughed. I calmed down to give my son some conditions to his new chore.

"You can burn the trash, son, but only when I am at home and with plenty of water under the barrel. Okay?"

Grayson nodded, but I could see the excitement in his eyes at being given the chore of an older child. He jumped up the few steps to the porch and hugged me. Valora threw her small arms around me and we all laughed. I glanced at the clock on the counter and saw that it was past the time for William to fetch us. I pulled loose from Grayson and Valora with a feeling of dread. I turned a smile on them.

"Okay, y'all, enough of these shenanigans. Let's go sit in the living room and wait for Dr. William."

Grayson and Valora nodded and raced past me to the living room. I swallowed the feeling of dread and walked through to sit with my rambunctious children.

An hour later, I let a very restless Grayson and Valora outside to play. I knew in my heart that William was at the hospital like Aunt Hallie said. I wasn't angry that he hadn't come by to tell me because he was the best doctor in Carson. It was routine that the hospital would call him for something like a stroke. I sat in my doldrums for a spell until I heard Grayson and Valora speak to someone. Alarmed that a stranger may have stopped on the highway, I ran out the door to be greeted by my mother's sedan as it pulled into the driveway. I walked down the steps slowly and tried to calm myself. Tess stopped the car and opened the door. I saw Grayson rush to help her out of the car. Tess thanked Grayson, turned, and beckoned for me to come closer. I noticed that she gave Valora only a cursory glance. I frowned and moved to meet her by her car.

"Hey, Mama, are you alright?"

Tess' face looked solemn. I wondered had Betts kicked the bucket yet and felt horrible for that train of thought. I clasped my hands together and waited for Tess to speak. She nodded at the children.

"Maybe you should send them away to play in the back."

I nodded in agreement because I didn't want the kids to hear any bad news. I caught Grayson's attention and tilted my head towards the back. He understood and grabbed Valora with the promise of a wild onion search. I smiled for a moment at Grayson's tactic. He knew Valora couldn't resist a chance to dig up something.

When the children ran to the back, I took Tess' rigid arm and led her up the steps into the house. She seemed to be in some sort of shock or daze. I covered her with the light shawl that I kept in the living room chest. She didn't seem to notice because her gaze was focused on her hands. I waited until she finally looked up at me. I wasn't prepared for the anguish and guilt that clouded my mother's eyes.

"Forgive me, please, Victoria. I need you to forgive me."

I stared at Tess in shock. Forgive her? Tess wanted forgiveness? For what? I shook my head because I didn't understand, and I guess that she thought it meant I wouldn't forgive her. She stood up and grasped my shoulders roughly.

"Victoria, you have to forgive me. I...I didn't know what I was doing to you. Well, I knew what I was doing, but I didn't want to do it. It was like something took hold of my heart and squeezed any love that I may have had for you out of it. When I was attacked in the field and everything that I did, well, now I know that it was from my choices. How I've treated you and my grandchildren, those were my choices. Victoria, please forgive me!"

Tess fell against me and slid down my body to sit on the chest while she sobbed. Speechless, I stared at my mother's salt and pepper curls and wondered what the heck was going on today. Betts came to my mind. She'd orchestrated almost every evil thing that happened in Allsville and beyond. Could it be that Betts' evil waned with her stroke? It was a thought that took hold and began to consume me. I knew that Valora's light held the darkness at bay. What if Betts' curses and evil went away with her illness? I needed to find out for myself. A plan formed quickly in my mind and I'd need Tess' help. I knelt down and grasped her hands.

"Mama, I forgive you. I forgave you a long time ago when Valora was born. I didn't want any more bad feelings, and I saw that you didn't either. I's okay, Mama. Everything is going to be okay."

Tess raised her tear-stained face and attempted a smile. I handed her a tissue and stood up while she wiped her face. I glanced outside at the car.

"Mama, is Daddy still at the hospital? Aunt Hallie came by and told us that Betts had a stroke."

I turned back and almost missed Tess when she rolled her eyes at the mention of Clyde.

"Yes, he left with your Aunt Pearl when the ambulance came to get Betts. I would have gone with him, but I felt under the weather until a little while ago. Why?"

I shrugged.

"I just wanted to know if he'd come back with word of Betts."

Tess nodded and sniffed into her tissue. I felt bad for a moment for what I was about to do, but it couldn't be helped.

"Mama, would you mind watching Grayson and Valora for a spell? I'd like to go see if everything is okay and pick up a few groceries."

Tess smiled and I thought to myself that my mother's age hadn't affected her dark beauty. She nodded and handed me the keys.

"Go ahead. I'd like to spend some time with Grayson and Valora. Ever since Leah and Gia have been coming to the house, I don't get to get over to this side of the creek too much."

I bobbed my head while she spoke, but my mind was on other things. She pulled the soft, white wool shawl from her shoulders and placed it over my red-checkered sundress.

"You'll need this for that cold hospital."

I squeezed her hand in thanks, grabbed my purse, and headed out the door. I called Grayson and Valora to me as I walked to the car. They ran from around the house. I shook my head at their dirty clothes and hands.

"I'm going to town for a little while. Grandma Tess will be here in case you need her, okay?"

Grayson and Valora said a quiet 'yes, ma'am' before they ran off to the other side of the house where an old fallen tree lay. I didn't want to think about what they'd dig out of it. I started the car, waved at Tess when she came out on the porch, and drove off toward Carson.

I walked into the front entrance of Carson General Hospital grateful for the cool air. Clyde and Tess' Chevy sedan didn't have an air conditioner that worked, so I'd ridden with the windows down all the way to Carson. The June heat had invaded the car anyway, so the wind hadn't done anything but mess my hair. I glanced in the window of the first office to see that a few strands were out of place from my bun. I smoothed them back in and straightened my dress.

"Victoria?"

The familiar voice made me spin around quickly. William stood there with a small smile in his white coat and stethoscope. A spark of anger lit within me that he didn't come by to tell me that he'd be late. I opened my mouth to blast him when he stepped closer. His nearness took my breath away for the moment.

"I'm very sorry that I couldn't come by to tell you that I'd been called to tend to your grandmother, Victoria," he murmured.

I cast my eyes to the clipboard in his hand so that I wouldn't have to look into his handsome face. I nodded, and he chuckled. I glanced up to see the smug look on his face, and frowned at him. He reached out and tried to smooth it away.

"No, no, no. You promised that you'd stop frowning at me, remember? Although, your frown lines are just as beautiful as the rest of you."

I felt my frown deepen at his mention of the slight lines on my forehead. William stepped back quickly from my wrath and held up his hands. He sighed.

"Alright, alright. We'll table that for another day. Anyway, are you here to see Mrs. Roberts?"

I nodded and felt my heartbeat start to race. Yes, I wanted to see Betts. William took my elbow and guided me down a long hallway to the right of the entrance.

"I'll take you to her room. I need to drop off this chart and head to the house to clean up for our picnic."

I glanced at William in surprise that he still wanted to attend the picnic. He saw me and chuckled.

"Oh, we're not going to miss that picnic. Anytime that we have a chance to celebrate our ancestry, we will. I don't care what my mother says."

I snorted quietly because I figured that Ms. Constance would have tried to stop William from celebrating the Juneteenth holiday.

William kept up the conversation until we reached a large waiting area. I saw Aunt Pearl and Clyde in the corner with their heads bent low. They looked up when we stopped. Aunt Pearl shot out of her chair. My father followed at a slower pace. Neither of them greeted me. I chalked it up to grief and worry.

"Dr. William. How is Mother?"

William pulled the chart to his chest and looked down at Aunt Pearl and Clyde.

"Ms. Pearl, Mr. Clyde. Your mother scared us for a while, but with rehabilitation, she should be fine. She won't function like she did before, but she'll live. You can see her whenever you're ready, but one at a time."

Aunt Pearl collapsed against William's chest in relieved sobs. Clyde thanked William and pulled my aunt from him. They walked back to their seats. I started to go over and offer my comfort, but there was something that I had to do first. I looked up at William with a bright smile. He looked surprised for a moment before he returned it. Gotcha.

"William, could you stay with my family while I visit my grandmother?"

I felt bad that I used my womanly wiles on William, but I needed to get to Betts without interference. William nodded and walked over to Aunt Pearl and Clyde. When he sat down and begin to speak to them, I hurried to the nurse's station and asked for Betts' room. The friendly Black nurse pointed to the last door on the left. I thanked her and almost ran to the room.

The sounds of machines and monitors greeted me when I entered the room. Betts lay in the center of them with tubes in her arms. I walked closer to see that her skin looked scaly with an orange tint. Now, she looks like the snake that she is, I thought to myself. I waited for the guilt or remorse to hit me, but it didn't. I stepped closer to the bed and tapped Betts' cheek with my finger. One of her eyes popped open while the other looked stuck. I leaned over the good eye so that she could see me. I could see when she recognized me, and fear soon replaced the recognition. I felt the malevolent smile curve my full lips. Yes, I liked seeing Betts this way.

"Hello, Betts. Well, well, I guess you escaped Death this time. It must be all the evil in you, Grandmother."

Betts eye widened at my statement. I chuckled low and glanced at the closed door.

"Yes, I called you Grandmother, but maybe I should call you Demon because that's what you are."

Betts' eye narrowed, and I felt the anger and hate in her glare. I grinned at the puny push of evil.

"I guess you don't have it like you used to, huh, Betts? You know, I used to be deathly afraid of you and that little room of yours. I'd pray and pray that you wouldn't come get me in my sleep. I never forgot what you did to me, Betts. I've forgiven you, but I've never forgotten."

Betts' tried to move her lips, but she could only utter a grunt. I shook my head at her.

"No, Betts. I will have my say, and you can only sit here and listen."

Betts narrowed her eye at me again and I saw that she tried to reach for the call button. I reached over and moved it away from her. I held it in front of her face with a wicked smile.

"Is this what you want? Well, you told me once that we can't always have what we want. Remember, Betts? It was my wedding day, and I'd caught Harlan and Shirley conspiring against me. You used my weakness to try to make me like you. I used your voodoo ways to bind that hateful, horrible man to me, Betts. I could have been happy with the love of my life, but your evil and my stupidity kept me from it. My children and I lived through terror until Harlan's own evil took root and freed me. Ha! You tried to stop me from ending this family curse, but you didn't. The darkness will end with my child, Betts. You are nothing to me now, and I'll pray for your miserable soul. Too bad that you can't speak to repent for your black sins."

"Victoria! What are you doing?"

I whipped around and saw William's pale face in the doorway. I'd been so wrapped up in telling Betts my mind that I hadn't heard the door open or the machine beeping wildly. I stepped away from the bed, but not before I saw the malevolent glee in Betts face. William hurried to the bed and took off his stethoscope to examine Betts. I moved toward the door to leave.

"No, Victoria. I want to speak with you. Now," William snapped.

I cringed at his tone. I watched while he tended Betts and pulled a syringe out of his pocket. He murmured something to Betts as he injected the IV. I saw Betts eye close and knew that she slept. William turned toward me with thunder in his eyes.

"She'll sleep well with the medicine, and she probably won't remember what you said. I, however, cannot forget it. What is wrong with you, Victoria? How could you use me to keep your father and aunt occupied while you terrorized their mother? And, the things that you said to her? Are they true?

Did you use voodoo on Harlan? Were you so superstitious that you used that as the reason why you denied our love after Victor's death? Well?"

In his anger and hurt, William grabbed my arms and shook me. I pushed against his strength. He let go of me with one hand to grip my chin. I tried to avoid his eyes, but he held me still. My own temper began to push its way into my mind at his heavy-handed treatment. I returned his glare and let my anger loose on him.

"Yes, William, in a moment of weakness, I allowed my grandmother's evil ways to cloud my judgment. I used voodoo to bind Harlan to me. It is not superstition. When I came that summer, I wanted to escape Harlan's abuse of my children and I. Victor's life and death brought us together, but for what? I wanted to leave with you, but not at the expense of my life or my children's."

William's eyes filled with disbelief and tears. My heart ached at his pain, and I twisted my head to glare at Betts. A sob escaped my throat as years of pain and torment crashed into me. I pointed at the bed.

"Betts is the cause of it all! She is the reason why my parents hated me! She is the reason why they beat me and put me to work as a child! She is the reason why I stayed married to that monster!"

William tried to hug me, and I broke loose from his touch. My fury unleashed on him.

"I loved you, William! I loved you from the time that I was a young girl, but you left me! You rejected me to live a White lie! Now, you sit here trying to judge me for exacting my revenge on Betts? Give me a break!"

Tears fell from William's beautiful blue eyes. I saw my anger reflected in them. I wiped a hand down my face and stepped back from him. William glanced toward the bed and turned a frown on me.

"Your grandmother isn't responsible for your mistakes or mine. You chose to stay with Harlan because of a stupid "voodoo" curse. You chose to have three more children with him. Those are your choices, Victoria."

My mouth opened and closed while I tried to absorb the shock of William's words. I decided not to respond and pressed my lips together. William's face told me that he knew that he'd hurt me, but he remained silent. He stepped around me and opened the door. I didn't turn around even when I felt a light touch on my back.

"I love you, Victoria. I always will. I know that you love me too. I thought that we could forget the past and make a life together, but I guess there's too much water under the bridge for now. I'll give you some time to sort out what you want to do about it."

The soft swish when the door closed echoed deep inside my heart. Wait, how did William know I'd only had three more children with Harlan?

8

I returned to the waiting area to find both of my aunts, Hallie and Pearl, with my father. One look at my face told them that the worst had happened to Betts. I smiled weakly and reassured them that she lived and would be fine. Aunt Pearl said that she would visit her next and left the room. Clyde left to smoke a cigarette, and Aunt Hallie sat down next to me when I sat down in the nearest chair. She smiled and patted my hand.

"See, I knew you were really upset this morning. It must have been the shock talking. Pearl and Clyde said that Dr. William took good care of Mama and that she's going to be all right now."

Numb and hurt, I nodded absentmindedly while Aunt Hallie rambled. Suddenly, I heard an overhead announcement. I sat up with a feeling of dread.

"Incoming ambulance! Available OR Nurses to the ER, Stat!"

Aunt Hallie squeezed my hand.

"Oh, my, I'm glad that wasn't for Mama."

I began to feel a chill as if someone turned the air conditioner to full blast. Aunt Hallie shot me a strange look.

"Are you alright, Victoria?"

I tried to say 'yes, ma'am', but my teeth chattered. Aunt Hallie made a noise and got up to ask the nurse for a blanket. The nurse became concerned and handed Aunt Hallie the blanket while she picked up the ringing phone. Aunt Hallie placed it on my shoulders, but I still felt cold. The sound of running feet made me look up to see my mother hurry towards us. I knew then that something was terribly wrong. I dropped the blanket and met Tess halfway. She grabbed my arms and started to pull me.

"Victoria! Come with me now. Valora is sick. Leah and Gia came home after you left. I was in the kitchen when I heard Valora scream in pain. She started to vomit and hold her stomach. I called the ambulance right away. Victoria! Snap out of it! Come with me now!"

I walked on lead feet while Tess spoke. Valora's sick? She can't be sick. She was just at home with Grayson digging up plants and worms. I felt Tess pull harder and I almost tripped. She stopped and turned around with a frown.

"Victoria!"

Slap!

I reeled from my mother's hard slap across my face. I stared at her for a moment and felt her impatience. Her panic sunk in quickly. My pumpkin was sick! I nodded and followed Tess down another hallway. The urgent need to be with my baby took over, and I began to run. Tess slowed down and shouted where to go. I nodded and turned the corner to the emergency room waiting area. Grayson, Leah, and Gia sat against the wall. Grayson and Leah were in tears. Gia looked smug and satisfied. I wanted to slap her, but I had to get to Valora. I told the children to stay put and went through the double doors. A White nurse stopped me as soon as I'd stepped through them.

"Excuse me, ma'am. You're not allowed back here."

A faded memory of Victor's time in this hospital crossed my mind, and I shook my head at the nurse.

"I apologize, however, I've been told that my daughter is here. I want to see her now."

The nurse's face held sympathy and understanding. I avoided looking at her because I didn't want to know why she looked at me that way. She took my arm and guided me down a short hallway where I could hear Valora cry and scream. I breathed a sigh of relief. She was alive! The nurse took me around the corner to an observation room. I could see Valora's face and writhing body on a table surrounded my nurses and a doctor. Terror filled my heart, and I wanted to be with my baby. I turned on the nurse beside me. I felt my hands itch to scratch the patronizing look off of her face. I decided to use the knowledge that working at William's practice gave me.

"I want to be with her. I am her mother, and I did not approve any treatment."

The nurse, whose name badge said Sarah Smith, offered me another look of condescension and shook her head.

"I'm sorry, ma'am. You can't go in there until the doctor has finished his exam. I'll say it will go faster if she stops fighting."

A memory of a dental hygienist who said the same thing crossed my mind. I shook it free as another scream of pain escaped my Valora's lips. My heart dropped when silence followed the scream. I turned and threw my hands against the cold glass to see the doctor leave her side. I stepped into his path when he came through the door.

"Doctor, that's my child in there. What is going on? Why is she quiet? I want to see her. Now," I demanded.

The short White doctor sighed and held up his hand. I frowned with impatience.

"I'm Dr. Clark, and you daughter seems to have acute appendicitis from my examination. I need to operate as soon as possible. I've given her something for the pain and to help us finish checking her. One of the nurses will be out in a moment to get your consent for the surgery."

Shock ran through my body that Valora needed surgery. My poor baby would be cut open and in pain for weeks. No, it couldn't have been her appendix. She'd been fine with no stomach ache or fever. I touched Dr. Clark's arm when he turned to leave. He glanced at me in frustration.

"Yes? Your daughter doesn't have time for more questions, ma'am. I need to get prepped for the OR."

I frowned at his haste. I put my hands on my hips and pointed toward my baby girl.

"I apologize, Dr. Clark, if the shock of seeing my child on a table surrounded by nurses and a doctor that I don't know anything about, is too much for me. Valora has been fine all day with no pain or fever. I do know that much. Please do not think that I'm not educated to know as a mother when my child is ill."

Dr. Clark narrowed his eyes at my sarcasm, but I wasn't through with him.

"Furthermore, I'd like a second opinion before you open my child up because you think that she has appendicitis. What if you're wrong?"

The short White doctor puffed up his chest in anger, but I held up my hand to stall his ire.

"I meant no offense, Dr. Clark, but I don't want to put my daughter through any more pain."

"And you shouldn't have to."

I spun around to see William's grim face glaring at Dr. Clark. I glance to see that Dr. Clark seemed to shrink in William's presence. Heck, even I wanted to melt away at the thunderous look on William's face. I watched as he took the chart from Dr. Clark's hand and scanned it. The scowl that he turned on the short doctor became even fiercer.

"Jonathan, this isn't appendicitis. She presented with no fever or swelling, only pain. There's no nausea or vomiting either. You would have cut open that child for nothing. Your inexperience would have cost this hospital thousands."

Dr. Clark seemed to find his courage and glowered at William's rejection of his assessment.

"Now, see here, William, you know that I could be right."

William placed his hand on Dr. Clark's shoulder. I watched as the short doctor winced when William squeezed.

"Could be right and being right are too different things, Jonathan. Her mother just asked for a second opinion, and I'm going to give it to her after I examine Valora."

William let go of Dr. Clark and went into the emergency exam room. Dr. Clark glared at Nurse Sarah. She looked stunned at the exchange between William and Dr. Clark.

"Go prepare the surgery consents. He's going to see that I'm right."

Nurse Sarah looked at me sideways while she hurried to do Dr. Clark's bidding. I turned toward the glass window and watched William gently touch Valora's tummy. Dr. Clark reached up on the wall and pressed a button. All of a sudden, we could hear everything in the exam room. I smiled to hear William speak in a light singsong voice.

"Valora? Valora? Or perhaps you'll wake up to, Princess Valora? Remember that game that we played with Grayson last week. Yes, I'll bet you do. He and I were so busy fighting monsters that we almost forgot you in the tree. You were so angry. Well, not as angry as your mother when she found out that you'd been in a tree all afternoon."

William chuckled, and I smiled at the memory. William looked up and waved me into the room. I shook my head and pointed to the nurses in the room. William nodded and sat on the stool by the bed. I swiped at the tears that flowed down my cheeks. I saw Dr. Clark roll his eyes in the reflection of the glass. I turned and frowned at him. He returned my scowl and turned back to the room. I followed suit when I heard Valora's small husky voice.

"Dr. William? Where's Mama?"

William brought Valora's hand to his mouth and kissed it. He nodded and laughed.

"Yes, it's me, sweetheart. I came as soon as I heard the nurses talking about how beautiful you are and that you were really sick. Your Mama is in the other room, and she'll be here soon to see you, but I have to make sure that you're okay so she won't whip me."

Valora's head shifted in a tiny nod. She didn't even respond to William's attempt at humor. She looked to be falling back to sleep. William patted her cheek.

"No, Valora, you have to stay awake because I have to ask you some questions. Okay, sweetheart?"

I saw Valora nod again. William's chest moved in a loud breath. Dr. Clark harrumphed. Worry and fear fueled my anger. I whipped around and glared at him.

"Dr. Clark, don't you have something else to do? I'm sure that you have other patients. You need to see to them because my daughter will not be your patient today. Thank you for everything that you have done. Have a blessed day."

Dr. Clark looked fit to be tied. He clenched his fists and leaned close, but he didn't know that I knew how to handle that kind of intimidation. I smiled and turned my back to him. I heard him grumble something and leave. I let out a pent up sigh of relief, but it was short-lived when I heard Valora answer one of William's questions.

"Valora, I don't think that I heard you correctly. Please say it again."

"I ate sour grass today with Grayson, and then we played in the old tree. I dug up three grubs for us to fish tomorrow. Grayson went to get some dirt from the shed to keep them damp when Gia and Leah came home. Leah went in the house, but Gia came to play with me."

Valora's voice faded into a sob. She grabbed her stomach with both of her small hands. William shushed her and nodded to the nurse. Valora saw the needle and screamed. She began to fight, but William raised her up and held her still while the nurse gave her the shot. I clenched my hands to keep from running into the room. I didn't want to distract Valora from her story. William patted her back until she calmed down to hiccups. He gently put her back down on the narrow bed and beckoned the nurse to him. He whispered something in her ear, she nodded, and left the room. I barely acknowledged her when she passed me. I kept my eyes on that room. William smiled at Valora.

"Now, I'm sorry that the shot hurt, but it doesn't hurt that much anymore, does it?"

Valora shook her head, but she gave William a wary look. William chuckled.

"I'm really sorry, Princess Valora. Can you finish telling me your story now?"

I unclenched my hands and tried to control my emotions. Disbelief, anger, and then rage filled me as Valora finished her story. William's face echoed how I felt.

"Gia brought me some little bottles and a plate to play kitchen. She even helped me make it into soup. It smelled like Mama's food, so I tasted it. She said if I dipped the china berries in it that it would taste like salt and plums. I ate some, but it didn't taste like salt and plums, Dr. William. After that, my tummy started to hurt really bad."

William nodded and gathered her into his arms. He turned and told the other two nurses who'd listened to Valora's story as well to leave the room. When they'd passed me with sympathetic glances, I went into the room with as big a smile on my face as I could muster. Valora saw me, and her face lit up with a smile. I rushed to the table to hug her before she could see my tears. I wanted to squeeze her, but I was afraid to cause her more pain. William saw the tears and handed me a tissue behind Valora's back. I smiled my thanks, but he just nodded. I closed my eyes and held on to Valora to deal with the pain of William's distance.

When I'd gathered myself together, I gently laid Valora down on the bed. I lifted my chin and faced William.

"Can you help her, William?"

I'd whispered my question because Valora's slept. William turned his back and remained quiet. I frowned at his backside and wanted to kick it. I took a deep breath to calm my scattered wits and my rising anger. It would not help my baby if I lost what little temper that I had left. I touched his rigid back.

"William, please. I know that we are at odds, but this is for my daughter's sake."

William whipped around with his blue eyes blazed with anger. I stepped away and waited warily. It only took a moment.

"Did you really think that I wouldn't take care of Valora because I'm angry with you? Surely, you can't think that of me, Victoria. She's been poisoned, and I sent the nurse for the charcoal pills and the tubes. I'm going to have to empty her stomach and put the pills down the tubes because she won't be able to swallow them. That should take care of whatever she ate."

Relieved, I plopped down on the stool and leaned my head against Valora's arm. I felt guilty for thinking that William wouldn't take care of Valora. Of course, he would. He loved her. I closed my eyes and said a prayer of thanks. William's hand on my arm brought my head around to look into his angry gaze. I frowned in question. He beckoned me the corner. I rose slowly and followed him. I wanted to know why he was still so angry. I stopped before I came too close.

"Do you know that if I hadn't been here or seen this before, that fresh out of med residency doctor would have butchered Valora? Victoria, why have you allowed Gia's behavior to almost kill her sister? We could have lost her like we lost..."

William's voice faded when he almost mentioned Victor. My beloved baby boy had died in this very hospital. I felt the familiar ache and rubbed my chest like a physical pain. I saw the remorse replace the anger in William's eyes, but it only brought out my fury. How dare he question me, and the way that I raised my children? I stepped closer to William and pointed my finger at him.

"Don't you think that I'm glad that you came when you did to save my baby, William? What do you want a bucket of gratitude? Well, I only have a handful right now because your highhanded manner questioning of my motherhood doesn't sit well with me. For you information, I usually don't leave Gia alone with Valora. I know that she's jealous and bitter with her own sister, but how I deal with it is none of your concern now. You made that choice in Betts' room an hour ago. What would you know about children anyway? You don't have any."

William's head snapped back and his eyes filled with hurt as I spoke. I immediately regretted what I'd said. William's eyes glazed with the unshed tears, and he pressed his lips together. He nodded and bowed to me. I reached out for his sleeve. He evaded my touch and stepped to the hospital bed. He stroked Valora's brow and spoke.

"It just keeps getting worse, doesn't it, Victoria? I throw a rock, you throw a bigger one and vice versa. I don't want to be this way, and I know that you don't either. It's a mystery to me as to how we got like this."

I wanted to tell him that it was Betts' evil. I just couldn't open my mouth to say it and hear his denial that it existed. I remained quiet and watched while he fiddled with Valora's blankets.

"I'm going to tell you something that I've never told anyone else, Victoria. About seven years ago, after my wife died, I wanted a child very badly. We tried before she passed away, but nothing happened. I thought about marriage again, but I didn't want to try to love someone else when I still loved you so much. I thought that perhaps it was my punishment for rejecting you when we were young. Anyway, the urge to have a son or daughter became worse when I'd go to the parks or pass a school. It became so bad that a colleague of mine took pity on me and told me about a friend of his that needed smart professional men for some tests. He said that it would give me something to do to keep my mind off of children, so I went to an office in downtown Dallas."

Something in William's tone made my heart began to beat faster. I waited until he was ready to speak again. He didn't keep me waiting long.

"It turned out to be an experiment to test for fertility. I took a few of the tests, and then I stopped going. I decided that maybe I was meant to take care of people instead of being a father. I vowed to never question God's path for me on the last day that I went to that place. I never returned and I never looked back."

My legs felt weak, and bees started to buzz in my head. Downtown Dallas? Fertility? William's words wound their way into my mind until I could almost see them. I looked from him to Valora and back again. Their hair was the same dark brown. They both had full lips like a bow. Cheekbones? Stubborn chin? William picked up Valora's hand to kiss it, and I grasped my throat! Even their hands looked the same? I reached out blindly in my shock and turned over the metal tray. William twisted around with a frown. When he saw my distress, he rushed to me and sat me in the chair in the corner. He pushed my head between my legs. I almost fought him, but the dizziness forced my eyes closed. I shivered until he leaned closer. His body heat kept the shock at bay. William clicked his tongue.

"Victoria, you'll make yourself sick if you don't take better care of yourself. I'm sorry if I upset you. I just wanted you to know how lucky that you were to have children. I also apologize if I stepped over the line. I didn't mean to question the way that you raised the children. They're good kids, Victoria. My concern for Valora is my only excuse."

I couldn't answer to tell William that I forgave him. I needed time to think about his revelation and if it was true.

William sighed at my silence. I heard the door open.

"Is Mrs. Sams alright, Dr. Herbert?"

William stepped away from me. I felt lost without his warmth. I caught myself from making a sound of protest. William took another step to the bed and touched Valora gently on the cheek.

"She will be, Claudia. Please assist her to the waiting area. Here comes Rena with the charcoal pills and tubes."

Claudia strode across the room and helped me to stand. William nodded in my direction but didn't turn from Valora. I didn't want to leave her even with William.

"William, can I stay? I know it's going to be rough, but I want her to know that I'm here."

"It will be bad, Victoria, but in the end it's going to be all right."

9

"Vicky, did you see what Nina had on today? I swear that she thinks she's so much better than the rest of us. Mama told me that Aunt Pearl said that Nina has a new job at the hospital in Tharkin."

I barely listened to my cousin Belle talk about our other cousin, Nina. Aunt Hallie and Belle offered me a ride to town to buy groceries since the old Plymouth gave out last month. I didn't have enough money for another car since I'd quit working at the home health agency last year. I stared out of the window and contemplated my situation.

The kids and I lived off of the stipend from Aunt Alice's estate. Sometimes that wasn't enough to get by so I applied for government assistance. I had pride but not when it came to my children. Valora, Grayson, and Leah were all that I had left at home. Mark and Willie enlisted in the Army because there just wasn't enough work for young Black men in the area. Willie went right after he graduated. It took Mark a while before he decided the Army was the best way to go. Even though, he'd graduated from the truck driving school three years ago, there wasn't anywhere that paid him for his education or experience.

The sad part was that everywhere I looked around in the country town of Carson, there weren't good jobs for most Black people. Period. I'd looked for myself after I'd quit William's practice, but there was nothing. William. My mind stopped on his face. My heart sunk when I thought about how much I still loved him. His letters told me how much he still loved me too. I tried to shake the thoughts away and pay attention to Belle, but the memories of that awful summer rushed in like a flash flood.

After William knew that Valora would be fine, he walked out of the hospital. He closed his practice and accepted another job in Dallas within two weeks. I hadn't known he'd left until I received his first letter in the mail. I'd looked at it so much that I could still see William's black scrawl on the heavy stationery:

My Dear Victoria,

What can I possibly say that will make us right again? So many things have crossed my mind at how we went down the wrong path, but none of them felt like they were the cause. I am so sorry if I hurt you in any way because that is not how I want to love you. I knew it would be difficult for us, but I thought that our strength was more than the obstacles. I still think that it is, but I also feel like we have to build a good foundation to find our way back to each other. I know that we will because I have faith in you, Victoria. I have faith in us, and that this time and distance will make us stronger.

As you probably know, I've closed the practice and accepted a Chief of Neurology job at Great Hope Hospital in Dallas. I've hired Sarah Smith to take care of Father and Mother.

I don't want you to think that I've abandoned you or the children. It's just that I can't be around you and the children and not be a part of your lives. Please tell Valora that I will miss her and that I love her. She is a very special little girl. All of your children are special. I'll miss them all.

    Please know that I love you, Victoria, and I always will.

    William

"Vicky?"

I blinked away the sting of tears and turned my head to see Belle frown into the backseat. I blinked again and drew upon my patience.

"I'm sorry, Belle. I was thinking about what I need to buy at the store."

Belle nodded with exaggerated understanding and turned around to look at a quiet Aunt Hallie.

"Mama? Since Aunt Pearl helped Nina get that new house built, we should build onto our house. We need more space anyway."

I rolled my eyes at the back of Belle's head. I never understood why she needed to one-up anyone in the family who got something that she didn't. I wanted to tell her so bad that we were all in the same boat. I sighed and looked out of the window as Carson came into view.

When I walked out of the store, I saw my daddy's El Camino in a front parking space. He leaned against it smoking a cigarette. I glanced around and saw that Aunt Hallie's Ford was gone. Clyde saw my impatient look and grinned. He threw the cigarette to the ground and stomped it.

"Your Aunt Hallie saw me at the gas station and asked if I could take you home. Something about you were acting funny in the car to Belle. I don't cotton to Indian giving, so I'm glad that I came back from Greensdale to see Mama. Otherwise, you might be pushing that cart all the way to Allsville."

Clyde chuckled. I rolled my eyes and nodded at my aunt's whimsy. I'd deal with that another day. I was more tired than usual, so I let Clyde take the cart of groceries and load it into his car. I got in and almost choked on the smell of cigarettes and cologne. My daddy got in the car and started it up without another word. I was still apprehensive around him. I decided to let him speak first if he wanted to keep up conversation. Apparently, he did.

"Victoria, Tess told me that it hasn't been going well since the older boys left for the military. She said that your big gal don't help you with the house or chores. If it were me, she'd feel the end of a belt because she needs to be helping you. You could have one of those spells like you had last year when your baby girl found you. It's not right."

I slowly turned my head to stare at Clyde in disbelief. He was concerned and giving me advice on whipping my children? Anger sparked with the memory of his "discipline".

"In all respect, Daddy, I'm not you. I don't want to beat my children into submission. I helped from the time that I was seven and still felt the end of your belt. I won't have my children cowered like I was. You had no right to treat me like that, and I swore a long time ago that I would never treat my own children like you and Mama treated me."

Clyde stayed quiet after I spoke my piece. I wished that he'd drive faster so that I could just get away from him. I began to scoot closer to the door when he cleared his throat.

"You're right, Victoria. You are right. I had no business treating my own flesh and blood the way that I treated you. It wasn't your fault that God saw fit to test my mettle. I failed. I failed badly when it came to you, Victoria," he said thickly.

I shook my head and stared out of the window. His apology seemed sincere, but I didn't understand what good that he thought it could do now. I pressed my lips together and kept my eyes on the passing scenery. I jumped when he cleared his throat again.

"Before Mama had her stroke a few years back, I had no plans to leave Allsville or Carson. Then one day, I woke up and Tess looked like a stranger to me. Terror filled my heart because I felt like I didn't know the woman who I'd married and had children. I was lost and didn't understand why. I tried to find my feelings for her, but I couldn't. Every day was torture to live with her. I felt stifled, so I told your mama how I felt. She surprised me and said that she'd felt the same way! I almost couldn't believe it. We came to an understanding that we'd stay married, but I would leave to figure myself out without Mama and Daddy. I made my peace with Marcos. Then, I wondered around for a bit until I came across this piece of land in Greensdale. It didn't take long for me to know that I needed to use the money that Mama gave me from the sale of the back ten of the ranch to buy my own land. I put a trailer on it and made a life for myself. The only thing that keeps me tied to Allsville is my family, Victoria."

Clyde reached out and grabbed my hand before I could move it from the seat. I held it stiffly while he squeezed it. He let it go and laughed.

"I don't blame you for being cautious. I'd be wary of me too."

I almost laughed with him. I relaxed and changed the subject.

"Marcos is teaching Valora Spanish. She goes fishing with Grayson, and they always end up at Marcos' house. He says that she's very good, but she can't practice at home because no one else speaks it."

Clyde chuckled.

"She's a bright one that baby girl of yours. I haven't seen her in a month of Sundays. I've got a tackle box full of fishing stuff for Grayson. Tess told me that he liked to fish. He'll be able to catch a mess of channel cats with these lures."

I smiled and nodded. Clyde stayed quiet for the rest of the trip home while I wondered what could have caused him to change.

The phone rang early the next morning. It wasn't time for the children to get up for school, so I grabbed it off the hook. I peeked back to see if Valora awakened, but she rolled over on her side.

"Hello?"

"Victoria! Victoria! Betts is dying! You have to come!"

I cringed away from the hysterical screeches coming from my cousin, Belle. I raised up and pulled my robe from the bottom of the bed. The room was cold when the stove died down, so I grabbed another short quilt to wrap around me. I took the phone through to the living room and sat my aching body into my easy chair.

"Belle, you have to calm down. You know that I don't have a car. It's going to be all right. Betts has been sick for a long time."

"Mama said that you wouldn't care!"

Belle began to cry in earnest at her perception of my feelings. She became incoherent in her ramblings and shouts. I stayed quiet so as not to antagonize her, but it was so hard. If this was a movie, I could just slap her a few times, I thought to myself and immediately felt guilty.

Belle's cries and tear slinging grated on my nerves after a few minutes. I waited patiently for her to collect herself. Finally, her cries reduced to sniffles.

"I'm calm now, Vicky, but you need to stop being so heartless. Betts is our grandmother. I'll come by in a half hour to pick you up on my way to be with Mama."

I stared at the phone after my cousin disconnected. She had some nerve, and she wondered why most of the family didn't come to Aunt Hallie's house. I shook my head and got up out of the chair to see that Valora stood in the doorway. I smiled and limped over to her. She looked at me with concern.

"Are you okay, Mama? Can I get your footies and help you put them on?"

My smile widened into a chuckle.

"It's 'May I' not 'Can I', pumpkin. I'm fine. I just get sore like this on the cold days, remember? Now, it's time to start getting ready for school. Can you go wake up your brother and sister?"

Valora smiled and ran through the curtain to the rest of the house. I smiled with pride at how she'd conquered her fear of the dark. She was such a special girl. She'd been sorely tested by Gia before she'd left to live with Tess. The ache in my hand felt similar to when I'd slapped the mess out of Gia when I caught her telling Valora that she hated her. I could almost see Valora's light dim at Gia's spiteful words. Grayson and I worked hard to bring Valora's loving nature back. I'd been so grateful to Grayson because he'd heard what Gia said too, and he'd taken Valora fishing right after I'd slapped Gia. He was so like Mark.

It didn't help that her fourth grade teacher, Ms. Hamilton, tried to crush her lively spirit and bright intelligence. After our parent-teacher conference, I don't think that Ms. Hamilton will ever try to reign in Valora's talents or any other child's ever again.

I broke out of my meanderings when I heard the children move around to get ready for school. I looked at the clock to see that Belle would be outside soon. I dragged my sore bones through the heavy curtain to my room. I laid out Valora's clothes and pulled some jeans and a sweatshirt out of the drawer for me. I barely glanced at Valora when she came into the room with her damp towel.

"Pumpkin, I've got to go with Cousin Belle this morning. Your great-grandmother, Betts, is really sick. Let me look at your hair. Yes, it looks fine. Your clothes are on the bed. If you get ready now, you can go in the living room and have a short nap before the bus comes, okay?"

"Is Betts going to die, Mama?"

I stopped and turned to see that Valora sat on the side of the bed with her head cocked to the side in question. I didn't want to lie to her. Besides, Valora would know.

"Yes, she is going to die, but we don't know when. Only Father God knows when people are going to die."

Valora nodded and pulled on her shirt and jeans. We got ready in silence until Valora made a noise and went still where she stood. Alarmed, I limped the few steps to her and grabbed her arms. Her face looked blank and her eyes glazed.

"Valora? Valora? Can you hear me, Pumpkin? What's wrong?"

She remained still and quiet. Frustrated and worried, I snapped my fingers in her face. She didn't blink. I tapped her cheeks. She didn't move. I shook her, and her head bobbed back and forth. Nothing.

"Valora!"

I shouted right into her face. I heard the sound of running footsteps.

"Mama? Are you okay? What's wrong with Valora?"

Grayson's deep voice echoed in the quiet room. His concern washed through me. I pulled Valora to me and hugged her. I hugged her and murmured that I loved her. After a few moments, her body softened. She shook her head and began to cry. My heart ached at her sobs. I held her until she quieted. I heard a honk outside, but I ignored it. My daughter was more important. I pulled her away from me and raised her face to mine with my finger under her chin.

"Pumpkin, tell Mama what happened? Why do you cry?"

Valora's lip trembled, but I watched as she brought herself under control.

"I put on my shoe and stood up. All of a sudden, I felt cold. Then, I was in another place. It looked like Aunt Pearl's den. I sat on the floor playing with Diana when Betts asked for a kiss. I thought that she was talking to me, so I got up to give her one. She grabbed me with a hand that looked like a claw and said, 'No, not you! You are my death!' I was scared so I pulled away, but she grabbed me. I screamed and Diana tried to help me. It was when a tall man in Black with a Black hat passed by the window and grabbed Betts that she let me go. It was so scary, Mama!"

Valora leaned into me, and I grabbed her into a tight hug. Betts had the power to torment even on her deathbed. I'd have to thank the schoolteacher when I next saw him venture past Tess'.

Valora's visions weren't a surprise to us anymore. If it hadn't been for one of her visions, I would have laid on the floor in a sick spell for a lot longer than I did last summer. I just prayed that she kept them quiet like I told her to while she was at school. I patted Valora's back and let her go. I looked up at Grayson and Leah's shadowed faces in the sunrise from the window.

"Belle is waiting for me outside. I want y'all to finish getting ready for school. Valora, since you're already ready, go sit on the sofa with your book bag. Grayson, I know that you have basketball practice, but I'm going to need you home. Leah, go ahead and go to work at the Dawson's. I'll have someone fetch you if we need you. All right, I'll see y'all later."

I hugged Valora and patted the other children on the back. Belle's honk sounded again in impatience when I walked through the door. The beam of her headlights almost caused me to trip over our dog, Sam. He sent me an injured look and went back to sleep. I knew that he waited on Valora to run around with him before school. I hoped that she skipped it today.

I felt each jarring step deep in my bones. I gritted my teeth and reminded myself that Betts was my grandmother. As I limped to the car, I prayed that Belle didn't feel the wrath from my pain. I opened the car door and sat down slowly. I could hear Belle's sigh of frustration.

"What took you so long? I told you that I'd be here in half the hour. It don't take that long to get ready, does it? I'm sure that the kids can get themselves together for school. And why are you limping? Are you having one of those sick spells again?"

I waited until Belle finished her questions before I began to answer, but my pain kept me silent. She turned the car onto the highway and put the metal to the pedal. I grabbed the strap and the seat belt to keep from moving around and aggravating my pain. Belle slowed down once we got past Lee's Grocery. I released my grip on the strap and rubbed the welt in my hand. I sent Belle an annoyed look. She glanced at me and laughed. I guess she remembered our purpose because she sobered quickly.

"You'll be fine, Victoria. Betts won't. Now, are you going to answer me or keep acting funny?"

I rolled my eyes in the early morning darkness. I loved my cousin, but sometimes, I wanted to just pinch her lips closed. I sighed and looked out of the windshield.

"I think that I am having a sick spell because I'm sore all the way down to my bones. I have a doctor's appointment next week. I hope they figure it out and fix it before it gets worse. It always takes me awhile in the wintertime to get my blood pumping. I guess it took a little longer this morning."

I shrugged, and Belle nodded. I sat back and thought about how I'd left out Valora's vision. I didn't want Belle to start in with any foolishness about it. Anyway, it's probably best to keep that information quiet. No one knew anyway except Grayson, Leah, Gia, and me. At least, that's what I hoped. I listened to Belle talk about our other cousin Nina. I sighed again because I had grown tired of the mess and drama between our families. I said a prayer that one day, it would be a thing of the past.

We got to Carson General Hospital to find most of the family in the waiting room. Clyde, Aunt Pearl, and Aunt Hallie sat on one side while Uncle Dean and Uncle Frank sat across from them. I looked at my uncles and realized that I didn't know very much about them. They'd been away in the Army for most of my life. If they hadn't looked like Clyde and my aunts, I would have thought that they were strangers.

Belle and I greeted everyone and found seats in the corner. I waved at Nina when she walked in with a tray of coffee and doughnuts. She smiled and beckoned towards the tray. Grateful for the breakfast, I nodded. She came over to where we sat and offered us the food. I grabbed a steaming cup and two donuts. Belle took a donut.

"Hey, Vicky, Belle, when I take this tray back, can I sit with y'all? I don't want to disturb the brothers and sisters."

She nodded toward my father and his siblings. I smiled and gestured to the chair beside me.

"Of course, Nina. You're more than welcome."

Nina grinned and left with the empty tray.

"Why did you do that? Now, she's going to want to talk about how much her life is better than ours."

I whipped my head around and frowned at Belle. I wasn't going to have any mess right now.

"Belle, you don't know that. Besides, we are cousins and our children play together well. We should take a page from their book."

Belle huffed and sat back. Nina returned and sat down in the empty chair. We chatted for a spell until the doctor came in the room. Everyone stood. I recognized Dr. Clark even though he'd grown a beard. He recognized me too, but he ignored me and went straight to Aunt Pearl.

"It won't be long now. Your mother's organs have begun to shut down. I'm so sorry. Would you like to see her?"

Clyde and my uncles answered yes for Aunt Pearl and Aunt Hallie because they held each other in silent tears. Dr. Clark glanced at us in the corner and gave us a sympathetic look. I forced myself to keep from narrowing my eyes in surprise at his humanity after what he tried to do with Valora. He walked over to us and held out his hand to Nina.

"It will be all right for everyone to be in the room. I'm sure that your grandmother would want that. Please follow me."

Nina thanked him and looked back at us. I shrugged and we got up to follow our parents and their brothers to Betts' room. Aunt Pearl and Aunt Hallie hurried to the bed and began to cry and talk to Betts. I looked at her and felt a twinge of pity. She looked to be in a lot of pain. Dr. Clark took a syringe out of his pocket and injected it into Betts' IV. She seemed to relax a bit. I backed into the corner and let everyone else say their goodbyes. Aunt Hallie ran from the room with Belle rushing behind her. Uncle Dean and Uncle Frank kissed Betts' forehead and left. Clyde sat down in the chair beside the bed and Aunt Pearl took the one beside it. Tears ran down their faces as they gazed at their mother. Nina glanced at me and tilted her head toward Betts. I shook my head and gestured for her to go ahead. She walked to the bed and said a teary goodbye. She blew a kiss to her mother. Aunt Pearl's sob echoed through the room when she grabbed Betts hand. Clyde patted her back and drew her into his arm. I kept my surprise to myself because I'd never seen my father give such open love and comfort.

"Paul? Is that you?"

Betts raspy voice sounded loud in the room. I saw Clyde and Aunt Pearl lean towards her in shock.

"Paul? What do you mean I'm not going with you? You're still such a fool."

Betts' breathless tone sounded a little like her old hateful self.

Aunt Pearl stood up and leaned over her mother.

"Mama, Daddy isn't here. He's waiting in Heaven for you."

Betts' raised a claw-like hand and pointed towards me.

"Stupid gal. He's over there by that little witch. Don't you see him? He said I'm not going to Heaven."

Aunt Pearl and Clyde twisted to look my way. I stood still and felt for the warmth of my grandfather's presence. When tingles went down my arm, I knew that Betts spoke the truth. I looked at her in sympathy. He'd come to tell her that she wasn't going Home.

"Mama, there's no one in the corner but Vicky, and she loves you."

Betts began to cough. Aunt Pearl and Clyde leaned over and tried to pat her back. She reached up and grabbed Clyde.

"I'll be seeing you soon, son," she growled.

Clyde tore away from her grip and stumbled backwards in shock. I watched in shock as Betts turned her head and vomited black liquid. The stench was foul. I covered my nose and walked towards the door. Aunt Pearl's cry stopped me in my tracks. I turned to see the black sludge bubble as if it boiled. I followed the trail of bubbles to Betts open mouth and empty eyes. She was gone.

10

"Mrs. Sams?"

I opened my eyes to see the White OR nurse, Eve, bent over me. A wave a nausea hit me and I turned my head to vomit.

"Get me a wet towel. Stat," she ordered.

A moment later, I felt the wet warmth gliding across my mouth and face. I closed my eyes and leaned into it. I groaned when it went away. The nurse chuckled.

"I'm sorry to take it away, Mrs. Sams, but I've got to get you ready to go upstairs. Can you open your eyes for me again, please?"

I opened my eyes again and saw that the nurse held a vomit pan to my mouth. I glanced at her smiling face.

"Just in case."

I smiled back at her before my heavy eyelids drifted closed.

"She's going back to sleep, Eve. You need to keep her awake until the doctor get here."

I recognized the nasal voice of the pinched face, White nurse who'd dug into my arm to find a vein during pre-op.

"Shh, Liv. She's probably not all the way sleep. Besides, she's going to be in a lot of pain when she really wakes up from this surgery," Eve replied.

"I don't care. It's the doctor's orders, Eve. Besides, she acts like she's White throwing around big words and asking questions when I tried to get her ready for surgery. She acted like I really hurt her when I set her IV and threatened to tell my supervisor. I hate Black people like her!"

I heard Eve pause. I wanted to let that hussy, Liv, know that she did hurt me, and I didn't like people like her either. Sleep almost pulled me under, but I struggled to stay awake. I heard a movement and someone squeak. I barely raised one eye to see Eve holding Liv by the shoulders. Eve looked angry enough to spit nails.

"You listen here, you stupid witch, you are supposed to care for all patients the same no matter what color they are. This woman has been one of the best patients that I've had and I won't allow you to treat her badly because of her skin color or your insecurities at doing your job right. I can't believe that people still think like that, but I guess it's because I'm not from Texas."

Liv snatched away from Eve with an angry glare.

"Don't you ever put your hands on me again or I will report you."

Eve shrugged.

"If you ever mention that trash again about color or hurt another patient failing to set an IV correctly, I'll report you. Now, I've got to help my patient because I refuse to let her awaken in pain."

I slid my eye shut and frowned at the mention of pain. I was so tired of being in pain. I awoke everyday now in excruciating pain in my bones. I went from a cane to crutches, and the doctors in Tharkin told me that this exploratory surgery of my knee would help them to find out what was wrong with me. Anger at Nurse Liv almost pulled me from my drug laced sleep. Almost. I made a note to address her when I awoke.

Drowsiness came over me and I drifted off with a prayer that Nurse Eve was wrong about the pain.

"Mrs. Sams, we've looked at your bone samples and we're afraid that we don't have good news for you."

I looked up in pain and fear at Dr. Kelly and Dr. Ren. The shock must have shown on my face because Dr. Kelly took a quick step to the side of the bed and snapped his fingers in front of my face. I shuddered and shook my head. I leaned back on the pillows to show him that I was fine and took a deep breath of relief when he nodded and stepped back to his position at the bottom of the hospital bed. He gave Dr. Ren a superior look that I wanted to wipe off his face by telling him that his hands smelled like our dog, Old Sam's, butt. Insane laughter bubbled up but I quashed it quickly to listen to what the young doctors needed to tell me.

"Mrs. Sams, when we looked at your medical history, we saw several episodes of high fevers, bone and joint pain, and weakness. Old Dr. Herbert's diagnosis of rheumatic fever was correct, however, what he didn't know was that it correlates with rheumatoid arthritis. You have one of the worst cases that we have seen after looking at the scans, blood tests, and tissue samples from the surgery."

I barely heard the bad news because my heart ached at the mention of Dr. Herbert. He'd passed on the year before, and I'd been sick and unable to attend his services. He'd been good to me all of my life, and he'd been very vocal about William and I messing up his chances of having grandchildren. Tess told me that William left right after the service. He hadn't even come by the homestead. No, I didn't have time for that pain right now. I narrowed my eyes at the doctors to focus on them again, but a feeling of déjà vu came over me. Somehow, I knew that this illness was my path, so I'd bear the pain while I underwent treatment to get rid of it once and for all. I nodded to myself. Dr. Ren's voice petered out when he saw me nod. He glanced at Dr. Kelly and they turned a look of confusion on me. Dr. Kelly voiced his.

"Why are you nodding, Mrs. Sams? Are you okay?"

He looked like he would come to my side again, and I knew that my nose couldn't take that. I raised a shaky hand to stop him.

"Actually, Doctors, Old Dr. Herbert did know what would happen to me. I vaguely remember him telling my Aunt Charlotte when I was a girl. I am aware that this is severe whatever this rheumatoid arthritis stuff is. All I want to know about is the cure, and where I can get it."

Both of the doctors looked faces turned pale and they remained quiet. My stomach took a small dive.

"What is it? Please tell me. Am I going to die?"

Panic filled every inch of my body, and I wanted to yell at the young doctors of the injustice of my life. I clenched my hands and opened my mouth to do it when Dr. Kelly spoke.

"I'm sorry, Mrs. Sams."

Dr. Kelly paused and stepped closer to the bed with concern on his face. Fear crept into my throat. He dropped his head, glanced at Dr. Ren, and turned back to me.

"There is no cure for this type of arthritis, but we can give you pain management and therapy to help you stay limber. Unfortunately, this disease or disorder, however you want to look at it, it is aggressive."

A sharp pain pricked my hand. I looked down to see that my fingernails broke the skin from my grip. Dr. Kelly tsked at the tiny drop of blood and reached for the gauze on the shelf. He turned and blotted the spot for a moment. He avoided my gaze, but I didn't mind. The knot in my gut told me that there was more to this diagnosis. Dr. Kelly stood up straighter and held my hand.

"Ms. Sams, you will eventually lose the cartilage in your joints. After some time, you won't be able to walk at all."

Dr. Ren reached to the bedside table and handed me a tissue from the box. I looked at it and knew that there were tears ready to fall. I took the tissue but refused to wipe my eyes. These young doctors had to be wrong. There must be a cure. I would not be an invalid. I narrowed my eyes again at them. They looked to be fresh out of medical school and probably didn't know as much anyway.

"Thank you, Doctors. I know that you've done your best, but would you please tell the attending doctor to look at my chart? I mean no offense, however, this is a bit much to take in and I'd like someone with a little more expertise to ensure a correct diagnosis."

I smiled at them while I issued my request. I could see Dr. Kelly getting ready to puff out his chest, but Dr. Ren touched his arm and bowed his head to me.

"Yes, ma'am, you are entitled to a third opinion because between Dr. Kelly and myself, we are the first and second. I will ask Dr. Max, our attending supervisor, to look at your chart and come to visit you. I know that this is hard for you to digest right now, Mrs. Sams, but believe me, we have to move quickly to avoid further loss of movement."

I turned my head to the bland window curtain and nodded. I heard Dr. Kelly furiously whispering as he and Dr. Ren left the room. I looked at the closing door and for a moment, I thought that I saw myself in a wheelchair coming into the room. I blinked and the image was gone. I shook my head at the power of the pain pills and closed my eyes to escape the words of the doctors in my dreams.

"Mama, are you alright?"

I swung around on my crutches to see Valora come through my room curtain into the kitchen. I smiled at how my beautiful pumpkin was growing into a young lady. She stood at almost my height, but I knew that she would be an inch or so taller. Her face still carried the baby fat of youth, but the promise of her beauty showed through it. I raised my eyebrows when I took in her figure. My words of long ago stuck in my craw because her young body showed signs of budding maturity that I wasn't ready for at all. I made a mental note to talk to her about boys again. Her dark brown hair held red and blond highlights from the sun, but it was her eyes that caught my breath every time. They changed from light brown to hazel to green depending on her mood. Today, they were green and in the dim light of the kitchen, they seemed to glow. I shuddered as memories of a similar same glow squeezed my heart. No, I didn't have time to dwell on those thoughts.

I took a deep breath through my pain and smoothed a wayward strand of hair back into her ponytail. I clicked my tongue and shook my head at the dirt on her cheek. Valora loved the outdoors so much that I had to threaten her with a whipping to come inside most evenings. She smiled at my scolding.

"Aw, Mama, it's just a little dirt. I went spice hunting and found a mess of wild garlic, greens, and onions. We can have greens tonight!"

Valora pulled her treasure from behind her back like a magician and held it up for me to see. I laughed at her excitement, but it died a quick death when a lizard ran out of the greens and dropped to the floor. I squeaked and tried to move out of its way. The abrupt movement jarred my painful body and almost made me fall. I lashed out at Valora.

"Valora! That was the stupidest thing that you could have done! You know that I can't move that fast and it hurts like hell when I do! Why didn't you shake all that mess out first before you brought it in here?"

Valora looked hurt and disappointed at my dressing down. Guild flooded through me because I knew that what I said was unfair. I felt as bad as the day that I'd spanked her because she'd wanted to go to church and we couldn't find her shoe. I chalked it up to the pain and shifted on the crutches. I wanted to apologize but the words wouldn't form on my tongue.

Tears filled her eyes, but Valora looked down at the floor as she usually did when she became emotional. I knew that she wouldn't cry. She refused to show anyone that weakness and most times, she would get angry to avoid tears at home and at school.

Valora had a sense of justice and fairness that didn't sit well with some people. I'd tried to help her see that the world didn't work that way from my own trials, but she kept getting hurt, especially by the small-minded people of Carson. I prayed for God to help the people who hurt her feelings because instead of tears, they would get burned by her hot anger or frozen out with her silence. I stopped myself from rolling my eyes at memories of her confrontations in Carson. Even at her young age, she dealt with prejudice head on and sometimes refused to back down. I shook my head at her stubbornness. It never crossed my mind that she'd learned that from me.

I looked at her bowed head and turned away to avoid the emotions on my eleven year old daughter's face. I knew I wouldn't see anger or silence because of her love and respect for me. I also knew that I'd been unfair, and I knew that Valora did too. The pain kept the apology behind my lips.

"Valora, can you go tell Grayson that it's time for dinner?"

Valora nodded quietly without looking at me and went through the back door. I sighed and released a breath that I didn't know I'd held. I steadied myself on my crutches and turned around to fix the dinner plates. I shook my head to silence the voice that whispered, "at least she's obedient, just like her father."

The next day, I opened the mailbox with the hope that Mark or Willie's stipend checks would be there. The shelves were almost bare and it wasn't even the end of the month. I'd used almost all of Aunt Alice's monthly gift on Grayson's graduation packet and Valora's oboe. I didn't know how I'd feed Grayson and Valora if one of the checks weren't in the mail.

Gratitude at my sons' generosity began to fill my heart and made me want to cry. My mind wandered to the day that both of my oldest sons became the good men that I worked so hard to raise.

"Mama? It's so good to hear your voice!"

Mark sounded so happy, and his voice was very deep. I smiled into the phone.

"Yes, son, it's good to hear yours too! I'm sorry that I missed your army graduation, but I got the pictures yesterday. I've been showing them off to anybody who comes my way!"

Mark and I both laughed. Joy and pride rode on my shoulders because Mark received such high marks in basic training that he'd been selected for the elite airborne Army Rangers. A swell of pride for Willie flowed through me too because he'd done even better and was sent overseas to a private communications base. I was one proud mother. Gia and Leah's escapades in Houston crossed my mind, but I pushed them away to listen to Mark.

"Mama, I talked to Willie and we both think that you need some help. Stuff is getting more expensive and with Grayson and baby sis growing up, well, they need more than we had. You can't help it that you're sick and can't work. I know that you applied for disability, but that might take a while. Anyway, I looked into it and my sergeant said that if you sign a paper, I can take Grayson and Willie can take Valora as our dependents. You'll get a check whenever we get paid, Mama. Can we do it, please, Mama?"

I sat down in shock. Mark and Willie offered a way to make ends meet just as I'd been depressed with the knowledge that Aunt Alice's money wasn't enough. Tears of happiness began to flow and I laughed out loud. Ha! Take that, Satan! You won't get the best of me!

"Mama, are you okay?"

I stared at the phone for a moment while I caught my breath. I returned it to my ear to reassure Mark.

"Yes, son, I'm fine now. Mark Sams, you don't know how much I needed help, but I know that God put it on your heart. Thank you, son, and yes, please send me whatever paper to sign. I'll tell Willie thank you when he calls next time."

I chuckled when I heard Mark whoop loudly. He promised to call me with the next steps and hung up the phone. I bowed my head and closed my eyes.

"Thank You, Father God, for all that You do. Thank You for blessing me with Mark and Willie's generosity. You *know the plan even when I don't and I know that with faith in You, anything is possible. In Jesus' Holy Name, Amen."*

I opened my eyes and got up on my crutches more easily than I could in a long time."

I smiled at the memory and breathed a sigh of relief when I saw an envelope with the government seal on it. It wasn't the familiar envelopes that the checks came in, but the thought crossed my mind that they'd probably changed it to keep down theft. I kissed it and tucked the rest of the mail in the pocket of my apron before I turned to slowly cross the highway to the old homestead.

I stopped in the front yard and stared at the house and land around it. A spark of pride flared at how far we'd brought the old place. There were trees new and old on either side of the front yard. The old farmhouse still looked run-down but not as much as when we first moved into it. A glance at the house planks and window shudders told me that they'd need a coat of paint soon. Last year, Juan and my baby brother, Will, fixed the porch up with short steps to help me get in and out of the house. I looked at the sunflowers, posies, and Aloe Vera that grew in abundance in the flower beds around the steps. Valora's gifts included gardening and it came in handy. I glanced toward the small crops of vegetables and strawberry vines by the fence. Yes, Valora's green thumb came in real handy.

I made it to the porch and sat down on the edge where I could stand up again. I pulled the mail from my pocket and separated it. My mouth opened in surprise when I saw not one but two letters from the Army. I tore open the first envelope and started making a list of what needed to be paid first. Instead of a check, there was a letter.

Dear Mrs. Victoria Sams,

The Army has reassessed the Sibling Dependent Program, and at this time, Grayson Sams does not qualify as a sibling dependent of Pfc. IV Mark Sams under our new program rules. We apologize for any inconvenience these changes may cause. If you have any questions, you may contact the Army's Bureau of Personnel Control.

Sincerely,

The United States Army Command

My hands shook as I reread the letter to make sure that I'd read it right. *New program rules. Does not qualify.* My mind wrapped around those words and they began to spin like they were in front of my eyes. I leaned over and emptied my stomach in Valora's Aloe Vera. There would be no money for Grayson. I glanced at the other envelope and started to reach for it when I realized that it probably said the same thing about Valora. I felt the hot tears course down my face and I gave in to my despair. I laid back on the porch and allowed my sobs to wrack my aching body. What was I going to do?

After my porch pity party was over, I sat up with painful difficulty and glanced over to Valora's crops. I knew that we'd have to eat from it for the next two weeks if I couldn't make some money soon. I stood up on my crutches and grabbed the rest of the mail. I'll go through it later, I told myself, but I already knew that most of it was letters for Grayson. A tiny voice told me to open them and take the gifts to feed us, but I would not do that to Grayson. He'd taken on more responsibility than an eighteen year old should have. Now, it was his time to shine. I sat down at my beloved antique writing desk and wrote my weekly letters to Aunt Charlotte and Aunt Mary. I refused to mention anything of our situation.

Grayson came home early that afternoon and found me trying to pull okra and tomatoes from Valora's patch. He ran over and helped me stand upright.

"Mama, you can't be picking at the patch. Let me help you to the house and I'll do it," he said gently.

I smiled at my tall handsome son and nodded in agreement because my body felt like all of my bones were broken.

"All right, son, I'd appreciate that. Mama is a little worn out today."

Worry filled Grayson's face. He turned and looked around the homestead while he helped me limp across the gravel packed yard.

"Mama, you and Valora can't stay here after I graduate. It won't be safe and Valora is still too little to take care of everything. Maybe I should put off going to the Army?"

I whipped around on Grayson and frowned.

"Grayson Damien Sams! You will not delay your enlistment! You have been looking forward to joining your brothers in the service."

Grayson winced at my tone and I let out a big sigh. Even through my pain, I raised my hand to his face and patted his cheek.

"Your sister and I will be fine. Your Uncle Will and Grandma Tess come once a week to help out anyway. I'm sure that I can ask them to come more often when you leave."

Grayson's eyes teared up at the mention of his impending departure. I felt the same way, but I would not let my son know how much I would miss him. I'd raised him to be responsible and respectful, so I knew that he'd find a way to get out of following through with his enlistment. I reached forward and hugged him. I felt his pause of surprise because I wasn't always outwardly affectionate. William's departure from our lives changed that part of me, I thought bitterly. I shook my head as those thoughts tried to burst into my mind. I pressed my lips together and ruthlessly pushed them away. I put a big smile on my face and pulled back from my son. He kept his gaze down until he regained his composure. Just like Valora, I thought to myself. I waited with that big fake grin until he looked up at me.

"I'm sorry, Mama. I guess it just dawned on me that in three weeks, I'll be headed toward basic training."

I felt my smile slip a bit, so I turned toward the porch with a dismissive wave.

"Yes, and after basic training, you will get your station and start to build your own life, son. Everything will be fine, so don't worry."

I glanced to see that Grayson still looked skeptical, but he remained silent. I nodded to myself that I'd convinced my son to follow his path. There was nothing but trouble for him if he stayed.

Grayson helped me to the porch as the long yellow school bus rumbled to a stop on the highway. It pulled away and Valora stood there for a moment before she crossed the road. I cocked my head and narrowed my eyes because something wasn't quite right about her. Her head was lowered and she held her books closely to her chest. I waited to feel Valora's light as she approached and frowned when I felt a heavy thickness in the air around her. I looked at Grayson to see that he frowned at Valora's bowed head as well. He glanced at me and I beckoned toward his sister. Grayson reached Valora's side just as she collapsed on her knees in sobs. My heart jumped into my throat and my mind begin to think that the unmentionable had happened to my Pumpkin Pie. Grayson tried to help Valora up off of the rough gravel, but she pushed him away. Helpless, Grayson looked to me for help. Shock that Valora had been hurt or violated ran though me and kept me still. Her deep sobs tore at my heart and broke through my trance. I shifted up on my crutches and silently asked Grayson for the rocking chair on the porch. He ran to get it and had it in place before I made it to where Valora sat on the ground with her dog, Mutt, who'd ran to his mistress' side at her cries. I sat down in the rocker and leaned forward to touch my baby's hair.

"Pumpkin Pie? Valora? Tell Mama what's wrong. Tell me what happened?"

I used a gentle tone, but I felt the darkness rise with my anger that someone had hurt my baby girl. Valora's only response was more tears. Frustration and anger got the best of me.

"Valora Sams! You will tell me what is wrong right now! Stop sniveling!"

I saw Grayson's start of surprise at my hard tone. I shrugged his reaction away because Valora's sobs slowed and she lifted eyes filled with despair and tears. I held myself still and waited.

"I wanted to be popular like the other girls, Mama, so I told one of Diana's friends, Kami, about Dr. William and how he was like my dad. She told another girl, Dalia, who's really mean and bullies everyone. She and Kami came up to me while I waited on the bus and called me a liar. When I spoke up and told them that it was true and to leave me alone, Dalia started making fun of my hair, clothes, the way that I spoke, and everything! The other kids heard her and started chanting with her! My friend, Laura, held my hand and whispered nice things to me because she knew that I wanted to cry. I wanted to cry so bad, Mama, but I just kept remembering what you told me about jealous girls and being strong. The buses came, and I thought it was all over, but Dalia shouted names at me through the window when she sat down. I ignored her and got on my bus. The other kids that heard Dalia wouldn't leave me alone and kept calling me names. They pulled at my hair and shot spitballs at me until the bus driver finally noticed and made them stop. I didn't cry though, Mama, I didn't cry!"

Valora collapsed against me and I held her to me while she cried her adolescent tears of pain and rejection. I wanted to find a belt, go to Carson, and beat that Dalia girl and her mother. What kind of parent would raise such an ill-mannered and ignorant child who could inflict such pain on others? As I crooned and caressed my baby girl's head, I thought back to the tortuous years that I'd spent at Carver Middle School. I would not have my daughter treated the same way. I would fight for her whether my legs worked on not.

When Valora's sobs became hiccups, I signaled to Grayson to help her into the house. Once they were inside with the door shut, I took a deep breath and looked out over the swaying grass in the field. Mutt, Old Sams' son, came over and sat by my side with a whimper. I looked down at him and smiled with sadness in my heart.

"She has the sharpest and the most creative mind that I have ever seen, Mutt. We can't let her forget that she is special, and we won't allow anyone to dim her shine."

Mutt looked up and woofed as if he understood. I chuckled and twisted my head to see an angry Grayson come out of the house flipping through the mail.

"Mama, Valora is sleep. I don't know how she fell asleep so fast after what she just went through at school. Valora is no angel, but she didn't deserve to be stomped into the ground like that. I want to go into town right now and find those kids to teach them a lesson. Nobody is going to mess with my little sister."

I nodded my understanding of Grayson's feelings. No child should have to come home to their parents with that much hurt in their heart. I knew that I raised my children to know that they were just as equal to everyone else regardless of color, background, or money, but they also knew to treat others with respect. It's just too bad that not all parents thought the same way.

I sighed at the injustices of the world and turned to see Grayson hand me two envelopes. I looked down to see that they were from the disability department. I frowned and almost threw them to the ground. I couldn't take more bad news today, and the letters were probably denials of my claim and the appeal that I'd filed after the first denial. I decided to open them because I might need to request another application. I opened the longer one first.

"Victoria Sams,

We have completed the assessment of the disability claim and appeal that you filed twenty months ago. We have found that your disability is eligible for payment under U.S. Eligible Disabilities Code 719§1943 from the medical history presented by your attending physician. Your date of eligibility begins from the date of your application. Your first check includes a lump sum amount from your date of eligibility. You will receive a check on the 1st of each month thereafter in the standard amount set forth for disabled persons by the U.S.

Disability Department. If there are any changes to your condition or if you have any questions, please contact us.

    Sincerely,

The U.S. Disability Department

    My hands began to shake and I dropped the letter to the ground to pick up the shorter envelope. With special care, I tore open the envelope to see the lump sum check. I blinked at it and sat back in my rocker to stare at the amount. A lightness filled my body until I felt like I floated in the air. The check fell from my hand, and I heard the alarm in Grayson's voice as I slowly slipped into the inviting darkness.

11

The next few years passed by quickly. Grayson had been right about Valora and me living in the homestead alone. We'd come home from a few weeks with Aunt Charlotte one summer to find the homestead in disarray with several heirlooms gone. I'd felt violated and helpless, so I petitioned the local housing assistance group to help us find a house due to my disability. It hadn't taken them long to find us a house 'across the tracks' in Carson. I didn't appreciate that they hadn't looked any further than the 'Black' side of town, but I also felt more comfortable because several of my cousins and high school friends lived in the neighborhood.

I heaved a sigh at the memory of the burdensome move. We'd lived in the homestead for so long that we'd accumulated a lot of junk and memorabilia which caused the transfer to be harder. However, it was the relief to feel safer and more secure in town that was worth more than the difficult move.

Gia and Leah came from Houston and gave us enthusiastic help to move all of our belongings. It came as a surprise to many that they started frequently visiting, but I appreciated the help all the same. The move would have been too much on Valora alone. Guilt stayed on my heart that she'd taken on so much responsibility of taking care of me and the house. Whenever I got the chance, I gave her money to go buy herself treats. I knew that it spoiled her, but I didn't care.

Gia seemed to be less hateful, but she still pushed Leah's buttons and Valora's when she felt slighted. Valora had grown taller than Gia and it was hard to keep her from retaliating when Gia unleashed her bitterness. Gia just didn't know that if I didn't have firm control over Valora, she'd have been black and blue as soon as Valora turned fifteen.

With Tess' help and my disability lump sum, I'd bought a used Buick sports sedan so that I wouldn't have to ask anyone else for a ride. The only problem was that my legs didn't work like they used to anymore, so after a year of struggling to drive in Carson, I sold the car to one of my brother Steven's classmates. Valora hadn't been happy because she'd thought to drive the car, and she'd moped around the small house on Love Street until I wanted to slap her. She acted so spoiled about it that I refused to tell her that the money from the sale was in a savings account to buy her one when she came of age.

Thoughts of Valora's stubbornness made me frown at the rosebush outside of my window. I sighed at its fragile beauty but knew that the sharp thorns were there for protection. Valora was the same way. She'd blossomed into a beautiful young woman, but she had a unique way of dealing with any negativity that she suffered at the hands of the children and teachers at school who didn't know what she went through at home with me. I knew that she wrote everything in her journal to shake off bad things that happened, but she lashed out when pushed too far. I also knew that her strong-willed and prideful personality hid her pain and leached away some of the Light that she carried as a child. It didn't help that she was also competitive and refused to allow the small-minded people of Carson to put her in the same box as most of the other Black children. She commanded respect and attention and when it wasn't given, she hardened her heart against those who slighted her.

Through the years, I encouraged her unique talents and extensive intellect, and I'd been able to temper her obstinate attitude. Since I'd become an invalid, all I wanted was to express my gratitude that she hadn't abandoned me like her sisters, so I allowed her to become an adult before her childhood ended.

Another sigh escaped my lips when I heard the front door shut. I waited patiently for Valora to come greet me before she went in her room, but after several minutes, I didn't hear her come down the hallway. She must be in one of her moods, I told myself. I shook my head and picked up my Bible to read one of my favorite verses.

"Be still before the Lord and wait patiently for him; fret not yourself over the one who prospers in his way, over the man who carries out evil devices! Refrain from anger, and forsake wrath! Fret not yourself; it tends only to evil. For the evildoers shall be cut off, but those who wait for the Lord shall inherit the land." Psalm 37:7-9.

I closed my eyes and said a silent prayer to not be angry with my daughter when she finally presented herself. I opened my eyes and a wave grief and nausea came over me. I touched my fingers to my mouth and a hand on my heart as if that would stop anything. I took several breaths through my nose and when the feeling passed, I exhaled heavily. I leaned back on my pillows and shifted my legs painfully. A grunt escaped my lips at the pain.

"Mama? Are you okay?"

I looked up to see Valora with a handful of teacakes in one hand and a glass of milk in the other. Uh oh, she's about to start her cycle, I told myself. Valora's monthly times were filled with excruciating pain and anger that rivaled a wounded bear. Aunt Charlotte took her to a specialist in Houston last summer who'd said that her condition would only worsen as she got older. He'd prescribed birth control to help, but I refused because I would not have my baby girl on pills that basically said she could have sex. Nope, nope, nope. Aunt Charlotte had agreed and bought Valora a big bottle of pain pills from the drug store. They didn't help much and she almost always had to stay home one day every month. It was better than have her be one of those loose girls at the school. She'd be fine, and it was all part of being a woman anyway.

"Mama? Is something wrong?"

I shrugged away my errant thoughts and concentrated on my baby girl. Her face held fear and alarm. Valora worried about me all the time. Even though, I had a home health aide to help me in the mornings and most afternoons, she still worried. I chalked it up to all of the sick spells that I'd had last winter. I refused to think it was anything else, so I smiled to allay her concern.

"Yes, Pumpkin, I'm fine."

Valora relaxed and took a bite of her cookie. Something about the way that she refused to meet my eyes concerned me. I narrowed my eyes to really see her and started in surprise when she cocked her head at me. Her eyes were the darkest that I'd ever seen them and filled with hurt and anger. I forced myself to stay calm.

"Valora, what's wrong, Pumpkin? Did something happen at school?"

Valora lowered her head and remained quiet. I breathed out in frustration at her silence. My openly sharing little girl wasn't so open and sharing anymore. Her teenage years took that away. I held myself still and silent until her head popped up to reveal unshed tears. My arms itched to go to her and hold her, but my legs refused to work. I didn't know what else to do in the face of her pain, so I clicked my tongue at her tears.

"Valora Sams! I didn't raise any cry-babies, so swallow those tears back and tell me what's wrong!"

Valora looked shocked for a moment at my hard tone before she wiped her hand down her face. It took only a second for my baby girl to regain her composure. She looked into the distance in the window behind me and spoke so softly that I had to lean over the bed to hear her.

"They assigned awards today in band. These awards are different, Mama, because you get to go to a picnic in the park with everyone else who received an award in other classes. It's a really fun day with no school. I was so happy because I knew that I would get the award in band because of my medals in first band and my solo excellence award. Everyone knew that I would get it too, but when Mr. Allen announced the awards, he didn't say my name. Everyone got really quiet when the boy that got my award came to the front."

Valora paused and walked over to the sofa beside my bed. She flopped down and stared out of the window at the rosebush. She became so lost in her thoughts for several moments that I was about to interrupt her stillness. She turned to me with dull and defeated eyes.

"Mr. Allen is prejudice, Mama. When Jamie came to get his award, he tried to give it back because he didn't feel like he'd earned it. Mr. Allen told him that he'd been helpful during marching season and since he played two instruments instead of perfecting one, the award was his. When class dismissed, I asked Mr. Allen why I didn't get the award. He smiled and I thought that he was going to tell me that it had been a mistake. I didn't feel right because his eyes looked really mean. He told me to come in his office and sit down. I didn't want to, but I had to know, Mama. I really wanted to go on that picnic. When he turned around, Mr. Allen's face was all screwed up."

Valora's own face twisted and she shocked me with a perfect mimicry of the band director's voice that I'd heard from a phone call.

"I'm so tired of you Black people getting free rides because of your so called "talents". Do you think that because you can play a simple instrument like the oboe and sway all of the contest judges that you should get every award, girl? You don't really have any talent that I can see. Let me give you a piece of advice. You need to quit setting yourself up against White students because you'll lose every time. You're Black and you'll never be anything else but Black, and it won't make a difference how great that you think are."

I stared at Valora's hurt and angry face and felt the fury fill my veins. How dare that hateful and prejudice piece of White trash crush my daughter's feelings. My hands clenched and I could feel his neck between them. I forced myself to relax, but I couldn't shake off the small bit of darkness that flooded in with my anger.

The ring of the phone in the heavy silence startled us. I glared at the black handset as if it would obey my mental command to cease, but it persisted to ring. I glanced to see Valora's shoulders slump in resignation.

"It's okay, Mama. It might be important."

I nodded even though she couldn't see me and picked up the phone.

"Hello?"

My tone was abrupt and I heard silence for a moment before a deep sob came across the line. My heart jumped that one of my children may be hurt.

"Victoria? Is that you?"

I gripped the phone at Ruth's distressed voice and answered shakily.

"Ruth? Yes, it's me. What's wrong? Is it Greg or one of the boys?"

Greg was my favorite brother-in-law and a good man. He took good care of my sister and their sons even when I knew my sister gave him fits and starts. I said a quick prayer that they were all right while my sister gathered herself.

"No, it's not Greg or the boys! Don't you know what's going on?"

Anger sparked at my sister's sudden spurt of temper, I pulled the phone from my ear to look at it for a moment. God give me strength, I told myself and put the phone back to my ear just in time to hear Ruth catch her breath to explain.

"Victoria, Mama should have called you, but I'm sure she's busy trying to find a way to get to Greensdale. Daddy is really sick. That woman that he's been living with, Serla, called Clyde Jr. and told him that Daddy vomited black blood all night long. She didn't even take him to the doctor, Victoria!

She pretended that she just thought he ate something bad, but it's like I told y'all all this time, she hoodooed Daddy to take him away from Mama all these years. Poor Mama, she's tried to stay respectful, but..."

"Ruth, hold on."

I had to know if my sister was right, but she wouldn't stop her tirade.

"I know that we haven't always seen eye to eye with Daddy, but I'm worried, Victoria. It's all that woman's fault..."

She won't stop until she's ready, a quiet voice said. I looked at Valora to see if she'd spoken, but she sat quietly reading one of her teen romance books. A sliver of fear at the unknown voice ran down my back. I shook it off and rolled my eyes at Ruth's stream of anger. I have to know about Clyde, I told myself, as the feeling of grief and nausea returned. Ruth's voice faded and I closed my eyes to reach for my gift. It awakened slowly like a sleeping child. I emptied my mind of everything and pushed at it to find Clyde. For a moment, I saw my father on the backseat of a car writhing in pain. With his arms wrapped around his stomach, Clyde turned his blood soaked face toward the window and screamed. My eyes popped open with a gasp. The phone slipped from my numb fingers.

"Mama, are you all right?"

My body trembled with chills and I felt my teeth chatter. I tried to answer Valora, but my tongue stuck to the roof of my mouth. More cold seeped into my body and I fell back onto the pillows of the bed. My eyes drifted closed.

"Mama! Please answer me! What's wrong?"

I wanted to answer my daughter, but I couldn't. My father's tortured cries echoed through my mind. My gift shifted back to the scene of horror to see Clyde in a pool of his own blood – pitch, black blood. I couldn't concentrate to cut off the sight of my father's death spasms and a moan escaped my lips.

Suddenly, Clyde twisted like he'd heard me. He lifted a trembling hand from his grip on his stomach. Blood bubbled from his lips as he whispered.

"Mama, you were wrong, and this is my price for helping you do your evil. God forgive me, please!"

Clyde began to thrash about in a seizure and I heard a woman scream. The noise freed my mind and I fought to return my gift to its place. My body felt hot and I couldn't catch my breath.

Whispered voices made me open my eyes to see that Valora and Old Man Hawkins, the volunteer fire chief, stood over me. Valora's pale worried face relaxed a little to see me awake. I wanted to tell her about my vision, but Old Man Hawkins spoke first.

"Victoria, you gave us quite a fright. Your daughter says that you'd been unconscious for almost an hour before we got here. That may be a little bit stretched out, you know how impatient kids are with time. You do look a little peaked, and your blood pressure is through the roof. The ambulance is on its way, and I suggest that you head on to the hospital."

Before I could say anything, Valora gently sat beside me and grabbed my hand. A slight frown touched her forehead and her beautiful hazel eyes widened when she turned to look into mine. I nodded at her unspoken question and tipped my head at Old Man Hawkins and the young fireman behind him. Valora nodded and stood up with a big smile.

"I'm so sorry to have scared y'all. I forgot that Mama took her medicine and it sometimes makes her sleep really deep and have bad dreams. I guess I allowed my impatience to get the best of me. Would y'all like some of the teacakes that I made last night on your way out?"

The young fireman perked up at the mention of the old fashioned cookies, but Old Man Hawkins scowled at Valora and shook his head. Valora ignored him, picked up his bag, and put her hand in his elbow to lead him from the room. Old Man Hawkins looked back at me and frowned. He tugged his arm from Valora's hand and turned around to face me with concern.

"Victoria, I promised my good friend, Old Dr. Herbert, to look after you, and you don't look so hot right now. I know that you're going to do as you please, but I think that you should go to the hospital to get checked out by the doctor. It's not right for you to let your young'un be so grown and make these kinds of decisions for you."

I shook my head at Old Man Hawkins because he didn't understand. No one knew how much it hurt me every day to see my child take on the responsibilities of a household and an invalid. Last year, Gia and Leah argued the same thing, and even went so far as to try to get me declared unfit in court to have Valora sent away. Luckily Aunt Charlotte, Tess, and Steven intervened to help us. Valora and I couldn't help our situation, but we did our best for each other. People just needed to understand that my body didn't work, but my mind was just fine.

I saw Valora's face darken with anger. She drew herself up to her full height, which wasn't much taller than me. I knew that Old Man Hawkins needed to go. Now.

"Mr. Hawkins, I just had a little spell and Valora didn't know what to do. I'll be just fine. Now, I'm a little tired and would like to get some real sleep. Would it ease your mind if I called my doctor tomorrow?"

Old Man Hawkins saw that I wouldn't be move. He pressed his lips together with a curt nod. I let out a sigh of relief when he turned to leave the room. Valora looked like she would still unleash her fury, so I intervened before Old Man Hawkins got his behind handed to him.

"Valora, please show the gentlemen out and please bring me a glass of water. I really do need to take my pain pills."

Valora's attitude changed to one of concern, and she left the room in hurry to do as I asked. I leaned over on my pillow and rubbed my face. Tears of regret and sorrow began to flow from my eyes. I glanced at the phone and knew that I'd have to call Ruth back before she called out the countryside to check on us. I just didn't want to tell her what I saw in my vision. I didn't want to break it to my sister that our father was dead.

Clyde left very specific instructions about his burial, and Tess tried to follow them all. It wasn't easy because he'd left the strange requests that he didn't want a viewing and to be buried before noon at a measured and exact six feet. There was also the fact that he'd left plans. It was almost as if he'd known he would die for some time. I wanted to ask Tess if she'd known anything, but she seemed consumed with the funeral details. When she became overwhelmed by grief, Ruth, Steven, and I took over to finish the plans. I felt pity for my mother because everyone knew that Daddy had left her and openly lived with another woman in Greensdale. To have to plan an estranged husband's funeral and save face was too much for anyone to bear. If it were me, I'd tell them to just throw Harlan in the creek.

Mark, Willie, and Grayson took leave and came home for Clyde's funeral. They looked very impressive in their military uniforms, and many of the single women in Carson attended the burial in Allsville to get a glimpse of them. I almost laughed aloud at their disappointed faces when they realized that Mark and Willie's wives had come home with them.

Marcos, Grayson, and Valora seemed to have the hardest time of anyone in the family as they dealt with my father's death. Juan and his oldest son, Pedro, had to escort a grief-stricken Marcos from the funeral. Disapproval crossed some of the Roberts' family's faces at Marcos' display of emotion during the services. I frowned at each of them to let them know what I thought of their silent reproach. Marcos had a right to his sorrow. What they didn't know was that for several years, Marcos and Clyde worked together to return the ranch to its former glory after Betts sold off so much of Grandpa Paul's land. When my father came to terms that Betts' anger and greed kept him from the enjoyment his brother's company, they'd grown close. I also knew from my talks with Marcos when he came to visit that he'd forgiven my father and thought of him as a brother.

My own heart ached in regret at my father's passing. I'd tried to find a middle ground after our talk in the car, but some parts of my childhood were tough to forget. The sorrow that I felt was more for what could have been, and that's what Clyde must have felt when he began to visit my younger children after he moved to Greensdale. The time that Clyde spent with Grayson and Valora had been his way to bridge the gap between our relationship, and I'd appreciated that he'd made the effort, but to watch my babies suffer at his loss was as painful as my aching bones.

"Aunt Victoria? Can I get you anything?"

I looked up from my thoughts to see that Lacey's daughter, Gladys, stood by my wheelchair. Gladys looked more like my younger self than Gia and Leah. Her freckled peach skin and deep auburn hair matched my own. She had my Coke bottle figure and was a very sweet young woman. A memory of Lacey calling to tell me that Gladys would look just like me when she grew up crossed my mind. I hadn't believed her because my sister could sometimes be a little light in the head. I sighed to myself and made a mental note to apologize to her.

"Aunt Victoria?"

I shook my head to clear my scattered thoughts and looked up at Gladys' lovely face with a wide smile.

"Thank you for asking, sweetheart, but I'm okay for now. I'm so glad that you spend so much time with Valora now that you're back from college. She needs someone to talk to besides Diana and Samantha. Have you seen Gia and Leah? I remember that you used to follow them around all the time at your Grandma Tess'."

Gladys' smile slipped just a bit, but I noticed the change and became concerned.

"Is something wrong, dear?"

Gladys' eyes welled with tears, but she pressed her lips together and shook her head. Yes, definitely something wrong, I told myself. I glanced around the ranch's living room to see that Gia and Leah sent hateful glances our way. I narrowed my eyes and frowned at them. Leah turned away chastised, but Gia threw me an arrogant frown and walked into the hallway. I rolled my eyes at her back and promised to have a little "chat" with my stubborn and bitter daughter. I looked up to see that Gladys followed my gaze. She turned back to me and shuddered before she caught herself. Her eyes flew down in embarrassment. I chuckled quietly and reached out to take her hand.

"Gladys, Aunt Victoria knows how difficult Gia and Leah can be when they feel envy or jealousy of someone. They try to do the same with Valora, but don't you let them make you feel less than your worth. You stand right up to them and tell them off when they try to get at you with their ugliness."

Gladys nodded but she wouldn't look up from her black pumps. I chuckled and squeezed her hand.

"Do you know that your Great-Grandpa Ed told me once to always hold my head up with pride? No? Well, he did, and he was a very smart man. Now, I'm going to tell you the same thing, Gladys. Lift your head and walk with the pride of our Egyptian ancestors. You can't see the world with your head down. Besides, your cousins are probably jealous because all the available men in the room are staring at you instead of them."

Gladys' head popped up and her eyes flew around the room to see that I was right. She giggled and looked back at me. I smiled, nodded, and let go of her hand when a tall, handsome Mexican boy appeared at her side with a glass of lemonade. Gladys looked up at him shyly and took the glass. She thanked him and took his offered arm to go sit by the fireplace. I chuckled when several other young men made a beeline for her chair.

"She reminds me of you so much at that age."

Aunt Charlotte limped around my wheelchair and sat down on the sofa with her aged but elegant hands folded over the silver eagle of her cane. I watched while she shifted her legs to recline on the old blue sofa. She sighed and relaxed against the old fashioned velvet. Aunt Charlotte watched the room for a few moments. She cleared her throat and rolled her head towards me and smiled. I couldn't help but let out a low laugh at the mischievous look on my aunt's face. She laughed as well but sobered quickly.

"Victoria, I'm very sorry about your father. When you told me that he'd tried to mend fences after Betts died, I didn't know what to think. Your Aunt Mary told me that she felt that he meant you no harm, so I left it to your good judgment. I didn't want you to get hurt especially in your condition. I just pray that Clyde's soul was ready."

I nodded at Aunt Charlotte's condolences and looked across the room to Valora who stood alone in the doorway. She stood with the bearing of a queen looking over her court. Aunt Charlotte followed my gaze and smiled.

"She is wonderful young woman, Victoria. I know that she is hurt over Clyde's death much like she was when Harlan's Aunt Julia passed last year. I also know that she is practical. She'll accept the loss and move on because she knows that's the right thing to do. You've raised her well, Victoria."

I turned toward Aunt Charlotte with a sad smile at the mention of Aunt Julia. I missed her too. I missed her a lot more than I missed Ms. Dorothy, a little voice chimed into my mind. Guilt flooded my body and my face. Aunt Charlotte saw my blush and cocked her head to the side.

"I wonder what caused that rose to bloom," she murmured.

I shrugged and glanced back at Valora to see a dark shadow hover next to her. Alarm and fear replaced my guilty thoughts. I knew that we shouldn't have had my father's luncheon so close to Betts' closet I scolded myself. Aunt Mary had left early because she hadn't wanted to come into the ranch house. She said that it didn't feel right, but I'd just thought she was tired. I opened my mouth to call to Valora, but a wash of uncomfortable cold ran through my body. I bit my lip to keep from making any noise, but Aunt Charlotte sat up with concern.

"What is it, child?"

I shook my head weakly and tried to smile, but Aunt Charlotte wasn't fooled.

"Victoria, you are not well and should be at home in bed by now," she scolded.

I shook my head again and another wave of freezing cold rushed through me. We needed to leave this house, especially Valora. I tried to call out, but I felt frozen. A memory of Valora telling me that she'd being stuck in the family graveyard in the same way crossed my mind. I hadn't believed her. Now, I knew that she spoke the truth.

"Victoria, what's wrong?"

I cut my eyes at Aunt Charlotte and tried to raise my hand to signal my distress. Aunt Charlotte frowned for a moment and leaned forward to touch my arm. She pulled her hand away as if she'd been shocked. She looked around quickly and waved at Mark and his wife, Cindy. Mark excused himself from his conversation with Clyde Jr. and came over to us. Aunt Charlotte beckoned him to sit beside her and leaned over to whisper in his ear.

"Mark, something is not right with your mother. I don't want to cause a scene, but we need to leave. Now."

Mark glanced at me with concern. I looked into his eyes to try to signal to him that I wasn't worried about myself. I glanced at Valora and back at Mark. Mark's brow wrinkled and then cleared in understanding. He got up quickly and walked toward his baby sister. Aunt Charlotte frowned at his back and opened her mouth to call him. She turned around to me and saw the relief in my eyes. Confusion and fear chased each other across her face, and she looked around the room. Her gaze stopped on the dark curtains that were made darker by the dreary, wet day. I saw her shudder and she grabbed her cane to stand. She watched as Mark grabbed Valora's arm and moved toward the front door. When they didn't reappear, Aunt Charlotte limped as fast as she could to Grayson and I could see her gesture toward me. Grayson took no time to stride across the room and kneel by my wheelchair.

Half of the room of mourners seemed to notice that something was wrong. Embarrassed at the attention, I pressed my lips together and willed my body to move against the bitter cold. I glanced around the room with a small smile to cover my torment. Grayson moved closer to whisper.

"Mama, are you all right?"

"I'm just a little tired. I wanted to stay for Mama and my brothers and sisters, but I think that I'm ready to go, son."

I frowned at the stiff sound of my voice.

Grayson nodded and shifted to move behind me to push me out of the room. Tess moved into the path with a frown. Grayson stopped with a deep sigh that echoed Aunt Charlotte's, who walked beside us. Disappointed to see a glimpse of the spiteful woman of my childhood, I frowned back at Tess. I glanced around to see that most of the guests weren't paying us any attention. I sat back in weakness from my struggle with the darkness and waited for Tess to speak. She glanced at Aunt Charlotte with glazed eyes of anger and envy. I felt Aunt Charlotte shift to stand straighter and step towards my mother. Tess ignored her and looked back at me with a raised eyebrow.

"Where are you going, Vicky? Surely, you're not leaving your father's funeral luncheon. That is bad manners and I know Charlotte taught you better than that," she hissed.

We and those around us didn't miss Tess' sarcasm. Aunt Charlotte took another step and touched Tess' arm. Tess looked at Aunt Charlotte's hand like it was a stinkbug. Aunt Charlotte didn't move her hand but stepped closer to Tess to whisper to her.

"Tess, can't you see that Clyde's loss is taking a toll on Victoria. She's not well, and I'm sure the memories of this house don't help either. We apologize for it, but we have to leave."

The nasty look on Tess' face didn't change at Aunt Charlotte's explanation. In fact, she looked a lot like the woman who'd almost broken my spirit with a switch so long ago. The memory of that day gave me the strength to push the darkness away. I lifted my chin and frowned at my mother.

"Mama, I will not embarrass myself or my family by having a spell at my Daddy's funeral luncheon. I know that you are hurt by Daddy's death. I understand because I'm grieving too, but you are not going to treat Aunt Charlotte or me like punching bags for your guilt and shame. Now, if you'll please forgive me, I need to get home to take my medicine and rest."

I nodded to Aunt Charlotte who signaled Grayson to push me out of the oppressive room. I glanced back to see Clyde Jr. and Will walk over to Tess and comfort her. I spun around with fear in my heart because all I could see was a circle of dark shadows.

After we got home, Valora helped me get into the bed. She put pillows under my knees because the rheumatoid arthritis had eaten away the cartilage and I could no longer unbend them. I watched her with a small smile of pride while she efficiently helped me into my nightgown and robe, straightened the room, and went to fix dinner. Aunt Charlotte, Mark, and Grayson made sure that I was okay and left.

I reclined back on the pillows and switched on the new remote control television that Grayson brought me for Mother's Day. One of my favorite detective shows was on, but I couldn't concentrate enough to watch it. What was in my grandparents' ranch house? What happened to me today and why? All of those questions went around and around in my head until I felt dizzy. I had no answers and I was afraid to use my gift because of what happened with Clyde. A glance at the phone told me that I should call Aunt Mary. She might be able to help me find the answer. I looked outside at the twilight and knew that I needed to make my call before dark. The windows seem to mock me and I wished that I'd told Valora to close them.

"Oh, well, she'd be in with dinner soon, and she can do it then," I whispered into the dead silence and turned back to the phone.

I started to pick up the black handset when Valora's tabby cat, Pepper, sauntered into the room with a loud meow and startled me. I shook my head at my jumpiness and frowned at Pepper.

"Pepper, you old tomcat, what do you want?"

Pepper was usually a spoiled and fickle cat whom spent more time eating and sleeping than he did being petted by Valora. She'd raised him from a kitten and he was extremely loyal to her. Pepper rarely ventured away from Valora which brought a frown to my face. He meowed again, turned, and stood in the doorway as if on guard. The hairs on the back of my neck stood up straight. I tried to look into the hallway to see what caused Pepper's defensive stance, but it was too dark. Something wasn't right with that darkness. Fear for Valora made me call out to her.

"Pumpkin Pie? Are you okay? It's been a long day. Why don't you come in and watch T.V. with me?"

I waited for a few moments and only heard silence. Pepper turned his head to me and my heart sped up at the glint in his green eyes.

"Pepper, I'll be fine. Go find your mistress."

Pepper meowed loudly and turned around to slowly walk down the hallway. I lost sight of him when he got about halfway. A bead of sweat dripped onto my cheek and I wiped it away with a trembling hand. The silence seemed to thicken while I waited to hear Valora greet Pepper. I wanted to call out again, but the darkness shifted and I finally felt the malevolence of it. Tears of frustration and helplessness gathered at being unable to face it on two legs. A rush of cold air flowed through my body and sorrow filled me. A sob escaped my throat and I closed my eyes to avoid the feel of the icy breath on my neck.

"I am not here for you, Victoria Sams. Not yet. I wanted you today, but you no longer embrace my black will. Your mother and brothers on the other hand..."

It lies, I told myself, but unbearable sadness filled my heart. No, I will not be fooled. I shrank away from the gravelly taunts and felt for my Bible. I reached a shaking hand under the pillow and touched the worn pages. My favorite Psalm popped into my head and off my lips.

"You are a liar. The Lord is my light and my salvation; whom shall I fear? The Lord is the strength of my life; of whom shall I be afraid?"

A hiss of cold skittered across my skin.

"Me, you should be afraid of me. You have not escaped me. I have the heart of two of your children and I will have another soon. Her Light is already dim from ridicule, hate, envy, and prejudice. The weight of responsibility is heavy for her young mind and makes her weak to me. Yes, she may have broken the Line, but she has the power to create another. Ha, ha, ha, what say you now?"

My heart clenched for a moment at the evil cackle, but the feel of God's Word gave me the strength to sit up and face the darkness.

"I say, curse you, foul demon. You will not conquer this child of God nor any in my house. I rebuke you in the Holy Name of Jesus Christ! Yea, though I walk through the valley of the shadow of death, I will fear no evil, for God is with me!"

A loud screech came from behind me. I sat up with my fists clenched and eyes open ready to fight. The room was filled with the light of the late evening. One look around the room and into the hallway told me that everything was fine. Valora's voice hummed a tune and Pepper meowed with her. The smell of meatloaf and cabbage wafted through air. I slumped back against my pillows with a deep breath and realized that I'd fallen asleep. I patted my pounding heart and picked up the remote to turn the television. It was only a nightmare. The phone rang just as I found an old war movie to watch. I sighed at the interruption and put the phone to my ear.

"Hello?"

"Victoria? It's your Aunt Charlotte."

I frowned because Aunt Charlotte sounded like she'd been crying. She'd also said that she would call tomorrow to check up on me.

"Yes, Aunt Charlotte, it's me. Are you all right?"

Aunt Charlotte exhaled heavily. A sliver of fear crept into my heart and panic began to set in at her silence.

"Aunt Charlotte?"

"Victoria, there's been an accident. Your mother, Clyde Jr., and Will were going around the corner by the creek. That Adams boy, Tim, was going too fast again and hit them head on," she sobbed.

I gripped the phone and waited for her to tell me that they were in the hospital. My patience ran out at her silence.

"Aunt Charlotte, are they okay? Are y'all at Carson General?"

Aunt Charlotte took another deep breath.

"No, child. No one lived including the Adams boy."

I dropped the phone and gripped my arms in horror, as my nightmare became reality.

12

"Valora Elise Sams."

The crowd erupted into thunderous applause and cheers. Shocked, I looked back to see that a host of Roberts', Daniels', Sams', and more stood and cheered for my daughter as she walked across the field to take the diploma from the Carson High School Superintendent. I turned around to see Valora's big smile and wave to the crowd. Everyone laughed, well, everyone except for Gia. She sat there filing her nails and rolling her eyes at her sister's triumph. It didn't help that her friend, Celeste, sat pointing and giggling at people. I bit my tongue to keep from dressing them down on Valora's special day. I wouldn't allow anyone to steal her joy after all of her struggles to graduate with honors.

I could finally breathe in relief that Valora finished high school. It hadn't been easy for her after that disastrous year when Clyde, Tess, and my brothers, Will and Clyde Jr. died. Valora became overwhelmed by caring for me and keeping up with her grades, competitions, and academic events. She'd wanted to quit band after that bigot, Mr. Allen, degraded her talent, but I wouldn't allow her. My adamant attitude about her remaining in band, caused a strain on our relationship and on

Valora. Her Light dimmed a little more and I became afraid for her. Eventually, her best friend, Faith, talked her into staying in band with her. I'd wanted to kiss Faith, but instead, I invited her over that Halloween, ordered them pizza, and told them ghost stories. Faith loved it, and it made Valora happier than she'd been in a long while.

In Valora's junior year, the stress began to build as she saw more and more how the White children were given opportunities that she was denied or ignored. For a while, I felt that she wanted to drop out of school, but she didn't say anything to me about it. I ignored the feelings until Valora's intentions came to light. If one of her mentors, a vibrant White woman, Christine Melbourne, hadn't taken a special interest in Valora and come to me to find a solution for the weight on her shoulders, I don't know what would have happened.

A knock sounded at the door. Valora left her room to go answer it. Her greeting sounded surprised but happy. Low voices made me lean over to peek down the hallway. When I heard footsteps, I leaned back over and looked at the television. I looked up at Valora's knock.

"Mama? Christine Melbourne is here."

I looked at my daughter and narrowed my eyes. She nervously fidgeted with her hands for a moment. What was Valora up to bringing that nosy White woman in my house? Christine Melbourne was always trying to get children from the neighborhood into her nutrition and leadership program. To most people, she was just another White woman with an agenda. Valora and her son were friends and classmates, so it wasn't a surprise when she enlisted Valora in her program. I'd thought it great until Valora had to go on trips and events. Sometimes, I was left alone for hours while she ran off to be with "Chris". I tried to be grateful that she was doing things that made her happy, but what about me? When Valora went to one of Christine's camps, she came back talking about boys and traveling in the program when she finished college. At least, that's what I'd heard on the phone extension. I looked at my daughter's bowed head again with a frown. She probably wants to go to some dance or something with a boy. Well, it's not going to happen. No, ma'am.

I opened my mouth to ask her why the woman was in my house when Valora raised her head. My harsh and angry thoughts folded in the face of my daughter's tears.

"What is it, Pumpkin Pie?"

Valora shook her head and I saw a shadow approach behind her. My heart jumped in fear only to relax as Christine Melbourne slid her arm around Valora's shoulders and led her into the room. I sat speechless while Christine settled Valora on the sofa. She turned to me, picked up my hand, shook it gently, and sat in the chair next to the door. A gentle smile touched her lips as she took in my shock.

"Hello, Ms. Victoria. I know it's been a long while since I've dropped by to see you."

I recovered my composure and narrowed my eyes at her.

"Yes, it has, Ms. Melbourne. What can I do for you?"

I nodded curtly to her, and she grinned.

"Now, I know where Valora gets her strength."

A small smile escaped my lips. I didn't want to like this woman, but I could feel the Light in her spirit. She glanced at Valora's hunched shoulders and sobered.

"As much as it's good to see you, Ms. Victoria, I need to talk to you about Valora."

I looked at Valora and frowned. I turned back to Christine with my eyebrow raised.

"Yes? What about my daughter?"

Christine took a deep breath.

"One of the boys in my program came to the office and told me that he'd heard Valora in the band hall crying. She was making plans to quit school and stay at home to help you."

Surprised, I looked at Valora and back at Christine.

"Surely you're mistaken, Ms. Melbourne. My daughter would have told me something like that."

A sad smile crossed her face.

"*I talked to Valora just now, and she confirmed what she said.*"

Valora turned from the window and looked me straight in the face. The sheen of tears in her eyes glistened in the afternoon sun.

"*Mama, I'm so sorry. I just want to be here to help you. I heard the lady from the home health service say that you're going to need more care after your last doctor's visit. She said that you might have to go to a nursing home, Mama! I can't let that happen not when I can quit school and take care of you. I can always go back and get that GED thing!*"

Tears sprang into my own eyes at my young daughter's thought to sacrifice herself to care for me. I couldn't even feel angry or embarrassed that Christine was there. My heart felt heavy while I listened to Valora's sobs. Christine got up and sat beside her on the sofa to comfort her, but Valora twisted away and knelt beside my useless legs with her head in my lap. I raised a hand and stroked her hair much like I did when she was a small child. I felt guilty for putting so much on my daughter and encouraging her independence so that it would benefit me. I'd groomed her to be almost a mirror image of me without allowing her to shine in her own Light. Suddenly, I knew the solution to our problem.

"*Ms. Melbourne, please excuse our show of emotion. Thank you so much for coming to tell me what Valora planned and forgive me for my bad manners. May I ask a favor? I'll understand if you refuse.*"

Christine wiped her eyes with a tissue from a little packet and handed me two. She moved closer to me and patted Valora on the back. She looked up at me and nodded.

"*Yes, ma'am. What can I do for you?*"

I smiled sadly down at my daughter's head and rubbed my hand across her beautiful hair. I spoke without looking at Christine and swallowed my pride.

"*Can you help us? I have put too much on Valora and she was too young to handle it. I know that you care for my daughter and want what's best for her. Can you help us find a way so that Valora doesn't have these thoughts of quitting school anymore?"*

Without another word, Christine Melbourne pulled out a pad and made it possible.

I blinked out of my memories to glance over and see Christine blow a kiss at Valora. I frowned when a twinge of jealousy reared its head. Valora adored Christine, and I knew that Christine felt the same way. I shook my head at the foolish envy and watched Christine beam with pride at the sea of burnt orange robes. She ignored ugly looks from the White people around her and showed her joy for my daughter and her own son, Alex.

After the school board president accepted the graduates, they all ran to the center of the field and celebrated while saying their goodbyes. Valora told me that several of her classmates were to leave for college in the next couple of weeks, some would go to the military, and some would stay close to home. Valora had been accepted into the Dallas University's pre-law program. She almost hadn't accepted the university's offer because she didn't want to leave me behind in Carson. I'd been shocked that Leah spoke up to encourage her to enroll because we could live with her. She'd relocated to Dallas the year before for a position with an attorney. She'd explained that the university wasn't far from new her apartment and Valora could commute. I'd jumped at the chance to stay with Valora while she studied for her law degree. It never occurred to me that I needed to give Valora a chance to spread her wings.

The moment came for the family pictures and Grayson rolled me down the ramp to meet an excited and teary-eyed Valora. She gave everyone hugs including Gia. I held up a hand and she grasped it for a second. I looked up in surprise at the familiar zing of Valora's Light. She nodded and smiled when I met her eyes. Now, I knew why everyone seemed to stare at Valora when they passed by her. They could feel her amazing spirit.

The photographer snapped a couple of pictures and moved away to another family. I smiled and leaned forward to tell Valora how proud that I was of her. Valora shifted to the side and my smile died a quick death. I'd seen that face in my nightmares, and I couldn't believe my eyes that he was here now. I sat back and watched him approach with that same smug look on his face from the past.

"Hello, Vicky."

Harlan Sams stepped into the present from my nightmares.

It was a sad day when we left Carson for Dallas. Since Leah's apartment couldn't hold all of our belongings, we put everything except the necessities in storage in Carson. Valora started school in the car that Harlan bought her. I knew that he'd bought it out of spite and that it was a lemon, but Valora loved the freedom of having her own car again. The car that I'd bought her in Carson had been totaled in a bad wreck when Valora was on her way to a competition one day. By the grace of God, she'd lived and her injuries healed with time, but the car was beyond repair. The police told us that it was her fault even though the firemen knew that the other driver had been drunk. I knew that they blamed her because he'd been a good ol' White man and she'd been a poor Black girl. Valora tried to make a fuss, but I told her to leave it alone. Besides, I didn't care because she'd lived. I hadn't the money to buy another, so Valora had been without a car until Harlan stepped back into the picture.

Harlan. He was such a piece of work. I narrowed my eyes at the television screen and felt the hot anger build in my heart. He was the reason for so much that had happened in Dallas ever since he showed up to Valora's graduation all those months ago with lies of wanting to be in his daughter's life. I frowned when the memory of that night rushed in before I could stop it.

"Harlan, what are you doing here?"

Harlan raised his eyebrows at my angry tone and looked at the sea of family faces that surrounded my wheelchair. I smiled when I imagined that all he could see were frowns. Harlan shrugged his shoulders and stepped closer to Valora who looked shocked. He grabbed her in a big hug and laughed out loud.

"There's my honey! Daddy has missed you so much! I'm so glad that your sisters called you last summer so that we could finally talk. It meant so much to me to talk to my baby girl this past year! I'm so proud of you!"

Stunned at Harlan's revelation, my eyes flew to where Leah and Gia stood. Leah lowered her head, but Gia raised her chin and smiled. My hand itched to slap her, but I narrowed my eyes and turned my gaze back to see Valora pull away from Harlan. She avoided my glare and fidgeted with her graduation cap. Gia walked forward and hugged Harlan. She stepped back and stared at Leah for a moment until she hugged Harlan as well. Mark came from around my chair and pulled Valora back to my side. Grayson stepped to the other side of my wheelchair. I smiled at my sons' protective stance. I glanced around to see that people stared at us as they walked past. Aunt Charlotte noticed too and limped forward with a graceful smile.

"Harlan. What a surprise to see you here in Carson. How ever did you know that Valora graduated today?"

Harlan's smile didn't quite reach his eyes. He looked from me to our sons to Aunt Charlotte and Aunt Mary who now stood beside us. He put an arm around Leah and Gia and grinned.

"Well, I hadn't heard from Valora in a while, and she usually calls once a week. I called Leah and she told me that Valora was busy with graduation stuff. She didn't give me any details, so I called Gia and she brought me the invitation. I couldn't miss this day."

I glanced up at the guilt and embarrassment on Valora's face and knew that Harlan spoke the truth about the phone calls. Hurt, betrayal, and fear twisted themselves into my heart. A knot of tears formed in my throat, but I refused to shed them in front of Harlan. He had no more power over me, but Valora's duplicity and deceit cut me deeply. I wanted to rail at the pain and injustice. Instead, I lifted my chin and smiled at Valora. I felt her start of surprise and almost narrowed my eyes to show my real displeasure with her. I would ignore Leah and Gia for now.

"Pumpkin, Grayson and Mark have to get me to the transport van. Aunt Charlotte and Aunt Mary rode with us as well. I'm sure that you want to find Faith before your senior party."

Valora's eyes bulged for a moment in shock before she saw the anger in my eyes. She knew that I'd told her she couldn't go to the senior party. Now, I just wanted to keep her away from Harlan by any means. Valora nodded and turned to Harlan and her sisters.

"Thank you, Daddy, for coming all this way. I apologize that I can't spend more time with you, but I've got to go find my friend for our senior party. It's a big party where they lock all the seniors in all night after graduation and it's supposed to be a lot of fun."

Harlan chuckled and came forward to give Valora another big hug. I cringed at that monster with my Pumpkin. I glanced over to see Aunt Mary wrinkle her forehead in a frown too. Valora pulled away from Harlan, gave us all a hug, and ran off to find her friend. Harlan tipped his head mockingly to me. I narrowed my eyes at him. He laughed and turned to walk away. Harlan paused and looked back at me.

"I heard Valora chose Dallas University. I wonder why?"

I signaled Grayson to push me away without any further acknowledgement of Harlan. His question stayed on my mind all night while I waited for Valora to get out of the senior lock-in party. Why did she choose Dallas University?

The sound of the key in the lock brought me out of those memories. I blinked and a tear fell on my cheek. I hadn't even realized that I'd been crying. I took off my glasses and wiped my eyes before Leah or Valora walked in the door.

"Hey Mama, look what I brought you."

I looked over to see Leah with a large vase of flowers. I smiled at her and shifted my legs to sit up on the sofa. Leah walked over and handed me the flowers. I breathed in their pungent sweet smells and promptly sneezed. We both laughed and Leah took the vase to place it on the fireplace mantel. She nodded at their position and turned to go in her bedroom. I picked up the remote and flipped through the channels until Leah returned to the living room changed from her office clothing. We sat in silence for a bit and then she spoke. Her abrupt tone made me shift to face her.

"Mama, I know Valora has been running wild since y'all got here. No, you don't have to deny it. I can see it for myself that taking care of you is almost an afterthought to her now. She's got college, a job, friends, and that so-called boyfriend of hers. Maybe this move wasn't a good idea. I mean, maybe you should have stayed in Carson with some family or went to Houston with Aunt Charlotte. You can't live like this."

I narrowed my eyes at Leah because Gia said the exact same thing to me a few days before when she'd called to speak to Leah. It was true that Valora seemed to enjoy her freedom a bit much, but Leah and Gia didn't understand our bond. They didn't understand what Valora and I sacrificed to stay together. She knew how to take care of me when no one else did. I sighed.

"Leah, everything will be all right. It's okay that Valora has some freedom. She didn't have much growing up taking care of me, her studies, and the house. She's unique, that's all. We have to realize that and give her some space. The move to Dallas just has her overwhelmed. She'll come back around to her responsibilities."

I nodded and turned back to the television. I glanced over to see Leah's lips twist. She looked at me with such anger that I almost shrank away from her in surprise. I steeled myself for her unusual fury.

"What is it about Valora, Mama? It's like she can't do any wrong in your eyes. I remember when she was born. You acted like she was a piece of gold, and all while we were growing up, you'd tell us she was "unique". 'Valora is going to have my figure', you'd say. Valora this and Valora that! You had other children, Mama. Children who needed you just to tell us that you loved us too! You weren't the only one that was hurt by your marriage to Daddy. You didn't even think about anything but staying with him and have more bastard children while he was married to another woman! How do you think that made us feel? And the move to Allsville to that run-down house and that horrible school? You even pushed away Dr. William when he would have made us happy! That was the worst time of my life, Mama, but you still only cared about Valora and what she needed because she was so "special"! Even now, I can bring you flowers that make you smile, but you don't compliment anything that I do! Valora ignores you, Mama! You have to call her beeper just to get her to come feed you or change your bed pads! You never ask me to do it! You just call your precious Valora! Well, my dear little sister has until Friday to pay her portion of the rent or both of you will be out on the streets!"

I looked at the rage on Leah's face in shock until my own anger ignited. I raised my eyebrow at her and spoke through clenched teeth.

"You think that you had it so bad, Leah? You have no idea. You have no idea about my marriage to Harlan. How dare you? You don't know what I've gone through with Harlan and what I went through to raise y'all on a fixed income and with my illness getting worse because I'm standing out in the cold waiting for rides to and from town, picking pecans, cutting firewood, and anything else that I needed to do to help us survive. And William making us happy? Carson wasn't the type of town and his mother wasn't the type of woman to let us be happy together. I came to that conclusion a long time ago."

I paused to swallow the sob that threatened to escape at the mention of William. We'd written each other for years to keep our love alive until my legs stopped working. I realized that I'd be a burden on him like I was on Valora. I didn't want him to protest like she did that I wasn't, so I stopped writing. After a few letters to ask why I didn't respond, the letters stopped. I cried for days because it felt like he'd left me again. Yes, I knew it was my fault, but it didn't stop the pain of a lost dream. Valora's Light helped me through that pain. She'd comforted me and brought me out of my heartbreak with songs, food, and gossip. I couldn't tell her why I was hurt, but I told her how much her love meant to me.

I felt my nostrils flare in anger that Leah would say such hateful things about her sister. I didn't care if there was even a drop of truth in her words. I only saw Gia's influence on her twin sister, and it made me angrier. I stared at her until she dropped her head. Maybe she feels like she's in control because you're vulnerable, a voice said in my mind. I narrowed my eyes at her bent head, and a plan came to mind. I didn't think about from where the idea came. I just wanted to be free from my daughters' criticism. I grabbed the phone and punched the keypad in anger. Leah glanced up in surprise, then she pressed her lips together in a sarcastic smile. I knew what she thought, and I wanted to tell her to go to the devil. The phone rang twice before a deep voice answered.

"Hello?"

"Mark, is that you?"

"Mama! It's so good to hear your voice! How are things in Dallas?"

I paused for a moment to get a hold of my emotions, but my intuitive son knew better. I heard Leah shift on the sofa to eavesdrop, but I refused to look at her.

"Mama, is everything all right?"

I took a deep breath for courage.

"Mark, do you remember when you said that I could come to Kansas for a while when Valora got settled? Is that offer still open?"

I smiled when I heard Mark whoop in excitement. He'd tried to get me to come to see his family for a while.

"Mama, you don't know how happy that you just made me! Cindy is going to be so thrilled to have you here with the new baby coming. I can finally have some coconut chess pie! When do you want to come?"

I thought about Valora and knew that I'd instilled enough wisdom in her to resist any environment that she found herself. Harlan wasn't paying attention to her anymore since she started college and found a boyfriend. I knew that he cared to spite me more than he cared for Valora. After all, he knew the truth. She would be fine, and I wouldn't be a burden to her or anyone else. I swallowed the apprehension and fear that climbed into my throat.

"When can you come get me, son?"

Mark whooped again and told me that he had to talk to his job first. He ended the call with the promise to come pick me up no later than the next Monday. I told her that I would be gone from her space in four days. I didn't get an answer, but I smiled in satisfaction. No one was going to dictate to me after what I'd gone though in my life.

I thought about my decision and felt that it was for the best. If I wasn't at Leah's, she nor Gia could continue to blame me for their mistakes. They wouldn't be able to take out their jealousy and anger on Valora. Valora, My Pumpkin Pie. My eyes misted and I lowered my head in sadness. It never occurred to me that I should have spoken to her first. She'll be fine, that same voice whispered. I raised my head and glanced around to see who'd spoken, but I knew that it was all in my mind. I wiped my face and picked up the remote. Yes, she would be fine, I told myself, and changed the channel.

Several years after I left Leah's apartment, my life changed tremendously. My time with Mark opened my eyes that my son's marriage had a dark seed within it that may grow into trouble for him later. Valora ended up pregnant by that good for nothing boyfriend, Michael. She dropped out of college and struggled to take care of herself. I rushed back from Kansas to make sure that she received medical care and wouldn't be homeless.

The thought of my baby's child made me happy, but her choice of man disappointed me. After Velise was born,

Michael left Valora and returned home to his mother. Valora picked up the pieces and moved on with the promise to her baby girl and me to rise above the challenge of single motherhood. The problem came with her feelings for Michael as her first real boyfriend. They clashed and butted heads about Velise until Valora met Tom. Tom seemed to adore Valora, but I could see that he didn't care for her child. It made me uneasy when I saw him disrespect her intelligence and put her down in front of people. He wouldn't even call Velise by her name. I brought it up to Valora, but she wouldn't listen.

"Pumpkin, you know that you don't need a man to raise your child. Times have changed, and women are doing it by themselves."

Valora looked at me like I had grown two heads. She shrugged and avoided my eyes.

"I don't know what you mean, Mama."

I frowned at her, but she couldn't see me because she left to get Velise a cookie. I looked at my beautiful grandchild and sighed.

"I just don't want her to make my mistakes, Velise."

Velise gurgled and showed her dimples. I smiled and reached into her playpen beside my bed to rub her dark, silky locks. I sighed again at my daughter's blindness.

"Maybe she'll figure it out soon."

Tom stayed around a few more months after he finished truck-driving school. He told Valora that he had to take a job in Missouri, but he'd send for her when he found a place for them. I rolled my eyes because the whole thing sounded murky. Valora found out that she was pregnant with twins later that month. She called Tom in excitement to be put off by his bad attitude. It depressed for a while, but I continued to support her in way that I could. Gia and Leah had a fit and didn't talk to me for almost two years. I didn't mind it so much, but Gia had a son that I wanted to see very much. I tried to ignore the hurt that the separation between my children caused but I would not abandon Valora again.

After the loss of one of the twins and a prolonged hospital stay, Valora delivered a beautiful baby girl that looked exactly like me with dark red hair and blue eyes. She named her Velea and began to pick up the pieces of her life from Tom's desertion. She returned to school and began to work as my personal aide to be at home with her children when she wasn't in school. I was so proud of her progress and would tell anyone off that said anything bad about her. She took care of me even when she was sick. Her determination to keep me from the nursing home and Leah and Gia's clutches matched mine to see her return to her path.

Valora's Light began to shine brightly again, and it wasn't long before a handsome young Mexican boy, Israel, noticed and captured her heart. Israel was very respectful to me and I loved that he treated Velise and Velea like his own. Valora was smitten, and I felt happy for her. There were a few times that I felt a twinge of jealousy because I didn't get to have with William what Valora and Israel had. I stamped out the envy with the realization that I'd pushed William away. I thought about reaching out to William often, but I didn't want to disturb whatever life he'd made for himself.

Eventually, Valora and Israel married. Valora gave birth to a son three years after Velea, and I knew that God had sent her the baby that was taken away. Again, I felt a twinge of envy but I ignored it. I didn't allow anyone to rain on Valora's happiness, and I certainly wouldn't do it myself. After all, she made sure that I had a room in their house and always gave me credit for raising my children as a single woman.

I tried very hard to mend fences with Willie, Leah, and Gia, but they were still bitter about the past and that I didn't turn from Valora or throw her to the wolves like they wanted. Whenever they visited me, they'd wait until Valora was gone to unleash their venom. Gia enjoyed stoking the fires of envy and anger in her siblings. She'd stand by with an unholy glee on her face when Leah would rant at me for past hurts. Most times, she wasn't satisfied with Leah's anger, so she'd rage at me as well. I fought hard not to show any emotion, but it was so hard. One day, I couldn't help it and I burst into tears as soon as Valora walked in from the store.

"Mama! What's wrong? What happened? Are you sick?"

I couldn't even answer her in my distress. I flinched away when she walked over and sat beside me on the bed. She reached out her hand and touched me with eyes closed. I calmed down and smiled to see Valora use her gift. Her hand tightened and her eyes popped open to frown at me. I knew that she'd seen Gia's dark arrows in my heart. She stood up and strode to the door. Panic filled me because I knew that she wanted to find Gia and why.

"Pumpkin, it's not worth it. I'm fine. Your sister is just bitter, and it doesn't help her to see you do well."

Valora paused and looked back at me with her temper in her burning light brown eyes. The stubborn set of her chin told me that there wasn't much that I could say to sway her.

"Mama, I love you. I want your other children to come see you whenever they want, but this is my house and I won't have Gia upset you. You can't stand up and confront her and she knows it. She takes advantage of your condition. You just had a stroke last year, for God's sake! Your diabetes is finally under control with that new pill and the anti-inflammatory arthritis medicine leveled out some of your pain. You don't need or deserve this kind of treatment, not after you sacrificed so much to take care of us. I won't have it! She's always smiles and giggles when I'm around but attacks you when I leave. She's a bitter and cowardly witch, Mama. She reminds me of Betts. I know it was her or her prodding Leah to call that complaint in to adult and child services on me. She wants everyone to be miserable because of her choice to use Betts' ways to get a man, and it backfired on her. I just pray that she never learned anything that could really harm any of us."

I nodded in agreement and kept silent instead of telling Valora that I'd done the same thing with Harlan.

After that day, Valora always stayed around when Leah or Gia came to visit. Sometimes, they argued, but it was always

Gia encouraging Leah to get in Valora's face. I knew that Valora wouldn't back down from them. I also knew that she'd listen to me when I told her to treat her sisters with patience and peace. I told her to bite her tongue or lip and pray for her sisters. Valora almost developed a lisp from biting her tongue so much that sometimes, all we could do was laugh about it.

My body started to betray me, and I fell ill several times over the next year. Each time, I always lost a little more of my strength. My heart and mind told me that I may not see my grandchildren grow up, but I felt pride that I'd raised their parents to fend for themselves. I began to express my feelings to Valora and tell her stories of the past. Sometimes, she got a kick out of them, and sometimes, she stayed silent while tears rolled down her face. I tried to let her know that there was always a rainbow waiting to shine after the darkness of a storm.

Israel tried to convince Valora to put me in a nursing home, but she refused. She didn't tell me until after their marriage fell apart that her care of me was one of the reasons why he'd left. She revealed that he also had affairs and he didn't want her to attend college. I felt shocked and dumbfounded because I'd been so blind to my daughter's marital problems. She hadn't confided in me because of my illness. I almost cursed my useless body, but I realized that everything happens for a reason. Israel wasn't the man for my daughter or the father for my grandchildren. I looked at Valora and how beautiful and strong she was. She may have been hurt, but she was a survivor like me. I vowed that as long as God blessed me to live, I would be there for my baby girl.

"It's called the Tale of the Cat and Dog, Velise and Velea. Did y'all like it?"

I looked at the eager faces of my granddaughters and smiled when they nodded that they'd liked the story that I'd written. It was one of three that I'd sent off to a publisher. I received the rejection letters in the mail, but I didn't care. One day, my stories would be famous and make my family enough money to take care of them. I tried to smile again but a harsh cough escaped my mouth. I held a tissue to my lips and saw the familiar red tinge. It's just a bad cough, I told myself. I glanced down at the sweet faces of my grandbabies and ignored the lingering ache in my chest.

"Do you want to hear another one?"

They hopped up with a loud whoop, and I shushed them. They immediately fell silent. I looked toward the back of the small apartment house to make sure that they hadn't awakened their mother and new baby sister. I glanced to the couch across the room to see Vincent turn over to continue his afternoon nap. I unfolded another packet of papers and put my glasses on my nose. A wave of dizziness hit me and I dropped the papers. I tried to pick them up, but pain went through my shoulder to my hand. I couldn't help but cry out in agony.

"Ahh!"

Velise jumped up and put her hand on my shoulder. The weight of her small hand felt like a brick and I cried out again. She turned to Velea.

"Go get, Mama."

Velea took off to the back and returned with a sleepy Valora. Valora took one look at me and reached for my insulin counter. I flinched at the tiny prick and waited for the beep. Valora's eyes widened, but she stayed calm.

"Mama, you sugar is still high. I've done everything that I can to bring it down to your range. Are you still coughing?"

I glanced away from my daughter's direct gaze and nodded. Valora sighed.

"I'm sorry, Mama, but we have to get you to the doctor. I'll call the ambulance."

I shook my head at her.

"No, I'll just go to the doctor Monday."

Valora pressed her lips together and put her hands on her hips.

"Velise, Velea, take your brother to the room and close the door."

The girls got up quickly, grabbed Vincent, and retreated to their bedroom. Valora waited to hear the door shut before she spoke in an unexpectedly gentle tone.

"Mama, I know that you don't want to go to the hospital or in the ambulance, but we have to go. I'll ask Maria, the neighbor, to watch the children while I go with you. Does that make you feel better about going?"

It didn't because I still didn't want to go, but I knew Valora needed assurance that I'd be fine. She was still a little scared since my last bout of sickness when I'd written Ruth, Lacey, and William letters to have a reunion because life was too short. My siblings responded that they'd try to get with their families to schedule a date, but no reunion yet. I tried to shift my legs a bit, but I had to bite my lip at the piercing agony. I guess it wouldn't hurt to go get a shot to stop all this pain.

"Ms. Sams? Hello, I am Dr. Alexander and this is Dr. Patel. We are part of the oncology team here on staff at Great Hope Hospital. We'd like to speak with you about your blood work."

I frowned at the older Black doctor. Oncology? Wait, they were cancer doctors. My heartbeat began to race and the machine beeped along with it. Dr. Alexander pressed a button on it and turned to me with a small smile.

"Please calm down, Ms. Sams. Is your daughter still here?"

I nodded and tried to swallow, but my throat was dry. I started to cough, and Dr. Patel moved forward with a tissue. I took it from his hand and wiped my mouth. I refused to look at it. Instead, I looked up at the doctors.

"What is wrong with me? I've been poked and prodded for two days. My pain is worse than its ever been and this cough won't go away. No one would tell me anything except that I needed overnight observation. Well, gentlemen, it's been almost two nights now."

Dr. Patel looked at Dr. Alexander. Dr. Alexander took a step toward the bed and opened my chart. Valora walked in with a cup of coffee and a bag of potato chips. She smiled at the doctors, and I almost snickered at the stunned looks on their faces. Even though, my daughter had four children, she still looked like a teenager with the figure to match. She walked forward and introduced herself.

"Hello, I'm Ms. Sams' daughter, Valora Perez. I'm so glad that I caught you. What's going on with my mother? My children are anxious to have her home."

Dr. Alexander's head lowered a bit, and Dr. Patel turned his head to avoid Valora's gaze. She looked at me, and I tried to shrug. Searing pain shot through my shoulders. I frowned at the doctors.

"Doctors, I am in a lot of pain. Please tell me what's wrong, how to fix it, and when I can go home."

Dr. Alexander approached the bed again and adjusted his glasses. He nor Dr. Patel would meet my eyes. Fear crawled up my spine like the Daddy Long Legs Spider that Velise scared Vincent with last week.

"Ms. Sams, you have a rare and aggressive lung cancer. When you were here four months ago, we saw a spot and sent the films and labs to your primary doctor. I don't know what happened there with the lapse of care, but the spot has spread. Since you didn't receive any treatment, the cancer has spread to your bones and caused them to metastasize. This is why your pain has increased."

Dr. Alexander paused. I felt lightheaded in the silence. He lifted his misted eyes to me. I saw sympathy in the depths of the dark brown irises.

"To break it down, you are beyond Stage 4 cancer, Ms. Sams. You may have four, maybe six months to live."

I fell back on my pillows in shock, and I heard Valora protest and request a second opinion. A memory of doctors and my original diagnosis floated through my mind. Surely, this isn't true. God, please don't let this be true. Lung Cancer? I'd never picked up a cigarette in my life. I'd only ever been around Harlan. Harlan. Everything was his fault. If I'd never met him, I wouldn't have felt so desperate to cross the *line*. I could have run away with William and pretended like him to be White. No, my choices were my own. I looked at the doctors trying to console Valora and knew that I'd make the same choices all over again for my children. I was dying, but it would be on my terms.

"Valora, hush. This is one of the best hospitals in the country. William wouldn't have chosen to come here if it wasn't. I don't need a second opinion. What I need is to go home and be with my family."

Valora shuffled forward and knelt beside the bed. Her tears almost broke my heart.

"Mama, they could be wrong. It's happened before to others. Please don't just accept this. It's not fair."

I smiled and lifted my hand to her cheek. She closed her eyes and leaned into it for a moment.

"Valora, no, it's not fair, but I've lived enough in this lifetime to put others to shame. God makes no mistakes, and if it's my time, it's my time."

Valora raised up and pushed her stubborn chin out mulishly and I knew I had to touch her inner compassion.

"I'm tired, Pumpkin."

Dr. Alexander stepped closer and pulled Valora from the floor.

"We won't tire you out any more, Ms. Sams. You need your rest. We can discuss home care and hospice with your daughter since she holds the Power of Attorney."

I hadn't meant that I was physically tired like Dr. Alexander thought, but Valora knew what I meant. She bent and kissed my forehead.

"I understand, Mama. I'll call the others," she whispered before she turned and walked away.

Dr. Alexander smiled at Valora's proud back. He turned to me with tears falling down his broad cheeks.

"I hope and pray that when my time comes, I have the love of someone like your daughter."

I swallowed the tightness in my throat and nodded. Dr. Alexander patted my shoulder and left the room. Dr. Patel nodded to me as well and turned to leave. He paused and turned back with his head cocked to the side.

"Ms. Sams. You mentioned a William that worked here. What is his last name?"

I shifted on my pillows and smiled at the young doctor.

"Herbert. Dr. William Herbert. He was a good friend of mine once upon a time. I wish that I could see and talk to him again," I replied wistfully.

Dr. Patel nodded again, snapped the light off, and left the room.

I turned toward the window and allowed the unshed tears to finally fall.

The next day, I stared at the watery powdered eggs on my tray and pushed it away. My appetite left when they started the morphine. It took away the pain, but it made me dizzy and slow. I sighed and picked up my Bible that Valora brought me from home. I flipped to Job and started to read of his trials. A quiet knock interrupted my study and commiseration with Job.

"Come in, please."

The door opened and the page I'd been reading was forgotten. Shock held me still until I heard the familiar chuckle.

"Hello, Victoria."

I stared at William's beloved smile, and I felt my lips curve. William Herbert was alive and well in my hospital room. He grinned and walked closer. I took in his sun-weathered and handsome face. He was still tall and handsome with not one iota of stooped posture. He wore a stethoscope around his neck, and he was dressed in a suit. All the years and distance slipped away as my love for this wonderful man almost burst from my heart. I met his eyes with a grin of my own.

"Well, Dr. Herbert. It looks like you've done well for yourself."

William bowed his head and sat down in the chair next to the bed. He leaned forward and took my arthritis-deformed hand. Embarrassed, I wanted to snatch it away, but he held firm. I looked down at the blanket to avoid his gaze, but he grasped my chin and turned me back to see the pain in his blue eyes.

"Why do you avoid looking at me? Dr. Patel came to see me, Victoria. He told me that you wanted to see and talk to me. I know that I've wanted the same thing for many years. Why did you stop writing to me or tell me that you've been in Dallas all these years? You let yourself suffer when you didn't have to, Victoria. I'm a doctor, but you still didn't trust that I loved you enough to care for you, even for your condition."

William's words twisted through my heart, and I cast my eyes down. Tears threatened to fall, but I had to tell him everything. His grip on my chin lessened, and I lifted my eyes to his.

"William, I know that I've caused you enough pain and heartache. After my diagnosis, I wanted to reach out to you. I started to write to you so many times that I ran out of paper. I picked up the phone to call the number from your letters and allowed fear to stop me. When my legs stopped working, I knew that I couldn't and wouldn't be a burden to you. You deserved so much more than I could give you, William. Harlan may have messed up my trust of men, but my choices destroyed what we could have been."

Tears fell down William's face. He swiped at them roughly and his lips curved into a sad smile. He leaned his forehead to mine and put his arms around me.

"Victoria, I have loved you since the day that I saw you sitting in your grandparent's truck. I will love you until the day that I take my last breath. You're the only woman that I've ever loved this way. It's not fair that I finally have you in my arms and you're going to leave me. Again."

William's words cut through me, and it became more real in that moment that my time would come soon. We sat there and cried tears of regret and heartbreak. When the storm was over, I knew that it was time. Fear inched into my heart, but I pushed it out because William needed to know. I took a deep breath and started to cough. William tsked and patted me on the back. I nodded to let him know that I was all right. I cleared my throat and looked him in the eye.

"William, years ago when Valora was sick, you told me that you envied me for my children. You said that you'd went to an office in downtown Dallas that turned out to be a fertility clinic. Do you remember the name of the doctor there?"

William frowned at me in confusion.

"Yes, I remember that I told you that. Why do you ask, Victoria?"

I frowned at him for being so nosy.

"William, please. Do you remember his name?"

"I think his name was Martin? No, Massey. No, it wasn't that, but it was something that started with an M."

My heartbeat started to race. I took another deep breath.

"Was it, Michaels?"

William snapped his fingers.

"Yes! Now, that I think of it, his name was Dr. Michaels. Very smart man. I heard that he became well known in scientific circle for genetics. Wait, how do you know his name?"

I pulled my hand from his so that William wouldn't feel my trembles. I looked away for a moment and gathered my courage. Now, I knew for certain. I turned my head and met William's confused blue eyes.

"I know Dr. Michaels because I've reported to his partners on his implant's progress for the last twenty-eight years. An implant that I provided the eggs and body to produce."

I sat and waited for William to understand. I knew that he did when he stumbled from his chair to lean on the tiny sink. He wiped his hand over his face. When he looked back at me, I saw more questions. I held up my hand and answered before he could ask.

"Yes, Valora is twenty-seven. No, I suspected but didn't know for sure until just now. I didn't tell you because I didn't want to raise your hopes to just be disappointed if it wasn't true."

William raised an angry eyebrow.

"What is this, some deathbed confession? Who the heck are you to decide if I wanted to be disappointed or not, Victoria? It goes back to trust. If you'd trusted me to love you, our path would have been different. You deliberately kept this information from me. I always had a connection to Valora that I couldn't explain. I thought that I was grasping at straws to be with you when it was real all along."

"I'm so sorry, William. I didn't do it on purpose, and I thought the same thing. I wanted to have a connection with you so bad. Every time that Valora smiled or looked at me, I would see you. I didn't know what to do. Now, I'm leaving her alone," I sobbed.

The pain of my heart outweighed the pain of my body to see the cost of the choices that I'd made in my life to William and myself. Tears of regret, anger, and fear poured from my soul.

The anger left William as quick as it came. He sat down and took my hand. He put a finger under my chin and lifted my face to meet his gaze. William's eyes darted across my face and he smiled.

"I know in my heart that you didn't do it on purpose. I promise you that I will watch over Valora for as long as God blesses me to live. I won't tell her who I am because I don't want to hurt her. There's been enough hurt in this family."

I nodded and William released my chin. It was just in time too because Valora walked in the door. She held little Vivienne in her arms and didn't see William until she moved further into the room. She gasped and almost dropped the baby.

"Dr. William!"

William laughed and got up to hug her.

"It's been a long time, my sweet. You have grown into a beautiful young woman. Actually, you look almost exactly like your mother at that age. And who is this gorgeous young lady?"

Valora laughed and shook her head. Her eyes twinkled when looked towards me.

"No, Dr. William, I could never be a bombshell like Mama was back in the day."

We all laughed, and Valora handed William the baby. Well, she let Vivienne go because William had her almost all the way in his arms. He started to coo and crow at Vivienne, and I smiled at the pride on his face. Some of my fear at leaving my loved ones behind lessened in the face of William's love for his daughter.

A few months later found me weak and racked with pain but I refused to give up when I looked around and saw how devastated my children and family would be at my passing. I tried to be brave and act normal, but it was difficult. Gia and Leah came around to the apartment and started to gang up on Valora. Valora didn't say a word until the day that they came hunting for my life insurance policy and anything that they could claim as their own. Valora barely contained her rage, and I knew it was because she didn't want to upset me. I saw then that she would receive little to no support from her sisters when I was gone. That realization almost pulled me into the abyss, but I held on to my strength to stay with my baby a little longer. The fight made me even more tired. I called Ruth and made arrangements. I wrote letters with the help of the hospice volunteer and put them where Valora would eventually find them. She would not be alone.

When I knew that my time was near, I called Valora to my side and told her that I'd left a special book for her on my antique desk. She barely listened to me because she'd turned to her volatile relationship with another Mexican boy named Tony. I watched her begin to fall off the path but I was too weak to do anything about it. I knew that her grief was great, but she looked to the wrong place for comfort. I prayed that she resisted the darkness that hovered on the edge. I told her over and over that God would be her comfort. I told her to take care of her precious little ones, especially Vincent. He would have the biggest obstacles in his way as a Black man in a world of prejudice and envy. I did not want that for him or any of my grandsons.

I told Valora more about my life so that she would learn from it and not suffer like I did. I knew that I wouldn't have enough time to tell her to remember her blessings and her gifts. She would need them to be the strong and successful woman that I knew that she would become one day. There just wasn't enough time.

William visited often and I knew he would be there until the end. So, I found the courage to send him away again because he didn't deserve to see me die.

I closed my eyes when William caressed my cheek. He sniffed and I opened my eyes to see his full of tears. I smiled and held out my hand. He grasped it gently and brought it to his face. His brow creased in concern when I grimaced.

"Are you alright, my love?"

I nodded.

"I'm fine. The medicine keeps me asleep, so I told Valora not to give me too much today."

William frowned.

"Victoria, you're supposed to take it so that you won't have pain. Where are the pills? I'll give it to you."

William moved to rise and I tightened my hand. He stopped but the frown stayed. I smiled.

"I wanted to be awake to enjoy our time. I'm tired, William, and I don't know how much time I've got left."

William's eyes misted again and he sobbed. He looked down and shook his head.

"This isn't fair. I love you and you're finally here with me. After all that we've been through, I haven't been broken, but this is going to break me, Victoria."

William's words pulled at my heart. I saw his pain and knew that his shoulders bowed a little more with each visit. I moved my hand and he gripped it like he didn't want to let it go. He raised his head and I saw grief in the blue depths of his eyes. I knew what I had to do. I smiled at him.

"William, do you remember that song that I used to sing? You'll Never Walk Alone?"

William frowned in confusion and nodded. I turned toward the window.

"My life has been filled with hardships and pain, but you and my children gave me the love that I needed to be strong. I have to be strong now for both of us."

William's eyes narrowed and he began to shake his head like he knew what I was about to say. I tightened my grip on his hand again and tried to push my love and understanding into him. Tears fell from his eyes and he quieted. I smiled at him gently.

"William Herbert, I love you and always will but I forbid you to return to this house. I will not allow you to watch me die. You promised that you would take care of Valora and her children and you have to be strong do that. Yes, you will mourn my passing from this earth but don't dwell on it. William, I want you to know that my soul is ready to meet my Savior and one day, we will see each other again."

William sobbed and leaned over the hospital bed rail to hug me with such tenderness that the tears that I tried to hold back fell anyway. We held each other like that until William kissed my forehead and cheek. Then, he looked me in the eyes.

"I won't say goodbye, Victoria, only I'll see you later."

He gently kissed my lips and walked out the door.

The next week my siblings and family came to see me and say goodbye. I heard their tears of sorrow and wanted to yell at them that I wasn't gone yet.

"She has maybe two or three days. I'm so sorry," a voice whispered.

I raised my heavy eyelids to see the hospice nurse speak to my sister, Ruth. The kind White nurse gave me a sympathetic glance and walked out of the door. I tried to open my mouth to tell her that only God knew when I would come home. My lips refused to move and I groaned in frustration.

"Mama? Are you all right?"

I tried to open my eyes to look at Leah but they wouldn't open all the way. I was able to nod but it took so much strength. She let out a relieved deep breath and moved away. Suddenly, I heard angry voices and tried to turn my head to listen.

"You just want to be the center of attention like you always have, Valora. It's not your decision to call the family and update them on Mama's condition. You're not the oldest or the oldest girl. I am."

I flinched at Gia's bitterness. She couldn't even wait for me to die before she started in on her sister. I tried to make my lips work to tell her to leave Valora alone, but they wouldn't move.

"Gia, you don't know anything. I promised Mama that I wouldn't keep her family in the dark. They were her family first, and I know Mama better than you ever would."

Valora sounded like she'd been crying and I wanted to so bad to comfort her and tell her that she only made things worse for herself. She'd need her sisters when I was gone. I heard Gia laugh with genuine delight.

"Oh, you think that you know Mama. Girl, please. She spoiled you and raised you to be just like her. A woman with a houseful of brats that she can't take care of without welfare."

Slap!

I rolled my eyes over to see that Gia pushed Valora too far. Valora stood over her with her fists balled. She looked at Leah with fury when she stepped forward to help Gia.

"Leah, I've never really had a problem with you because I know that Gia influenced you with her hate and ugly nature. I will tell you one thing and one thing only. If you move to help her while I give her the ass-kicking that she deserves, you won't leave this house alive," Valora growled.

Leah took another step and Valora did too. No, Valora, please stop! They want you in jail and helpless! Just let it go! I screamed in my mind and hoped that I could reach her gift. I pushed the words to her. It took almost all of my remaining strength, but it did no good. I saw Ruth grab Leah just as Gia kicked Valora in the thigh. Valora grunted in pain and fell on her knees on top of Gia. She slapped her several times and then stood up with a hold on Gia's bloody shirt. Gia tried to scratch and pull at Valora, but Valora was too strong for her. She balled her fist and slammed it into Gia's jaw. Gia hit the floor hard and Leah ran to her while threatening to call the police on Valora. Valora stood breathing heavily. Ruth went to Valora's side and frowned down at Gia and Leah.

"No, you won't call the police, Leah. Your mother is dying and all you can think of is to punish your sister for sacrificing her childhood and life to take care of your mother. Gia got what she's deserved all these years, Leah. Remember that Valora is your sister too. What is it that bothers you more, you mother's death or the embarrassment that everyone knows what Valora did for her? Get over yourselves and leave if you want to, but I'm staying here with my sister until she..."

Ruth's words ended on a sob and she collapsed onto the sofa. Valora comforted her until she saw my eyes open. She walked over and sat in the chair by the bed. She picked up my hand and began to sing as I'd trained her. The words of my favorite song, "His Eye is on the Sparrow" moved my lips into a smile. I looked in the corner and saw Big Mama Chandra, Grandpa Ed, Aunt Alice, and Grandpa Paul. They smiled and beckoned me to them. I knew why they'd come and I wasn't afraid. I felt their love and wanted to go to them, but I didn't want to leave Valora. Big Mama Chandra came closer and took my hand. I stood and looked at the tears that slid down Valora's face as she sang, Ruth sobbed on the couch, and Leah on the floor with Gia in her arms. I let go of Big Mama Chandra's hand and walked to Ruth. I hugged her to give her comfort and she quieted some. I knelt beside Leah and Gia and hugged them too but they didn't notice. When I turned back to Valora, she had her head down. I stroked my hand down her beautiful auburn hair and let her feel the warmth of my love. She shifted her head and smiled back at me as if she could see me.

"It's okay, Mama. I'll be all right. I couldn't have asked for a better mother. You kept me in God even when I'd lost my way. There is no more darkness in the Light of your love for us. Please don't worry because you were the best of mothers and I'll carry your wisdom all the rest of my days. I swear that I'll make you proud. I love you, Mama, and I'll see you again one day," she whispered.

I felt no sorrow at Valora's words, only joy. Yes, she would be fine. I turned to Big Mama Chandra and took her hand. My journey was at an end.

Epilogue

"Mom?"

Valora turned towards the knock and her oldest daughter's voice at the closed bedroom door. She sighed and closed her new laptop. Maybe later, she told herself. This was the fourth interruption this morning. First, Vivienne, Vincent, and Forrest wanted to play outside but couldn't get along with each other. Then, Vance asked could he go with his friend to the ice-cream shop. When Valora thought she'd finally have some peace, Velea appeared to complain about Velise's side of the room. Valora closed her eyes and counted to ten before she got up and swung the door wide. Velise jumped at the sudden movement, and Valora rolled her eyes.

"Yes, Velise?"

At the sight of the impatience in her mother's face, Velise decided to hurry her explanation for the interruption.

"Mom, I really don't want to share a room with Velea anymore. She's messy, and she has too much attitude. Can we please get a bigger house or something? I swear I'm going to stick her in the face. She's always..."

Valora tuned out the rest of Velise's words and rolled her eyes again at the same argument that she'd heard from Velea. She interrupted me for this, Valora asked herself. She sighed loud enough to stop Velise in mid-tirade. Valora stared at her beautiful daughter for a moment and recognized her mother in her features. A twinge of sadness crept into her heart. Velise squirmed under her mother's gaze until she couldn't take it anymore.

"Mom? Did you hear me?"

Sadness forgotten, Valora's eyes narrowed at Velise's tone. Velise realized what she had done and quickly sought to placate her mother.

"I'm sorry, Mom. It's just that Velea makes me so mad! I'm really sorry."

"I understand that you're upset, Velise. However, not now or ever, will you use that tone with me. Do you understand? I don't care with whom you are angry. You are the oldest, and I expect you to be more mature than this. Velise, you and Velea are going to find a way to get along, or I will find it for you. Comprendé?"

Velise nodded and backed away with a quiet yes ma'am. Satisfied that her daughter had returned to usual respectful self, Valora smiled. Velise looked confused by her mother's change in mood.

"Now, since you and your siblings are determined to keep me from my task, how about we take a trip to the gym? I'm sure everyone could use some space and have some fun too."

Velise's light brown eyes lit up with excitement.

"Yes, ma'am! I'll go tell everyone. Is Mr. Jack going? He just got back from the store and is outside with the little kids."

Valora nodded and smiled at her daughter's new attitude. Velise took off to tell the other children to get ready. Valora stepped back into the room and shut the door. She looked at the closed laptop and decided to type a few more words before she got ready for the gym. Valora lowered her lush curves into the chair behind the antique desk and opened the computer. She worked for a few moments then got up and readied herself for the punishment of the elliptical machine. Her husband, Jack, came in after she finished. Valora smiled at her tall, handsome husband and waited for the perfunctory kiss. Jack gave her the usual quick "hello honey" peck on the lips and turned to get ready for the gym.

"Velise said that we're going to the gym. I guess you're done for the day?"

Valora grinned at Jack's lowered head. She knew that he'd told the children to leave her alone, but he'd also escaped to his favorite tools store. Six blended kids were too much for her husband to handle alone.

"Yes, I'm done for the day. Actually, I think I'm all done."

Jack's head popped up in surprise.

"Really? You're all done with the whole thing?"

Valora nodded and laughed. Jack followed suit, stood up, and grabbed his gorgeous wife in a bear hug. He pulled back and kissed her forehead.

"I'm so proud of you! After the gym, let's celebrate. I'm going to go tell the kids."

Valora tried not to laugh as Jack grabbed his duffle bag and almost tripped in his excitement to tell the children the good news. Valora picked up her gym bag and turned toward the door. Something warm touched her arm, and she turned around to see the bright laptop screen.

"I must have forgotten to close it," she murmured.

She walked over and put her hand out to shut the lid when she noticed her work was on a specific page. Valora dropped her bag in shock because she knew that she didn't leave it on that page. She felt the warmth again on her shoulder and closed her eyes. Tears formed, but she smiled through them.

"I hope I did you proud," she whispered.

The warmth moved across her back like a hug. Valora closed her eyes again to feel as much of it as she could. In the next instance, the warmth was gone, but she didn't feel distraught.

"Honey? Are you coming? I wrestled all of the kids into the car, but I don't know how long that's going to last."

Valora glanced back at her wonderful husband and smiled.

"Here I come. I just needed to close a door."

Jack nodded absentmindedly and left the room.

Valora stood up and reached for her discarded gym bag. She took a few steps and forgot to close the laptop again. Before she closed it, she read what was on the page:

"I dedicate this book to my mother, Victoria Alicia Sams, who gave everything and asked for nothing."

PLEASE VISIT
WWW.BREAKINGTHELINEBOOKS.COM FOR
BOOKS, EXCERPTS, INFORMATION, AND RELEASE
DATES OF MORE BOOKS FROM BREAKING THE
LINE BOOKS SMALL PRESS

FOR DOMESTIC VIOLENCE PREVENTION
INFORMATION PLEASE VISIT
WWW.INDYGIRLWORLD.COM AND
WWW.DEYJAY.COM

VICTORIA'S OXTAIL STEW (makes 6 servings)

Oxtail stew has been a staple of good old country eating for a long time. It is a comfort food and best served with hot water cornbread or biscuits. Passed down through four generations, nothing has changed. Please do not substitute the ingredients as this stew is meant to be hearty and made with love. Enjoy!

Ingredients:

2 ½ lb. oxtails, cut half if preferred (pork neckbones may be used as a substitute)
2 tbsp. oil
1 Cup chopped onion
1 Tbsp minced garlic
2 (16 oz.) can tomatoes
1 Tbsp Salt
1 ½ tsps black pepper
3 Large white potatoes, peeled and quartered
2 carrots, pared & quartered
2 can green beans
Salt & pepper to taste

Directions:

Brown meat in oil in large stew pot. Add onion, garlic, tomatoes, ! Tbsp salt and 1½tsps pepper. Cover and simmer for about 2 hours. Skim off fat. Add potatoes, carrots, and green beans. Cover and simmer for 1 hour. Skim off fat. If desired, thicken broth with 2 tsps cornstarch mixed with water to make a thin paste for desired thickness. Simmer for additional 30 minutes. Allow to cool to desired temp and serve with cornbread or biscuits.

VICTORIA'S HOT WATER CORNBREAD (makes 10 cornbread patties)

Hot water cornbread is another staple of country life. Because there milk and eggs sometimes were scare, people began to find ways to make bread from their dry goods. Hello, hot water cornbread. It is a delicious addition to any meal or by itself. Passed down through four generations, nothing has changed. Please do not substitute the ingredients Enjoy!

Ingredients:

2 cups corn meal
3/4 cup flour
3 Tbsps sugar
1 ½ tsps. salt
1 1/2 teaspoon Clabbergirl baking powder
1 Cup Crisco oil
Cast iron skillet or equivalent

Directions:

Preheat oil in skillet. Too much oil will cause splatter and too little will cause the patties to separate. Start a pot of water to boil on the stove. Bring to a rolling boil. Sift all of the ingredient together in a large bowl Add boiling water while stirring constantly until you get a thick batter. The meal must be moistened but not too wet.

Let the cornbread mix cool to where it can be handled. Make patties slightly larger than an egg and about a half inch thick. You may want a bowl of cool water near to wet your hands with water while making the patties.

Drop in hot oil and cook to a golden brown. Separate them with a spatula or large fork. Allow patties to drain but not cool down too much. Serve warm with butter.

BIG MAMA CHANDRA'S BISCUITS (makes 10 biscuits)

These biscuits are a flaky and mouthwatering breakfast addition. Passed down through four generations, nothing has changed. Please do not substitute the ingredients as these tasty treats are meant to be buttery and full of goodness. Enjoy!

Ingredients:

2 1/4 cups all purpose flour
3 tsp Clabber Girl baking powder
1/2 tsp Salt
1/2 cup melted butter
1 cup whole milk
3 Tbsps shortening(Crisco/Butter flavored Crisco preferred)

Directions:

Preheat oven to 400°F. Lightly grease a large mixing bowl. Sift together the flour, baking powder, and salt in the bowl. Cut the shortening in with a large fork. (I use a pastry cutter now.) Continue cutting the shortening in until it has a course look and feel. Add the milk slowly while stirring the mixture into a ball of dough. Lightly flour a wide space on the counter and place the dough in the center. Knead the dough into a smooth ball. Roll out to a fingertip thickness or ¾ in. Cut the dough with a 2 in biscuit cutter or an empty medium sized cup/glass turned upside down. Place on an ungreased cookie sheet and brush tops with half of the melted butter. Bake at 400° on the top rack for 10 to 12 minutes or until light brown. Brush the tops with the remaining butter. Serve hot with butter and jelly, honey, or preserves.

MS. SADIE'S TEACAKES (makes 2 dozen cookies)

Teacakes were a special treat during my childhood. They are sweet cookies that can be baked soft or hard to your preference. Please do not substitute the ingredients as these tasty treats are meant to be sweet and full of goodness. Enjoy!

Ingredients

1 1/4 cup butter
2 cups white sugar
2 eggs
3 cups all-purpose flour
1/2 tsp Clabber Girl baking soda
1 tsp salt
1/4 tsp ground nutmeg
1 tsp vanilla extract

Directions:

In a medium bowl, cream together the butter and sugar until smooth. Beat in the eggs one at a time, stir in vanilla. Sift together the flour, baking soda, salt and nutmeg. Slowly stir into the creamed mixture. Flour a baking board and knead the dough until smooth. Cover and refrigerate until firm. Preheat the oven to 325 degrees. On a lightly floured surface, roll the dough out to a fingertip thickness for thicker teacakes and ¼ inch thick for thinner teacakes. Cut with cookie cutters or a medium sized cup/glass turned upside down. Place cookies an inch apart on ungreased cookie sheets. Bake for 8 to 10 minutes in the preheated oven. Allow cookies to cool on baking sheet for 3-4 minutes before transferring to a wire rack to cool all the way for storage. Serve with any beverage or alone for a quick snack.

VICTORIA'S COCONUT CHESS PIE (makes 8 slices)

Chess pies are a mouthwatering finish to any meal. This recipe for coconut chess pie has been passed down through generations and perfected by me as the Texas Pastry Diva. It is absolutely delicious. Enjoy!

Ingredients:
Crust
1 ½ Cups All-purpose flour
½ tsp. salt
4 oz. (1/4 lb.) butter flavored Crisco or unsalted butter
1 egg, beaten
1/4 cup cold water
½ tsp. white vinegar
Custard
1 Cup white sugar
2Tbsps Cornstarch or All-purpose flour
1/3 Cup Sweetened coconut flakes
2 eggs, beaten
1 stick of unsalted butter or margarine, melted
½ cup evaporated milk
1 tsp vanilla extract

Directions:
Crust: Preheat oven to 400°F. Lightly grease a large mixing bowl. Sift together the flour and salt in the bowl. Cut the shortening in with a large fork. (I use a pastry cutter now.) Continue cutting the shortening in until it has a course look and feel. Mix the egg, water, and vinegar in a small bowl. Add to mixture slowly while stirring into a ball of dough. Lightly flour a wide space on the counter and place the dough in the center. Knead the dough into a smooth ball. Roll out to a ½ in. thickness. Place in pie pan and trim crust slightly over edges. Pinch or score edges with butter knife to design. Bake at 400° on the top rack for 4 to 5 minutes. Remove and let cool. When cooled slightly coat the crust with butter and set aside.

Custard:

Sift together sugar and flour. Add melted butter and eggs. Stir well into a thick mixture. Add coconut flakes and stir well. Stir in milk and vanilla extract. Place pie crust on oven rack and while stirring, pour custard into crust. Bake for 30 to 45 minutes until pie has risen and golden brown. Remove and allow to cool. Serve warm with whipped cream or Blue Bell vanilla ice cream.

www.ingramcontent.com/pod-product-compliance
Lightning Source LLC
Chambersburg PA
CBHW061504020726
47502CB00006B/1923